I0772748

The Human Inside: Adaugeo

Book 1

By

Y.T. CHENG

For my mom and dad.
Thanks for not giving up on me.
I love you.

Table of Contents

Prologue vii
Chapter 1: Unexpected Inception 1
Chapter 2: Decisions, Decisions, Decisions 23
Chapter 3: Shots Fired 45
Chapter 4: Disorganized Hot Zone 55
Chapter 5: We... Are... Family?? 95
Chapter 6: Gotta Stay Sharp 130
Chapter 7: Emotional... Old-Manhunt 152
Chapter 8: Phantom Limb Retaliation 170
Chapter 9: Cities Underneath 196
Chapter 10: Your "Presents" is Requested 224
Chapter 11: A Dangerous Trap 272
Chapter 12: Moving Forward 299
Chapter 13: Super Sibling Squabble 316
Chapter 14: Inner Cyberspace 345
Chapter 15: Cyber Rumble in the Bronx 370
Chapter 16: Meeting Friends 391
Chapter 17: Blitzkrieg Beginning 407
Chapter 18: Amborg Texas Two-Step 426
Chapter 19: Humanity's Future 445
Chapter 20: The Not-So-Great Escape 478
Chapter 21: Wait, Watt Now?? 500
Chapter 22: Convenient Miracle Mile 514
Chapter 23: Hurricane Serina 43 531
Chapter 24: A-"maze"-ing Nightmare 546
Chapter 25: Grand Showdown 563
Chapter 26: We Have Vacation Days? 578
Chapter 27: Future Aspirations 591
Chapter 28: Finding Their Own Path 602
Chapter 29: Legacy 619
Chapter 30: Peace 626
Epilogue 635
Inheritance of a Generation 640
A.I. Industries Database Personnel Files.................................... 672

Prologue

Amborg Industries, or A.I. Industries for short, was initially and still is a place dedicated to science. There are several things that aren't known to the public, though, despite its popularity. For instance, no one knows where it's actually located and everyone there would prefer to keep it that way. It is kept a secret by every single person on the staff and their security list. It makes Congress look like a preschool. Employees are personally interviewed by Dr. Kendrick himself, who greatly values loyalty. Remember that name. His name is probably the very reason this story is written. Anyway, anyone affiliated with A.I. Industries live onsite, room and board, all expenses paid. The job applications keep coming in from every college graduate around the country and overseas. If you somehow manage to land a job, then you enter a new world where you'll be working with an incredibly unique group of individuals. These individuals are not exactly normal. Not anymore. Dr. Kendrick prefers to call them a very special group of... children. Young adults or teenagers would probably be more politically correct. They are not affiliated with law enforcement or any private military organization, but they were created for a few important reasons. It's all about taking evolution to the next level and fighting for humanity. Although that might not be specific enough for most audiences, let us return to the specifics at A.I. Industries and what the company does. We will get back to the special individuals, the characters of this story, in a bit. Promise.

The first thing that I would say to describe what you need to learn about A.I. Industries is that it's not a school. It isn't a retirement home, a factory, or has anything to do with artificial intelligence production. The company's name is Amborg Industries, which makes up the acronym A.I., and Dr. Kendrick thought it'd be clever to make us say, "Industries Industries." Despite the fact that one section of the complex is made up entirely of classrooms, it isn't a place that common high schoolers can attend. One might assume that it's a private school, like Hogwarts or Professor X's mansion, and they would be partially correct. The curriculum there covers just about everything. Well... everything about the known world that is. These classes range from philosophy, art, and music, to physics, and so on. Pretty much, any class elective you can think of, there is an eighty-six percent chance they teach it. If you're wondering what the students there are like, well, then you're about to find out.

They are known to the public by classification, known to each other by their name and numbers, and known by their own individual stories. Quite remarkable, in my opinion. If you had the time to sit through their life stories, which would literally take forever, then Dr. Kendrick would be able to explain how special each of them are. What are their names? They have regular first names, but their last names are numbers. I know that sounds a little complicated. These individuals are named for the company that made them. They are known as, you probably already guessed it, the amborgs.

It does sound like a weird name to give to a group of people that are and have been special for generations. Dr. Kendrick, when he came up with the idea, hoped it would be iconic while admitting it was a peculiar but unique name. In fact, it wasn't even spelled the way it is now. It was a typo; can you believe that? Originally, the word amborg was a combination of the words anthropological cyborg. It was supposed to spell "anborg" but thanks to a news reporter that misheard, a typo was put into the broadcast making the word amborg. Interestingly enough, the name just stuck, and everyone got used to the accidentally edited title. Several of the leading scientists in the world prefer it that way. My friend John Kendrick eventually agreed that amborg is actually a lot easier to say. They don't care what you call them.

If it hasn't been made clear already, an amborg is a step up in human evolution. When you combine anthropology and cybernetics together it results in a half-human half-robot hybrid. Dr. Kendrick created the world's first cyborg. Over a short period of time, he organized a team, and now they call themselves a family. The amborgs look human but are equipped with the advanced capabilities of a computer with minimal flaws. Plus, they possess the typical strengths and skills of a cyborg—speed, intelligence, and strength. It's a bit terrifying, but also an awesome demonstration of their power. Initially, there were problems with the First Group amborgs. But eventually, with the coming of the second group amborgs, they overcame these issues. This is that story. Where to begin though, that is the real question, isn't it? So have fun. Welcome to a new world. The future is here.

The not too distant future:

Most of the staff were not on duty during the evening hours, which made it fairly convenient for Mandy Walker, one of the senior instructors and technicians at A.I. Industries. Night classes were her favorite because most of the time, it was silent. She disliked being interrupted by loud noises or any distractions when she was about to give lessons. Her footsteps echoed across the hallway as she walked to her designated classroom. She spotted one of the guards down the hall chatting with a custodian. They both looked at her and smiled, acknowledging her presence, to which she smiled back before entering the classroom. It was labeled 312 next to the door.

The door hissed open and she stepped inside. When she was clear, it chimed as it closed. As it slid across the frame, the door clicked as it secured in place, and she took a moment to survey her surroundings.

The classroom was designed in a tiered fashion, resembling a miniature auditorium. Mandy walked forward and began to descend some steps towards the front. On her right, there were curved tables shaped like crescent moons, while straight desks lined her left side with every step. The classroom was spacious enough for at least 50 students, but tonight, she only needed to talk to one.

She strolled by the podium on the ground floor, right in front of the large display screen. Her lesson plan was saved on her computer tucked away in the corner of the room.

As she made her way over to her desk, her monitor detected her presence and lit up. She allowed the camera to look at her face. Once it acquired her in the camera frame, her facial ID unlocked the first security measure. A black bar appeared and her keyboard popped out of the desk. Mandy entered her password into her computer and the screen unlocked.

She checked the time on her watch and the clock in the room as she took her seat. She was exactly five minutes early for her private tutoring session. Mandy turned her gaze across the room to one of the cabinets that sat at the other end. Perhaps she could brew some coffee. She had a personal coffee machine hidden in the back for whenever she needed some emergency caffeine. One of her students had given it to her as a gift when the cafeteria coffee grinders had malfunctioned and died for a few weeks. Without coffee, she had gone through a rather small type of hell. The gifted machine was one of her favorite presents that she had ever received. It certainly saved her a lot of time and also was a nice way to get around any long lines or crowds in the cafeteria attempting to hog the drink machines. The temptation had her standing up as she felt the cravings for a cup. Unfortunately, before she could even step away from her chair, there was a chime at the door, halting her in her tracks.

"I guess I'm not the only one who likes being somewhere early," Mandy let out a sigh of dismay as she stared at the door. Her shoulders drooped as she cleared her throat and spoke loudly. "Come on in!"

The door opened, revealing a tall figure. Mandy smiled as a young woman walked in with a very neutral expression. She had glowing green neon stripes that stretched from her shoulders all the way down her arms. Another stripe started at her neckline, running straight down and wrapping around her waist. Her pants featured stripes that trailed down the sides of her thighs to her ankles. A bright, glowing "A" adorned her breast pocket, signaling one thing: this young woman was an amborg. Mandy, on the other hand, opted for an outfit with darker color schemes. Her business jacket and long office skirt were completely devoid of neon stripes, highlighting the contrast in their statuses. Having mentored, trained, and supervised so many of them, she always found herself admiring their bright, glowing uniforms.

There were times when she couldn't help but feel a bit envious of one particular physical trait that set them apart from normal humans. The amborgs managed to look young no matter how long they lived after their cybernetic enhancement. When Dr. Kendrick created the very first amborgs, they had discovered an unexpected side effect. Not only did their new cybernetic upgrades extend their lifespans tenfold, it also slowed their aging.

Shoving that thought aside, Mandy redirected her attention to the reason they were both in her classroom. She gestured for her student to take a seat in the front row instead of her usual spot in the middle. The young amborg hesitated, glancing between her regular seat and the one in front. After a moment, she quietly complied, her footsteps making soft thuds down each step as she made her way over and settled into the new chair.

"Good evening Mrs. Walker," she said without even flashing a smile.

This made Mandy sigh a little. Not this again. She shook her head and let out a soft groan. The young amborg tilted her head slightly, wondering if what she had said was wrong.

"How many times have I told you Sarah," Mandy spoke cheerfully, "one, call me Mandy. You can do that when it's just us. Two, remember your human etiquette classes? Always remember to smile every now and then. But, to continue with a proper response, good evening to you as well."

"I apologize," Sarah looked downwards but then shifted her eyes back up to Mandy. "Everyone refers to you as Mrs. Walker during your classes. Personally, I also believe that smiling is redundant as I can find no correlation with that action to happiness at all. Perhaps my programming is malfunctioning."

Even if she was trying to give her a proper answer, Sarah sounded like such a robot.

This was how they always talked. Cybernetic enhancement seemed to do a pretty good job at wiping out their personalities, leaving only the bare minimum. It would take a lot of time for their emotions to return to normal levels.

"No one's perfect Sarah, even when someone has an advanced supercomputer in their brain," Mandy said as she grabbed a data pad and synchronized it to the screen at the front of the room. The projector turned on and the wall lit up. "In the classroom setting, yes, it's Mrs. Walker. I agree. But, when it's just us, I'd prefer it if you used my first name. The conversation is more personal and I want to be your friend, not your teacher right now. I use all of your first names because they make you who you are. Dr. Kendrick does the same for all of you."

"But our first names are informal," Sarah frowned. "Amborgs have numbers which are shorter and faster to say."

"Also true. Yes," Mandy said. She had learned to be patient with the amborgs' observations and continued to smile. "It is, but I feel it's a much better way to get to know you if I use the names you were born with instead of just using your numbers. Your numbers are cool and a nice way to distinguish all of you but so are your names. I completely understand that among the amborgs, your numbers camouflage your last names but I happen to be one of the few oddballs who likes calling out your names and not the numbers. You mustn't forget who you've always been. Even with a high powered mind and superhuman strength, you were still born as a human."

"Very well. If that is your choice. Also there is a flaw within that statement. Amborgs do not forget. Our long-term memory is entirely accurate."

"It's a play on words Sarah," Mandy smiled, her eye twitching slightly, "but then again, that was always something I dealt with the early generation amborgs when I was still only a technician. And actually, it's one of the minor subjects I'm hoping to be able to teach you in this lesson. The subject is amborg David 117."

Sarah perked up at this name. The way her eyes seemed to glint with recognition made Mandy nod her head. His name was legendary.

"David 117," she stated, "Second Group amborg. Records show that he was the first amborg you were partnered with."

"I chose to be his technician," Mandy corrected Sarah's statement. "Many years ago."

"His reputation is very well-known and he has a list of many great accomplishments in the history files of A.I. Industries," Sarah replied. "There are possibly thousands of data files that hold all of his deeds, his merits, and stories, all contained in terabytes of information."

"Very good," Mandy opened the file that she had prepared on her screen and made sure it was connected to Sarah's monitor. "Nice to see that long-term memory working perfectly."

The blank but curious expression that Sarah displayed made her clear her throat and she turned back to the screen.

"Anyway," she said confidently, "I thought that a look into some of the video files and reports that 117 and I made so long ago would give you some insight into how even the slowest of amborgs could re-discover their full personality and arsenal of human emotions. You remind me so much of him that in a way, I have a hunch this might help teach you something. Computer, unlock files and begin the presentation please?"

As the files began to play, Mandy looked up quickly at Sarah who was waiting curiously for the files to run the playback.

"Alright," she said to the silent amborg, "let's begin."

CHAPTER 1

Unexpected Inception

A.I. Industries
2135 September

"So what model drone are you? You don't seem like one of the new ones that the military uses. Uh... hello?"

Footsteps echoed through the hall as two individuals strolled to their destination. A high school senior followed the mechanical figure in front of him as he tried to get its attention.

Brad had seen almost every make and type of drone that was in service. He had always heard the stories that A.I. Industries employed older ones in their security division. It was really strange that the company didn't like to use the current models. Brad let out a sigh when he was ignored.

"Never mind," he mumbled. "I don't think it's your job to care about someone like me."

"On the contrary..."

The drone abruptly stopped and eerily turned around to face him. A soft and warm yellow light shining from its vertical faceplate gazed back at him.

"I am under orders to ensure that your visit with us is the highest priority," it stated politely. "High school senior Brad is to be protected, cared for, and given the highest level of service at all times during his time here. As instructed by Dr. John Kendrick himself."

"He said that?" Brad gazed at the drone in amazement. "For real?"

"I did not stutter."

The drone turned around and proceeded forward without another word. Brad felt excited as he eagerly ran to catch up with it.

Reinvigorated, Brad couldn't help but smile as they arrived at their destination.

"Dr. Kendrick has set aside this conference room for your time," the drone informed him as it courteously opened the door. "Please wait here."

Brad stepped over the threshold and looked around. The door hissed shut behind him as he made his way to the center of the room. There, a large, elongated circular table stood with a glowing blue stripe running along its edge. The chairs positioned around it were marked with neon square outlines, indicating where people were meant to sit. Noticing some photos on the wall, Brad decided to check out the other cool things on display.

Video screens hung on the walls, and as he approached them, a holographic overlay materialized in front of him. Floating in midair were left and right arrow keys, and he curiously pointed a finger at the right arrow. Without touching it, a sensor somewhere in the wall behind the video screen sensed his motion and changed the image. As he continued to "press" the right arrow key, photos of A.I. Industries appeared before him.

When he moved to the next video screen and began playing with the arrow keys, a collection of photos featuring staff members from various departments popped up. The next screen displayed some beautiful scenery, but it was the final image, just before the end, that snagged his attention.

As Brad neared the last video screen, he noticed it was positioned right next to a rather luxurious office chair that occupied the head of the table. This had to be Dr. Kendrick's designated seat for meetings or discussions. The same holographic interface appeared in front of him, and he began to sift through the images.

Unlike the previous video screen that displayed pictures of A.I. Industries employees without any names or text, this one was notably different. It featured a wider array of staff members, including George Ramirez, the head of PR, and Security Chief A. Malayno. She must have put in a request to have her first name concealed from public view. As he continued to sift through the images of a few more rather important-looking A.I. Industries figures, he found himself fixated on two particular pictures.

In a classic portrait-style photo, a striking woman with long, straight brown hair and glasses exuded charm in her business attire and white lab coat. She beamed at the camera, radiating beauty. Brad couldn't help but notice that her last name was missing from the display—only her first name, Melissa, was visible in the image, leaving her last name a mystery.

"Must be important," Brad muttered as he continued on to the next photo. "Oh, who are these two?"

The next photo featured a man and a woman, both smiling pleasantly at the camera. However, Brad couldn't shake the feeling that they looked oddly familiar. He glanced at the names printed at the bottom of the photo. How

"Dr. Ethan Kendrick and Dr. Susan Kendrick," Brad read the names out loud. Then his eyes widened as he realized who these two had to be. "Wow. I know these names."

Ethan Kendrick had a stern but polite smile as he held himself in a rather dignified and proper pose. Susan, on the other hand, seemed to give off a rather gentle and warm vibe as she cheerfully grinned.

"Having fun?"

Brad jumped and whirled around to see that someone had stealthily entered the conference room. The door had slid open and closed so fast that he hadn't heard it at all. A man stood in the entryway, smirking. Looking closely, Brad noticed that he bore similar features to the couple in the photo he had just been admiring. He had Ethan Kendrick's cheekbones and the same kind of glasses, but his smile looked just like Susan's. This had to be their son, the man he had come to see, Dr. John Kendrick himself. The man, the myth, and the legend. Well, that's what his classmates had always said.

Dr. Kendrick strode confidently into the room, his lab coat billowing with each purposeful step, which made Brad shrink back in awe. While he didn't give off an intimidating presence, the class difference between the two was colossal. Now that he was in the same room as him, Brad noticed another interesting detail: they were nearly the same height. He had always imagined Dr. Kendrick to be taller.

"Uh, I... I was just..."

"Curious?" Dr. Kendrick raised his eyebrows and chuckled. "It's perfectly natural. Especially in a place like this."

Brad nodded, feeling uncertain about where to put his hands. He instinctively reached for the straps of his backpack, contemplating whether to take it off his shoulders. After a moment of hesitation, he clasped his fingers together. With a hint of nervousness, he introduced himself.

"I'm Brad! I'm a senior trying to do research!"

"I am aware of that," Dr. Kendrick let out another soft chuckle. "You're the one who sent over 500 emails, called us 200 times, and sent in a lot of fan mail."

"Yeah..." Brad mumbled sheepishly. He began to blush as he lifted a hand behind the back of his head. "I kind of went overboard."

"You look like you're about to fall over," Dr. Kendrick gestured to the table. "Have a seat."

Brad managed to make it over to the table and grabbed a chair. He let his backpack drop to the floor and unzipped it. As he rummaged through his stuff, he felt some of the pressure disappear when he looked away from Dr. Kendrick. He fished out his data pad and, sitting up straight, placed it on the table, swallowing hard.

He had expected Dr. Kendrick to come around to sit at his side or at the big chair. This would help him avoid making direct eye contact during his interview. Instead, Dr. Kendrick had chosen to sit in the seat directly across from him. He immediately began to feel himself sweating profusely.

"You're not going to sit in your... big chair??" he asked nervously.

"I figured that this would be the best way to talk to you," Dr. Kendrick smiled. "Not as a CEO or one of the most powerful scientists on the planet. I thought you were here to talk as a friend. I think this chair is less intimidating than my big chair."

Brad nodded. This answer did make him feel a little relieved. If Dr. Kendrick was willing to be casual with him, maybe this wouldn't be so bad after all. He had cleared the entire day so he could begin his project. He cheerfully picked up his data pad from the table, switched it on, and pulled the stylus out. He began to jot down notes and nodded.

"May I call you John, sir?"

He clamped his mouth shut. Brad had looked away and tried to make that question sound casual, but his eyes widened when he realized how nonchalant he had delivered his words. The atmosphere of the room wasn't supposed to be intimidating at all, yet he still found it nerve wracking to be there.

"I can't believe..." he stammered as he felt the blood rushing to his face, "...I just asked that."

Dr. Kendrick let out a laugh.

"Well, I did suggest that we try talking to each other as friends," he smiled. "Do you mind if I call you Brad?"

"Of course!"

"As for calling me John," Dr. Kendrick lifted a hand and began fiddling with his glasses. Pondering quietly, he let out a quiet murmur, "We'll see about that. For starters, why don't you tell me what you're writing about? This must be one important homework assignment for you."

"Yes it is! It really is sir, uh, Dr. Kendrick... Oops!"

Brad fumbled and dropped the stylus, which made a mildly loud tap on the smooth polished floor. He clambered out of his seat and bent down to pick it up. Upon retrieving his tool, he rose too quickly and smacked his head into the edge of the table.

"Ack!" he exclaimed.

Rubbing his head, Brad sheepishly sat back in his seat as Dr. Kendrick watched in amusement.

"Huh...Do I look that old?"

Dr. Kendrick raised his right hand and examined it carefully as Brad bowed his head forward and continued to massage where he had hit his head.

"Hmm, curious. I see a few wrinkles starting to show but I doubt that's a definite sign."

Brad nodded apologetically. He wasn't sure if it was from the pain but he tried to regain his composure. In his tense state however, he fumbled and the stylus fell onto the table. This was not that great of a start.

"Uh no sir. I meant…" he stammered as his eyes quickly tried to follow the stylus and he leaned forward to try and catch it. He only succeeded in launching it towards Dr. Kendrick. "Shoot!"

Dr. Kendrick patiently smiled as he lifted a hand and put it down. Catching the stylus and pinning it to the table, he curled his fingers and held it up in his hands. He gently tossed it back to Brad.

"Calm down," he said reassuringly and motioned for Brad to sit back in his chair. He was still nervous, but at least he had managed to stop fidgeting. Dr. Kendrick looked him over once before continuing. "There is nothing to be nervous about. Forget for a moment of what I do for a living. Treat me like you would anyone else you meet."

"Begging your pardon, sir, ha ha…" Brad let out a shaky laugh, "but you are one of the smartest scientists in the entire world. You own and run A.I. Industries. I don't think I can really look past all of that."

"Try," Dr. Kendrick replied softly. "Then you'll see how there's no need to be on edge. Take a deep breath. Just… talk to me as if you're speaking to your parents or someone you enjoy hanging out with."

Brad took a deep breath and coughed a few times. He straightened up and prepared to write.

"Thanks Doctor."

Dr. Kendrick looked Brad over a few more times, then turned his head to look past his shoulder and out the window at the skyline. He decided to ask a question before the young student could.

"Before we begin, I'd like to ask why you decided to write your essay about my work. Sure, it's flattering but not normally what someone of your age range is typically interested in."

"Really?" Brad stared curiously.

"It's usually college kids who really have the levels of enthusiasm that you have displayed," Dr. Kendrick nodded. "Never before have I met a high-school student as passionate as you. Especially one with such entertaining and very excellent credentials."

"You... looked up my transcripts??" Brad's eyes widened.

"We do a lot of background checks around here. I can't claim responsibility for looking into your academic records. One of my A.I. programs did," Dr. Kendrick chuckled sheepishly. "They were checking up on you to make sure you weren't another crazy person. Clearly, since we allowed you to be here, that seems pretty definitive."

"That's very... thorough," Brad blushed.

He felt slightly insulted that other people at A.I. Industries would consider the possibility of him being another psychopath. However, as he began to think about it, it was understandable from Dr. Kendrick's perspective. He probably had to deal with a lot of unusual people before.

"Thank you," Dr. Kendrick nodded. "So, what interests you about A.I. Industries?"

"Well," he fidgeted a bit more but looked at the Doctor's silhouette, "I think that your work in cybernetics is truly incredible. I think that your work in cybernetics is very amazing. Not a lot of my classmates really care, but I do because what you do is bigger than all of us and I want to be a part of that. Most of my friends just want to make it to graduation, but I was hoping to get better insight into what you do so I can show them how what you've done has helped the world they live in. Everyone knows how famous you are, but they just don't know about you and the amborgs at a personal level. There are only the stories. The real inspiration to me is seeing them in action. Teenagers that look almost like me doing great things and I want to hear it all directly from you. It was like someone granted my wish when you agreed to let me come here. Opportunities like this are like gold, but it's really making me edgy because I want to savor everything about this."

"Well, I did have to reply to you at some point," Dr. Kendrick admitted bluntly. "Reading your letters was a nice way to pass time. After your eighty-seventh letter, I figured I knew you to the point that it merited a response. You mentioned in several of them that you were hoping to one day sign on here after your schooling was finished. Which position are you considering? Artificial Intelligence Development? Drone Research? Technician Placement?"

"Umm, actually I was hoping to be submitted for cybernetic augmentation. To be one of them."

Dr. Kendrick's smile faded. His eyes narrowed as he tilted his head forward. Brad felt uneasy again. The mood changed quite drastically as Dr. Kendrick seemed to be burrowing into his soul with a sharp and piercing gaze.

"No," he declared firmly without taking his eyes off of Brad. "Don't take this the wrong way but unfortunately, I refuse your request. Ask me again and this meeting is over."

It was probably the fastest that Brad had ever been turned down. Even faster than when he got rejected by Vivian Becker, one of the most popular girls at his school. He gulped, feeling his heart begin to pound. Everything felt hollow as each beat in his chest echoed in his mind. Did he already mess this whole thing up before it even began?

Dr. Kendrick sighed and placed his elbows on the table. Clasping his hands together, he rested his chin on his thumbs and shook his head.

"I know you're going to ask why," he said in a calm and polite manner. "That look of confusion in your eyes, I've seen it before, and I'm going to tell you it's dangerous. I appreciate the fact that you're willing to volunteer for it, but I refuse that here and now."

"But why?" Brad wrote the word 'dangerous' on his notepad. "I figured that the augmentation procedure was perfected after the Third Group's success."

"True," Dr. Kendrick nodded, "but still, no. The reason being that you have other priorities. Mmm, or rather, you have more important responsibilities, and you shouldn't throw your life down a path that is, in my opinion, irreversible."

"More so than an amborg's responsibilities? What could be more important than being a scientifically enhanced robotic organism capable of... a lot?? They are the strongest human beings in existence."

Dr. Kendrick nodded and pushed away from the table. The chair slid back and he stood up. Brad followed his movement, watching as he slid his hand across the headrest of the CEO's chair. When he came around to his side, he let out a soft chuckle.

"An excellent question, actually, but there's a really complicated answer that comes with it," Dr. Kendrick said, placing a hand on Brad's shoulder and gestured towards the door. "I can tell you for sure that it won't be easy to explain here. Why don't we take a walk and make it a personal tour? You good at taking notes while walking?"

Brad froze, nearly dropping his stylus. His eyes widened in disbelief, and his jaw fell slack. That was not what he expected during this visit.

"Into the facility?" he rapidly glanced between the door and Dr. Kendrick, his expression lighting up. "Seriously? THE facility itself?! You're kidding! You mean I'll be allowed to see them in person?"

"Well... not too much, just enough for you to understand what we've created here."

As they left the room, they proceeded left and walked down the hall. Brad's gaze fell upon the wall, where he noticed something intricately carved into the surface. It was something he had overlooked until now, but as he concentrated, he realized there was a myriad of tiny numbers etched in various spots. Before he could ask the significance, Dr. Kendrick and activated a console that immediately lit up.

"Who's online?"

He hadn't spoken to anyone in particular, but his voice had been picked up by the screen. The console beeped and a female voice filled the hallway.

"Greetings Dr. Kendrick, CEO of Amborg Industries, representative to multiple law enforcement detachments worldwide, official consultant for the United Nations and Creator of the Amborg. Artificial Intelligence Serina is available and reporting to you shortly."

The console flashed a brilliant bright light from a projector which caused Brad to wince and shield his eyes. When he lowered his hand, he watched in awe as a floating holographic image began to form in front of them thanks to the miniature light show. Pixels began to form and solidify immediately in the form of a small three-dimensional figure. As it came into view, they could see that it was a doll-sized human, an artificial intelligence with a holographic visual form. She was also a little cute. A young dark haired girl in average clothing appeared and smiled.

After a bit of time and effort, an A.I. program could manifest a visual representation of itself if it chose to. Unlike a standard virtual intelligence with limited functions, an A.I. was much more advanced and had a stronger self-awareness, which is what made them so unique and powerful. In a lot of pop culture and portrayals in film, tv shows, and other media, there always seemed to be depictions of A.I. as mankind's doom. In their world, it was quite common for large corporations and businesses to have them on hand. A.I. Industries was one of those companies.

Brad stared wide-eyed at a light blue silhouette of the A.I. in front of him. She beamed up at him with a warm and kind smile, even though she was partially see-through. Dr. Kendrick looked extremely pleased to see her.

"Ah Serina! Perfect! I was going to ask for you anyway," Dr. Kendrick smiled. "This here is Brad and he's going to be coming along with us on a special tour."

He pulled Brad forward, who had begun to slink backwards. He straightened up and extended a hand. But then he remembered he had just offered his hand to a holographically projected figure and retracted it quickly. She dipped her head courteously and stifled a laugh.

"Wow... Uh I mean," he gaped at Serina as she pulled a holographic top-hat out of nowhere in particular and tried it on. "You're an A.I.?"

"Bingo! Aren't you the observant one?" she winked.

"Serina is one of our best A.I. programs living here," Dr. Kendrick explained. "She has a rare design in her code."

Serina gave a slight look of disgust and threw her hat away. The hat disappeared in a flash of pixels and she looked back at the two of them with a huge grin.

"Oh, really?" Brad asked with concern. "Life-saving code? Or end-of-the-world code?"

Serina let out a chuckle, and Brad couldn't help but stare in surprise. An A.I. was casually laughing at his response? He suddenly thought about how the drones he had interacted with always spoke in a really dull monotone. Serina was very different in comparison. It felt as if he were conversing with an actual human being.

"The short answer is my personality was flash-cloned from someone else!" she replied.

"The... technology where someone creates a digital carbon-copy of their brain?" Brad asked. "Who was your original host?"

"Oh, she's been dead for a while," Serina replied, lifting a finger up to her mouth, as if keeping a secret. "I am all that's left."

Brad felt goosebumps across his body. Chills shot up his spine as he glanced nervously at Dr. Kendrick.

"Isn't that technique of creating an A.I. illegal?" Brad whispered.

"I can still hear you," Serina interrupted casually, "no matter how much you lower your speaking voice."

Brad turned his attention back to Serina, who had put her hands on her hips. They watched as she began to impatiently tap her foot in annoyance as she floated in midair. Bright lights flashed from her toes.

"I'm sorry!" Brad apologized quickly. "It's just...! Isn't there a law that prohibits artificial intelligence programs from copying real people?"

"I think the one that you're thinking of is Temerson's cyber accords. I believe it's the Ninth rule," Dr. Kendrick informed them. "It advises all A.I. and V.I. programs to never impersonate, steal, borrow, or abuse anyone's identity."

"I can read all of the Ninth if you'd like," Serina offered pleasantly. "It's only four pages."

"Uh, no thanks," Brad chuckled nervously. "But... Doesn't that mean...? Did you just admit to violating the Ninth rule?"

"Nope," Serina shook her head optimistically. "My personality profile came from a real person who eventually died but this visual appearance that I have is formally registered. I'll spare you the boring bits and let you know that I am completely legal."

Serina blinked and then looked away in embarrassment. Brad watched her glowing figure turn a deep shade of blood red.

"That sounded wrong..." she mumbled. Then she changed to a light green color. "Or was it?"

"She sure is unique," Brad nodded slowly as he glanced at Dr. Kendrick. "Just like you said. Is Serina always this outgoing?"

"Yes," Dr. Kendrick replied bluntly, biting his lip and nodding firmly. "Before her original host passed away, I managed to accumulate as much data about her to convert her personality into an A.I. She's one of a kind."

"That's... interesting?" Brad shuddered.

Dr. Kendrick gave him a reassuring smile as Serina created an orb of light in her hands and juggled it around playfully. She looked up at Brad and tilted her head.

"He doesn't look too thrilled about my origin story," she noted.

"It's alright Brad, we're not trying to scare you off," Dr. Kendrick added, also noticing Brad's anxious expression. "But just be aware of a few things. Becoming an amborg or having your mind copied to create an A.I. requires a huge sacrifice. If things don't go the right way, you could find yourself in an early grave. That's one reason you need to think carefully about augmentation. Even if successful, if you have second thoughts, it will be next to impossible to go back. Now, I think we've lingered here long enough. Don't you agree?"

"Umm...," Brad stared at the floor and looked at his data pad. He had stopped writing, unsure of what to put down. "I'm not sure..."

"Say yes! I'm kinda getting bored here," Serina piped up after the awkward silence. She turned her eyes down in embarrassment when Dr. Kendrick gave her a look. "Heh, sorry. It's just that we rarely get visitors. I mean, visitors on the younger side. Seeing someone new is always a nice change. No offense to our security guards, the other scientists, and the janitorial staff of course."

"Yes!" Brad piped up, "I mean, yes, I'm ready. I've been waiting my whole life for this."

Dr. Kendrick motioned for Brad to follow, and he led them down the hall. Brad realized that Serina didn't have to walk, instead she floated alongside them like a little fairy guide. He realized that there were thin strips of neon lights along the walls that contained small projectors. These light strips matched Serina's colors as she moved with them. As they continued down the hall, the projectors in the wall lit up in sequence to keep Serina from disappearing. It was like being followed by a classroom projector on a cart.

"Is that how you travel?" he asked curiously.

"Yes," Serina smiled. "Normally, I can go much faster than this when I disappear from view. But, over time, it's considered rude to zoom off when we have company."

"The A.I.s all seem to behave like ghosts in our walls," Dr. Kendrick joked. "They can just pop up anywhere as long as they have a strong signal to broadcast."

"It must be fun," Brad commented.

"It is," Serina grinned. She lifted both hands and pointed in various directions. "I love being here, here, here, over there, there, up above, behind you, below, anywhere. I see everything!"

"Serina," Dr. Kendrick said in a cautious tone.

"Kidding," Serina replied cheekily. "I can see everything but... I respect your privacy at all times. That's why there are a lot of quiet rooms built here."

Before Brad could ask what those rooms were like, Dr. Kendrick stopped them at a closed door. There was a sign that said "Residential Common A" on the panel next to the door frame, along with a keypad and some kind of scanner with a bright red indicating it was locked.

"Ok Brad," Dr. Kendrick waved at it and the sensor light shifted from red to green. With a loud hiss, the door slid open to the right. "Once we go through here, you're going to see something really awesome. I hope your heart is prepared for what you're about to see."

"Residential Area A," an automated voice announced as the door hissed open. "Amborg housing, data storage, and family center."

Dr. Kendrick and Brad stepped through while Serina followed. She floated along the hallway with them as a light emitter on the other side of the door activated and allowed her to maintain her form.

"Here's my favorite part of the tour," she said enthusiastically. "Or rather, all of it is my favorite."

Brad could not believe what he was seeing. He was actually in the place where the amborgs lived. A real behind-the-scenes up close tour just for him. He wasn't sure whether to feel excited or faint as he struggled to absorb everything around him. There was one question building at the forefront of his mind, one that he had hoped to ask Dr. Kendrick since he was a child, but his mind was flooded with countless other thoughts. What should he ask first?

"Dr. Kendrick," he said, taking several breaths to clear his head. "All of this is amazing. I have a million questions!"

"I'd assume so, otherwise I'd think you're crazy if you claimed you only had one," Dr. Kendrick winked. "What's on your mind?"

"Well, for starters, where did you get the inspiration for all of this?"

"Would you believe me if I told you I had a dream about it? If the spirit of Dr. Martin Luther King would permit me to use that type of phrase under these circumstances, then that's the simplest answer I can give you for a start. It was because I had a dream."

Brad scribbled the word 'dream' onto his data pad but then found himself drawing a question mark next to the word. Was this the whole truth?

"So, you're saying that the reason that the amborgs exist today," he spoke, lifting his stylus and pointing it at Dr. Kendrick, "is entirely because you dreamt about it? That sounds like a cliché right out of a children's storybook. They have been helping the world for so many years and this all started from a single thought?"

"How else is it supposed to manifest into something great?" Dr. Kendrick replied with a curt smile. "All of the most brilliant ideas and scientific achievements were created because someone thought of it. Dreams are one of the best ways to come up with creative ideas."

He gestured toward a nearby window as they moved along. As Brad glanced through, he noticed a lab of some kind on the other side of the glass. It looked relatively small compared to the larger ones he'd seen earlier. Inside, an amborg was collaborating with a security guard, instructing one of the caretaker drones on a few things.

He recognized the figure as an amborg because of the distinctive uniform he wore. Neon blue stripes ran down the sides of his sleeves and pants, and another traced the center of his jacket. Brad's eyes were drawn to the glowing number 227 on his left breast pocket. There was a shoulder patch on the uniform too, but the boy labeled 227 was moving around, making it difficult for Brad to make out what it was.

Brad observed as amborg 227 reached for a coffee mug resting on a table in front of him. The drone attempted to grasp its own mug, but it shorted out and fell over. The loud noise drew the attention of the two people inside, who stared in dismay. 227 looked at the guard, who appeared equally baffled. They both turned to the window and made eye contact with Dr. Kendrick. Feeling a bit uncomfortable, Brad shifted his gaze to Serina, who was clearing her throat, and then to Dr. Kendrick, who let out a nervous chuckle. He casually motioned for the group to keep moving.

"There were rough patches and there still are to this day, but thankfully, my ideas came to light and became a reality when people said it couldn't be done," he said as they entered another hall. "It did start from something small. All big things start like that. Look at the way people or animals are born, how we design buildings, go traveling somewhere, assemble armies, start families, go to college, make money, or help others. These are all things that start from the most basic and abstract thoughts in our mind. It just takes a great deal to develop it into something fantastic for the world to idolize. If you're motivated, you will pursue it."

"You're not going to write that down?"

Turning around, Brad noticed Serina staring at his data pad. He had only written a few notes before pausing to listen to Dr. Kendrick's lengthy explanation. It was as if he had just wrapped up a podcast, with a calming British voice narrating a sweet bedtime story. It had temporarily distracted him.

"Uhh," he muttered. "Can you repeat that again, Doctor? Any of that?"

Dr. Kendrick looked a little crestfallen at the notion.

"I have that all recorded if you need to listen to that again," Serina whispered. "He's not really good at repeating inspirational quips that he just came up with."

Dr. Kendrick let out a sigh and smiled kindly.

"Just write down 'dreams inspire outcomes,'" he replied thoughtfully. "It is the choices of every single individual, be it amborg or human, that decide the final outcomes of whatever it is they put their minds to. Good things, yes. But always remember that there are bad things in the world too. I would be lying if I told you that we live in a perfect world. Even with all my contributions."

"What exactly did you see in your dream doctor?" Brad asked as they stopped outside another room.

"Well, it's better to show you a tidbit of what I dreamt."

There was a bold gray number on the door, illuminated by neon lights. Brad read the number 33 on the metallic surface. Dr. Kendrick raised his hand and knocked on the wall just to the right of it, leaving Brad puzzled about why he would knock there instead of on the door itself. Before he could ask, the wall vanished in an instant, and Brad gaped in awe. In its place was a window frame of transparent glass, revealing the room on the other side. Behind the glass stood a taller than average teenager, who smiled and waved back at them. Brad quickly realized this young man was also an amborg, dressed in a similar jacket with glowing stripes. His was light green with the number 33 printed on the left chest pocket.

"This is amborg 33," Serina said as the amborg inside turned away from the window. They watched him sit back down at his desk and resume his activities. "He seems to be enjoying some downtime."

Dr. Kendrick watched as 33 lifted a model car in his hands and held it up for them to see. Both he and Serina gave him a thumbs-up, and 33 returned to his modeling kit.

"Years ago, the amborg was a fresh idea in my mind," he explained as he motioned for Brad to step closer to the window. "I wanted to change the way we were treating the world and its inhabitants. So I thought, why not give it people who could be the change? I figured, why not put electronics inside someone and upgrade them? Unfortunately, several people said that this was too radical. They were right. After all, at the time, I was limited by the technology that was available to me. But I believed in what was possible despite the risks."

He nodded to Serina, who flashed a bright blue. A set of images appeared on 33's window. It revealed a young boy lying on a table, surrounded by specialists who were preparing some surgical machines. The images faded before it could reveal anything gruesome, which was good since Brad was starting to feel queasy.

"33 was one of the lucky ones, you see," Dr. Kendrick explained as they watched 33 slowly grab different parts and meticulously glued them together. "Then again, every amborg is lucky after they undergo a successful enhancement. Obviously, my original proposals for these projects weren't well-received. Naturally, I was on my own for a while. Nowadays, everyone is falling over each other to try and get in on the action at A.I. Industries. Almost all of the ethical concerns brought up back then have mostly or completely faded into the history books. Almost."

"But Doctor, if no one wanted to support you in your proposals, how did you get where you are now?" Brad asked as he kept writing down notes. Every now and then, he would look up to peer into 33's room to make sure he wasn't missing anything. "I mean, A.I. Industries is one of the biggest companies worldwide. It was the amborgs that kick-started all of the popularity and pretty much made this place what it is now."

"Very true," Dr. Kendrick agreed. "Before, however, it was definitely not a similar story. Which is why I have to give credit to my ancestors and my parents. When you're a third generation scientist, there was much to live up to and a lot that came from my family. Most of the initial research, equipment, and funding came from my own personal expenses and family fortune. I would have been broke if the amborg projects hadn't succeeded. Also, my reputation was seriously questioned."

"How so?"

Brad's question was answered by Serina.

"Well, because of the death rates."

Brad turned to look at Serina's solemn expression. Her luminescent hand came up and she scratched her cheek. She cleared her throat and looked down, avoiding the stunned gaze from Brad. Ashamed, she looked up nervously at Dr. Kendrick, but he merely smiled.

"Sorry," she said quickly. "You really didn't need to know that."

"It's alright, Serina. Sometimes the best way to tell the truth is to say it like it is," Dr. Kendrick shrugged. "You just saved me from having to find the words for it."

"Death rates?" Brad said questionably. "I was under the impression the death rates were extremely low. Well obviously, you can't make someone cybernetic without drawbacks but wasn't it ok? When the First Group amborgs appeared, we were told that all of them had survived the procedures with minimal negative effects."

"The media never really changes does it?" Dr. Kendrick said amusingly. "It has been a while since I last stepped off the grounds. Do they still say that sort of thing?"

"Seventy-eight percent of the statistics I found claim that the Second Group had no casualties whatsoever," Serina pointed out. "I just love when people assume they know the truth. News and media usually have a habit of posting first and never questioning anything correctly."

"The point in this case, Brad, is that you shouldn't be so quick to get your information straight from secondary sources," Dr. Kendrick added. "As much as the news likes to make it sound family-friendly, the unfortunate reality of it is much more harsh and upsetting. Not everyone accepts the truth for what it actually is. There was a high risk for failure and the public didn't care about dead test subjects. They only saw what they wanted and censored the rest. But here, too many lives were lost."

"If it was so bad..." Brad started to speak but was interrupted.

"Why did they all do it?" Serina asked with a smile.

"They all chose to," Dr. Kendrick answered promptly. "Once the public saw who they were, the Amborgs became a symbol of hope to a very chaotic time in this country and now we're making our mark on the world. What people don't really know is that they also carry a heavy legacy in order to honor the fallen."

"They chose to do it?" Brad asked with concern. "Sounds very harsh."

"Oh yes," Dr. Kendrick admitted. "As more and more amborgs came into being, I developed the ability to safely keep them alive. At great cost. Other scientists accused me of defying ethical codes of conduct. Many claimed I was manipulating human lives in order to accomplish my goals like a tyrant, but that wasn't so. Every person I found for the amborg projects were orphans, children that the world had turned their back on. Crippled, too young to be cast aside and struggling for their own survival on the ground they lay upon. I took it upon myself to offer them an opportunity to have a life different from their current one. Of course, I couldn't take in all of them, which was an added consequence. I offered these teenagers the opportunity to advance forward and gave them all the chances to do many spectacular things. I interviewed them myself and asked them if they wanted to volunteer. Every one of them who have survived to become an amborg or who died, accepted these terms. They knew the risks, had nothing to lose, and clung to their hope. I admired, even to this day, the courage they showed me. The human will inside of them was strong, which was heartbreaking, but something I could respect."

An eerie silence filled the corridor as Dr. Kendrick looked down sadly. The only thing that could be heard was the sound of their footsteps echoing off the walls. Serina stopped smiling, closed her eyes, and bowed her head.

"They will be remembered," she whispered. "Brothers and sisters who will rest in peace. Their memories will not disappear."

"Thank you Serina," Dr. Kendrick nodded as he pushed his glasses up his nose. Brad was filled with remorse.

"You interviewed them, understood them, and really learned about who they were," he said. "It must have been very personal for you. I'm sorry."

"It's alright. You should have seen when the government brought me in for a hearing," Dr. Kendrick explained. "I was initially charged with intended manslaughter... but then my amborgs fought for me. Not literally, of course. They banded together and argued about how their lives were better and that they chose this kind of life for themselves voluntarily. They absolutely refused to allow me to be locked away. Now that I had amborgs with me, they claimed that the future would be worth the costs inflicted. My biggest regret was trying to mass produce them. It's still a regret but seeing them in action makes me feel better. Remember kid, life is precious. We don't really notice that until we lose it."

"Wasn't there an incident with the military as well?"

Brad stopped. He'd remembered something he had read about a few years ago. Something about the amborgs appearance and performance in the field had led to the U.S. military coming about. Dr. Kendrick merely nodded when the subject was brought up.

"Yes there was Brad," he said. "Although, let me correct you. It wasn't actually an incident. It was more of a rebellious choice. The top brass in the government wanted the amborgs to be commissioned into service with the military. They figured the amborgs could be used to bring down some of their toughest enemies."

"What was wrong with that sort of thinking?"

"They wanted to use them like cannon fodder," Serina said with a huff. "There aren't a lot of military people that I trust and I have tons of code that draws the line whenever we get labeled as weapons."

"Blunt as usual Serina," Dr. Kendrick shook his head with a small chuckle. "From my perspective, I said at the time that their descriptions of them as weapons was demeaning and I refused to let them take control of the kids. The military witnessed their strength, skills, and abilities and wanted to exploit that without even trying to understand that amborgs continue to retain their feelings about humanity. They aren't mindless machines that just take orders. They have the capabilities of a commander leading an army but individually, that's their choice."

"But, the amborgs have fought with the police and military on many occasions?"

"We've maintained a steady alliance and friendship over the years," Dr. Kendrick nodded. "A couple of other events have taken place that have not been revealed to the public that almost shook the hornet's nest."

"Really? What kind of events?"

"The classified kind," Dr. Kendrick winked. "All I will say is, the amborgs each operate at their own discretion and I don't ever want the government to come in and try a rug pull on us."

"Ah. So that's where you draw the line," Brad stated his thoughts aloud.

"One that must never be crossed," he explained as he nodded again. "Well, it's a line that I personally drew and it serves as a guideline. Amborgs have their own individual free wills and choose what they want to do. They can set their own boundaries and then choose to do whatever their hearts desire. It really depends on what you ask each of them individually. Believe me, they do have their opinions."

As Brad listened, Dr. Kendrick pulled a small hand-held rod from his pocket and pressed his thumb onto the end. It lit up and showed a few video postings and newspaper articles. Several of them were about the amborgs and what appeared to be personal media interviews of them.

"Nowadays, there aren't that many conflicts for the amborgs to resolve anymore. If the military had taken them, I shudder at the idea of what would have happened to them in peacetime," Kendrick scrolled through all of the different videos and stopped at a certain clip. Brad watched a video of an amborg carrying two crates to a transport. "But I'm glad they have lots of fun working on their hobbies and doing other things for society in their free time."

Another video popped up, showing a few amborgs feeding homeless people sitting on the sidewalk. Brad then saw the image change to a video of an amborg working in the hospital. The scene quickly transitioned again, revealing a team of amborgs assembling a small building faster than any construction crew he had ever seen. He was about to ask Dr. Kendrick what sort of things they did for recreation when the videos abruptly switched to a different scene. This one showed an amborg who looked like they had just been set on fire, while another amborg with a fire extinguisher laughed in the background.

"Ah, that would be 8 and 9," Dr. Kendrick said, rolling his eyes. "They've been pulling pranks on each other for as long as I can remember. And their devious little imaginations continue plotting up another humorous stress reliever. It surprisingly doesn't get old."

The video image changed again and revealed a female amborg trimming a few flowers. Then it revealed a male amborg flaming a steak. Another image showed a pair of amborgs fixing a car engine. Then it showed an image of a familiar face.

"That's 33 right?" Brad said excitedly and pointed at the amborg who was in the middle of assembling a model with one hand while piecing a puzzle with his other. "He really does love puzzles and complicated set-ups."

"Yes he does," Dr. Kendrick smiled. "Watch this next part."

Brad watched as 33 picked up a piece of tubing, looked at the instructions, and carefully attached the piece to another and began to slowly glue it together. He set the pieces down to dry and grabbed a lego set. He rapidly took it apart in his hands within seconds and slowly began to piece it back together as if he had just opened the box.

"Do you notice how slowly he is building the model?"

Brad nodded as he watched 33 smile at his handiwork.

"When he first started on the models, he'd always build them so fast that it took all the fun out of it. Eventually, he learned patience and gradually found the fun in working slower, the way model toys were designed to be made."

"Wow, that's really neat," Brad said in awe as the three of them continued on. The trio found themselves at another fairly large door. The word 'GYM' was printed in bold black ink on the door frame.

"Welcome to the training facility!" Serina piped up as the three of them stopped outside another door. Smiling again, she bowed and waved her arm towards the entrance as it slid open to allow them inside.

"Amborg Industries Gymnasium," a small bodiless voice announced as they stepped inside. "Welcome Dr. Kendrick, A.I. Serina, and VIP guest. ID confirmed."

"I'm not all that special though," Brad muttered in embarrassment as they stepped inside.

The door opened to reveal a massive gym. Brad looked straight up at the ceiling and was amazed at how high it was. There was probably room to fit a small five-story office building. Mats lined the walls and there were a few crash test dummies on the floor. Some of the equipment along the walls included hand to hand weapons for training purposes. Apart from the few vacuum bots scooting across the floor, there wasn't anyone in sight which made it convenient for Dr. Kendrick.

"Hmm," he said observantly, scanning the area, "it doesn't look like we have anyone using the gym. For starters, Serina, go and find him."

"Him?" Serina floated towards the two of them. "Who are you referring to? There are tons of guys in the facility, doctor. It'd be helpful and I could save eight whole minutes of scanning the entire database."

"Number 117, Serina," Dr. Kendrick chuckled. "Just checking to see how well you're paying attention. Also, be a dear and request some refreshments. I'm guessing we might be here awhile."

They headed to the corner of the gym where there was a large stack of fold-up chairs. He pulled out a chair and motioned for Brad to grab one as well. Serina responded to the doctor's instructions and then did a loop de loop in the air, emitting sparks of light from her palms. The light show illuminated the gym brightly, like a star erupting in the night sky, causing Brad to gaze in wonder as he followed Dr. Kendrick towards the center of the gym.

"Absolutely doctor! Number 117 it is!" she squealed delightfully and disappeared into the wall.

A blue light emanated off the panel where she had practically jumped into. The panel connected to similar light projectors that ran through the hallway corridors. With a flash, she moved from one emitter to another and then the light flew off towards an exit on the other side of the gym. The light reached the door and then disappeared like magic.

"Now Brad, have you ever met any of the amborgs?" Kendrick turned to look at Brad who was still gaping in awe at what he had just observed.

Shaking his head to gather his thoughts, Brad sat down slowly with one eye focused on the wall panel where Serina had disappeared.

"No, I can't say that I have," he replied calmly without looking at the Doctor. He began to scribble a few notes again. "I think one visited my school once but that was a few years ago. Do they make a lot of time for public appearances?"

"They try their best," Dr. Kendrick took his glasses off and wiped the lenses using the edge of his jacket. "They manage their schedules very efficiently and they can do wonders that would leave you drooling."

"I'll say," Brad chuckled as he wrote a few notes about Artificial Intelligence and described Serina in his data pad. "If Serina is that eccentric, I assume the amborgs are better?"

"Mmm, I'd say that Serina surpasses them greatly," Dr. Kendrick placed a few fingers under his chin. "It depends on what circumstances you wish to compare an A.I. or an amborg to. Some things are best handled by an A.I., some... are best with the amborgs. Not that the amborgs are inferior to an A.I. but... Serina is probably one of the best ones that ever existed on this good planet. Adventurous, full of humor, brave, quick... those don't even begin to describe what other features there are about her."

"I can tell," Brad stopped writing and immediately remembered something else. "You keep steering the conversation back to her. Is she as special as 117?"

"Nice guess. Why do you ask?"

"Well," he stared at Kendrick and continued his observation, "you specifically asked for him or her, and with such intensity that I don't think it was by random choice. Seems like that amborg made a huge impression on you."

"Very good," Dr. Kendrick applauded. "He is a very special amborg indeed. Actually, he's made an impression on a lot of people. Even though all the amborgs are special to me, I have great admiration, err, well, everyone has great admiration for him."

Dr. Kendrick looked over his shoulder at the door but nothing happened. He sighed patiently and turned back to face Brad.

"But I think to really connect with that story," he smirked, "I believe he can tell you that himself. Want to hear his story personally directly from the mouth?"

"Directly from his mouth?" Brad's smile faded. "I thought that amborgs could only communicate with us through the specially designed wrist bracelets. Aren't their speech patterns gone instantly after the cybernetic augmentation?"

"Yes, that is very true, but 117 specifically learned how to speak again."

"Verbal speech??" he exclaimed. "How?? They don't have use of their vocal cords! I thought the augmentation disabled them permanently!"

Dr. Kendrick didn't respond right away. He merely smiled as he watched Brad's excitement. The silence pretty much confirmed his own thinking.

"Still true, no matter which way you say it," Dr. Kendrick let out a laugh.

Embarrassed, Brad realized that he had indeed repeated the same thing twice.

"What happened was unexpected," Dr. Kendrick continued the explanation. "You see, when I first met 117, he had a very sincere voice. All of the amborgs, their voices were recreated electronically through their special gold bracelets. It always felt strange to me, hearing the robotic and endless monotone."

Dr. Kendrick looked over his shoulder again but the door remained shut. Was something holding up 117? Brad couldn't help but feel like he was missing something.

"Is something wrong?"

"No," Dr. Kendrick shook his head innocently. "Anyway, so imagine my surprise when I first heard his voice again. It wasn't the computer-like monotone that broadcasts from the transmission of their bracelets. After a whole year of being an amborg, and fighting the bad guys, he found his actual voice and shocked me. Actually, he shocked everyone. Not even any of the First Group amborgs could believe what was going on. Imagine that. Not being able to speak with your real voice for a year and then suddenly, sound was coming out of his throat."

"So, did you manage to figure out what happened?"

Dr. Kendrick leaned in with enthusiasm, a broad smile lighting up his face at Brad's question. At that moment, he seemed less like a world-renowned scientist. Instead, Dr. Kendrick resembled his best friend when he got excited or passionate about something.

"His vocal chords adapted and by some miracle, they restructured in a way that I never anticipated," Dr. Kendrick said with a look of glee on his face. "It truly was something amazing that I never saw coming. Complete and total immersion with his upgrades and suddenly, he was talking again. To all of us. Soon after, they all began developing their voices again as well. He was the first one... and he started something different. Even after the First Group had been operating for years before his time."

Dr. Kendrick then checked over his shoulder again. Finally, Brad felt compelled to ask since this had become a regular occurrence.

"What are you looking for?" he asked skeptically. "Is there a reason why you've started to act so jumpy?"

"Oh."

Dr. Kendrick turned to face Brad and looked a little uneasy. However, he shook it off and smiled confidently.

"It's a reflex," he explained. "It's difficult for me to sit still sometimes."

"But... weren't you doing alright when we first met in the meeting room?" Brad tilted his eyes upward and tried to rack his brain.

"I think you were slightly distracted," Dr. Kendrick tilted his head, indicating the data pad in Brad's hands. "But, I was also glancing over my shoulder when you were struggling with your stylus."

"Oh," Brad looked at his stylus and let out a nervous chuckle. Changing the subject, he cleared his throat. "So, may I know why you look over your shoulder?"

"It's simple. When I sit down, I always feel a little..."

Dr. Kendrick had begun to answer when a sudden noise interrupted him. A whooshing followed by the sound of hydraulic whirring echoed through the room. They glanced over to see the door opening, revealing two people stepping inside. Actually, it was technically only one since Serina was a glowing miniature floating light next to who she had arrived with. She waved her arms majestically and pointed at the man behind her.

"Well, say hello to amazing!" she exclaimed with a wink.

She stepped aside and the amborg walked forward. Brad gaped at the six to seven foot tall cyborg. The number 117 was printed into his jacket on his chest, which glowed a bright green. Slowly, he raised his arm forward and extended it for Brad, who continued to stare upward at the modified human being before him.

"Pleasure... to meet you," 117 said slowly.

Speaking from the mouth did take a toll. Brad noticed 117 was wincing with pain and his neck twitched with each word. In order to remedy this, 117's wrist bracelet lit up, flashing in a sequence of lights and another voice with a more electronic tone came out, finishing his introduction.

"I'm David 117." The lights on his wrist flashed as the words projected out for everyone to hear. "At your service. Speaking is very strenuous. I was in the middle of attending an amborg seminar when Serina called. May I inquire about your designation... correction. Sorry. I mean... What's your name?"

CHAPTER 2

Decisions, Decisions, Decisions

Amborg Evaluation Center: Observation Wing
2127 July
Eight Years Earlier

"But I want to go with mommy! Why can't I go with mommy?!"

George Ramirez let out a sigh. He was already losing an uphill battle emotionally. This wasn't a great start to his day, and he had a full schedule. He looked at his wife, Marina, who reciprocated a light and reassuring smile. It was a warm gesture meant to comfort their daughter Thalia, but George could sense the underlying sorrow she was trying to mask.

He quickly took charge and redirected their daughter's attention to him. Kneeling down, he raised his arms and motioned to her.

Thalia wore a sleeveless square neck dress with a flower pattern on it past her knees. Underneath, she had a white short-sleeve crewneck shirt with a small silver chain necklace. The white colors of her outfit greatly contrasted against the dark business suits that her parents wore.

"We talked about this," George spoke softly, and Thalia focused on him. He smiled and let her step forward so he could place his hands on her shoulders. "Thalia, mommy needs to go to her appointments and meetings without us. It's like when I have to go on trips."

"I don't like it when you go," Thalia mumbled.

"We know," Marina said, causing Thalia to turn her head to look at her mother, "but we need to sometimes go away. One day, when you're older..."

"That's what you said before!" Thalia stamped her foot. "But I'm older now!"

"By the second, yes, but still not enough," George laughed, which made Thalia look at him and pout. "You have to be patient a little longer. It will all make sense someday. Now, I have a surprise for you."

Thalia's pouting expression faded as her eyes widened. She seemed to perk up as George rose to his feet and her eyes followed.

"Do you want to come with me to a selection session?"

"With the amborgs?" Thalia exclaimed. "Really?!"

"Yes! Do you know where to go?"

This question was redundant since Thalia already did know. She spent most of her free time exploring A.I. Industries. That is, the parts where children were allowed to be.

"Yes!" she said excitedly.

Thalia eagerly ran off down the hall. Once she turned a corner and was out of sight, George's smile disappeared, and he felt a light smack on his shoulder. Wincing in pain, he jumped and one hand immediately flew to his right shoulder.

"You do realize that Dr. Kendrick has a few activities here on company grounds that he prefers the actual children stay away from, right?" Marina sighed. "And the selection is one of them?"

"Sorry," George shrugged apologetically. "I didn't really have a better option."

"Really?" Marina raised an eyebrow. "There wasn't a better one? Unless... you were already planning on playing that card?"

"Well, you heard her," George gestured down the hall. "She's growing up. It's getting harder and harder to protect her childhood by the day."

"You think we should tell her?"

George glanced at Marina. Her smile was completely gone, replaced with worry. George nodded and pocketed his hands.

"We've been dreading this day for a long time," he said, letting out a sigh.

"After my next few sessions," Marina spoke softly, "I'll start thinking about that conversation. Better yet, perhaps I should ask the doctor and see what they recommend."

"Good idea," George whispered as he nodded his head slowly. "Want me to tell Dr. Kendrick?"

"Please."

George briefly hugged Marina and they both shared a quick kiss. Once they parted, she smiled and walked in the opposite direction. As he briefly watched his wife walk away, he tilted his eyes and admired her from afar. He then turned to go after his daughter. If he had taken a few more seconds to check out his wife, he would have seen that she had also turned to gaze back at him.

The gravity of their situation was much grimmer than they had let on to Thalia. Even though Marina was dressed for work, that was in fact just to keep up appearances so that no one would be suspicious. She was actually sneaking away from the company in order to make a very important personal appointment. Their daughter was definitely starting to pick up on these weekly trips as it was George's responsibility to keep her in the dark.

Unfortunately, they had to take it one day at a time. George straightened his jacket and glanced at his reflection in the wall, making sure he looked presentable. He entered a room and saw his daughter sitting patiently in a lounge chair.

"Observation lounge," he heard an announcement declare as he stepped over the threshold.

"Hi Thalia," George smiled. "There you are!"

Thalia looked up. She had made herself comfortable in one of the chairs in the lounge, waiting patiently for her father. She eagerly leaped to her feet and ran over.

"Hi papa! Can we go see the amborgs?"

Fortunately, the idea of seeing the selection had kept her mind occupied with something else entirely. George felt her small hands clinging onto his sleeve. For the moment, he could focus on the upcoming inspection tour.

They stepped out of the lounge and into a waiting room. The father-daughter pair entered and found a group of people chatting among themselves. This room lacked chairs, which left everyone standing and towering over Thalia, but she was excited to see them all.

"Remember," George looked down at her as he tugged on her hand, "please remember to be on your best behavior."

"Ok!" Thalia chimed.

He straightened up and cleared his throat. A few people had already noticed them and turned to greet them but everyone in the back was still casually chatting.

"Excuse me!" he boldly declared. "May I have your attention please?"

A chime echoed across the room, which silenced the entire crowd. George couldn't help but smile. In a corner, he saw a holographic teenage boy saluting him with a ghostly pale orange arm. One of the A.I. programs had decided to help him out. He watched the little figure disappear from sight before facing the crowd.

"Thank you!" he nodded, and he felt all eyes on him. "Welcome! Thank you for being part of this tour. It is our hope that by the end of this visit, you will have a clearer understanding of what it is we are trying to accomplish here. My daughter will be joining us and we have planned some exciting things for you to see. Thalia?"

Thalia eagerly stepped forward and waved at all of the executives in the room.

"Hello everyone! My name is Thalia. Tall-ee-uh. You spell it with an 'H' after the T and before the first A in my name. This is my daddy and we're both going to be your tour guides for the afternoon!"

A few of the executives chuckled and waved back. Some of them clapped for Thalia's introduction as she gestured for her father to speak up. George stepped forward, bowed his head in acknowledgement, and then spoke.

"Please, follow us to our first stop. It is the amborg selection process."

"Mr. Ramirez," someone raised their hand excitedly, "are you saying that we get to select...?"

"No," George replied immediately with a gracious smile. "The selection process is when an amborg meets a trained and certified technician to be partnered with."

He briefly saw the person lower their hand in embarrassment, but they pleasantly smiled as George turned towards the exit. He and Thalia led the tour group down a couple of halls until they arrived at an observation room. It had a long, angled panel of windows that drew their attention. Everyone took a spot and peered through the glass.

On the other side was a room down below. Many people in the A.I. Industries lab coats mingled with several executives dressed in formal business attire. From their vantage point, George cleared his throat, and Thalia joined him at the window, leaning in closer and pressing her hands against the glass to get a better look.

A sudden announcement spoke overhead.

"Would the following amborgs report to the selection room, please? Technicians are standing by. Numbers 35, 82, 27, 43, 297, and 117. Prepare for social interaction in your designated mingling session."

George couldn't help but smirk a little as he surveyed all of the younger employees down below. Although Dr. Kendrick's orders had stated that these selections should be like a casual pot-luck setting, most still felt it necessary to look their best. It seemed less casual and more like they were about to meet with a congressman or someone of similar significance. He could understand why. A few of the new technicians were about to meet their first amborgs. Theoretically, all of them were about to select their future cybernetic partners after this event. It was a very important occasion.

"Daddy, can I pick an amborg?"

George glanced down at Thalia, and she looked up at him with her big brown eyes.

She continued to lean on the windows of the observatory and peeped down. The amborgs hadn't arrived yet and she was just as anxious to see them just like everyone else was.

"No sweetheart, only technicians get to pick an amborg," George said to his little girl. "I'm afraid you're not old enough for that job."

"But you said I could come with you today," Thalia murmured.

"I did," George replied with a gentle smile. "But you're going to have to talk to Dr. Kendrick about being a future technician."

"I want to be a technician!" Thalia said eagerly.

Maintaining his smile, George looked at the rest of the tour group. Some were watching them curiously, listening to their conversation.

"Well, you heard it straight from the child's mouth," he announced. "As you can see, ladies and gentlemen, my daughter is already ready to start her career. Let's give you the local rundown of what we have happening today. Now you already had a tour of the research division and production labs with Dr. Kendrick but now he's currently unavailable for the rest of the day. It is my pleasure to introduce you to the golden crown of A.I. Industries. Please keep looking and you'll get to see the amborgs for yourselves."

Everyone fell silent and peered into the room. They watched as a door opened and a group of amborgs entered. Six of them strode in confidently and obediently lined up in front of the employees. The technicians and everyone in the observation room quietly stared for a few seconds. Finally, one technician took the initiative and stepped forward to introduce himself, breaking the silence and prompting the rest of the crowd to join in, one by one. As they interacted, one of the executives coughed for attention. George turned and noticed someone raising her hand.

"So, what exactly is the selection, Mr. Ramirez?" she asked, which prompted everyone to face George.

"This is the event where a technician is assigned to an amborg. Or rather, an amborg is assigned their human partner for operations in future endeavors," George explained. "A moment where the amborgs are allowed time to interact with normal human beings who are prepared to be friends and their partners, in a sense. One key component to an effective team is to allow them to bond with each other."

"Why pair one of the amborgs with a human technician?" another person asked. "Isn't that supposedly less efficient? Like ehhh... asking a janitor to keep a supercomputer oiled and properly maintained?"

"To answer that sir," George chuckled, "first, a supercomputer is never oiled, it is liquid cooled. At least that's what I know about the one at the Leibniz Supercomputing Centre in Germany when it first debuted in the year of 2012. Second, pardon me for saying it like it is but they are not maintained by janitors the last time I checked."

Everyone laughed, including the man who asked the question. Bashfully chuckling, he muttered an apology and then George continued to speak.

"Nevertheless, that is a fair comparison, and it also generates many questions," he said, nodding in agreement. "Why put an ordinary human at the hub of another human being with the calculating speed of a supercomputer at all? The reason is it's because the technician is able to provide human instinct into what an amborg sees. The amborg takes to the field while the technician remains here on the A.I. Industries compound and monitors them carefully. The technician is in charge of monitoring the amborg's well-being, mental state, physical prowess, and occasionally, helping them with basic human behavior and decision making."

"Why would the technicians need to help the amborgs with... basic human behavior? Amborgs are superior to us in so many ways. Aren't they?"

George anticipated this particular question. It was frequently asked in each of these inspection tours. He confidently answered.

"That is actually partially untrue. Surprisingly, most of the amborgs have trouble dealing with certain issues," he explained in a loud and clear tone. "It used to be that someone was torn between two choices. Should they save the bus full of children or defeat the person causing the destruction to escape? Normally an amborg is actually capable of doing both. But several of them have actually developed significant problems making difficult choices. They sometimes become indecisive, the calculations don't compute to them emotionally, or in the time it takes for them to map out every possible contingency, because they actually do think about it, it's most likely too late. That's also why the technician is there for the role of being a guide. A support system. The person who provides hints if the game becomes too difficult. They keep an eye on their choices and become a little voice in their heads. A mentor, teacher, or the manager of the buddy system. Many of the amborgs lose or are slow to use their own instincts in certain situations. Therefore, the technician helps them adapt and undergo a type of therapy or whatever they choose to call it in order to make it easy for them. After making the ultimate sacrifice to become the next level of humanity, as Dr. Kendrick describes it, it was discovered that abandoning certain aspects of being human is more of a disadvantage."

"Is the selection random?" another woman inquired.

"Why would it be random?" her friend nudged her slightly. "He just explained that they're down there trying to bond."

"Ladies!"

George called for their attention. The two women fell silent. From their expressions, it looked like they were coworkers who didn't mesh well. He was relieved when they all paid attention to him again and the pending argument was averted.

"No, it is not," he answered the question. "Random assignments to the teams aren't that feasible. The technicians end up choosing which amborg they'd like to be paired with. Like I said earlier, this is when they are allowed to bond. A time for them to get to know one another, both the amborgs and our technicians. They'll become a team when they go into the open world. We try to teach the amborgs to feel secure and comfortable with whoever they feel close to. Or rather, the technician most compatible is the way they like to describe it."

"So why not have a team of technicians working with a single amborg?"

The same woman looked at George, who smiled back. He remembered how difficult it was when the First Group amborgs were all individually micromanaged by teams of people at A.I. Industries. In a nutshell, it was a total disaster. However, if he answered it that way, he knew they would inquire more about the matter. So, he took another deep breath.

"Picture yourself as an amborg," he explained. "You can't speak through your mouth due to broken vocal cords after augmentation — another sacrifice that they volunteered for. Instead, a signal from the CPU in your head travels to a bracelet and then transmits a reproduced version of your voice. That's all you have in order to communicate. A basic walking computer with several outlets, but technically you only have two ears and one brain."

George pointed at the room below. The people closest to the glass glanced down. They shuffled around so that those in the back could also get a turn. He didn't know if all of them could see, but the amborgs were in fact talking to the technicians.

Each of them had silver bracelets on their left wrists. Small lights were blinking and pulsing in short sequences. Their mouths weren't moving but George could see that they were engaging in light conversations. The technicians all had the same kind of silver bracelets, but they were deactivated. If the amborgs had lost their own, they could send a signal to another bracelet close by. George continued his explanation as they watched.

"Do you really want fifteen people talking into your head at the same time?" he asked. "It's already annoying for the rest of us when large groups of our friends try to ask us questions or feed us information simultaneously. Too much activity on any computer system will increase the chance of an overload or a crash. In the mind of an amborg, it's a similar principle because it's not good for them mentally. It is also difficult to describe or even imagine. You do have to admire the bravery they have to submit to such a sacrifice."

The woman who had posed the question closed her mouth, nodded in understanding, and turned back to the window to look back down below. Thalia was still looking through the window. She wasn't really able to understand what her father was talking about, so she just silently observed. As she quietly scanned the room below, George began to describe some of the amborgs.

"Below us," he said, "you'll see these amborgs are from the Second Group. Except for 27 over there. Regretfully, he lost his technician in an automobile accident a few weeks ago, so he's attending the selection sessions. He actually requested time to grieve for his lost partner, but now he's back for another one. Came back pretty fast, that boy."

"What do you mean by Second Group? Is 27 different from the others?" someone interrupted. "What are these groups you keep describing?"

George looked carefully at the person who asked the question. This particular executive appeared to be younger than the rest of them. His suit was much shinier and newer compared to the two people he stood between, whose attire looked older and more worn out. Definitely someone not aware or knowledgeably experienced. Whatever company he was with, he was a newbie, just like an amborg in one of their shiny, brand-new jackets.

"Our project began years ago with over one hundred people and two volunteers specially selected by Dr. Kendrick. Forty eight survived the initial augmentation process. But we lost eighteen more soon after, leaving only thirty survivors who became official amborgs. These thirty survivors are referred to as the First Group."

Several of the executives began to mutter and whisper amongst each other. Many of them turned their heads when George finished and a wave of fear and uncertainty spread. Realizing he had everyone's attention again, he spoke up.

"Several months ago," he continued, "we successfully made another thirty amborgs. For security reasons, I won't say out of how many. The death toll still hangs over us, but now we have developed safer methods to ensure a lower casualty rate. These next amborgs have been designated the Second group."

Everyone murmured and began to trade glances with each other. George knew that even with some details being omitted, he was starting to lose their trust. He was going to have to reel them back in with some positive facts. Thankfully, he had planned a presentation later in the auditorium to ease their concerns.

"Today will be the day. I am expecting a favorable outcome today."

Down in the selection room, 117 stood in earnest. He looked at 43, who stared back. Although both showed no emotion or made any response, they were secretly having a private chat in the back of their heads, transmitting to each other on their own separate channel.

"I don't agree," 117 replied to her in a dull monotone. "The previous sessions that we have attended have not yielded the desired outcome."

As long as they were in range of each other, they could send messages back and forth without the possibilities of anyone eavesdropping. Unless another amborg was allowed into the loop, they could talk to each other as long as they wanted without being interrupted. 43 stared at 117 and, without opening her mouth, her voice rang clear in the back of his mind.

"After plenty of failed sessions, perhaps it is time to think differently than before," she stated. Her tone was the same as his but she spoke with a rather warm inflection. It was difficult to explain as he observed her giving him a tiny smile. "Is there something distracting you?"

"In our previous selections," he answered while tilting his gaze downward, "I didn't sustain my conversations long enough. 23 past conversations have been for naught. The probability of being selected during this one remains the same. A minimal chance to find a partner. Perhaps I have no appeal."

"Do not be negative 117. A technician will select you today," 43's voice rang clear as day in his mind. "During preliminary exercises and training, you have met the qualifications set by Dr. Kendrick."

Her attempt at reassuring 117 was unsuccessful. He continued to replay his memories from the last selections to figure out where it had gone wrong. He did admit that he was quite as capable as the others, but even with his passing scores and qualifications, why was it an issue for him to secure a partner?

"Apologies," he replied while shifting his mouth into a frown. "I don't share in your optimism. This will be my fourth selection and still, no one has chosen me. I calculate a low chance of being selected today."

At that moment, 43 side-stepped and put herself on his right. He turned and looked at her as she continued to face forward, but leaned towards him. He realized that she was imitating someone who was silently requesting a private word, as if she was about to whisper in his ear. Since she was slightly shorter than him, 117 turned at an angle and courteously dipped his head forward.

"Calculations do not factor for them. Perhaps some patience will benefit your situation," she said. Her voice spoke in his head as she lifted a hand and gestured to the crowd. "I know someone will choose. This is... a prediction. From what I have perceived in human behavior."

"Since when do you make predictions?"

"We're amborgs aren't we?" 43 shrugged her shoulders. "It's in our programming. We make thousands of calculations and predictions per second. That last one was a calculation for you. It was an attempt to assist your current mentality."

"I see," 117 stared blankly at a technician who was interacting with 27.

He watched the technician placed a hand on 27's shoulder, who reacted with a smile on his face. From what he could guess, this technician was possibly exhibiting sympathy, however it felt so unfamiliar that 117 disregarded this notion. As he did so, he heard 43 speaking to him again.

"Do not feel alone," she said. "After all, I too am without a partner."

"True," 117 nodded.

"Perhaps if the circumstances were different, I could be your technician," 43 suggested.

"But you cannot be," 117 replied. "You are an amborg; the same as I am."

"Do you not agree that if I hypothetically was still fully human," she said, "would I be a suitable candidate to be your partner?"

"I agree with your statement," 117 said confidently. "However, we cannot focus on unrealistic hypothetical scenarios."

"Then shift your focus on the fact that if I could have been a suitable partner for you," 43 smiled, "then someone will choose you to be partnered with."

117 processed her words and his eyes widened slightly. Her argument wasn't entirely wrong. There had to be someone here who would be willing to try and communicate with him.

"43," 117 suddenly realized something. "I would like to submit an inquiry."

"Yes?" 43 responded formally.

"A personal inquiry," he declared.

"Of course," she answered.

"Why did you say that I shouldn't feel alone? I don't feel loneliness."

"It was an effort to reinforce the idea that I am here as your friend," 43 replied casually. "While we remain on the subject, there seems to be someone watching you."

117 blinked and peered across the room. Unfortunately, he couldn't see anyone looking his way. She gently tapped his shoulder.

"Look up in the observation room, 117," she informed him. He glanced up when she gestured upwards. "It would appear that you have a young admirer."

117 tilted his head back and he gazed up at the room. He could see many people watching them. In the middle of the crowd, his eyes met those of a little girl that was staring right at him.

"Daddy, that one looks sad."

George saw Thalia point a finger at the glass. She spoke loudly enough for several of them to hear as he knelt down next to her.

"Do you see?" she pointed again, poking her finger against the window. "The boy amborg who's talking to that girl amborg."

George looked closely. A couple of the executives, overhearing the conversation, turned to see where Thalia was pointing. Despite her age, George couldn't wrap his head around how she could pick up on that type of feeling.

Must be from her mother's side, he guessed.

He let out a sigh and rested his hand on her shoulder.

"Amborgs don't get sad Thalia," he said plainly. "They don't have the same feelings as us. So emotions aren't really a priority in their programming."

Thalia turned to face him. She had an insistent look in her eyes that made him slightly uncomfortable. Without a word, she began pouting. George glanced to the side and noticed a couple of executives staring. So he conceded and decided to ask.

"Alright," he sighed. "Why do you think he's sad?'

She made a small humming noise which meant that she was thinking really hard about her answer. After a couple of seconds, she spoke again.

"Because he hasn't been chosen," she replied softly. "That's how mommy looks when she's sad. Look at his face. He's waiting for someone."

George looked at 117. If he remembered correctly, from Dr. Kendrick's files, he was a quiet one. Before enhancement, Dr. Kendrick had theorized that whatever his personality was before, it would be amplified when he woke up with his new abilities. Since he became an amborg, George remembered that he was a lot more soft spoken than before. He didn't really have many opportunities to make friends. Thalia was probably able to spot that.

Now that she mentioned it, he was beginning to see what she was talking about. He looked around briefly and realized that the whole room had gone quiet. Everyone had stopped to listen to the conversation, too. George glanced through the window again and noticed that 117 was looking back up at them.

He must be wondering why we're singling him out, he thought. I wonder what's on his mind?

"It would appear there is more than just one."

Noticing the number of eyes that were trained on him, 117 nudged 43 to point out his correction. Seeing three pairs of eyes fixed on him with his peripherals, he didn't have to guess that all of them were watching. Without making a noise and standing perfectly still, he concentrated and tuned his audio input. After calibrating his ears, he could hear the exact number of people sitting up in the booth above. By his count, there were about 15 people possibly staring down at him.

"43, perhaps returning to your original position will be appropriate," 117 said as he tilted his head towards her. "Multiple individuals are now monitoring me."

117 looked up at a little girl who was pointing at him. Running a facial recognition within his personal database, he realized it was Thalia, daughter to George Ramirez. He had seen George before but never Thalia. It was already curious that she was up there.

While he gazed at Thalia, who appeared to be smiling at him, he ran a search through the personnel files that he had access to. George and Marina Ramirez had been with the company for over a decade. However, what got his attention was the fact that George seemed to work more than his wife. Apparently, some of her files were locked when he tried accessing them to learn more about her. A red warning light appeared in the lower right corner of his HUD. The lock was put in place by Dr. Kendrick. 117 assumed that this was because he had accidentally tried to invade the privacy of the Ramirez family.

He remembered his ethical programming and a yellow prompt appeared. When he accessed it with his mind, he read a long disclaimer about the code of conduct for amborgs. Thanks to his cybernetic processors, he was able to just skim through the entire thing in seconds.

Once he was done, he focused back on Thalia.

"Curious," 117 said. "I wonder if Ms. Thalia is selecting me? That would be a first. A child technician for an amborg."

"117, it is quite impossible for a child to qualify for such a role."

"I was attempting to enhance my sense of humor. It is well-known to the public that child labor is illegal."

117 turned to look at 43, who was tilting her head in confusion. Suddenly, she arched her head back slightly and then nodded.

"Oh. Pardon me. I failed to recognize the attempt," she replied dubiously.

"No apology is necessary," 117 said promptly. "There has been no insult detected."

The pair were about to initiate another private conversation when there was a small commotion that snagged their attention. A few other people noticed, but ignored it. With their enhanced senses, 43 and 117 both turned their heads to the entrance on the opposite side from where they had entered.

A door suddenly swung open and a teenage girl burst through as if she was being chased. Despite how young she looked, she wore the same uniform that the other technicians were sporting and entered the crowd. The lab coat that she had on was disheveled and falling off one of her shoulders while she tried to catch her breath.

"I'm so sorry!" she exclaimed to one of the security guards. "I got held up! I'm glad I made it!"

She took off the lab coat and set it on a table nearby before adjusting herself. 117 saw that she was wearing a business suit with dark slacks. On their private channel, 43 made a comment that she could probably pass for one of the executives on the inspection tour.

"That is a young technician," 43 noted observantly at the late arrival. "Although, I have been wrong on a few occasions. She might be older than she looks."

The new arrival continued to take a lot of deep breaths as she joined the other technicians. 117 continued to watch while she introduced herself to the others and began to circulate around the room. Over the course of the next twenty minutes, she walked around and took a deep look at each amborg. No introductions or any kind of greeting at all. She merely silently observed each amborg present for the selection. When she got to 43, the two women exchanged courteous nods and smiled. Without a word, 117 continued to stare until he realized that he was the next person she was about to approach. Before he knew it, she was right in front of him, smiling.

Puzzled, he tilted his head and continued to gaze at her in curiosity. Just as he was about to initiate a facial recognition scan to look for her in the employee database, she cleared her throat and opened her mouth.

"Well?" she asked in a plain but demanding voice.

117 stared blankly back at her.

She was obviously waiting for a response. But her one word question confused him slightly. What should he say? Her tone of voice clearly indicated that she was expecting him to answer, but she had also used a strange word that didn't make sense to him. He stared at her and thought hard about what he wanted to say. Finally, he opened a connection from his CPU to his wrist bracelet and spoke.

"Apologies. I do not understand," he admitted as his voice projected out of his silver bracelet. "'Well?' A word of inquiry to examine one's physical or emotional well-being. If that is indeed the context you are indicating, then I am...well. Is my response satisfactory?"

He casually glanced to his side and noticed that 43 was watching him intently. He couldn't figure out if she was trying to tell him if his response was the right one.

Instead of using a private channel, 117 faced the lady in front of him, who was staring back at him. Suddenly, she began to laugh, confusing 117 even more. He had never encountered such a strange person. This behavior was highly unexpected.

"Pardon," he interjected. "Did I say something humorous?"

After a few moments, the technician stopped laughing and composed herself. She continued to smile pleasantly, making it clear that he hadn't said anything wrong.

"I was under the impression we were introducing ourselves," she remarked, giving him a strong pat on the shoulder that left him staring at the spot she struck with a look of bewilderment. "In that... context, was it? You amborgs really do speak so technical and formally. I admit, I was trying to see what kind of response you'd make. I'm Mandy. What's your name? One hundred seventeen?"

"That is incorrect."

"Pardon?"

Mandy raised an eyebrow. 117 repeated his answer.

"That is the incorrect pronunciation," he stated. "My number is one-one-seven."

"What's the difference?" Mandy asked.

"It is what Dr. Kendrick first called me when I... woke up from augmentation. It is my designated amborg number," he explained.

"Oh, I see. Alright then. One-one-seven it is. What's your name?"

117 paused. Why was she repeating the question when it had already been answered?

"Amborg designation number 117," he replied. "It is a pleasure to meet you, Mandy."

Mandy had extended her arm, but 117 didn't move. He was still contemplating what the pat on his shoulder meant.

"No, silly!" she said with another laugh. "I was asking for your name. Your real one? I know you have a number but you have a name, too. Don't tell me you don't know how to shake hands. Do you?"

117 held up both hands and shook them rapidly at a tremendous speed. A small buzzing noise began to sound from the rapid movement. A normal human would have shaken their hands clean off, but for an amborg, it was a very simple feat. Unfortunately, 117 knew this was wrong when Mandy placed a hand to her forehead and shook her head.

"No no no," she chuckled. "Copy me. Take your right hand, hold it out and hold my hand. Now close your fingers but don't do it too hard or you'll crush mine. I know how strong you amborgs are, so be careful."

As 117 slowly laced his fingers with hers, he looked directly at her.

"Before I chose 117 as my number, I was designated with the name of David. Last name: Classified."

"It isn't classified David," Mandy sighed. "We just respect your privacy and your family names which is why it is not mandatory for you to share your last name. Don't act like we locked it away from you."

She released his hand. He allowed his arm to casually drop to his side.

"Another thing, 'was'? What do you mean you were designated as David?" Mandy asked. "You still are David. I know we just met but we'll be doing many things together. After all, 117 is going to be weird to say consistently when you're in the field. Which is why I like David more. It suits an amborg with your looks. A six foot tall human being cybernetically upgraded. It's interesting how you have not been chosen in four selection sessions. To me, that makes me think you're someone unique. Am I going too fast?"

"When I am in the field?" 117 repeated for clarification. "Who are you referring to? Someone unique?"

"I'm talking about you, David," she replied happily. "I'm standing here and I've made my decision! From now on, I'm your technician. David 117, you and I are going to be a team! And we got a lot to learn together! But for an amborg, you sure are surprisingly slow..."

"Slow?" 117 repeated skeptically. "My programming operates at full capacity, enabling rapid calculations in the exabyte range. If my calculation speed is not in question, I am perfectly capable of withstanding or exceeding normal human parameters in the field based on training simulations. My speed is equal to that of the other amborgs."

"Yeah David," Mandy sighed, "but I am talking about a different version of slow. But we'll... slowly get to that later. For now, I'm your technician and you'll be taking instruction from me. Does that work for you?"

"Understood," 117 nodded once.

"Understood? I'm asking if this arrangement is acceptable and works for you."

"Understood Ms. Mandy. Your terms are acceptable."

"Just call me by my first name, David. I prefer just Mandy."

"Very well... 'Just' Mandy. Request acknowledged."

Mandy's eye twitched slightly. She casually glanced at 43, who gave a small grin. Her eyes widened when she noticed that 43's expression was forced and exaggerated. She looked like she was in a little pain as she struggled to give an encouraging smile.

"Oh boy," Mandy groaned. "No, David, please just use my first name."

"Understood Miss Mandy."

43 stopped smiling and patted 117 on the shoulder in the same way that Mandy did. Her physical strength was five times greater than hers and, instead of reducing her power, the force of her slap actually caused 117 to shift slightly.

Mandy flinched at how close 43's arm had swung to her. How much strength did she use? That felt like it could have decapitated her.

"I am very pleased with this outcome," 43 stated as her voice transmitted from her own bracelet. "Thank you, Mandy."

43 approached Mandy, causing her to shrink back a bit. Standing so close, she noticed that 43 was much taller than she had initially thought.

"For what?" Mandy asked nervously.

"Earlier, 117 predicted that the selection would not yield positive results," she stated. "Thank you for being part of that change."

"Oh, you're welcome! Uh... amborg Four-three."

"Incorrect. I pronounce my number as forty-three," 43 explained.

"Right," Mandy let out a sigh. "That's going to take some getting used to. What's your first name?"

"Oh," 43 blinked, her eyes widening slightly in alarm. "My apologies. If you are 117's technician, then that means I am the last amborg here that doesn't have a partner. Please excuse me!"

Mandy was left hanging as 43 pivoted and strode off to chat with a few technicians that seemed available for a conversation. 117 merely watched with an impassive look as he stood next to his new and energetic partner.

"Aw, I was hoping to get to know her a little more too," Mandy looked crestfallen. She turned to glance at 117. "If you don't mind my bringing this up, I read in your files that both of you were childhood friends? Before cybernetic enhancement?"

"Correct," 117 stated.

"Well that certainly sounds quite... unique," Mandy nodded as they both watched 43 greeting a woman with a polite wave. "Are you two close?"

"She is no longer within my physical proximity, the distance between us is about 15 feet."

"No, David," Mandy let out a sputter as she tried to contain a laugh. "I didn't mean literally."

"May I ask what your intention was?" 117 asked.

"You can just say, 'what do you mean?'" Mandy replied casually. "Try asking me that way."

117 blinked, pausing for a second. After he processed her request, he decided to say exactly what she had said.

"What... do you mean?" he asked slowly.

"It's probably nothing but..." Mandy shrugged. "43 seems to like you. I haven't seen an amborg express that much emotion before."

"She had no emotion," 117 reported. "We don't display or express the same kind of emotions that humans do."

"You're still human, David," Mandy sighed. "Anyway, do you know what 43's first name is?"

"Yes," 117 replied.

There was a short silence, which prompted Mandy to turn and look at 117 again. He stared at her blankly.

"Oh right."

Mandy nodded when she realized how the conversation had ended. She awkwardly chuckled.

"Do you know her name?" she mumbled as she repeated her own words. "He said yes because that was the direct answer to my question. He didn't say the wrong thing."

117 remained silent. He was starting to feel confused again. Mandy seemed to have an odd habit of repeating a lot of things.

Mandy looked 117 in the eye and pleasantly bowed.

"Can you tell me her name?" she asked politely. For good measure, she reworded her question. "May I know her name?"

"Yes," 117 nodded. "She has preferred to be called by her amborg number ever since we were enhanced. This is because one of the A.I. programs here shares the same name as her. To avoid confusing many people, 43 would like to be addressed by her amborg number."

"So she shares the same name as an A.I. with this company?" Mandy asked. "Well that narrows it down to over 40 possibilities... David, I feel like you're avoiding my question."

"Pardon me," 117 replied, "I was simply explaining the context."

Back in the observatory, Thalia's cheerful smile caught her father's eye. They had been observing 117 as he engaged in conversation with a woman who had chosen to introduce herself. It looked like it was going really well.

"Look daddy, he's happy now," she smiled. "They're friends! It's going to be alright for him now."

"You know sweetheart," George replied, a small smile forming on his face, "I think you might be onto something."

He straightened up and turned to the others. All of the executives, satisfied with this portion of the tour, appeared to be ready to move on as they all began to huddle around the exit.

"So, would everyone like to continue the inspection? It looks like we're all finished here," George addressed all of them. "Dr. Kendrick would like to meet with you once we finish the tour to give a concluding statement. Our next stop is the medical center."

The large group of executives began to file out the door. George glanced back and motioned for Thalia to follow. She turned away from the glass to walk toward her father but then hesitated. In a burst of energy, she dashed back to the window and waved at 117. Down below, he noticed her, tilting his head in curiosity. The woman beside him also looked up and began waving at Thalia. Thalia saw her give 117 a gentle nudge, prompting him to wave too. Having successfully signaled her farewell, Thalia turned away from the glass once more and hurried over to her father.

"George?"

George suddenly froze on the spot. The executives were already out the door and heading towards the next destination, leaving him and Thalia as the only ones left in the room. There was no mistaking that voice that had called out to him.

"Oh!" Thalia exclaimed. "It's Dr. Kendrick! Hi!"

George heard footsteps approaching from behind. The same voice pleasantly spoke again.

"Hello Thalia," George heard Dr. Kendrick say. He remained rooted on the spot and refused to turn around. "Did you unexpectedly join us today?"

"Yes!" Thalia answered cheerfully. "My daddy let me see the amborgs!"

George gulped. His own daughter's honesty was brutal. Forget getting fired, it was time to arrange for his funeral.

"Really? Wasn't that nice of him?"

Dr. Kendrick sounded amused and the forced optimism only gave George chills.

"George," Dr. Kendrick cleared his throat. "There's something we need to discuss. Could you please face me?"

George managed to get his hands working again as he brought them up to his neck and straightened his tie.

"J-John," he stammered as he turned around. "I wasn't expecting you!"

Dr. Kendrick held his hands behind his back as he gave a sly grin. George had been caught red-handed. No escape now.

"I think you should know by now that you should always expect me even when you don't expect it," he declared. "After all, I own this company."

"Yes sir, you choose where you go and what you do whenever you like!"

Dr. Kendrick nodded as he glanced at Thalia.

"Thalia," he said cheerfully. "Your father and I need to talk. Could you go ahead and wait outside this room?"

"Do I have to?"

"Yes please," George spoke insistently. "I'll be right there, sweetheart."

"Ok!"

Thalia eagerly turned away and left the observation room. George wished that she had put up more of a fight to remain at his side. How did Dr. Kendrick get her to agree to his demands when he and his wife struggled earlier?

"George," Dr. Kendrick spoke in a soft, but stern tone. "You realize we have rules here?"

"Yes sir, John."

"Doctor," Dr. Kendrick snapped.

"Yes sir, doctor!"

"Do you know why I prefer that children of my employees – children of a certain age, are not allowed to watch the selections?"

"Yes doctor," George nodded his head. "It's because at this phase of their training, the amborgs are readjusting to new social situations."

"With how unpredictable their behavior is," Dr. Kendrick crossed his arms, "it is not good to expose a child like Thalia to them. She'll ask questions. A lot of questions that the amborgs will provide answers to. Answers that a child like her might not be ready to hear."

"Yes sir," George nodded again. "It was a foolish mistake. Won't happen again."

"I don't think any punishment is necessary in this case," Dr. Kendrick gave him a satisfied nod. "Just be careful with any future promises."

"Sure."

Dr. Kendrick looked at the window and glanced into the room below. The amborgs were all mingling properly. He noticed that 117 was paying close attention to Mandy as she carried the conversation.

"How's Marina?" he asked George while observing the crowd below.

"Oh, she's doing great!" George replied nervously.

"You realize that, as your boss, I know when you lie to me," Dr. Kendrick spoke softly. "Talk to me. Do not hide the truth from me, George."

George then realized that Dr. Kendrick had sent Thalia out of the room so she couldn't hear this. There was no putting this past a man like the CEO of A.I. Industries.

"She's been lashing out," George whispered. "Her weekly appointments have been helping but every now and then, she has a sudden episode and then doesn't remember it after it happens."

"Has she hurt any of you?" Dr. Kendrick asked. "Crossed any lines?"

"No! No, of course not!" George replied hastily. "It's just that... it's getting harder to keep it from Thalia. We were talking about it the other day and... Marina thinks that we need to resort to..."

"Ah ah ah!" Dr. Kendrick interrupted him. "Let's... not go there. Perhaps we should discuss this after the inspection tour is done for the day."

"Sure," George nodded.

"I'll treat you and Marina to dinner when she returns," Dr. Kendrick said. "Let's go. We still have work to do."

"Yes sir," George nodded. "Doctor."

"George... Now you can call me John again."

Both men headed towards the door that the tour group and Thalia had gone through. When the door opened, George saw his daughter waiting patiently for them. Dr. Kendrick smiled as he watched his friend scoop his little girl up in his arms, and they left the observation room together.

Present Day
Classroom 312

Mandy hit the pause button and the video stopped. Sarah looked up from her screen with a blank expression. Evidently, it was time for a little bit of commentary.

"Is there something wrong, Mrs. Mandy?" she asked. "That was a video log of you all those years ago wasn't it?"

"It really was, wasn't it? A long time ago I mean," Mandy smiled just as she did in the video, which caught the attention of Sarah who recognized the similarities. "Some things still haven't changed either in the present. That's why I stopped for a bit. Did you notice anything that caught your eye so far?"

"This lesson focuses mostly on amborg 117, like you mentioned previously," Sarah said observingly. "But I fail to understand. You also clarified before the presentation that he was the first amborg you paired with. That is common knowledge to everyone. Why show the footage of your first meeting during that selection?"

"Because you just had the opportunity to see what you've heard about all this time," Mandy smirked. "Tell me something Sarah. What is the difference between hearing stories about someone versus being there to actually see it happening?"

"Wouldn't the experience of being there as a full on witness increase the genuine feeling of what really happened? Exaggeration of certain details is a variable that occurs when one tells a story, which mostly results in very inaccurate misunderstandings."

"Yes absolutely."

Mandy scrolled the video back a bit and it showed the picture of her shaking hands with 117. She appeared very enthusiastic, but the same couldn't be said for 117. Sarah looked at his confused and innocent expression and began to see what Mandy was trying to teach her.

"He was helpless wasn't he?" she said presumptuously.

"Not entirely," Mandy corrected her. "I would say he was a little lost when I first met him. You see, all the records portray his accomplishments. His profile tells you all about his personality and what he's like. But when you see him interacting during our first meeting, you get another piece of the puzzle that makes him... him."

"When you first met him, was he not living up to your expectations?"

"Actually, when I first met him, I thought he needed someone to guide him," Mandy replied, zooming in on 117's face. "It wasn't that he wasn't living up to my expectations. It just felt like he acted differently.

Sure, the Second Group had all the same equipment installed inside their cybernetics as the First Group, but he had this aura about him that just made him stand out to me. It felt like he was stuck between trying to be an amborg and himself. Naturally, all the other amborgs had difficulties adjusting and they all coped with it at their own pace. But with 117, I chose him because I felt that he was the one who needed my help specifically. His pace was... a little off. Now do you see why you remind me of him so much?"

"Am I failing the exams in your class Mrs. Mandy?" Sarah asked with a little bit of concern in her voice. She suddenly began to look afraid.

"No of course not," Mandy quickly reassured her. "You're one of the best students in the class. But sometimes you just have that aura that tells me you're a little lost. Caught between your upgrades and your normal life. We don't have technicians paired with amborgs anymore, which is a disadvantage with amborgs who exhibit problems. At the same time, they all can cope and so will you. Is that clear, Sarah?"

"Yes ma'am," Sarah said with a sigh of relief. "Are we continuing the lesson? I would very much like to proceed to the part of the lesson where you talk about the high school student, Brad."

"All in due time Sarah. Commence video log again at the last pause."

The computer chimed once and the video began to play again.

CHAPTER 3

Shots Fired

A.I. Industries Gymnasium: Temporary Weapons Testing Site
2127 July
2 Weeks Post Selection

"Attention all personnel. Next stage of testing will now commence. All personnel stand clear of the temporary firing range. Next group of amborgs, stand by for ballistics testing please."

Mandy scowled as she watched 117 take his place among the other amborgs that were in line. Whoever came up with this idea was an absolute barbarian.

"This is insane," she muttered angrily.

The gymnasium had been retrofitted for many different uses. Today, the vast room was being used to conduct experiments and physical exercises. The Second Group amborgs were undergoing multiple tests with their technicians on hand. This was a massive evaluation of performance under certain conditions. After weeks of physical therapy, rehab, and rest from their post augmentation, they were now being physically tested for possible field work.

Practice dummies and sparring bots stood in various spots while a large shooting range occupied one corner. However, instead of dummies or paper targets, the targets were the amborgs. Mandy had walked with 117 over to the range, but she had to stand at a safe distance since it was a hazard for her to step into the potential line of fire. She stood with several other technicians, and all of them continued to watch as army soldiers grabbed various weapons and firearms to the shooting stands.

She couldn't believe what she was seeing. Mandy let out a huff and crossed her arms. The sight of watching their own security guards and military personnel shooting at unarmed people for test results was simply not what she called a good day.

"It's sick what they do to you in order to get results," she pouted. "Why on earth do they have to shoot all these guns at you? I get that all of you are willing to do this, but it feels like assisted suicide..."

117, from downrange, heard her and looked her way. His bracelet was too far away for her to hear. So, he transmitted his voice from her own bracelet.

"Do not be alarmed Ms..."

Even from downrange, 117 paused and noticed how angry she was. At least his eyesight was still good.

"...Mandy," he quickly corrected. His voice spoke calmly but she could almost detect a hint of fear. "An amborg's exo-skeletal structure is designed to withstand every known weapon in existence from a standard firearm minus a superheated concentrated blast or tactical nuclear explosion. In theory, explosives and high-yield bombs cannot severely harm us, but it is inadvisable to perform those tests indoors. It is highly improbable that I will be destroyed from a simple ballistics test."

Before she could respond, the officer in charge of the drills suddenly bellowed his orders.

"Shooters! On the line! Safeties off!"

117 stood in line with nine other amborgs. The ten of them each kept to their own individual lanes and stood their ground against one shooter. There were five army soldiers wearing green B.D.U.s. The other five in dark body armor were part of the A.I. Industries security team.

117 faced a soldier aiming his weapon, standing firm. Mandy scowled as she and everyone nearby that weren't wearing hearing protection immediately raised their hands to cover their ears. The officer in charge was preparing to give the order.

"You are only firing one round for this test!" he commanded. "Take aim! Fire!"

Each shooter fired exactly one shot. Ten shots simultaneously rang out in the gym. All ten amborgs were hit center mass, but barely flinched. Unfazed, 117 turned to look at Mandy and nodded reassuringly, but this didn't appease her.

"You know that's not what I mean, David!" Mandy called out to him in annoyance. She whirled to the technician next to her. "Come on! Back me up here! Are you seeing this?!"

"Uhh..." he turned, giving Mandy a bewildered expression as he kept his ears covered. "Isn't this procedure?"

"Forget it..." Mandy groaned.

What happened next riled her up even more. The soldier in 117's lane had taken another shot. A bullet from his pistol hit 117 squarely in the forehead, but he showed no reaction. To everyone's surprise, 117 simply appeared as if a fly had landed on him, completely unbothered. This left Mandy furious.

"What the hell?!" she yelled. "What was that for?!"

The man who had shot 117 turned slightly and slid his hearing protection off his ears. He saw her approaching and set his weapon down.

"All shooters!" his commanding officer barked out. "Safety your weapons and holster! Civilian entering the range!"

"You!" Mandy snapped.

"What?" the soldier sneered. "He took that bullet, and nothing happened. These amborgs sure are built like tanks."

"I'm talking about how you fired an extra shot when he wasn't looking!" Mandy got in the soldier's face and pointed a finger towards his throat. "You just shot him when we were having a conversation!"

"I'm j-just following orders," he stammered.

Mandy glanced at the name on his uniform. His name was Henderson. She examined the striped chevrons on his shoulders. There were two of them. If she remembered correctly, this man was a corporal.

"Fuck your orders," Mandy snarled.

She turned and glanced at the officer in charge.

"You in charge of this dumbass?!" she yelled.

117 and the other amborgs downrange were all staring at the drama unfolding. Each shooter in their lanes shifted uncomfortably, awkwardly turning to watch as well. The officer in charge was taken aback. Mandy was shorter than almost everyone at the range, but she radiated intimidation, looking ready to strike.

"Ma'am," the officer said calmly. "Corporal Henderson is one of my best soldiers. We're just here administering the tests that Dr. Kendrick contracted us to carry out."

"Your target practice is turning into a violation of human rights!"

The two silver bars on this officer's collar told Mandy that he was a captain. His nametag read, 'Cobb'.

Excellent, she thought, Captain Dumbass it is.

As Mandy tried to confront Cobb, he merely scoffed and turned to the shooters on the range.

"Keep firing!" he commanded. "We have a schedule to keep."

The army soldiers nodded and faced the amborgs downrange. They picked up their weapons and prepared to fire again. However, the five A.I. Industries security guards stood in place. They were not members of the U.S. army, so they weren't technically under obligation to follow Cobb's orders. Instead of continuing the test, they defiantly kept their eyes on the confrontation between Cobb and Mandy.

"Oh sure!" Mandy shouted sarcastically. "Keep your stupid schedule! Well, I'm trying to keep their rights from going out the window!"

The soldiers resumed firing. As 117 felt the bullets hitting him and bouncing off, amborg Ryan 35, right beside him, leaned over and publicly broadcasted a message.

"What window is your technician referring to?" 35 asked curiously.

"Unclear," 117 replied as he felt a bullet strike his stomach. "Mandy is quite… proficient when it comes to metaphors."

Mandy looked down the line and saw all the amborgs obediently standing still as bullets plastered them. She noticed the five security guards who had refused to resume the test were standing in place, observing. Downrange, the amborgs that were supposed to be their targets were patiently waiting and staring straight ahead. In her eyes, this wasn't a shooting range. It looked more like a gallery at a carnival.

"This is what we're supposed to do!" Cobb protested.

"From where I'm standing…" Mandy pointed to 117 and lowered her fingers, "all I can see is a line of unarmed human beings getting shot at repeatedly. How can you just shoot them so easily?! If you wore a bulletproof vest and I had a gun, would you be ok if I shot you?!"

"That's not the point…" Cobb sighed.

Suddenly, Mandy's silver bracelet lit up and they heard 117 speak.

"But I am not human Mandy," he interjected. "None of us on the shooting range are. I am an amborg and so are they. I am confused how this is still making you feel angry."

This didn't make Mandy feel better at all. She stared at him and made sure he could see her expression clearly. It didn't help that Henderson was still shooting him.

"Will you stop that?!" she barked. "You've got plenty of results! Stop shooting David!"

Henderson lowered his gun and set it on the table. He turned his head back to look at Mandy and Cobb. It was actually quite impressive how much her voice carried.

"You've named him?" Henderson asked, once again looking bewildered. "I thought he was just a number."

"He always had a name, you ignorant jarhead!" Mandy fired back. "And you!"

Mandy rounded on 117. She pointed her finger at him fiercely. More people in the gym were starting to notice her outburst. Steve 92 and Jon 93, twin brother amborgs, both displayed identical wide-eyed expressions as they enjoyed the show.

"I know you are an amborg," she snapped. "But from my own eyes you should be aware that I have concerns about this. You should be able to at least understand the ethical implications and morals currently in place right now. Also, you should… HEY!! What do you think you're doing with that?!"

While she was busy lecturing 117, Henderson had decided to pick out another weapon. The room fell silent in disbelief when everyone caught sight of what he picked up from the weapon rack. For some reason, he switched from a small handgun to a ridiculously huge rifle. Scratch that — it resembled a massive cannon, yet somehow small enough for a single person to carry.

Her outburst had caused Henderson to flinch. Taken aback, he clenched the fifty-caliber sniper rifle in his hands and looked from her to 117.

"Following the proper testing procedures miss," he said nervously as he turned to look at Mandy and Captain Cobb. "All amborgs need to be tested if they can withstand even our most powerful guns. Those are my orders."

"Will you stop ignoring me and just listen?!" Mandy roared.

Marco 125 and Jesse 274 were in the middle of lifting weights. They gently set down their 1000-pound dumbbells and quietly watched.

"Corporal," Mandy said angrily. She had had enough. "Are you always blindly following orders like this?? Can't you grab some of the material used to make their exo-skeletons and shoot at THAT!?"

From downrange, 117 watched, startled as Mandy stared straight into Henderson's eyes. Despite the huge rifle in his hands, she was definitely intimidating him. She pointed at the rifle and then at 117.

"Can't you see how wrong it is to purposely use... that," she said, "that weapon on an innocent looking biologically enhanced human? A fifty caliber would blast a regular person's head off... as well as the ones behind them for Christ's sake!!"

"I'm sorry you feel that way, but I'm under orders..."

Corporal Henderson stole a glance at 117, then looked back at Mandy. Captain Cobb had shut his mouth and was listening intently.

"It's not like this is the first time I've seen someone else feel this way before," he explained as best as he could while trying to hold his own composure. "And it's not like I haven't done this only once. I've fired every known firearm they've given me and these amborgs take it. No emotion, no damage, no nothing. Of course, it's wrong to do it just for test results but they can withstand it."

"Did you hear what you just said?" Mandy asked. Unfazed, she stared hard at him and shouted, "They aren't playthings for the military that you can abuse!"

The other soldiers along the firing line had lowered their weapons and were now listening to the argument. They joined the A.I. Industries security guards and observed quietly. Although her gaze did not stray,

Mandy was now aware of how much attention she was drawing. The rest of the Second Group, their technicians, and every other individual had put a pause on their activities to look their way.

117 continued to stare. Instead of a look of confusion, he was contemplating hard about what Mandy was arguing about. Out of his peripherals, he saw Carter 297, Katie 57, and Luis 777 stop their two-ton medicine ball exercises and were now facing his way.

"Get Dr. Kendrick here and he'd agree," Mandy said very sternly. "Frankly, I don't know why he authorized this sort of thing when there are better ways to test their durability. They aren't just machines. Not entirely. They are humans who have changed. You still need to treat them equally. They're not livestock that you can just send in to be slaughtered."

With their enhanced hearing, the amborgs picked up a soft creaking noise on the other end of the gym. 117 shifted his glance and saw amborg Alice 999 stop doing her pushups and was now looking up at the shooting range. Her spotter, amborg Jack 917, placed a hand to steady the cargo container she had resting on her back. It was clear that all the amborgs of the Second Group were directing their attention to Mandy. A few drones and employees allowed the weights they were carrying to fall to the ground with a clatter, and the gym fell eerily silent. Several were whipping out their phones.

Henderson took a breath and looked at 117, who didn't say anything. All of the amborgs being tested on the shooting range kept silently staring. It looked super ominous as they stood like expressionless mannequins. Each of the technicians, employees, and security guards in the gym were curious about the outcome of this turn of events. Finally, Corporal Henderson sighed and faced Mandy with a nod. He shot a quick glance at Captain Cobb, too.

"Well what would you have me do?" he asked politely. "If I don't do my job, I'm screwed. I have to provide results. Captain Cobb is going to yell at us if we don't follow orders. What can I do to fix this?"

Mandy's answer was immediate and direct.

"Ask him."

"What?" Henderson blinked. He shook his head, unsure of what she meant.

"Ask him how he feels," Mandy repeated firmly. She pointed at 117. "Before you take the next shot, you ask him how he feels about getting shot at without trying to dodge the bullet like the freaking Matrix. Get his permission and make sure he's ok with it. Go on."

She enunciated, putting a great deal of emphasis on her next words.

"Ask David what it's like to be a target for the rest of his life."

Henderson didn't respond. He looked downrange at 117 and then at his fellow soldiers.

Baffled by this request, the sergeant lowered his rifle and turned to face 117.

Henderon placed the rifle on the stand, the barrel aimed downrange, but before he leaned forward and put his eyes to the scope, he stood straight and called out to 117.

"Amborg... David 117," he said respectfully. "Permission to discharge a fifty caliber rifle round for ballistics testing? Am I clear to proceed?"

117 stared back with a little twitch in his head. The other amborgs next to him looked at him curiously. After a brief pause, a response came through, out of both Mandy's and Henderson's silver bracelet for both to hear.

"Permission to proceed, granted," 117 nodded. "You may fire when ready, Corporal Henderson."

"Stop!"

Mandy and Henderson both pivoted around to see Captain Cobb stepping forward.

"Corporal," he commanded. "Stand down."

"Sir?" Henderson looked confused.

"I'll take this one," Cobb stated. "You and I are both qualified to handle the fifty cal."

"But sir," Henderson protested. "I can finish this test."

"I agree," Cobb let out a sigh as he stepped up to the rifle and put on a pair of safety glasses. "However, this technician is right."

Cobb glanced at Mandy, then turned to Henderson.

"You're right that the amborgs are bullet-proof," he explained his reasoning promptly and in a commanding tone. "However, you fired extra shots when I only cleared you for one. So, why did you shoot at the amborg more than once?"

Henderson shut his mouth, straightened up, and backed off.

"Sorry sir," he mumbled.

"Not to me, corporal..."

Henderson looked at Mandy.

"I'm sorry," he stated.

"And?" Cobb gestured downrange.

Henderson turned to face 117 and called out to him.

"I am sorry for firing excessively, amborg 117!"

Cobb put on his hearing protection and leaned forward. He readied himself and positioned the rifle butt next to his right shoulder.

"Corporal," Cobb declared.

"Sir!" Henderson answered.

"Stand aside," Cobb stated. "I'm taking the shot."

As Henderson stepped away, Cobb looked up at Mandy for confirmation, who reluctantly but quietly nodded.

Cobb grabbed a magazine full of ammunition and loaded the rifle. Once it was secured and in place, he pulled the charging handle back. Once he heard the loud snap and click of the bullet being chambered, he released the handle and it flew forward.

"Range is hot!" he called out. "Live ammo in play!"

Mandy lifted her hands to her ears again in preparation for the noise, but a drone quickly handed her a pair of earmuffs. She slipped them on and clenched them over her head tightly.

Captain Cobb took a deep breath, looked through the scope down the sights, and took careful aim. The safety was switched off and after a few seconds, he pulled the trigger.

A massive bang rang out through the entire gymnasium like cannon fire. It seemed louder now that everyone wasn't going about their own business. The bullet instantly struck 117 directly in the chest, creating a giant puff of smoke. The force of the impact caused him to bend a couple of inches forward, and Mandy saw him get pushed back. With the smoke dissipating, all that remained was a blast mark all over his A.I. Industries jacket. Looking carefully, Mandy saw a small hole torn next to where 117's heart was, but there was no blood or any sign of penetration. It didn't look like he was hurt too badly. Aside from having a strong bulletproof body, the amborg uniforms were also built to withstand bullets. Seeing that hole made Mandy wish that they wouldn't encounter guns this powerful out in the field.

Captain Cobb switched the safety back on, unloaded the magazine, stood up, and called for a ceasefire, even though no one was shooting anything. Everyone watched as he walked over to 117, who was straightening up from taking the full force of the shot.

"Are you all right?" he asked calmly.

117 eyes were downcast, but then looked up at Cobb as if nothing had happened.

"Damage assessment; struck by fifty caliber sniper round at a velocity of three thousand feet per second," he recited slowly. "Force of impact at twenty-three thousand four hundred and thirty-two pounds. The result of the impact has pushed me back roughly three inches from my original position. Structural integrity and circuitry undamaged. All systems functioning within the proper parameters. Thank you for asking."

Cobb almost laughed a little but he kept a professional composure.

"Next time, just say you're fine," he smiled and then walked back to the firing line. "I think that certainly concludes this test."

Once the show was over, everyone else went back to their own business. As noise flooded the gym again, Mandy brushed past Cobb and ran up to 117. She heard him yell that a civilian was on the range. No weapons or tests until she was clear.

"You should always have your own voice David, always," she stated firmly. "Don't let anyone take your right to defend yourself away from you. You're not a complete machine that just runs entirely from your programming. You have feelings too. I want you to use them."

"Accessing my feelings is a little difficult," 117 stated, then asked her a question, "Have I offended you Mandy?"

"No, it's all right David, I... accidentally made a scene," she sighed as she led him aside, away from the line of fire.

Once they were clear, Mandy heard Corporal Henderson, the other army soldiers, and their security guards asking for permission from the other amborgs. After they got consent, they began preparing for the next test, which made her feel better.

"By the way, when that jarhead asked you for permission, did you really think about your answer?"

117 nodded before delivering his response.

"Of course Mandy, after hearing your discussion, I took all of the factors into consideration: the alloy that our exoskeletons are made of, the maker and designer of the rifle, the amount of force that I could expect from the bullet, the captain's previous records, your tone of voice, and Dr. Kendrick's reports on all of the test subjects. This is only the first of a few factors I thought of before reaching my decision."

"How many factors did you think about?" Mandy stared.

"Approximately 82 different ones."

Mandy let out a laugh and started to grin.

"How long did it take for you to think of all that?" she asked curiously.

"About 3.72 seconds," he replied. "And that is a long time for an amborg."

Mandy didn't know why but she found his response quite funny. As she began to laugh, they heard an incoming transmission. 117's bracelet flashed and another man's voice spoke out through it.

"Hey 117!" 917 said, interrupting their conversation. "You want to do some pushups? 999 says she's done and will let you have a turn with the cargo container. Just tell us how much weight you want us to load inside."

117 and Mandy watched as 917 slid his hands under the container and held it up as if it weighed nothing. 999 crawled forward and straightened up. When she was clear, he lowered the container and set it on the ground with a loud clang.

"You still need to finish your physical test on the relay race too," 297 added as he ran by. "My technician and I are done calculating my fastest time."

117 looked at Mandy, who sighed. After a moment, she gave him an encouraging smile.

"Go finish what you need to do," she replied. "Don't keep your family waiting."

CHAPTER 4

Disorganized Hot Zone

Los Angeles, California
2127 September
The Second Group's First Deployment

"Date: September 8th, 2127. This briefing is directed to amborg 117 and his technician. Attention, an emergency amborg deployment was requested by several key officials from the city of Los Angeles. Urban and rural districts are reporting an increase in gang-related activity. Local police forces have been unable to contain the surge in crime. The National Guard is assembling, but their response time has been delayed. All available amborgs are mobilizing. The state of California is under emergency status. Stand by and prepare for deployment."

117 firmly gripped his armrests as the computer's initial pre-deployment briefing concluded. He stole a quick glance out the window of his deployment pod, noticing a scattering of clouds drifting lazily by. However, his attention was quickly drawn to the columns of smoke rising along the skyline.

The quickest vehicles at A.I. Industries were their drop pods. They were a neat invention that Dr. Kendrick and the research team had come up with using modified rocket booster technology from NASA many years ago, just around the time that the First Group saw action. Each amborg had one built and assigned to them, and they could take them just about anywhere. The trip from A.I. Industries to Los Angeles only took about 24 minutes, when normally it would take an hour by any other form of transportation.

His memories of his old home were fuzzy, but he knew that this was the type of setting that he'd lived in before Dr. Kendrick found him. Now here he was, getting ready to step back out into the world for the first time as an amborg. Saving innocent people caught in the crossfire was on the forefront of his mind. Mandy's voice spoke in the back of his head a moment later.

"Ready for your first operation David?" she asked in a loud and clear voice. "I suppose it's technically our first operation together. But luckily, you get to do the heavy lifting, and I've got my coffee back here in my cubicle."

"Isn't questioning my readiness redundant?" 117 answered as he tilted his head. "I have been ready for this and am operating under normal parameters. After finishing all of the required qualifying tests, this is what I've been preparing for. I predict many positive outcomes as well."

"David, just say you're ready..." Mandy mumbled bitterly. "I'm already nervous enough."

"Did I say something to make you nervous?" 117 asked.

"Obviously, yes 117," Mandy answered as the pod's thrusters activated and its speed began to drop. "It looks like both of us are asking redundant questions today."

The pod began to tilt upwards and 117 felt himself returning to an upright position. As it began its descent, he felt the pull of gravity as he dropped towards the ground. Suddenly, a muffled roar echoed from beneath him. The landing thrusters activated, gradually slowing their descent. A resounding boom filled the air as the pod touched down. The door clamps hissed and unlocked, allowing the door to swing outwards. 117's harness automatically unfastened itself, and he leapt out, landing on his feet as he surveyed the immediate area.

"Whoa," Mandy exclaimed. "I'm sure glad I don't live here."

His landing zone was in the middle of a parking lot with a few battered and worn out vehicles. Taking particular note of a group of children playing in the wreckage of a destroyed car, 117 nodded and waved a hand at their stunned faces. He stepped forward and transmitted a signal to his pod.

The engines roared and with a loud burst of flames, it flew up like a rocket and shot back off into the air. 117 watched it shoot out of sight before beginning his walk. His HUD, which was on almost all the time, began to chime. Mandy's face appeared in the upper right corner of his display as she began a live video feed.

"Alright David," she said. "Checking your sensory data. Eyesight, hearing, taste... All good! Well, only if you actually eat some food. Uhh, implants are running really well since your last checkup. Primary CPU and main functions are green. Perfect as usual. Sensor and GPS are running right... about... now. Sound systems, video connection is streaming. Great graphics. I now see what you see. A set of eyes and voice in the back of your head. Standard procedure says I have to ask this even though it's obvious... Can you hear me?"

"I am reading your communication line loud and clear Mandy," 117 replied. "All systems are green."

"Oh good," Mandy replied, "I was afraid I'd have to check the volume control."

"Sarcasm is still not my strongest suit," 117 replied in his neutral tone. He looked around, not noticing anything suspicious. "What is my current objective?"

The kids nearby all stared at him in awe as he began to leave the parking lot. Several pedestrians noticed him and scurried away. This got his attention.

"Curious," he transmitted to Mandy. "The people seem to be afraid of my presence."

"Well, it's probably because they know there's a lot of trouble in the city," Mandy explained. "Seeing the police, military, or the amborgs in person is probably their signal to get out of the area. Be careful, someone could try to ambush you."

"Understood," 117 replied as he watched a few cars drive by. "Where should I deploy?"

"Right, your current objective. Ok David, here's what's up," Mandy said informatively. "Heavy assaults from gangs all over the West Coast are flooding in like crazy. Los Angeles is one of the worst places to be living in right now. Not really a surprise. A large influx of violence and outbreaks have been happening over the last few months. The precincts here have requested more amborg deployments than usual to help calm the situation, which leads to more bad news. A great deal of major cities are flooding A.I. Industries with help requests faster than we can process them."

"All of those distress calls... That totals to over one hundred cities," 117 immediately calculated as he turned a corner. He could hear several shots now as he progressed slowly and voiced his conclusion. "There aren't enough amborgs to respond to so many deployment requests."

"That's right David," Mandy replied grimly, "which is also why you're being deployed today instead of one month from now. It's so bad that Dr. Kendrick authorized the release of the Second Group early, even with the First Group working overtime. But it also might mean we'll be sharing that same workload soon. So far, the First Group amborgs are scattered up in Washington and Oregon. If we're lucky, maybe we'll encounter a veteran who has time to kill, and they'll decide to come south. Until that happens, we will take care of California, which is the state that has the highest record of amborg deployments so far. Hopefully that's not too intimidating or stereotypical. It's actually not an entirely bad place to live once you get past all the violence and other horrible things."

117 approached another corner and peered around it cautiously. The street was deserted, possibly because people were hiding in the safety of their homes or had already evacuated. He could hear the sound of loudspeakers over thirty meters to the northwest blaring out a series of alarms. From what he knew from the city emergency plans, the broadcast alarms were signaling for the people to remain indoors and to keep out of sight.

From A.I. Industries, a flood of data surged into 117's HUD from Mandy's computer system. Mandy was typing furiously, her fingers a blur on the keyboard, as a continuous flow of information was entered and displayed from 117 in perfect synchronization.

As he followed her directions, he made his way to the nearest police station.

"Who is it that I am seeking out Mandy?" 117 asked as he spotted the entrance.

"Calm down you walking GPS," she replied with a chuckle. "I'm getting to that. We need to focus. I got a ton of stuff to go through and the cops are really flooding the com-lines. They urgently need our help and it's my job to prioritize where to guide you. According to this, you're looking for the captain of the precinct. Dr. Kendrick wants you to report to her before you go running around. Her name is Bradley."

"What is your assessment of this operation?" he asked as he scanned the area in front of the police station. Seeing no one around, which puzzled him, he walked up the steps to the entrance, which was badly boarded up. "How is my current performance?"

"Well, you've been deployed to Los Angeles for your very first op," Mandy said with slight discomfort as he stepped inside. "Sending you out now would be good experience for you. You're doing fine so far, David. Watch the ceiling."

117 looked up and stepped aside as one of the ceiling tiles fell down, shattering on the ground next to him. He was suddenly aware of the smattering of bullet holes and several make-shift barricades sitting in the middle of the entrance hall. Mandy chuckled from the back of his head.

"Wouldn't want a decapitation by tile now, would we?" she said. A moment later, she brought up a picture of someone on his HUD. "Now let's see, according to these files, Captain Marsha Bradley.. Wait a minute..."

"What is it?" 117 asked as he glanced around, trying to find an officer.

"It's weird, the system is telling me that she's the current chief of police," Mandy mumbled in confusion. "But... she's a captain. I don't know how the ranking system works with the LAPD..."

"Bradley is the Chief of Police for all of LAPD," 117 replied promptly. "Then there would be a Deputy Chief, commander, and then a captain. I also have questions about her rank in our files."

"Thanks David," Mandy sighed. "Yeah, then you would have lieutenants or detectives, a sergeant and then your basic officer ranks at the lowest part of the chain. She's not even the head of the metro division, the best unit in LAPD. How strange..."

117 heard footsteps ahead. From behind a door, two officers in full tactical body armor walked out. They saw him and stopped.

"Whoa, an amborg," the man in front said. "Glad someone heard our cries for help."

117 stepped aside politely as the officer brushed past him. The second one acknowledged him and gave an encouraging smile.

"You must be a new one, right?" he asked.

"Yes," 117 nodded. "I am amborg 117 of A.I. Industries. Second Group."

"About time, let us know if we can provide you with any backup."

"My technician and I could use some assistance," 117 stated as his bracelet flashed and transmitted his words. "Could you direct us to... Chief Captain Bradley?"

"Ask him to confirm what her actual rank is," Mandy reminded him in the back of his head.

"We were also wondering what her rank is," 117 added quickly.

"Sure," the officer nodded. "What's left of her office is upstairs. Third floor. It's the fourth one down that's missing a door when you enter the main office."

"Thank you," 117 nodded. "But what is her rank?"

"Oh, the commander? We just follow her orders. She's in charge of us."

"I don't think he knows either," Mandy stated. 117 could see her dumbfounded expression and agreed with that assessment.

"Hey," the officer looked outside and dipped his head apologetically, "I got to run. Damn good to see you buddy. Wherever you go, you kick ass alright?"

The officer rushed out after his partner and was gone before 117 could even say a proper farewell.

"Mandy? Why would I kick ass? That doesn't sound like the most effective method in combat," he surmised.

"It's an expression," Mandy replied. "Save it for later, alright?"

"Understood."

Following the man's directions, 117 walked up the stairs to the third floor while Mandy looked through Bradley's official records again.

"Wow, she's got quite a rep. Check this out, David. Apparently, she's been dealing with a gang called the Splatter-Bugs – how original – for the last five years, so I'm assuming she'll tell you where to go to take on these guys. If you ask me, she'd probably give us the worst part of the mission to take care of. Ha. Ha. Oh shit. There goes my coffee."

117 heard the sound of a mug falling over on a desk in his head. Disregarding the noise, he kept walking.

"Hmm," he muttered as he looked around. "Shit. A slang term and noun for feces or a contemptible worthless person, object, or thing. Where do you see shit Mandy? I cannot identify anything in the area to associate with that term. A rag would also be sufficient in wiping up the mess."

"T-that's not what I meant David," Mandy stammered. "Ouch! That's hot! Oh, never mind. Just go find the chief, commander, or whatever her rank is."

"A curious name for a gang," 117 stated. "Splatter-Bugs."

"After a quick read," Mandy's voice shuddered, "they like to take their victims up to really tall buildings or other high places and drop them to the ground. Apparently, some of the earliest gang members that were part of this group many years ago loved using gravity to incite fear. That's just messed up."

When he reached the third floor, he encountered more people. Some officers were resting on whatever furniture they had left. They all looked up and nodded to him, but casually went back to lounging around. Carefully, 117 walked past them and entered the main office.

Several police officers looked his way when he walked in. But things were so hectic, they ignored him and promptly went about their business. Every single officer was walking around in body armor, which caught his attention. Were they regularly dealing with fighting inside their own station? Nevertheless, he continued on down the aisle through the middle of all the chaos while everyone continued scrambling around. Despite there being so many empty desks, it seemed like there were already enough people running around to fill the whole room, including damaged police drones.

Phones were ringing, people were shouting, and sirens were blaring from the garage, which sounded like it was coming from below. For normal humans, 117 was amazed anyone could hear each other through all of this. He promptly adjusted his hearing to mute out the noise and continued his search for Bradley's office. The officer downstairs had said to look for the fourth one with a missing door, but it was interesting to see that almost all of the doors were missing from several offices. Anyone that required privacy probably wasn't going to get it in here. 117 made his way to the fourth one as directed and suddenly heard a woman yelling from inside.

"I don't care if it's dangerous! I was born in the middle of this, raised and molded by this municipality, and I'm going to keep fighting! I've been in the field against orders because for the last week, there hasn't been time for anything else! We can't stop all these damn raids because I keep getting a whole bunch of academy noobs who've barely graduated with average skills! Everyone is getting their heads shot off after being here for only a couple of hours! Participating in the streets with all of my officers is risky but I'd rather lead my officers than stay in my office! Stop telling me a lucky crook is going to get me because of my recklessness. I'd like to see them try! I had one woman show up who survived at least a week, and I'd finally learned her name, but that went south because I just found out we lost her twenty-two minutes ago! So, excuse me if you hate my attitude and total disregard for your orders, but I have to be on the streets three minutes ago to make sure I don't lose another one of L.A.'s finest! I need you to get in touch with the National Guard and have them relieve my officers! We need to try to save city hall, which I still think is on fire!"

There was a loud thud as 117 heard someone's hand slam down on what he assumed was the phone, or at least what was left of one in this place. He looked at the office without a door and peered inside. He immediately knew he was in the right place when he saw the name Marsha Bradley poorly smeared in black ink on the side of the wall. It almost looked like someone had crudely dipped their fingers in ink and painted it on without the brush. The name was written just above a destroyed bulletin board, which held requisition orders for several miscellaneous items, including a new door, new wall, new stationery, and more jars of black ink. His attention then drifted over to the middle-aged woman standing over her desk or rather, half of one, who looked up at the doorway.

"Well FINALLY!" she shouted. "Look who's finally here!"

117 immediately detected the thick layer of sarcasm and false joy she forced into her voice. He stood there, completely bewildered at her appearance. She was wearing body armor just like the officers outside, but there was a bandage on her right cheek. Her left cheek, as well as her hands, were covered in black ink, and there were several holes in her shoulder sleeves from what looked like fire damage. 117 only had a

moment to speculate about what this woman had been through when she marched around her desk and made an exaggerated welcoming gesture.

"You'll have to pardon the blown-up door," Bradley said with a look of irritation. "A Splatter-Bug raid is what we have to thank for no privacy nowadays. Can I get you anything? How about some motor oil or whatever you guys eat? Come in, come in and take a break! God knows I haven't lost any more people while you've been taking your time getting here!"

Taken aback by her questions, 117 quickly linked his CPU to her bracelet before she could comment about why he hadn't said a word yet.

"I do not require anything Chief Bradley," he said, hoping that this would pacify her apparent rage. Seeing that it wasn't working, he quickly continued, "It was my understanding that you requested an amborg and you needed tactical support. Have we misinterpreted your request?"

From the back of his head, he heard a slap and a groan from Mandy. He briefly looked at the upper corner of his HUD and realized that Mandy was still on the line.

Strange, he thought, hadn't she hung up temporarily to clean up the coffee?

From what he could tell from the slap, he concluded that Mandy had done a face palm. People did that whenever something stupid happened. He concluded that he had said the wrong thing because Bradley didn't look pleased at all.

"No shit wise guy," she said, growling under her breath. 117 detected sarcasm again and listened without saying another word. "I sent that request an hour ago for crying out loud! What'd you do, stop at the drive-through?! Shut up. I don't want to know. Come here, look at this map, and let me show you where you can be useful!"

He silently followed her over to the wall where a holo-map was shining. However, it was sputtering and barely able to maintain its image. To fix it, Bradley slammed her fist into the side and the image cleared up. It displayed the area around the precinct, with several red dots blinking throughout it. As 117 observed the dots, he privately sent Mandy a message.

"Have I offended her, Mandy?"

"No David, she's just stressed," Mandy replied reassuringly. "Women at her age can get really tough when they're pushed, especially with what she's been through. But she's fairly tough based on what I can tell about her initially and her records. Just follow her instructions and don't worry about it. You'll learn how to interact with tough people soon enough. But I definitely don't think she likes it when you ask rhetorical or dumb questions. Be more direct and don't let her catch you saying anything stupid."

"Hey tin-head! Bring whatever's going on in your head back to now!"

Shifting his attention away from Mandy, 117 immediately turned back to the chief and casually perused the map for a third time.

"Where is my presence required?" he asked.

"Right here, bozo!" she answered, extending a finger and pointing it at a location on the map, which was at least a few miles north of the station. "Splatter-Bugs have got this area pinned down from the north, a couple civvies are down, five of my men wounded and two of my nut-jobs are taking on a whole goddamn mob with low ammo three blocks east from that position. If we try to move in to help, we get sent back with more people hurt or killed. Some officers and emergency crews have set up a barricade here, but they can't hold. Every block we take, I lose good men and women and... Where do you think you're going?"

117 was already heading to the door before she had even finished.

"Situation understood," he said. "I'll handle it. Or as everyone else says, I got this."

"Wait a minute," Bradley called, following 117 out of her office and waved her hand to signal someone. "Take Johnson here with you, he's kinda new but he needs experience on these streets. I'd rather have him fight next to an amborg rather than get killed with another clean gun they send my way."

A young officer in a safety vest holding two assault rifles ran up a moment later. One of the rifles slipped out of his hand and fell to the ground with a clatter.

"That is..." Bradley said, shaking her head, "if his own clumsiness doesn't get him killed."

We are both new at this, 117 thought silently as Johnson struggled to pick up the other rifle.

"Anyway, he'll do the job right, I hope," she said while Johnson straightened up, placed the rifles on another desk and smiled, which didn't reassure her at all. "But... while you're here, try to keep him and everyone else alive. That's asking a lot but I'm sick of seeing too many new faces and writing condolence letters. Johnson, I want you back here by tonight."

"Yes ma'am," the young officer replied.

"It's Captain. Or Chief."

117 and Mandy both got their questions answered and unanswered at the same time. Bradley was a police captain, but she had also declared that she was chief.

Bradley nodded grimly as Johnson obediently fell silent. She gave a thumbs-up to 117, who dipped his head in acknowledgement. With that, she snatched up a shotgun from a nearby desk and headed down the hall where she was immediately flanked by a pair of officers. Left alone, 117 and Johnson weaved their way out of the office and descended the stairs.

"So, your number is 117?" Johnson asked.

"Correct..." 117 glanced at the stripes on Johnson's sleeves. He was surprised to see there were three stripes. "...sergeant Johnson?"

"Oh, yeah," Johnson nodded. "I'm a sergeant."

"How?"

Mandy's voice broadcasted from 117's bracelet.

"He looks barely older than me," she said loud enough for Johnson to hear. "Didn't Bradley just say that he's a new guy?"

"It was a mistake," Johnson replied sheepishly. "I came here, and they gave me sergeant's stripes and apparently I jumped up on the chain of command in my first week."

"How long ago was your first week?" 117 asked.

"13 days ago," Johnson answered with a nod. "Also, to whoever just talked out of your bracelet, hello!"

Johnson then looked at 117 skeptically.

"Unless you like to talk like a woman every now and then?"

"Incorrect," 117 stated. "That was my technician, Mandy, who just spoke to you from my bracelet. She is my partner and follows along with everything I see."

"Oh, neat!"

"Is that the reason why Bradley has... well, multiple ranks? The system is just that messed up?" Mandy asked.

"Unfortunately, yes," Johnson admitted as they reached the first floor. "The casualty rate in Los Angeles is dangerously high. Veterans like Captain Bradley try their best to keep us safe, but a lot of us here are being forced into positions that we're not ready for."

"So, she's the Chief of Police for all of the LAPD because..." Mandy's voice filled with dread as she and 117 listened to Johnson's explanation.

"They're all dead," Johnson shuddered. "In the entire city, the captain is one of the few highest-ranking officers still around, so she got the title."

"That explains the confusion," 117 nodded. "Her position in the police department is due to a lack of options."

Johnson nodded as he checked that his sidearm was secured to his belt. Once they reached the lobby, he stopped by a counter where a police drone and another officer handed him an assault rifle.

"Pretty much," he stated.

"Well," Mandy gulped, "things are much worse than I thought."

Once Johnson was armed and 117 helped him with a thorough check of his equipment, they made their way out of the station and onto the streets. Finding north, the two of them began to run at a slight pace. Seeing that Johnson was struggling to keep up, 117 eased his speed to match Johnson's.

"Sorry we don't have a vehicle," Johnson panted as he struggled to maintain a good pace. "But with the way things are, most of our vehicles have been destroyed or already have been taken from the motorpool."

"It is alright," 117 stated. "Unless it is a vehicle custom made from A.I. Industries, riding in a public vehicle is actually a disadvantage."

"Really? You know, now that you mention it, I've always wondered about that."

117 and Johnson stopped at an intersection and looked in all directions for signs of trouble, then quickly ran across the road.

"Why do the amborgs not drive their own cars? Or ride with normal people?"

"It actually slows them down," Mandy's voice explained from 117's bracelet. "Want to demonstrate for him, David?"

"What?" Johnson asked.

Without a word, 117 looked around and spotted an abandoned vehicle with broken windows. The front hood had been removed and the entire engine block was missing. Someone must have looted it. He noticed that the tires were blown out and rusted as he approached the nearest door.

"Each amborg has a physical problem if they get into a vehicle that's not built to withstand them," Mandy explained as 117 reached for the door handle.

With a loud creak, he swung it open and leaned forward to sit down on what was left of the front seat. There was a loud thud. Johnson watched with wide eyes as the suspension on the abandoned car gave out and the entire thing collapsed, hitting the pavement with a resounding crash.

"Holy s-shit..." Johnson stammered.

"That's what I said when I first watched him do that," Mandy's voice let out a laugh from 117's bracelet.

117 climbed out of the car and brushed himself off. As he walked back to Johnson, the young officer stood still, staring at the wreck with a mixture of pure shock and awe. Only when 117 began to pass him did Johnson realize that he was spacing out.

"Wait!" he exclaimed. "So, the augmentation of your cybernetic implants makes you heavier? How much do you weigh?"

117 paused and looked at Johnson.

"I am approximately 352 pounds," he stated bluntly.

"Just don't go asking that question to the girls at A.I. Industries," Mandy reminded cheekily. "You might find yourself in an early grave."

Johnson's mouth hung open, his eyes widening just a fraction more. Politely, 117 raised his arm and with his index finger, gently closed Johnson's mouth. He turned away in order to keep leading them to their objective.

"Three hundred..." he mumbled.

"Let us proceed, Sergeant Johnson," 117 stated over his shoulder.

"352 pounds," he repeated. After a few seconds of contemplating, he hurried after 117. "Well, hey, you all look great!"

Mandy had to remind 117 to give Sergeant Johnson a polite thank you.

The noise in the background grew louder as the two of them drew closer to their objective. 117 was perfectly alright with running to his destination. Every amborg had strength, agility and stamina. Although, he had concerns as to why Johnson was having trouble.

A recent graduate from the police academy should give him strong physical and aerobic training. His physical condition should be up to date, he thought.

"Since you submitted an inquiry with me, may I reciprocate, Sergeant?" 117 spoke as the two of them stopped at an abandoned store.

"Oh, sure!"

Johnson nodded as they examined the broken glass window, taking note of the disarray inside. Every shelf and display had been overturned and looted.

"Are you physically fit to be in law enforcement?" 117 asked candidly.

"Wow," Mandy's voice blurted out from his bracelet. "Very tactful, David..."

"I am simply surprised," 117 said before Johnson could even reply. He looked at the young officer and nodded to him. "You are struggling to maintain a pace which is effectively exhausting you even though police academy training focuses on endurance and physical training."

Johnson blinked a few times. 117 heard Mandy sigh in the back of his head. Her connection to his bracelet had been terminated, so he only heard her voice on a private channel.

"We really need to work on teaching you how to talk in a... simpler fashion," 117 saw her shaking her head in his HUD.

"Was my reasoning unclear?" he asked.

"Hey, pay attention to him!"

117 had looked away to speak to Mandy privately. Under her direction, he noticed that Johnson was ready to answer him.

"Oh, well that's easy to answer. It's all because of how fast they've been rushing us out into the field," Johnson explained. He glanced inside the store, taking in all of the damage, and sighed. "To be honest, I was only halfway through the academy when I was sent back to L.A. The whole time I was at the academy, what we should have learned in the classrooms was instead devoted to training for field operations. It's almost like they were teaching us to skip all the legal stuff and just wanted us to kill the criminals because there are too many to arrest. I did do a lot of running but I always hated it. It's funny, even after how intense the training was, nothing could ever prepare me for this."

"Perfectly natural feelings," 117 stated observingly. "Especially since both of us are participating in our first mission."

"Actually, this is my third."

117 and Johnson cautiously moved away from the abandoned store. With Mandy's assistance, 117 scanned the area and tuned in to the background noise. He picked up on the sounds of gunfire, fighting, and ambulance and police sirens. The combination of noises blared in the distance and the shouts of people filled the air. Despite all of that, Johnson still felt optimistic.

"What were your other missions like?" Mandy asked from 117's bracelet.

"My first mission," he said slowly to 117, "it was with... amborg number... 5. Do you know him? I think his name is Johnny. He's really funny."

"5 is humorous?" 117 asked. "In what way?"

"He liked to joke around a lot," Johnson grinned as he reminisced. His smile was filled with warmth, despite being in a risky environment. "He always liked making us laugh."

"For morale," Mandy whispered in 117's head.

"Mandy and I have only heard of his exploits," 117 admitted. "Never met him before."

As he thought about it, he realized that he'd never met any of the other First Group amborgs. He had probably passed by their individual dorm rooms multiple times. They were just so busy that it was rare to see them in person.

Many of the First Group Amborgs had already accomplished a great deal while he'd still been recovering from cybernetic enhancement. Before 117's initial training, several amborgs already had amazing reputations that were often discussed by many A.I. Industries staff. But with so many distress calls, they were often away for long periods of time. They only returned when they needed to recharge their implants and equipment.

"The amborgs don't really have a lot of time to interact with each other except for when we collaborate about our mission reports," 117 explained. "Because of how many amborgs there currently are, we are limited from many social activities most humans typically participate in. Although we are kept away from each other, we are always busy helping around in places where we are needed."

"That's pretty amazing." Astounded, Johnson stared in awe at 117. "I bet you guys wouldn't mind a vacation anytime soon though right? It must get tiring doing what you do all the time."

"We do not have vacations," 117 said with a puzzled look. "If we are not in the field, we spend time recharging our energy levels and working nonstop."

"But that's pretty unhealthy even if you're only part-human," Johnson stated matter-of-factly. "I'm all human and already wish I was on vacation instead of being here."

"Your feelings are precisely what we were built for," 117 replied. "So your fear of death can be alleviated."

"Well, if you're ever in L.A. more often, then we need to teach you how to relax."

"Amen to that," Mandy broadcasted.

Soon, they arrived at a makeshift barricade and found a crude but small tent, which 117 noticed was a triage center based on the torn Red Cross on the side of the canvas. It was sitting behind the wrecks of several destroyed cars piled on top of one another, making a perfect barricade from all the flying bullets.

Mandy did a quick analysis of the stacked pile of scrapped vehicles and guessed that it had to have been the handiwork of another amborg from before. It was highly unlikely that a construction crew would have gotten this close to a warzone with heavy machinery or mobile crane systems to make this temporary fort.

117 peered briefly into the flaps of the tent and saw paramedics helping a group of civilians, but there didn't seem to be any other officers guarding the wounded. He now understood Bradley's dilemma. There were many innocent lives risking it all with virtually no help. All of the training and experience could easily be gone in seconds with how exposed they were out here.

Automatic fire filled the air along with shouts coming from police, the EMTs, civilian refugees, and possibly gang members. At least his noise filter was working. 117 immediately knew what his first task was. He ran to the edge of the barricade and peered around the corner. As he did so, he felt someone bump into his back, which meant that Johnson had followed him.

"Sergeant Johnson," 117 leaned forward and immediately withdrew his head when bullets began to strike at his cover. "I can hear four civilians trapped down the street. If you look over my right shoulder," 117 pointed in that direction, "they are on the other side of the road behind that wreckage. They are being suppressed by gunfire twelve meters in that direction. We need to pull them back behind this area."

117 felt a hand grip his shoulder. Johnson stared at where he was pointing and then ducked down.

"You're nuts! How am I supposed to get over there? I mean, I know you're bulletproof, and I can hide behind you to get there but you can't block all the bullets with four people behind you coming back," Johnson looked in disbelief at the ground between the barricade and the trapped civilians. "What if after we got over there, I lay down some suppressing fire to give you cover?"

"David," Mandy instructed, "let's try what we practiced last week! Remember when I told you to give me cover?"

117 knew what to do. While Johnson brainstormed and voiced his ideas, he dashed towards an abandoned car nearby. Without any windows, he easily reached inside and lifted it. He flipped it onto its side with a loud crash, causing Johnson to whirl around. Grabbing the chassis, 117 lifted it up and made his way back to the gap in the barricade. Johnson stared as 117 jogged back as if he was merely carrying a wadded up piece of paper.

"It would possibly be more ideal if I cover you, sergeant. There are too many weapons firing at us and you would hardly be able to shoot anything," he said, preparing to move the car out into the open. "I will use this as a shield and draw their attention. You make sure no one strays into the line of fire."

"Oh right, we can do that," Johnson said, wide-eyed. "I'll follow your lead."

The lack of effort from carrying the car had him in a daze, but he snapped out of it and waited for 117's signal. Suddenly, there was another flash from his bracelet as 117 gave his next command.

"Walk with me."

The instant they stepped out into the open, the car-shield was instantly struck with a barrage of bullets. 117 knew that the top was being shredded to pieces, but it didn't matter. They eventually made it to the trapped civilians. 117 held the car in place while Johnson began rounding up the terrified people. Johnson immediately urged them to their feet and soon, they all huddled around 117. Checking to make sure they had everyone, Johnson tapped 117 on the back.

"Ready!" he shouted, and 117 nodded.

At the signal, he carefully raised the car, and they all started their journey back. The return trip seemed longer with 117 carrying the car as slowly as he could, ensuring that those following him didn't lag too far behind. Johnson kept an eye on the civilians, making sure they stayed close to 117 and away from the car's edges. Once they reached the safety of the barricade, some paramedics escorted them to the triage tent while 117 lowered the shield and carried it back to where he picked it up. Johnson looked at the car and noted the extensive damage; the entire roof had been shredded all the way down to the chassis, leaving only the wheels and a couple of seats intact.

"Man, I hope that guy's insured," he joked as 117 lowered the car.

Just before it touched the ground, there was a slight snap and 117's arms shot up, leaving him only gripping a piece of metal. The wreck slammed into the ground with a loud crash. He examined the fragment in his hands for a moment before casually dropping it, where it clattered on the pavement as he inspected what was left.

"Insurance accommodation for bullets. I doubt they will... cover this much damage," 117 said as he took note of how many hits the shield had taken.

Johnson opened his mouth, then abruptly shut it, staring in astonishment. 117 had made a joke. He had no idea how to respond to that. He had said it in such a stoic manner that it caught him off guard.

"That was a pun," 117 said when he noticed the young officer staring with a questioning look. "Was that not effective?"

"It was not bad," Johnson shrugged. "Maybe work on the delivery?"

"I thought that was clever," Mandy spoke cheerfully as 117's bracelet glowed brightly.

"After a quick analysis," 117 gestured to the wreck, "all of these bullets were fired by over a dozen hostiles. Their accuracy, even though it did hit us, was not very centered."

"Most of these gang members prefer quantity over quality," Johnson explained. "They're so hopped up on drugs that when they pick up anything that has a large ammo capacity, they're a danger to themselves and the public. We should be glad that none of them are trained snipers."

"Then I believe I will begin an attack on the enemy position that was suppressing the civilians we just rescued," 117 stated. "Sergeant, please remain here. Call for any available officers to reinforce this position."

117 activated a projector on his bracelet. A square image of a topographical map of Los Angeles appeared. Using his HUD, and Mandy's assistance, he highlighted a position two blocks away from their current location.

"I shall clear the area," he said.

"Alone?"

"I am much faster by myself," 117 nodded. "You would not be able to keep up."

"Right," Johnson replied in a concerned voice. "I'll take your word for it. Hey, are you sure about this?"

117 turned to look back. He was already walking away towards his next objective.

"Defend the area and protect the civilians," he ordered. "After I stop the hostiles from attacking this checkpoint, I will proceed to support the cut-off officers. Once I have ensured their safety, I will send them here to support you."

"Good plan," Johnson nodded. "Thank you."

"You are welcome," 117 replied. "I would very much like to continue having conversations. Once this mission is over."

"Sounds good. Thanks again, David 117."

117 moved towards the entrance of the barricade.

"Aw," Mandy said, "you made a friend!"

"I believe that Sergeant Johnson is merely an acquaintance," 117 replied.

"Yeah, but it's nice that you've taken an interest in seeing him again," Mandy said, sounding quite pleased. "Having conversations with more friends or allies will greatly help with giving you more perspective."

"That is a very... pleasant sentiment. For now, I need assistance, " 117 decided to focus on the task at hand.

"What's up David?" she asked as 117 moved beyond the barricade, immediately coming under heavy fire and taking several hits. He was able to identify where they were coming from based on the trajectories of the bullets. "You do realize you're getting hit a lot, right?"

"Yes, that is obvious."

"Please help me set up a proper route to clear out this area," he said. "I need to complete my objectives here and proceed to rescue the stranded officers."

"Sounds good," Mandy replied. "Get some good footage of you taking out the bad guys for me."

"My eyes are recording and broadcasting live Mandy," 117 pointed out as he neared the enemy. "You are able to see what I see. Are you planning to disconnect or step away from your cubicle?"

"That was me being sarcastic," Mandy sighed. "Just pretending to be lazy. You going to do anything about the bad guys shooting you?"

"I intend to stop them from doing any more harm."

A couple of bullets struck 117 in his head, but he shrugged them off and kept walking. Mandy chuckled and then spoke to him calmly.

"Great!" she said. "But, dodge the bullets at least. You can't let your reflexes get sloppy while learning how to develop people skills. I still haven't gotten over you letting yourself get shot so many times for test results..."

"Understood," 117 nodded. "Send calls for back-up to arrive at this location, multiple civilians unprotected, and we need transports to pick these people up."

"Roger that David," Mandy replied. "Oh by the way, 43's tech just notified me. She's in the area if you need or want some help."

"I am fine Mandy," 117 responded. "Unless 43 wants to help. Then I have no objection."

"Alright Mr. Teenage Mutant Ninja Terminator," Mandy sighed. "Less talking, more ass-kicking."

Several blocks away

"This is 7-Adam-15! I need backup now!! Do you hear me?! I have Splatter-Bugs pinning us down!! A lot of hopped up addicts with guns!!"

As bullets pelted the hood of the car he was sheltered behind, Officer Joe Harrison fired off one last round before instinctively ducking for safety. He heard a response from control as he struggled to stay alive.

"7-Adam-15! We copy Harrison... but right now there's no one to spare! If you can hold for a few more minutes, we'll get you help! What's the situation now?"

He knew that the people working dispatch were trained to handle situations calmly and professionally. For some strange reason, whoever he was communicating with only pissed him off even more.

"I told you!" he panted as he heard the sound of glass breaking and covered his head. Pieces of the car window dropped on him. "It's just down to the two of us!! Officers down! Can you hear the noise and the intensity of my voice?! We're not going to last a few more seconds!"

Harrison looked over his cover, took aim, and fired three more shots. He realized his gun was empty and ducked back down to reload.

"7-Adam-15, we have help coming. Please hold on as long as you can!"

"Did you not hear me?!"

Harrison loaded his gun and straightened up to take aim. He fired two shots.

"Our situation is extremely hostile! Please hurry! I need backup to defend this position and I need medical assistance to my location!"

A bullet suddenly struck Harrison's radio. He immediately took cover again, feeling like his soul almost left his body. Pieces of the radio burst and flew everywhere, the bullet barely missing his flesh. The shot had destroyed the microphone. His frequency selector and whip antenna were still intact, but it was useless if he couldn't transmit to anyone else. Static came out of the receiver. Furious, Harrison pulled his radio out and tossed it. It was only going to be distracting with all of that noise. Thinking fast, he stayed low and ran back to his colleague, who was desperately checking his pockets. Several more bullets began raining down on them as they huddled together.

"Lewis!" he shouted. "How's Murtaugh?!"

Harrison gestured towards a wounded officer sprawled on the pavement beside his partner, Paul Lewis. A few minutes ago, Harrison had seen Lewis trying to provide medical assistance while they were under fire. Now, Lewis was desperately trying to defend their position.

"U-unconscious!" he stammered as he pulled a clip out of his belt. "But, the good news is he's alive!"

"You got any ammo?" Harrison panted as they huddled together.

"Harrison, I'm almost out," Lewis said, peering over the hood of their damaged squad car. "This is my last clip. How much you got?"

"12 rounds left and my revolver," Harrison informed him as he stood up, quickly took aim, and pulled the trigger. The trigger stuck in place and failed to fire. "Shit!"

"That's not good," Lewis exclaimed. "Jammed?"

"It's jammed!" Harrison nodded.

Harrison tapped the bottom of the gun hard, where the magazine was stored. Quickly, he tried to rack it. But the slide was stuck and he couldn't move it. Lewis watched carefully as Harrison struggled.

"Double jam?" he asked curiously as the barrage of bullets made them cower lower.

"What?!"

"Are there two bullets trying to feed into the chamber?!" Lewis asked in the middle of all the noise.

"Uh..."

Harrison ejected the magazine and pulled the slide back. The bullet in the chamber ejected perfectly. As he let it drop onto the street, he pulled it again but there was no other bullet. Both officers stared at each other in confusion as Harrison loaded the magazine back into his gun and racked it. He stood up and tried firing again, but nothing happened.

"This is useless!" he yelled.

By now, the enemy Splatter-Bugs had to have noticed that they weren't firing back. They were probably aware of their situation and getting ready to come in for the kill. They were likely done for at this rate.

When he failed to clear his gun, Harrison decided to leave it on the street as he quickly took his revolver out of a secondary holster in his belt.

"I think you're the only cop I know that carries a working antique like that," Lewis stated.

"I swear!" Harrison glared at his partner. "You make fun of how old I am one more time and I'll kill you myself! Our standard issues are useless! Looks like this is it for us Lewis!"

Lewis took a breath to take in the moment and grasp his partner's words. He gave the veteran cop a nervous and cheeky smile, but it faded when more bullets hit their cover. Harrison pulled back on the hammer of the revolver and inhaled deeply.

"Harrison?" Lewis gulped. "Partners to the end. Right?"

"You kidding?" Harrison said with a smirk. "I always hated you kid."

"Thanks sir," Lewis chuckled as they both lifted their weapons. "You always were an old windbag."

"Always... Now. Lewis. On three ok? One... Two..."

"WAIT!"

Lewis suddenly grabbed Harrison's hand, interrupting the count. Startled, Harrison glanced at the younger officer nervously.

"What's wrong?" he asked in alarm.

"Is it one...two...three... and then we jump out?" Lewis asked, confused. "Or do we jump out on three?"

"Does it matter?" Harrison stared at his partner in disbelief, then suddenly realized how serious he was. He quickly dropped the question and said, "Fine! We'll count to three and then jump out."

"Oh ok... phew. So it's on four then?"

"Lewis!"

"No, I got it! Thanks."

"You're welcome," Harrison nodded. Both maintained heavy eye contact as they bobbed their heads in sync. "Now...Together...One...Two..."

"Wait!"

Harrison flinched but managed to stop himself from leaping up for the second time.

"What now?!"

Lewis pointed at the silver revolver in Harrison's hand.

"I know we've only been partners for a few months but... why do you carry that?" he asked curiously. "It's older than most of the standard weapons we have in our armory."

Harrison rolled his eyes.

"It's sentimental! I got it from my old man, damn it!" he snapped, but he couldn't help but show it off a bit. "Still works perfectly. Useful in a pinch. Now will you shut up and let us do this?"

"Ok, got it."

"Are you ready? For real?" Harrison double-checked apprehensively. "I swear to God, I almost want these gangsters to shoot me... Or blow me up before you at least."

Lewis shrugged once, thought silently for a moment, then nodded. Harrison didn't count but continued to stare at his partner as more bullets struck their car. Lewis nodded his head once more, paused, nodded a third time, but stopped to think again, causing Harrison to glare silently.

We're so dead, he shuddered, letting out a sigh.

In his mind, Harrison was already unsure if he wanted to die with such a mediocre partner. Finally, Lewis nodded much more firmly for a fourth time. Harrison prepared to give the count again.

"One...Two...Three!"

The two of them jumped out from behind the squad car, giving off the loudest war cry they could muster. Just as Harrison managed to fire one shot out of his six-shooter, many more shots rang out.

The sound of an automatic rifle echoed in the distance. As the two officers sprang into action, they quickly noticed a swarm of at least 20 gang members charging toward them. To their shock, each and every one of the Splatter-Bugs dropped to the ground in an instant, either screaming or dead silent. After a few seconds, the officers cautiously moved further from their cover to observe the mess.

"WHOA," Lewis exclaimed in awe. "Did you do that? What kind of ammo was that? Nice shooting."

"I only fired one shot..." Harrison shook his head slightly. He eyed his revolver curiously, then at the bodies sprawled across the street. "That... was definitely not me..."

"What's that up there?" Lewis pointed towards the top of the nearest building and grinned. "Oh hey! It looks like our back-up came."

Both gazed up at the figure perched atop the building. Suddenly, it leaped down three stories. Their savior touched down with an almighty thud, sending tremors through the ground and creating massive cracks in the street, forming a small crater. The two officers stood frozen, completely dumbstruck. Lewis' smile vanished, and his mouth hung open in utter disbelief.

"N-nice entrance," Lewis stammered.

"Uhh, Lewis, I think our back-up isn't human..." Harrison said to his partner, who closed his mouth but still stared wide-eyed at their savior. "It's an amborg."

Based on the iconic glowing neon stripes, the amborg uniform of A.I. Industries was a very notable design. A standard police drone or military robot could also pull off a fall from that high up, but Harrison could definitely tell that this cybernetic man before him looked human.

The amborg stood up, revealing the number printed on his jacket, number 117. Harrison hadn't seen this number before. He knew that there was a group assigned one through thirty, so did this mean that this amborg was a new one?

They watched as it... he straightened up and walked over, waving his hand. The rifle he'd been holding fell to the ground. Lewis continued to stare, realizing that it had somehow gotten crushed when it clattered onto the pavement.

"Greetings," his bracelet flashed brightly as an electronic voice spoke to them. "What is the current situation?"

"Well..." Harrison began to explain, but quickly was interrupted.

"No, David... ask them if they're ok."

117's bracelet flashed again, and they heard a girl's voice come out of it. Confused, Harrison and Lewis glanced down at 117's left wrist and then up at 117. Had he changed voices?

"Unnecessary," they heard a male voice speak as 117 looked away. "I scanned them as I approached and did not detect any injuries."

"Who was that?" Lewis asked.

"My technician, Mandy," 117 answered, turning back to them and nodding his head. "She is overseeing my deployment."

His voice spoke to them, but neither of the two officers saw his mouth move. This wasn't surprising since they had seen the older amborgs broadcast their voices on their silver bracelet projection devices before. But it seemed odd that this amborg was having a separate casual conversation right after he saved them.

Finally, Harrison stepped up and greeted 117 with a warm smile with Lewis following alongside.

"Well, I wanted to say thanks..."

Suddenly, 117 pivoted, his expression sharpening with focus for a brief moment. Harrison was left hanging, at a total loss for words.

"...for saving us?"

117 turned his head to acknowledge the officers again.

"My apologies," 117 said. "My technician was just privately informing me of my lack of manners. I forgot to introduce myself. I am amborg 117."

"Oh, uhh well, I'm Harrison," Harrison nodded, and then pointed at his partner. "And this is Lewis. Nice to meet you. Always a pleasure meeting you upgraded kids."

"Introductions aside," 117 continued, "what is the current situation?"

"Better now that you saved our necks," Lewis smiled.

"Strange," 117 tilted his head, "I was under the impression that I was trying to save your entire body."

"W-what?" Lewis stammered.

"David..." Mandy's disappointed tone drifted out of his bracelet. "Remember how I told you that sometimes you must think before you speak?"

Harrison and Lewis exchanged awkward glances as 117 fell silent. He lowered his gaze, seeming to be pondering something deeply. They guessed that he was having another internal private conversation.

"Well, uhh, we have five wounded, and some dead civilians we didn't get to in time... We weren't able to sweep the area properly for survivors," Harrison cleared his throat and began to explain what had happened. "We got ambushed when we arrived in this area, you see. A lot of people here… Well, as you can see, we almost got killed."

"Thanks for helping us out," Lewis added with a sigh of relief. "We owe you big time. Otherwise, we likely would've ended up like everyone else here."

"You are welcome," 117 answered curtly. "I took the liberty of running bio-scans on the two of you to check for any injuries, but I have been told that it is more reassuring to ask directly."

"Oh yeah," Lewis let out a laugh. "Thanks for asking."

As they chatted, Harrison turned away and headed back to where they had hidden. He holstered his revolver and crouched down to pick up his jammed gun from where he'd dropped it.

"Just a few scratches… but we're fine," Harrison said quite comfortably as he walked back to 117. "Hey, you wouldn't mind checking up on my nicotine intake from my bio-scan, would you? My wife always tells me that smoking will kill me, but I keep telling her with all these raids, who has the time to light up? Am I right?"

"Pft, that's funny," Mandy's voice spoke from 117's bracelet.

Lewis and 117 both fell silent as they stared at Harrison.

"Oh well," he shrugged, "at least one person thought that was funny, and she isn't physically here."

"I am in spirit," Mandy said in a reassuring and friendly voice.

"Your weapon is jammed."

117 lifted a finger and pointed at Harrison's gun.

"Oh, yeah it is, I couldn't get it fixed."

117 leaned forward and examined the gun. Then he looked up at Harrison and held out his hand. Harrison gently handed his weapon over. With rapid precision and speed, 117 disassembled the gun, then put it back together within seconds.

"Whoa…" Lewis' eyes widened.

"Wow," Harrison shook his head in disbelief, a huge grin appearing on his face. "Kids these days."

"I have fixed the problem," 117 declared.

Harrison looked down at the reassembled weapon. It looked the same as before. He was absolutely impressed. He couldn't even tell that it had been taken apart at an impossibly high-speed seconds ago.

"The spring in the magazine was short," 117 explained. "I assume that when it was manufactured, it was defective and caused the weapon to jam unexpectedly."

"I don't think we would have caught that," Harris nodded as he reached forward to take his gun back. "You're really good at this."

117 tilted his head and didn't respond.

Oh right, Harrison just remembered, they aren't too good with small talk.

Before 117 could say anything, he turned his head sharply to the right. He got into a defensive stance, still holding Harrison's gun.

"Stand firm! Three hostiles still remain," 117 said as he whipped around.

A heartbeat later, a gunshot rang out. In an instant, 117 extended his arm, positioning it protectively in front of Harrison's face. The two officers stood motionless, hearing a sudden thump. At the same time, 117 took aim with Harrison's gun and pulled the trigger. A deafening bang reverberated as he fired a shot toward the source of the gunfire.

The sound of a scream echoed in the distance, causing both Harrison and Lewis to do a double take. Lewis was still processing the situation when he glanced at his partner. Harrison's eyes were locked onto 117's hand. As Lewis leaned in for a better look, he understood why. Tucked between 117's left thumb and forefinger was a bullet. The way it was positioned suggested it could have struck Harrison directly in the head. Thankfully, 117 had intercepted it just in time, but the chilling possibility of what could have happened sent a shiver down Lewis' spine.

"Correction: Make that two," 117 reported. "One second late and officer Harrison would not have to worry about dying from smoking anymore."

117 threw the bullet away and handed the gun back to Harrison, who apprehensively took it in silence. 117 stared at them, puzzled by their expressions.

"That was a joke," he explained to the officers. "Was that poorly timed?"

"N-no no! I-it wasn't at all," Harrison stammered, looking blankly at where 117 had cast aside the bullet that almost claimed his life. "I owe you one again it seems. You kids sure know how to do things with a flair."

"You are welcome again," 117 nodded. "Thank you for the compliment, officer Harrison. Excuse me for a moment. Initiating scan. Completed. Two hostiles are in retreat, but the area is secure temporarily. Support units may now proceed to your location. Estimated time to arrival, approximately four minutes. Forgive me for leaving but I am needed elsewhere."

"Leaving already?" Lewis asked nervously.

He looked around at all the wrecked buildings, as if a python was about to suddenly strike from above.

"I am more efficient with making the city secure if I return to my mission parameters in other parts of unresolved combat zones," 117 said reassuringly. "You are safe, officer Lewis."

"Well, thanks again," Harrison said. "Lewis, let's go check on the wounded. We need to get them ready for the paramedics when they get here."

"Got it partner."

Without hesitation, Lewis ran off and knelt down by a wounded officer, who was beginning to stir. 117 bid Harrison one last nod before turning away to leave. Suddenly, Harrison called out to the amborg's retreating figure.

"Hey, wait a moment 117," he called. "You need a weapon?"

"Concern appreciated but unnecessary officer Harrison," 117 smiled. "I am well prepared. However, you might need to fix the trigger on your gun. I believe I bent it by mistake. Stay safe."

117 ran off as Harrison glanced down at his gun. The trigger actually was bent out of place. His cybernetic strength was immense. As he looked up to say goodbye, 117 was gone. He had disappeared around the corner in a matter of seconds.

"Damn," he muttered as he jogged over to Lewis, who was checking the pulse on an unconscious officer. "Kids get the best stuff these days."

"Next time David... remember to say thank you. If someone is trying to offer you help and you refuse it, acknowledge that at least. Don't get cocky."

"Oh. I will try to remember that. Sorry Mandy."

117 approached another intersection and stopped. The gunfire was now further away. Checking his GPS and listening to the surrounding environment, he slowly walked forward and tried to scan for the two people he had been tracking. If they managed to escape, it would be a problem.

"Mandy," he said in his mind, "Requesting secondary support. Those two hostiles seem to have disappeared. I might need to switch to infrared."

"Careful, just remember that it hurts your eyes after a few minutes."

"Perhaps I should restrategize," 117 paused, thinking carefully. "With so many potential heat signatures, I could identify the wrong criminals."

"That's why I'm also on it," Mandy replied. "You just need to look carefully at their body language, the way they move, and find the two signatures that don't look like the civilians."

"Very well," 117 took a deep breath and accessed his HUD. Once he made the selection, he closed his eyes. "Activating infrared scanner."

The scanner was in his eyes. When activated, an amborg's vision could pick up on thermal readings. If he was looking for the two gang members that had tried to ambush Harrison while they were having a conversation, then identifying them according to Mandy's guidelines should be quite simple. Although, one question did pop up in his mind.

"Mandy, is there a reason why prolonged use of the infrared can hurt us?" he asked as he turned his head. "This method is quite effective. There are many signatures."

"You mean aside from the fact that you look like a creepy and terrifying Terminator if you were in a dark room?" Mandy chuckled. "Seriously, when your eyes turn bright red, it makes me want to run away as fast as possible. I need to show you what you all look like when you have infrared turned on, I'll text you a photo."

"Your light-hearted comments do not seem like a suitable answer to my question," 117 stated as he moved forward and noticed some signatures huddled together in a building. "Are there any examples that correlate to the rules?"

"Well, there is one story I heard," Mandy replied seriously. "I suggest turning your infrared off in about 40 seconds. Anyway, do you know that Leonard wears glasses?"

"Amborg 1? Yes, I have noticed."

Mandy was talking about the boy that became the world's first cyborg. Leonard 1 was a legend among the First Group amborgs.

"Do you know why?" Mandy continued her explanation. "It's because during a mission, he had his infrared on for too long. Standard protocol states that infrared should not be used for more than three to nine minutes. Using it longer than that begins the countdown to pain."

"Countdown?"

"1 burned out his eyes when he had to use his infrared in a rather precarious situation," Mandy said in a grim tone. "I read a lot of after-action reports from the First Group in my spare time. He had his infrared on for over 47 minutes. Since then, after he had his eyes fixed, he's needed to wear glasses."

"When I met him," 117 said, "I always assumed it was because he just wanted to look more human."

"I think glasses suit him."

117 continued walking and when he made it to the next street, he stopped focusing on heat signatures on the ground floor of each building he passed. Perhaps the two gang members he was searching for had

decided to go upstairs. As he lifted his gaze, Mandy provided support, helping him focus on the sights above.

"Strange, if they came this way, they probably would have hidden somewhere," she murmured. "Splatter-Bugs do have a tendency to seek out elevated positions. Wait, do you hear that David? I'm picking up something. It's faint. Let me filter it out. It sounds like... DAVID! Incoming!"

Her warning came too late.

117 heard what sounded like a loud whoosh, but before he could identify the noise, he felt something strike his chest. An explosion followed a split second later.

Blasted off his feet, 117 was launched backward and hit the pavement hard. Heat washed over every part of his body, but it quickly dissipated. He blinked once and sat up slowly. His HUD was blaring warnings, which he immediately muted. He took a moment to assess the damage. The heat from the explosive had seared his jacket, but his endoskeleton structure had successfully protected him. Glancing at his left wrist, he noticed that his bracelet was cracked and damaged. That wasn't good.

"David!" he heard Mandy cry. "My screen is scrambled! Answer me! Are you alright?!"

"Diagnostic check initiated," 117 replied as he got to his feet. "An RPG missile launcher. Struck in the upper abdomen at a force of three thousand pounds at a velocity of two hundred and ninety one meters per second. Point of origin located. It would appear that the weapon caused minimal damage. I have lost my bracelet."

"Would you please just say you're fine next time David?" Mandy snapped. "Finally, the video feed is restored."

"Perhaps I should have these burn marks examined," 117 said, taking note of the hole in his jacket. The skin underneath was badly burned but he didn't feel too much pain. "Permission to retaliate against the hostiles Mandy?"

"Well, I'd be pretty pissed if someone tried to get away with shooting an RPG at me David."

"Noted," 117 nodded. "Engaging hostiles."

He traced the location of the shooter to a building on the corner straight ahead. The second floor window from which the rocket had been fired was boarded up, but he could identify a hole just large enough to shoot through. The gangsters had to have taken careful aim through a hole that size.

To do so with such stealth to avoid my senses is very impressive, 117 thought as he analyzed the footage of the attack moments before. Were these gang members really high on drugs? How did they even get their hands on an RPG?

This attack seemed different in comparison to all of the other reports he had reviewed from this area. However, given the circumstances, he would have to report his findings later.

He approached the entrance to the hideout and gently pushed the door open. The sound of two people arguing and desperately trying to come up with a new plan drifted down from the floor above. Stepping into the dilapidated structure, he began searching for a way upstairs.

"Aw man," someone shouted. "It didn't work!! Quick, give me another one!"

"That was the last one idiot!" the other one snapped.

"We're in trouble man, how do we beat one of these guys?! They're unstoppable."

Moving cautiously through the building, 117 lifted his head to scan the room above. The sounds of clattering and voices led him to their exact position. He activated his infrared vision and found them huddled together, frantically trying to assemble some furniture into a makeshift barricade in a desperate last-ditch effort. They definitely didn't seem like they were on drugs.

"Perhaps I should have accepted a weapon from Officer Harrison, Mandy," 117 said in his mind. "At least I could incapacitate them from down here to avoid walking into a trap."

"True," Mandy replied. "But from what I can hear, they'll probably just scream and make more noise if you shoot them from below. You could just walk up and ask them to surrender nicely."

"A very polite plan Mandy but... I do not have the means to do so," 117 nodded and proceeded to walk towards the stairs.

"Why is that? Oh."

Mandy's eyes widened as she glanced to the side. Through his HUD, 117 noticed that she had figured out what the problem was.

"Your bracelet is broken," she said. "That's not good. Neither of us can say anything to them. They should really redesign those..."

"I can still attempt to ask them politely."

"How? Are you going to use sign language or something?"

"An excellent idea," 117 nodded. "Accessing the ASL database."

"Wait, that's not what I meant!"

He heard Mandy sigh as he began heading upstairs.

"We really need to work on your sarcasm detection when you get back," she groaned as he reached the second floor. A thought suddenly crossed his mind.

"Mandy, I am noticing a slight problem," he said.

"What is it?"

"What happens if they don't understand sign language?"

A brief silence passed between them, then Mandy responded.

"Well, I guess things just became much harder," she sighed impatiently. "You can try to communicate with them but it might not make sense. It could escalate into a fight."

"If I am attempting to offer a surrender... do you think they'll accept?"

"In a perfect world?" Mandy pondered her words slowly. "Yes. But in this case, most likely no."

"I shall try," 117 nodded. "Can you issue a distress call? I may need assistance."

"Copy that."

"The right thing to do is offer the enemy a chance to surrender," 117 said observantly.

When he reached a closed door at the top of the stairs, he paused. He put his hand on the frame, sliding it to the door and resting it there. He wasn't ready to enter just yet; he needed to assess the situation first. On the other side, it was completely silent. Both sides were waiting for the other to make the first move.

"Without a bracelet in close vicinity," 117 explained to Mandy, "I cannot, using my voice, ask them to peacefully surrender."

"You can try sign language... but you also need to remember that these people chose this path," Mandy said after a few seconds. "Sometimes when you are deciding to accept the hand of surrender, it means turning over your life into another's hands. They then have to hope that they can help you. People don't like to take that hand because they're afraid or their pride makes it difficult to admit the consequences of their life choices. Some people are beyond redemption."

"But you have taught me before that redemption is possible for everyone," 117 stated adamantly. "Everyone and everything deserves help of all forms."

"I did," Mandy sighed in agreement. "But, you have to be careful of those who may betray your trust. There's a lot of things you need to consider. So use your own instincts and judgements about what you feel is right. Now go get them. Understood? Let's talk more about this later. I strongly suggest you get these two off the streets and prevent them from harming anyone else."

"Understood."

Initially, 117 considered breaking the door down, but he quickly decided that being cordial would serve him better. He gently opened the door, and it immediately bumped against a cabinet that had been hastily shoved there as a barricade. With his super-human strength, he easily pushed the door open with a loud scrape. As he casually stepped into the room, the occupants inside immediately began panicking. 117 noticed that they remained huddled together, each holding what looked like wine bottles with rags sticking out of them, and they were lit.

"Hey! Stay back!"

Molotov cocktails, he thought, *primitive but effective.*

"Ok you stupid amborg," the gangster on the left shouted. "Can you handle the heat?!"

117 lifted both of his hands and motioned them downwards so the two could see them clearly. He softened his facial expression and tried to look less aggressive to ease the tension, but as he originally thought, the gangsters couldn't understand his silent game of charades.

"What are you doing? What's that mean? Don't play with us! We will burn you! We'll burn this whole building down. If we die, then we die our way!!"

No one has to die though, 117 thought.

"*Please*," 117 used sign language in an attempt to communicate. He signed slowly and kept his hands relaxed, hoping they would understand his meaning. *"I am here to offer you an opportunity."*

"The hell are you doing?!" the man on the right screamed. "This is a trick!"

"Stay back! Damn robot!" the other cried.

Realizing that things weren't getting any better, he decided to try something different. He opened his mouth and made an attempt to speak. But no words came out. The air that he expelled from his lungs only made a quiet whine, which only sent the gangsters into a deeper state of panic.

"Hey man! Quit messing with us! We aren't afraid of you!"

Sensing that there was no hope for continued negotiations, 117 prepared for their attack. Suddenly, the wall behind the Splatter-Bugs burst open, and someone leaped into the room. In a frenzy, the Splatter-Bugs spun around and hurled all four bottles at the newcomer, who instantly went up in flames. Despite becoming a raging inferno, the burning figure stood up, completely unfazed, and advanced toward the two of them like a demon straight out of hell.

The new arrival made their move, lunging at the criminals. Shrill, high pitched screams tore out of them as two fiery hands grabbed them by the necks.

"F-fiery entrance," Mandy stammered.

"Indeed," 117 agreed.

117 and Mandy already recognized the attacker based on the obvious fact that they were still moving, given their current state. Both gangsters were hurled across the room, hitting the wall with a loud crash. They fell to the floor in a crumpled heap, both knocked out from the force.

117 turned his head sharply and saw a fire extinguisher sitting in the corner. He moved over to it, picked it up, and immediately aimed it at his savior. A stream of foam sprayed over the flames, dousing them. The fire had charred and darkened the texture of their whole outfit, but once it was out, their neon stripes glowed brightly, along with a familiar amborg number.

"Thanks 117. I didn't know they were armed with molotov cocktails until after I burst in. Oh well. Guess I should have kept my infrared on."

43 gently patted her shoulders, ran her hands along her arms, and wiped her mouth. Glancing around, she spotted a broken mirror and inspected herself. Although the flames could have scorched her skin, her enhanced resilience protected her from severe burns. She took a moment to assess the black ash and soot smeared across her face but simply shrugged it off.

"It's great to see you," she turned and smiled, throwing him off-guard. "Oh, one second."

43 reached behind her and pulled out a small pouch from the back of her belt. She unzipped it and withdrew a small tin. Unscrewing the lid, she dipped her fingers in it and began spreading what looked like lotion on her face. 117 quickly identified it as a specialized burn ointment designed to heal within minutes. 43's skin would look good as new in a short period of time.

"Ah, I love how cold and refreshing that is," she stated as she walked up to 117. "How are you? We have not had much contact since the selection."

"The feeling is mutual 43, it has been... empty without your optimism and praise," 117 replied warmly. He set down the extinguisher and quickly scanned her. "Those were severe burns. Are you all right?"

"I am perfectly fine," 43 replied calmly. "I'll visit the medical bay when we return home. Nothing they can't fix. Maybe 6 will help and let me keep some of this damage I've received as battle scars. That will make me look slightly more badass, right?"

43 smiled, a small laugh broadcasting from her silver bracelet. 117 watched as she reached up and undid her ponytail. Switching her style, she straightened her hair and began tying it up in a bun. While doing so, she glanced at 117's torso. Her smile faded, replaced with concern.

"I think you had more of an experience than I did though," she observed. "What was it? Ah, wait... An RPG?"

She put her hand to his chest and examined the area where the blast had hit him. From 43's quick analysis, it pretty much spoke for itself. 117 nodded as she retracted her hand and finished tying up her hair.

"It was," 117 looked at her uniform. Most of it had been burned, but it could be fixed. Several black marks marred it from where the flames had made contact. "Why are you here?"

"I was actually right behind you after you saved those two police officers," she explained with a grin. "You were moving around so fast... I couldn't keep up. Those two guys, Harrison and Lewis, kept raving about you when I asked them what happened. About how you swooped in, killed all of the Splatter-Bugs and saved the day. I am paraphrasing though."

"An overstatement 43," 117 replied with his neutral tone. "The day is not over and one cannot necessarily save a day specifically. Unless the scientific community perfected time travel."

"I made the same observation. Still, it was humorous."

As both of them walked out of the building, 117 couldn't help but notice something different about 43. It had only been a couple of months but she was exhibiting many different patterns of new behavior he hadn't seen before.

"I can tell that you're staring," she said without looking at him. 117 saw her reach into her pocket. "Penny for your thoughts?"

117 saw her hand whip something out and tossed it to him. He quickly lifted his arm and caught a small object with his quick reflexes. He gazed down at what she had given him and paused.

"Huh," Mandy spoke thoughtfully, "she actually had a penny for you."

"Where did you find this?" 117 held up the antique copper coin in the light. "This one is dated from the year 2055."

"It was a present from my technician, Sherry," 43 answered as she turned and smiled at him. "For deploying on our first mission."

"Ok..." Mandy said slowly, "not my first choice for a gift but to each their own, I guess."

"Sorry for interrupting you," 43 shrugged as 117 returned the penny. "What's up?"

"43," 117 said, "this might be just a visual malfunction, but I believe your posture and movements have changed. Also your speech pattern has altered slightly. Is this a wrong assumption?"

"I think the phrase is, correct me if I am wrong," she replied. "And yes. Your assumptions are correct. You noticed."

She paused and turned on the spot in a three hundred sixty degree spin, then stopped to face him. Her movements were much more extravagant than before.

"My technician is the one responsible," 43 winked. "She has been educating me. Or rather, she has and is providing plenty of etiquette and explicit instructions on how to behave as a woman."

"Ah, ah, ah."

43's bracelet glowed as another voice joined the conversation. In 117's HUD, another video screen appeared and a bright, enthusiastic face waved at the camera. Mandy waved through her own screen in response.

"Hey Sherry," she smiled.

"Sup?" Sherry chuckled. "Kinda funny considering you're just a few cubicles away from me. Hope you don't mind if I crash this party."

"Well, remember the rules," Mandy sighed. "As much as I enjoy the company, this is too many people in both our amborgs' heads."

"It is no trouble," 117 pointed out casually, noticing 43 nodding in agreement. "Sherry is not causing any problems."

"Aw, you're sweet," Sherry dipped her head respectfully. She had a rather relaxed and casual vibe in comparison to Mandy. "Anyway, the only reason I butted in was because I wanted 43 to correct her earlier statement. Sounded too formal. Now, I should exit this group chat. Both of you are technically still in an active combat zone."

"Wow," Mandy rolled her eyes. "Look who's following the rules for once."

"See ya around 117!"

Sherry waved as her screen disappeared from 117's HUD. Her voice broadcasted from 43's bracelet once again.

"Oh wait," she laughed. "I can still see you! Now, 43?"

"Right," 43 nodded. "My friend Sherry has been teaching me how to behave as a growing young female teenager progressing to adulthood. Very insightful."

"Oh. Mandy has also been educating me since the selection," 117 said as enthusiastically as he could. "So far she has been repeatedly pestering me in an attempt to teach me to speak normally with a decent and fairly basic vocabulary. Unfortunately, it is not succeeding."

"No kidding," Mandy muttered from the back of his head.

"I can tell," 43 said softly. "You always were a strange one, 117. Tell me, what do you think of my hair?"

117 took a casual glance and replied.

"Your hairstyle selection is that of what is commonly referred to by humans as a low hair bun. Worn occasionally by women or girls with the appropriate length in which some, most, or all of the hair on the head is pulled away from the face, gathered and secured at the back of the head with a hair tie, clip, or other similar device, and allowed to hang freely causing minimal swaying."

"If you like it, 117, just say so," 43 rolled her eyes and placed a hand on her hip.

"I believe I was," 117 said, flustered. "Although your ponytail was much better. I prefer that style."

"Agreed," 117 saw Mandy nodding in the viewscreen in his display.

"Really? You might be right," 43 nodded. She reached up and undid her bun. "This was a really fast and crude attempt anyway."

As her hair fell down, she grabbed her hair band and tied it up. She pulled the ponytail and let it dangle over her right shoulder down her front for 117 to see.

"What do you think?" she asked again.

117 stared, then replied a second time.

"Your new selected hairstyle: a ponytail. Worn frequently by women or girls in which some, most, or all of the hair on the head is pulled away from the face, gathered and secured at the back of the head with a hair tie, clip, or other similar device, and allowed to hang freely from that point. Its resemblance to an actual horse/pony's tail is where the name derives from. In your case, 43, the ponytail removes most of the hair from covering or obscuring your facial features. And it also provides you with a high sense of fashion."

43 beamed, looking amused. She gently walked ahead while twiddling her hands behind her back.

"So you included those last two sentences because you prefer this hairstyle?" she asked in an amazed voice. "Wow. I need to wear ponytails for you more often."

"You appear to have already assimilated proper human speech," 117 said, crestfallen. "But while we are on that subject, I will alter my earlier answer. Yes I do like it this way."

"Thank you 117."

As she thanked him, she walked up and kissed him on the cheek. Dumbfounded, he lifted a hand and ran it where her lips had been. It felt warm but the air had made it dissipate fast.

"Ooh," Mandy brought a hand up to her face and tried to hide a mischievous grin. "That was cute."

117 blinked.

"What was that for?" he asked.

"Well, I had two reasons to thank you. One was for the lovely and long descriptive complement," she said as she began walking up the street, "and the second was for putting me out when I was on fire. I had just remembered and wanted to do that. Sherry told me a kiss was an acceptable thank you reward for heroism. I hope that wasn't disrespectful."

"Y-you are welcome 43..." he stuttered as he transmitted the message to her head. "No disrespect was detected. I am alright with the circumstances."

"Hey 117," Mandy interrupted. "I have a distress beacon from 917 and Alice 999. Public altercation."

43 and 117 both looked at each other and nodded. They began to run. In his map, Mandy highlighted a beacon for them to navigate to. He assumed that Sherry had done the same for 43.

"Public altercation? Let's go help," 43 declared. "Then we can wrap up this mission."

Unlike when he ran with Johnson, the two amborgs could jog at a constant and balanced pace. Thanks to their cybernetic abilities, they were able to run abnormally fast. At that point, Mandy decided to chime in.

"Well don't mind me," she joked in a very obvious tone of sarcasm. "I'm just a third wheel in the back of David 117's head, forced to witness Sherry who apparently can get 43 to learn seduction faster than I can teach 117 how to speak basic english. Having fun, lover boy?"

"I hope that watching all that hasn't made you uncomfortable," 117 replied on their private channel.

"That was unexpected, but cute," Mandy admitted. "Now if you two need to get a room, I'll just be sure to take a lunch break."

"Unnecessary," 117 replied hastily. "It is not... well, it isn't supposed to look like that."

"Huh," Mandy continued to smile as she looked at him in her camera. "David 117 is getting flustered. Is there a story you want to tell me?"

"43 is my friend."

"Looks like she wants to be more than that," Mandy smugly let out a soft chuckle.

"Now is not the appropriate time..."

"I'm in my cubicle being the annoying voice in your head, David," Mandy declared. "We've got time. Besides, I've always wondered about you two."

"What about?" 117 asked.

"Well, you were both pretty close when I first met you," Mandy stated. "Literally. I know that most of your personal records are kept sealed for privacy but... did you know her before cybernetic augmentation?"

"Yes I did," 117 answered honestly. "We were both close friends."

"Were? What's with the past tense?" Mandy asked. "You're making it sound like you fell apart."

"We are still friends," 117 corrected his statement. "I have missed her."

"Ah, you did do some training sessions for a while after the selection," Mandy nodded sympathetically. She suddenly appeared excited as she continued to work from her station. "Well, I think it's really nice that you have someone like her as a friend. She's pretty special, even though I barely know her. Are you going to ask her out?"

Even though he wasn't fully human, he could feel the blood rushing to his head. It seemed to burn hotter than the RPG blast. His temperature monitor was spiking at abnormally high levels.

"Whoa," Mandy exclaimed in wonder. "I can see your temperature readings going up. Is that a yes?"

"No comment," 117 mumbled.

"Right," Mandy scoffed. "I'm your technician. I watch and listen to everything when you're deployed. I think you have more pressing issues besides the fact I'm in your head, 117. It looks like someone's got a crush on you."

117 slowed slightly and glanced up at the sky. 43 hadn't seemed to notice what he was doing and continued to run at a brisk pace. He didn't see anything out of the ordinary except for a few wispy clouds drifting by.

"I cannot see anything that might crush me, Mandy. Please clarify."

"Eyes down and front."

117 tilted his head back down and quickened his pace.

"Basically, she likes you David," Mandy said teasingly into his head. "Looks like Sherry is pushing her to make the moves on you. Definitely has got you hooked."

"Improbable, there is no chance of attraction. Amborgs don't have feelings," 117 looked at 43, who was now ahead of him.

"Ah, denial. Classic. You want to explain how there's so much blood flowing to your head?" Mandy snickered. She let out a sigh, which caught his attention. "David, 43 may be an amborg but both of you still have human qualities. You guys are not total machines. Feelings are bound to pop up and I think it's kinda cute. You two were found together by the good old doctor, underwent the same procedures together, and... who knows? Maybe one thing will lead to another."

"I am uncertain though, Mandy," 117 said slowly in his mind. "I cannot determine whether or not I have a similar interest in her."

He began running some serious calculations about the conversations and the relevant data, but it wasn't helping. Mandy sighed and then spoke again.

"Ok... well, take a direct approach. What do you think of when you look at her?" she asked. Perhaps changing tactics would help. "If you feel uncertain, then what is it about her that you think of if you just focus on her?"

117 took a quick glance and then formed a statement.

"Her ponytail aforementioned with the description I used earlier. Her posture and her methods of walking are very fluid and very different from what I remember. Less rigid. Now, it seems as if her motion helps her to blend in as a regular woman. She has also adopted the human capacity to smile, which also attracted my attention. Among humans, it is an expression denoting pleasure, sociability, happiness, or amusement. Upon listening to the way she speaks, her speech patterns and use of vocabulary have drastically changed. She has progressed to the point where she probably has become close to perfect."

There was an awkward pause.

"David," Mandy said slowly, "How long did you look at her??"

"1.84 seconds," he reported, checking the time index. "Shall I continue?"

"No thanks, 117. You can keep that to yourself. Still, close to perfect. That's quite a compliment."

From her monitor back at A.I. Industries, Mandy watched as 117 stopped talking and continued following 43. She could see his built-in radar, GPS tracker, and vitals on her systems just like a regular first-person video game, only through the eyes of another real person. Just as Mandy was about to take a brief break from the operation, she heard someone shuffling behind her cubicle. Frantically, she attempted to straighten everything out as she turned to look at who had dropped by. She grew more flustered when she realized it was her boss.

"Oh... hello Dr. Kendrick," she mumbled meekly. "Can I help you? You'll have to pardon the mess. I don't get visitors and well, it's not like there was a routine inspection today."

"That's quite alright," Dr. Kendrick replied with a chuckle as he watched Mandy continue to straighten her desk. "I actually came to see how you and David 117 were doing. I've always noticed he was a late bloomer in certain fields with his cybernetic upgrades. Any problems whatsoever?"

"So far, I can list several," Mandy sighed as she looked back at the monitor. "The current one being that he clearly likes her and can't talk about it properly. Sherry sure seems to be having a lot more success at this than I am."

"In time Mandy, in time. You can't force him to know what to feel. Everyone develops their own thoughts and feelings by themselves."

Dr. Kendrick looked at the monitor and assessed 117's readings, which seemed to be in order. He adjusted his glasses and then patted Mandy on her shoulder.

"You two are a compatible team," he said solemnly. "117 listens to you fairly well, so I don't think it'll be long until he gets a good grasp on certain issues."

"Thank you doctor."

As Dr. Kendrick turned to leave, he suddenly stopped and looked back to ask one more question.

"By the way, how's your fiancée?"

Mandy glanced at Dr. Kendrick and then back to her own monitor. She turned her chair and faced him.

"He's fine," she said with a dim expression. "I just haven't heard from him in a few weeks. They haven't notified me if anything has happened so that's good news for now."

"He's military, isn't he? Will this affect your performance?"

Mandy let out a large sigh as her gaze flicked from her monitor and back to Dr. Kendrick, who's eyes were still on her.

"No," she stated firmly. "I used to worry about him every day. Now that I'm here, I can help the amborgs and be part of the action. He and 117 are both fighting to protect the world."

"And you also wanted to do something rather than sit at home," Dr. Kendrick nodded in understanding.

"We understood the risks," Mandy replied. "There are many things that are bound to happen. And I know in my heart that I have prepared myself for the worst. So, I will not let it get in the way of my job and with 117."

"After seeing you panic when David was hit by that RPG," Dr. Kendrick pondered, "I find it difficult to believe you."

"That was..."

Mandy tried to respond but couldn't find the words. When she fell silent, Dr. Kendrick nodded again.

"That wasn't weakness, Mandy, it showed me that you do truly care about him as a friend," he explained, "but you should know that no matter what you read about or watch in the films, nothing fully prepares you for the worst until it happens. Trust me, I know. Also, I have studied psychology... a lot of it. I can tell when someone hides behind words. It's ok to share what's really on your mind."

"Easy for you to say, sir," Mandy said in a soft and disappointed tone.

"Trust me, it is easier that way," Dr. Kendrick nodded. "Give 117 my regards."

"You're the boss," Mandy replied with a smirk. "I'll be sure to tell David that."

As Dr. Kendrick began to walk away, a thought suddenly crossed her mind.

"One last thing!" she called out. He stopped and turned to look at her again.

"Yes?"

"Please don't psychoanalyze me, sir. The amborgs already do that enough around here."

"I guarantee nothing," Dr. Kendrick winked, leaving her cubicle.

"After what you've been through, Dr. Kendrick," Mandy whispered, "I know exactly what you're talking about."

She hit a few keys on her keyboard and reopened the communication channel with 117. A green light flashed in front of the microphone to show that he had picked up the call. Her video camera caught her, broadcasting her face to him in his display.

"Ok 117," Mandy said into the tip of the microphone. "Keep this in mind when you get back. We have some social skills that need practice. Now get back in the game. It's not over yet."

117's voice suddenly replied from the speakers.

"What game are you referring to Mandy?"

"Nothing. Just carry out the mission."

"Affirmative."

CHAPTER 5

We... Are... Family??

A.I. Industries: Technician Monthly Review Board
2127 November
Two months later: Twelve successful operations

"Alright everyone, now that we've covered the post action report for the last week, let's move on to personal updates."

Mandy was seated at a table surrounded by a group of technicians. The room hosted a total of 30 people, split into five tables of six. Each person was designated as the official partner to a member of the Second Group.

The entire review board was a special event for the team to come together to share insights and noteworthy accomplishments their amborgs had achieved. It was also a place to discuss any issues, request advice, and collaborate on strategies that needed to be implemented or revised. Mandy was, of course, representing and reporting to her colleagues about David 117.

"Anyone want to go first?" she heard someone ask.

Mandy turned her head to look at Sherry, who was shrugging.

"You know," she smiled, "we can do it alphabetically or by numerical order."

"How about highest number first and then in descending order?"

Mandy glanced at a man wearing spectacles that looked similar to Dr. Kendrick's. This was James, the technician that worked with amborg Carter 297. He meekly lowered his shoulders as the table shifted its attention toward him.

"We never did that before," Mandy said encouragingly. "Let's do it."

"Well, then that means Aaron is first."

All eyes fell on Aaron. Sherry grabbed a little squishy, blue stress ball and rolled it across the table. The technician leaned forward, effortlessly catching it with a cheerful smile.

"Thank you!" he answered enthusiastically.

"This should be good," Sherry snickered.

"I haven't even said anything yet!" Aaron exclaimed with a laugh.

"Neither has your amborg," Mandy chuckled. "Well, not that we've heard."

The entire table burst out into small fits of laughter. Aaron shook his head, joining in with a hint of forced sarcasm.

It was funny because Aaron was the technician assigned to Alice 999. She was making quite a name for herself among the staff members at A.I. Industries. If anyone fit the bill for the quietest human being on Earth, it would be her.

"Alright, alright!" Mandy waved her hands, signaling for the room to settle down. "Let's let him actually talk about Miss Silent-But-Deadly."

"I'll have you know that she actually said something recently," Aaron smirked.

"Ooh, do tell."

Mandy glanced at a girl sitting on her right. Meilin, amborg 917's technician. She seemed rather excited to hear more.

"The only other person she really likes to talk to is 917," she explained with a fascinated gleam in her eyes.

"She asked me to look into records of some orphans that we passed on the street when we deployed in Chicago," Aaron described, sharing his story for them. "She asked for first responders to find them a place to shelter and had me coordinate it."

"Was that when 917 wasn't nearby?" Meilin asked. "Because we had to coordinate with firefighters about that structural fire with the twins."

"You mean the 22 minutes that they were apart from each other? Yeah," Aaron nodded.

"Aw, that's progress!" Sherry interjected. "It's so interesting to hear about the fact that the lone wolf has something to say..."

Sherry eyed Meilin mischievously.

"...other than to her best friend."

"That's another question I still have..." James spoke up. "Why are 999 and 917 considered best friends?"

"Because they are?"

Everyone looked at Prajit. He was Ryan 35's technician. James shook his head and crossed his arms.

"I understand that but... why?" he clarified his question. "He has such an inviting and open personality..."

Then he glanced around the table and shrugged.

"But she's... so cold and distant."

"I'm pretty sure you'd be that way too if you knew what she's been through," Aaron replied courteously.

"Why? What has she been through?" James asked.

"You really need to read the other amborgs' files," Sherry snickered, "the ones that are available to the public."

"There's a rumor that Alice 999 was recovered from a slum district in Oregon," Meilin explained to James when he scowled at Sherry. "She was a former child slave for the local mob. As far back as her earliest childhood memory, she was exposed to a really terrible and inhumane life."

"Wait, as in, child trafficking...?" James asked, his eyes widening as his look of annoyance faded in seconds.

"The worst parts," Aaron nodded grimly. "Basically."

This particular topic gave Mandy chills as well as a huge knot in her stomach.

"Hence," Aaron added, "that is why she's so quiet. She doesn't like to open up to anyone."

"This subject just became pretty heavy..." Mandy shuddered.

"Yeah," Sherry patted Mandy's shoulder sympathetically. "Let's move on. Meilin?"

Meilin smiled warmly at the rest of the table. James nodded politely and adjusted his glasses as they all turned their attention to 917's technician.

"Of course," she announced, "I have a personal update about 917. He has chosen a first name for himself!"

Each person in the room perked up, their interest immediately piqued. Mandy smiled and her eyes widened in excitement.

"Really?" Sherry clapped her hands. "That's so nice! He finally picked one!"

917 was another unique case. Until he had picked a number, he was often known as the nameless one.

According to what Mandy had heard about him, Dr. Kendrick found him in a hospital, deep in a coma. The story goes that he brought the boy back to A.I. Industries, where he was cybernetically enhanced. As a result, when 917 eventually woke up, he became the first amborg in history to be augmented while completely unconscious. His transformation ignited a fierce debate among the technicians who'd learned about his origins. One of the major repercussions of 917's awakening was the severe amnesia he faced; while he realized he was one of the strongest humans on the planet, he couldn't remember anything from his life prior to being admitted to the hospital. He had no idea what his name was and no one had been there for him, until Dr. Kendrick strolled into the picture.

"What did he pick?" Mandy asked curiously.

"Amborg 917 has elected and settled on the name, Jack," Meilin answered with a bright smile.

"Amborg Jack 917," Aaron beamed. "I like it."

"Good for him," Sherry said excitedly.

"You didn't pick it for him, right?"

"Damn it James, read the room," Aaron sighed.

"No," Meilin said, exasperated. "Jack 917 picked it after thinking about it for several days. He told me that it was inconvenient referring to him by number only. This meant a lot to him so he took his time."

"Speaking of time," Aaron cleared his throat and jutted his chin towards James. "I think you're next."

"Not much to report," James shrugged. "Carter 297 has continued to excel at every task that he has undertaken."

"Wait a minute, why did you say it like that?"

Sherry leaned forward and raised an eyebrow. James responded with a look of bafflement.

"You said two ninety-seven," she stated, "not... two nine seven."

"Oh, well, that's actually quite simple," James nodded to confirm that they had heard him right. "297 has asked that you pronounce it that way. He talked about how saying 97 is faster than nine seven."

"Oh, so it's just like Katie 57."

Mandy looked over at another bright young colleague, Ariana. When she'd picked Katie 57 to partner with, they had begun referring to the duo as AK-57. It was a funny joke in reference to the design of a rifle still used by armed military groups worldwide.

"Katie likes her number to be pronounced as fifty-seven instead of five seven," Ariana said, making eye contact with Sherry. "Like 43 wants to be called forty-three."

Sherry gave a slight tilt of her head to confirm Ariana's statement.

"Pretty much," James nodded. "297 just wanted me to make that clear so that we can address him with the correct pronunciation."

"Sounds like most of the amborgs are settling on some pretty important preferences," Sherry turned to glance at Mandy. "When is David going to ask us to call him one hundred seventeen? Or Jack nine hundred seventeen?"

"Fat chance of that," Mandy replied smugly. "It's always one one seven with David."

"Same with Jack," Meilin took Mandy's side. "I think 297 is the only one out of all of our amborgs that wants to steer away from singular number pronunciations and join 57, 43, and 35."

"What about Alice?" Mandy smirked as she leaned forward on her hands and joked with Aaron. "Has she explained why it's just nine nine nine?"

"Do I look like I have a death wish?" Aaron retorted.

The room erupted in more laughter.

"Isn't she half German or something?" Sherry asked. Without wasting a second, she put on her best German accent, straightened up and boldly exclaimed, "Nein nein nein! Has anyone ever said that in front of her?"

"And lived to tell the tale? I'll get back to you on that," Aaron shook his head uncomfortably as he slunk down into his chair. "You're so lucky the amborgs don't participate in these meetings."

"Why don't they?"

The entire table shifted towards Mandy. She leaned forward again, crossing her hands and resting them on the table.

"Wouldn't it be better if they did participate?" she asked, noticing she had everyone's attention. "I just feel like having our amborgs here would allow them more time to connect with us."

"That's the whole point..." James shook his head. "They're not supposed to be here because we're sharing updates and our opinions about them."

"It just feels like every month... we're gossiping behind their backs," Mandy replied. "Am I the only one that feels weird about that?"

"Well, I do, but probably not for the same reason."

Everyone looked at Meilin. She smiled sheepishly.

"What does that mean?" James asked.

"Oh, I'll tell you," Sherry eyed Meilin mischievously. "It means that Meilin here has a crush on her amborg."

"Isn't that against the rules?" Aaron asked.

"Actually, there is no official rule with entering a relationship with your amborg."

Everybody's attention shifted toward Prajit, who had been listening quietly the whole time. He tilted his head forward, breaking eye contact. He looked down while adjusting his glasses.

"Really?" Mandy asked, eyeing Prajit in fascination. She shook her head and focused on Meilin. "Wait a minute. Back up. How did I miss this? Meilin likes 917? I mean, Jack? How did I not know this for the last two months??"

"It's because you spend so much time babysitting 117," Sherry casually blurted out. "Meilin is attracted to 917."

"I don't babysit him," Mandy retorted.

"Mandy, honey..." Sherry said in a gentle but mocking tone. "You do."

"You are ten years older than most of us!" Mandy exclaimed. "If anything, you're the one babysitting 43 too much!"

"Well, yeah... I'm her technician."

Prajit cleared his throat. "Uh, aren't we going off the rails here?"

He was right. This meeting had spun out of control in just a few short seconds.

"Sorry," Mandy spoke first, breaking the silence. "That was my fault."

"How about this?" Sherry sighed. "James, any other updates about 297?"

"None," James shook his head.

"Well, then it's Mandy's turn," Sherry nudged Mandy in the shoulder and grinned. "Let's talk about Meilin after we get through the last three technicians. So, what's up with 117 these days?"

Mandy nodded but had to pause for a moment while the rest of the table stared back at her.

"He's... unwavering?" she replied.

Her colleagues continued to wait in silence.

"Pft. Why are you talking like 117?" Aaron sputtered out a laugh.

"I have no idea..." Mandy groaned.

"You've spent so much time with each other, that you've started adopting each other's habits," Sherry laughed.

"He's just moving at a slower pace than the others," Mandy sighed. "I don't really know what to tell you."

"To be fair," James interjected, "he is a top-performing amborg in the field, despite the emotional obstacles that seem to be hindering his human side. All of his missions with Mandy have been successful."

Everyone murmured their agreement. Their praise and supportive words of approval seemed to help Mandy relax slightly.

"If things keep going well for you," Sherry winked, "you could spend more free time hanging out with him to speak with him properly. We could always put together some files or come up with ways to communicate certain experiences to him."

"Is there more?" Ariana asked Mandy.

"No," she answered politely.

"Alright! My turn then. So, here's what 57 did the other day..."

Mandy found it a little difficult to focus. While everyone else seemed to be more lax about their own amborgs, she was struggling to come up with examples from her own life experiences that 117 could possibly relate to. The only one that seemed to have made the most progress educating their partner was Sherry. Compared to her, Mandy was more comfortable sticking to the rules, whereas Sherry was actively going around telling everyone to toss the rulebook out the window.

Why does everyone else make it sound so easy? Especially Sherry? It feels like I'm... trying to climb uphill, even with all of David's accomplishments."

Mandy smiled and nodded along, pretending to listen to Ariana's update, but uncertainty clouded her thoughts. She missed most of what her friend was saying, because as she tried to shift her focus back to the group, Prajit was already in the middle of sharing a story about Ryan 35.

Fortunately, the meeting wrapped up quickly, and the technicians began to rise, preparing to return to their usual tasks. As Mandy got up from her chair, it was no surprise that Sherry was the first to approach her, eager to strike up a conversation.

"Spaced out there towards the end?"

Mandy nodded. There was no hiding the guilt as she dipped her head forward.

"Don't feel discouraged," Sherry smiled reassuringly. "You really have done a phenomenal job being 117's technician."

"But how do you do it so well?" Mandy asked. "Everyone seems to connect with their amborgs so strongly, which is what I've been trying to do. It feels like 117 and I aren't at that level."

"Ever heard of this expression?" Sherry shrugged. "Sometimes there are both right and wrong ways to get the correct answer?"

Mandy nodded, prompting Sherry to finish explaining.

"Well, no one's saying you're in the wrong," she said. "From my perspective, you're so focused on adhering to the rules that 117 doesn't prioritize any sort of time for his human side."

"So, have I been doing this wrong for the last couple of months?"

"If that were the case, then you and 117 wouldn't have had so many successful missions," Sherry said confidently. "You've been doing things the Mandy way. Nothing wrong with your approach. But if there's still something that makes you feel unsure, then perhaps you need to upgrade your methods."

The two of them exited the meeting room together along with many of the other technicians.

"I don't know what I should do," Mandy admitted softly.

"It's not like you need to know all the answers," Sherry replied.

"So says the technician of the best amborg in all of A.I. Industries," Mandy scoffed.

"Oh, come on," Sherry waved her hand, shrugging it away, "that's just people exaggerating."

"Have you not heard the stories?!" Mandy exclaimed. "Look at your reports! 43 is the best amborg. You helped her get that title."

"*Un*-official... title," Sherry replied, enunciating her response.

"Still, you have to admit, she's progressed much faster and established her human emotions really well."

"Well, at the rate she's going," Sherry smiled, "she might not need me anymore."

"What do you mean?"

"It means, I'm considering retirement if 43 becomes a fully independent and self-sustaining human," Sherry let out a peaceful sigh of relief. "I will bet you a whole month of my salary that Meilin hooks up with 917 the instant he finds the need for romance."

Mandy held up her arms and shrugged. "How can Meilin be attracted to an amborg?"

Sherry paused, eyeing Mandy sternly.

"What's wrong with that?"

"Nothing!" Mandy answered. "I'm just curious what she's thinking about."

"It's a Florence Nightingale situation," Sherry said bluntly. "Jack 917 is the first amborg in history to be enhanced out of a coma. Meilin was one of his nurses that looked after him when Dr. Kendrick and his team discovered him. Apparently, it wasn't easy for him. He was falling behind just like 117. But she helped him with a ton of physical therapy, and he was cleared for active duty during the Second Group's big debut. I can totally see why she'd develop a fondness for the guy. Poor guy literally woke up with superpowers and a whole new life."

Mandy fell into an awkward silence as she thought about Meilin. From the sound of it, 917 also had his own share of difficulties. Maybe they weren't exactly the same as 117's problems, but he had almost fallen behind too.

"But if you look at him now," she murmured, "you couldn't even tell that was how he got his start."

"Exactly! Just keep at it with 117," Sherry said, giving Mandy another big pat on the shoulder. "Just keep working together and he'll find a way to be more human."

Sherry left Mandy as they split off in different directions at a hall intersection. After exchanging goodbyes, Mandy decided to head for her cubicle. One of the best ways for her to think was going over paperwork. She still had some files on her data pad that she could look through when she relaxed in her living quarters.

The technician's offices were empty for the first time in a while. Things around the country were probably slow and that's why the amborgs didn't have any emergency calls. It was pretty nice that the bad guys were taking the day off.

Oh, of course, Mandy let out a soft groan as she reached her desk and picked up the data pad she needed. *I probably just jinxed us all.*

After leaving the office, she began to walk back to her room. On quieter days, she preferred taking the scenic route through the amborg residential area, finding solace in the longer walk. Something about it had a calming effect on her. Normally, she would just breeze past the rooms belonging to the cybernetic teens but today, she took her time, taking in her surroundings. Maybe it was the rather interesting direction the technician meeting had taken that had her deep in thought, or perhaps she was mentally exhausted. As she clutched her data pad close to her side, she formulated a plan. She considered hopping on the next shuttle to her real home off-site for a little downtime. A visit with her family could be just what she needed after a long stretch of nonstop work. Of course, that was assuming World War IV didn't break out or something as soon as she left.

As she stepped into another corridor, her gaze drifted to the right and she peered through the windows. The afternoon sun illuminated the courtyard outside, and she caught sight of the main complex on the opposite side. This was the center of research and development, all under the direct supervision of Dr. Kendrick. Unless given permission, no one, not even the amborgs, were allowed there, which meant a lot of the work inside seemed ridiculously classified.

While considering what she wanted to pick up from her room, Mandy made her way into the amborg residential area. The distance to the transport pad was short, but she chose to go at her own pace to pass the time slowly. Part of her wanted to return home quickly and catch up with her real family but for some reason, she felt reluctant. It felt as though something was anchoring her here.

"This place feels like home," she muttered. "I spend almost every day here. We're all just one big family living in a high-tech country house with thousands of cool toys and jobs to keep us all well-financed and entertained."

"A very astute analogy. May I use that in potential future conversations of interesting subjects?"

Mandy startled at a sudden voice from behind. She whipped around and found herself looking up at a familiar face; one of the first amborgs she had met when she was still just starting out.

"Johnny 5!" she exclaimed happily. "It's so nice to see you again!"

"It's a pleasure Mandy," 5 nodded cheerfully.

The first group amborg smiled pleasantly as his bracelet lit up and recited his thoughts.

"Aren't you off work? Or something like that? You should be on your way home by now. The Thanksgiving holidays are approaching. Unless you really believe that this place is also your home now."

"Uh, there was a technician meeting," Mandy suddenly shuddered as she remembered how twisted the discussion had been. "It was... very informal."

"Oh, I remember those," 5 smiled with a glint of excitement in his expression, as if he was reminiscing the memory. "My old technician used to tell me that I would always make him cry."

"Huh?"

5 winked when he saw Mandy's puzzled look.

"Because I made him laugh too hard on several occasions," he explained.

"Oh."

If Mandy remembered correctly from what she had read in 5's public personality files, he had an amazing sense of humor and wit. He and many others had suspected that the cybernetic augmentation of his mind had enhanced his wit and charm. He was quite the conversationalist as a result. Maybe if he had spare time, she could ask him to try hanging out with 117.

"Speaking of Thanksgiving," Mandy suddenly remembered what he had said earlier. "Are the amborgs doing anything?"

"I'm working," 5 answered with a smile.

"Why?"

"So, everyone else can enjoy their holiday."

"Why does it always seem like you never like to relax?"

"We do," 5 answered confidently. "Just not the same way that you do."

"You mean like normal human beings?" Mandy sighed.

"We are anything but normal," 5 winked again.

Mandy could have continued this debate, but given how long the amborgs could draw out conversations, this would likely go on for hours if she continued pursuing the matter.

"I'm never going to hear the end of the conversation, am I?"

5 grinned when Mandy stared up at him with a look of disappointment.

"I can do this all day," he snickered. "All eternity, if your lifespan keeps up with mine."

"I think I should head home for now," Mandy shook her head, rolling her eyes.

"An excellent idea," 5 replied sarcastically. "Going to see family for the holidays?"

"Yes. I'm really grateful for the time off," Mandy nodded, "but at the same time, it feels strange getting ready to leave after working with 117 for a while. Time flew."

"It certainly has," 5 nodded sympathetically. "It seems like yesterday when the First Group was working overtime. Now, with more amborgs, my colleagues and I can enjoy some respite."

"Happy to help," Mandy forced a laugh. "Anyway, I shouldn't keep you. I'm going to review some things before I head home."

"Of course. Are you planning on taking work home with you?" 5 inquired humorously. "That's not exactly an ideal vacation."

"You won't believe how many reports I've been filing and how many more that aren't finished," Mandy slouched her shoulders but continued to show determination. "This is the best way to report 117's successes in the field so that we can look at them later to see what to improve on."

"Sounds like an ordeal."

"Look, since I can't do the heavy lifting like you or David," Mandy shrugged as she waved the data pad for him to see, "then I will do my best work; organizing the paperwork after 117 fills them out."

"Seems fair," 5 smiled. "I guess it isn't a surprise that your reports are enormous. 117 has been accomplishing quite a handful of tasks. You two really are an excellent team."

"Thanks. How exactly do you know this?"

"I like reading the after-action reports in my spare time," 5 answered with a playful tilt of his head. He beamed brightly. "They are all entertaining to me."

5 then began to walk away from Mandy.

"See you around Mandy," he waved. "I hope one day, I can have the privilege of fighting alongside 117 in the field. He is a remarkable amborg. Be sure to tell him that for me next time you see him, ok?"

"Ok. Thanks 5," Mandy said, blushing a little. She raised her hand and bashfully stroked the back of her head. "That really means a lot."

"Well, he has a very supportive technician. Giving you credit for taking care of him is also important."

"I don't think I deserve that level of praise," Mandy murmured.

"Please," 5 raised a hand, waving goodbye as he casually walked away. "You both function well as a team in your own unique way. Also, you may call me Johnny next time."

Mandy smiled and waved as 5 continued on his way. The bright neon orange stripes of his jacket, marked with the number 5, glowed vividly as she watched him disappear around the corner. She was really glad that they had accidentally met. Hearing a First Group amborg's praise certainly was very helpful.

Ever since the technician meeting, the others had made her feel like she wasn't on their level. For some reason, Johnny 5's praise seemed to reinforce Sherry's words. She was a capable technician. The main thing she had to focus on was that she was on a level that was unique to her style and that was what benefited David 117.

"That's twice you've helped me... Thanks Johnny," Mandy murmured to herself.

She remembered the day she met 5. It was by accident. When she first arrived at A.I. Industries, she struggled to learn the layout. After getting lost and attempting to follow the various directions given to her, she ended up late for the amborg selection—the event where she would meet 117.

Luckily, after bumping into Johnny 5, he helped to point her in the right direction. As a result, she got a rare opportunity to chat with him and even briefly saw a few other First Group amborgs. Normally, they kept to themselves whenever they returned to A.I. Industries after their missions. It was difficult to meet one, but she had said hi to about four of them. According to her coworkers and those from other departments, there was a special informal prize for anyone that was able to successfully meet all of the amborgs from the First Group. It was like a game of amborg bingo.

What was the prize? Mandy thought. *Everyone makes such a big deal when you tell them that you met a First Group amborg.*

Mandy paused. It actually was a big deal. She had read every single one of the First Group amborg's files over the last month. Giving herself insight into the amborgs that she had always seen as legendary heroes kept her fascinated with A.I. Industries. When she got hired as a technician, her curiosity, along with her access to their public files, was too good to pass up.

Amborg 3 pursued an interest in cooking in her spare time. Maybe it was the snacks in her room that triggered Mandy's thoughts of her. For some reason, her mind couldn't conjure up 3's name. Her stomach grumbled, her hunger likely the culprit for her clouded thoughts. The closest Mandy and her coworkers had come to interacting with her was when she was in charge of the mess hall. It was said that whenever she returned from deployments, 3 would often cook for everyone at A.I. Industries, whether it was breakfast, lunch, or dinner on one random day of the month. Each time she took over the kitchen, the food she made transformed into a culinary experience that rivaled the finest dining establishments, the kind the rich class often boasted about.

"Great, now I'm hungry..." Mandy groaned as she resumed her walk back to her room. "But if I stop for lunch... I'd have to text my parents that I'm running late."

As she passed another hall intersection, she briefly caught a glimpse of some custodians cleaning up a mess. Stan, a short man with grey hair, was giving instructions to a couple of drones while he and the human custodians swept and carefully removed debris. Mandy noticed dark burn marks from some kind of miniature explosion. She immediately recognized it as the handiwork of amborgs 8 and 9. Known as Stuart and Christy, they had gained a notorious reputation as pyrotechnic experts. After 117's first mission in L.A., both First Group amborgs had been relentlessly pestering him about the incident involving Molotov cocktails. At first, Mandy thought their questions stemmed from genuine concern, but in reality, they were more interested in hearing 117 recount what it was like to be on fire. They had a strange obsession. When they weren't burning stuff, the two of them had a penchant for playing pranks on each other, which happened on a consistent and unnecessary basis.

"I'm glad they target the bad guys and themselves instead of us," Mandy muttered as she walked on, leaving the custodians to their work.

She continued going through the roster. If her memory was right, she only needed to meet amborgs 1, 2, 4, 6, 7 and 10 in person. It wouldn't complete the amborg bingo card, but she would meet the requirements of "The Top Ten" employee achievement, a program initiated by Dr. Kendrick. Meeting the first ten people to be the first cyborgs in history was definitely significant.

"Let's see..." Mandy muttered, "I think 3's first name is Missy. A real southern belle type of name. Amborg 7... he had a lucky name... No, 777's name is Luis so... what was 7's name?? I know that 4 goes by... Katrina? Kat? Amborg 1 is Leonard, just like my cousin."

As Mandy struggled to recall their names, something caught her eye. At the far end of the passageway, she noticed two figures standing by what seemed to be a massive memorial.

When did this get constructed?

Mandy changed direction and headed toward it. Looking closely, she examined the decor and realized it was a huge collection of photos. Some were framed and holographic, with special light projectors casting images into the air, creating a chaotic yet captivating display. There were a lot of them, scattered and disorganized, as if dozens of people were using the space. There were even printed pictures glued or stuck onto the wall in some way. Someone actually taking the time to develop physical photos was impressive. Mandy couldn't help but notice that several of them had been torn and mended, while others bore burn marks around the edges, making it difficult to recognize the faces. It didn't take long for Mandy to piece together the identities of the people captured in those images.

As she gazed at the photos, she soon approached the two figures at the end, who turned out to be a couple of amborgs. As she drew near, they both faced her, revealing the glowing neon numbers on their jackets: 35 and 57 of the Second Group. It was a remarkable coincidence, since Mandy had just been in a meeting with their technicians.

The same group as David, Mandy thought. *Aside from me, they're also close friends with him.*

Although the two amborgs before her were enhanced at the same time as 117, she realized that she never really bothered to learn about them. It was understandable, considering there were a lot of amborgs roaming around, but this still managed to hit her heart with a twinge of guilt. Mandy began feeling bad for zoning out when Prajit and Ariana had given their updates about 35 and 57 during the meeting.

Perhaps now was the right time. Mandy decided that this could be the moment to change that. She walked up to them and gave them a kind, warm smile. Neither of them showed any change in expression as they quietly stared at her.

"Ryan," Mandy looked at 35, then to 57, "Katie. It's good to see you."

"Good evening, Ms. Mandy," 57 greeted her.

"You can just call me Mandy," Mandy laughed. "You don't call Prajit or Ariana, mister or miss, right?"

35 and 57 turned to face each other, their eyes meeting in a shared moment of unspoken thought. Were they having one of their "internal" conversations? They tilted their gazes back to Mandy in a fast but creepy robotic swivel.

"Mandy's words do have merit," 35 declared, his bracelet flashing as it broadcasted his voice. "I am not formal towards my technician."

"Apologies," 57 added, dipping her head politely. "I do not say Ms. Ariana. I shall remember for future conversations to just say 'Mandy.'"

"Don't apologize!" Mandy said casually as she waved her hand, clutching her data pad in the other, and continued to smile. "It just feels weird being called 'miss.' Anyway, what are you up to? What is all of this?"

"We were posting additional photographs on the memorial in honor of... our friends."

The mood suddenly dimmed as 57 fell silent. No more lights flashed from her bracelet as the tall amborg looked away. Mandy examined her expression closely and saw that she appeared crestfallen.

Before Mandy could say anything, 57 gave her a slight nod and turned away. She hurried off, leaving Mandy in a state of confusion. 35 followed her movement with his gaze, not saying a word. He turned and uttered a quick goodbye, the light from his bracelet fading as he disappeared too, heading in the same direction as 57. Mandy couldn't help but feel concerned, hurt, and lost all at once. 35 paused at the corner, casting a detached glance at Mandy, then continued on, vanishing around the corner. That certainly made things awkward.

"They are mourning, do not feel guilty."

Mandy jumped at the sound of another voice from behind. It was so close that she thought Johnny 5 had snuck up on her again. Whirling around, ready to have words, Mandy paused when she realized she was looking up at 117. How did all the amborgs move so quietly?? Her hand flew up to her chest, checking to make sure her heart was still beating.

"David!" Mandy exclaimed, nearly dropping her data pad. "Don't do that!"

"Do what?" he asked with an innocent but puzzled expression.

"The sneaking around thing," she replied in a very aggravated tone. "Even when you're home and not deployed, do you guys always have to be so silent?"

"Sorry. It is a part of our nature," 117 tilted his head inquisitively. "Very effective too. 917 believes many of us are possibly descended from ninjas."

"You mean Jack?" Mandy sighed.

"Ah, yes," 117's eyes widened slightly and he nodded firmly. "He recently informed me that he had selected a name. Many of us are happy for him."

Mandy stared at 117's neutral expression.

"You? Happy?" she said.

"Yes, it is a very important moment," 117 replied casually.

"You certainly don't look happy," Mandy observed in a skeptical tone.

"Oh," 117 looked down, "I shall try to correct my behavior."

Mandy groaned.

This is going to be difficult Sherry, she thought, *but I will absolutely keep at it.*

Obviously, this was something they needed a lot of time to work on, but for now, she wanted to hear from 117 what was going on here with this beautiful yet dreary hallway. She leaned forward and focused on the picture that she had seen 57 hang up. It was a picture of a teenage girl who bore a striking resemblance to the female amborg she had met a moment ago. A smile was etched onto the figure in the frame.

"Who is this?" she asked.

"That is 57's sister," 117 stated as Mandy looked deeply at the photo. "I believe she was younger by a year. Or... I don't know for sure. 57 doesn't like to talk about it. All she's told us is that both of them were in the streets of L.A. when Dr. Kendrick first found them, and that she didn't survive the biological enhancement process. She spent a long time protecting and taking care of her sister. They grew up here at A.I. Industries until they were old enough to volunteer to be amborgs. 57 woke up, but not her sister."

Mandy looked along the wall, where every picture depicted someone smiling or teenagers with determined looks on their faces. Several more frames held images of some of the amborgs, before their transformations, with their family members. The display also included children and a collection of knick-knacks—family heirlooms and personal belongings of the like. The whole memorial was dedicated to people that were related in some way to the surviving volunteers that were now amborgs. Mandy thought of 35, who'd gone silent and run off, just like 57.

"What about 35?" she asked.

117 pointed at another photo to her right. It showed three boys all with their arms around each other's shoulders. In the middle, 35 was easily identifiable, a wide smile on his face. Taped over this image was another photo of a couple, whom Mandy assumed was 35's parents.

"His older brother developed a serious and violent reaction to the bio-enhancement," 117 explained. "Dr. Kendrick failed to anticipate this and there was nothing that could be done. We discovered that some of the formulas contained ingredients that he was allergic to. As for the younger brother... 35 is still looking for him."

"What do you mean?" Mandy asked softly.

"A long time before he came to A.I. Industries, his younger brother disappeared and went missing," 117 explained. "35 says that he hopes that he can find out what happened so that he can gain closure. A few of us have spent time working with him on this missing persons case."

Mandy struggled to hold back tears, taking a few deep breaths. The atmosphere grew heavy, and she felt a lump forming in her throat. She sniffed and turned her gaze away from the memorial.

How? She wondered. *We're supposed to be living in the future.*

How was it possible, with all the technology and the brains that went into this idea, that so many of humanity's potential saviors still lost their lives? All of these photos and decorations of the memorial were the last known memories of everyone who volunteered and didn't live to see the future that they were making a tremendous sacrifice for.

"How do you do it?" she asked 117. "How are you ok with shutting out your feelings? Just like that?"

117 paused briefly, averting his eyes to think. A moment later, he faced her again and replied.

"I don't know if I am completely ok. As for the others, every amborg tries living their lives as best as they can. Officer Johnson once asked me why we never rest or take time off. Most of our spare time is utilized thinking about many subjects. We may never know our true feelings again."

"Sounds a little depressing," Mandy stated. Then she realized what she had said, and her eyes widened, "I mean! When I pause from my normal activities, I suddenly find myself thinking about feelings and wondering about a lot of things too. Not knowing your true feelings just makes me feel sad."

"But we do remember everything."

117 stood before the memorial, taking in the array of faces displayed in pictures, holograms, and brief video clips. Each video, though only a few seconds long, gave the impression that the people in them were truly alive. It was a lot like watching snippets from social media, with a wholesome and uplifting vibe.

"I don't currently feel the same way as I used to or how you can Mandy," 117 explained. "The emotions don't factor into my daily life. Sorrow, anger, envy, remorse, guilt. Even positive emotions are difficult to interpret. Dr. Kendrick encourages us to try over and over again even though it feels like our emotions have been forced into a tight corner. He says our feelings are not shut out, as you say, but we are constantly working to unlock them again. I don't believe we close ourselves off from them entirely. It is difficult to express or recall how we felt before our lives changed. But I can confidently reassure you that we're learning."

Mandy, barely understanding a quarter of what he said, nodded in understanding anyway. 117 spoke of emotions as if they were nearly in his grasp, but it seemed as if the amborgs could never fully understand them one hundred percent. They could only experience them from a cold, hard, and new perspective. What was it like to fully devote yourself to becoming an amborg? When you had nothing to lose? It was a pretty impressive but scary lifestyle. Mandy decided to change the subject.

"Have you lost anyone?" she asked calmly. "Anyone you cared about or knew?"

Mandy caught 117's eye, but he quickly looked down before meeting her gaze again. She wasn't sure if her question upset him. Without answering, he gestured toward another photograph a few feet away, and Mandy stepped forward to take a closer look. In the image, a man and a woman stood together, appearing far too old to be amborg test subjects. They were locked in a joyful embrace, beaming at the camera. As Mandy reached out to brush an overlapping picture out of the way, something extraordinary happened.

The photograph transformed into a small video screen, and the image began to move. The man leaned in and planted a kiss on the woman's cheek, making her blush and close her eyes with a smile. This was the only scene that played, and she saw it restart from the beginning, entering another loop. Mandy glanced back at 117, who stared at the moving image with a dazed look. He appeared sad, but she couldn't tell. Turning back to the video, she noticed several more photos beneath it, showing the same man and woman in what appeared to be A.I. Industries outfits.

"My parents," 117 explained as they watched the couple embrace each other again.

"They used to work for Dr. Kendrick?" Mandy politely inquired.

"Correct," 117 nodded. "My father was part of the research team. Unfortunately, no one has told me what he was working on."

"What about your mom?"

"She was a nurse," 117 answered. "She worked back in Chicago and moved out to the West Coast when she married my father."

"If you'd like," Mandy spoke awkwardly, "can I ask you more questions about them?"

"Of course."

"Dr. Kendrick doesn't usually accept volunteers if they have biological relatives or family that are still alive," Mandy thought carefully and tried to remember what the official rules were. "So, how were you allowed to join the training program to prepare for augmentation?"

"Both my parents passed away when I was eight," 117 answered. "Same as 43."

"Wait, what? 43?"

"Her parents were also employed here at A.I. Industries," 117 glanced around, making sure there weren't others in earshot. "We both went through the same experience."

"Her parents died too?"

"Dr. Kendrick found us and took us in," 117 noticed that the coast was clear and nodded. "When we were both 18 years old, we volunteered to become amborgs."

"So... if my math is right," Mandy mumbled, "you two have been here at A.I. Industries since the First Group became active?"

"They were activated in 2115," 117 stated. "43 and I were brought to A.I. Industries two years after. Dr. Kendrick told us about our parents and how close they were. It's how 43 and I have been good friends for so long."

"When you legally became 18," Mandy nodded in understanding, "both of you wanted to become amborgs. That's still a risky sacrifice. I'm surprised that Dr. Kendrick agreed to it."

"43 and I argued that it would be the best way to take care of ourselves," 117 described in a pleasant tone. "Dr. Kendrick made a promise to take care of us after we lost our parents. When we reached adulthood and were allowed more opportunities to choose what we wanted to do, I wanted to become an amborg. So did 43."

"Do any of the others know? No one's accused you or brought up any issues of nepotism... have they?"

"Before we were enhanced, several of the others voiced their displeasure about us," 117 admitted. "I remember someone referring to us as 'entitled spoiled brats' that got in with exclusive connections instead of merit."

"I've seen your training records," Mandy declared, "you and 43 have great results!"

"Both of us have endeavored to work hard and dedicate our lives to be here," 117 nodded. Mandy could almost see a bright gleam in his eyes as he attempted a faint smile. "Anyone who learns about our past will know, but we also want to show everyone that is not the main reason we are amborgs."

"Well, this makes sense."

Mandy glanced at the pictures of his parents and then faced him with a smile.

"I think your parents would be proud of the fact that you're one of the strongest humans in the world," she said. "Even though they're gone, I think you made a difficult but brave decision. Same with 43."

"Thank you," 117 nodded. "I am also glad that 43 and I remained firm in our choices with Dr. Kendrick."

117 and Mandy began to leave the hall.

"This all took place just this last year?" she asked.

"Yes, for both of us, it was a new beginning," he explained. "I was... happy to see that 43 survived. But we were also both... very quiet when we found out how many didn't survive. Friends that we knew and trained with were gone. I wish they were still here. But we stand here alive, and we fight for our memories and for them."

"I think that's the coolest thing I've ever heard you say since we became partners."

"I wasn't aware that my words could have a low temperature..."

"And there's the David 117 I know," Mandy let out a slight chuckle.

Getting to her room to pick up some things, her primary objective, had suddenly disappeared completely from Mandy's mind. She was enjoying the time spent with him, and with each new detail she learned about him, her confidence as his technician grew. She made a mental note to text her parents later about running late. Eventually, their casual conversation ended when she stood in front of 117's door. This was the first time she had seen where he lived.

"Would you like to come in?" he asked politely. "Unless you have other plans?"

"Sure!" Mandy nodded as she gazed at the glowing neon text on the nameplate.

David 117, Second Group.

Mandy then read a quote underneath the name.

It takes courage to become who you really are.

"Nice quote," Mandy smiled at 117. "Who said that?"

"I think the person who engraved that just picked a random positive quote," 117 shrugged, indicating that he didn't know. "It is a nice quote."

The door slid open with a soft hiss when 117 pressed his finger up to the green button on the side. He politely gestured for Mandy to head inside first.

It was a simple room. Mandy glanced to the side and noticed a small closet filled with uniforms and civilian clothing. She felt confused by his choice of outfits. When did 117 even wear casual clothes? She had only ever seen him wear his amborg jacket everywhere he went. Perhaps those were his before augmentation.

In the corner, there was a standard A.I. Industries computer terminal. She didn't see a keyboard anywhere and realized it was one of those models without a holographic interface. The thought made her smile—how did 117 even use this thing?

Maybe he links his own CPU to that computer and just sits in front of it like a statue while browsing online, she guessed.

Everything else in the room looked like a standard amborg's layout. There was a tall circular chamber with "117" written on the glass sitting across from the closet in the corner. It was a charging capsule for... actually, she wasn't sure what it was for.

Mandy noticed a small single bed along with some other standard furniture. A few photos hung on the walls, adding a personal touch. All in all, it looked perfect, immaculate and well-organized.

"Wow. It looks nice," she nodded approvingly.

"Thank you."

"It sure looks better than the dump I live in."

"Your listed address for your family outside of A.I. Industries does not indicate that you live in a garbage dump," 117 looked at Mandy with concern. "Have you forgotten to make a change of address?"

Mandy stared at 117 with dim eyes. He took one look at her and nodded silently.

"Oh, that was just another expression," he stated, figuring out why she looked at him skeptically. "Excuse me."

117 lifted his hand and waved it around, showcasing the room.

"Please, make yourself at home."

She smiled a little at his attempt to change the subject. It was a relief to see that he was actually learning, and that she didn't feel the need to explain everything like she did a few months ago.

Mandy graciously walked up to a picture and examined it as 117 headed to his computer. He raised his hand and placed it on a scanner positioned beside the monitor. The lights flickered on, and the screen powered up. A camera activated, and a ray of light scanned 117's face. His desktop unlocked after confirming his facial recognition and palm scan. When he was in his system, 117 initiated a link to his computer and remained there for a few seconds.

"Data transfer complete," the computer responded. "Welcome back, David 117."

"Data what?" Mandy curiously looked at the screen. "What did you do?"

"A few of my friends have been helping me obtain old movies and films from the 20th century," 117 said as a holographic keyboard appeared in front of the computer, and he began hitting a few keys. "There is one in particular that I have taken a liking to."

The computer screen lit up and various images appeared. Mandy noticed that several of them looked vintage.

"Do you know the television series, Star Trek: The Next Generation?" 117 asked.

"I think so," she replied thoughtfully. "My dad is a huge collector, so I think he knows that show and I might have watched several episodes when I was a kid. There was a famous actor named Sir Patrick Stewart, and he was... Captain Picard or something."

Mandy kept her eyes on the screen as 117 sifted through the pictures.

"My dad showed me lots of those old shows from back then. He was really into records and lots of historical stuff like that. He always told me that there's so much that people have forgotten about. A few hundred years ago was a different but really great time period."

"There were several wars and military conflicts in the 20th century."

"I didn't say it was an entirely good segment of history," Mandy shrugged.

117 changed the subject and got them back on track by pulling up the record of an actor named Brent Spiner. As Mandy read his file in the historical database, 117 spoke again.

"I am very fascinated by the character they refer to as Lieutenant Commander Data," 117 said as he swapped the photo. It changed from the actor to the character that he portrayed. Mandy assumed it was from the show. "Brent Spiner put on an amazing performance by my understanding. An android completely built by humans and his main programming is that he wants to learn from humans. His desire is to be human. His observations over the years aboard the Starship Enterprise. In my spare time, I have been trying to monitor and learn by example from him. There are so many thematic and social themes from shows like this one."

"You know," Mandy suddenly had an idea, "Why don't you come visit my home sometime? My parents would probably love to meet you on a day off. Hangout and watch old classic movies or television shows with my dad."

117 perked up. Mandy could have sworn she saw his eyes light up.

"This is an unexpected proposal," 117 tilted his head but eagerly nodded in response. "However, I will accept this offer. If your family agrees, then I will say yes. Upon consent, I will submit arrangements."

"Maybe a day leading up to Christmas?" Mandy suggested. "I would invite you for Thanksgiving but... it might be too short notice."

"It's alright," 117 replied casually. "I'm scheduled to be on duty for the upcoming holidays. But I am grateful that you considered me in your plans."

"Of course, David," Mandy smiled. "We're partners. The rate at which we're going, we're family. And we always look out for each other."

"When were you planning to leave for your vacation?"

Mandy's eyes widened. She suddenly checked the time, realized how much time had actually passed, and frantically turned to leave.

"Where does the time go?!" she exclaimed. "Sorry! I was supposed to pack a few things from my room! I wasn't paying attention to the time! My parents are probably going to text me soon and ask what's taking so long."

"One moment Mandy."

Just as she was about to open the door, she glanced back and noticed 117 quickly pulling something up on the computer. She tried to look at the screen, but was unable to see it from her angle.

"What is it?"

"It is a quote that I've been studying," 117 replied. "One moment please."

He activated a projector from his computer and a light shined on the wall behind it. Mandy saw a highlighted quote in cursive bold letters.

Where belief is painful, we are slow to believe. -Ovid

"Studying?"

"It's a hobby," 117 replied. "I found this quote by a long forgotten roman named Ovid."

"Interesting quote," she remarked. "Are you looking up all these things in your spare time? Don't you sleep?"

"I won't be taking a sleep day for another five days," he replied earnestly. "Can you please assist me in interpreting this?"

Mandy sighed. Who could resist helping a teenage cyborg with the curiosity of an infant? She shrugged but nodded her head.

"Sure, why not? But make it fast."

"Thank you," he said, standing up. "Mandy, is it alright for people to develop their own beliefs?"

"Of course it is. It's perfectly alright."

"But Ovid's quote puzzles me," he looked at the screen in confusion. "If a belief is painful, how does it inflict pain? And how would people be slow to believe?"

"First, don't think of it so literally," she replied, laughing a little at how he had tried to begin his interpretation. "Is there anything online that explains what the quote means?"

"One definition I found was this," 117 straightened up and recited his answer. "This phrase means that when believing something is difficult or causes pain, people tend to hesitate or resist believing it, often because it challenges their existing beliefs or comfort zones."

"See? It's not talking about actual pain," Mandy explained. "At the time, Ovid was saying that forming new beliefs is hard, especially when you're in the minority who believe in it. Not a lot of people like change, which is why we're slow. Or the fact that, if something bad happens, we don't want to believe it because of how painful the truth could be. At least I think that's what he meant."

"Can you think of an example?"

"Uh..." Mandy paused for a moment. "Oh, there was an incident with my uncle a while ago. The entire family was hesitant to believe that he had an affair and cheated on my aunt. When we found out that he really did cheat on her, she was slow to believe it because it was too painful to accept."

"That is a good example," 117 looked down and continued to think. "Is it also fair to use this as an example? When the First Group amborgs first appeared to the public, people were slow to believe in them and that caused many problems."

"That's another good one," Mandy nodded. "When I first saw what the amborgs were capable of, I thought they were heroes. But a lot of other people saw you as overpowered vigilantes. Nowadays, most people are happy to see you in public and they support A.I. Industries more."

"In that case, may I share something with you?"

"What is it?"

"I wish to be more human," David stared calmly at the photos on the wall. "It is my belief that I can learn to be fully human again while achieving a state of symbiosis with my cybernetics. I know that you and the other technicians talk about me during the meetings, the other amborgs have told me."

Mandy awkwardly glanced away and focused on a random spot on the wall behind him. She let out an uncomfortable groan.

"Well, David, you do know that when I bring it up, it's not anything against you."

"Thank you for clarifying," 117 nodded. "We pay attention to a lot of rumors and gossip, and we spend plenty of time analyzing your words. I am glad to have talked about this with you."

"Me too," Mandy smiled. This was obviously important to him so she didn't mind making herself more late if it meant taking care of her friend. "Is there anything else?"

"Commander Data was an android built from scratch and he is working to become human. In a way, I sympathize with him as an amborg. I was remade and reborn with a superhuman ability to learn fast, and I believe I can be like him when he pursues his goal to be human."

"Well David," Mandy smiled and placed a hand on his shoulder. "That's something I can believe in too. I can't speak for everyone else but maybe, they'll believe in you too."

"Did I interpret the quote correctly?"

"Heh. I don't know David. Hehe, I don't really know."

A chime sounded from the door, snagging their attention. Upon hearing the bell, 117 called out.

"Yes? Come in!"

The door slid open and heavy footsteps crossed the threshold. Another amborg arrived, and Mandy looked at the number on his jacket.

297 of the Second Group walked in. Mandy remembered that he was not two-nine-seven. James had said that he preferred that people say it a specific way.

"Hello 297," Mandy waved, "Carter!"

297 seemed pleased when he heard her say his number the way he preferred. He had blond hair and was the same height as 117. Aside from the fact that his neon stripes were a shade of orange, Mandy was wondering what 117 would look like if he went from having dark hair to the same shade of blond as 297. They would probably look like brothers.

"It is nice to see you, Mandy. 117, how are you?"

As 117 eagerly stepped forward and the two amborgs casually exchanged a special handshake. Mandy couldn't help but look closely at the other Second Group amborg in the room.

297 kept a reserved but strong look on his face. What caught Mandy's eyes slightly unnerved her. There was something in his eyes that seemed devoid of life, like he was fixated on something troubling. Sure, his interactions with 117 were pleasant but his expression appeared way more intense than the other amborgs. It was like he was focusing on something and nothing at the same time. If it was something serious, James had left it out of the meeting on purpose or didn't think it was a big enough deal to mention it. She decided to shrug it off since it wasn't her business to pry into 297's personal business.

From what Mandy had heard in previous technician meetings, he was slowly making a name for himself. 297 was a skilled marksman and also had a flawless record that mirrored 117's. Off-duty, the two had become great friends when they first went into service cybernetically.

"117," he greeted them with a curt nod. "I apologize for interrupting. I actually came by to tell you that dinner was ready."

"You guys actually eat food?"

117 and 297 both stared at Mandy, who coughed in embarrassment.

"S-sorry," she stammered. "It's just that I never see 117 stop even for a simple snack break when he's in the field. Whenever I see him off-duty, it doesn't seem like he has an appetite."

"That is understandable," 117 replied with a nod. "Amborgs don't consume food at the same times that humans usually do."

The cybernetic implants that sustained and kept the amborgs endowed with their superhuman abilities had some rather unusual but effective side effects. One amborg could go days, weeks, or even a few months without sleep, food, or rest, which was cool, but seemed really terrible. The average human needs water, food, and sustenance on a daily basis to function properly. Dr. Kendrick's augmentation procedures were awesome and terrifying at the same time. Hearing 117 describe his abilities so nonchalantly was scary.

"You make it sound like you just vaporize your meals and absorb it in some weird magical way," Mandy shuddered.

"We consume food just like you," 297 replied. "Just not as often."

"For special occasions, there are many benefits," 117 said, straightening his jacket. "Food is a very nice pastime for us."

"3 is cooking dinner tonight," 297 stated excitedly.

"What?" Mandy whined. "3 is here? Back onsite? Cooking dinner? I'm going to miss it?"

"You could cancel your prior engagement?" 297 suggested.

"I'm supposed to be heading home to my family for the holidays…" Mandy mumbled in response.

"Oh," 297 looked away sheepishly. "My apologies. Perhaps it isn't a good idea to cancel plans with your family."

"But I want 3's cooking…" Mandy said in a dazed voice.

"I believe she is experiencing an ethical conundrum," 117 observed in a concerned tone.

"Noted," 297 nodded and crossed his arms. "I'll shut up now before I suggest any other ideas."

"Perhaps I can help get her back on track," 117 said.

Mandy blinked and focused on 117. When she was fully paying attention, 117 brought his fist up to his mouth and made the sound of clearing his throat through his bracelet. Mandy stared in fascination at his imitation of human behavior.

"3, 7, 9, and 13's skills are excellent when cooking food," he announced. "Stimulating our olfactory and gustation senses provide nice results. Our data analysis and study of the culinary arts constantly improves due to their expertise. If we end up going to a restaurant for food on a mission, for example, undercover, it can provide us with proper camouflage. Many have suggested it may help us blend in if we are out for a long period of time. To the public, we will appear normal while eating our favorite foods."

Mandy shook her head in disbelief and tried to focus on what he had said. Instead, her eye twitched and then she erupted in laughter. 297 and 117 watched as she doubled over, shaking from a fit of silent giggles. When she finally attempted to straighten up, they noticed that her mouth was open, her laughter barely audible.

"What...? I don't... David..."

"I think you have made it worse," 297 said with concern as he leaned towards 117.

Mandy was trying to regain control of herself but her laughing confused the two amborgs. Mandy looked from 297 to 117 and could tell that they were transmitting to each other privately. Obviously, they had no idea how to respond to the current situation.

"Sorry," she cleared her throat and coughed. She let out an involuntary giggle as she caught her breath. "I was just laughing because... only you, David... could make dinner sound so interesting and boring at the same time."

"Based on previous patterns on our missions together, it would appear that you have reached a state of clarity," 117 replied confidently.

"Oh, that's what you did?" 297 raised an eyebrow.

Mandy smiled at 297.

"Don't let James rope you into any mind games, ok Carter?" she chuckled. "David and I have our own unique method of communication."

"Noted."

Mandy then turned to 117.

"Even when you guys try to blend in when you're deployed, it doesn't work," she sighed. "I mean sorry, I can still spot you guys from a mile away even if you tried to hide in the open."

"Our performance seems to be lacking more than we thought," 297 noted observingly. "Perhaps we need to have another eight-hour discussion."

"I agree," 117 nodded.

Mandy let out another sigh, prompting both of them to stare at her silently.

"Next time," she added, enunciating her words clearly, "you should include some actual humans who know how to teach whatever it is you're discussing during your meetings. And... really? Eight hours? Wow you guys have too much time on your hands."

"To this day, it is our shortest meeting time," 117 stated.

Mandy sighed.

"Well, I won't get in the way of that then," she said, trying not to burst out in another fit of laughter. "I think I'll head home now. Carter? Will you go on ahead and give us a minute? I have something to ask David."

"Certainly," 297 nodded courteously, signaling his farewell. "But make it quick, the main course is spaghetti tonight."

Without another word, 297 turned around and exited 117's room.

"What did you want to ask?" 117 asked as the door closed.

There was another thing that she had never really bothered to ask. Now was probably the best time. Otherwise, she'd forget about it.

"Well, it's about your numbers," she looked at the number 117 on his jacket. "The first group is all numbered one through thirty. But then they allowed the second group the choice of picking their own numbers. Well... can I ask why you chose the number designation 117?"

117 nodded and his reply was quick.

"That is part of the number of an apartment building that 43 and I remember living in with our families before we came here to A.I. Industries. Therefore, in memory of our old home, we chose the number 43117."

Mandy nodded, then paused when something dawned on her. If there were five digits in that building number, how did 43 and 117 decide who would get the middle digit?

"So, when you chose your numbers," she said slowly, "43 almost became amborg 431? And you would have been... wait, that couldn't work..."

"Correct," 117 nodded, "43 would have most likely chosen 431 and I would have settled with 71 since we already have an amborg 17 that is actively using that number. We decided it would be easier if I became 117 instead."

"Oh, I see," Mandy nodded as she prepared to leave his room. "Funny, I thought it was because you were a Halo fan."

"I have spent time playing that game series," 117 replied. "It is a very good game, Mandy."

"I got a bit of a tiny confession David," Mandy cleared her throat and spoke quietly. "I'm not a gamer girl so I'm not going to really be able to share a connection with you if you talk about video games."

"Yet, you have an awareness of the Halo games."

"I'm not a gamer but I do like reading stuff in the archives in my spare time. A lot of historical entries in the database provide some interesting things to read about. Even the internet is a great place to look for classics from the past."

"Yes," 117 agreed. "It is very… fun when I like researching past relics."

"And you know what, you have fun during the next week," Mandy gave 117 one more smile. "I'm going to go home. See you when I get back."

"Of course, Mandy. Unless trouble breaks out," 117 replied with a small grin.

Mandy paused and stared at 117. His smile was forced, making him appear a bit rigid and intimidating.

"Was that a joke David?" she asked, slightly off put.

"Yes… was it a good attempt?"

"Not bad, but… I think your smile is a little too stiff," she said, holding up an a-okay sign with her fingers. "For homework, try working on smiling."

117 watched Mandy exit the room. He looked down at the floor, taking her words to heart, then headed to the restroom. When he stepped in, the light turned on automatically when it detected his presence, and he walked up to the mirror.

"Too stiff," he repeated her words to himself as he gazed at his reflection.

Through his HUD, he pulled up a display screen and replayed footage from the past few minutes. Mandy had laughed and smiled several times during her visit. With the video data that he had, perhaps he could try and replicate what he had seen.

He paused the footage, and the image on the screen captured Mandy looking up at him with a bright, natural smile. Changing the overlay, he switched to an x-ray view of her jawline. How difficult could this be? 117 attempted to replicate her smile, concentrating on his zygomatic muscles. Her facial nerves tugged in an unfamiliar way, but eventually, he managed to hold a smile in the mirror for a few minutes. He blinked, activated his camera, and took a photo. 117 wanted to analyze it later, or at least show it to someone else to get their input.

"I shall reattempt if this image fails to convey happiness," he declared as he exited the bathroom.

Keeping this in mind, 117 left his room and proceeded to the mess hall. Showing his smiling picture to anyone there was sure to provide him with plenty of feedback and constructive criticism.

As he stepped through the doors, he was greeted by an abundance of noise. It was evident that 3's cooking had attracted many staff members.

Mandy had either lucked out by avoiding such a huge dinner rush or was probably going to be mad when she found out how popular it was. He glanced to the right and saw Dr. Kendrick sitting with a few others at one of the round tables. From the look of it, they were all enjoying the amborg-cooked spaghetti served in a communal style. Someone had laid out a massive bowl in the center and they were passing food around so that everyone had something on their plates. Even the security guards had decided to join in, momentarily setting aside their weapons while still in uniform, clearly allowed a break to enjoy the meal. 117 scanned the crowd and spotted the face he was looking for, just as Dr. Kendrick approached him.

"David, my boy!" he happily clapped his hand on 117's back. Then he retracted it and winced from the pain, but continued smiling as he shook his hand furiously. "I was afraid you weren't going to show up! You have got to try this! Out of all the food that 3, 7, 9 and 13 have made, I believe they may have truly outdone themselves with this recipe! Not that their other recipes were bad, of course, but I haven't eaten anything so scrumptious in my entire life!"

117 looked down at the plate in Dr. Kendrick's hand. The noodles definitely appeared to be quite fresh and tasty. After a careful and brief scan, he picked up on a few details. From how Dr. Kendrick was raving and chewing on them, it was clear that the noodles were made in house. Soft and with a thick texture, but not like the firm and rigid spaghetti noodle packs he had seen in public grocery stores.

While he was analyzing the food and developing positive expectations about when he would grab his own plate, Dr. Kendrick suddenly spoke again.

"Anyway, I wanted to tell you that I'm currently working on something in R&D that I think you'll enjoy. Also, if you have time during the holidays, stop by the motor pool. The mechanics there want to consult with you about a few things. Oh, and stop by the armory too! Wow, everything seems so busy lately. An early look at Christmas, I guess."

"Of course, Dr. Kendrick," 117 replied. "So aside from the motor pool and the armory, should I also visit R&D? Is there any particular destination that should be prioritized first?"

"Hmm, maybe set up an appointment and see when they'll fit you in," Dr. Kendrick thought carefully as he twirled his fork through his spaghetti. "Every department wants to have an opportunity to consult with every amborg in the Second Group."

"Every amborg?" 117 asked. What was so important that everyone needed to consult with all of these departments? "Pardon me but... may I ask...?"

"Hey Doc!"

Interrupted, Dr. Kendrick and 117 turned to look toward a nearby table where a security guard held up his plate while all the other people at the table cheered.

"We should make Friday spaghetti night!" he shouted, which made a few people nearby laugh, drowning out 117's words. "We need food like this on a weekly basis instead of every month!"

As the room erupted in whoops and cheers and everyone returned to their meals, Dr. Kendrick gazed apologetically at 117.

"Sorry David!" He raised his voice in order to make himself heard. "It'll have to wait! Go grab something to eat! We'll talk later!"

"It is nice to see you Dr. Kendrick," 117 answered respectfully, but it didn't seem like he had been heard. The noise deterred 117 from continuing the conversation, but he still tried to give Dr. Kendrick a proper goodbye. "I'm also... glad to see you too."

If he was being totally honest with himself, 117 didn't feel as grateful as he tried to convey. Seeing everyone else laughing, smiling, and enjoying themselves began to make him feel slightly alienated, like an outcast.

Discreetly, 117 made his way to a line leading to a lengthy table where four amborgs were serving up meals. Directly behind them was a counter bustling with activity, and a large expo window revealed a team of cooks hard at work. Food runners darted around, collecting plates and dishes to deliver to the table where people eagerly waited to be served. Everything was proceeding smoothly, and before long, 117 found himself at the front of the table, a plate in hand. The amborg cooking team greeted him as he approached.

Amborg 3 was the first one to greet him. She wore a cute and bright apron over her amborg jacket, which seemed like a rather odd fashion choice. It made her seem out of place, but he wasn't going to say that.

"Ah 117" 3 exclaimed. "Glad you arrived! We have been very successful with this particular recipe. Today 13 learned how to make individual pasta strips for the noodles. He has never been so fascinated by the methods the Italians use to make the dough just right. I guess that mission to Livorno last week really left an impression on him."

She passed him a plate and a fork. 117 immediately dug into the noodles and scooped them into his mouth. The four amborgs paused briefly to observe as he chewed and swallowed.

"After he got back," 3 smiled, "I convinced Dr. Kendrick to let me spend a couple of days traveling in Italy. They were very kind and sent me home with a lot of secret techniques."

"I always thought that secret techniques were passed from generation to generation within Italian families," 117 said as he continued to eat his spaghetti. "How did you acquire their techniques?"

"If you volunteer for more of the international deployments," 3 winked, "you'll find that many people around the world will befriend you if you spend enough time with them. Now, what do you think of the food?"

"Very impressive," 117 said after finishing his first plate. "The sauce is slightly acidic, and the spices cause a great feeling of warmth throughout my circuitry. Also, the textures of the noodles are not too thick or soft but very filling. After personally tasting it and comparing it to my visual scans of Dr. Kendrick's plate, it is very fresh and definitely home-made. The metal on the fork probably altered my initial taste-test so I cannot be entirely certain, but the taste is very promising."

"Look at him!" 7 piped up. "He still cannot work up the basic grammar to even tell us flat-out that he likes it."

"Oh, give it a rest 7," 3 replied, slapping his shoulder.

"He does sound a lot like we did many years ago," 13 chuckled.

"Exactly," 3 nodded in agreement. "7, if I remember correctly, it took you a year to even get a basic understanding of the differences between peppers. One time, you made the mistake of feeding 22 a chili pepper containing extreme levels of capsaicin. The results were amusing and otherwise fantastic, but she swears her performance has faltered by point zero two one percent ever since that incident."

"I remember that perfectly," 7 responded innocently. "You would think that with all the biological enhancements and upgrades, the vanilloid receptors in our mouths would be able to resist the pain that the capsaicin ingredient elicited. Strongest human in the world and she can't handle spicy food?"

"22 already had severe allergies to certain spices before she went through the biological enhancement!" 3 retorted with a very annoyed look. "Clearly, it translated and adapted after cybernetic enhancement. She still hates you."

117 was effectively shunted out of the conversation again. Leaving the two of them to their quarrelling, 117 grabbed his plate and held it up to the other two amborgs. 9 and 13 added some more noodles and drenched them in sauce. They thanked 117 for his initial thoughts and turned to help the next person in line.

As he carried his plate, he proceeded to the table where 43 was sitting. She was chatting with a floating A.I. and smiled when she noticed him approaching.

"Thank you, Serina," 43 smiled. "I really appreciate your advice."

117 glanced down at the little A.I. and nodded. Serina turned to look back up at him.

"Hello David," she said in a soft and warm tone. "Good to see you again."

"I am pleased to see you too," 117 replied.

"If you'll excuse me, I have to calculate a few itineraries."

117 and 43 both nodded politely at the A.I., who turned around and began to walk away. Once she was a few feet away, she disappeared in a small flash of light.

As 117 took a seat next to 43, he suddenly felt warmer when he looked at her.

"Did I interrupt your conversation?" he asked.

"It's ok," 43 smiled. "Serina was just killing some time before heading back to work."

"Aside from sharing the same name as her, you two have become quite close," 117 said as he resumed eating.

"I don't know what it is about her," 43 shrugged. "Both our names are Serina, and we've really been bonding the more that we talk. The way she speaks makes it feel like you're not talking to an artificial intelligence. She seems like someone who is alive and really caring."

"That is quite impressive coding," 117 remarked. "Her operating system and main structural matrix must have taken a long time to perfect."

"I tell you," 43 whispered, "Dr. Kendrick's team in the main programming department has some certified geniuses working here. I know you barely see them come out of their hidey holes, but it'd be great to meet them. I really want to know how they raise their A.I. programs."

Since she had brought it up, 117 began thinking about the A.I. programs that roamed around A.I. Industries. This only added to his disappointment when he realized that most of them had better personalities than his.

His glum and sour expression when he fell silent caught 43's attention.

"Busy day? What's on your mind?" she inquired as she twirled her fork into her own spaghetti. "I guess maybe we should focus on enjoying our time off rather than talking about work."

"I thought about the day when Dr. Kendrick brought us here," he replied, taking another bite. A stray noodle flung sauce onto his cheek.

43 picked up a napkin and wiped his face.

"What brought that up?" she asked.

"I showed Mandy the Hall of Commemoration," he said, setting his fork down. 117 then reached out, taking her hand in his. "We had a conversation about personal matters."

"Oh..." 43 stopped, turning to him with a serious look.

"I'm sorry if that initiated any residual memories," he apologized quickly.

"No no it's fine," 43 turned and stared at her plate again. "I just haven't really thought about the day we lost our parents. Not for some time."

They both paused for a few minutes as the atmosphere between them became a little awkward. 117 glanced around, watching the joyful chaos around him.

"I miss them," he sighed.

"Me too," 43 nodded.

"Mandy has taught me that moving on with our lives is not a mark of shame," 117 replied. "It demonstrates perseverance."

"I think if Sherry was here, she'd say the same thing."

43 and 117 both continued to people-watch as they ate in silence. Feeling bad for killing the mood, he decided to bring up what he had tried to do earlier.

"I would like to request a favor 43," he said.

"Just one?" she perked up and smiled cheekily.

"For the moment."

"Ask away. Anything for you."

"Can you teach me to smile 43?"

"What?"

43 raised her eyebrows.

"Well," 117 looked around, "I think it would be convenient to finally educate myself in that manner. You are aware of how terrible I am with that process."

"Same old 117," she sighed. "Always making the simplest objectives the most complex ones. Let's see what we can do. Try to say something funny."

"What?"

"I don't know," 43 shrugged. "Make me laugh."

117 didn't have anything to say. Nothing came to mind. Well, there was one thing.

"I took a photo of myself attempting to smile in my bathroom," he declared. "May I send you the photo?"

"Uh... sure," 43 nodded cautiously.

He linked up with her CPU and transmitted the image. Within seconds, her eyes widened and her smile faded.

"Ohh... uhh... w-whoa," she stammered.

"That is not reassuring..." 117 stared blankly at her.

"N-no it's...! Fine! Really! Um, like... the Joker getting... an aneurysm!"

117 heard the forced optimism in 43's tone and sighed. She let out an awkward laugh.

"It's not that bad," she smiled pleasantly. "I just need to... delete that image from my brain and... well, we've got a lot of work to do."

CHAPTER 6

Gotta Stay Sharp

Los Angeles, California
Five Days Later
Giuseppe's Cucina di Nonna

"Welcome to Echo Park, 117."

"Quiet!"

Sergeant Johnson's mouth snapped shut, his eyes widening as he realized he'd forgotten what they were doing. Captain Bradley raised a finger to her lips, signaling for silence from her subordinate while she moved ahead of him.

"He's not supposed to be talking!" she hissed as she motioned for 117 to follow.

"Right," Johnson looked down guiltily.

"It is alright," 117 lowered the volume on his bracelet so only they could hear him. "Thank you for welcoming me to this part of Los Angeles."

"Shut it, Tinhead..." Bradley glared in his direction. 117 quickly pulled his sleeve past his bracelet, hiding it from view. "Do you want the entire neighborhood to know who you are?"

117 silently shook his head.

He'd deployed to Los Angeles when the police requested assistance from A.I. Industries for an amborg to help with a stakeout, which meant they needed to blend in by wearing civilian attire.

117 noted how different Sergeant Johnson and Captain Bradley looked out of uniform. He hoped that all the practice and training he'd done over the last five days would pay off.

Mandy had stated that even if he tried to disguise himself as a regular person, she could still spot him a mile away. The goal of accepting this mission was to make sure that he could plausibly hide in plain sight. So, he decided to pretend that he was deaf. Every amborg, due to damaged or impaired vocal chords, were highly proficient in sign language. Since speaking out of his bracelet would give away his identity, he had to resort to visual communication methods instead.

The three of them peered across the street toward their next stop. 117 quietly gazed up at the sign of a nice restaurant called "Giuseppe's Cucina di Nonna." Maybe they would have some spaghetti on the menu. 117 had been thinking about checking out other recipes to see how they compared to 3's version.

They crossed the street and made their way to the entrance. 117 watched as Captain Bradley opened the door by pulling on the handle. He cast a curious glance at Johnson, who began signing and speaking simultaneously.

"Giuseppe's family doesn't like automatic doors," he said.

117 nodded in understanding.

As they entered, a human host greeted them with a warm smile and a friendly wave. Beside the host, a humanoid drone waved as well, its yellow faceplate grinning back at them. 117 glanced at the drone, impressed with its appearance. Its entire body chassis was spray-painted to resemble a tuxedo, giving it a shiny and formal look.

"Buongiorno!" the host bowed her head forward. "Welcome to Giuseppe's!"

"Hi!" Johnson smiled pleasantly. Captain Bradley quietly nodded while 117 waved his hand. "We're a party of three!"

"It's about a 30 minute wait for three," the host replied with a kind smile. "Or do you have a reservation?"

117 cast a glance at Johnson, who looked concerned, but Captain Bradley stepped ahead of them.

"Yeah," she said, "it's under the name, Marsha."

The host and her drone companion tilted their heads toward the screen behind their podium. After a brief pause, they looked up and smiled.

"Of course!" she said. "Bud will show you to your booth!"

The drone stepped forward and politely gestured for them to follow.

"Right this way," Bud's robotic voice buzzed as it began to march inside.

117 let Captain Bradley take the lead while he and Johnson followed. After double-checking her files through his CPU, he confirmed that her name really was Marsha. Rather than looking through Johnson's file, 117 tapped him on the shoulder. When he turned around, 117 signed to him.

"If the Captain's first name is Marsha," he said, *"What is your first name?"*

"It's Joe," officer Johnson replied casually. "Some people call me JJ."

"Since we are friends," 117 tried to smile but he felt his face stiffen, *"may I use the name JJ since we are in civilian disguises?"*

"Sure! That sounds nice!"

"What are you two talking about?"

They pivoted, noticing that Bud had stopped at a comfortable looking booth. Captain Bradley was standing there, waiting impatiently.

"Hurry up and grab a seat!"

She discreetly glanced to the side, where a few people were sitting nearby. It didn't seem as though they'd heard her. She cleared her throat and spoke normally.

"I'm... really starving," she coughed. "Can we please just sit already?"

Johnson looked at 117, and they both settled into the booth. 117 chose one side, while Johnson took a seat across from him. Captain Bradley joined them, sliding in beside Johnson. Bud's arm and servos whirred as it handed them a menu.

"If you require an additional menu, there is a screen on the wall. Either order from one of your servers or on the monitor. If you need further assistance, please signal an employee or hit the service button. Enjoy your time with us."

Bud turned and headed back towards the entrance.

"Ok," Johnson slid over to the monitor and looked at the screen. "Want anything to drink... Marsha?"

Captain Bradley's eye twitched, but she maintained a cool composure. 117 guessed that she wasn't accustomed to anyone addressing her so casually, but since they were still undercover as regular civilians, she had no choice but to play along.

"Yeah, Maui Splash," she frowned as she leaned back to rest her head against the wall of the booth. "The cocktail."

"Uh," Johnson gazed at her with a questionable look. "Are you sure? That's the alcoholic version..."

He eyed 117 carefully. It was technically against the rules to consume alcohol or any drugs while on the job. Johnson was likely going to subtly remind her that it was also illegal since they were police officers.

"It only has a small amount," Bradley stared annoyingly at Johnson. "It's fine."

She looked at 117.

"Order what you like," she stated. "It's on me."

117 nodded and slid over to the screen that Johnson was examining. He eyed the drink menu curiously, trying to find something that would seem appealing. One specific drink caught his eye, especially considering it was featured in an Italian restaurant.

117 lifted a finger and tapped the screen, highlighting his drink in green. Johnson read the description.

"You picked a... virgin strawberry party bowl?" he asked in mild bewilderment. 117 nodded eagerly.

The party bowl came in what resembled a large, wide wine glass, large enough for a group of five people. 117 wasn't interested in the alcoholic version, he just liked strawberries and wanted to know how it tasted.

"Do you drink?" 117 heard Bradley ask. "Anything at all?"

117 turned and responded enthusiastically.

"Yes, I do! I am constantly drinking water and various other drinks to refresh my body."

"No," Bradley shook her head, rolling her eyes. "I mean, do you drink alcohol?"

"No, I personally do not find alcohol appealing," 117 replied, shaking his head in response.

"That just sounds incredibly depressing... Are you and your family even living a full life?"

117 nodded politely but Bradley scoffed and folded her arms. Had he said the wrong thing?

"I think I messed up..." he signed to Johnson, who smiled sympathetically.

"No you didn't," Johnson answered cheerfully. Captain er... Miss Marsha just likes relaxing in her own way."

"You did not just call me Miss Marsha like how this deaf numb nut calls his... best friend."

Bradley's disgruntled tone was immediate as she glared at Johnson, who looked like he wanted to evaporate on the spot. 117 assumed that when she referred to his best friend, she was probably pointing out how the amborgs would sometimes address their technicians like they were teachers in elementary school.

Taking their current environment into consideration as well as the ambient noise, 117 decided to violate the rules of their undercover mission.

"Captain Bradley," he spoke as his voice softly transmitted under his sleeve, "you may want to consider changing your expression to something slightly more pleasant. Otherwise, you risk drawing attention to us if you wish to berate Johnson."

Bradley's eyes widened as her face contorted with rage. She glared at 117 with a sharp, penetrating stare that felt like a laser beam aimed straight at his forehead.

"Shut up tin-head," she grumbled, "you're not supposed to be talking... at all!"

"Captain...!"

Bradley shot Johnson the same look, causing him to flinch.

"I mean, Marsha! Please calm down!"

"I'm perfectly calm!" Captain Bradley snapped. Then she muttered under her breath. "Completely calm... dumb shits."

Despite her loud retort, the other diners around them continued their meals and conversations, completely oblivious. The restaurant was bustling with activity, which allowed the three of them to maintain a low profile. Suddenly, someone approached their table. 117 glanced up, assuming it was a server, but the man's outfit didn't match that of the staff. At first, he appeared to be just another patron in casual wear, but 117 quickly noticed the small electronic tablet and the empty tray he was carrying.

"Ah Ms. Bradley, going undercover again?" he spoke casually. "Mr. Johnson, good to see you again."

"Hi Giuseppe," Johnson waved, but was silenced when Bradley cleared her throat.

"What is it with everyone undermining this stakeout?" she grumbled.

Giuseppe set his tray on their table and nonchalantly tapped the little screen of his tablet.

"Maybe because it's the fact that whenever you select my restaurant for these... stakeouts, nothing happens? They always end up being luncheons or free dinners for the LAPD."

117 glanced at Bradley who fumed while Johnson looked down at the table, stifling his laughter.

"Oh shucks, and I tried so hard to look like a damn civilian," Bradley looked back at the owner angrily.

"Well, he does have a point," Johnson said calmly. "Nothing ever happens here."

"Your tone suggests sarcasm Captain..." 117 stated.

117 felt someone kick him from under the table. The primary suspect had to be Captain Bradley.

"Very well, I shall act the part." 117 replied coolly. He pretended to lean forward and acted like he was in pain. "Ouch."

"Quiet."

Unconcerned, Giuseppe dragged his finger over the mini-screen and stole a glance at 117, who offered a friendly wave. His demeanor became much more receptive when he saw him.

"It'll be the usual then," he muttered cheerfully. Then he gave his undivided attention to 117 and smiled brightly. "So! Who do we have the pleasure of joining us? You can't be LAPD."

117 nodded.

"Oh, ok. Don't tell me," Giuseppe said, eyeing 117's outfit. "I thought I heard your voice coming from your wrist bracelet under your sleeve. It also sounds just like the robots on my staff. You're... hmm, an amborg from A.I. Industries?"

"No," Bradley replied sarcastically, "he's from Mars."

"That is incorrect," 117 replied.

"Nice to meet you," Giuseppe said pleasantly, ignoring Captain Bradley entirely as he extended his hand towards him. "What's your name?"

"David 117, Second Group," 117 grasped Giuseppe's hand and shook it.

"If the bad guys can hear you," Bradley shook her head again and sighed, "we're blown."

"Oh relax," Giuseppe laughed. "Let me go check on your food and drinks."

Giuseppe turned and headed toward the kitchen at the back of the restaurant. Moments later, Bradley stood up from the booth, causing Johnson to flinch again.

"I'm going to the bathroom to...freshen up," she said very sourly. "You two keep an eye on the place. If there's any trouble, just scream real loud. That means you, Johnson."

As she stalked off, Johnson let out a huge sigh of relief. A server passed by their table, placing three cups of water in front of them. Once alone, Johnson lifted his cup and took a drink, while 117 watched intently. He noticed beads of sweat trickling down the young officer's forehead, a clear sign that he was under a lot of pressure.

"This does not seem like a traditional undercover operation," 117 said quietly.

"You're telling me," Johnson sighed. "I think the captain just likes coming here for her lunch breaks. The food really is good here. Filing this as an undercover stakeout is probably the only time that she gets away with taking it easy."

"Is she always angry about something?" 117 looked in the direction she had gone.

Johnson turned and glanced around, then leaned forward and whispered back.

"Since I've known her? Yeah, she's always been like that. She's tough as nails. I'm telling you, if looks could kill, then the captain gets the prize."

"I believe I know someone in the Second Group that could compete against her for that particular title," 117's thoughts rested on amborg 999. "Should I tell you about my friend Alice?"

"Ok, first, yes. I've heard about her. She's like this really quiet badass cyborg? I mean, all of you are. But second, there's something I've wanted to ask about."

117 nodded, granting Johnson permission to proceed.

"Sometimes I hear you or the other amborgs refer to each other as brothers or sisters," he stated. "Do you really consider yourselves that close of a family?"

"We all have the same cybernetic implants that provide us with our abilities," 117 explained. "We have spent so much time training and working together that it is like having a family that we can relate with consistently. Would you agree that it feels similar to how you interact with your colleagues?"

"Actually, when you put it that way, yeah, that makes sense."

Giuseppe returned, balancing a tray full of glasses, and set them on the table. It was far more than they had anticipated. 117's eyes were drawn to the party bowl he'd chosen, recognizing it from the photos on the wall's menu screen. He looked curiously at the vibrant lights dancing inside the red strawberry-flavored drink. It really looked like a party in a glass bowl. He glanced up at Giuseppe as he placed a tall, clear glass filled with a yellowish orange glow at Captain Bradley's seat. It had a tropical vibe, filled with honey, and resembled a smoothie, though he knew it was the Maui Splash that she had asked for. Lastly, a medium glass was set before Johnson, and 117 noticed it looked similar to the Maui Splash, but in shades of pink and purple. If he had to guess, Johnson had probably ordered a passion fruit fizz, as it showed clear signs of bubbly carbonation.

"I love fruit soda," Johnson declared as he accepted a straw from Giuseppe and eagerly tore off the paper wrapping. "They make it so delicious here."

Johnson began sipping on his drink in delight as 117 grabbed the end of a curly straw from his party bowl. The moment he tasted it, a wave of cold and refreshing flavor burst onto his taste buds, instantly registering and causing his synapses to relax. As his brain processed the data from his brief euphoria, he noticed Giuseppe placing a martini glass on the table beside him. 117 and Johnson paused to take a closer look at it.

"Uh," Johnson pointed, "we didn't order that."

"An unidentified concoction," 117 observed as he checked the restaurant's menu that he had downloaded in his display screen. "It is brand new... and green."

"Correct! And it's a present for you!"

Giuseppe lowered his tray to his side and graciously gestured to the martini glass like he was presenting a brand new car fresh off the assembly line. He certainly looked proud of it.

"All right, my indestructible friend," he said cheerfully. "Try one of these new formulas that I just invented. I want to see if you like it."

Giuseppe's Italian accent thickened along with his excitement. 117 wasn't sure if it was true for everyone, but he recognized a certain pattern. People's accents seemed to reveal themselves whenever they were excited or passionate about something. Another person he knew who fit this category was Marco 125, an amborg who had Italian ancestry. Even though the amborgs utilized their bracelets to broadcast a replicated substitute for their voices, 125 always appeared to have a different inflection when he was excited. An Italian accent mixed in with his usual monotonous robotic voice was quite unique. Johnson's voice suddenly snapped him out of his internal thoughts.

"Hey, is that alcohol? Is it ok for a... 'Cough' person of your type to drink alcohol?" Johnson said, concerned. 117 merely shrugged.

They looked at the drink and watched as it fizzed softly, like Johnson's soda. It was a bright, electric lime green, as if someone had created some sort of a plasma-based gel and poured it in a glass. Was it carbonated or something? Normal cocktails didn't do whatever this was doing.

"Filtering out alcohol is an added benefit," 117 stated confidently. "It is extremely difficult to become intoxicated."

117 reached out for the glass and lifted it. It looked like goo but when he tilted it, the drink moved like a normal liquid. Although, he could see that it definitely had some high viscosity which made it appear... thicker than water.

"It is also polite to... accept presents when they're given," 117 said courteously, raising the glass and nodding his head at Giuseppe. "It would be rude to turn down Giuseppe's show of kindness."

"Yeah, but... that doesn't look appetizing or... appealing..."

"Well," 117 raised the glass to his lips, "there is always a first for something."

Without delay, he downed the whole drink in mere seconds. Nothing seemed to happen at first. Giuseppe waited with eager anticipation as Johnson stared in silence. Suddenly, 117 let out a cough, causing them to inch away. With a quick jerk of his neck, 117 turned and grimaced. He gagged and tried to identify what he had just downed. It felt as if he had been hit by a hammer. Johnson gaped, then nervously glanced around to check if anyone had noticed what was going on. Thankfully, everyone remained oblivious to what had just happened.

"Are you crazy?" he whispered harshly to Giuseppe who starting to laugh. "You killed him!"

"That statement is... incorrect," 117 burped as he felt air in his stomach flow upwards and out of his mouth.

"Was... that a burp?" Johnson asked. "That's the most noise I've heard straight from your mouth."

"Normally, I would have scanned the drink but some of my amborg functions have been shut off temporarily to maintain my human disguise."

Giuseppe laughed harder. It was impressive that his chortling wasn't drawing any attention.

"So, that's what happens when you consume alcohol?" he chuckled as he regained his composure. "I wish I had a camera."

"What if someone had seen?" Johnson asked. "We're supposed to keep a low profile during a stakeout!"

117 coughed again and a smoke ring came out of his mouth. His eyes drooped.

"I am fine sergeant," he said reassuringly out of Johnson's bracelet. "Although that drink was... more potent than I anticipated. Also the ingredients were... strange."

"So what did you think? You like?" Giuseppe looked at 117 with great interest. Clearly, he had never seen anything so amusing before. "Your sister, 18. I believe she was the one who asked me to make some special drinks for you kids."

"Actually," Johnson pointed at 117, "he looks like he hates it."

"That is correct," 117 replied as his eyes continued twitching abnormally. He politely smiled. "I hate it."

"More?" Giuseppe asked.

"Please," 117 nodded.

Johnson looked at 117 in disbelief.

"Why do you want more??"

"The drink has triggered strong negative impulses throughout my circuitry," 117 explained casually. "I believe it has elicited an emotional response which is worth studying further."

"Oh right," Johnson groaned, "you're really into learning how to act normal. But, does it have to be a drink that tastes like... whatever it was that caused you to seize up like that?"

117 looked up at Giuseppe, who was listening intently.

"I believe the taste resembles tar. As the owner of your restaurant, it is my recommendation you do not distribute this to the local population. Reviews of your restaurant could be catastrophic."

Giuseppe chuckled again.

"Don't worry son! It was just a joke! Besides, I did put tar inside that drink," he smiled. "Combined with large amounts of alcohol."

"Why would you purposefully feed a terrible drink to an amborg?" 117 glanced at the empty glass with concern.

"Because I've been trying to find something nice to feed you little lab rats!" Giuseppe explained. "Every time one of you amborgs comes in undercover with some cops, it's very important that you look inconspicuous. But you'll draw attention if you don't order food or even look like you're enjoying a drink. So lately, I've been trying to find a drink formula that you amborgs might like so you will fit in. And if normal alcohol does not work, then I improvise."

117 held up the empty glass to Giuseppe.

"You could have just given me a plate of spaghetti," he said as Giuseppe grabbed the glass. "But I'll have some more of this formula. I am... not driving home tonight."

"Another tartini and one plate of spaghetti it is!" Giuseppe said joyously and walked cheerfully into the kitchen.

As they watched him saunter off, Johnson turned to 117 and took the opportunity to speak up.

"Hey buddy, is it safe to be talking?" he leaned forward and whispered. "I mean, won't it give you away if you keep talking out of your bracelet? Maybe we should go back to our sign-language thing."

"Do not be alarmed Sergeant. I took that into consideration," 117 looked around. "The restaurant is creating enough ambient noise so that our conversation cannot be heard. Everyone is far too distracted with their own matters."

Johnson relaxed his shoulders and smiled. However, after a moment, 117 saw his eyes veer to the side and he gazed in a direction outside of their booth.

"Oh yeah? Tell that to the guy in the corner."

117 looked at the reflection in Johnson's water glass. In the corner of the restaurant, to his five o'clock, was a man facing their booth from a corner seat near a window. His face was obscured, and he wore an urban hooded cloak.

"Oh," 117 glanced at Johnson, "I cannot perform facial recognition. This person you have pointed out is wearing a hooded cloak, which masks his physique and features perfectly. Very peculiar and highly suspicious in a public restaurant."

"He looks like Strider from Lord of the Rings," Johnson mumbled as he kept darting a few glances. "Well, can't you have your tech do something? A computer scan or 3D construction from the security cameras? Something advanced? Anything?"

"You have seen too many movies, Johnson," 117 looked at some of the photos on the wall above the menu screen. He found them quite fascinating as he continued to make small talk. "Besides, we do not have evidence to suddenly arrest a man for just wearing a hood in a restaurant. Also, I am afraid that communicating with my tech is impossible as Mandy is not at her cubicle."

"Wait...what?" Johnson looked at him with shock. "You mean, you're operating in the field without your tech?"

117 nodded casually, leaving Johnson stunned.

"Yes... Mandy is away for the Thanksgiving holidays," he stated. "She is spending time with her family. I believe her fiance is there too."

117 held up his hands and made finger quotes, except it appeared robotic and rigid. 117 had to glance down at his middle and index fingers to make sure he was doing it correctly, like how he had been taught by 43.

"A... 'real looker' according to her exact description," he said as Johnson stared at the finger quotes. "It is very nice to know that she is spending time with her loved ones."

"But... why?"

"Dr. Kendrick ordered her to use her vacation days."

Johnson shook his head.

"No, that's not... I mean, I get that but... why are you here?"

"I thought that the police department requested an amborg to assist," 117 stared at Johnson with a puzzled expression. "Thus, making your question redundant. However, since we are friends, I shall provide exposition."

"N-no," Johnson stammered, "T-that's not..."

"I am here assisting in a stakeout based on an anonymous tip submitted to the department. You told me that this would most likely end up being a free lunch for us. Provided that I maintain my character role of the 'deaf friend' visiting from Long Beach."

"...necessary," Johnson sighed. "I guess I walked into that one."

"Incorrect," 117 stated. "You are in a seated position."

An awkward silence passed between them as Johnson looked at him with a dim and dumbfounded expression.

"That was a joke," 117 declared promptly.

"You know... I think I get why the captain gets mad most of the time," Johnson looked around cautiously. "But, why you specifically? I mean, did you do something wrong and now you're here because of something you did? Did you spill something on Dr. Kendrick and your punishment is working without a tech? Or maybe you sat in the wrong person's car?"

117 was quite impressed with Johnson's creative thinking under pressure. His instincts as an officer made him quite investigative. This prompted a few questions in his mind. Was this supposed to be a casual lunch, a mission, or an interrogation?

"You have quite an active imagination, Joe," 117 said with a curt nod.

"Thanks," Johnson smiled with a prideful tilt of his head. "Still didn't answer my question."

"It was my turn. To be specific, I didn't cause any trouble," 117 answered directly. "Your examples, however, were quite specific. Care to elaborate?"

Johnson replied suspiciously fast.

"Not really. So you all take turns?"

"Affirmative."

"How does that work?"

"We've started brainstorming a schedule for every amborg," 117 explained. "Everyone deploys a fair and equal number of turns so that no one gets under or overworked. It was my watch and I was standing by when I received the call from LAPD. This resulted in me visiting."

The sound of footsteps snagged their attention before they could continue the conversation. Johnson and 117 both glanced up and froze. They were expecting Giuseppe, but instead, the hooded figure had approached their booth. The man towered over 117, causing him and Johnson to instinctively recoil. He had moved with such speed that 117 was amazed no one else had noticed. There was definitely something wrong. As 117 cautiously raised his gaze, he caught sight of a bearded man with a mischievous glint in his eye. Beneath the hood, a subtle smirk played at the stranger's lips. Then, they heard him speak.

"So, it's you then? Alright, keep up with me if you can."

His tone was deep and gruff. 117 could tell that this was an older man but before he could fully process it, the hooded figure suddenly lunged at them. With one hand, he grabbed Johnson by the shoulder. 17 watched with wide eyes as the young officer was lifted and effortlessly thrown from the booth. Johnson let out a shout as he flew into another patron nearby, causing a loud crash when the table collapsed under him, sending both him and the unsuspecting bystander to the ground. Reacting quickly, 117 tried to escape the booth, but the old man swung his arm and delivered a powerful backhand to his chest, slamming him back against the seat.

The sudden uproar attracted the attention of every customer in the restaurant. Numerous gazes were fixed on 117 as he tried to get his bearings. The blow had hurt way more than he thought it would, which was a bit surprising. Mildly irritated, he got up from the booth, and the hooded figure backed off.

"You have hurt my friend," 117 spoke sternly.

The old man noticed that 117's sleeve had rolled back slightly, revealing the bracelet on his wrist.

"Ha, guess your secret's out!"

This guy had thrown Johnson around like it was nothing, demonstrating his incredible strength. Now he was mocking 117? No way he was going to let this slide. As he prepared for a fight, a deafening boom echoed through the air.

The hooded man and 117 glanced to the side and saw that someone had fired a shotgun. It was Giuseppe, who'd quickly armed himself from the back of the kitchen or wherever he had come from. They noticed that he had fired the first shot with the gun pointed up, but now he was lowering it so the barrel was aimed at the hooded figure.

"I'm not afraid to use this," Giuseppe shouted bravely. "Leave the customers alone! My family is ready to fight back if you continue to make trouble! Police!"

The old man let out a loud, raucous laugh that brought everything to a standstill. Confusion spread among the crowd, and 117 furrowed his brow, realizing the laughter was a tactic to throw them off. Giuseppe was momentarily taken aback, which gave the hooded man the chance to pivot and sprint toward the exit. As he bolted out of the restaurant, several patrons scrambled to avoid him. In the chaos, they inadvertently crossed into Giuseppe's line of fire, forcing him to quickly raise his shotgun and aim it upward to avoid harming anyone. 117 sprang into action, weaving through the crowd in pursuit, catching a fleeting glimpse of Captain Bradley running out of the restroom.

"What the hell?!" she demanded. "I was gone for five minutes!"

She hurried over to Johnson, who was feebly stirring from the wreckage of the dining table. Noticing that he was injured but still conscious, she shifted her focus to the man he had crashed into. The others seated at the table were a little boy and his mother, whom 117 assumed was the man's family. The mother was anxiously checking on both Johnson and her husband to make sure they were alright.

"I will deal with this," 117 was already out the door. "Take care of the Sergeant."

Once he was outside, he radioed dispatch and contacted A.I. Industries.

"This is 117," he reported. "Officer involved in an unprovoked assault. Center on my location. Please send assistance. I am in pursuit of one suspect."

117 burst out of the restaurant and immediately checked his surroundings, startling several people passing by. He quickly spoke to the nearest pedestrian.

"Did anyone see a hooded figure exit this building?" he asked urgently.

"Uh, yeah, that way."

The man he spoke to lifted a hand and pointed toward the other side of the street. Thanking him, 117 sprinted across the street, dodging and leaping over the slow moving traffic. Once on the other side, he dashed into an alley. That's when he heard a familiar, gravelly voice call out to him.

"Follow me if you dare, boy, we have much to discuss. Think of this as a test. I'm curious about whether or not you will succeed or fail."

Following the sound of the voice, 117 lifted his gaze and pressed forward, but as silence enveloped the area, he stopped. An unsettling feeling washed over him. Something was not right. His analysis of where the voice was coming from indicated that he should change direction and go straight up. Just as he was about to figure out where to begin his climb, a loud noise suddenly broke the stillness.

A dumpster came barreling toward him. Before 117 could process how it had come to be flying in his direction, he instinctively raised his hands to stop it. Planting his feet firmly and crouching into a defensive position, he managed to bring the heavy object to a halt with a thunderous crash. However, that wasn't the end of it.

Swift movement caught his attention as several hooded figures descended around him. He was surrounded. Steeling himself, 117 gripped the edge of the dumpster tightly and forcefully shoved it back the way it came. It careened down the alley, and he watched as three hooded figures nimbly sidestepped it. They were quite fast if they were able to avoid such a heavily thrown object with that much ease. Once the dumpster was out of the way, 117 was able to concentrate on the attacking assailants.

Hearing footsteps close behind, he pivoted sharply, attempting a high kick. The hooded figure darted in, dodged it, and tumbled backward.

Just then, 117 noticed an arm lunging toward his face. He blocked it and quickly countered, but a sudden hit to his back caused him to lose his balance and stumble forward.

117 zeroed in on the swarm of attackers. They all aggressively converged on him at once. It was unlike any thugs he had faced before. Without Mandy there to help him spot threats, he felt at a slight disadvantage, but he didn't let this hinder him. First, he needed to figure out how many there were.

Six opponents surrounded him, launching their assaults from every direction. As he endured the impact of shoes striking his side, punches bouncing off his elbows, and a few lucky blows to the chest, 117 initiated a counterattack.

When an assailant tried to kick him from the front, 117 reacted quickly, lunging forward to grab the attacker's leg and pull him in. Without losing momentum, 117 swung him like a baseball bat and spun around. One person on his left couldn't escape in time and was struck by his buddy, falling hard onto the pavement. 117 let go of the enemy's leg, sending the attacker crashing into a brick wall, which buckled under the impact, creating a deep crater. The hooded man crumpled to the ground, unable to get back up. With two down, 117 expertly blocked another attack and delivered a fierce elbow strike to the sternum. The attacker gasped in pain, clutching his chest as he fell to his knees.

117 curled his left hand into a fist and struck at the thug's head. The blow was so forceful that it sent the man sprawling backward. Without hesitation, 117 dropped to his knees and whirled around, closing the gap between him and another attacker. There was no escaping 117's reach as he raised his fist and aimed for the attacker's kneecap. He dislocated the person's joint, eliciting a sharp crunch and causing him to cry out in pain. Rising to his feet, 117 punched him in the throat to shut him up. He slumped to the ground without another peep.

117 turned around again, eyeing the last two hooded figures still holding their ground. They glanced at each other and then back at 117, who was getting into another defensive stance. Before anything happened, they unexpectedly turned and bolted.

"Ok, that was pretty good."

117 gazed upward when he heard the voice again.

"Surely, you're not done yet, are you?"

Crouching low, 117 launched himself upward, gripping the fire escape railing, and climbed up towards the roof. In a matter of seconds, he had scaled an entire five-story building. Upon reaching the rooftop, he was met by more enemies.

Three figures instantly charged at him. The first one aimed a punch at his chest. 117 retaliated by dodging, avoiding the attack, and lunged to grab his shirt. With a quick pivot, he hurled him off the roof. Such a reckless attack would be their literal downfall. 117 felt a twinge of guilt for adopting a technique the Splatter-Bugs would have approved of. Two enemies moving in to attack quickly erased any remorse he felt as he shifted his focus to them. The second person seized the moment after 117 threw his buddy off the roof to deliver a powerful blow to his head. The strike landed just as 117 kicked him away, causing him to stagger back and nurse his cheek. The impact took him by surprise; the force of that single blow left him momentarily disoriented. Shaking it off, he swung his arm and managed to hit the third enemy, sending him off his feet and crashing to the ground. When he didn't get up, 117 turned to look for the old man from the restaurant, all the while trying to piece together what that guy did when he struck him in the head.

"What's the matter?" the old man called out, the sound of his voice seeming to ring out in every direction. "Dazed? I thought you were more durable than that."

117 pivoted toward the source of the voice. His guess was spot on as he caught sight of someone vaulting across the rooftops ahead of him. He immediately went after him, clearing each rooftop with ease, timing his jumps carefully as he leaped after the figure. Finally, after he crossed what must have been the fifteenth roof, the voice spoke again.

"Not bad!" the man called. "Alright! You do have skills."

As soon as 117 landed on the neighboring rooftop, more assailants surged toward him. Calculating fast, he turned to face the closest one and opened his arms. The first attacker, unable to slow down in time, was caught in a bear hug. In one fluid motion, 117 tightened his grip and executed a suplex, arching backward to send his enemy crashing headfirst into the floor of the roof. A loud thud and a sickening crunch sound followed as the man's skull met concrete. Maneuvering quickly, 117 rolled away and got to his feet. As he straightened up, the last two attackers stopped and exchanged uncertain looks. Using this to his advantage, 117 picked up the unconscious guy and hurled him at both attackers. Rather than engaging them further, he sprinted after the old man, who shouted back at him.

"What's the matter?" he shouted. "Can't take the pressure? There's no points for skipping a test! I thought you'd be better than that! Looks like we got to add some punishment!"

As he landed on the next roof, he was met with the sharp sound of gunfire. A handful of hooded attackers, armed with rifles, had entered the fight. Ignoring the bullets pelting his uniform, 117 charged forward and engaged in close combat. He noticed a few women among them, backing away while attempting to shoot at him. One of them lunged at him with a bayonet attached to her rifle, trying to stab him. With a quick sidestep, he dodged the attack and brought his arm down, tearing the weapon in half. As the woman watched in shock as her weapon crumbled before her eyes, 117 swiftly lifted his foot and delivered a hard kick to her chest. She was sent flying backward, skidding across the ground. Without missing a beat, 117 seized the barrel of another assailant's rifle, and crushed it effortlessly with his bare hands. With a fierce yank, he wrenched it from their grip and swung it, striking two more gunmen squarely in the head. Just then, a sudden blow to the back of his head sent him reeling, leaving him momentarily disoriented. Concern began to creep in as he struggled to comprehend where these guys were getting this much strength. The old man leading them commanded a formidable team of fighters.

It became increasingly clear as the fight went on. While 117 continued to engage the hooded attackers and defend himself from their bullets, fists, and kicks, he realized he was being corralled to the edge of the roof. With nowhere to go, a sharp kick struck him in the stomach. A flurry of punches to his head followed, and before he knew it, he was looking up at the sky, lifted off his feet. 117, wide-eyed, realized he was plummeting off the roof. He desperately activated his distress beacon. Since it would be the first time he had ever switched it on in the field, he hoped that the nearest amborg would respond quickly. As he fell, the windows rushed past him, gravity accelerating his descent toward an inevitable and back-breaking landing. When he finally crashed into the pavement, the impact was jarring, but he felt no pain as he tried to get back on his feet. A normal human would have died from a fall like that. He raised his head, scanning his surroundings for any signs of help.

"Situation unfavorable," 117 muttered as he tried to transmit a message to the dispatch. "I have never encountered these gang members before. Probability of defeat is increasing. I repeat, to anyone listening... highly skilled assailants encountered. I must... retreat."

"All right, that's enough of that now."

117 slowly stood up and glanced towards the end of the alley. Conveniently, the old hooded man stood there, watching. This man was the right one for sure.

He threw my friend, 117 thought.

The man was already assuming a defensive stance. It was a showdown.

"You got past all that a lot better than I originally thought," the man called out to 117. "But you're definitely not good enough against me and my people as you've already realized. Against me, you won't be able to win."

117 walked forward. The man lifted a hand and beckoned to him with his fingers, taunting him, then readied his fists. 117 mirrored the old man and assumed an attack stance as well.

"Show me what you got, amborg."

117 charged toward his target. As he closed the distance, he raised his right fist and aimed for the man's head. Remembering how fast and powerful his followers were in the fight moments before, 117 realized he had to ramp it up. His cybernetic implants gave him unnatural strength and speed but if used on normal people, he would risk inflicting too much damage. There was a reason why the amborgs had strict rules and training protocols to prevent causing irreversible harm. However, now was probably the best time to set aside those particular limitations.

Given how formidable his followers were, 117 concluded that the old man had to be equally powerful, if not stronger. He had to try and land a hit.

"Come on...!"

The hooded man dodged 117's punch. This was bad. As the old man sidestepped his right hook, 117 noticed a flash of movement before a sharp pain struck his rib cage. For a brief moment, it seemed as if the old man had vanished into thin air. No, it was just that he was that fast, his movements too quick to follow. To his shock, he felt pain for the first time since becoming an amborg. Clenching his stomach, he tried to look for the mysterious attacker.

His speed and power... This man is too fast for me to track, he thought as another blow struck his back, causing him to stumble forward. *I'm at a disadvantage.*

117 heard the man cry out in annoyance.

"This is the best you can do? After Dr. Kendrick gave you all of this power... and you call yourself an evolved human being?"

Was this man trying to kill him or prolong the inevitable? 117 straightened up and faced the hooded man.

"Why don't you stop trying to hit me... and just hit me!" he snarled. "Give me all you got!"

"That would be inadvisable," 117 replied as he wiped his mouth and tried to focus. "Unless you want to be shattered into pieces."

Under his hood, the old man nodded and let out a laugh. 117 saw him smirk as he motioned for him to come at him again.

"That's more like it," he grinned.

117 funneled more power to his arms and lunged again. The old man quickly outmaneuvered and sidestepped his attacks as 117 tried to analyze any potential weaknesses. Each punch that he threw was being deflected, dodged and avoided with ease.

"Ok. I. Admit. You're. Doing. Better," he said nervously as 117's fist came dangerously close to his nose. "But you're not going to win at this rate."

"Is this a fight or a lecture?" 117 panted as he kept his arms up.

"Right now, it looks more like an old man is kicking your ass."

117's attacks slowed as he began to back down, unable to land a single hit. The old man crossed his arms and sighed disappointedly. Shaking his head, he stepped forward, prompting 117 to shift back into a defensive stance.

"You know what your problem is?"

The old man swung at 117, who tried to block the attack, but felt a sharp blow to his left wrist. 117 winced as he began to step back.

"You've worn yourself out too quickly and now your strength is being tested!"

117 was too slow to block the next attack and suffered another blow to the head.

"Dr. Kendrick designed you to be powerful and fast! So show me how powerful and fast you are!"

This was really becoming less of a fight and more like he was training back at A.I. Industries. Except, the training drones and the other amborgs weren't this cruel.

117 felt dizzy and exhausted. If one man was able to back him into a corner, then who knows what would happen if this man encountered his friends or fought the other amborgs? They had to be warned. Was it even possible to run from this fight?

Running isn't favorable, 117 thought, fighting to stay awake. He shook his head and tried to keep his arms up. *Continuing to fight will buy me time for help to get here. What happens if someone else comes and they don't stand a chance against this gang? I would have called more people here and led them into a trap.*

117 gulped and tried another tactic. Perhaps a desperate but diplomatic approach would work. It couldn't hurt anymore to try.

"I surrender," 117 admitted as he lowered his hands. "I cannot win this fight. I am outmatched and you are clearly unbeatable."

"You would give up so easily? Just like that? What a disappointment!" the old man said furiously, shaking his head.

"You're an augment," 117 stated. "Your group of followers are too. All enhanced. I can't fight you all."

"Glad you figured that out, because I think it was pretty obvious."

He lifted his arms and rolled up his sleeves. 117 could see metal titanium braces surgically wrapped around his wrists, going all the way up his forearms. He also had cybernetic implants, except his were on the outside, worn on his body. If 117 could see what was under his hood and cloak, then maybe, there was more to him than what he had already faced. Keeping all of that concealed under his mysterious attire was impressive.

"Maybe one of your friends will be tougher than you," he scoffed. "If you're going to chicken out like a coward."

Anger surged through 117. Sure, he was afraid that he would lose his life if he continued to fight, but he had offered his surrender in order to find a reasonable way to discuss a solution out of this mess. However, the old man's comment about tracking down one of his friends only heightened his fear. The image of 43, his best friend, facing guys like this in the field made his blood boil. He couldn't let anything happen to her or the other amborgs.

"You stay away from them," 117 said slowly, lifting his hands and assuming a kung-fu stance.

"No," the old man replied as he lunged forward. "I don't think I will."

117 watched as the hooded man picked up speed, moving too fast for him to react. 117 knew he had no time to dodge it. His eyes widened as the old man brandished a knife, and the next thing he knew, a sharp, agonizing pain shot through his abdomen. Stunned, 117 gasped and slowly glanced down. According to his database, Dr. Kendrick had told them that only one type of metal had the capability to do this. He tried to run a scan, but the pain was messing with his HUD, causing everything in his eyes to flicker. Blood seeped from the wound where the knife remained embedded. He needed to escape, but the old man was forcing him down onto his knees while keeping a tight grip on the small blade.

"Do I have your attention now? This is what you get when you give up in front of someone who wants you dead."

117's vision blurred as the knife twisted, setting off a barrage of alarms in his display. He wanted to cry out in pain, but couldn't.

"Don't... kill my... friends," 117 transmitted desperately from his bracelet.

"Listen well," the old man said, forcing 117 to look up into his eyes. "I'm not going to kill you here and now... but if you don't get your act together, you and your friends will die."

The moment the knife was pulled out, a searing pain shot through him, leaving him gasping for air. A knot formed in his throat, making it hard to breathe. Panic set in as he clasped his hands over the wound, feeling warm blood spilling out. The old man pulled his hood back, revealing a beard and scattered gray hair. He leaned forward and put a hand on 117's shoulder.

"This knife is one of the only weapons capable of inflicting severe damage to the amborg exoskeleton," he said smugly. "I'm sorry I put you through all that. But, you needed to know that these weapons are in the open. The amborgs are no longer the invincible beings that everyone thinks you are. The rats have found a way to fight the exterminators now. Fortunately, I'm a rat-lover. And I'm giving you a sample of what's coming."

He eyed the wound carefully and backed away when 117 tried to grab him. Struggling to keep his eyes open, he fought with every ounce of strength he had left.

"I bet you're really surprised," he said, "still don't recognize me?"

For the first time in his life, 117 was seething with rage and in more pain than he could have imagined. He looked right into the man's eyes, opened his mouth, and drew in as much air as he could. Then he let out a loud cry.

"WHO..." he wheezed, "...Arrrree.... You!?"

The old man drew back in shock when he heard 117 talking from his mouth and not his bracelet.

"He speaks again," he exclaimed. "Isn't that something?"

He smacked 117 right on the head, pushing him past his limits. 117 collapsed onto his side, landing on the wet pavement, acutely aware that he was still bleeding out. His readings were so scrambled that he couldn't run a system diagnostic. Lying there on the messy pavement of the alley, he felt utterly powerless.

"The amborgs are in danger," 117 heard the old man say. "It would be wise to take whatever measures you can. David, give this warning to the fair doctor from an old acquaintance of his. Demons from the past are about to wage war and this city will be caught in a massive crossfire. You must warn everyone and prepare. From an old man to his grandson, I really hope you'll make the right choice."

"What?" 117 murmured weakly.

"Ah, I believe your friends are coming now. See you around kid."

Before 117 closed his eyes, he saw the old man's feet retreat into the darkness. Grandson? What was that he said? No, 117 had definitely heard correctly. But it wasn't possible. He had no family. As he faded from consciousness, he saw someone else step over him, yelling. Blue and red lights flashed and gunshots were heard. He could make out the loud voice of Captain Bradley.

"Hey! Stay with me! 117! Dispatch, I need medical assistance at my location! Link this emergency call to the nearest amborg! Secure the area and get me A.I. Industries on the line! We have an amborg down! Repeat! Amborg down!"

"Someone," 117 whispered, hoping anyone could hear him. "Someone help... me."

Captain Bradley was still shouting orders, but that's all that 117 could hear. Feeling exhausted, he shut his eyes and everything went dark. Without any calculations or any way to stay awake, 117 fell unconscious for the first time as an amborg.

CHAPTER 7

Emotional... Old-Manhunt

A.I. Industries
Gymnasium
2135

The sudden blare of an alarm made everyone jump. Brad's stylus slipped from his fingers, clattering to the floor from the unexpected noise. He quickly bent down to pick it up. Meanwhile, 117 remained seated, unperturbed, looking around the room with a calm demeanor. Dr. Kendrick sprang to his feet, his eyes darting to Serina, who had been comfortably perched on the armrest of his chair. Unfazed by the alarm, she merely blinked out of sight and reappeared, hands clasped behind her back, and looked up curiously.

"Serina, go find out what's going on," Dr. Kendrick said, adjusting his glasses. "How strange. That's an internal breach alarm..."

"I'm on it."

Serina flashed a quick thumbs up, turned bright blue, and leaped into the wall. She transformed into a beam of light, racing along the wall panel and vanishing out the door.

Dr. Kendrick looked at Brad with a reassuring smile.

"Don't worry," he clarified, "one of the amborgs is probably dealing with a slight inconvenience."

"That was an alarm. Are you sure it's only a slight inconvenience??" Brad asked nervously as he instinctively moved and slid his chair closer to 117.

He had paused his storytelling of his encounter with the mysterious hooded man when the alarm went off. Now he appeared lost in thought. Casting a quick glance at Dr. Kendrick, he gave Brad a casual nod, who returned the gesture with a smile.

"Negative," he said reassuringly.

The strain of talking with his real voice made 117 cough, prompting him to switch to his bracelet instead. It was then that Brad noticed 117's A.I. Industries bracelet. It looked different than the one that they had talked about in their story.

"What kind of bracelet is that?" he asked, pointing.

117 held up his left wrist and the lights flickered as his voice was broadcasted through it.

"This is a standard gold bracelet that Dr. Kendrick designed for the amborgs," 117 said as he allowed Brad to lean closer for a better look. "The old silver ones that everyone had were not durable. The design of it would lead to many of them shattering or being destroyed in the field."

"It took many tries but eventually, we created a much better version," Dr. Kendrick nodded approvingly. "It's nice that the amborgs know sign language. Except, it's a major problem when a lot of people don't know about it. So, to make it more convenient for everyone, these custom bracelets are for the amborgs. A little more expensive than I wanted it to be but at least they hold up better than the first designs."

"They're really neat," Brad said with a fascinated gaze.

"Thank you," Dr. Kendrick shrugged and gave a modest grin. "I don't mean to boast but, it was the best invention of that year."

117 brought his fist up to his mouth and cleared his throat, grabbing their attention. While Brad appeared curious, Dr. Kendrick looked disgruntled.

"Yes," he groaned sarcastically, "I am aware of the fact that not everyone else thinks so."

"As much as I do enjoy having a very strong and durable bracelet," 117 looked at Brad and playfully shrugged, "I actually prefer my car as my favorite invention."

"Invention? Of a car?" Brad raised an eyebrow.

"Remember when 117 told you about his first mission in L.A.?" Dr. Kendrick reminded him.

"Oh right. You sat down inside a broken car to show him how... heavy... you were... are!" Brad recalled, catching himself.

Brad's eyes widened as he averted his gaze. He shifted uneasily in his seat, suddenly aware that his words could be misinterpreted as an insult. In his excitement, he had let his words slip out before his mind had a chance to filter them.

"I think Brad managed to call me fat," 117 stated with a cold and unamused expression. "As well as all of the others."

"Oh no!" Brad immediately sputtered as he waved his hands and tried to explain. "I didn't mean that! It's just that... your cybernetic implants are so strong and powerful; I wish I had them so I could also punch through walls and shatter buildings! It's great leaping over tall buildings and performing superhero landings."

Brad nodded encouragingly, but Dr. Kendrick and 117 merely stared.

"Now you see, that is why you wouldn't be a good fit to be an amborg," Dr. Kendrick shook his head. "If anyone suddenly had superhuman abilities, then the world would be doomed from all of that unnecessary destruction."

Brad looked at them in dismay. That didn't make things better.

"117," he almost pleaded, "you understand, right?"

"Actually," 117 exchanged a worried look with Dr. Kendrick, "we try to actively avoid jumping or falling from tall places. What goes up, must come down. Amborgs come down extremely hard... due to our circumstances."

Brad awkwardly shut his mouth and fell silent. Not only had he managed to offend Dr. Kendrick and 117, but he had probably shamed the rest of the amborgs and A.I. Industries. The back of his neck and his cheeks burned as he thought about being kicked out at the rate he was going.

There was a flash of light as Serina suddenly appeared between them.

"Well, that was exciting!" she grinned and looked around. "I'm happy to report that... hey, what's with all of you?"

Serina suddenly disappeared, then reappeared in front of 117, Dr. Kendrick, and then Brad, startling him. He leaned back in surprise.

"Oh, hi," he said.

"Hmm."

Serina then popped up in the center and pointed a glowing holographic finger at 117.

"You made fun of Brad, didn't you?" She accused 117 and Dr. Kendrick.

They both grinned, and Dr. Kendrick let out a chuckle. Brad blinked in surprise.

"What?" he tilted his head.

"They're messing with you, Brad," Serina let out a sigh. "Also, I just double-checked the security footage and listened to the audio files in here while I was gone."

"Guilty," 117 declared.

"Oh, come on," Brad also sighed in relief. "That was nerve-wracking!"

"But it was amusing," 117 winked.

"How about we get back on track?" Dr. Kendrick suggested. "Serina, what was the alarm for?"

"There was another explosion in the amborg residential area," Serina stated.

"Oh," Dr. Kendrick nodded. "That's fine then."

"Fine?" Brad stared in bewilderment. "An explosion is fine?"

"This happens quite frequently," 117 nodded. "Excuse me, I'm going to make a call."

Brad was still a little concerned, but impressed at how relaxed everyone was during an emergency. From the way they were talking, was it even that big of a problem?

"If you'll excuse me," Serina chuckled, "I'm going to go see if I can help supervise the cleanup. Oh, and Brad?"

"Yes?"

Brad gazed at Serina, who cheekily floated next to him and smiled.

"Lighten up and have a little fun," she said as her small form appeared to radiate a higher brightness. Brad realized she was increasing her light settings. "Dr. Kendrick and 117 love teasing visitors!"

"Really?"

Serina nodded.

"I mean, if you want to talk about the amborgs' weight," she snickered, "I do it all the time! Especially since I have nobody."

"But you're an A.I. program... how can you be alone?"

Dr. Kendrick cleared his throat.

"Brad, she just used a pun," he explained.

"Get it?" Serina winked and floated away. "Weight isn't an issue for me because I have no body."

She laughed, and in a flash of light, she disappeared. Brad sat there with his mouth agape as Dr. Kendrick burst out laughing. 117 stood there quietly and focused on his internal phone call, ignoring them while Brad took a few moments to realize what Serina had said.

"Wow," Brad sighed dejectedly. "I think I just got punked by the world's most powerful CEO, an amborg of the Second Group, and an A.I. in less than five minutes."

"To be clear," Dr. Kendrick said, patting Brad's shoulder, "Serina was more annoyed that we started joking around without her. She hates it when she has to work and misses out on certain conversations."

"But she can just watch the past recordings of it, right?"

"Sometimes, listening to someone directly, laughing with them, or being there in the moment is much more meaningful. Serina has a lot of time on her hands, but she also wants to fit in."

Brad looked at 117, who continued to stare off into space and ignore them. There was something ominous about the look in his eyes, as if he were frozen in place. He then remembered what they were talking about previously before he fell victim to their jokes.

"So, what was 117 talking about when he mentioned his car?"

Dr. Kendrick nodded.

"There's only so much one genius such as myself can do," he admitted. "I focused on creating stronger bracelets for the amborgs and many other members of my staff were concentrating on their projects, too. Our motor pool and auto mechanical department fashioned special custom vehicles for the amborgs. They had to be able to carry them wherever they needed to go. Sometimes, their drop-pods aren't the best way when it comes to maneuvering on the ground."

"Oh, I see," Brad nodded as he took more notes.

"When 117 was stabbed," Dr. Kendrick stated, "the news spread like wildfire and many people were afraid. Naturally, a lot of tools, inventions, and research projects were kicked into gear so that we could continue figuring out ways to support or keep the amborgs safe."

"So, that day that 117 got stabbed..." Brad glanced at 117, "Was he actually being serious when he said that it was his grandfather? I thought he said that he had no living relatives at the time."

"From his point of view, that is correct," Dr. Kendrick stated. "He didn't know because it was kept secret from him."

"His grandfather was some long-lost old man that showed up like someone out of Assassin's Creed?" Brad asked with uncertainty. "How does that make sense?"

"Don't you have any relatives that partake in vigilante justice from time to time?"

"No," Brad replied bluntly with a firm shake of his head. "Dr. Kendrick, I should kind of remind you that I don't live here at A.I. Industries."

"Oh," Dr. Kendrick looked down in contemplation and chuckled awkwardly. "Right."

Brad smiled.

"When you have a large adopted family of the most powerful human beings on Earth, then it makes sense that you would have connections with all sorts of people."

Brad wrote a note about 117's incident during the stakeout, but his eyes kept darting back to the part where the old man had introduced himself as his grandfather. His smile was replaced with skepticism as he glanced back at Dr. Kendrick.

"So, what was that old man like? Or what was up with that?? Was 117 ok after...?"

"Hold on a second, Brad."

Dr. Kendrick held up a hand, and Brad stopped talking. They both turned to look at 117.

"Let's wait for 117 to finish his call. It isn't right to forget about the person who was actually there. He was about to get to that part of the story when we were interrupted."

After a moment of silence, Brad saw 117 blink and then turned his head to face them. Seeing 117 moving helped Brad relax a little. During the phone call, 117 had remained completely still, his gaze fixed ahead and unblinking. It was like watching a puppet suddenly come back to life.

"My apologies," 117 replied promptly. "I was in a group chat. According to amborg 8, he explained to me what had happened."

"Let me guess," Dr. Kendrick sighed, "Did 9 pull another prank?"

"It would appear so."

Brad looked at Dr. Kendrick, who shook his head and let out a sigh.

"Out of all of our amborgs, those two are the most chaotic. They love following crude but amusing behavior patterns," he explained to Brad. "You could describe them as our own residential pranksters."

Before Brad could ask a question, 117 suddenly turned his head, staring blankly, and fell silent. The two of them continued to watch as 117 sat quietly.

"What is he looking at?" Brad whispered to Dr. Kendrick.

"He's not actually looking at anything," Dr. Kendrick replied softly. "That's just their expression when they're concentrating. Quite fascinating."

Dr. Kendrick then realized that Brad appeared concerned.

"Of course," he added with a reassuring grin, "I can understand why it's rather uncomforting."

After a few more minutes, 117 turned his head slowly in a creepy robotic fashion. He gazed at the two of them again and his bracelet flashed.

"It appears that 9 has set 8's sheets on fire and set up a miniature mud volcano outside the entrance of 8's quarters," he reported. "Hang on, the feed is a bit fuzzy. Ah, it looks like 8 has pulled the fire alarm and also drenched himself in fire suppressant foam. He declared an internal breach and activated the alarm while he was being soaked."

As he explained, the flashing warning lights on the wall suddenly stopped. Everything was quiet.

"So..." Brad muttered, "How does the rest of the story go?"

117 politely smiled.

"I was rescued and returned home."

Brad lifted his stylus and pointed the end at 117.

"If you don't mind my asking," he said, "Were you in a lot of pain when you were recovering from that stab wound?"

"Yes, I was," 117 admitted. "It was very unexpected to go through that kind of situation. It did turn into quite the learning experience. Not just for me."

"Wow, I feel like this is one big story that has gone far beyond the requirements of my essay," Brad said in a tone of wonder and inspired awe. "Perhaps I can write an article or publish my essay to scholastic journals. This is something exclusive that I believe should be shared."

117 dipped his head politely, but Brad noticed that he looked troubled.

"My apologies for straying from your assignment's subject parameters," he stated.

"Oh, that's ok!" Brad smiled encouragingly. "This is really great information!"

His reaction made 117 light up, and a genuine smile appeared as his lips curled in a very human fashion. Judging by the stories and lessons he shared while imitating human behavior, it was clear that 117 had overcome a significant amount of challenges over time. His smile appeared much less robotic and stiff than he had described. It looked like he had perfected the art of smiling quite nicely.

As they talked, they failed to hear the door open, where someone called out to them.

"Hey guys! How's it going?"

Everyone's gaze shifted to Johnny 5 as he entered the room. His clothes were marred by heavy stains, most likely the result of the earlier disaster. Brad was quite impressed with the uniform's design. The glowing number on 5's jacket pocket was still visible.

"Johnny!" Dr. Kendrick exclaimed and waved for him to come closer.

"Holy crap, t-that's Johnny 5!" Brad stammered as his mouth dropped open.

"Very astute," 117 smirked.

5 strolled over to where the folding chairs were, grabbed one, and brought it over. He unfolded it with ease and took a seat in their little group circle. Dr. Kendrick eyed his clothes in amusement.

"I take it you were just at 8's residence?" he asked.

5 waved back but then his brows furled slightly. He looked at them in confusion.

"I am afraid you are mistaken, doctor," he replied. "I actually just got back from a deployment and the people I arrested laid a trap for me. It involved a basement, then a massive tank of mud that was connected to the structure, and they tried drowning me. I am quite happy to report that they failed when I managed to swim out. But what happened to 8?"

"Well..."

5 observed everyone's expressions, then nodded in understanding. He already knew within a second.

"Right," 5 chuckled. "Whenever you mention 8, I can tell the culprit had to be 9."

"I think there was an explosion," Brad piped up.

"Those two never quit," 5 let out a sigh, which didn't sound like disappointment. His grin indicated that he was quite pleased with hearing this news. "I swear, all these years, they keep coming up with new ways to humiliate each other. It does not really affect us since we've stopped worrying about them so much. I find their methods to be funny, but it only makes me feel a little unproductive."

"Is that a hint of envy in your tone? How surprising," Dr. Kendrick raised an eyebrow.

5 returned his gaze and it slowly turned into a soft and mischievous smile.

"Well, yeah, I am," 5 said with a presumptuous tone. "Sometimes I just wish I had their creativity. You know how hard it is trying to keep up with their combined chaos?"

The four of them broke out in a fit of laughter. Brad noticed that when 117 and 5 were laughing, their upper chests and shoulders shook like a normal person's would, yet no sound came from their mouths. Instead, their laughs projected from their bracelets. 117 attempted to laugh with his real voice, but a few coughs slipped out, hinting at some discomfort. He wasn't letting that stop him from continuing the conversation like normal, so Brad decided not to broach the subject.

"Why do they keep pranking each other?" he asked once they had calmed down.

"It's a little hard to say. Who knows?" 5 shrugged. "They change their reasons all the time."

"There's a new insult, new strategy, and new explanation every time you choose to interrogate them," 117 let out a gentle cough as he explained carefully.

"Ah yes," Dr. Kendrick nodded thoughtfully, "last month, 9's excuse was that 8 was a stuck-up...dirt-bag."

The way Dr. Kendrick stressed the last word sent Brad into another fit of laughter.

"If you think that was funny Brad, wait till you hear about this one," 5 said cheerfully. "I remember this one time when 8 soaked all of 9's underwear in meat. When 9 deployed into a combat zone later that day, practically fifty dogs were all chasing and attacking her. Everyone stopped fighting to watch. Police and gang members were all in a daze from trying to figure out what was happening."

Brad's mind immediately conjured up the image of an amborg being chased as 5 had described. While some details might have been exaggerated, the story sounded genuine. The idea of an amborg actually scheming and humiliating another was a little cruel, but it still struck him as quite hilarious. The laughter went on for a few minutes. Finally, after what sounded like a giant expulsion of air, 5 calmed down before speaking again.

"Anyway," 5 sighed as he dusted off a bit of mud from his sleeve, "I believe we should continue with 117's story. Brad seems anxious."

"Am I?" Brad took a couple of breaths and put a hand to his chest.

"Well, you keep looking at 117 in anticipation," 5 remarked.

"I think I'm still jumpy from the alarm," Brad shrugged. "But... are you ok? 117?"

117 lifted the back of his hand to his mouth, cleared his throat, and nodded.

"Thank you for asking," he gently replied. "I sometimes just have a cough whenever things get too funny. I am ready to continue sharing my story."

117 looked at Dr. Kendrick and dipped his head.

"Dr. Kendrick," he said, "would you mind sharing what happened when I was unconscious?"

"Of course," Dr. Kendrick leaned back and relaxed in his seat. He pondered for a moment about what he was going to say next. "After 117 left for that particular mission, we received a distress beacon. His first one in the field. It didn't help that Mandy wasn't at her post due to her Thanksgiving vacation but we scrambled a few amborgs to David's last known position. Once reinforcements arrived, we recovered him and brought him back home. After that, I had a lot to tell him..."

Brad eagerly listened as he took notes again.

"...and now," Dr. Kendrick smiled, "I'm going to share some pretty surprising details."

Amborg Medical Facility
2127

117's eyes slowly opened, adjusting to the soft glow of a pristine ceiling above him. Groggily, he attempted to sit up, but he wasn't able to move. His whole body felt heavy as he tried to run a system diagnostic on himself. As he struggled to figure out where he was and assess the damage, he began to pick up on the murmurs of voices nearby.

"Is there a status update?"

"Mandy, it's alright. He is safe here and is recovering."

"I shouldn't have left him..."

117 tried to tilt his head. As his eyes focused, he checked his surroundings and identified the voices speaking in the background. It was Mandy and Dr. Kendrick. She had returned to A.I. Industries, since she was listed as 117's emergency contact. Getting the news of his particular defeat while deployed on a mission must have been shocking. He figured that her vacation had been interrupted when someone contacted her about the situation.

"Please listen," 117 heard another girl's voice speaking softly. "His wounds weren't fatal and after Dr. Wildman's and my assistance, he will make a full recovery."

117 recognized the other girl's voice. It belonged to 6, a First Group amborg who was highly skilled in the medical field and well known for it. There seemed to be a whole discussion going on nearby. He heard Dr. Kendrick speak up.

"He'll be fine. Once he wakes up..."

"Why do you sound so concerned?" Mandy asked.

"There's something I need to tell him," Dr. Kendrick replied. 117 picked up on a heaviness in his tone. "Something I need to tell you too."

"What is it?" Mandy said hesitantly.

"When he wakes up," Dr. Kendrick stated firmly in annoyance.

117 heard a chuckle from 6.

"How cryptic," she mused playfully. "I'll give you a friendly lesson, Mandy."

"Vanessa..." Dr. Kendrick said warningly. "Please don't."

"I've known Dr. Kendrick for many years," 6 explained. "In that time, we've learned a lot about each other. Whatever's going on, he's acting quite calm despite the fact that one of his prodigies from the Second Group has been stabbed."

Silence fell over the room. 117 listened closely. Then Dr. Kendrick spoke again.

"If everyone witnessed me panicking," he huffed angrily, "then it wouldn't set a good example."

"Neither is lying to Mandy," 6 countered in a casual and soft tone. "If I had to guess, it almost seems like you knew..."

"Vanessa!" Dr. Kendrick sharply cut her off. "You're dismissed. That's an order. Thank you."

"Intense," 6 replied with a charming and playful voice. "Well, looks like my time is up. I'll go and check the inventory or something."

117 heard the sound of footsteps growing fainter as they moved away. He recognized the distinct, heavy tread of 6's steps as she left the hospital wing.

"When he talks like a stern dad," 6 called out to them, "it's super serious. This is interesting stuff."

Another moment of silence passed, then Mandy spoke up.

"What's going on?" she asked.

"Not until David wakes up," Dr. Kendrick repeated.

"Damn it doctor..." Mandy spat out in a soft but determined voice. 117 heard a foot stomp on the floor. It sounded like Mandy was throwing a tantrum, or something along those lines. "David almost died. And I wasn't here to help him when he needed us! You can tell me what's going on! I'm his technician, which means I'm responsible for him."

"I am responsible for him too," Dr. Kendrick declared.

"I wasn't invalidating you," Mandy replied, "I know you raised and took care of him. But he isn't going to be entirely fine. Not after something like this."

"Then wait a moment longer," Dr. Kendrick said. "43. Serina. I want you to..."

"Deploy? Yes sir."

117 heard 43's voice. She was here too? Then again, it didn't come as a surprise.

"No," Dr. Kendrick countermanded 43's statement.

"Let me out there and join the search!" 43 protested.

"This concerns you just as much as it does for David," Dr. Kendrick replied sternly. "I need to be here in person when he wakes so I can talk to both of you."

"W-well," 43 stammered as her voice fell, "I do appreciate that but I have to try to help! What would 117 say if he knew that I stayed here the whole entire time protecting him?"

"I'm sure he'd be happy?" Dr. Kendrick replied, confused.

117 let out a weak cough. A soft warm light appeared above him and he looked up. He found himself looking at an upside down miniature holographic face of an A.I.

"Hello 117," she smiled, whispering gently to him.

"Hi... Serina," 117 opened his mouth and mumbled weakly.

"Listen to me."

117 saw Serina do a gentle flip in the air. Like a gymnast, she somersaulted and spun around, "landing" softly right in front of him. Although she was technically floating, she carried herself like a nurturing mother tending to a bedridden child.

"You must have heard them outside, right?" she whispered, leaning forward and bringing a hand up to her cheek.

117 nodded in response.

"If you like," Serina smiled gently, "I can pretend you're still asleep so that you can rest."

117 shook his head. He drafted a text message and quietly sent it to the glowing green A.I. hovering in front of him.

It is alright. I would like to talk to Dr. Kendrick. Everyone has been waiting for me.

"Ok," Serina nodded politely. "Hang on a moment."

Instead of disappearing in a flash of light, Serina glided over to the curtain. Like a ghost, she poked her head through the fabric. Without a physical form, she was able to phase through without any problems, like she was sticking her head out of a window that wasn't there.

"Doctor, he's awake," 117 heard Serina calmly announce.

Within seconds, someone pulled back the curtains, and the room brightened noticeably. Suddenly, the headrest of the bed began whirring as it lifted him into an upright position. 117 saw Mandy rush inside with 43 right behind her. Dr. Kendrick soon followed, along with Sherry.

The four of them gathered around the bed, with Mandy and 43 positioned on either side, while Dr. Kendrick and Sherry stood at the foot of the bed. Serina hovered above them, and 117 noticed her reach out. A handlebar appeared, and she pulled a holographic folding chair from thin air, unfolding it easily. She sat down, and a holographic book materialized in her hands. What was she doing? 117 decided to text her again.

You have very peculiar habits for an artificial intelligence. Why put so much effort into public appearances when you're capable of performing specialized tasks discreetly?

117 received a notification in his mind a moment later.

Pay attention, she wrote, ***I think you have other matters to worry about.***

117 turned to look at Mandy.

"David, can you hear me?" she asked, expressing concern.

"I think so," 117 broadcasted from his bracelet.

Even that sounded a little weak. 117 transmitted a reboot function to the bracelet and it reset. He tried talking again.

"I need to update everyone on the current situation."

"Don't worry!" Mandy replied gently. "We watched the footage and saw what happened."

"It's going to be ok," 43 smiled. "Dr. Wildman and Dr. Kendrick both were here to oversee your treatment. You suffered minor damage but it wasn't fatal."

117 smiled at everyone. He gazed at 43 and extended his hand towards her, and she gently wrapped her fingers with his. Her touch was soothing and warm.

"I overheard you," he admitted. "You would rather be out there. I appreciate your dedication so do not feel guilty about being here. I am glad I woke up and knew that you were here."

"Well," 43 awkwardly tilted her head from side to side. "I was technically ordered to."

She turned and glanced at Sherry, then at Dr. Kendrick.

"But I really am happy that you're awake," she said.

"Did they find the man who did it?" 117 asked.

"A few amborgs are in L.A. right now," Mandy explained. "They and their technicians have been looking the entire time you were out."

117 checked the clock once it updated. When his internal clock was synchronized to the one next to his bed, he could see the current time and date. He had been stabbed yesterday. It was already the following morning.

"What if the amborgs out there also get ambushed?"

117 tried to get out of bed but everyone quickly protested.

"It's alright, David. Please calm down," Dr. Kendrick motioned for 117 to settle back into his pillows. "If you heard me earlier after you woke up, please be patient and let me share some things with you and 43."

"Uh, us too, right?"

Sherry pointed a finger at herself. Dr. Kendrick let out a sigh and nodded vigorously.

"Of course," he replied. "I know that everyone has a lot of questions after seeing the recordings of what 117 saw."

He shifted uncomfortably, feeling the weight of everyone's gaze. 43 seemed the most annoyed, turning to him with an apprehensive look.

"Is it true?" she demanded, "What that man said?"

Dr. Kendrick gave a silent nod, causing everyone to stare in disbelief. The instant he opened his mouth to say yes, the entire group cut him off.

"What?" Sherry raised her eyebrows.

The others murmured in surprise.

"How... is that possible?" 117 asked.

"The man who stabbed you is your paternal grandfather," Dr. Kendrick stated. "He is your last living relative on the planet."

"Why would you even know that information?" Sherry asked.

Mandy however, suddenly remembered.

"David's father," she said, glancing at 117, who nodded. "He worked for A.I. Industries!"

Dr. Kendrick nodded in confirmation.

"He was one of my best researchers," he explained, looking 117 in the eye. "That's when I learned about your grandfather."

117 sat up straighter. This was definitely not something he expected to hear. He had never known anything of what his father had done for A.I. Industries. When he became an amborg, he'd hoped it would grant him access to certain records, but there were a lot of classified and heavily guarded secrets.

Listening to Dr. Kendrick offered some great insight into the past.

"From how he spoke of him," Dr. Kendrick recalled, "your father always made it sound like your grandfather was dead. After he was killed in that tragic accident with your mother... I went looking for you and brought you in."

Dr. Kendrick then activated the bracelet on his arm and an image appeared before 117. The others leaned in to get a closer look, whereas 43 and 117 could just zoom in and enhance the image with their eyes.

"Is this the man you saw? Can you confirm?"

117 saw that the photo was timestamped around ten years ago. There were two men standing next to each other in the photo. One looked just like his father and the other seemed familiar too. He didn't have a cloak or hood covering his head, but there was no mistaking that beard.

"The hooded man!" 117 declared. He suddenly felt anger bubbling up from within. "That is him! I am positive!"

"Easy David!"

Dr. Kendrick's voice rose sharply, causing everyone to pull back in alarm. Mandy and Sherry exchanged worried glances, clearly shaken, but 43 remained still. 117 took a moment to breathe and focused on the picture in front of him.

"Thank you," Dr. Kendrick cleared his throat.

"S-so..." Mandy stammered, "are you telling us that 117's only surviving relative revealed himself to us by stabbing his own grandson? What kind of psycho does that??"

"I don't know," Dr. Kendrick shook his head. "That's why finding him is top priority."

An eerie silence loomed over the five of them. 117 stared in disbelief at what he had just heard.

"He didn't try to kill me," 117 stated.

Mandy whirled around and stared wide-eyed at 117.

"I think he did," she stated.

"No," 117 looked down at his stomach, which was concealed by the sheets. "The stab wound wasn't fatal. He let me live for a reason."

"Well, once we find and catch him, then we'll interrogate him."

117 looked at 43. It was pretty obvious she was itching for a fight.

"There are amborgs already out there," Dr. Kendrick reminded them.

"Well, we should join them!" Sherry stated confidently. "If 43 deploys, we'll have this wrapped up in no time!"

"Wait," 117 said, "I have a few more questions."

117 turned to Dr. Kendrick after Sherry politely stopped talking. She nodded respectfully, granting him the opportunity to speak.

"Why did you not tell me about my grandfather?"

"Like I said, I thought he was dead," Dr. Kendrick replied. "Clearly, based on yesterday's events, this isn't the case. I don't believe that he and your father were on good terms. He described him as arrogant, naïve, and was quite brash in his methods and problem solving. I also think 'untrustworthy' was a commonly used phrase as well."

117 felt a twinge in his abdomen. The ache in his wound suddenly got worse. That description definitely fit with what he had encountered.

"From what I dug up from your parent's records," Dr. Kendrick explained, "he was a veteran of the third world war. He is a survivor. His actions were very unorthodox and not always within, shall we say, proper codes of conduct. Now, he's revealed himself without so much as a warning."

"Well we can add 'stabbing grandchildren in the back' to that list of actions," 117 replied grimly. "It is very comforting to have a family reunion where one gets stabbed as a greeting."

"Now you use sarcasm properly?" Mandy asked in surprise.

"Please Mandy," 117 replied, "I'm not having a good day..."

"Sorry," Mandy apologized and nodded her head.

"Anyway," Dr. Kendrick interrupted, "He's made an appearance which tells me he wants to reach out to you. I don't know why he decided on this but you're right, he hasn't killed you. But we must be careful because we don't know what he's up to."

"Uh, question," Sherry raised her finger and then pointed it at 117. "What I want to know is how a knife was able to penetrate 117's exoskeleton. Aren't they bulletproof and resistant to sharp objects? I know that their skin can withstand a certain amount of pain and damage but they can still get hurt from minor things like that."

"Because the armored exoskeleton of an amborg can only be penetrated by a weapon made specifically of the same material," Dr. Kendrick replied. He brought up an image of a knife on one of the wall monitors. "And we have found traces of LTO alloy left from the knife deep in the wound."

"A new weapon that can kill us is out there," 43 looked horrified at the thought.

Lutetium, Titanium and Osmium were the strongest metals on the planet. The combination of the three was what made up their inner armor. Remembering certain bits of history, 117 knew that the concept for it was originally meant for construction. Scientists had found a way to actually mix them together, which created a newer and stronger metal. All hopes and dreams of improving building infrastructure in the construction industry were tarnished after the initial experiments.

There was a scarcity of resources, low funds, and poor stability rates, making it unviable for large scale projects. After Dr. Kendrick learned about this, he incorporated the idea of implanting this metal into human bodies, which was the basis for how the amborgs had such strong armored bodies. This eventually would provide them with great defensive capabilities that made them walking tanks.

"Doctor," 117 sat up once again. "If there are knives that exist that can kill us... Does that mean?"

He looked at 43 with a concerned expression. They didn't have to text each other privately to know what the other was thinking. 43 knew right away.

"Bullets too?" she asked, turning to look up at Dr. Kendrick.

"I don't know," He said, shaking his head dejectedly.

"They could put pieces of shrapnel inside a bomb," Sherry looked around worriedly.

"It is possible but... past studies and experiments have found that using the LTO formula to make a bullet is just not viable," Dr. Kendrick answered with a shrug. "The shrapnel idea, Sherry, is more than likely. But, I think there's nothing to be gained from wasting so many resources on crafting bullets that won't work."

Dr. Kendrick took off his glasses and fiddled around with them. Mandy and 43 fell silent again. Shocked at the revelation, it felt as if everything had just changed. 117, however, decided not to sit around and wait for a worse outcome. The fact is, there was one man who could answer the questions burning in his mind.

He transmitted a signal to the TV monitor across from him. When it turned on, it requested his user ID and password. He entered his information, appearing as simple circular dots across the bar, which was standard protocol. When it accepted his credentials, he brought up a huge map overlay. The U.S. was displayed in full view with seven orange dots blinking in various places. Each one represented an amborg, his friends away from home. He zoomed in on California, where there were two dots.

"Doctor, who is that?" 117 asked, trying not to look at the area where he'd been wounded.

Dr. Kendrick quickly surveyed the map. 117 zoomed in more, revealing the numbers of the amborgs out there: 917 and 5.

"Johnny and Jack are both there now. They volunteered to remain in the area to search for your grandfather or any sign of his hooded followers."

"Call them back now."

"What?"

Moments after Dr. Kendrick asked the question, one of the dots on the map flashed and turned dark red. 43 put a hand up to her head and concentrated. Serina rose from her little holographic chair and tossed her book away. It dissolved into pixels as she floated above them, fully alert.

"Amborg distress beacon," she announced. "Johnny 5 is calling for help."

"How close can 917 assist?" Sherry asked.

Another alarm pinged on the map and they saw 917's dot also turn a deep shade of red.

"Second distress beacon detected," Serina replied. "Houston, we have a problem..."

"Never mind," Sherry replied, "I'm going to report to my station."

Sherry turned to leave as 43 suddenly stood up.

"Doctor," she said, "I'm receiving numerous reports of attacks in Los Angeles. Extremely heavy assaults across the lower districts. Requests for military support have been confirmed. We need to go."

"We need to go and rescue them," 117 commanded. "If there are weapons out there that can kill or wound us, then the amborgs who don't know of this information need to be warned."

117 immediately got out of the bed and began to stagger to the entrance. Mandy and Dr. Kendrick attempted to stop him, but it was no use. They couldn't exactly stop a heavy set man like him. Fortunately,

amid their protests, 43 stepped forward and blocked his path. He stopped, face to face with her.

"What do you think you're doing?" She demanded.

Sensing that she wasn't going to budge, 117 looked right into her eyes. "We're going to L.A. Don't try to stop me."

He tried to move forward again but she remained rooted between him and the entrance.

"You're injured," she protested as she gently put her hand on his cheek. He ignored the look on her face, which had begun to sadden. "Let me handle this."

"No," 117 said firmly, taking her hand off his face. "We need to do this together."

43 nodded, and 117 turned to Mandy and Dr. Kendrick. Suddenly, they heard the sound of footsteps approaching, and they saw amborg 6 and a couple of nurses making their way toward them. It was obvious they had noticed he had detached himself from the medical bed and monitor and were now rushing over.

"Mandy, Dr. Kendrick..." he said, and then looked at 6, "I am discharging myself from the hospital."

"If it were up to me," 6 sighed, "I would not allow this. But I doubt stopping you and 43 would end well here."

She glanced at Dr. Kendrick.

"Does he have permission?" she asked.

Dr. Kendrick turned and cautiously gazed at 117 and 43. He conceded and let out a sigh.

"Granted," he nodded. Then he sharply spoke up. "But I want you to take at least two other amborgs with you. Take Alice and Carter. Notify their technicians."

"Yes sir," 117 nodded.

117 and 43 walked out of the hospital. He needed to put on his uniform and get to the drop-pod hangar.

"What's the plan?" 43 asked.

"I'm going to get some answers and there is only one man who can do that."

"So we're winging it?"

117 answered her with a firm and silent nod.

CHAPTER 8

Phantom Limb Retaliation

Los Angeles Rural District Fourteen

"Help us! Help! We're trapped in here!"

In the middle of a battle-torn street, desperate cries for help caught the attention of one single U.S. army officer navigating his way through the destruction. Drawn by the sound, he moved toward what seemed to be the voices of children. Lowering himself, he crawled through the remains of a bombed out home. He reached a door that was stuck shut and hammered on the surface loudly.

"Hello?! I'm an army officer! I'll try to get through!" he shouted as loud as he could. He looked around for something to help him force his way in, but couldn't find anything. "I need to break down the door!"

"We're in here!" someone cried from the other side.

A sudden crash echoed from outside. The officer whirled around and heard heavy footsteps approaching.

ar"Oh crap," he mumbled as he backed up against the door.

He relaxed when he saw who had ducked through the front entrance, his neon stripes glowing in the dim light. He couldn't see the guy's face clearly, but he recognized the uniform. It was one he knew well.

"Oh! Thank god! I sure am glad to see..."

He was interrupted when the amborg suddenly leaped toward him menacingly and barked an order.

"Move!"

A commanding voice blared from his bracelet. He watched the amborg raise his fist, aiming it right at him—or was he? In a flash, he dodged to the side just in time to see the amborg's fist smash right through the door, creating a massive hole. He hooked his arm in and yanked it back, ripping the door off its hinges and causing some plaster and dust to drop from the ceiling.

Explosions outside rattled the whole building. The ground trembled violently, knocking the soldier off his feet. He hit the ground hard as more bombs went off in the street. As he struggled to pick himself up, he looked up to see the amborg offering him a hand.

"Get up soldier," he spoke insistently. "We need to get inside."

Not questioning the command, the soldier lifted his arm and grabbed his hand, only to be yanked upward. He shouted as he was suddenly flung into the air and sent flying right through the broken door.

"Oof!" he exclaimed when he hit the ground.

The impact with the floor sent a jolt of pain through his body, and he groaned as he tried to get up. Just then, he heard the sound of tiny murmurs. Propping himself up on one of his elbows, he glanced up and realized that he'd landed right in front of a group of children, all staring at him in silent, wide-eyed bewilderment. Noticing their frightened expressions, he flashed a grin and began to push himself up on his knees.

"Cavalry's here kids," he stated as positively as he could while trying to ignore the pain in his chest. Fortunately, his chest armor had absorbed most of the fall. "We're just going to wait here until it's safe."

A heartbeat later, they heard a heavy thud near the door. The amborg had jumped inside and landed in a clumsy heap next to the small group.

"Whoa, you ok?"

"Not really," the bracelet transmitted.

Something long and heavy fell to the ground, but the lingering darkness and dust made it difficult to see what it was. The two men crawled to the wall, resting against the rubble for support. Outside, the sound of explosions continued, the vibrations from the blasts sending tremors through the building. The officer focused on the amborg next to him, struggling to make out the number on his jacket through the layers of dust and mud. He looked down to see what he had brought. His stomach lurched when he realized what it was. It was a leg. A human one.

"What?" the amborg asked casually with a shrug. "You've never seen a detached prosthetic before?"

"Sweet mother of god," the officer let out a sigh of relief. "I almost thought you were carrying someone's leg."

"Don't worry, it's mine. Johnny 5 at your service."

Amborg 5 dusted his hand off on his clothes and extended it to him. The two of them shook hands as they introduced each other.

"My name's Tom, Lieutenant Palmer, U.S. army. And... are you ok? That's your leg? And it's not attached to you?"

"It looks more painful than it actually is," 5 answered reassuringly. "Now smile. We still need to be positive for the kids."

"Pardon me for staring," the soldier replied. "I'm used to seeing you guys with all limbs attached."

"Well, now I'm a cripple. So, you get a very special rare moment."

Palmer glanced at the kids and gave them a thumbs up as well as a forced smile.

"Everything's ok kids!" he declared.

"I said, be positive," 5 said impatiently. "That sounded cringey. Don't force it or they'll realize you're being a total chicken. Relax."

Annoyed, Palmer turned his back on the kids and frowned at their one-legged savior.

"Flow naturally?" he whispered in a tense voice. "Have you seen the immediate surroundings?"

"I'm just saying," 5 replied casually, "if the kids realize that you're psychologically manipulating them, it'll hurt their development."

"It isn't psychological manipulation when we're in the middle of a warzone!" Palmer spoke through gritted teeth. "I'd say that I'm being as natural as I can be!"

"No one's perfect," 5 shrugged.

5 suddenly leaned forward and lifted his leg up. For a minute, Palmer thought that he was going to attack, but then his bracelet flashed again. 5 looked at the kids cheerfully.

"Hey kids!" he playfully announced. "Want to see the leg of an amborg? Don't be concerned. The bad guys and I just had a disagreement and they tried to steal my leg, but I got it back!"

The kids, who had remained silent the whole time, moved forward slowly, and then 5 passed his leg to them. They all stared in wonder at the cybernetically altered body part. Fully distracted, 5 leaned back to relax and resumed his conversation with Palmer.

"So... what's up?"

"Where do I even begin?" Palmer grumbled as he crossed his arms. He checked his radio and all the equipment he still had. "I got cut off from my unit when we were on patrol here. I lost my rifle and I've been trying to make my way back to the outpost."

Palmer glanced at 5's other leg. It looked like the pant leg had been torn when his prosthetic had been separated from his body.

"What about you?" he asked.

"I was out here looking for someone who hurt a really good friend of mine," 5 answered. "Next thing I know, I walked into an ambush. They came out from all directions and when I fought them off, I felt something stab me in the leg."

"Stabbed? Is that even a thing for you?" Palmer looked at 5 in disbelief. "Should we try to get you some medical help when we get out of here?"

"I'm fine," 5 motioned for Palmer to keep his voice down. "Like I told you earlier, it doesn't hurt so much anymore. But that's twice in my life now that someone has taken my leg from me."

Palmer glanced back at the kids, then examined the leg. It was all robotic. No bones, blood or regular human anatomical parts. It really was a completely well-built robotic prosthesis.

"So, that's not a human leg?" Palmer clarified with 5, who nodded. "That was built for you?"

"Yes," he replied with a proud smile. "Custom-made and machine manufactured at A.I. Industries!"

"How did you lose it?"

"I lost it when I was a kid. Spent a few years walking on whatever I could make into crutches. That leg is one of the greatest gifts from Dr. Kendrick that no money can buy. At least, it is a very treasured gift that I can never repay."

"Oh uh," Palmer awkwardly pointed at the kids. "I mean, how did you lose it just now?"

"Oh," 5 paused and then laughed a little. "Splatter-Bugs rushed me and I got stabbed. The next thing I knew, they pulled it off... I really hope it can be fixed."

"Is there anything I can do?"

Palmer instantly began checking his pockets for something that might help, but 5 held up a hand. What could he do in this situation?

"No thanks. I'm good," 5 said reassuringly. "They didn't get any vital arteries or other biological parts. My right leg is a complete machine attachment. They just tore it in the right spot. Actually, they used some sort of special knife. I was surprised when they got in close and managed to stab me."

"At least you're not bleeding," Palmer remarked.

"Yup," 5 smiled. "I activated my distress beacon so someone should be coming for me soon. We'll be ok."

Some slight movement cut off the conversation. They turned to the side and noticed that one of the kids had crawled over to them. They both smiled welcomingly to the boy.

"Mr. Amborg? Could you show us how your leg works?"

5 let out a soft chuckle.

"Hang on a second, ok kid?" he said gently and held up his index finger.

5 turned to give Palmer a bright and energetic smile.

"You call for your backup," he recommended in a kind tone. "Once you get out of here, I'll wait for my friends."

"You don't want to evacuate with us?" Palmer asked, concerned about 5's casual demeanor.

"Nah," 5 replied. "If I have to stay behind to get you out, I can buy you time."

"I'd feel much better if you let me help you out."

"Suit yourself," 5 shrugged. "Can't exactly get rid of your free will."

He then shifted around and crawled over to the kids. While 5 distracted them with a presentation about his leg, Palmer decided to take the opportunity and call for help since it looked like they would be stuck here a bit longer. He grabbed his radio and tried to transmit to any allies nearby.

"Mayday, mayday, can anyone copy?" he said softly. "Transmitting on military emergency frequency alpha four."

Glancing over at the children, he saw that all of them were still fixating on the leg, which gave him a sense of relief. He didn't have to worry about them trying to understand what he was saying and starting a panic. Suddenly, a response came crackling through the radio.

"Alpha four acknowledged," someone replied. "Please identify yourself."

"Lieutenant Palmer, 79th of the 40th ID," Palmer replied.

After a few seconds, the radio responded.

"Confirmed, thank you Lieutenant. SIT-REP, please?"

Now we're talking. Palmer felt hopeful as he spoke again.

He pulled up a small map from his watch and read the coordinates of his location. When he made sure his beacon was active, he transmitted it to the person from dispatch.

"I need an immediate evac right now from my location," he stated slowly and clearly. "Gridzone bravo three. We were ambushed in rural district 14 and I got separated from my teams. I'm hiding with some children here. Track my location from this transmission and send help."

"Copy that Lieutenant," the radio answered promptly. "We've isolated your signal and are tracking you. Looks like you're twelve clicks out from our nearest unit. How many to evac?"

"I have five kids who need to be extracted along with an amborg. It's Johnny 5 of A.I. Industries."

The radio static suddenly intensified. Palmer tuned the radio, trying to clear it. Finally, he heard a response from dispatch, but he could barely make out their words.

"Lieutenant... if there's an amborg, I'm pretty sure you're fine if you hunker down for a while," the person on the other line replied calmly. Palmer kept trying to tune it so that he could hear their instructions more clearly. "We will reprioritize your evac to another location if you're holding with one of them. There are others in less fortunate conditions that can be evacuated before you."

"Listen. We kind of are the less fortunate," Palmer exclaimed, raising his voice. He held the radio closer and briefly glanced at the kids out of the corner of his eye. Luckily, they hadn't heard his growing anxiety. "Amborg 5 is crippled and we are on the defensive. Repeat, we are completely on the defensive and are hiding from Splatter-Bugs. We have no weapons and no way out of here. I could really use something here!"

The static interference continued to intensify, making it harder for Palmer to make out the words coming through. He gave the radio a small slap and concentrated harder. The kids were now playing tug-of-war with 5's leg.

How much fun are they having? he wondered.

As he continued to fight a losing battle with the radio, he could make out a few words coming through from dispatch.

"...fzzt-say again? zzhh-amborzz... crippled? Repeat-kzzt... Support-zzft...ot...available! Hold... zzpt...urrent position! If you read...zztth-we will try to reach you!"

Before Palmer had the chance to send another transmission, a hand materialized out of thin air and snatched the radio. With a giant crunch, 5 clenched his fist and destroyed it. The sudden silence that followed left Palmer wide-eyed and speechless.

"What did you do that for...mmmph?!"

5 held up a hand and placed it over the Lieutenant's mouth. With his other hand, he drew his index finger up to his own lips in a gesture for silence, then pointed outside the doorway. Palmer, disgruntled at being forced to keep quiet, listened carefully.

A few voices could be heard from outside in the other rooms. The look on 5's face indicated to Palmer that they weren't friendly. Splatter-Bugs, he guessed as 5 removed his hand. They both ushered the kids to come closer, then got in front of them. As silently as possible, Palmer slowly drew his knife while 5 motioned for the kids to quiet down. Nobody dared to make a sound as they listened to whoever was in the other room.

"It doesn't look like anyone's here," they heard someone say. "Let's head over to the next place. Nothing to hunt for here."

"Come on, there's got to be something! Our bombs would have sent someone ducking in here. Right? I thought I heard something when we passed by," another voice spoke.

"We're tearing it up out there bro. All the fun stuff is out there!"

"You telling me I'm imagining shit? What the... hey, check this out!"

"Sup? It's just a stupid photo. Whoa! She looks hot! Wonder where this one's hiding?"

5 and Palmer quietly glanced at each other. Palmer could see 5's brow furrow a little. He couldn't tell what he was thinking, but he noticed that 5 was looking down at one of his pockets. Following his gaze, Palmer's eyes widened when he checked his left breast pocket. It had come undone and it was empty!!

Shoot, he thought. *I lost Ellie's photo! I gotta get that back!*

He immediately tried to surge forward, but 5 grabbed his shoulder, holding him back with superhuman strength. Outside, the two gang members continued arguing over the photo. They were still hidden from their antics.

"Well, don't hog it all for yourself, give it here!" the first voice spoke again. "Don't clench it! She's a hottie."

"Finders keepers," the second voice taunted. "She looks like someone I would..."

"Achoo!"

Palmer froze. Both he and 5 whirled around to see one of the little girls with her hands over her mouth. Even though it was absolutely unlikely, he held onto an extremely thin strand of hope that the two strangers outside hadn't heard. The little girl who sneezed clenched her hands tightly as she looked up at them with wide eyes.

"I'm sorry!" she whispered in a horrified voice.

5 and Palmer listened and realized they had been made. There were footsteps running towards them.

Damn! Palmer thought angrily as he lifted his knife.

Someone came around the corner, peered into the hole of the wreckage, and saw them hiding in the opening where the destroyed door had been earlier. A wide grin appeared on the gangster's face.

"Hey! What do you know?" he said cheerfully. "Looks like we got some lost birds! Hey, Joey, I found some people here! Fresh kills for us today!"

"Yeah, that's great," the other Splatter-Bug joined the fray. "Kill them and let's get out of here already! We got to find that amborg that got away. Boss said we wouldn't get any good hits tonight if we don't finish that stupid cyborg."

Despite his protests, the second gang member, Joey, followed his friend into the room, both with weapons out and pointed right at Palmer and the children.

"Oh sure, ignore the amborg," 5 muttered.

Palmer immediately lowered his knife and tossed it towards the two gangsters. He held his arms up in a peaceful gesture and slowly inched closer to the kids, trying to shield them as best he could.

"Smart move, soldier," the Splatter-Bug who found them smiled as he grabbed Palmer's knife, throwing it behind him out the door, and out of anyone's reach. "I love it when the smart ones know they're about to be thrown off a roof. Saves us so much... trouble."

The gangster faltered, choosing that moment to look over and finally noticed 5. He cheekily waved a hand and greeted them.

"Yo," he chimed.

The gangster's face lit up in excitement, whereas his companion, Joey, appeared dumbfounded. The look on his face suggested that this was the last place he'd expected to see 5.

"WHOA! Are you kidding me?!!" he exclaimed gleefully. "We fucking found him! Hey Joey! And you wanted to skip this house!"

"Shut up Iva," Joey replied annoyingly. "You were right one time!"

"Seriously? Iva?" 5 asked. "That's the most intimidating name you came up with? So uncool."

"Hey! I spent a lot of time thinking about my name!" Iva snapped, pointing his gun at 5.

A gunshot rang out as he pulled the trigger, causing Palmer to flinch. The children shrieked in terror, clustering together for safety. In a moment of panic, Palmer glanced at them and checked himself, relieved to find that none were injured. 5, however, took a bullet to his forehead, which had bounced off. Palmer could hear the bullet clatter to the floor, along with the empty casing from Iva's gun.

"Why are you pissing them off?!" Palmer hissed at 5.

"I'm just saying," 5 replied, ignoring the fact that he had gotten shot, "if you want to be intimidating, name yourself anything except Iva. You need something strong, menacing and... I don't know, something that sounds memorable. I mean, Joey gets it."

"You can't talk yourself out of this one," Joey replied, but was cut off when Iva let out a sputter.

"That's not fair!" Iva complained. "Joey is his actual name! He didn't have to choose a new name!"

5 looked at Palmer and they blinked in confusion.

"Uh," 5 scoffed. "So, why did you?"

"He's new," Joey answered quickly. "We might have said it was part of the initiation."

"You lied to me?!"

Iva whirled around to Joey, who had a mischievous grin on his face.

"You fell for it," he chuckled.

"I thought we were friends!"

"I think you should focus on the fact that this amborg is trying to distract us."

Joey focused his gun back on Palmer. Iva did the same while pouting as he fired another shot at 5's chest. Again, he sustained no damage as he took the next bullet like a champ.

"What can I say?" 5 shrugged calmly. "My distractions are quite effective. Especially against stupid people. You should try it sometime."

5 rolled his eyes as Iva fired more bullets.

"Temper... Temper," 5 said mockingly as he was pelted mercilessly. "I love how you're shooting the only bullet proof body in this entire room. You're doing such a great job at being an idiot."

"Iva! Cut it out!"

Iva's gun clicked empty as he continued to unleash his pent-up frustration at 5. Palmer realized he was trying to draw all the focus to himself. With each passing moment, the danger to themselves and the children they were protecting decreased. 5 was stalling for time by trying to annoy the hell out of their enemies. It seemed to be working on Iva, who clearly had some anger management issues, but Joey stayed remarkably level-headed.

"Iva," Joey holstered his gun and began to speak in an eerie, sing-song voice. "You gotta kill them the right way. Forget dropping these ones off a roof. Let's make the amborg watch us work on the others."

"That is so creepy," 5 replied, "I am more than willing to recommend professional help for you. You like getting high and killing unarmed people? Or you only do kids?"

"Nah," Joey eyed Palmer with great interest. "I think soldier boy over here is the one I want to get rid of first. Then I toss the bodies of these kids at your feet. Or... your one foot."

"You realize that I am quite capable of taking both your asses down, right?"

5's questions made Joey laugh, while Iva looked bewildered. His frown disappeared as he lowered his gun and waved at the entire room.

"You're missing one leg!" Iva replied in a condescending manner. "You don't scare us!"

"Ok ok. You take the kids," Joey suddenly stopped laughing, then pointed his gun at Palmer's head and snarled at 5. "You take that knife that they gave us and take out the amborg. This is for all my friends that you stupid robots locked away and killed. We are living free lives and you guys don't like that? Well, how do you like me now?"

The bracelet 5's wrist lit up once more as he responded.

"Trust me pal, you're risking your life," he said smugly with a smirk.

"What are you talking about?" Joey asked, confusion sweeping over his features.

5 smiled.

"I'm saying it's not nice to point guns," his voice lowered to a whisper. Palmer suddenly pivoted to him with a look of concern. "Besides, I could have taken you..."

Iva yelped as something grabbed him from behind and hurled him toward the door. Palmer realized that someone had snuck in during the entire conversation. Iva was slammed against a wall, losing consciousness immediately. As he hit the ground, Joey barely had time to look before a hand grabbed his gun, crushing it in seconds, and he too was thrown towards the door. He hit the wall hard, a loud crack echoing as he slumped into Iva's body. Neither of them got up.

"...but," 5 smiled, "I was letting him get into position."

"I appreciate the distraction."

Palmer caught sight of another amborg turning to face them. He looked... different for some reason. The neon stripes on this one's uniform suddenly lit up, revealing a number. He hadn't realized they could do that with their uniforms. The glowing number 117 stood out prominently on his chest.

"For an amborg without a leg," 117 spoke, "it is very strange that you did not engage them sooner when you clearly could have. You would have solved the problem."

"Well 117," 5 shrugged as he waved his hand cheerfully. "I was not about to give away your position by telling them. It would have been an even bigger waste of time. Savor the fact that you just rescued us like a total badass and enjoy the moment."

117 looked around and gave a thumbs up to 5. Once the coast was confirmed to be clear, Palmer stood and walked over to the two unconscious Splatter-Bugs. 117 sauntered over and knelt down to pick up his knife. Palmer ignored this and went straight for the first body and searched his pockets.

"Asshole," Palmer said angrily as he rifled through Iva's pockets. "Targeting kids..."

He heard footsteps approaching and, without looking up, he knew that 117 had joined him. 117 had turned Joey's body over and was now checking his pockets. While Palmer was still rummaging around, he glanced up as 117 held something in front of his eyes. He snatched it out of the amborg's hands and inspected it. Sighing in relief, he inserted it back into his own pocket upon confirming that it was the right photo.

"Objective retrieved Lieutenant," 117's voice spoke out softly. "You should consider not carrying personalized materials that will easily fall to the ground during combat. I suggest not carrying them at all."

As Palmer double checked the clip on his pocket was secure, he glared at 117 in the eye.

"Look mister 'I don't have feelings,'" he said, tensing up, "when you're about to die, the last thing you probably want to see or think about is something pleasant. I don't know how you stay calm but for those of us who have actual feelings..."

He pointed a finger at his pocket for 117 to see.

"...it helps sometimes."

He shoved 117's hand away. 117 merely watched quietly as he reached over and picked up the gun laying next to Iva. Then, he retrieved a few clips of ammunition tucked in his belt while 117 turned to look at 5.

"Might as well," Palmer muttered as he reloaded the gun. There was probably going to be another fight and he wasn't sure how long it'd be until he could make it back to base. "I think we should wait in the next room."

"I agree," 117 nodded. "This room is not entirely safe."

Palmer put the gun in his holster. It felt a little heavier than a standard issue, but there wasn't really any time to complain. He then walked over and helped 117 lift 5 up off the ground. They all motioned for the kids to follow them outside.

The three of them stepped through the open doorway, the kids following closely behind. When they made it into the other room, Palmer stopped, which made 117 and 5 pause and glance at him. A flicker of guilt burned in the back of his mind as he let out a sigh.

"One seventeen, was it?" he muttered quietly.

"Correction," 117 replied. "It's pronounced one one seven."

"Sorry, 117," Palmer stated. "Thanks for helping us back there. I shouldn't have snapped at you like that. I guess I owe you."

"You're welcome," 117 nodded. "How interesting."

"What?" Palmer asked.

"Everyone says they owe me but do not specify what I am owed," 117 replied humorously.

"Wow," 5 chuckled in amazement. "The first joke that I've ever heard from him and he sounds like an extorting capitalist."

Palmer managed to get a signal from his radio. Dispatch reached out to them, confirming that an evacuation unit was en route to their location. After ensuring that 5 was properly balanced and secure, with his leg in his hands, literally, they made their way outside. The kids stayed silent, but at least they felt safe now.

When they stepped out into the light, Palmer and 117 both looked down at where 5's leg was supposed to be attached.

"You look... great," 117 commented as they made their way down some steps. "Mandy also says hi."

Palmer shifted uncomfortably while 5 let out a laugh.

"It looks like you took a beating too," he said enthusiastically. "When I heard what happened to you, I came out here because I couldn't believe it at first. I stayed alert but, you can see that I also took a hit. I certainly wasn't expecting to hop around like this today."

Palmer then decided to ask.

"What happened?"

117 leaned forward and glanced at him.

"I was stabbed," he explained. "An LTO knife."

The small party heard a rumbling in the distance and looked to the right. A pair of vehicles were heading their way.

"LTO? In the shape of a knife?" 5 said in surprise. "That's not good."

"It was in the report when I was hospitalized," 117 said, taken aback by 5's reaction. "Why do you sound so skeptical?"

"Like I said," 5 shrugged, "to me, it sounded a little unbelievable."

He glanced down at his detached leg.

"Now that I've also been through the same thing, I know that I was wrong. Who could have the technology to keep the reaction of forging those metals together and keep it stable? Especially with a tool so small?"

"That is what I am here to find out. Mandy has been scanning for patterns the whole time since I arrived."

The rumbling grew louder as they watched two military transports approach. They rolled to a stop a few feet away, kicking up dust and dirt into the air. The vehicles opened their doors and two squads of soldiers disembarked, fanning out and securing the area.

Palmer asked to take care of the kids, and 117 agreed with a nod. He slipped out from 5's arm, letting both amborgs hold on to each other and immediately ushered the kids inside the armored jeeps as fast as he could.

While they waited, 117 set up a private communication with 5.

"Also, there is one more thing," 117 said informatively. "The person who stabbed me is... my grandfather."

5 blinked, staring at him in disbelief. It was probably the first time that 117 had ever seen 5 at a sudden loss for words.

"What?" 5 finally forced out. "Now that's an interesting twist. Is he a long hated relative?"

"Not exactly," 117 replied. "His methods were unorthodox, but he is apparently alive and we have to find him. So, I wanted to ask if you see him, please don't kill him. He might do more damage to you even if he notices your current state."

"Let me get this straight. You want me to help you catch the guy who stabbed you..."

5 lifted up his still detached leg for 117 to see. Then he tilted his hand so that his foot was pointing down at the ground.

"...while I'm currently like this? You think a crippled amborg is the best backup for that?"

"No," 117 replied firmly. "We can do this as a team."

A beacon suddenly popped up in 117's HUD, closing in fast.

"Neat," 5 exclaimed. "Now there's three of us."

From a nearby roof, they saw someone leap off the top of a building and land on his feet in the street with a massive thud. Mud and dirt burst up and around him in a plume of debris. The arrival stood up and dusted himself off as he walked over.

"917," 5 smiled. "Good to see you."

"Likewise," Jack 917 nodded.

117 smiled, but his eyes widened when he glanced down at 917's right arm. His jacket sleeve had been ripped through, revealing a severe stab wound.

"Whoa," 5 said, staring at him in concern. "Are you ok?"

"I was ambushed," 917 sighed. "Meilin suggested I regroup with you."

"Where is 999?" 117 asked.

"Evacuating and protecting civilians," 917 replied promptly. "I'm surprised that 43 isn't with you."

"She is also in a different zone doing search-and-rescue. I am very sorry to see that both of you were hurt."

"Don't be," 917 smiled reassuringly. "Both of us are here because we chose to be."

"He's right," 5 nodded. "When we heard you got stabbed, we were under orders to redeploy but we really wanted to seek out and enact justice for you."

"Thank you," 117 smiled. "I think all three of us will have a much higher chance of finding the one responsible."

"Right," 917 held up a fist and pumped it up in front of his chest confidently. "We're going to kick that old man's ass and take him down."

5 and 117 both exchanged a look. 917 noticed this and his brazen smile faded instantly.

"What?" he asked suspiciously.

"The old man who stabbed 117 is his grandfather," 5 stated quickly. He then turned to look at 117. "Am I allowed to share that?"

"It would appear so," 117 sighed.

917 tilted his head for a moment, processing the information. He looked like he was about to speak again, but paused a second time.

"We know," 117 spoke when words failed him. "It's complicated."

"Your grandfather... whether or not that's true," 917 said slowly, "...is quite different from any other foe that we've encountered. Based on the footage, he is incredibly strong and abnormally faster than a normal human."

"How does he get so much strength? Steroids?" 5 asked.

"No," 117 answered. "Older cybernetic implants. Primitive but effective."

"Badass grandpa. Never thought we'd be hunting one down," 917 remarked. He casually glanced at 5's leg, amusement dancing in his eyes. "Are you going into battle looking like that? Must have cost you a leg."

"Very poorly phrased," 5 rolled his eyes. "If I lost my arm too, then the joke would have worked in its entirety."

"Ah. Of course. It must have cost you an arm and a leg," 117 recited from the standard joke database. "I'll try that joke again some other time."

Minutes later, Palmer ran back to them and reached out to help carry 5 again, but was turned down. 5 smiled in gratitude as the amborgs faced the transports.

"Hey guys," Palmer said optimistically. When he saw 917, he uttered a quick greeting. "The three legged race is over. We loaded most of us onto the first transport and 5 can ride in the other one without exceeding the weight limit. If you're ok with running, 117 and... Nine seventeen can escort us and we'll have you back at the F.O.B. safe and sound."

Palmer caught himself, looking at 917 apologetically.

"Sorry, I assume you prefer nine one seven?"

917's eyes widened in surprise. He gave Palmer a pleased smile. He eagerly glanced at 117 and 5.

"I like him," he declared. "A new friend of yours?"

"Yeah," 5 nodded.

Palmer appeared flattered, flashing a light smile. It was replaced with confusion when he realized that the amborgs weren't moving to the transports. They remained in place.

"Actually, lieutenant," 117 shook his head. "That won't be necessary. We are remaining behind to finish another important objective."

"You can't possibly stay out here!"

Palmer's protests were cut short when one of the soldiers approached them, speaking urgently.

"Sir! Sorry to interrupt but we have to leave now! Reports are saying this area is about to get overrun! Our drones are picking up heavy enemy contacts! Too many incoming. We're sitting ducks. We need to evac!"

"Go!" 5 said urgently. "We will stay behind and distract them."

"Are you sure?" Palmer eyed 5's leg with concern.

"I am still combat ready," 5 winked. He held up his leg. "This does make a great club, and I'm not alone this time."

"They may have injured and wounded us when we were by ourselves," 117 declared, "but now we can take the fight to them."

After a few moments, Palmer looked at each of them and conceded, then turned to the other soldiers on the perimeter.

"Fall back!" he commanded.

Like clockwork, those remaining lowered their weapons and quickly boarded the transports. Palmer, being one of the ranking officers, also moved to climb in, making sure he was the last one aboard. Just before he ducked inside and shut the door, he nodded in thanks to the amborgs.

"Good luck!" he called out.

917 gave the army transports a thumbs-up as the door slammed shut. Once secure, the drivers revved their engines and the vehicles drove off. 117, 5, and 917 were left behind. When the transports were out of sight, the three of them readied a defensive formation.

"Just so you know," 5 warned, "based on the number of enemies I am detecting, this is exactly how they cornered me. When I tried fighting them off, in the chaos, one of them managed to get close enough to knife me."

117 and 5 shifted around so they were back-to-back. 917 walked up to one side and they arranged themselves in a triangle formation.

"Well, like you told lieutenant Palmer," 117 looked down and discovered that there was a rifle in the rubble. "You aren't alone this time."

917 glanced down and noticed the same rifle lying there. Both of them scanned it, seeing that it still had ammunition and was functional. 917 raised his right hand face-down and opened his palm. A radiant blue light

shown as a magnet in his hand activated, drawing the rifle up from the ground. Catching it effortlessly, he passed it to 117.

"You take this," he said.

"But you're unarmed," 117 replied. "Will you be ok?"

"Yeah," 917 grinned. "I think the bad guys need a nice close-up meeting with my fists."

117 nodded as he aimed his rifle around at a 180 degree angle. With his field of view set, he scoped the area in front of him while the other two amborgs focused on their sides.

"Enormous group of hostiles detected. They are surrounding us," he reported. "I can hear some assembling in the nearby streets. And the ones I can see moving between each building and sneaking around the rubble are definitely carrying knives. Confirmed Mandy?"

"Got it David," she replied. "I'm coordinating with the other techs and we are now presenting to you data on the Splatter-Bugs' locations. Uhh, wait a minute..."

"What's wrong?" 117 asked.

"David... I don't think it's just them. Can you ask 917 and 5 where they were when they got ambushed?"

117 snuck glances at the other two amborgs, who were watching their respective sides of their triangle formation.

"5? 917?" 117 spoke quickly. "Where exactly were you when you were attacked?"

"Meilin was watching my back when I did some recon in an eight story warehouse. Turns out, I accidentally discovered it was a hideout for the West Coast Slugs."

"WCS?" 5 asked. "Lucky. I got ambushed by Double Helix."

"Wait," 117's eyes widened. "The Splatter-Bugs, DH, and WCS are all prominent gangs in this area. They all have weapons capable of killing us?"

"Oh, I am so glad I don't work in the field," Mandy said with a shudder in her voice.

"Mandy?" 117 gulped. "5, 917... I would like to formally declare that my confidence is wavering."

"Come on," 5 scoffed. "This is not the worst thing I've been through."

"Name one other time," 917 countered.

"Ok, nothing's really coming to mind..." 5 chuckled nervously. "But seriously, how did you get ambushed by WCS? Those gang members are nothing but crazy teenage stoners."

"Correction," 917 stated. "Teenage stoners with crazy adrenaline highs that lose all sense of themselves. How did you get taken down by

Double Helix? You always told us those guys were a small-time motorcycle club. Why did they target you?"

"Let's just say we might have a history."

"Both of you," 117 cleared his throat. "Focus please? Do you hear that?"

They could faintly hear the sounds of celebration in the distance, a chorus of whoops and cheers ringing out. The roar of engines soon followed, indicating that a large group of motorcycles were rapidly approaching their position.

"I guess we're about to become extremely popular," 5 sighed.

"Meilin is opening lines to your technicians," 917 declared. "We need to coordinate a defense."

"Can we do this?" 117 asked.

"Hey," Mandy's voice spoke in the back of his mind. "David, are you ok?"

"I'm just..."

117 turned to look at 5.

"5, could you take over?"

"If both my legs were attached and I had full mobility, maybe," 5 glanced towards 117. "What's up?"

117 ignored 5's question and turned to 917.

"917, perhaps you could...?"

917's response was quick and encouraging.

"Uh, sure. Of course. But... what's the matter?"

117 took his left hand off the rifle and felt the place on his stomach where he had been stabbed.

"I uh... I feel..."

"Scared?" Mandy asked. "It's ok, David. I am too. But we need to focus! Bad guys are coming in and they're not going to let us have a spare moment to think about our feelings."

"This was a mistake," 117's breathing quickened as he tried to inhale and exhale.

"You admitted yourself out of the hospital a little too soon," 917 stated. "Alright, let me take this one then. 117, you use that rifle and the last of the ammo to cover us. I'll focus on my side but I'll watch both of your backs. 5, you be the bait and draw them in."

"Sure... is it because I'm stationary?"

"Precisely."

117 wasn't fully in the right headspace to lead the three of them. The knife wound from his grandfather still lingered, and pushing himself could lead to even more complications. 5 was dealing with his own limitations,

concentrating on keeping his balance on one leg. He was still able to defend himself, but only from a fixed position. This meant that, despite his own injured arm, 917 would need to take charge as they braced for the fight ahead.

"Listen," 917 said to them, "they got the drop on us because we were alone. Now I got both of you here with me. The odds are much better if we coordinate everything as a team."

"Data confirmed," 5 stated. "All three of us are more or less in one piece. Synchronizing with 117 and 917's neural link... complete. I'm ready for this."

"It isn't exactly a textbook ambush," 117 remarked. "This is just unfair bullying."

"Three of us against all of them?" 917 asked sarcastically.

"Yes," 117 nodded. He took a deep breath and focused on what Mandy had said to him earlier. They were about to go against three gangs that would show no mercy. He gulped and steadied his hands as he took aim. "That's what makes it fair."

"There's the 117 I know," 917 replied.

The first Splatter-Bug appeared ten meters away and let out a whooping cry, a signal to attack. In response, a throng of them surged forward, ready to strike. On 917's side, the gang members of West Coast Slugs added to the noise with adrenaline-fueled cheers and screams of their own. On 5's side, motorcycles sped up, revving their engines as they sped into the chaos.

"If we could just fly upwards," 917 sighed, "it'd be funny if they all just collided into each other."

"So, 117, are you going to ask them to surrender?" 5 asked in a serious tone.

"No," 117 replied. "I really shouldn't have shared that story..."

"Unfortunately," 5 chuckled, "it's available for us to read in your after-action report. Very noble trying to ask for their surrender in sign language."

"This time," 117 gritted his teeth and prepared his stance, "I will fight first. We just need to grab my grandfather's attention. If we live, then perhaps he'll find us."

"How do you know he'll even show up?" 917 asked. "Why would he?"

"I don't think he would have left the area," 117 answered. "But I don't fully know. Both of you have been searching for him since I was stabbed. My guess is, he chooses when he wants to appear. So, I don't know if my presence will change anything."

"You decided to break out of the hospital without allowing yourself to heal completely without confirming if your objective was going to be here?" 917 asked. "Those are Meilin's words, not mine, by the way. I am inclined to agree with her that this is suicide."

"David," Mandy spoke in the back of 117's head. "You can tell Johnny and Jack that what he just said is pretty spot-on."

"Well," 117 sighed, "it's too late now."

"And if we die?" 917 grumbled.

Several bullets pelted them as several gunshots rang out from the incoming attackers. 117 began to take aim, preparing to return fire.

"Take as many as you can with you."

"I guess if we're going to be the first amborgs in history to die... we might as well do it in chaotic combat," 917 said shakily. "117, if we make it through this, you're the team leader on the next assignment."

"Noted," 117 found his first target and pulled the trigger.

The first person went down instantly. With Mandy's assistance, 117 focused on the nearest enemy, and she marked them on his screen with a red silhouette outline.

Most of the Splatter-Bugs charging at him brandished the same type of knife that he had been stabbed with yesterday. The large number of them—more than a dozen—made it all the more intimidating.

Some Splatter-Bugs took to the high ground or emerged from windows, unleashing a barrage of fire at the trio of amborgs. At first, their attempts appeared ineffective. That is, until 117 suddenly felt a relentless hail of bullets pelting him in the head. While none of the shots inflicted any real harm, the sheer force of the automatic fire created significant vibrations. The Splatter-Bugs, attacking from afar, weren't aiming to kill; instead, they aimed to distract so the ones wielding knives could close in to finish them off. This was a new tactic, completely different from their usual M.O.

Letting out their crazy war-cries, the knife-wielders charged ahead. As they closed in, they launched their attacks. 5, using his severed leg as a baseball bat, sent several gang members sprawling or unconscious. Despite resembling the Pixar lamp, he balanced on his one good leg, swinging fiercely at anyone who dared to approach. Meanwhile, 917 unleashed a flurry of punches and kicks, while 117 fired off the last rounds from his rifle.

For a few minutes, this was how they held their ground. LTO knives and the lifeless forms of gang members from each group littered the street around them. 5 and 917 protected 117 as best as they could, stopping anyone that came within reach. If anyone with a weapon or firearm got too close, they would steal their guns and pass them to 117. Out of the three of them, 117 had the best accuracy.

Eventually, after taking down at least 41 thugs, they finally grasped the current conditions of the fight. No gang member armed with a handheld gun or rifle dared to approach after they figured out that 117 was stealing their ammo and weapons while systematically taking out their long-range fighters.

117 soon found himself down to his last magazine. The gang members carrying them were staying out of reach, and the others were unable to retrieve any more. Now, he had no choice but to help 917 and 5 in close-quarters combat. He fired off 5 rounds, each one finding its mark. But just as he aimed for a sixth, the rifle jammed.

This was the signal that they had to switch it up. Without a long-range weapon in their arsenal, he needed to adapt his role in the fight. Fortunately, with other amborgs close by, he was able to transmit his plan without alerting the remaining enemies.

"Weapon gone," he reported to 5 and 917. "I'm bringing the fight to them."

917 and 5 acknowledged this and the triangle formation continued fighting.

With the jammed rifle, 117 quickly hit the release and ripped the magazine out. He tossed the rifle into the air and, with his other hand, threw the magazine at another gangster. It smacked the man in the face with so much force that he was knocked over, collapsing in a heap on the ground. 117 then caught the empty rifle and whirled it around, wielding it as a melee weapon. Imitating 5, 117 began swinging it, swatting at anyone who was unfortunate enough to get too close.

The three of them fought hard, continuing to battle against what seemed to be an endless swarm. They had predicted that after creating so many casualties, they would scare away the rest. Unfortunately, they were completely wrong.

"I think. That all the. Video games we play," 917 said in between punching and wrestling attackers. Despite his ferocity, they were totally on the defensive. "Are wrong! Normally. At this point! They start running for the hills!"

"I think that went. Out the window... oof! Maybe... 36 bad guys ago?" 5 called out as he smacked someone upside the head with his leg in a golf swing.

"I believe. Uh. 5? 917? I am. Not. Not feeling well."

A moment later, it became clear that things were beginning to go south. 117's rifle had been torn apart after engaging with a multitude of enemies. Without hesitation, 5 signaled to 117, who acknowledged it right away.

117 threw what was left of the rifle over the back of his shoulder. 5 caught it easily and passed him his leg in exchange, giving each other a different advantage. The motorcyclists attempting to target 5 were slowly moving around their position like wolves circling their prey. On 117's side, there were more Splatter-Bugs attempting to move in to stab him, which was what prompted the decision to swap weapons.

5 ripped the barrel off the rifle and chucked it at someone's head with great accuracy. There was a comedic "plink" as the gang member fell off his bike, followed by a tremendous crash. Everyone riding behind him had to break formation to avoid driving into the wreckage. He lifted the rest of the rifle over his head with his right arm and brought it down to the ground, smashing it in half. A piece of it was sent flying off from the intense force, and with his left hand, 5 picked it up and threw it towards another motorcycle passing in front of him. It caught on the front wheel, tearing it apart and resulting in another violent crash. With the other half of the rifle, 5 took aim again and hurled it at another rider. 5 had managed to disrupt their momentum easily as the Double Helix formation was broken. It would take a minute for them to regroup, which would give 5 a few seconds to take an extremely short reprieve.

It felt bizarre for 117 to use 5's severed leg as a weapon against the enemy. However, after a few vigorous swings, he realized it was not only delivering physical blows but also inflicting psychological damage, causing the charge of the remaining gang members to start to dwindle.

While 117 took on the Splatter-Bugs, 917 dealt with the West Coast Slugs. One of the gang members came at him with a knife, but 917 was ready. He blocked the strike, captured the knife in his left hand, and unleashed a series of blows to the Slug's head with his right. With a powerful kick, he sent the thug sprawling, then snatched up one of the LTO knives and began slashing back.

After a few more bouts and clashes with the diminishing ranks of the combined force of gang members, 117, 917 and 5 looked around and realized it was over. Their time logs indicated it had been 17 minutes since the battle started. 117 took a deep breath, feeling the weight of fatigue settle into his muscles. The fight felt as though it went on for an eternity, exhausting and never ending. The ground was littered with bodies, some dead and others unconscious. As the amborgs returned to a passive state, they scanned their surroundings, inspecting their handiwork—except for 5, who was still staggering on one leg.

"How many was that? In total?" 5 looked around as he held onto his leg. They all surveyed the area, searching for any other signs of movement. "What's your count? I need to double check."

"I counted 104," 117 said. "In total."

"Any of them alive?" 917 asked. "I'll ask Meilin to scan for life signs."

"I'll do it too," Mandy spoke up. "Wow..."

"Are you ok, Mandy?" 117 asked privately on their own channel.

"That was really intense," Mandy replied shakily. "I know that when we first started working together, I would get front-row seats to the action... but that was so much more than I was expecting... and there were three of you."

117 suddenly looked up and spotted something. He reached out his hand to 917, signaling for assistance. In response, 117 felt him put a small metallic object in his extended palm. It was the knife that 917 had borrowed from the enemy.

"Hang on a moment."

117 leaned back slightly, tilting his head up, and checked the wind. He took careful aim as he calculated the angle, direction, and energy he needed. Once his calculations were set, he threw his knife into the distance. Moments later, they all heard someone scream.

"Correction. 105."

"Showoff," 5 chuckled.

"Not bad," 917 complimented.

"Anyway, my tech and I agree with 117. We have the same count."

After 5 confirmed the total, 917 expressed his agreement with a firm nod.

"An amazing number," 5 noted, "but there's a chance that we only dented a small fraction, since there are hundreds more in each gang."

"Hopefully, it was enough to send a statement," 917 sighed.

"There is one thing that makes me nervous," 117 said as he scanned the area again. "It is strange that they pressed their attack when they had no hope. Why bother continuing to fight when this is the result?"

"When you give powerful weapons to highly motivated people, then retreat is no longer an option. They won't stop. Not until they feel the playing field is in their favor."

117 and 917 both whirled around. 5 could only turn his head to look in the direction they faced. As the two Second Group amborgs readied themselves, 5 let out a sigh and hopped a few times to properly turn around.

"I got to say, you boys did a really impressive job."

117 clenched his fists as he locked eyes with the newcomer. Immediately recognizing the voice, a wave of anger washed over him. As his facial recognition software activated, it confirmed the identity of the person he had seen in yesterday's footage.

"You!" he stated.

"I'm guessing that's him," 917 muttered.

117 nodded. Everyone stood in place as they faced the hooded old man.

"So that's the one?" Mandy stated on their private channel.

"It is," 117 privately transmitted back.

The old man smiled at them.

"Here's the thing David," he said. "When you give free-to-play players the right equipment to take down the boss, they will keep using that premium subscription and gifts to keep fighting. Also, most of them are hopped up on drugs and crazy half the time."

"Uh..." 917 glanced at everyone skeptically. "Was that a videogame analogy?"

The old man ignored his comment as he continued his explanation.

"I did warn you. Who knows what would have happened if I wasn't there last night? Your 'brothers' or any of the other amborgs would have lost their lives by now. Even you might have calculated that the situation had escalated to a terrifying degree."

"How was stabbing me your best way of informing me of... all of this?" 117 asked aggressively while he gestured to the entire area. "You could have just said so."

"Well, I figured," the old man sighed, "I doubt you would have believed me if I came forward in the first place. Have you ever tried to warn people about a threat? Most of the time, they refuse to accept it and don't take you seriously."

"Actually..." 5 raised his hand and chuckled nervously. "I do know how that feels."

117 turned to glare at 5.

"But you know, 117 getting stabbed," 5 quickly amended his statement with an apologetic smile. "Still bad."

"By the time you figured out the truth in those... calculations, I probably couldn't imagine what would have happened. You needed to face the reality of it, and I felt it was best to use a reasonable show of force."

"By stabbing your... grandson?" 917 asked.

"He's clearly not dead," the man indicated to 117, which only intensified his anger.

"You're clearly delusional!" 117 snapped.

"Hey, I wanted you to feel scared. Enough to the point where you'd become furious and motivated to seek out the truth. Don't underestimate the fear of death. I made sure that you would stay alive so that you could realize that you're not invincible! The enemy would have shown less mercy."

117, still suspicious, glared at the hooded man, trying to comprehend what he had just said.

"Maybe I believe you," he said. "But you better answer my questions and get to the point now."

"Done," the old man smirked. "But lower your fists, ok? I come in peace. It's not worth getting beat up again."

"This time, I have my friends."

"Oh, come now," the man chuckled. "Surely you've realized that I brought my friends too."

More hooded figures appeared silently behind him. 117 felt a gentle tap on his shoulder from 917, causing the amborgs to turn their heads. As if by magic, they were surrounded again. The old man's hooded gang had materialized like ghosts.

"I think we should surrender," 5 held up his hands, his leg still in one of them.

Several of the hooded people spotted his leg and began to murmur amongst themselves.

"Whoa," the old man exclaimed. "They sure did a number on you, didn't they?"

"We can probably stick with 'I was one of the amborgs who found out too late,'" 5 said cheekily. "A lucky hit from an ambush."

"We can fix that."

As the old man approached, 117 held up his hands, halting everyone in their tracks.

"Are you really my grandfather?"

Everyone heard the question loud and clear. The hooded figures standing directly behind the old man remained still, their expressions stoic. Out of the corner of his eye, 117 noticed other hooded figures beginning to murmur amongst themselves. He caught snippets of astonished comments and reactions to his question, revealing that not everyone was aware of this particular situation.

"Yes, I am," the old man nodded.

917 and 5 stared quietly as more murmurs and shocked reactions spread among the hooded gang members. The lie detector that the amborgs had wasn't going off. The statement was true.

"I have more questions," 117 spoke softly.

"All right boy," 117's grandfather said after pondering it for a few moments. "Smart decision. It's time you learned about what's happening underground. There are many weapons being circulated amongst all the gangs. Not just here but everywhere. I don't know who it is, which means they have a heavily secured network that's much stronger than my own. With the amborgs to help us, however, we may be able to save L.A. and possibly the whole country from total chaos and destruction. We won't be able to stop the initial thing from happening. It's already too late, but we can still do what we can to build a dam before the flood arrives. Now let's get moving."

117 pulled 5's arm around his shoulder again. 917 took a position on his other side. The two of them would keep him in the center to better protect him.

"You take point," 117 said to the old man.

The old man laughed.

"Still don't trust me?" he smirked.

"Negative."

"Well, you'll have to, starting now," the old man sighed. "Come on. I know a place where we can shelter. You also might want to tell Mandy to stay on the line and hold off on the next bathroom break. I really would rather not repeat any important information."

"How do you know her name?" 117 asked suspiciously, stopping suddenly.

5 and 917 glanced from him to his grandfather with matching looks of concern.

"I have ways. By the way, I don't think you knew about this but that lieutenant Palmer, the officer and that charming man you saved? That was Mandy's fiancée you just saved. Thought you should know. But it looks like that blank expression on your quiet and obvious face tells me that you didn't know."

117 blinked. He didn't recall showing any indication of changing the expression on his face. Somehow, this old man was reading him just like a children's book.

"How do you know this?" he asked. "The lieutenant referred to that lady in his photo as Ellie."

"Why didn't you just do facial recognition on the photo when you looked at it?"

"I was being polite and respecting his privacy," 117 replied casually. "It is not usually our business to do facial recognition scans on personal property of civilians or military personnel."

"But you have high access to records at A.I. Industries, right?" 117's grandpa asked with a hopeful look. "You would have seen that her full name is Mandy Elizabeth Walker."

917 looked at 117.

"Is that Mandy's actual middle name?" he asked.

117 didn't get a chance to answer.

"Ok seriously..."

117 heard Mandy begin to freak out.

"I don't care if he says he's your grandpa David," she said. "But he's starting to scare the living daylights out of me..."

117 didn't reply. His grandfather stared back at him, his smile eventually fading.

"Let me guess," he said, stroking his beard. "You haven't bothered to even look at your own technician's file."

"To do so would breach a basic level of privacy and trust," 117 responded harshly. "We are programmed..."

"I get it," the old man sighed. "You kids have basic moral and ethics programming. Man, that just sucks the fun out of everything. But you're going to have to grow out of that sometime."

The old man turned to lead them away.

"David, you wanted answers, and you're going to get them," he said as he led the large party up the street and into an alleyway. "In return, I need your help along with Kendrick and the other amborgs. Let me introduce you to my own security group. You thought you were the only group fighting to protect the world? We're not as strong or fast as you kids but we get the job done at the end of the day."

CHAPTER 9

Cities Underneath

The Underground
LA Isolated Survival Refuge: The Forgotten Labyrinth
1 Hour Later

"You come from a world with rules, of laws. This place is different from all that."

"You really do like classic video games and tv shows."

117's grandfather laughed at 917's response.

"I'll admit," he called back to them as he turned right and led them around a dimly lit hall, "it sure is nice to know that someone gets my references."

"917..." 117 grumbled.

"What?" 917 shrugged as they continued at a leisure pace. Eventually, they began to descend at a downward angle. "He's quoting Fallout. He's very well-versed in history."

"So are we..." 5 spoke up from behind them.

"Yeah, but, 117... No one really likes listening to us talk about this kind of stuff. It tends to put a lot of people to sleep."

5 had been provided a hoverchair, and it turned out to be surprisingly durable, easily lifting him a few feet off the ground despite his full weight. He felt a wave of relief as he settled into the seat and took control of the joystick, granting him the ability to follow 117's grandfather and his team of vigilantes down a really complex labyrinth. At least they didn't have to carry him.

To pass the time, there was a bit of small talk going on, much to 117's annoyance. On the other hand, 5 and 917 were quite interested in the ongoing chat. His grandfather appeared pretty laid-back, behaving as if he'd never stabbed 117 at all.

"You know, my team and I were watching you," the old man turned, beaming at each of them. When his eyes met 117, he awkwardly averted his gaze and faced forward again. "You all have some good skills. Could be better, but you do live up to your reputation."

"Thanks," 5 smiled.

"But you Second Group boys..."

917 glanced at 117, who remained quiet. His smile faded when 117's grandfather's tone turned slightly judgemental.

"You two look so... young," he commented. "Inexperienced."

"But that's inaccurate," 917 stated. "We've been on several missions. Every amborg of the Second Group..."

"Weak," the old man interrupted. "You're all weak."

117 felt a sharp sting from his wound as he glared angrily at his grandfather. He took notice and eyed 117 with interest. The entire group paused to see what would happen next.

"Touched a nerve, eh?" he chuckled. "Looks like your emotions aren't totally gone."

117 advanced with a menacing stride, but 917 quickly raised his hand, placing it firmly against his chest. 117 glared at him fiercely, yet 917's resolute shake of the head communicated a clear message: it was better to avoid further conflict.

"If I might ask," 917 turned away from 117, speaking calmly. "What do you mean?"

"Look, you kids are good fighters," the old man replied, "but you're too by-the-books. Once they all learn about any of your weaknesses, they'll exploit you."

"What weaknesses?" 117 muttered.

"For starters," his grandpa looked down at 117's stomach, "you got stabbed. A young amborg, in his prime, was stabbed by an old man."

"Hey."

917 removed his hand from 117's chest and pointed back at him with his thumb. The old man lifted his eyebrows, appearing surprised by 917's unexpected display of anger.

"I admit that when we received the news that 117 was stabbed, I was shocked," 917 stated. "Could you please elaborate your thoughts clearly? You have been making him uncomfortable this entire time."

The tunnel system that they were in was not on any of their known maps or charts. As they ventured deeper, the amborgs diligently documented every twist and turn, measuring the distances of each hallway they passed through.

"Look," 917 said, calmly looking between the old man and 117. "We came down here with you because you said you were going to give him answers to his questions. You can carry a decent conversation, but how do we know that you're not leading us to a trap?"

"Because if there was another trap," the old man rolled his eyes, "then the entirety of A.I. Industries and law enforcement would already be after us."

The old man forged ahead, a signal to the rest of his followers to continue on. The ones at the back began urging the amborgs to start moving, so they did.

"Besides," he informed them in a kind tone, "I already know that you three left homing beacons when we stepped through the entrance down here. You've also been discreetly leaving markings on the walls. I know that you already called for backup. You want them to find you."

"Well, can you blame us?" 5 grinned cheekily. "It is a little creepy following a bunch of people that look like cultists underground to a dark and gloomy place."

"Actually, I thought they looked like the characters from Assassin's Creed," 917 chuckled. "117, your grandfather looks a bit like an older version of Ezio."

"I haven't played that game yet," 117 grumbled.

The group pressed on, trailing behind the hooded figures as they wound their way through the shadowy passage. After several more minutes of maneuvering through the dimly lit corridor, they reached an enormous door marked with faded writing.

"What's it say?" 5 asked 917, unable to see over everyone's shoulders.

"The New Vernon shelter," 917 read. After a brief moment of contemplation, he looked at 117's grandfather. "So gramps, is this a fallout bunker?"

"You can call me Mark," the old man replied casually. "Seriously, call me Mark. 'Old man' makes me feel really old."

"That's not happening," 117 lowered the volume on his bracelet, delivering his response bitterly.

"Er," 917 stammered.

Two of Mark's followers approached an ancient keypad. Instead of pressing the buttons, they tore the panel off and reached into the mechanism. While they worked to unlock the door, 917 fixed his gaze on 5. Both amborgs shrugged and turned to 117, their expressions filled with unease.

"Grandpa... Mark?" 5 raised a hand.

The old man flinched slightly. Under his hood, they saw his eye twitch at the mention of his name.

"Ok, that still feels weird but I'll allow it," he mumbled. He tilted his head up and looked at 5. "Yes?"

"Is this place an old shelter from the third world war?" he asked.

Mark perked up at 5's question, appearing excited as a spark ignited from the panel where his two followers were busy. Just then, a low rumble echoed in the background, signaling the machinery powering up as the door slowly creaked open.

"Remember what I said about where you come from?" he smiled. "A world with rules and laws? Well, this is my world. Nice and hidden away."

917 and 117 noticed 5 bouncing eagerly in his chair. He leaned in, covering his mouth with a hand as if he were about to reveal a closely guarded secret. With a playful wink, they saw his bracelet light up. Each time he spoke, his words danced like a cheerful light show.

"That's not a no," 5 whispered excitedly to them. "This is going to be amazing!"

When the door was open, everyone began to move inside. 117 hesitated, but he knew that his grandfather's guards were going to urge him to step through. He trailed after 5, who zoomed ahead in his hoverchair, his attention drawn to the vibrant neon lights reflecting off 917's jacket as they passed through the massive door. He sensed his grandfather's watchful gaze but resisted the urge to glance back.

His mind was racing as he tried to process a whirlwind of emotions rushing through him. Had this been a mistake? Did he rush into this too soon?

He couldn't talk to Mandy. None of them could. When they began their descent into the tunnels, his grandpa had warned them that there was no signal down there and that their connection to A.I. Industries would be blocked. Virtually cut off, 117 was left without Mandy's voice or the guidance he needed from her. 917 and 5 were in the same boat and yet, they appeared to be handling the situation with far less anxiety than he was experiencing.

"Whoa," 917 exclaimed, looking upwards. "117! This is so cool!"

As 117 listened to his fellow amborg's awestruck tone, he shifted his eyes up. When he took in what he saw, his jaw dropped slightly.

"There's a whole city under here," 5 remarked. "All these years and we never knew."

It was evident that a significant amount of resources, time, and effort went into the design and construction of this place. It was a massive hall, appearing several hundred feet across and reaching a height of at least 100 feet, its vaulted ceilings held up by massive pillars. The entire place was lit with what looked like old and rundown chandeliers. Narrow streets and walkways separated each dwelling, which resembled small, makeshift concrete bunkers.

"It's the year 2127 and we just discovered the Great Halls of Moria?" 917 exclaimed excitedly.

"You like it?"

117 nodded, forgetting his anger from earlier. Mark laughed as he walked ahead of them.

"Well, don't just stand there gawking," he said, motioning for them to follow. "I'm going to give you boys a proper welcome."

A few kids ran by waving enthusiastically, but kept their eyes fixed on the amborgs, likely mesmerized by their glowing uniforms. Aside from a few people wearing the same hooded cloaks as Mark's guards, many civilians were dressed in casual clothing. They didn't look like soldiers at all, instead, they appeared clean and unscathed by the violence happening above.,

"There were always rumors about places like these," 5 said with a huge grin on his face. "I can't wait to tell the others!"

"Rumors?" 117 asked.

"Yeah, underground communities!" 5 nodded. "When I was growing up, I heard these stories about people that felt that humanity's survival was at risk, so they went underground, literally. This must be one of those places!"

"Someone who knows their history," Mark grinned, "or, the dark shadows of our planet's history."

"It's an isolated community?" 117 asked. Then his eyes widened. "Wait, are we allowed to even be here?"

"Well, they did permit me and my vigilantes to establish a base here for whenever we needed to lay low," Mark stated. "David... son..."

117 looked at the old man as he pulled back his hood. Now that his face was fully visible, he took note of his features. There were a few gray strands in his beard, yet his brown hair appeared strikingly vibrant. It dawned on him that his grandfather had intentionally colored his hair to seem younger.

"Ready to talk?" he asked, extending his hand.

117's face fell slightly. He didn't know what to say.

"Hey, you," Mark turned to 917. "917, right?"

"Yes?" 917 raised an eyebrow.

"I thought that he had questions," Mark pointed at 117. "Why's he so quiet?"

"If I had to venture a guess," 917 answered politely, "I'd say that 117 is taking in a lot of information and trying to process it. After all, your first meeting was a rather violent one."

917 then turned and stepped closer to 117, resting a gentle hand on his right shoulder. 117 looked up to meet his friend's eyes.

"If you need some time alone, collect your thoughts, or ponder your questions," he said, "I could always speak to your grandfather for you."

117 contemplated it for a moment, but shook his head. Focusing, he nodded with a determined look in his eyes.

"It's ok," he said as 917 lowered his arm. He glanced at 5, who was giving him a reassuring smile. "I want to try. Could you both perhaps stick close?"

"Not like we've got anywhere else to be," 5 laughed. Then he paused and glanced down at his detached leg. "Actually, if anyone here could help me out with this, I'd be really grateful. Kinda want to stand up again on my own."

Mark turned around and eyed one of his vigilantes. Silently, he nodded, acknowledging his nonverbal orders. The amborgs stood there, watching with curiosity as the stranger strode ahead, 5 trailing closely behind.

"Silent and mysterious," 5 stated cautiously. "If you guys hear me scream, come get me."

Mark motioned for 917 and 117 to follow. They came up on a large table sitting on what appeared to be someone's front porch. A few of the hooded vigilantes lounged nearby, and one of them gestured for 5 to climb up onto the table. He eagerly hopped on, and someone provided him with a pillow to lie down on.

Mark strolled across the narrow street to grab a lawn chair and took a seat. 117 and 917 watched questionably, while Mark's guards quietly withdrew, vanishing from sight.

"This way, you can watch him from a short distance," the old man explained.

"117," 917 said as the two of them grabbed their own chairs. "Do you want to go first or should I? My questions probably aren't relevant, but if you need some time..."

117 let out a sigh and nodded. Mark and 917 both exchanged a glance. To break the tension, 917 asked his first question.

"What is this place? Who are all of these people?"

"This?" Mark gestured up towards the ceiling. "It's a forgotten relic. Someone's last attempt to save humanity before we destroyed it."

"But we didn't," 917 declared.

"Son..." Mark crossed his arms and exhaled slowly. He shook his head mournfully, his eyes downcast. "If only I could believe you. Everytime someone says that..."

The old man shifted his gaze to observe the inhabitants of this hidden community. His hooded vigilantes were stationed throughout, keeping a watchful eye on everyone, guarding and protecting them. Some of them participated in various activities, a few with their hoods on and others without, revealing a very different side to them.

"...it makes me think about all the friends that I wish were still with me today."

"Sir," 917 spoke softly as his face fell. "Were you a soldier? In World War 3?"

"I'm a survivor," Mark replied. "Just like everyone else here."

"How did you find this place?" 917 asked.

"Fell down a rabbit hole," Mark replied cheekily.

117 and 917 exchanged confused glances before turning to look at Mark again.

"This is New Vernon," Mark answered in a serious tone. "It's an underground safe haven where I've set up one of my bases of operation."

"This is an old underground city," 917 exclaimed. "Wasn't this established decades ago in the events of total annihilation on the surface? It should have been abandoned!"

117 was curious how 917, someone who was very close in age to him, was so familiar with this particular part of history. Yet, he chose to remain silent while his grandfather laughed and began to respond.

"There are many of these places all across the country. Hell, the whole world for that matter. This is one of the few that time has forgotten about... and my organization keeps it safe. We've taken measures to ensure it remains impenetrable."

"And these people haven't seen the surface before?"

"I don't think there are many left here that can remember," Mark answered. "A lot of the younger folks here don't really know that there's a bigger world outside of these walls."

A flurry of footsteps grabbed everyone's attention, and they turned to see a couple of vigilantes approaching them. 117 noticed they were carrying a couple of small tables, which they set down near their seats. A few other people appeared with pitchers of water and plates of what looked like snacks. Mark thanked them and began to pour himself a glass of water while 117 and 917 hesitated. They exchanged wary glances, eyeing the snacks skeptically as if they were possibly poisoned.

"This place is part of the Los Angeles Underground. There's about 10 of them in the Pacific Northwest. Six were abandoned when the world didn't nuke itself out of existence but somehow... four didn't get that memo. I'll be honest with you, David. I really did set up a base under the city just so I could say cool stuff like that."

917 snickered, but 117 stayed silent, sitting stiffly.

"It is pretty cool to hear something like that," 917 replied.

117 transmitted a private text message to him.

Perhaps you'd like to have him as your grandfather? he wrote with a stoic expression.

917 kept smiling courteously, but 117 noticed the discomfort as he shifted in his seat.

Oh come on, 917 responded, ***you need to say something to him. It's the only way you can move past your problems.***

Unfortunately, because Mark wasn't included in their private text channel, he continued talking, not realizing that they were only partially paying attention.

"During a skirmish, my unit was ambushed, and I collapsed somewhere near the entrance to the tunnel system," he said. "Someone must have dragged me all the way here. When I woke up, I was being patched up. I discovered that this place is filled with numerous small bunkers designed for VIPs and rich families. New Vernon was sponsored by a rather generous tycoon who relocated many people here. I was one of the few outsiders they chose to take in, so... once I recovered, I decided to form my own group of vigilantes."

"You protect them?" 917 concluded.

"They saved my life," Mark nodded. "They let me stay here whenever and however long I like. Least I can do."

917 turned to 117. Instead of a private text, he spoke aloud.

"I think I'm starting to like the guy."

Mark beamed. He cautiously glanced at 117 with a hopeful look, but there was no kind reciprocation.

He stabbed me, 117 texted a reminder.

Agh, 917 responded while maintaining a straight face, ***I don't know if I like being torn between the two of you...***

"Anyway," Mark awkwardly looked back out towards the people of the underground community. "As you can see, this place is a little worn out, but it still serves as a suitable home for them. They can continue to stay here and flourish for decades despite all the destruction and turmoil raging above."

"Why did they decide to stay here?"

"Well, the war ended," Mark answered. "Everyone celebrated and most of the communities were shut down as people returned to the surface. In my travels and discoveries of these other underground shelters, I've met people who don't want to go back up."

917 turned and gestured toward another one of the hooded vigilantes standing guard on the roof of a nearby bunker.

"So, how did you find all of these people? Kinda looks like you've got quite an army here."

"I appreciate you not using the word 'mercenary' but in reality, that's technically what we are."

Mark's eyes sparkled with admiration as he glanced over at the vigilantes that were helping 5 reattach his leg. 5 was giving them instructions as they attempted to make repairs.

"I have drones that guard the entrances to the labyrinth," he said. "Everyone else is just like you kids. I've been following the same path as Dr. Kendrick with the amborgs—taking in all the poor bastards out there and enjoying my itsy bitsy nations of control to maintain security around the world. Or in this case, below it."

117 stared at him silently. There was no way that he was going to believe that his grandfather, that this old man, was the same as Dr. Kendrick. How could he even sit there and try to make that comparison?

"So," he breathed, speaking in a raspy voice, "Is this where... *cough*... you've been? For years? Did you leave... our family?"

Mark and 917 spun around in surprise when 117 unexpectedly used his real voice. 917's expression shifted to one of concern, while Mark's smile fell. A wave of sorrow clouded his eyes as he looked down.

"Oh... boy," 917 gulped, hunching down slightly.

Mark glanced up and spoke earnestly.

"I promised my son... and my daughter in law... in order to keep you safe."

"What kind of reason is that?!"

117 switched to his bracelet and pointed at his stomach. He winced in pain but continued to stare defiantly at the old man.

"Keep me safe? When the first thing you did was the complete opposite?!"

An uncomfortable silence hung in the air as 117 released his pent-up feelings. Mark stared at 117 quietly for a moment, then glanced over his shoulder and gestured with his hand. 917 and 117 turned to see the vigilantes, who had been working to reattach 5's leg, abruptly stop when they heard 117's raised voice. 5, looking worried, shifted to a sitting position. He propped himself up on his elbows to get a better view of the situation.

"Your dad didn't like what I was getting into."

117 pivoted and gazed sharply at his grandfather, who appeared crestfallen.

"Believe me, it really was the best decision we could make," he let out a defeated sigh. "The police and the military were falling short of what was needed. After the war ended, the streets were plagued with chaos and despair. I survived a horrific war, only to come home and end up participating in more conflicts, whether in politics or on the streets. Eventually, it became too much, and I realized I couldn't just sit back and wait for change. I took matters into my own hands, tried to get involved more directly. But, that meant skirting around rules and dangerous corners, which left a dark stain on the work your parents were doing."

117 watched as his grandfather shifted uncomfortably. His eyes dimmed as the memories of the past surfaced and began to haunt him.

"When you and Serina were children, your dad told me to stay away," he stated grimly. "I agreed because it prevented you from knowing about what we did. But, tell me how you're any different?"

"What?" 117 asked.

"I fight everyday and I do things that no normal human would ever do," Mark said. "Every single day. The amborgs also wake up, go wherever they're needed, and they fight too."

"We are not the same," 117 retorted.

"Don't be so sure," Mark scoffed. "You, 917, and 5 just took on three of LA's top criminal gangs. If you hadn't chosen to be cybernetically enhanced, you wouldn't have been able to take them on. My crew and I all have cybernetic implants as well, but not as fancy or advanced as yours. You might be stronger but you lack the intuition and speed of my entry-level recruits."

917 sputtered at the last words in Mark's sentence. "What are you, like, the manager of superheroes and thugs-for-less incorporated or something? How do you even have access to these cybernetics? The designs are old but they almost seem just like ours."

Mark nodded and smiled at 117.

"You can thank your dad," he said, which made 117 blink in confusion.

"My dad?" 117 asked.

"I still think it's ironic how he disapproved but still chose to support me. Err... indirectly that is," Mark explained. "Even though I couldn't be part of the family, he convinced Dr. Kendrick to provide us with equipment. Most were experimental prototypes, but he also found ways to provide us with blueprints and schematics for early cybernetic tools and devices. To you, it's probably all outdated stuff, but we've been able to hold our own against everything we've faced."

That certainly explained how despite his old age, 117's grandpa was able to overpower him. The amborgs had the best equipment that Dr. Kendrick's research and A.I. Industries had to offer, but it was a past generation's technology that had managed to exploit his weakness and resulted in his failure.

"And... well... God, now that I think about it," Mark suddenly glanced up towards the ceiling and sighed again. "I miss him..."

He looked down and smiled at 117.

"Very much," he finished the statement. "Honestly, it's great to see him again in you. You've grown into a man that strongly resembles him."

"I'm curious," 917 asked. "When was the last time that you saw 117? Or your son?"

Mark glanced at 117 once more. The two amborgs noticed that he appeared happy on the surface, but there was a veil of sadness in his eyes. It was a bittersweet moment; looking at 117 was both heartwarming and damaging to his soul.

"After you were born," he answered softly, "the last time I saw your dad in person... was around then."

117 gulped, feeling a lump in his throat.

"What was he like? What kind of person was he?"

117 struggled to keep his emotions in check. Anger had faded away, replaced by a growing curiosity to learn more about his parents. Sitting right in front of him was the last living link to his past. His grandfather surely held a wealth of knowledge about his mom and dad. Mark smiled sympathetically, clearly willing to share stories about his family.

"Your dad was... a great man... I loved him and I was so proud. I just never got the chance to say it that often to him. The thing is, we weren't enemies. He just didn't want any part of how I took care of things, you know? Our whole family was fervently dedicated to what we believed was best for our world. Your dad and I just... we didn't share the same ideologies, and we just had completely different methods for achieving peace."

117 blinked, his next question flying out the window. He glanced at 917, who shook his head and shrugged.

"Don't judge me," 917 smiled nervously, "but I think that was rather moving."

"Really?" 117 asked.

"117," 917 admitted with a firm nod of his head, "you know if there was a chance, I'd want to know about my parents too. Hell, I'd settle for any memory of them. I think it's lucky that your grandfather is here, alive and willing to... integrate himself in your life."

117 paused as a fresh wave of guilt hit him. The lump in his throat grew tighter. He immediately felt ashamed for not trying to figure this out sooner.

"Well," he sighed. "I have less questions but there is the issue of familial trust."

"117, I am not your biological brother."

117 pivoted to 917, eyes wide with surprise. 917 was looking at him with a rather harsh and stern expression.

"I know," 117 nodded. "We are not related by blood."

"I say this as someone who does consider you to be like a brother to me," 917 rolled his eyes annoyingly. "Because I woke up and became part of a nice group of superhuman teenagers. But can you please... just... get over it?"

117 and Mark both stared at 917, who looked so done.

"We get it," 917 grumbled as he crossed his arms. "He stabbed you."

"Nonlethally," Mark added.

"Exactly!" 917 pointed at Mark while nodding at 117. "Yes, I do agree that using a knife to introduce yourself is ludicrous, but does it have to be repeated consistently?"

117 paused.

"It hurt... a lot," he mumbled.

"Here's an easier solution."

917 suddenly pointed at Mark, which caused the old man to lean back slightly. He looked as though an invisible knife had been thrown in his direction, but remained calm and collected nonetheless.

"Old man!" 917 declared.

"A little rude but I'll allow it," Mark acknowledged him with a nod.

"Whatever," 917 snapped. "Do you apologize for stabbing my friend, David 117?"

Mark nodded vigorously.

"I apologize," he took a deep breath and spoke clearly.

"For?" 917 put strong emphasis on the word.

"For stabbing you," Mark gazed at 117 and nodded again. "And putting you in the hospital."

917 abruptly turned to 117, who flinched when 917 suddenly pointed a finger at him.

"How do you wish to respond?" 917 asked.

117 looked between 917, his amborg brother, and then his grandfather. He realized that 917 was actually allowing him a few seconds to decide on an answer. He was acting pushy because he really wanted the two of them to get over this particular hurdle.

"I... choose to forgive you," 117 stated.

Mark's smile widened with excitement.

"Sweet!" he clapped his hands together and almost bounced out of his chair.

117 blinked, his eyes darting around, causing the others to stare at him in confusion.

"I do not understand..." he replied casually, "I detect nothing in the vicinity affiliated with or that contains any sugar..."

917 brought his hand up and leaned his head into it.

"And he is back," he said.

"Boy," Mark stared, dumbfounded, "when this is over, you have to learn how to properly hold a conversation..."

A couple of people ran by, but 117 ignored them. His gaze remained fixed on his newly forgiven relative while trying to adopt a more serious expression. His grandfather fished a cigarette from his pocket, searching for a lighter.

"That's bad for you," 117 pointed out.

"Sticking your nose in my business is also bad for you," Mark replied.

117 glanced at 917.

"No, 117," he replied immediately, "we are not doing the anti-smoking recommendations protocol. Your grandfather would probably kick both our asses if we tried."

"I think three..."

117 and 917 looked at Mark.

"Three... what?" 117 asked.

"Three amborgs in a fight," Mark shrugged as he found his lighter. "That's my limit. Fortunately, I'm not in the mood to really fight anyone."

"So, even an old man has limits?" 917 mused.

"Ok kid," Mark said, holding up his cigarette and pointing it at both amborgs. "Don't be so wound up. Wound up... Hehe get it? Because you're like wind-up toys?

Another bout of silence filled the air as 117 and 917 remained unresponsive to the joke. His grandfather eagerly waited for a reaction, but his face fell. He sighed as he lit the cigarette and held it to his mouth.

"Nothing?" he asked, raising an eyebrow. "Ok, come on, I admit that that was a bad joke from someone my age but we're family. I mean, I am entitled to say stupid things with relatives of... a certain modern nature. We should be getting to know each other and talking about... familial bonding? Or something like that."

"It wasn't funny," 117 muttered. "How do you know that you wouldn't be able to take on more than three of us?"

"Well, if I was motivated, I could easily do four or five," Mark took a puff of his cigarette, blowing a stream of smoke upwards. "I can read you kids better than you think."

117 raised an eyebrow but watched as Mark lifted his arm and pointed behind them. Without taking his eyes off him, 117 knew that he was gesturing to 5.

"Johnny 5," he spoke informatively, "First Group amborg. He has more experience than the two of you boys combined. When he's serious, he is brutally efficient. Even on one leg, his hits, swings, and attacks were precise and accurate."

"How did you...?" 117 started, but Mark was already interrupting him.

"Body language," he answered. "He's got a great sense of humor but in reality, he covers up his sorrow and pain by massively overcompensating. It's how he handles all of the trauma and the dangers of the job. He's a good man and a good person to be friends with. Sticking with him will make any situation much lighter than normal."

The old man scratched the back of his head, thinking about what to say next as he focused on 117 and 917. The two Second Group amborgs were eager to hear his criticism about their methods.

"917... it's clear that he's lived on the streets for a long time," he muttered as he took another puff. "The way he moves, it's all about survival. Your form is loose, unpredictable and a little wild but effective. You... also have amnesia?"

"He's good," 917 remarked.

"I can see the scars on the back of your head," Mark tilted his head towards 917. 117 turned curiously. "And I apologize if this is rude but... are you using a holographic projection to cover the left side of your face?"

117's eyes widened as he stared at 917 closely.

"What?"

"He favors the right side when he's in combat," Mark stated. "It's like he's shielding his left from danger."

"Right again," 917 sighed.

"You didn't tell any of us about..." 117 began, but 917 raised his hand, cutting him off.

"Because I wanted to keep it that way," he spoke calmly. "Your grandpa's right."

"I apologize if I overstepped," Mark stated in a low voice.

"No, it's fine," 917 said. "It's true. I'm the first amborg in history to have amnesia and was enhanced while in a coma. I don't know who I am."

"I know who you are," 117 said quietly.

917 glanced back at him, hope glimmering in his eyes.

"You're my brother," 117 declared. "It doesn't matter that we don't look like it, but I value you as a friend."

917 smiled warmly, his words seeming to make him happier.

"I appreciate that," he nodded as the two of them refocused their attention on Mark. "However, your grandfather still hasn't talked about you."

"Oh no," 117 groaned.

Mark smacked his lips and nodded. There was a hint of mischief in his eyes. He flashed a deliberate grin but then paused, forcing 117 to brace himself. Out of the corner of his eye, he noticed 917 smiling in amusement.

"Cringey," Mark spoke sharply.

"Not good," 117 took offense immediately, but he swallowed his pride and sat up attentively.

"Seriously, David, you fight like a toddler or some kid that's throwing a tantrum and then backs down after baring your teeth," Mark replied bluntly.

"Those comparisons seem a little unfair," 117's eye twitched.

"You come across as someone from a desk job being forced into violent situations," Mark shrugged as he continued expressing his thoughts. "Sure, you have strength and speed, but you don't seem to know how to fully use them. Your training is good, but you fight like you're adhering to a set of rules that may not apply in the heat of battle."

"Are you saying that he's too... by-the-book?" 917 suggested.

"Actually, yeah," Mark nodded.

"917!" 117 exclaimed.

"I said what I said," 917 mumbled. "Sorry 117."

"Look, son," Mark started.

117 turned to look at his grandfather, giving him his attention once again.

"You act like you're evolved and that's fine," he explained. "But if you can't be comfortable breaking the rules more often, how can you be expected to break an enemy's spirit? Especially if they're about to kill you or your loved ones?"

"What you're describing is to be an anti-hero," 117 replied. "I can't just... be like you or do what you and your followers do."

"You can choose what you want to be," Mark stated. "I just need you to know that there are people out there that want to take advantage of you. Your kind and good nature helps a lot of others, but some will choose to exploit that. When that happens, and you do have to fight, what will you do?"

117 fell silent.

"Dr. Kendrick may have groomed you kids and filled your heads with all these thoughts of accomplishments, hope, and dreams, but you're still your own selves."

"I think your methods are a little too extreme," 117 argued. "It is not the right way to constantly use force to enact change."

"Great! That sounded like an answer from your heart and not your CPU," Mark stared into 117's eyes and grinned. "You almost sounded like your dad."

117 felt a surge of pride fill up his chest when Mark brought up his father.

"Your dad was like that as well whenever someone ticked him off," Mark nodded as he reminisced. "I always told him that you had to use your fists if words couldn't get the message across. He'd say that violence isn't always effective. Only that it was a tool for fear and oppression."

"Have I... broken a nerve? Grandfather? Acting like my dad?"

"It touched a nerve, son, and... you know what? My name is Mark. Try using my name, David," the old man replied casually. He set his cigarette down on the arm of his chair and pulled a screwdriver from his pocket. He began to tinker with his own arm. "If you don't feel like calling me old man or grandpa, then I hope we can have a fresh start at least knowing each other's names."

117 nodded.

"Mark," he repeated. "Grandpa Mark. Old man Mark. I'm not sure that name actually suits you."

"It's the only one I've got," Mark shrugged. He twisted his hand a little and examined his arm brace.

"How do you have all of this information?" 117 asked curiously. "Or where does it all come from? For a normal human, it should be restricted."

"Not only do I have tools through my connections with Dr. Kendrick, I'm also well informed because I have eyes and ears everywhere."

Mark clenched his fist a few times. Once he was satisfied, he put the screwdriver away and looked at the two of them.

"Remember boys, I am not bound completely by the law," he explained informatively, pointing at the ceiling. "This place was forgotten for some reason, but you think I'm going to just report their existence? It's a nice place. I live here occasionally. They want to be left alone. Boom. Simple as that. I hate to sound condescending but even an amborg with sophisticated calculations constantly running through your mind should be able to work out the fact that I have a system."

"You have many contacts then?"

Mark chuckled.

"That's an understatement," he said. "Nearly half of the states' police forces are giving us info. I have contacts spread across the globe, including some at A.I. Industries who are keeping an eye on Dr. Kendrick. You'd be surprised by how many people hate him."

"How many?" 917 asked.

"There's a watchlist."

A sudden thought struck 117. He had mentioned gathering information from police departments nationwide. He couldn't possibly be referring to who he was thinking of, was he?

"Police?" 117's head tilted to the side. "Are you possibly referring to..."

"Bradley?"

"Yes," 117 suddenly realized. "Did you... plan that whole entire thing with her... so we could meet?"

"Calm down," Mark held up his hands gently. "Yes and no. In her defense, I told her that there were weapons out on the streets designed to kill the amborgs."

"So, she knew you were coming," 917 said.

"When we knew that 117 was on call, she brought him out to LA. She might tear me a new one the next time I contact her."

117 scrunched his face as he tried to wrap his head around the fact that his grandfather and Chief Bradley knew each other. The whole undercover mission was a setup.

"I didn't know she cared," 117 spoke softly. "She always seems uptight and dislikes us."

"She also doesn't really approve of me," Mark admitted guiltily. "You already know why, but she considers me an ally from past encounters. She operates as the face of the LAPD, and I help her out on the side. I remember when she told me about how you met, and I knew I wanted to eventually meet you. She's probably going to blow a gasket if she knew that you came back out into the field without properly taking care of yourself."

"Captain Bradley? Are we referring to the same one? The chief of police?"

"The full metal buh?"

117 turned to 917, who had raised his hand to his mouth. His bracelet flashed again as he gave an awkward smile.

"My apologies," 917 chuckled. "I almost said her nickname out loud. The one she doesn't like."

"I know she really doesn't seem the type," Mark sighed in agreement. He had stifled a laugh when 917 held himself back. "She really has a soft spot for you kids. When we discovered that someone was creating weapons designed to target the amborgs, it was clear that this was no small matter; someone means to do serious business. If this sort of thing had been kept out of reach from both the local police and even your common criminal organizations, then it's been perfectly concealed from A.I. Industries as well. Well... She had no idea about the stabbing part. She's still pissed at me for endangering your life."

"You believe that someone is planning to fight the amborgs?" 117 asked, but his grandfather shrugged.

"I'm one of the best information brokers in the underworld," Mark said bluntly. "If I don't have knowledge about the identity or even the complex details of this... plot, then I'm telling you to be careful David. But I have the feeling that things are already underway if common criminals are stockpiling weapons. It's as though someone is preparing their forces for something big. These small street battles across the country are no longer the main concern; they're merely a cover for something that even the U.S. military won't be able to ignore. Just look at what happened to Lieutenant Palmer earlier. We can't compare this to past instances where police needed military backup to handle typical riots or chase down drug addicts. That battle today was more than just a clash; it was a warning sign to something much larger. We have to be ready now."

This was surprising to hear even to 117. He had predicted the possibility that one day, a threat would emerge, but this was happening sooner than he had expected. He thought about the amborgs and their methods of handling situations much like what had happened earlier. Were they even capable of preparing for a war? It wasn't what they were built for.

"Even with all of this and our help," 117 said, pointing at Mark's arms, "the equipment my father provided isn't enough. This could potentially be too much for us to handle."

"I can take care of myself. I'm wondering if you can."

"I think our chances are still pretty good, even with your warnings," 917 said with a confident nod.

"Don't let your confidence get the best of you," Mark replied. "Back then, augmentation through implants and removable cybernetic equipment was the latest fashion. When your dad first gave me those experimental prototype braces, they were almost too much to handle, but I eventually adapted. The only thing I'm concerned about is leaving this world before I can see this fight through to the end. Honestly, you young ones have a much better shot at living a long life than I do."

"If you bested me," 117 said reassuringly, "then your chances are the same as mine based on what you have described to us. You have lived a full life, too. Perhaps you could purchase security drones and just relax through the whole thing when it happens. Stay safe and retire while you still can at your age."

"Funding for robotic drones was and still is expensive these days," Mark replied.

A smile crept across his face at 117's idea, and he leaned back, as if a sudden wave of exhaustion swept over him. 117 wasn't surprised. Even with cybernetic upgrades, he was still an old man. How old though? He hadn't really specified.

"Retirement is not for me I'm afraid," he muttered grimly. "Not now. I'd much rather enjoy one margarita at the end than spend the rest of my life lazing around and having one handed to me. It doesn't sit well with me to accept good fortune without earning it myself. Only the rich can afford vacations, proper security programs, and drones. No. As long as there are still people living off the streets, I'll continue to dedicate my time to helping them. Those margaritas can wait. Someday, David, you will come to appreciate those rare moments of true success. When they do come, cherish them."

"One day," 117 said with a small smile. "I will be able to completely trust you. One day, I will fully understand that you are possibly the last family I have apart from my brothers and sisters. One day, we will share that margarita together... Grandpa."

"I thought you kids didn't drink," Mark chuckled, looking up at 117 with a wide smile.

"If I am still going to be human," 117 shrugged, "perhaps I should partake in a few bad habits to boost my social skills."

"Sounds good to me son."

"There is still something I don't... get..." 117 said thinking about what was said earlier. "What is your relationship to Captain Bradley?"

Mark perked up, clearly eager to share.

"We go way back."

Mark pressed a button on his right arm brace and a holographic photo shone brightly from a projector. 917 and 117 stared, unable to look away.

"What?" they replied simultaneously.

The image showed a young man and woman dressed in formal attire. 117 recognized a younger version of Mark in what appeared to be a suit. And... that girl standing with him... That couldn't be her in a dress... was it? It looked like a younger version of...

"See?" Mark said cheerfully. "I took her to prom!"

"I-I'm afraid to ask how long ago this photo was taken," 917 stammered.

117 stared wide-eyed at the holographic photo. If he had only heard it, he wouldn't have believed it. As he examined the couple more closely, he realized however unlikely it was, his grandfather was telling the truth.

"I agree. But because I'm seeing this... how long ago was this?" 117 asked, feeling very unnerved and slightly disturbed at seeing such a young-looking Captain Bradley in a single shoulder-strapped dress and smiling. The smile was throwing him off. "You went to a high school promenade with the woman that refers to me as a 'tinhead'?"

"Yeah! Lucky! She was prom queen," Mark replied, winking. "Oh, it's been years now... several decades now, I think. With anti-aging technology, she sure doesn't look that old so it's hard to remember. Senile is definitely not in her vocabulary. Bless her heart. She still has a nice figure, but I do wish I was crowned King. There would have been a lot more satisfaction."

"As much as I do enjoy a romantic story..." 917 pretended to act like he was about to throw up. He leaned away, looking ill. "The thought... of the chief and your grandfather, 117."

117 agreed. They both let out a soft shudder as the mere thought of it sent chills up their spines. Slightly offended, Mark sighed and shut off the projector.

"Kids," he shook his head.

Mark suddenly glanced behind them. Something had caught his attention.

"By the way, David, you mind calling off your girlfriend before she kills one of my guys?"

A sudden shout from behind startled 117, causing him to whirl around. He and 917 sprang from their seats, the chairs clattering to the ground as they prepared for a fight. But, as they grasped what was happening, they both let their arms fall to their sides.

"Hey!"

5 had been knocked off the table and was now sprawled on the ground. His leg had already been reattached, but the table was now on top of him. The whole area had been upended, thanks to the arrival of someone familiar.

117 and 917 watched in disbelief as 43 sprang into action, fighting the people who'd been helping 5. Amazingly, she had managed to sneak into the area, bypass the security guards at the entrance, and found their little group. Her stealth skills were remarkable, but there was no time to waste. Without hesitation, 117 charged ahead and engaged.

Before anyone could even try to talk to her, she had jumped onto a platform above one of the huts and was already unleashing a flurry of punches and kicks at Mark's team of vigilantes. Her movements were efficient, quick, and deadly. Complete pandemonium ensued. In response to her sudden attack, several of Mark's hooded fighters emerged to confront her. As 5 fought to regain his footing and find safety, 117 and 917 shouted for 43 to stand down, but they were ignored. 43 held her ground, prepared to face anyone who dared to charge at her.

For a brief moment, 117 felt as if time had come to a standstill, mesmerized by her ferocity as she confronted her attackers. Either it was because he was in awe of her incredible strength or it was the twinge of fear of what might happen if he were to intervene.

Making instant calculations, 117 moved into the fray while 917 signaled to him that he would remain a safe distance behind him.

"Really?" 117 transmitted to him as he tried to figure out how he was going to fix this.

"Hey," 917 replied cautiously, "she's deadly. Remember the last time we sparred with her? I'm still recovering from the last time she punched me in the face."

117 concentrated and looked for his opening into the ensuing fight. 43 was holding her own against nine vigilantes, her movements fluid and precise. However, the sight of more people charging toward them sent a jolt of anxiety through him. This was beginning to remind him of the massive fight they had on the surface earlier. He began to worry; if all these newcomers targeted 43, it could result in her becoming overwhelmed after a drawn out battle, or a significant number of Mark's personnel would be severely injured. If she was in a bad mood, she might not hold back and could end up killing most of them. As 117 attempted to

close the distance, he was stunned to see several hooded figures hurtling toward him.

"She might tear them apart," 117 said in an agitated tone.

"We really need to stop her!" 5 cried out from the ground.

117 leaped into the air just as a vigilante was sent crashing to the ground, skidding across the surface. He narrowly avoided tripping over the body, glancing down for a split second to make sure they were ok. Another vigilante came barreling toward him, forcing him to duck instinctively. Sidestepping another person, 117 moved forward, eventually inserting himself into the whirlwind of people. Finally, after dodging a fifth vigilante, he saw his chance. He charged power to his legs and sprang forward, arms outstretched. He managed to wrap his arms around 43 and both of them fell off the platform. There was a resounding crash as the two amborgs landed in a large garden bed, shattering a small wooden fence in the process.

"Ow!" 43 cried out.

"Stop!" 117 shouted, then felt her fist slap his ear. "Ow!"

43 continued to struggle, but 117 was slightly stronger as they rolled in the dirt.

"They're not the enemy!"

"You've been missing for hours!" she protested angrily. "You go deep underground, further than we've ever been before, and had all of our techs worried! Why are you even defending these people?!"

"They're not that bad! They reattached my leg!" 5 shouted as he joined them. "Man, that was surprising..."

As 117 and 43 quit struggling, they glanced around. The vigilantes they'd been fighting had stopped moving.

Quickly getting to their feet, 117 turned and noticed his grandfather still seated in his chair, enjoying his cigarette with an amused look on his face.

Things calmed down a moment later as the combatants withdrew. 117 couldn't help but admire how fluid their movements were, as if there hadn't been a huge scuffle a few seconds ago. Well, except for the unfortunate souls who'd been beaten up.

"It's ok, we're fine!" 117 said reassuringly.

117 glanced down, and he realized his hands were still wrapped around 43's wrists. She quickly shook out of his grasp, and he immediately held up his hands and stepped back a few paces. 43 looked around cautiously. Then she saw Mark.

"That's him?" she muttered.

With a light jump, 43 leaped back up to the platform where 5 was slowly getting back on his feet.

"Careful," he said, flinching when she appeared right next to him. "I'm still calibrating my leg."

He massaged the upper thigh of his reattached leg and sighed.

"They put it back on, see?" 5 reported calmly. "It was all a misunderstanding. No harm no foul. I'm good as new! Almost."

43 awkwardly gazed at 5 and dipped her head apologetically. Then she faced Mark and began to march towards him. He remained seated as he quietly watched her approach. 117 quickly clambered back up to where 5 was standing.

"Uh, you handle this one," 5 said as he stepped aside. "I'm just going to sit over there and wait for my leg to reconnect. Give you lovebirds a moment."

"It might not be pleasant," 117 gulped nervously.

"You know, David?"

Mark looked 43 in the eye and nodded his approval.

"That's some girl you got here," he said. "Amborg Serina 43. Nice to see you again."

"I'm sorry," 43 replied warily. "I can't say the same for you. "How do you know me?"

"Uh," 917 spoke up. "He kind of knows all of us."

"Yeah?" 43 stared defiantly at Mark. "Then I don't need to introduce... her?"

117's breath hitched as he caught sight of another person emerging directly behind Mark. He recognized a head of blonde hair slowly rising, revealing a girl in an amborg jacket with a Second Group insignia standing dangerously close to Mark's shoulder. It was the perfect position to kill him if necessary. How had they missed her?

"Don't tell me," Mark chuckled as he tilted his head back and got a look at the new arrival. "The lone wolf of A.I. Industries?"

Amborg 999 had a knife drawn and was holding it a few inches away from his neck.

"If I give her the signal, she'll end you before you can blink," 43 said threateningly.

"Neat trick," Mark smiled at 43. "But uh, using yourself as a distraction so that she could maneuver into position? I've been doing that since I was a teenager myself."

With a slight gesture with his arm, more hooded vigilantes appeared behind amborg 999. She slowly turned her head, and her eyes shifted from side to side. After a brief analysis, she got rid of her aggressive stance and seemed to relax despite her expressionless and fierce gaze. She straightened up, withdrew her knife, sheathed it into a pouch on her waist, and raised her hands gently.

"Surrendering," 999's bracelet transmitted a cold and soft tone.

43 shot 999 an angry look as Mark gave them a smile of satisfaction.

"Smart," Mark replied as he gently stood up. "What do you say we call it a day?"

"I had 999 sneak behind you so that I could negotiate," 43 stated. She seemed annoyed that her plan had failed.

"43, there's no need," 117 said urgently. "Everything's ok!"

"Yeah, actually..." Mark let out a laugh, "we're all just wrapping up here."

43 glanced at 999. Silently, 999 shook her head, then looked to 917. He read her expression, nodded, and then glanced at 43.

"There's no need to fight," he translated 999's body language. "It's not a hostile environment."

43 looked at 999 again as if she had been betrayed. She shook her head in frustration.

"I don't trust him!" 43 replied. She faced Mark and spoke again. "Not after what he did to you."

117 nodded and stepped forward.

"I know," he said, "but you don't have to fight. I'll explain everything later."

43 shot a quick look at 117 before turning her attention to the rest of the group. The entire team of amborgs currently present appeared completely at ease, taking neutral stances. She was all alone in her current dilemma. Finally, she scoffed and crossed her arms. Mark signaled for his vigilantes to stand down and they all backed away. They remained in a formation surrounding them, but they visibly relaxed and hid all signs of hostility.

"I want to take the others home," 43 demanded in a soft but firm voice from her bracelet. "Give us safe passage out of here and back to the surface..."

Then she opened her mouth.

"...Or.... Else..." she rasped. "I will... *cough*... destroy you... and your followers."

"Whoa…"

5 said what all of them were thinking. A thick silence enveloped the group as they all tried to comprehend what had just happened. 43 had used her real voice, and now the spotlight was on her. 117 stared at her incredulously. He noticed Mark raising an eyebrow, looking equally taken aback. Just behind him, 999 clenched her fists nervously as she tensed up, though her face betrayed no emotion.

Mark held up his hands calmly and nodded compliantly.

"Fair enough," he said. Then he turned to look at 117. "You are welcome here anytime."

Mark gently smiled at 43, who averted her gaze angrily.

"Even you," he said kindly. "Hopefully, we can be friends."

"Don't hold your breath… old man."

43 let out a snarl through her bracelet, which flashed in a menacing glare. The others remained quiet. They hadn't realized their bracelets had that kind of setting. 43's bracelet lit up again as she turned to leave.

"I'll wait near the entrance to this place…" she said. "Let's go, everyone."

After she stalked away, Mark walked up to 117 and held something out to him. 999 followed closely and moved to stand next to 917.

"That's some girl you got there," he said.

"Indeed," 117 nodded and glanced down at the device in his grandfather's hand. "What is that?"

"It's a reinforced mobile cellphone," Mark replied. "It has my number on it so call me whenever you need me."

"Isn't that a… uh… military grade satellite phone?" 917 asked skeptically. "That's what you use to call nuclear strikes…"

"It's a new phone," Mark insisted. "It can reach me from almost anywhere on the planet. Don't ask me how I got it."

"I don't think I want to know…" 117 replied as he nodded and pocketed the phone.

"One more thing, David. You treat Serina well, ok?"

"I always do," 117 replied casually.

"She's got a thing for you," Mark winked. "You should ask her out. She's practically waiting for you."

117 felt a clap on his shoulder as Mark grinned. He sent him off with a smile as 117 headed over to 5.

"Ready to go," 5 smiled, giving everyone a thumbs up. "My leg should be fine until we get back for a full diagnostic."

117 and 5 turned to leave, but they heard Mark still conversing with 999 and 917.

"You don't talk much, do you?"

Everyone glanced back and saw that 999 was glaring up at Mark. He chuckled when she didn't say anything.

"If you don't mind my saying so," he added with a polite nod to her, "your technique was flawless. I almost didn't hear you until the last second."

Without a word, 999 gently blinked as her expression softened. She brought her hand up to her chin and with the back of her hand aiming at him, she lowered it down sharply, quietly conveying a brief thank you. Mark nodded and waved goodbye as she calmly followed 43. When she was out of sight, he looked at 917.

"She said thank you," 917 said, looking impressed. "That's probably the only sign of communication you're getting from her this week."

Mark snickered.

"You've also got quite the girlfriend there," he commented.

"She's not my girlfriend," 917 replied.

"Really? The way that she looks at you?" Mark seemed quite interested in 917's response. "That's quite an interesting relationship. Kinda feels like she wants you."

"It's a friendship," 917 stated. "She's my best friend."

"What's holding you back?" Mark pointed in the direction 999 went.

917 didn't have an answer. His gaze dropped to the ground, and he began to walk away.

"It was good to meet you," 917 said gently.

Mark stared at 917 intently, a thoughtful expression crossing his face. After a moment, he smiled, and 117 couldn't help but notice something peculiar about the way he was nodding, like he could see right through 917. Mark turned to look at 117.

"I can tell that 999 has issues," Mark replied, "but, pardon me for leaving you boys with one last piece of advice. She and 43 may act tough... but they're definitely reserving a soft spot for you two."

Mark gave 117 another mischievous smile.

"You're both quite lucky. In these times? Having badass women like them at your side? I wouldn't waste another second, if you catch my meaning?"

5 let out a laugh while 117 was at a loss for words. The next thing he knew, 5 was pushing him in order to get him to start walking to the exit. 43 and 999 were both waiting.

"Thanks for finding us," 5 smiled.

His grin instantly faded when he noticed the sour look on 43's face. 999 maintained a cold and neutral expression, but it looked more like she didn't care. She merely acknowledged 5 with a firm and quick nod while 43 steamed.

"Don't ever do that again."

She had directed this statement at 117, who shuddered under her stern gaze.

"You worried us!" she exclaimed.

"Actually," 999 crossed her arms and rolled her eyes, "you were the only one worried."

"I'm sorry," 117 stated. Then he had an idea. "Perhaps I could make amends with you?"

"You can just say, 'make up', 117," 5 spoke on the side.

"Right," 117 nodded. "May I invite you out?"

Everyone suddenly fell silent. He glanced around, wondering if he had said the wrong thing. 43 began stuttering and blushed, her face taking on a deep shade of red. This was an odd and unexpected reaction. Suddenly, a faint beeping noise emanated from each of their bracelets.

"Whoa... A temperature spike," 5 said observingly.

43's eyes widened even more as she quickly walked away. They all watched her offer a quick goodbye to the guard at the security gate. 117 noticed the others immediately turning to face him with incredible judgement.

"I don't think I've ever seen 43 that embarrassed before," 5 sighed.

999 shook her head and then swiftly departed to catch up with 43.

"Time and place, 117," 917 snickered. "Now was not the right time."

"But I thought that she would be pleased with my request," 117 replied.

"I think," 5 said as the three of them walked out the gate together, "you have a lot to learn."

"Why would she be mad?" 117 asked.

"Do we tell him?" 917 asked teasingly.

"We should," 5 snickered. "Otherwise he's going to wander around like an innocent puppy for days."

"But..."

"Don't even deny it 117," 5 smiled. "I am speaking directly to you. The cause of her supposed emotional malfunction."

"Sarcasm detected," 117 stated. "She didn't have an emotional malfunction."

"She did," 917 replied firmly. "Besides, it's not her that I think you need to worry about."

117 cast a worried glance at 917 as they stepped into the dark labyrinth to begin their trip back up to the surface. He spoke again with a cheerful grin, trying to lighten the mood.

"All of our technicians are probably going to kill us when we get back," he sighed. "We did worry them for quite a while."

117 felt his stomach lurch a little. If there was one thing he was not looking forward to, it was a lecture from Mandy. Hopefully, when they regained a signal and their connection back home, she wouldn't be too angry. 917 and 5's reactions, however, were not reassuring at all.

CHAPTER 10

Your "Presents" is Requested

A.I. Industries
Christmas Day

"So, what do you think?"

117 blinked and turned around. Mandy smiled at him from the backseat.

"David, are you ok?"

117 faced forward, snapping out of his daydream.

"Yes, I'm sorry," he stated. "My mind was preoccupied."

The man in the front passenger seat of the car they were sitting in chuckled in amazement.

"Well, that's not the reaction I was expecting for your Christmas present but I'll take it."

117 and Mandy were seated in a specially designed car. They'd been summoned to the motor pool a few minutes earlier by Drago Kolti, one of the lead auto mechanics at A.I. Industries. Renowned for his expertise and innovative techniques, Drago specialized in inventing and upgrading vehicles tailored specifically for the amborgs. 117 and Mandy were currently sitting in a Christmas present from Drago.

"Now, I remember you saying that you wanted something that could be strong, maneuverable and fuel-efficient," he said excitedly. "I still have to fix the suspension but I think you'll enjoy taking this out on the road."

117 gripped the steering wheel, feeling the smooth, clean leather as he admired the car's interior. It was a Suyota high-range jeep, equipped with armor upgrades, perfectly suited for navigating city streets or the toughest road conditions with ease.

"It can hold the weight of six amborgs," Drago explained excitedly. "It's really amazing! We gave the engine an extreme makeover. More horsepower and less noise. Everything is reinforced for a nice and leisurely drive, but able to handle moderate to severe amounts of combat."

"Thank you Drago," Mandy beamed from behind 117. "You got us a tank for Christmas! How fast is it able to go?"

"In optimal conditions, you can go up to 140 mph," Drago replied. "Obviously, the more amborgs that ride with you, the more it will decrease its performance, but you can't deny that it's strong, despite its appearance as a family-friendly looking vehicle."

"It is very impressive," 117 nodded. "How soon will it be ready?"

"It will be ready in three days," Drago replied. "You can test drive it then. I just thought you'd like to see it considering that today is the day for presents."

"Thank you for your gift," 117 smiled politely. "I am looking forward to the test drive."

"Oh, right, you do have a driver's license right?" Drago asked.

117 reached into his pocket and pulled out his ID. He passed the card over and Drago examined it. When he was satisfied, he nodded and gave 117 a kind smile.

"Ah, this was issued before you were enhanced," he noted, but then his look turned questionable. "Do you still remember how to drive?"

"Yeah..." Mandy said nervously from the backseat. "I haven't seen you behind the wheel since we first started working together. Are you a good driver?"

"If I remember correctly," 117 paused to do some calculations, "I had average skills."

"What does average skills mean?"

Drago and Mandy eyed 117 curiously. He continued to try to recall what his life was like before becoming an amborg. A smile spread across his face as he turned to them, exuding confidence.

"I have about 60 hours of driving experience," he declared.

"Wait..." Mandy gulped with wide eyes. "Usually, you need a minimum of 100 or more to take the driving test!"

"Yes," 117 nodded. "I decided to take the test sooner when I realized that 100 hours is a recommended guideline than an actual rule. I secretly took my driver's test at another DMV location and I passed."

Mandy gulped again.

"I-I don't think I want to ride along during your test drive," she stammered.

"But I'm an adequate driver..."

"I'm getting out," Mandy interrupted him.

Startled, 117 and Drago watched Mandy quickly slide out of her seat and slam the door behind her as she scurried out.

"But we're not moving," 117 stated.

"How interesting," Drago seemed fascinated as he examined 117's ID again.

They both got out of the car and strode up to Mandy, who was fidgeting with her hands.

"Is everything alright, Mandy?" 117 asked.

"How come you didn't drive more hours?" she asked.

"In my case," 117 shrugged, "I never had a lot of time to drive. I was usually training every day to prepare for the enhancement surgeries."

Mandy nodded but still eyed 117 warily. She knew that the training and physical requirements prior to becoming an amborg were strict, but even with that information, there was no way she was ready to get in the same car with 117 as the driver.

"Please promise me that you'll get more practice before I ride with you?"

"I can practice after Christmas," 117 nodded. "Are you... concerned about my driving habits?"

"Well... it would make me feel better," Mandy replied. "After you became an amborg and we first met... Isn't that like a baby being put behind the wheel right after they open their eyes?"

"I don't believe that I fit in that particular analogy."

117 and Mandy bid Drago a quick farewell. He summoned some drones to move his car to a nearby docking station in the garage, then walked them over to his console.

"You are coming to the party later?" Mandy asked him.

"I wouldn't miss it," Drago smiled. "I have a couple of motorcycles that are going to be completed soon and one more car to show to another amborg. Then my schedule is clear."

"Please do not overwork yourself," 117 reminded Drago promptly. "You have our thanks for supplying us with suitable vehicles for future missions, but we do not wish you to overextend yourself."

"Are you kidding?" Drago grinned as he waved at the empty garage. "This job is fantastic! I love taking these vehicles apart and upgrading them to carry the amborgs without any difficulties. Don't worry 117. I am looking forward to a nice vacation after the Second Group all acquire their custom vehicles."

Mandy and 117 waved goodbye and left the motorpool.

"On the bright side," Mandy let out a sigh, "I'm going to miss all of the footage of you accidentally crushing cars out in public."

"I am unsure why you find that footage amusing," 117 replied. "Most of those incidents document property damage."

"Watching you guys accidentally wrecking things is pretty funny," Mandy chuckled. "Someday, you might understand."

"I understand... Ellie."

Mandy halted, and her smile vanished just as abruptly. 117's heart raced as she spun around to face him, her eyes blazing with fury. This triggered unpleasant memories of their return from New Vernon, when they finally managed to get in touch with their technicians again. Mandy had given him an earful.

"David, please don't call me that. EVER. Only my fiancé gets to call me that."

"I don't understand," 117 said. "Your file says that your middle name is Elizabeth. So... Ellie is an appropriate nickname, is it not?"

"Yes," Mandy spoke through gritted teeth and pointed a finger in his face. "But, you need to understand that only certain people are allowed to know my nickname. Far fewer get to use it. The only reason Tom is allowed to call me that is because I love him. It's a very intimate and serious thing between us. If you start calling me by my nickname, it... just doesn't feel right."

117 swallowed and nodded vigorously.

"Understood," he said quickly. "I shall promise never to use your nickname or your middle name ever again."

"Geez David," Mandy sighed as she backed off and they began to walk down the hall at a slow pace. "You sure have been testing the waters lately."

Before 117 was even able to ask what she was referring to, she continued to grumble.

"First, you worry all of us by going underground. We lose all contact and then you come back with 43 pissed at you," she said. "Now you're using my middle name. Do you have a death wish?"

"No I don't," 117 replied.

"How's Serina?" Mandy chimed in a sarcastic tone.

An awkward silence hung in the air as 117 stared straight ahead. Out of the corner of his eye, he noticed Mandy was watching him with a smug look and a devious smile.

"I believe I see your point," 117 replied grimly.

"I'll see you at the party David."

"Is Lieutenant Palmer going to be there?" 117 asked cordially.

"He'll be here soon," Mandy nodded. "We're going to spend some quality time together before the party. So, I'm going to meet him at the landing pad."

"I shall meet with both of you then," 117 nodded.

Even though he had specifically requested some time alone on Christmas day, it was still a rather enjoyable experience looking at his new car with Mandy. Ever since the end of the Thanksgiving holidays, there had been a few more missions that required the amborgs to implement new policies or adjust existing protocols in the field.

In response to the emergence of weapons actually capable of causing them serious harm, the amborgs adopted a new buddy system that would apply to future missions. Each amborg would pair up with another or form a team, depending on the circumstances. Since meeting his grandfather, 117 had taken part in a few missions. A few days ago, he and 43 were assigned to protect a few large shopping centers during the busy season, but she had avoided talking to him the entire time. At Mandy's suggestion, she recommended that 43 be given some space.

Mandy had also promised him that she would speak to Sherry, who was 43's technician and the one most likely to know what was on her mind. With the two of them, she assured 117 that things would be fine.

Aside from the personal matter between him and 43, 117 couldn't believe that it was almost the end of the year. Time seemed to have passed rather quickly since he last spoke with his grandfather. He never forgot about it and was constantly on guard.

After the amborgs submitted their full report to Dr. Kendrick, which filled the gaps left by their technicians, a thorough review of their mission revealed what appeared to be a surge in energy. Along with the new protocols being implemented, every department at A.I. Industries worked tirelessly around the clock on their own projects. Everyone seemed fired up, determined to face whatever challenges lay ahead. It did help ease the tension and uneasiness that had developed since 117's stabbing.

Even though it was winter, A.I. Industries continued to maintain a strong presence across the country to meet the hectic needs of the holidays. 117 found himself keeping up a sense of security and constant vigilance. He was always on standby for mission alerts, but he took advantage of any opportunities to relax that came his way. 117 decided to visit his parents and made his way to the memorial hall.

As he turned a corner, he felt a small twinge in his stomach. He placed his hand briefly on the wound and checked his bio-scans. The scar from the knife would always be there to serve as a reminder of his first defeat. When he removed the bandages a week ago, 6 had asked him if he wanted her to perform an extra procedure to get rid of the scar, but he had decided to keep it. Hiding it from view wasn't going to make the pain go away, and he didn't want to waste time.

As he strolled through the corridors of the Amborg Residential Area, he passed several rooms belonging to the First Group. As he did so, he found himself in front of 8 and 9's quarters. Suddenly, a deafening explosion erupted in 8's room, stopping him in his tracks. Instinctively, 117 leaped to the wall farthest from the source of the blast, crouching low. The door across from 8's quarters flung open and amborg 13 darted out. He rushed by, ignoring 117's defensive stance and pretended as if nothing was going on.

"Hi 117. Bye 117. I don't want to be here to see what happens this time," he said irritably and quickly disappeared around the corner. "I'm going to help set up the party early! Merry Christmas and see you later."

117 calculated 13's speed and nodded approvingly.

"14 miles an hour," he muttered. "Good speed."

He sent a text to 13.

See you there 13.

Within seconds, 117 received a thumbs-up and a waving hand emoji in response.

"Unfortunately, it's too late for me to escape," 117 sighed as he straightened up.

Just in time, 117 saw the door to 8's room burst open. Stuart 8 dashed outside, head on fire, and was attempting to put it out by repeatedly smacking his head. 117 ran to the emergency panel and grabbed the fire extinguisher. This was a safety measure that had been installed there several years ago since 8 and 9 started living in this particular hallway. All the amborgs knew to use it whenever something like this happened. 117 pulled the worn out safety pin and began to press down on the nozzle while aiming the hose. A jet of extinguishing foam shot out and the fire on 8's head was put out instantly. The flames were gone but the extinguisher had coated his entire upper body in white frosty foam. While he hadn't taken too much damage, the look on his face was one of utmost fury. 117 did his best to stifle his laughter.

8 looked like a snowman. At that same moment, Christy 9 came out of her room and immediately took several photos with a large grin on her face. Not only did she use the camera built in her eye cybernetics, but she also had a phone in her hand which 117 assumed was recording everything.

"Annnndd... Merry Christmas to you 8!" she said cheerfully. "I was planning to take a picture of him on fire buuuut... this-works-too!"

8 didn't appear amused at all as 117 lowered the extinguisher and stepped aside.

"9! An incendiary grenade?! I just finished cleaning up for the Christmas party!" 8 shouted.

117 was quite surprised that 8 had actually fallen for the prank. Given all the years witnessing their shenanigans, it was hard to fathom how 8 hadn't somehow avoided this entire situation.

"Schrodinger's grenade," 9 stuck out her tongue.

Now it made sense.

117 placed the extinguisher back on the holder and radioed for a team of janitors as the two of them began to throw insults. This time, however, there weren't as many, which was a first.

"Always worrying for nothing. You won't be late," 9 reassured him in a teasing manner. "If you start cleaning up now, you'll make it in time for the start of the party!"

"You mean you could have made me late?"

"I chose not to," 9 winked. "Consider that a gift from my precious thoughts of you during this lovely yuletide."

With a grin, she went back inside her quarters, shutting the door behind her. A loud click indicated to the two amborgs that she had safely locked herself inside.

117 glanced over at 8, who was glaring furiously at her door. It looked like he was ready to unleash a torrent of words, but nothing came out. He looked to 117 for help, but all 117 could offer in return was a sympathetic smile.

"So, with all of your security and preventative measures," he chuckled softly, "how did she get a grenade past your defenses?"

"Schrodinger's grenade," 8 grumbled. "The mail drone delivered Christmas presents from everyone else to my room. When I got to 9's present, I immediately grew suspicious."

"Go on," 117 nodded.

"She has never given me a normal present in a box," 8 explained as he dusted his shoulders off. "So, I scanned the box, verified that her fingerprints were on it and carefully unwrapped the present."

"Why didn't you do it somewhere safe?" 117 asked.

"It IS safe in my room," 8 replied insistently. "I sat there for a few hours contemplating whether or not to open the present. In the end, my curiosity got the better of me."

"Did you have to open it?" 117 asked, raising an eyebrow.

"It's incredibly rude to leave a present unopened," 8 shrugged. "Besides, it's tradition. It wouldn't be a proper holiday unless one of us was involved in an explosion."

"A very morbid and chaotic response," 117 noted.

"I'll see you later 117. Glad to see you doing ok."

117 thanked 8, who turned and disappeared into his room. Once he was alone, 117 took a moment to inspect both doors for any further signs of activity. Satisfied that all was quiet, he nodded, confident that there wasn't going to be any more imminent trouble. At least, for the rest of the day. 117 scanned the floor and the hall to prepare an assessment for the janitors when they arrived.

Just then, a loud clatter drew his attention behind him. He turned to find a janitor appearing from around the corner, trailed by a team of drones, each equipped with their own set of cleaning supplies.

"Hello Stan," 117 said in greeting, then looked to both the drones behind the old man. "J-B12. J-B18. It's good to see you."

J-B12 and J-B18 flashed their eyes and dipped their heads politely to him before getting to work. 117 immediately moved forward and reached for Stan's tools, but stopped when the old man waved his arm.

"Ah 117, I may look old but I'm still capable of doing my job. It's great to see you though!" Stan said cheerfully, wielding his mop and clenching his bucket of tools tightly. "So what's the story? What happened between 8 and 9 this time?"

"Incendiary grenade," 117 explained as he pointed at the mess. "There are some remnants of the extinguishing agent in the hallway. Are you certain I cannot assist in any way?"

Stan brushed away 117's hand again, which had automatically begun reaching for the mop. The short old man clung onto his tools stubbornly and chuckled.

"Hey I told you, I'm not as old as you think. Remember, I can get the job done no matter how big it is," he smiled. "An incendiary grenade? Well it's a good thing you guys are indestructible."

"That is not entirely accurate," 117 smiled.

"I heard," Stan nodded in understanding. "Are you ok?"

"I am well," 117 replied. "Your praise and concern is appreciated. I do have time to help if you do change your mind."

"I'm fine David 117," the old man smirked and began mopping the floor. "Go find that 43 and make something of yourselves. Get some action while you're still young. Merry Christmas! And remember, you've been working hard. Whatever you face, just know that a lot of us believe in you, kid. That wound in your stomach will always be there, but there is only one thing anyone who attacks you like that cannot destroy."

"What is that?"

"The courage in your heart and the will to fight."

Stan smiled and went back to cleaning with the two drones. 117 stood there at a loss for words from his bold declaration. Instead, he walked away.

Although he'd planned to visit his parents and go directly to the memorial hall, another idea suddenly crossed his mind. 117 veered off in the opposite direction from his original destination and headed toward one of the research labs. The lab doubled as an information data center, functioning like a cozy library for both the amborgs and the regular staff. On quieter days, when he was sure she wasn't on an assignment, 43 would sometimes hide in here. She loved immersing herself in reading articles, books, and various published journals to pass the time.

He greeted the librarian at his desk as he walked in. A man with short light blue hair and a silver nose ring glanced up and smiled.

"David 117," he dipped his head politely. "Merry Christmas."

"Francis," 117 replied. "Merry Christmas."

"What can I help you with on this lovely day?"

"Did... 43 come in today?" 117 asked carefully, his eyes darting around hopefully.

"She did..." Francis looked up thoughtfully, but became uncertain. "Sorry, I'm not entirely sure. We had quite a few people visit the library so I couldn't tell if she left to get ready for the party."

Francis held a tablet up to 117. He glanced at it, noticing that it was an ebook.

"This murder mystery is pretty epic," Francis grinned, then let out an awkward chuckle. "But uh... it's been pretty easy to get sucked into it."

"I understand," 117 stated. "May I please take a look around?"

"Feel free."

117 smiled and dipped his head. After he bid Francis a kind farewell, he headed towards the first aisle. When he approached, he saw a familiar face, just not the one he was looking for.

"Hello 999," 117 said.

She wasn't facing him, but staring down one aisle. 117 stopped abruptly when 999's hand snapped up, signaling him to freeze in place. 117 watched as she tapped her bracelet two times with her index finger. Recognizing her signal, he began to text her.

What is the situation? he asked curiously.

Unclear, she responded instantly.

999 permitted 117 to move closer, allowing him to see what had caught her eye. 117 realized that she'd been watching a man standing in the aisle, who seemed to be perusing some hardcover books in the classic

collection. However, as they both observed him more closely, they noticed that he was quietly muttering to himself.

Who is that? 117 texted his next question.

He looks like a homeless man who broke onto company grounds and stole one of the researcher's coats, she replied.

117 turned his head abruptly and stared vacantly at 999. Another message alert popped up and he read her next text.

I said he looks like one, she added, *it doesn't mean he is one. He's just weird.*

How would you like to proceed? 117 asked.

Not me, she replied, *you.*

999 glanced at 117. He suddenly understood why she was directing this particular matter to him.

But… you were here first, he messaged back.

Clearly, that man is a talker, she explained as she turned to leave. *I am not. Happy holidays, 117. I am going back to my room.*

Wait!

999 stopped and turned back to him. When he had her full attention, he tried to bargain with her.

If I speak to that man, he wrote, *will you tell me what you were doing here?*

999's expression darkened as she glared at him. If looks could kill, 117 definitely would be dead by now.

My apologies 117, she replied sourly, *but did I give any indications that I was interested in sharing personal information?*

I suppose not. But I would like to attempt to be friends.

We are the same, 999 turned away, scoffed, and moved towards the front desk. *We are friends, 117. However, that doesn't mean I'm interested in having heart-to-heart discussions that you annoyingly like to have with everyone. Save your bandwidth for someone who cares.*

"It was worth a shot…" 117 sighed as he watched 999 walk away.

117 knew that socializing wasn't her thing, so it was perfect timing when he showed up, allowing her to pass this particular issue to him. Facing forward, he noticed the man still lingering, muttering fervently under his breath. When he got close enough, he made his presence known. As he did, he heard his name.

"…to 117. David… please."

117 blinked.

"Sir?" he announced.

The man froze, then twisted his head in a quick and unsettling way. 117 looked at him carefully and initiated a bio-scan. Mandy had always told him that doing so was a violation of someone's privacy, but this seemed rather peculiar. The man had spoken his name and number aloud, which was concerning. That alone was enough to give him probable cause to run the scan. Moments later, the scan results appeared in his HUD, indicating no drugs were present in the man's system. However, there were significantly elevated levels of adenosine, suggesting he hadn't had a proper night's sleep in quite some time.

As he drew closer, the man continued rubbing his hands and fidgeting. 117 noticed his ID on his chest pocket. The name written was Dr. Robert Kolaski. Before 117 could say anything, a red alert flashed in his eyes. Big, bold letters blared on his display screen as he shook his head in alarm.

Dr. R. Kolaski: Research Level: Maximum Clearance Highly Sensitive Company/Corporate Operations.

"Uh..." 117 stammered as more warnings popped up.

117 read them as more words flooded his eyes. It was almost seizure inducing with how many that kept popping into view.

David 117: Second Group Amborg: Clearance level unauthorized. Access denied to the Artificial Intelligence Division.

Do Not Engage Subject and allow Dr. Kolaski total privacy. Orders from Dr. J. Kendrick, CEO: A.I. Industries. Have a nice day.

117 struggled to make the warnings disappear, but they hung in front of his eyes as if someone had etched them onto a glass pane. Stumped and unsure of what to do, Dr. Kolaski approached him.

"Computer," he said shakily. "Please... disengage and mute warnings on David 117's... display, please? Authorization, Dr. Robert Kolaski. I would like... to speak... to him."

As if by magic, the big bold sentences on his display disappeared. The red alert messages were gone and no longer pestering him.

"Uh..." 117 stammered, "t-thank you? What happened?"

"Maximum clearance," Dr. Kolaski mumbled. "Has that happened to you in front of John? The warnings?"

John? Was he referring to Dr. Kendrick? 117 raised an eyebrow. Was Dr. Kolaski a close friend or something?

"I don't think so," 117 replied. "What is maximum clearance?"

Dr. Kolaski scanned his surroundings with a wary eye. His short brown hair danced around every time he turned his head. He seemed very uncomfortable in this place. 117 noticed the light stubble on his face, and a subtle hint of honey-scented shampoo from his hair, which was oddly pleasant. When he leaned forward, 117 realized that his clothes looked rather worn and smelled like they hadn't been washed in quite some time. He had to admit, 999's earlier observations held some truth; while he didn't appear homeless, he clearly stunk like someone without access to a washing machine.

"Some secrets..." he answered 117's question slowly and in a soft voice, "...are not meant to be shared."

"I saw the warning," 117 replied cautiously. "You have the same clearance level as Dr. Kendrick and Mr. Ramirez but I've never seen a restriction like that. Are you on the board?"

"It's an honorary... seat," Kolaski mumbled. "I don't... attend... those meetings."

117 brought up the employee database but couldn't find Dr. Kolaski on any of the general listings at A.I. Industries. Why would an honorary member of the board not be listed?

"You work in the artificial intelligence division?" 117 asked.

"I oversee it," Dr. Kolaski nodded as he brought his hands up and clenched his wrists nervously. "I program... I inspect the code... I see the unending flow... and I uh... I take care of them."

117 nodded. He could guess what he was hinting at.

"You take care of all of the A.I. programs."

"The artificial people," Dr. Kolaski muttered. "I raise them. I teach them."

"They... are not alive," 117 stated.

"They are sentient," Dr. Kolaski countered. "They are humanity's future... or our destruction. I want to understand them."

This line of thought sounded very familiar. 117 recalled a moment when Dr. Kendrick had shared a similar sentiment during their enhancement. He'd talked about how humanity's future rested in their hands.

"I see," 117 nodded with a friendly smile, even though he had no idea what the man was saying. "Is there a book here that you're looking for?"

"No. No. No."

Taken aback, Dr. Kolaski looked around and frantically shook his head.

"I heard from... friend... that," he pointed in a seemingly random direction. He suddenly turned on the spot, searching for something while appearing lost. "Serina... was here... 43."

"Are you looking for 43?" 117 asked curiously. "I am as well. I don't think she's here."

Dr. Kolaski glanced at 117, his shifty eyes appearing crestfallen.

"Oh, I should... go..."

"You... could see her at the party," 117 suggested sympathetically.

"Noo... No. No. I can't."

Dr. Kolaski looked like he was about to have a nervous breakdown. 117 realized that he was much like 999. Though, while her choice to avoid talking to strangers stemmed from a personal resolve, his seemed to come from a crippling social anxiety.

"Maybe..." 117 spoke firmly but in a gentle tone, "we should talk somewhere you feel comfortable?"

Dr. Kolaski's nervous shaking subsided as he focused on 117's words. A faint smile formed, suggesting that he found the idea quite appealing.

"Yes," he said. "You should come visit me."

"Uh..."

Dr. Kolaski suddenly sped past 117 and headed for the front desk. 117 hesitated briefly before deciding to follow. Dr. Kolaski rushed up to Francis and put his hands on the desk. Startled, Francis looked up, but his eyes gleamed as he recognized him and broke into a smile.

"Hey!" Francis exclaimed. "Good to see you Dr. Kolaski! Haven't seen you in a while!"

"I-I... am d-done here," Dr. Kolaski stammered.

"Well, you have a Merry Christmas, ok?" Francis nodded.

"Same... to you."

Dr. Kolaski headed towards the entrance. Francis and 117 watched as he stepped out through the doors and turned around. He waited expectantly for 117 to follow.

"I believe I am finished here as well," 117 said to Francis as he eyed the doctor.

"Find what you were looking for?" Francis said as he glanced down at his tablet.

117 shrugged.

"Unclear," he said. "What can you tell me about Dr. Kolaski?"

"He keeps to himself a lot," Francis muttered without looking up. "I think he has a social communication disorder or something. Someone with that much anxiety usually stays in their comfort zone to avoid having a potential breakdown. He is... trying his best."

"To do what?" 117 asked.

"Make friends," Francis replied.

117 understood but still wasn't too sure about Dr. Kolaski's character. He glanced at the front desk and began to head his way.

"Thank you, Francis."

"You're welcome, 117," Francis said cheerfully.

117 stopped suddenly and looked back.

"Yes?" Francis let out a sigh, looking up again.

"Do you intend to stay here the entire time?" 117 asked. "The Christmas party. You should join us later."

"It's not my cup of tea," Francis smiled. "Just a reminder, 117, but some people prefer to be alone. Me, for example. I'd rather sit here and read a book instead of dealing with other people. And I hope you'll respect my privacy and dig deeper."

"I understand," 117 replied. "I just don't believe you or Stan should be working on this holiday."

"Some don't celebrate like most people do," Francis replied.

"Of course," 117 dipped his head respectfully and turned to leave.

"But... for the record," Francis called out, "thank you for thinking of me. You have enough fun for both of us, ok?"

Dr. Kolaski took the lead as 117 exited the library, guiding the way into the R&D wing. It was the same hallway where he and Mandy had previously walked in from the motor pool after Drago summoned them to show off his new car. Instead of heading toward the garage, Dr. Kolaski veered off in another direction, and soon they reached the elevators. Except, Dr. Kolaski continued walking right past them.

"Uh... Doctor?" 117 asked, pointing at the elevator. "That's a dead end."

Dr. Kolaski ignored 117 and headed further into the corner. Curious, 117 followed and watched as he knocked on the wall. Suddenly, a retinal scanner popped out. He leaned forward, and the device glowed green once it scanned his eye. Then a microphone appeared.

"Robert Kolaski," he declared.

The wall slid open, and 117's eyes widened in surprise. It was a hidden elevator, small enough to hold no more than four people. Did Dr. Kolaski expect them both to squeeze in there together? Just as they were about to step inside, a security drone stepped out. 117 quickly raised his hands as the drone aimed its arm cannon, the laser sight zeroing in on his head. Where was this thing even hidden?

"...And guest!" Dr. Kolaski added as he spoke frantically into the microphone.

The microphone emitted a soft chime, retracting into the wall alongside the retinal scanner. The drone lowered its weapon and the red light in its eye socket shifted to green as it retreated into its hidden space in the elevator. 117, still staring, awkwardly lowered his arms.

"That was... extreme," 117 gulped.

"Sorry," Dr. Kolaski bowed apologetically to 117. "I forgot... I don't get visitors too often."

"There you are..."

Before they could enter the elevator, a sudden flash of light stopped them and an A.I. appeared in front of them.

"Serina," Dr. Kolaski smiled warmly.

"Dr. Kolaski," Serina sighed disappointedly. "You told me you were running out for some air. What took you so long?"

"I didn't find her."

117 noticed that Dr. Kolaski's speech became more coherent, and he didn't appear to be stuttering anymore. Perhaps it was because he was much more comfortable talking to an A.I. program that he was familiar with. It made sense considering he was most likely the one who created Serina.

"Well, I'm glad you're back," Serina frowned, "but please don't stay out too long. You know what happened the last time."

"I just wanted to see them. They went dark."

Serina glanced at 117 and nodded, acknowledging his presence, before turning her attention back to the scientist.

"I see you met David," she said. "How was it?"

"He's a good man."

"Thank you?" 117 said awkwardly.

Serina flashed him a smile before frowning again at Dr. Kolaski.

"You know he can't come down to your lab or your home," she stated in a soft tone.

"It's alright," Dr. Kolaski replied. "I just wanted to get him his Christmas present."

117 blinked. He had just met Dr. Kolaski less than ten minutes ago. He had a present for him? He didn't want to raise any issues, but this was certainly odd. Although, he wouldn't be surprised if Serina or Dr. Kendrick had shared stories about him before.

Serina turned and floated over to 117.

"I know that you and Dr. Kolaski had a nice and friendly meeting," she said with a kind smile, but then her gaze became rather stern as she crossed her arms. "However, I am under orders from Dr. Kendrick. I also must obey Dr. Kolaski's own rules."

"Maximum clearance?" 117 asked. It was the only thing he could think of to explain why she was being so restrictive. "Should I... wait here?"

"Thank you for understanding," Serina nodded.

Dr. Kolaski stepped into the elevator.

"I'll be back," he said as the doors closed.

When the elevator door slid shut, disappearing into the wall, 117 looked at Serina curiously.

"Why does Dr. Kendrick have such strict orders for Dr. Kolaski? Aren't they friends? Or colleagues?"

"He's a special case," Serina replied in a soft tone. "His research and work projects are extremely sensitive. Please don't ask him any questions."

"But... he has a present for me? I don't understand."

"He's wanted to meet you for a long time," Serina stated.

"Funny," 117 chuckled. "That certainly sounds familiar."

He and Serina shared a brief laugh, then 117 glanced at the wall where Dr. Kolaski had disappeared.

"Did he create you?" 117 asked.

"He did," Serina nodded. "My existence is because of him. Just like every other A.I. here at this company."

"How does he know Dr. Kendrick?"

"Question denied," Serina shook her head. "You don't have clearance for that information."

"How mysterious..."

"Yes, it is," Serina replied smugly. "Want to try another question?"

"I don't think it'll really be worth it if it turns out to be a maximum clearance requirement," 117 sighed.

"It depends on the question," Serina smiled.

"Ok."

117 thought about his next question. He factored in the fact that Dr. Kolaski knew of him and wanted to meet him in person. Also, he was originally in the library looking for 43. So, there was also a connection to her as well.

"He said he wanted to meet 43," 117 spoke thoughtfully. "Why is that?"

"Good question," Serina nodded, but then shook her head. She held up her hands and shrugged. "No clue."

"Is that a restricted question?" 117 asked.

"If it was, I would have denied it," Serina answered playfully. "In this case, I can't answer because I actually don't know. I'm not privy to what goes on in everyone's minds."

Another question then came to mind, whether Dr. Kolaski really did have a Christmas present for him. Right as the wall slid open and the elevator returned, he spoke out of his bracelet.

"Did he know my parents?"

"Yes, I did."

Serina looked down sadly as they both watched Dr. Kolaski step out of the elevator. His expression mirrored theirs as he held out a small, gift-wrapped box. The bright blue neon ribbon, though charming, was tied a bit clumsily. He turned it to reveal a label with 117's name on it.

"Was that restricted?" 117 looked at Serina.

"Not anymore," Serina replied courteously. "But I highly suggest that the questions stop here."

That was a very cryptic response. 117 held out his hand and took the present from Dr. Kolaski.

"May I open this?"

"It is Christmas," he nodded eagerly. "Also, be sure to give this one to 43. Please?"

117 saw Dr. Kolaski pull another similarly shaped box from the pocket of his dirty lab coat. It was wrapped in a different color of paper, also with a haphazardly tied neon ribbon, but it did look like he'd put in a lot of effort to get this one right, too. 117 took it and carefully put it in his own pocket, then began to tear through the paper of his own present. Once he revealed what was inside, he smiled.

"Chocolate," he mused.

"Do you like it?" Dr. Kolaski asked.

"I love these," 117 nodded. "Thank you for the present. I apologize for not having one prepared for you."

"It's ok," Dr. Kolaski shook his head. "Meeting you was a gift."

"What does that...?"

Serina flashed a bright red, prompting 117 to stop his question. Dr. Kolaski then waved goodbye and turned towards the elevator.

"Could you please tell... 43? Merry Christmas?"

117 nodded.

"Yes sir."

"Don't forget... to tell the other amborgs, too."

Then he was gone. It was just him and Serina now.

"Don't you have a party to get to?" she asked.

"Are you going?"

Serina smiled and nodded her head.

"Of course I'll be there," she said. "I can make time. I'm here, I'm there, I'm everywhere! Remember? It's easy for me to zoom all over the place, watching everything and hanging out with you."

"Could I see Dr. Kolaski again?" 117 asked, looking at the wall.

"Maybe," Serina nodded. "It depends on if he's socially up for it."

117 nodded and turned to leave. Then he remembered something.

"Serina," he said. "You know Stan, the janitor?"

"Of course," Serina nodded.

"Does he have family?"

"Yes, I believe he has a wife and two children," Serina held a finger up to her chin and pondered a moment. "This is a peculiar inquiry, David. Why do you ask?"

"I think he deserves the rest of the day off," 117 explained. "Can you call them from their residence and ask them to come over to the party? I think they would have fun being together."

Serina lit up brightly. She moved and began to float towards the wall.

"That sounds like a wonderful idea."

Then she disappeared out of sight.

"You're so kind and thoughtful, David 117."

That was the last thing he heard, which signaled to him that he was done here. He realized he shouldn't linger, or someone passing by might wonder what he was up to. He felt that his parents had probably waited long enough for him. 117's next destination was the memorial hall.

When he arrived, he took in the sight of the numerous photos and memorabilia adorning the walls, perched on the ground, or put on display. The Christmas decorations in the hall were suspended from the ceiling so as to not interfere with everything that had accumulated over time. 117 noted that there appeared to be more photos, artistic pieces, and significant personal items than before.

There were pictures that were clearly drawn by children and given to the amborgs as gifts. 117 noticed that there were a few missing persons/ children reports and posters added along the wall. On each of them, there was a bright red stamp that said "found" which indicated that it was a case that had been resolved by an amborg or employee of A.I. Industries. 117 knew that there were specialists that occasionally coordinated with their technicians to work on cold cases. Mandy had once explained that the reason people look into or continue investigating these cases was because it was a way of providing closure for people that had unresolved issues in certain fields of criminology. She also told him that every single case that was completed was a significant emotional victory and that the huge pile of unresolved ongoing missions shouldn't deter their commitment to what they do.

117 walked over to the section where he had set up a holographic frame of his parents. When he reached the photo, 117 stood there and watched as it switched to a holographic projection and began to play

its short video loop. As his parents danced happily in the holo-picture, a wistful smile crept onto 117's face. As the loop played, 117 began to ponder many questions. Had things between his dad and grandpa Mark already broken apart at the time that this video was recorded? If his parents had lived, would he have still wanted to become an amborg? 117 shook the idea from his head. Brooding over alternate outcomes in his life was probably not healthy. Once his parents stopped dancing, the hologram restarted again. 117 stood up and placed a hand on the frame of the photo while the image of his parents danced close to his chest. He opened his mouth, took a breath, and spoke the following words despite the burning sensation in his throat.

"Merry... 'cough'...Christmas," he managed to say. "I... love... you."

117 massaged his throat and sighed. Switching to his bracelet, he continued the rest of what he wanted to say by broadcasting it.

"There's so much that I wanted to ask you," he said. "I suppose Mark is now the best way to learn about our family. I don't know if this is something you would approve of but... I hope you accept my decision, dad, to make amends with grandpa on your behalf."

There was no response, obviously, as 117 watched the image of his parents continue to do their short dance in its holographic loop.

"I shall visit again soon," he said as he turned to leave. "Goodnight, mom. Goodnight, dad."

117 left the memorial hall and decided to head to the gym. Maybe they could use some assistance setting up. It was probably unlikely that they would need him, given the multitude of names on the volunteer sign-up sheet. If setting up the party wasn't an option, maybe he would request a bit of time to help clean up afterwards.

As 117 strolled past a window, something outside caught his eye. He turned to see a light snowfall, creating a bright and picturesque scene. Defense drones were on duty, either guarding entrances or making their rounds, just like they always did. A few human security guards were around, though not as many as usual. It was understandable, given the holiday season; many had likely taken time off. For some, however, the holidays meant no break at all. Christmas was just another work day.

117 watched a few children and their families joyfully playing in the snow. He recognized several of the researchers and staff members among them. These families had permanent residencies here at A.I. Industries. The way they interacted with each other brought a smile to 117's face. There was no violence or paranoia—just a peaceful space where worries and fears seemed to vanish. This was something that was worth

protecting. Suddenly, 117 blinked and felt tears welling up, leaving him feeling confused. He rubbed his eyes and dried his hands with his sleeve. Why did watching these families outside make him feel so sad? He decided to shrug it off and headed to the gym.

The party had just begun when 117 arrived. He was immediately awestruck by the transformation of the space. It had been completely redecorated to resemble a grand ballroom, complete with a sparkling dance floor and an enticing buffet. The DJs, who were actually drones, were adorned in themed clothing that added to the festive atmosphere. Among the crowd, he noticed several security guards in their uniforms enjoying snacks and drinks. A few of them were seen leaving with to-go boxes and drinks in hand, likely returning to their shifts or delivering refreshments to other guards still on duty.

Almost all of the employees of the company were there hanging around, mingling and sharing in the fun with their families they'd brought along. It made 117 happy to see so many people enjoying special moments with their loved ones. The children were particularly energetic, darting around with the most excitement. As he looked around, he admired the stunning gowns and outfits worn by the women. Most of the amborgs had all decided to dress up for the party and were wearing custom-made gowns and dresses. He felt a little awkward when he began noticing that some of the guys had opted to wear formal jackets. It was unusual to see his friends out of uniform and dressed in suits and tuxedos. Although he felt slightly underdressed, he found comfort in the fact that several others had chosen to wear their amborg jackets. Some amborgs were either on call for the holidays or absent entirely. When they weren't damaged or covered in mud stains, their standard outfits surprisingly managed to fit in with the formal atmosphere of the party. The neon stripes made it look like they were ready for a rave.

117 spotted Mr. Ramirez and his daughter, Thalia, approaching him. They greeted him with a handshake, and Thalia even topped it off with a hug, sharing her relief that he was feeling better. Mr. Ramirez then quietly explained that a cover story had been put in place. The children at A.I. Industries were told that 117 had the flu, allowing him to recover from his knife injury without alarming them. Grateful for this information, 117 thanked Mr. Ramirez for his support. It was reassuring that the public relations team had managed to keep the true events under wraps, especially since his hospital stay had drawn so much attention. Just as he was about to ask about Mrs. Ramirez, Thalia dashed off, which forced Mr. Ramirez to cut the conversation short. Left alone, 117 waved goodbye.

Feeling a little rumble in his stomach, he realized it was time to grab something to eat. Before he could, the door opened, and 8 and 9 strolled into the gym. They had shown up without any injuries and were behaving themselves, by the look of it. 8 appeared to be sulking, while 9 was grinning shamelessly. 117's gaze shifted to Dr. Kendrick, whose smile vanished at the sight of the two notorious pranksters, a look of suspicion creeping onto his face. It was clear he would be keeping a close eye on them. 117 smirked, finding the whole thing amusing, which distracted him from the person sneaking up behind him.

"Hello 117."

Without needing to turn around, 117 instantly knew who it was; the friendly amborg beacon flashing in his display made it clear. The computer-synthesized voice was also a dead giveaway.

"Hello," he answered, "Leonard 1."

Turning around, 117 shook hands with the very first man to become an amborg. 1, who was a few inches shorter than 117, returned the gesture with a warm smile. 1 had elected to nix his amborg uniform for the night, instead wearing a nice dinner jacket with a white button-down shirt. He adjusted his glasses and then they turned their attention back on the party.

"How are you?"

"I am well," 117 replied with a firm nod. "How about you?"

"I'm also doing good," 1 replied. "Well, I was notifying the janitor, Stan, to attend the party with me. Bumped into him on the way here."

"So did I," 117 replied. "He was cleaning another prank from 9."

"Yes indeed," 1 snickered. "I got all the details from Stan."

1 began eyeing 8 and 9, who were currently both drinking punch at the buffet. 3 was in charge of the food and drinks. She stood nearby with her team, keeping a steady eye on them. At her side, 117 noticed 7, who appeared to be holding a type of rifle that he'd never seen before. It looked like a prototype.

"I should have tried to invite him to the party," 117 sighed. "He said something positive and inspiring, which distracted me."

"He'll do that," 1 smiled. "If you hangout with him, he'll spend over an hour talking to you about not wasting time. He's very big on treasuring the moment."

"His work ethic is impressive. He works hard to continue providing for his family despite it being Christmas," 117 said.

1 nodded.

"That's not surprising," he said. "His wife having medical issues and raising their four kids must be incredibly stressful and difficult. Someone with that amount of dedication and loyalty probably would like to stay away from others."

"But, even someone like Stan would enjoy some fun together with his own family. Is this a fair assumption?"

117 turned to see that 1 was smirking at him.

"117, why do I get the feeling you're up to something?" he said suspiciously.

"I'm not up on anything," 117 replied smugly. He gazed at 1 and winked. "I am simply taller than you."

"Really?" 1 let out a laugh. "You're going to deflect with a 'high-ground' joke? Well played."

"Thank you. It is a surprise," 117 smiled and held up a finger to his lips. "You will know when you see it."

"Very well," 1 dipped his head in acknowledgment. "Then I won't question the matter further. I trust your surprise will be enlightening. Merry Christmas, David 117."

"To you as well, Leonard 1," 117 replied.

After the conversation ended, 1 slipped away into the crowd. 117 felt it was time to join in the festivities as well. Driven by his hunger, he made his way to the food area. 117 entertained at the buffet table, chatting with 3 and her team. Things were going smoothly until 8 and 9 decided to go at it again by starting a punch battle, which 117 could only assume resulted from a private argument. Cups of fruit punch were thrown, and 8 and 9 were nose-to-nose, which only incited more chaos from the kids who were witnessing the whole thing. The situation escalated when a group of children stormed the drinks table, sending cups of punch flying everywhere. Concern spread among the nearby adults and onlookers, who watched anxiously 8 and 9 continued their bickering amidst the growing noise from the kids.

117 knew he should intervene, but what would he say? Amborgs and children often did not make a good combination, even when it was a non-hostile situation. Although someone had already called security to dissuade the public disturbance, 3 decided to step in and take charge before they could respond.

She grabbed the rifle from 7's hands and fired a shot at the ceiling. A bright red light sparked from the weapon like a flare, and as it hit the ceiling, it exploded into a shower of sparkling red lights that scattered in every direction. The dazzling display faded just a few meters above the crowd, harmlessly missing everyone. The children erupted in cheers and begged for more, while the amborgs watched with wide-eyed curiosity. Even 8 and 9 stopped mid-fight to look.

"ALL RIGHT!"

3's voice rang out in the heads of every the amborgs in the vicinity, causing them to cringe. She had hijacked their internal messaging system and added them to a group chat to ensure her message reached them all. Through her wrist bracelet, even those who weren't amborgs could hear her loud and clear. Several adults approached the children, ushering them away while the amborgs remained focused on 3.

She brandished the rifle, pointed it safely up at the ceiling, and took her finger off the trigger. Putting her lecture face on, she looked at each of them sternly, even the amborgs that hadn't done anything.

"THIS thing here is something new from the armory!" she declared, voice raised. "R&D developed it! Actually, I came up with the design, and they let me keep the prototype after it was built!"

So it really was a prototype. 117 was happy to have guessed it, but remained quiet as 3 continued yelling.

"The safety is on! So, it is harmless but if it wasn't, then those sparks would have been seriously painful. You don't want to be on the other end of my pop gun! And that was the first setting out of twenty! Who wants to see setting two?!"

The children, completely oblivious to the loud scolding the amborgs had just been subject to, continued to cheer and ask for more of 3's fireworks, even as most parents were busy dragging or carrying them away from the buffet table. All the surrounding adults relaxed and things went back to normal. 8 and 9 ceased their little fight and started behaving again. The twins, 92 and 93, stayed close to them to ensure nothing else happened. 117 then turned to 3 and requested a drink. She looked at 117, sighed, and began to put something together.

"Those two!" she huffed as 117 watched her prepare a random mixture since he hadn't specified what he wanted. "I made punch to be consumed, not to be thrown around! This stuff is high quality, organic, straight from my kitchen, and they want to use it as ammunition."

She took a shaker, covered it, and began to shake it so fast that it became a blur.

"If they want to punch each other," 3 grumbled, "they can get a room."

She bent down and picked out a glass with one hand while the other continued shaking the mix. Finally, she began pouring the mixture as 117 spoke cheerfully.

"It is all right 3," he said reassuringly. "They probably made this party much livelier anyway."

"I'd rather they didn't if it means wasting food or drinks that we spent a lot of time preparing," 3 sighed as she held out a martini glass to 117. "Here you go. One drink recipe that I recently acquired."

The drink fizzed loudly, a sound that seemed strangely familiar to him. Forgetting to scan it, 117 tossed it back in one gulp. Just like the day he'd been stabbed, he turned his head sharply, pulled a face, and coughed violently. 3 was smiling, pretending not to laugh.

"You got this recipe from Giuseppe!" 117 coughed, tasting tar.

"8 and 9 are not the only ones who like pranks," 3 chuckled. "Giuseppe called me. He and his family hope you're ok. He sent me this recipe as a present for you because this was something you were familiar with. I can now make your special cocktail."

Then she grabbed a green bottle and a soda can. 117 set down the martini glass and watched as she cracked both open and began to mix another drink.

"A little soju and sprite. Here's a dash of grenadine," she said as she brought out a new glass. "With a lemon wedge. Try this."

117 picked up the new drink and sipped it. It tasted bubbly and sweet. It was significantly better and probably good for normal humans.

"That is delicious," 117 smiled.

"Merry Christmas 117," she replied.

As he enjoyed the drink, the music softened and the lights dimmed, snagging their attention. The atmosphere took on a more subdued tone. 117 turned to see what was happening, and it appeared that a wave of relief washed over the crowd. People began to drift away from the center, clearing a large space for dancing. A few people lingered, while those who wanted to dance paired up and started to move in a gentle rhythm. 3 gazed dreamily at the dance floor as a very old traditional song began to play.

"A slow dance!" she exclaimed, clapping her hands excitedly. "I've got to get in on that! Hey, 7? Let's take a break!"

The tartini taste still lingered as 117 kept trying to clear his throat. Her second drink was tasty but it didn't fully cleanse his system. Unfortunately, there was nothing he could do since she had run off to find a partner.

Looks like the buffet is self-serving, he thought as he burped out a ring of smoke.

117 glanced to the right and noticed an A.I. program hovering nearby. He immediately shook his head, and the A.I. returned a courteous smile before gliding off. His gaze shifted to the center, where he spotted several amborgs pairing up and dancing around the circle. Above him, the ceiling

was filled with the twinkling lights of many A.I. programs floating overhead, showering the party with sparkles and special effects.

117 noticed a couple on the dance floor moving a bit awkwardly, their movements clumsy and stiff. It was then that he realized one specific detail about himself: he didn't know how to dance. Getting an idea, he set out to find someone he knew would be able to help. In less than 10 seconds, he found her—Mandy, wrapped in the arms of Lieutenant Palmer. He made his way to their secluded spot and greeted them.

"Mandy," he grinned.

"Hey! There you are David," she said, pleasantly surprised.

117 looked at Palmer and nodded courteously.

"Lieutenant," he said. "Good to see you again."

"Same here," Palmer replied warmly.

Lieutenant Palmer extended his hand, which 117 took gently.

"What I have to ask won't be long, Lieutenant," 117 said politely, shaking his hand. "May I...cut in?"

Mandy and her fiancé exchanged a look. They both smiled as they faced 117.

"Why not? I'll go get some drinks," Palmer nodded.

He turned and headed toward the buffet table. 117 then placed his left hand on Mandy's hip and held her other hand with his right.

"Query," he looked at Mandy who was wearing a business jacket and regular work skirt. The standard clothes he always saw her wear. "You have not dressed for the occasion, Mandy?"

She shook her head as they slowly began to dance, but after a couple of steps, they didn't move at all.

"Didn't have the time," she sighed, lifting her shoulders. "All that matters to me is that Palmer is here. Having him here is the best present in the world. Besides, I don't think gowns are my style. Why don't we save the world first and then I'll go dress shopping?"

"Understood," 117 nodded.

Mandy let out a laugh.

"Aside from that," she said, "I didn't know you danced, David."

"To be quite honest, I can't," 117 responded sheepishly. "I was hoping you could teach me."

Mandy nodded, understanding immediately.

"For starters David, we should probably move again."

"Oh... that would be a wise solution," he replied and began to lead. "Here goes."

Unfortunately, it wasn't a good start. After about fifteen seconds of clumsily moving across the dance floor, he'd already stepped on Mandy's feet several times. He tried to stay light on his feet, considering how heavy he was, and managed to avoid completely crushing her toes but eventually, she had to call it. Mandy decided to stop him before the bones in her feet endured any more punishment. She probably could have withstood the pain a lot longer had she been dancing with a regular human, but an amborg practically weighed twice as much and she wasn't wearing protective footwear.

"Agh...Ok. David. Ow," she winced, hunching over. "I don't understand. You do so well in your regular classes in human etiquette! Didn't you have a dance elective course? What went wrong?"

"I am unable to mimic your movement unless I stare at your feet," he said casually. "In class, we always danced with each other or practiced with drones. I am used to practicing with another amborg or a robot. It is taking me some time to register you as a new dance partner."

"That sounded completely ridiculous," Mandy continued to wince as she shook her head. "And yet, it makes a lot of sense..."

Mandy took another breath and came up with a solution.

"Ok, this time," she said, "look at my feet and I will lead. Provided, the feeling in my feet ever comes back. Also, remind me later that we need to revise the dancing curriculum so it includes more human participants to partner with the amborgs. I knew I made a mistake just observing and not taking a more active role. There's a lot we fail at even though we're a famous company."

"What else are we failing at?" 117 asked curiously.

"Never mind."

They both raised their arms, setting themselves up to resume dancing.

"Alright," she took a deep breath and they listened to the beat. "One-two. Ready-steady-go."

117 focused intently on Mandy's feet as they began to dance. This time, there were no missteps. Even though he was fixated on the floor and Mandy looked as though she was steering a refrigerator on two feet, they managed to get the hang of it. When the song ended, Mandy had managed to work up quite a sweat, as if she'd just finished an intense aerobics session.

"Ok David," she panted, slightly winded. "Now, you lead."

"Lead where, Mandy?" 117 asked with a puzzled expression while Mandy took a couple of breaths.

"Look at everyone else. Do you see how I forced you to move in certain directions?" she asked, pointing around the room as they resumed dancing once more. "Did you notice when I led you in a turn? Here, let me show you at this column."

She led him to a nearby column and promptly turned so the two of them could avoid bumping into it. 117 observed their movement and nodded.

"Ah I understand now," he said. "I was looking at your foot movement during that sequence and I believe I have it."

Unconvinced, Mandy decided to test him.

"David, look up."

He lifted his eyes from the floor to the ceiling, which caused Mandy to shake her head and laugh.

"No David, look at me," she said with a giggle. "Look at your partner's eyes. The person you're dancing with, remember?"

Not saying anything, 117 fixed his gaze on Mandy. His CPU processor confirmed that her eyes were perfectly normal, just as he remembered them. But he decided not to bring it up, sensing that something else might go wrong. As he began to properly lead, she exhaled and relaxed. He guided them effortlessly and without error once around the floor, returning to their starting point, and that's when a bright smile lit up Mandy's face.

"Now that's how you take someone for a dance."

After the song ended, the two of them left the dance floor to find Palmer. They found him at the small bar where 117 had picked up his drinks. 3 hadn't returned yet so amborg 13 had taken over. To their dismay, they found Palmer sitting on the floor. 13 appeared frantic while 6 stood beside Palmer, attempting to conduct a scan despite his protests. Mandy rushed in as 117 asked for details. It turned out that Palmer had accidentally taken a drink meant for 22 and was now spitting out whatever it was into an empty glass. 13 quickly snatched a pail from behind the bar, and 6 swiped it, positioning it under Palmer's mouth, which he pushed away gently.

"If you vomit," 6 informed him, "then use this. Don't get sick near the food or drinks."

"Hey honey, are you ok?" Mandy said as she knelt down and patted his back. 117 began running a scan, too. "What's happened? Everything ok?"

Palmer nodded reassuringly as he straightened up. He pointed at a glass on the table across from him. 13 grabbed it, sniffed, and instantly poured what was left of it down the drain behind the bar. Palmer looked green, but kept trying to tell them all that he was ok.

"Oh yeah sure," he said cheerfully as he pulled a handkerchief from his pocket and coughed into it. "I was just enjoying a drink with 13. I grabbed the wrong one and now I'm paying for it. No seriously, it's fine. Can I have a drink without motor oil mixed into it please?"

"Motor oil?" Mandy said incredulously. "I thought you guys established safety protocols. Separate the amborg cocktails from the regular human ones so this doesn't happen!"

117 placed his hand over Palmer's throat and continued scanning. 13 offered an apologetic smile and ducked under the counter to look for something to help cleanse Palmer's throat. He stood back up and tossed a vial to 6, who caught it easily.

"Take this now," she instructed. "Even though most of it was thrown up, it was still a custom drink for Sarah 22. That blend of motor oil was slightly toxic but necessary for some of her cybernetics. We need to make sure you get it out of your system completely, so this is a neutralizing agent."

"He is in no danger," 117 said reassuringly as he lowered his hand. "Luckily the Lieutenant managed to eject the vile contents of the drink. Well done, sir, in your vomiting."

"Thanks? Can you guys stop with the scanning please? Thank you."

Palmer was lifted back to his feet with 6 and 117's help. Mandy took the vial and popped it open. After handing it to him, he immediately swallowed the contents and excused himself, with Mandy guiding him to the nearest bathroom. As they walked away, 117 turned to 13, who was watching them with concern.

"What did that drink contain?"

"Oh, it was nothing serious," 13 replied, the look on his face betraying just how nervous he actually was. "22 has a known allergy to certain spices. Remember that one time she had an allergic reaction and kept bringing up her performance issues? It turns out that reaction had some unfortunate side effects on a couple of her processors, and she hasn't been feeling well since. I was only trying to synthesize something she could safely enjoy, and you know how she likes motor oil."

6 let out a sigh and shook her head.

"If she was still human," she added, "that allergic reaction could have very well hospitalized her for a long period of time. 22 has been taking a prescription ever since but that mistake could have negatively affected the Lieutenant permanently. We're supposed to make sure that we don't cause any harm to others."

6 put her equipment back in her bag, a simple yet stylish purse that caught 117's eye. He admired her deep, rose red dress that hugged her

shoulders and cascaded down to her feet. The skirt flared, allowing her to move around without constraints.

"This isn't exactly a doctor's outfit," she explained, noticing other people nearby captivated by her dress as well. "I would like to enjoy the night off."

6 dipped her head to both of them and walked away. 117 turned back to 13, who chuckled nervously. Only one problem remained.

"13," 117 said, "you say that the mixture was intended for 22. But where is she? If she was here, this mix-up with Lieutenant Palmer might have been avoided."

13 looked around.

"Well actually," he said, "I was hoping she would stop by soon. I felt bad for her condition so I wanted to give her something to drink. I am not one of the servers though, so I cannot leave this station. That was reserved for her."

117 cast a suspicious look at 13, a sly grin creeping onto his face. 13 stared back, worry etched across his features.

"What is it? Is something wrong?" he asked apprehensively.

"Nothing 13," 117 said as he reached forward and gave 13 a pat on the shoulder. "Perhaps you could make another one. Maybe 22 will still stop by."

"Maybe," 13 said, grabbing some bottles dejectedly. "Thanks 117."

117 turned and walked away from the bar counter. Oddly enough, he found 22 sitting alone at a table, relaxing. Her seat was positioned just out of sight from where 13 was busy working. No wonder she hadn't seen the mix-up earlier. She glanced up when 117 approached.

"Hello 117, are you alone as well? Well actually, that sounded a little harsh. At least 43 will be here in a bit," she sighed sadly as she looked at the dance floor. "You can ignore me."

117 noticed that she had chosen an emerald green dress for the party, perfectly matching the decorations and lights around them. It was definitely a waste if she spent the entire evening sitting alone, missing a chance to show off her stunning dress on the dance floor.

"For the moment. But 22," 117 leaned forward, "if you are finding yourself in need of a partner, I believe the solution can be found sixty-eight degrees to the left."

She turned to look in the direction he indicated. Both of them noticed 13 at the drinks station, struggling with a mishap. He'd made a mistake with a concoction, resulting in a small explosion that drew the attention

of several onlookers. The blast had left his face covered in a pitch black residue, and he wore one of the most disappointed frowns 117 had ever seen. He was surprised that 3 hadn't come back yet to chew him out. 22's expression softened into a sympathetic smile. Rising from her seat, 117 offered her a handkerchief, which she accepted with a nod of thanks before heading toward 13. He wasn't able to see the end result, though, as someone else snuck up behind him. This time, a familiar, gentle feminine voice spoke.

"You seem to be having fun helping nearly everyone around you. How about you help me for a bit?"

117 turned and someone fell into his open arms. He recognized her immediately as he felt her wrap her arms around his back. He was stunned, but only for a moment, as he returned her hug.

"Merry Christmas 43, I have been searching for you all day," 117 smiled as they continued to embrace each other. "How may I be of service?"

"Do you remember that time you asked me out?" she said, without looking up at him.

117's smile faded.

"Uh... yes. I made you mad."

"It was only because it was terrible timing," 43 muttered. "But, I... didn't respond properly and I basically left you on 'read.' I wanted to say I was sorry."

43 stepped back as the two of them lowered their arms.

"Could we try that again? Maybe we could be each other's holiday date?" she asked.

"Yes," 117 smiled and nodded pleasantly.

43 grinned as she brought her hand up and brushed her bangs out of the way.

"So you've been searching for me all day? Really? Now that is a load of bull. I just saw you talking to a bunch of other people."

"There were complications," 117 explained.

He took a step back to admire her dress. It was a soft shade of green, with a single strap over her left shoulder. There was a slit in her dress stopping at the waist, revealing a glimpse of her leg. She twirled around, showing her bare upper back, and smiled brightly.

"You think this looks bad on me?" she asked, clasping his hands.

"Of course not. In fact, you are the most beautiful thing I have ever seen," 117 bowed his head and she curtsied in response.

"Thank you," 43's smile widened as she let out a laugh. "Sherry helped me pick this out before she went home."

"She didn't want to stay for the party?" 117 asked.

"I guess she has her own important one to go to," 43 replied. "I didn't ask. It seemed personal."

"Understandable."

"Well then, I guess you should tell me what I missed and what you've been up to," she said, linking her arm around his outstretched elbow as they walked side by side around the gym. "Also, are Mandy and her fiancé ok?"

"Yes. Why do you ask?"

"They rushed past me when I was coming here," 43 said. "He looked sick."

They strolled around the room and chatted about what had happened in her absence. He filled her in on the incident where Palmer nearly got poisoned, then shared details about the dance lesson he had with Mandy. Their discussion shifted to the trouble 8 and 9 caused, 13's crush on 22, and 3's new weapon. It was amazing how much had happened in such a short amount of time, yet it was still quite early.

"Wow," 43 nodded. "That might be a lot more activity and entertainment than we saw on our last deployment. All of us under one roof, causing mischief and finding our own ways to have a good time."

"Oh yes," 117 reached inside his pocket and pulled out the wrapped present from Dr. Kolaski. "This is for you."

"What is it?"

43 grabbed the package and smiled.

"It's cute!" she said as she unwrapped it.

"It's from Dr. Kolaski," 117 stated.

43 stopped what she was doing and blinked in confusion. Her expression went blank, as if she'd just heard something strange and outlandish.

"The... doctor that... lives in our basement?" she asked.

"You've met him before?"

43 shook her head.

"No," she said. "Serina told me about him. Dr. Kendrick has mentioned him a few times before, too."

"I met him in the library," 117 said.

"What's he like?" 43's eyes widened with curiosity.

"Do you remember how you once said that I was very introverted?" 117 asked with a grim expression.

"He's... just like that?" 43 chuckled softly.

"Worse," 117 answered. "He's much worse, except when he interacts with the A.I. programs here. I need more data to confirm that finding, actually."

"Social communication disorder?"

117 looked at 43 and nodded in agreement.

"I believe so," he replied.

"It does make sense," 43 murmured as she glanced at her gift, then continued to tear off the packaging. "The head of the artificial intelligence division is a shut-in? I wonder what he got me."

Instead of letting the shedded wrappings fall to the floor, a custodial drone walked by and took it to be recycled. 43 thanked the drone while 117 pulled out his own present, already unwrapped.

"Oh!" 43 exclaimed. "My favorite!"

"I wonder how he acquired these," 117 wondered aloud.

They each held identical boxes of chocolate. It was a special brand called Ferindor. A chocolate company founded over a century ago, they were well known for their iconic recipes. It was also a company that prided itself on selling its product at affordable prices, which was why their supply was always low online or in stores, making it hard to come by. The boxes 43 and 117 held were a limited holiday sampler with six pieces inside.

They eagerly ripped open their boxes, pulling out the trays containing the small chocolates, and broke through the plastic covers. As soon as they were unsealed, a delicious scent filled the air, and they immediately dug in. 117 cheerfully took the first bite of creamy milk chocolate, while 43 started with a piece of dark chocolate.

"I haven't had these in so long," 43 smiled gleefully as she savored the taste. "Remind me to send Dr. Kolaski a thank you card."

"I will do the same," 117 nodded in agreement.

117's eyes lit up as the gym door swung open. Spotting someone familiar, he nudged 43 in the shoulder excitedly. He pointed towards the entrance while they both savored the last bites of their chocolates.

"Look, 43!" he said. "There he is!"

"Dr. Kolaski??"

"No, another person I helped!"

917 was leading Stand into the gym. The old man entered without any of his cleaning supplies, sporting a festive bow tie and looking utterly confused as he followed his amborg escort. His expression brightened, though, when Dr. Kendrick greeted him warmly and ushered him in without a second thought.

"Stan is here? How sweet!" 43 jumped up excitedly. "I've only ever seen him working!"

They saw Stand give 917 a fist bump, who retracted his hand and waved it dramatically, feigning pain. They realized that he was joking around, pretending that Stan injured him. The two of them smiled and shared a laugh.

"Wait till you see the next phase of my plan," 117 leaned in close and lowered his volume to a whisper. "I hope Stan can now take the evening off."

The door to the gym opened a second time, and an elderly woman in a wheelchair rolled in, followed by a young lady and two teenage boys. Stan, noticing the new arrivals, turned around, his face lighting up with pure joy. Without a moment's notice, the entire family came together for a loving embrace. Stan wrapped his arms around his wife in a hug so warm it could melt the hearts of anyone in the vicinity. Meanwhile, 999, who'd been their escort, walked over to 917, and the two began to chat, while Stan's family joined in the lively festivities of the party.

"You got his family to come here?" 43 asked.

"All it took was a phone call," 117 said casually. "I asked Serina to help me."

"You called for them to be sent here?" 43 said as she placed a hand over her heart. "117, that is very considerate. On Christmas too! What a wonderful Christmas gift!"

With Stan's family fully immersed in the party, 117 took 43's hands and led her to the edge of the dance floor, where they began to dance. They glided past Mr. Ramirez, who had Thalia perched on his shoulders, swaying to the rhythm of the music. Nearby, Dr. Kendrick was entertaining a crowd, eliciting laughter from several guests, while the amborgs stood quietly, contemplating his jokes. As they continued their dance, they passed 917 and 999. 117 waved to them, but 999 only offered a slight nod. 117 could have sworn that she'd shot him a quick, irritated glance as they moved away.

"You ok?" 43 asked.

"I have this weird feeling that 999 hates me," 117 sighed.

"She kind of hates everyone," 43 laughed.

"I know that she doesn't trust everyone," 117 said. "It's not as if she's a terrible person. I'm just wondering..."

"Why Dr. Kendrick chose her?" 43 finished his thoughts for him. "I don't think we should question his motives too much. He has a way of finding people with unique perspectives. Maybe she piqued his interest when she first met him."

117 let 43 perform a twirl before pulling her back to him.

"I'm just glad to see her participating in the festivities," she said. "This is probably the only time I have ever seen her not so heavily on guard. Too bad she's not wearing a dress. I am actually a little curious to see how she would look."

"43, I did not know you liked judging people on their outward appearance," 117 said in an amazed tone as he spun her around again. "It isn't polite."

"I wasn't saying she's unattractive," 43 said gently. "I think that with her, it takes a lot more to get her to step out of her comfort zone. For instance, this is the first time I have ever seen her change her hairstyle."

117 looked again and noticed that 43 was right. Normally, 999 kept her blonde hair in a simple low bun, but this time she'd gone for a twisted bun with braids. The change made her hair stand out nicely while giving her a more casual, festive look at the party.

"You see it, right?" 43 asked. "It is my wish that someday, she'll finally decide to wear something that highlights her natural beauty. Sure, her start may not have been the best...But with more time spent with us, maybe things will improve for her, giving her the chance to be more herself. Once the world is at peace, we might be out of a job and actually have time for vacations. Frankly, I think 917 is the lucky one here. He's her best friend, and it didn't even take much to get there. It seems like 999 has a bit of a soft spot for him."

"Well, that is why she is known as a lone wolf," 117 remarked. "She is nearly as deadly as you are, and getting to know her takes considerable patience. Despite her rough looking exterior, 917 has always had a knack for seeing things in people and situations that most overlook. Maybe he was able to see past her fortified defenses. His relationship with 999 seems to be perfectly balanced. Very interesting."

"Do you think their relationship is similar to ours?" 43 asked as 117 dipped her.

"Possibly," 117 replied, pulling her back upright. "But, you are obviously more outspoken than she is."

"Do you prefer I not talk as much as I do?" 43 teased.

"No," 117 smiled. "I prefer hearing your voice all the time."

"Well, that's something I'm happy to hear you say," 43 chuckled. "You know, 999's stoic and quiet personality can be attractive to some people."

"Well," 117 shrugged, "as everyone always says, we aren't all the same. We aren't better than them but we have our own special relationship that no one can match. Precisely because it's unique only to the two of us. 917 and 999 have their close friendship. I have you."

43 paused, then turned her head away. He noticed that she was grinning, but she couldn't meet his eyes anymore. Was this too embarrassing?

Suddenly, his temperature scanner activated and he detected a heat spike from her. He quickly shut it off. It was an invasion of privacy to scan someone's readings without their consent.

"How can you say things like that so casually?" she asked with a deep blush on her face.

"Oh, did I say something wrong again?"

"No, not this time."

43 turned to look at him and smiled. Something about this one made his heart skip a beat. 117 felt his throat tighten, making it a little difficult to breathe. This was a new sensation.

"Are you alright, 117?"

43's expression shifted to one of concern as they stopped dancing, and 117's hands rested on her waist. He glanced down, a hint of uncertainty in his eyes.

"I am fine," he replied calmly. "Although, I am having a brief moment of heightened anxiety."

"Why?" 43 asked as her eyes widened. "Are you alright?"

"It's because I want to ask you something... but I don't know how."

117 took her hand gently and guided her away from the dance floor. They walked side by side to a quieter spot along the gym wall for a bit of privacy. Although a few people lingered nearby, their attention was mainly focused on the center of the room, allowing 117 and 43 to stay out of sight for the moment. 43 inched a bit closer to 117's side.

"You should never have to be anxious around me," she said empathetically. "I mean. We are at that stage where we can always tell each other what's on our minds... right?"

"Of course," 117 replied quickly. "It isn't that complicated at all. I am very anxious about what is next because I still need to give you my gift. I spent the last few days making preparations for it. So please 43, would you close your eyes?"

43 nodded and promptly shut her eyes. Once he was sure that she couldn't see, 117 reached into his pocket and pulled out a box. Just then, there was a loud "chink", causing him to look up. 43, having heard the sound too, tilted her head up but kept her eyes shut, patiently waiting. Someone had fired a dart, embedding itself in the wall a few feet above them. Dangling from it was a sprig of mistletoe. 117 quickly assessed the angle and looked for the point of origin based on its trajectory. In the distance, he spotted 297, 35, and 57 waving at him. The trio of amborgs beamed, giving him a thumbs-up. There was a tiny crossbow in 297's hand.

Oh, why not? 117 gulped and slowly inhaled. *Here goes...*

He glanced at the box in his hand, then back at Serina. With her eyes still shut, he knew he needed to speed things along. The more he delayed, the less likely she'd continue to go along with this.

Shifting the box to his left hand, he tenderly cradled her cheek with his right and leaned in for a kiss. As he closed the distance, 117 knew there was no turning back; he was now just inches away from her. 43 instinctively turned her head, sensing his proximity, and moved closer. When their lips finally met, he pressed against her gently. Although it didn't quite go how he initially planned, it would have to do. Doubts flickered in his mind about whether this was the right choice, and he considered pulling away, but 43 wrapped her arms around his neck, holding him in place. He'd anticipated her returning the kiss, but it was more enchanting than he had imagined. After a few moments, they reluctantly pulled apart, but remained locked in a warm embrace.

"About time."

43 and 117 turned to see Serina floating close by. She gave a playful wink and flashed a bright smile while waving at them enthusiastically. With a flourish, she executed a backflip before vanishing into thin air. 43 laughed when she noticed the other amborgs nearby, all clapping and cheering in excitement.

"Nice move with the mistletoe dart," she remarked as she glanced upwards.

"Actually, it wasn't me," 117 replied.

"I know," 43 nodded. "The sudden mistletoe hitting its mark and then prompting you to go for a kiss? Clever."

"Well, I felt anxious because I wasn't sure if you liked me enough for something of that level," 117 said. "But now I know for sure."

"Absolutely," 43 smiled. Then she looked down. "Now why don't you tell me what's in the box?"

Without hesitation, 117 opened the box, revealing a beautiful silver chain bracelet. 43 gasped as she picked it up, her fingers tracing its delicate links as it sparkled in the low lighting. The soft glow of the party's lighting highlighted the chain's texture, and the look of wonder on her face assured him that his hard work had truly paid off.

"This for me? David 117, it is beautiful! Where did you find this?"

"I made it myself," he explained as he slipped the chain over her wrist and secured it. "Now you know what I was in the middle of accomplishing during my spare time. I hadn't heard from you in a while so... I tried to find something to do. It is very durable but can shine even with the faintest light so remember to conceal it during stealth missions."

"You made this yourself?" 43 nodded in approval as she held up her wrist and admired the chain. "Why not just buy one?"

"Most stores are quite expensive," 117 admitted. "Even with the allowance we get from Dr. Kendrick, I don't think I could afford the ones you liked."

"117," 43 shook her head insistently, holding her wrist out to him. "This is perfect. I don't want you to empty your bank account for me. The fact that you learned to make this says enough."

"Thank you," 117 said, filled with satisfaction.

"Oh... if I had known, I would have gotten you something equally as good," 43 said glumly, looking a little crestfallen. 117 squeezed her hand. "I mean I did get you something, but you put so much work into yours..."

"I will love whatever you got me," 117 said confidently. "In all fairness, that kiss was really good."

"Not bad for a first kiss, right?" 43 smirked.

"Where did you learn how to kiss?" 117 asked curiously.

"Where did you learn?" 43 countered.

"Movies," 117 answered. "I was imitating a lot of actors' forms and methods."

"Same," 43 said enthusiastically. Then she looked over 117's shoulder and nodded. "Anyway, here's your present."

A waiter walked up to them and held out a tray with several glasses of drinks. 117 noticed a small box perched on the edge. 43 thanked the waiter and eagerly picked up the box. Carefully, she held it up to him, then pulled off the lid to reveal a delicate glass figurine of two swans gracefully intertwined.

"Do you remember that zoo we visited just after we were enhanced?" 43 asked. "I saw this in the gift shop and picked it up. I thought you might like it."

"I do," 117 smiled as he gazed at the glass figurines. "These are pretty."

"I always loved how swans moved so when I saw this on the store shelves, I thought of you," 43 smiled. "It was really fun being deployed to their natural habitat."

"But... that was a zoo..."

"It's still considered a habitat. Artificial but still a habitat. Heh."

Both of them chuckled. 117 carefully put the swans inside the box that had previously contained his gift to her.

"There, it is safe with me and I shall treasure this," he said pocketing the box. "It won't be as if I'm carrying this with me into combat."

"Of course not," 43 giggled. "I don't believe those swans are built for it."

She wrapped her arms around him again, and they continued to sway gently in their secluded corner, far from the rest of the party. Eventually, 43 decided to break the silence.

"117," she said. "David. Do you know... we sometimes refer to each other... amborgs... as brothers or sisters-in-arms?"

"Yes," 117 nodded.

"Well, you gave me a really passionate kiss," 43 stated and cleared her throat. "We... uh... passionately kissed each other. Is it safe to say that we're cementing a serious relationship?"

117 gulped and nodded his head.

"Yes," he said. "Yes we are."

"Great!" 43 smiled as she moved in close and rested her head on his shoulder. "I'm really glad we clarified that."

"It would be very disturbing to refer to you as a..."

43 snapped her head up and immediately put a hand on his mouth, even though he was speaking out of his bracelet.

"Oh, do not finish that sentence," she said frantically. "Don't say it aloud and don't even think it!"

117's eyes widened and he blinked, realizing that she was right. He nearly slipped and used the word "sister," which would have been incredibly awkward. Thankfully, 43 stopped him just in time.

"I just brought it up because..." she looked around, prompting 117 to do the same.

43's eyes wandered over the couples at the party. Most were normal humans, accompanied by their spouses, partners, or family. Meanwhile, several employees from A.I. Industries were busy flirting, mingling, and getting cozy with their colleagues. To her surprise, even a handful of amborgs were showing significant affection towards one another, while others were openly sharing romantic moments with their human counterparts.

"There are a lot of couples here," she observed.

"Yes, there are," 117 agreed.

"I just see the other amborgs...forming these deeper bonds with each other and even with normal humans," she said. "Sometimes, it's for a role when they go undercover. But honestly, a lot of those connections lead to real feelings."

43 looked at 117.

"I should have talked to you," she admitted, shaking her head with a hint of sadness in her eyes. "But the truth is, I was trying to figure out my feelings for you. You asked me out so casually after I worried about you and yes, it was what I wanted to hear you say but... it put me on the spot."

117 nodded quietly, listening intently.

"After taking some time," 43 nodded firmly, and it was her turn to take a breath. "I'm ready to tell you that we've spent a long time together. You're all I have. Remember when we said that to each other?"

"Yes," 117 nodded. "Right after we were told our parents died."

"We both survived together and we both lived through our augmentation," 43 said. "We've been friends for a long time and... now we're going to a whole new level. I need you to know that... I don't just like you..."

117's heart pounded in his chest like a marching band trampling him from the inside. He nodded vigorously as she trailed off. He was taken aback when 43 opened her mouth and expressed the rest of her thoughts.

"I... love... 'cough'... you," she said.

117 smiled as he held her hands. His fingers brushed the silver chain on her wrist.

"Well, I believe the proper response..." 117 replied, taking a breath, "is that I also feel the same."

117 opened his mouth and also used his real voice to speak.

"I love you... 'cough'... too. Ow."

43 let go of his hands and did a cute little dance, bouncing in place and clapping her hands. Even though she was trembling, 117 could tell she was excited.

"You have no... 'cough'... idea... ow, how 'cough' 'cough'... that makes me feel! Ow."

117 nodded but felt the pain in his throat catching up. Watching 43 continue to speak to him in her actual voice seemed to make it hurt worse.

"Could we change back... 'cough'... before we...ow... lose our voices?"

43's bracelet lit up.

"Yeah," she nodded, massaging her throat, "that was really stupid."

"But worth it," 117 grinned. "You have become strong, independent, and the most attractive woman I have had the privilege of growing up with. I know that without you, things would be very different. You are special to me."

"You couldn't have just said that last sentence?" 43 asked.

"I wanted to expand upon my thoughts about you," 117 shrugged.

"Definitely don't stop," 43 bit her lower lip. "That was pretty nice to hear."

The two of them smiled and gazed into each other's eyes. They shared another small kiss, then suddenly, the music stopped and they heard Dr. Kendrick's voice ring over the speaker.

"Sorry to cut the party off but I'd like to make an announcement."

They both turned around and noticed Dr. Kendrick up on the stage next to the DJ.

"Attention amborgs, ladies and gentlemen and children of all ages," he spoke loudly, "I wanted to thank everyone for putting their efforts into this party to celebrate the end of the year. It's been a pleasure working with all of you, old and new employees alike. This year was filled with many amazing and notable events. Everyone here, thank you all for coming tonight! Christy 9, Stuart 8. That's enough pranks for the evening. Cease and desist for a few minutes, please."

Laughter erupted when Dr. Kendrick shot a stern look toward the back. 117 followed his gaze and spotted 8 and 9 standing side by side, eyeing each other suspiciously. The room filled with applause, and Dr. Kendrick responded with a wave and a slight bow. Several people raised their glasses and took a hearty swig as he continued his speech.

"Now, I have several announcements to make before we continue the rest of the evening," he said. "The first is a minor one but I believe that it should be declared to the world! My head of medical staff here and my personal friend, Dr. Wildman, would like to perform a promotion ceremony in front of all of you as witnesses."

Dr. Wildman stepped onto the stage and joined Dr. Kendrick. He was shorter than him by a few inches, with closely cropped brown hair. They looked like they could pass as biological siblings, even though it was common knowledge that they weren't related. 117 knew that Dr. Wildman had been there while he was unconscious to treat him after he'd been stabbed. He had sent him a written thank-you card for all that he had done.

They wore similar lab coats, the only difference being that Dr. Wildman sported the iconic Red Cross symbol on his chest pocket. Dr. Kendrick handed the microphone over to him and he spoke quite enthusiastically.

"Yes, thank you John," he said, smiling. "Well, it was meant to be a surprise, but a little incident at a bar revealed this person's unique skills in action. It only proved to me again that this person deserves this recognition. Just yesterday, I completed the necessary paperwork, and I am thrilled to officially welcome one of the amborgs to our medical team."

Dr. Wildman scanned the crowd.

"She has shown great interest and dedication into the health and welfare of humans as well as her siblings among the amborgs," he continued, then smiled when he found who he was looking for. "Vanessa 6, this is my Christmas present to you. You have worked hard since you joined the First Group amborgs. You studied, learned, and educated yourself in this field for several years. Some of you might not know this, but her journey into the medical field was met with many obstacles that had to be overcome."

A spotlight shined down from the ceiling, illuminating 6. The crowd parted, giving her clear passage to the stage.

"Medical school was easy for her," Dr. Wildman gestured to her. "Unfortunately, people working for the license examination denied her petition repeatedly. They had the gall to say that because she was a cyborg, and that she's not fully human, she wasn't qualified to get her medical license."

Parts of the crowd erupted in boos and jeers in response.

"We took her case to court, and thankfully, they sided in her favor. With a perfect score, 6 surpassed expectations, and as a result, she was allowed residency here at A.I. Industries."

6 arrived on stage and stood beside Dr. Wildman.

"Vanessa 6," he smiled proudly. "Watching you persevere when people said you weren't human and unfit to be a doctor was amazing to witness first hand. Your unwavering dedication to the protection and preservation of life in the medical field is nothing short of inspiring. You have taught the other amborgs basic medical care and now you can continue to do so as a fully qualified doctor. I welcome you as part of my staff and I encourage you to continue expanding your knowledge. The journey of learning never ends, especially when it comes to caring for others and treating the most powerful and vicious plagues that lurk on the battlefield. I hope that you will consider this as your trade for a long time."

The audience erupted in cheers and applause as Dr. Wildman raised his arm and waved at 6, who appeared both surprised and delighted. The A.I.s floating above showered the crowd with brilliant sparks of multi-colored light while a spectacular mini holographic fireworks show lit up the gym. After wrapping up his announcement, Dr. Wildman passed the microphone off to Dr. Kendrick, then approached 6 and pulled her into a warm hug.

"Congratulations 6," Dr. Kendrick smiled. "We are all proud of you! Thank you Dr. Wildman! Well done! Now then, for the next present I have."

A research scientist stepped onto the stage, holding a tray with some kind of device on it, which he offered to Dr. Kendrick. With a nod of appreciation, he picked up the device and held it high for everyone to see. It looked like one of the standard issue bracelets that the amborgs wore to communicate with, but this one looked different. 117 noticed that it was gold instead of the usual silver.

"I would like to express my sincere apologies to all of the amborgs for the numerous problems they faced in the field," Dr. Kendrick said. "It was foolish to deploy them with outdated equipment. Initially, many of them managed well, but once their bracelets—their main method of communication—were damaged, they encountered significant challenges. Countless lives, both on the side of good and evil, could have been saved if the amborgs had their voices in these crucial moments. While the standard issue bracelets are easy to produce, they simply can't withstand the combat my children face. This has forced the amborgs to make difficult choices. Over time, some of them have regained their ability to speak without the aid of a device, but I find myself pondering one very important question. How long will it be before they can fully use their voices again? Well, until then, I will offer this."

He held the bracelet up a little bit higher.

"These are new bracelets forged from the hard working minds of my research staff," Dr. Kendrick said proudly. "Made to withstand the worst conditions known to man and completely built to suit the needs of the amborgs. It is my wish that you accept these golden bands with my apologies. They did not come when you needed them the most and I'm sorry it took so many wrongs to make this right."

"Hear hear!" someone shouted. "To the amborgs!"

The gym filled with more applause and cheers. The amborgs looked at Dr. Kendrick excitedly, and 117 and 43 smiled at each other as they joined in on the clapping. Amongst themselves, they didn't harbor any resentment at all. 117 felt a sense of relief knowing that Dr. Kendrick and his team had taken the incidents from his first operations to heart. This would undoubtedly make a huge difference in their future assignments.

"Finally! Research has provided us with new stuff!" 297 called out sarcastically. "About time!"

Dr. Kendrick turned sharply and gave him a sardonic look.

"Thank you 297!" he rolled his eyes. "Your impatience definitely contributed to the development of this project."

Everyone burst into laughter, and 297 flashed a thumbs up as Dr. Kendrick placed the bracelet back on the tray. The scientist carefully stepped away and excited the stage. Dr. Kendrick then leaned into the microphone to speak again.

"They have been specially designed for each amborg," he explained. "As you already might have guessed, they are much better than your silver standard issues. Capable of withstanding intense heat, braving deep-freeze scenarios, transmitting to other bracelets from exceptionally long distances; they are very strong. I hope that you will use these bracelets to the best of their ability. Learn how to wear them and continue to utilize them well. Also, to keep with the Christmas spirit, they come as nicely wrapped presents."

Dr. Kendrick took a glass of water from a small table behind him and chugged it. When he caught his breath, he continued.

"That is not the only news I have tonight. You are all aware that volunteers for the Third Group have been selected. Well, the deadline for their formal appearance was supposed to be after New Year's. That, however, was a rumor I asked my staff to spread. These amborgs actually came online after a purposefully falsified scheduling of augmentation two days ago and they have done magnificently in the testing centers. Which is why I give to you on Christmas day, the Third Group of amborgs! This time, all of the volunteers have survived the procedures!"

"All of them?" 43's eyes widened in excitement. "That's fantastic!"

At Dr. Kendrick's signal, a spotlight shown on one of the entrances to the gym. The doors parted and a small crowd walked in. Thirty amborgs entered the gym, all appearing as normal human teenagers and displaying nervous but intense looks of curiosity.

"Funny," 43 muttered to 117 privately. "If the crowd was not paying attention to them right now, they look a lot more inconspicuous in terms of human behavior than we did when our systems were installed and put online."

"Dr. Kendrick must be perfecting the augmentation," 117 remarked.

The Third Group amborgs stood in silence, their expressions contrasting sharply with the loud gasps of awe and wonder. They looked significantly younger than the older amborgs, even though the augmentation procedures didn't alter their physical appearances. Even 117 felt a little old watching the young amborgs despite his 18 year old appearance. Dr. Kendrick cleared his throat and spoke again.

"This will be my last announcement before we allow the party to commence. I would like to bring up an important piece of protocol that the amborgs have already implemented in the last few weeks," he said informatively. "It is unsafe for the amborgs to go out into the field alone.

We will continue performing our duties where we are needed and when we are needed, but we will not allow ourselves to be cornered. Therefore, based on recent events..."

With a careful glance at the amborgs, Dr. Kendrick continued to speak. His gaze settled on 117 and 43, and nodded to them.

"I would like to remind the amborgs of the First and Second groups that when deployed, you will be accompanied by one other amborg or more. I would like you to establish official teams. Our enemies have weapons that can genuinely harm you, so we will do everything we can to watch out for each other. Third group amborgs, I have brought you here to meet your new family. Mingle, have fun, bond with each other, and protect each other. Assemble your teams, coordinate with each team member, and work together. Merry Christmas. Thank you and have a wonderful evening."

Everyone broke out into applause.

"Play on my friends," Dr. Kendrick shouted to the robot DJs, and music began to fill the gym once more.

As the music ramped back up, the crowd dispersed. The amborgs began making their way over to the Third Group, who looked a little lost. The other employees and their families stepped aside, allowing the amborgs to socialize freely as they returned to their previous activities before the announcements.

"117, that announcement has me thinking."

43 inched closer to him as they moved with the rest of the amborgs towards the Third group's gathering place.

"Is it about being in a team together?" 117 asked as they slid past some security officers. "Because you already know what the answer is if you ask."

"No, of course," 43 said. "My point is that we will probably be mentoring the kids. They look so innocent, young and defenseless. Let's do our best together and be the best teachers for them!"

"Considering that you are the best amborg in the history of A.I. Industries," 117 smiled, "you would probably do a better job than I will."

"Come on, let's see if we can find someone to be part of our team."

As the two of them joined the First and Second Group to mingle with the newcomers, they noticed something. The presence of the older veteran amborgs caused many to hesitate, but as soon as the conversations began, they visibly relaxed and were welcomed warmly. The First and Second Groups were both astonished and moved by the younger amborgs' acts of bravery and the sacrifices they had made before Dr. Kendrick found them. Their backgrounds were roughly similar to those of the older amborgs. Teams began to form almost instantly among those who shared similar experiences.

53, 54, and 55 were triplets struggling to survive on the streets as beggars, barely scraping by on whatever scraps they could find. Their luck took a turn for the worse when they inadvertently attempted to steal Dr. Kendrick's lunch while he was incognito in New York. The Second Group twins, 92 and 93, took an immediate liking to the three.

345 was an orphan from the slums of San Francisco. From a young age, she showed an extraordinary talent for mathematics, becoming a prodigy that was unmatched, until tragedy struck and she lost her parents. As a result, she was sent to a decaying orphanage, where the owners, believing she appeared old enough, sold her to a brothel to make ends meet. Luckily, police had shut down the establishment and rescued her and other young children from their enslavement. 999, despite her hard stare, had come from a similar predicament, and began to listen to 345 intently. 917, of course, was the one who handled the introductions while 999 remained quiet.

922 had been struck by a speeding truck and was found by one of Dr. Kendrick's scouts in a Chicago hospital under dire conditions. The staff had no information on his family, which raised suspicions and prompted a deeper investigation. Dr. Kendrick soon learned that 922 was an orphan and had spent the last eight years living on the streets since his father's death when he was just nine. Due to his severe injuries, 922 was deemed crippled and unlikely to fully recover, which led Dr. Kendrick to offer him the same chance given to other amborg candidates. At that moment, 1 and 5 were both deeply engaged in conversation with 922. As they talked, 5 had a hand on his leg as 922 popped off the prosthetic hand from his wrist, holding it up for the two First Group amborgs to see.

The amborgs were bonding so quickly that it seemed like there was no one else left to talk to. As 117 and 43 were considering dropping in on another conversation, two specific amborgs caught their eye. 117 gestured toward them and 43 silently followed. They weaved through the crowd and approached the isolated pair, a boy and a girl, who appeared quite anxious, gripping each other's hands firmly. Both were wearing bright yellow neon stripes on their amborg jackets. 43 quickly sent a text to 117.

A couple to couple conversation might ease the tension, she wrote.

117 nodded in agreement. Although their amborg numbers were clearly displayed on their chest pockets, he was still eager to hear them introduce themselves.

"Hello! Designation?" 117 asked the two of them politely. "What are your names and numbers?"

It was the girl who spoke first. Her golden bracelet lit up as she replied.

"My designation is Carol 466," she said as she directed her attention to 117 and 43. "It is the short version of my full name, Carolina."

"Carolina?" 43 asked with a cheeky grin on her face. "Are you north or south?"

466 returned her smile with a curious and puzzled look. Obviously, she was making an attempt to understand 43's question but before she could answer, the other amborg interrupted.

"The one and only."

117, 43, and 466 looked at the boy, who sheepishly stared at the ground. A faint blush crept onto 466's cheeks as she tried to suppress a smile. 43 glanced at 117 before shifting her attention back to the two of them.

"Well that was unexpected," 117 chuckled. The boy and 466 avoided each other's eyes, their faces glowing a vivid crimson. "Blunt. But an honest answer. What is your name?"

"Dominic 501," the boy replied in 117's mind. He cleared his throat and extended a hand, which 117 shook. "My nickname is Donut."

43 sputtered, or rather, she didn't actually make any noise, she just made the movement and the sputtering sound went off in all of their heads as they mingled on the private channel.

"Forgive me, I couldn't help but laugh a little," she coughed, speaking in their minds clearly. "You are kidding? Right?"

501's silence indicated otherwise. 43 nodded in understanding, but she couldn't help but continue to smile.

"Well," 117 said, pausing awkwardly. "Would you be interested in telling us why you are named after... food?"

"Yes," 43 added as she forced herself to regain her composure and tried to be serious. "Dom would probably be a much closer nickname. I think a lot of Fast & Furious fans, the ones that you save and that still watch the franchise, will find that name much more appealing."

"It never stuck," 501 admitted, which was pretty much all he said as he turned to look at 466, who merely shrugged.

"Really?" 43 asked in surprise. "I have a strange feeling..."

"Which is her way of saying she has a hard time believing that is the whole truth," 117 pointed out.

"Exactly," 43 nodded as she continued with her curious analysis. "Are you really telling the truth?"

"What he means to say is," 466 interrupted, "it is a very long story. He was being serious about it not sticking. I've known him since grade school and there was an... incident that branded him for life."

"Well, hopefully you'll grow comfortable enough to where you would like to share that... incident with us," 117 nodded reassuringly. "But everyone else will probably be very curious now that the subject has been brought up."

"But we asked first so remember to tell us about it before the others, ok?" 43 added.

"Will do," 501 smiled meekly. "Are you two a couple? We've read your missions and after-action reports!"

"Yes!" 466 chimed brightly. "You are 117 and 43 of the Second Group! You're famous."

117 and 43 looked at each other.

"Aww," 43 smiled. "That's sweet! I don't think we're that famous..."

"But you are!" 501 stared up at 117 in fascination. "You're the first amborg who got stabbed! Is it really true that it was your long-lost grandfather?"

"Yes it was," 117 smiled nervously.

"So, he beat you? Fully kicked your butt?"

"Well, I wouldn't put it that way..." 117 could feel the phantom pain in his stomach again.

"501," 466 grumbled, "it's really rude to bring up something like that. Have some tact."

"Oh, sorry," 501 said shyly.

"Don't be," 43 replied hastily. "He really did get his ass kicked. His grandfather is old but is actually really badass."

"Thanks," 117 sighed as his shoulders drooped. "I thought you hated him."

"I'm kind of getting over it," 43 smiled cheekily.

"Since you put it that way," 466 eagerly spoke up, "could you share your thoughts about 117's grandfather? Will he perhaps be here at this Christmas party?"

"I don't think so," 117 shook his head. "The last time I spoke with him, he was quite busy. He had to decline his invitation to this party."

"Aww," 501 looked a little disappointed. "I really wanted to meet Grandpa 117."

"He's not... grandpa 117," 117 stared.

"Is it bad that I want to see what happens if 501 actually calls Mark that?" 43 asked mischievously.

"There's probably going to be another amborg stabbing," 117 replied bluntly.

"Perhaps that is not the best idea," 466 reminded 501.

The four of them then decided to continue this conversation with some food. Each of them knew, as they became friends, that this was going to be an interesting team dynamic.

CHAPTER 11

A Dangerous Trap

O.C.D.E. Task Force: Amborg-Police Operation
Kinzie District, Chicago
2128 January

"Mandy, what do you think so far?"

"Honestly? I've got a really bad feeling about this."

117 was seated at an old and worn-out computer console in an abandoned office room, the air thick with dust and neglect. He and his team were part of a police task force raiding a dilapidated industrial plant. Recent intelligence indicated that this site served as a base of operations for a local cartel. The military and police had enlisted the expertise of A.I. Industries to assist in the operation in order to thoroughly investigate any signs of criminal activity.

The moment they arrived, the response they received certainly confirmed it. Gang members instantly opened fire, and when the amborgs showed up, they began their assault. Due to the sheer size of the abandoned plant, a substantial contingent of amborgs had been deployed to assist in this operation.

117 and 501 had cleared out a warehouse earlier and were now investigating the area for any clues. After sending their team of police to scout ahead, 117 plugged into the computer, reconnected it to an energy source, and then began to look into its previous records.

"Why do you have a bad feeling?" he asked Mandy as he tried to figure out the most recent time the computer had been active.

"I hate abandoned places," Mandy shuddered in the back of his head. "They're so eerie. As much as I trust 18's reports, couldn't she have picked a location that felt less haunted?"

"There is no evidence to suggest that this location is possessed by spirits of the dead," 117 replied. When he found that the computer didn't provide any information, he transmitted the data back to Mandy's cubicle. "The criminal activity we found here is what's causing problems for the surrounding areas. Considering the hostiles that we have encountered, I believe 18's intel is accurate and that we are in the right place."

Amborg Kiden 18 of the First Group was well-known among all of the amborgs. She was exempt from the new buddy system protocol because of her unique skills. 18 had trained herself to be an undercover specialist and had spent the last 10 years infiltrating and taking down criminal organizations from the inside. She was also known for designing the combat training and exercise courses at A.I. Industries. She literally wrote the book and training programs that they participated in to hone their physical skills. In a way, she was a highly trained and wise teacher for all of the younger amborgs.

When she wasn't back home at A.I. Industries, she was often away for extended periods of time gathering intelligence. Most of her reports played a crucial role in coordinating their efforts nationwide.

"I don't think we're going to find anything here," Mandy said. "The data from this computer isn't helpful. I'll check with Sherry and see if 43 found anything."

117 and 501 were partnered up together, whereas 43 had taken 466 to another area. Just as 117 stood up from his spot at the computer console, ready to leave the office, he hesitated a moment, choosing instead to stay and communicate with Mandy a little longer.

"Anything?" 117 asked.

"Not really," Mandy replied quickly. "Sherry says that 43 just cleared another office just like the one you're in. Nothing. Oh, we got an update from Meilin. 917 and 345 found signs that people used to live here."

"People live here?"

"Used to," Mandy clarified. "This must be one of those places where the homeless took shelter after it was shut down."

"Curious," 117 said. "Why would a homeless community abandon this plant?"

"According to past records and news articles, emergency crews had to evacuate every person they found illegally using this place as a shelter," Mandy answered promptly. "Uh, looks like there was a leak in the basement which sent toxic fumes everywhere. Emergency crews found a way to fix it, but this place went back to being an abandoned shell. It doesn't seem like anyone has ever wanted to come back."

Their conversation was suddenly cut short when 501 called out to 117.

"117! 117! Help! I require immediate assistance!"

"What now?" Mandy sighed.

117 ran out of the office and into the warehouse, trying to track 501's beacon.

"If you just quiet down for a moment," 117 replied frantically, "I'll be right there!"

He spotted 501 on the other side of a worn out cargo container. He jumped onto the top of it to get a better view of where 501 was.

501 was backed against a wall surrounded by ten thugs, all brandishing LTO knives. Just before they had the chance to close in, 117 launched himself from his position and landed on one of the thugs. The man let out a loud yelp as he was crushed beneath 117's feet. He dashed forward and stood next to 501, who was hunched over in fear, and pulled him to his feet. The two of them readied themselves as the other nine assailants closed in.

"What happened?" 117 asked.

"I opened a container..." 501 replied. "These bad guys were hiding in there... hoping no one would notice them. Thank you for your help."

"Maybe wait until after we fight off these guys," 117 sighed.

"Right!" 501 nodded gratefully. "I am sorry if I started to panic."

"Is he for real?" Mandy asked.

117 shrugged and immediately grabbed 501's left arm. Not replying to Mandy, he lifted the Third Group amborg up off his feet and swung him at the gang members.

"What are you doing 117?!" he exclaimed as he was flung outward, his feet smacking into a few of the thugs trying to get in close. "Hey! Look out!"

501 had only struck four of them in the attack. Five were left standing, staring awkwardly at their felled companions. 501 looked around helplessly as he was hoisted up by his side while 117 continued to think of other battle strategies.

"117!" he cried. "Please put me down! I can take care of the last five guys."

"My thoughts exactly," 117 smirked. "Not a bad idea Donut. Get ready to land."

"Land where? Wha... hey wait!"

501's protests were cut off when 117 suddenly threw him with tremendous force at the gang members. 501 knocked over the remaining thugs in one massive body slam. Even though they'd all been knocked down, 501 still carried a great deal of momentum and continued to fly several feet across the room. Instead of landing on his feet, 501 ended up somersaulting into a pile of crates, adding to the collateral damage.

"I know that you were trained in teamwork," Mandy chuckled slightly, "but I don't think using another amborg as a weapon counts."

"He did a great job," 117 stated as he jogged over to check on 501.

"After you threw him," Mandy stated.

"The desired outcome was accomplished."

117 leaned forward and extended his hand to 501, who was slowly trying to get back to his feet. When he saw his hand, 501 grabbed it and 117 helped him back up.

"For an amborg," 117 said. As he approached, he punched another gangster who tried to jump him. "You have strange responses to hostile situations. Are you combat-certified?"

"I was just informed by his technician and the answer is yes," Mandy spoke in the back of his head. "Surprising, considering how sheepish he is."

"501," 117 looked at the Third Group amborg and sighed. "Is your technician suffering from any headaches?"

"You know," 501 spoke thoughtfully, "he has reported an increase in migraines ever since I was cleared for active duty."

"I think I'm going to get a migraine myself thanks to him," Mandy muttered.

117 switched their private line so 501 wouldn't hear him.

"Who has the worst headache?" 117 asked. "The amborg or the technician?"

He heard Mandy let out a sarcastic laugh.

"Very funny, David."

There was a sudden shout from behind, and 501 instinctively ducked behind 117 as he pivoted. He caught sight of another thug charging at him, but he deftly sidestepped the attack and delivered a sharp punch to the criminal's head. The blow sent the guy to the ground, and he didn't get back up.

117 turned and gazed sternly at 501. He smiled nervously.

"My system performance drops when I am in hostile situations," he muttered as he twiddled his fingers. "I wonder how 466 is doing. I'm starting to talk too fast and in situations like this, without her guidance, it is difficult to remain calm unless I hear her words of pulchritudinous perfection."

Rolling his eyes, 117 casually punched 501 in the ribs. It wasn't a heavy hit, but 117 did want to at least inflict some minor damage in order to snap him back to his senses. 501 bent forward as if he was vomiting. He straightened back up, blinked, and looked back at 117 with a completely normal and calm demeanor, all traces of the panicky state he was in gone in an instant.

"Thanks 117," he nodded in relief. "I needed that."

501 took two steps to the left and noticed a small emergency wall panel. Ripping it open, he pulled out the fire extinguisher inside and

threw it at another gangster who had just appeared around the corner. The enemy was knocked unconscious with a loud clang. He turned and glanced back at 117 with a small smile.

"My... pleasure," 117 said, eyeing the person who'd been hit by the extinguisher. "Did you really just use the word 'pulchritudinous' in a sentence?"

501 glanced around, scanning the area.

"Yes I did," 501 said, nodding casually. "I've always wanted to use that word. It's such a unique one, too."

"I think everyone listening to this conversation is jumping straight for a dictionary right now," 117 muttered.

"What do you mean?"

117 lifted his right foot and put it down inside a rust pail on the floor. With a swift motion, he flicked his leg up, launching the bucket toward another incoming assailant. A loud gong indicated he had hit his target perfectly. They watched the attacker flop backwards, knocked out cold.

"You know how our technicians are always watching our movements and actions?" 117 said as the two of them began walking towards another doorway. "Sometimes Mandy says I say things that could be considered outside this dimension. She refers to them as 'fourth wall jokes'. Except I never really know when or how I use them exactly."

"Perhaps I should give it a try some time," 501 said.

The two of them entered another room and stood back to back. Many of the human enemies they kept encountering as they went deeper in the facility were dwindling. Soon, they found themselves surrounded by a growing number of hijacked security drones, modified solely for combat. Without hesitation, 501 and 117 launched into a fierce fight with a small team of them.

"This is a lot of stolen tech!" 501 called out as he ripped a drone's arm off. He swung and whacked another drone in the head with it. "They must have their own personal drone army!"

"Hopefully after... this," 117 replied, crushing a drone's neck with his fingers, "we will be able to find out who is responsible for stealing so much hardware. The cartel based here probably attempted to replenish their numbers by stealing and reprogramming these drones to fight for them."

"Do you think your grandpa knows anything about this?" 501 asked. "You said that he doesn't use any robots or drones in his vigilante group, right?"

117 nodded as soon as the coast was clear. Drone parts were strung out across the floor.

"What I said was, he doesn't like to use the newer models," 117 clarified. "Mark likes to use older models because they are quite reliable."

"What is it about the new drone models that he doesn't like?"

"I believe he has stated that the newer models utilize one network to share data and transmit protocols to each other," 117 answered. "If anyone were to acquire this network and override it, then the newer drones are highly susceptible to sabotage."

Looking at his map on his HUD, 117 checked for 43 and 466's locators. They were on the other side of the complex, which meant that they needed to cut through an open courtyard. 117 felt it would be better to get outside, otherwise they would probably encounter more ambushes and traps if they stayed indoors. 501 would likely continue to have anxiety issues if they kept dealing with more drones or criminals popping out of the shadows.

They both proceeded into the courtyard and spotted the doorway they needed to go through. However, they stopped when they saw a group of officers under fire several yards from that entrance.

"Those SWAT officers will not be able to reach the main entrance to support us in their current situation," 117 looked to where the shooters were and identified four enemy riflemen up above. "Stay here and protect the police, 501. I will be back after I clear the way."

501 nodded as 117 got a running start and launched himself up to the second floor. He quickly scanned the room and climbed through the window as silently as possible. Thankfully, the noise from the gunmen masked the sound of his landing. When it was safe, 117 moved to the door and opened it slowly. He peeped through it and looked down the hall. He could see the four gunners opening fire down into the courtyard below. Silent as a mouse, 117 snuck out and began to creep up on them when his bracelet lit up.

"117," 501's voice said loudly. "I have a question."

117 opened his eyes wide in horror. 501 had accidentally used an open line. The four gunmen stopped shooting and pivoted to him as 501's voice kept coming through.

"Oh wait," he said as 117 awkwardly stood there. "Forget that I had a question, the gunmen have stopped firing on the soldiers. Did you take them out yet?"

Ignoring the question, 117 locked eyes with the first bewildered gunman. A slight chuckle escaped him and he smiled, showing his teeth. Without warning, he thrust his fist forward, landing a punch that sent the first gunman crashing into the second and third. As they all collapsed into a heap, unconscious, the fourth took one look at his fallen pals, dropped his gun, and scurried away.

"Smart," Mandy stated.

"Was it?" 117 rolled his eyes.

"Smart," Mandy stated.

"Was it?" 117 rolled his eyes.

"Well..." Mandy chuckled nervously, "that went well. We really need to get 501 to learn about proper battle protocol. I'll have a few words with his technician."

"At least you aren't required to work with him," 117 said with a sigh.

He climbed out one of the windows and dropped back into the courtyard. 501 ran up to 117, followed by the SWAT team who looked relieved to be out of danger. As they formed up and began to prepare for entry to the ground floor, 117 took 501 aside.

"501," he said on a private channel. "If you had a question to ask, why did you send it on an open frequency to my bracelet when it could have been done privately? You gave away my position!"

"Oh, so that was why they stopped shooting," 501 chuckled uneasily. "Well, at least you got them. Right?"

"How did you pass combat training? You're a hazard in the field. No offense."

"None taken. Whatever failures I make in the field I make up for in diplomacy, tact, and analysis. That's usually for problem-solving scenarios when we're not in combat," 501 shrugged.

"That doesn't make me feel better," 117 groaned.

As they made their way inside, the Chicago SWAT team they had rescued linked up and followed them inside. 501 and 117 escorted this small squad of highly trained officers as they proceeded on the shortest possible route to meet with 43 and 466. Pretty soon, they found themselves taking cover behind a large storeroom of concrete slabs. This room was quite large, but 117 could see second story windows above them. It was a perfect place for an ambush.

117 looked around and urged everyone to crouch low. Once everyone was perfectly hidden, he signaled for them to move on. If they weren't careful, they could be killed the instant one of them lifted their head to peek up. They stayed low and quiet until...

"117, why are we sneaking around?" 501 asked curiously out of 117's bracelet.

This time, he had whispered, but the squad immediately hunched down further, indicating it was still too loud. Luckily, no one else made a sound. Ignoring them, 501 lowered the volume and continued.

"I thought we had the advantage?"

The officer behind 501 looked livid. 117 assumed that he was probably the squad's leader, who was likely pissed off because of 501's recklessness.

If the situation hadn't demanded complete silence, 117 would have been ready to do exactly what the SWAT officer behind 501 looked poised to do. Rather than allowing anger to take over and getting into an argument, 117 counted to four, resisting the urge to yell, and instead just gave 501 a quiet look of disbelief.

"501," 117 whispered. He was too preoccupied to switch to a private channel, so he broadcasted it on 501's bracelet at the lowest volume. "Including the two of us and the officers we have accompanying us, there are nine of us altogether. We cannot afford to be detected. Especially since, forgive me for being blunt, the rest of us aren't exactly bulletproof. A firefight right now is the last thing we need."

"How bad could the situation possibly be?" 501 asked innocently as he stuck his head up for a look.

A loud bang rang out through the entire room as 501 fell to the floor with a bullet mark on his head. Despite all the intense and shocked expressions on the soldiers' faces, 117 looked on in utter amusement trying very hard not to burst out laughing.

"Situation updated... sniper," he noted. The soldiers began to crouch lower.

The SWAT leader crawled over to 117, who greeted the sergeant with a polite and courteous nod.

"Ok..." he breathed in a concerned tone. "Aside from your buddy taking one in the head, we kinda need to get to the main complex of the warehouse with as little setbacks as possible, set some charges, and blow this place up. We got a job to finish, and we'd rather not die today."

"I beg your pardon?" 501 interrupted as he sat up and leaned against the concrete slab. "Why are you trying to commit suicide?"

The SWAT sergeant stared. The other officers in his squad regarded him with bafflement and concern.

"What?" he blurted out.

117 brought a hand up to his face and sighed.

"Here he goes again," Mandy scoffed gently.

The sergeant looked at 117 and pointed at 501.

"Did he actually just say..."

"Yes," 117 interrupted with a firm nod. His head was still buried in his palm. "He did."

The officer shook his head and turned to face 501 with a look of dismay.

"Look pal," he whispered while 117 watched quietly. "I don't know where you got that idea but there is absolutely no suicide involved in this plan whatsoever!"

"Yes, there is!" 501 argued. "When you say to set charges, you obviously are referring to explosives, but then you said as a final instruction, you plan to blow the complex up WITH you and your comrades. Therefore, I conclude you are committing suicide and the intended genocide of your men."

The entire squad of officers continued to stare in silence. A few of them looked at each other, checking to make sure they had all heard 501 correctly. 117 groaned.

"Mandy..." 117 muttered privately. "Please tell me you're giving 501's technician a proper lecture. I'm this close... this close..."

"Hang on... please hold..." Mandy sighed. "Again..."

As 501 and the sergeant continued to argue quietly, 117 silently pointed to one of the officers. He noticed he was indicating his holster and took out his pistol. 117 nodded his thanks, grabbed it, stood up, took aim and fired twice into the distance. A pained shout rang out, causing the others to stop bickering immediately. They all peeped over the concrete slab and looked to where 117 had fired his shots.

"The coast is clear," 117 informed them.

The sergeant nodded in response. He turned and signaled to his squad. Everyone stood up, relieved when the threat was neutralized.

"Is your amborg buddy here for real?"

117 nodded to the sergeant.

"Unfortunately," he replied, handing the pistol back to the officer he had borrowed it from. "I work with him on a consistent basis. A literal answer would be yes, he is for real. He is also fairly new and it's how he processes information. I suggest that we should be as specific as possible. As you say, just roll with it."

The sergeant looked at 117 skeptically, accepting the information despite how he felt about it, and turned to 501 again.

"Look," he said, placing a hand on 501's shoulder. "There is not going to be a suicide. Not on my watch. We will set the explosives and then leave. Then we blow the place up after we're safely away from the blast zone. The men and women under my command as well as my brothers and sisters in arms are brave, and I am proud to be fighting alongside such individuals. I will never allow them to die in such a reckless manner. I will keep them safe because it's my responsibility. Just like it's yours to help us finish the job by protecting us. Then we all go home."

"I don't think the last half of that was necessary," Mandy muttered on the private channel in the back of 117's mind. "But that was a pretty good clarification."

"Hey sarge," one officer smiled cheerfully, "thanks!"

501 nodded in understanding. He smiled and then looked to 117 for instructions in the same way the SWAT officers regarded their sergeant. Everyone seemed to be satisfied with this outcome.

"If you don't mind," 117 said courteously to the SWAT team, "we will meet you at the final set of coordinates."

"You're not going with us?"

The officers began to grow worried. 117 smiled confidently.

"We are going to meet with the other members of our team. You will be fine."

The sergeant dipped his head and bid the two amborgs farewell. After the squad headed off in the other direction, 117 and 501 split off to rendezvous with 43 and 466, heading down another corridor towards their homing beacons. Eventually, they came across a locked door. As 117 got to work attempting to hack the door's security panel, 501 stood guard, keeping an eye out while 117 focused.

"All I'm saying 117, if the situation wants to get better, I should do it!"

"No."

"Ok, then can I try the next door? I know my performance has not been perfect, but I think you should give me the opportunity. I need to practice."

"No. Practice at home."

"But I really think I should do it in the field. How will I get experience if I don't get the chance? If you would just let me…"

"NO!"

117 yanked the outer cover off a security panel mounted on the wall after refusing a third time. The door was significantly tough to hack, which was interesting. An abandoned facility like this shouldn't have such high-level security. He had his doubts about 501's ability to crack it, but he figured it was worth a shot.

"Alright," he conceded, allowing 501 to look over his shoulder. "You want to try?"

501's eyes widened, and he backed away.

"Oh, no thanks…" he mumbled.

"What happened to your enthusiasm?" 117 stared at 501, who was smiling back cheekily.

"It went away when I saw that complicated code," he replied.

117 shook his head as he turned his attention back to the door panel and tried to figure out the password. With Mandy's assistance, he ran a decryption sequence while 501 kept a lookout.

"Hey, 117?" 501 asked as he reached into his pockets.

"Yes?" 117 said without turning away from the panel.

"Can we play Hot Grenades again sometime?"

117 paused and thought about 501's question.

"I suppose that would be fine," he started to say.

"With live grenades?"

117 turned and glared at 501.

"You know that it is a safety hazard. Wait... what is that??"

117's eyes widened when he noticed that 501 was casually tossing a grenade up and down, catching it over and over repeatedly. Had that been in his pocket? How long had he been keeping that?

"This?" 501 held up the grenade. "I picked it up from a bad guy I took out."

"You mean the bad guys I threw you at?"

"Well, yeah," 501 grinned. "I figured it'd be best to confiscate and hold onto it. Who knows, maybe we can use it? It got me thinking about live grenades for a game!"

Hot Grenades was an amborg-only activity they'd invented. Basically, a training grenade would be rigged on a timer and the participants of the game would pass the grenade around. Whoever had it in their possession when the timer went off would "explode" and they would be out of the game. 501 was talking about a version where the grenade would be an active one. An actual explosion would signal the player holding it to be out of the game, literally. 117 definitely knew that it wouldn't be something normal humans would like to play.

"Absolutely not," 117 refused instantly.

"Aww, why not?"

"No!" 117 repeated again. "Are you choosing to ignore the last time we gave you a live grenade? You threw it in the wrong direction and a whole supply of practice dummies went to pieces! Amborgs may be capable of withstanding a blast from a grenade but even we would agree to normal human standards."

"What standards are those?" 501 asked.

"That we do not behave idiotically just because we can."

"Well," 501 sighed, "it was just a thought."

501 sighed and threw the grenade down the hall. 117 began to protest, but it was too late. It had already left 501's hand and hit the wall. It

bounced and rolled out of sight, disappearing around the corner. Alarmed, 117 cleared his throat loudly.

"Be careful! That's a live grenade! Was it armed when you carried it in your pocket?"

501 didn't have time to answer the question. Seconds later, a deafening explosion rang out at the end of the hall. 117 stopped hacking and fixed 501 with a silent, furious glare.

"Uh... I thought it wasn't armed," 501 gulped, looking at 117 apologetically.

"Sorry," he added as his shoulders sagged. "I think I will just keep watch for real now."

117 sighed. He thought about saying something, but words couldn't describe how he was feeling. Instead of getting angry, he decided to go back to decrypting the code on the lock.

"Ok then," 501 muttered awkwardly. "Can I at least help with the lock?"

117 hesitated but figured it couldn't hurt. Perhaps 501 would stay out of trouble if they both worked on this together.

"Fine," 117 grumbled.

501 cheerfully crouched down next to 117. He raised his hand and stuck it inside the panel.

"What's that?" he asked.

"No, wait!"

It was too late. 501 had accidentally stuck his hand into a ground wire and was instantly electrocuted. He gurgled and yelled out in pain as he took several volts of power from the door. Alarmed, 117 watched as smoke billowed out of the panel. A moment later, 501 managed to pull his hand out. Inspecting the damage, 117 stood up and looked him over. 501 meekly gave him a thumbs up, his hair wild and standing on end. At that moment the access panel turned green, and the door opened. The outcome turned out in their favor, but 117 never would have guessed that would work.

"I didn't need help," 117 sighed, but he did chuckle slightly at 501's new look. "But I will admit, that was nicely done."

"At least I managed to get a compliment out of you on this mission," 501 coughed as he stood up. "Even if I suck at doing things right, I still get things done. I think I will take point."

"Sheesh," Mandy said. "Where did Dr. Kendrick find that guy?"

"I doubt it's the time to be stereotypical but I bet it's from someplace special," 117 remarked as he followed 501.

The two of them walked down the middle of a rather large hallway when the door at the other end opened up. There was a series of loud thuds as something enormous stomped in through the entrance. 501 and 117 both stared wide-eyed at what appeared to be the largest and biggest robot ever created. Its imposing frame was not only massive, but it was also armed to the teeth. A deep and menacing voice reverberated through the hall.

"Resist and you will be put down. Amborgs, prepare to be crushed."

"Whoa..." 501 exclaimed as he tried to scan the giant. "How come we don't have something like that? Because that thing is cool... except it wants to kill us."

"The better question Donut," 117 interrupted, "...is WHY they have something like that. Mandy? Please tell me you have begun analyzing the... murder bot?"

"I'm on it, David," she said urgently as the two amborgs stood their ground. The robot began to march straight to them. "Give me all the data you got, and I'll scan for any weaknesses. But you have to at least distract it for a few minutes. This isn't anything I've ever seen before."

"Unknown hostile," 117 declared. "Stand down!"

"Amborgs identified," the giant robot answered. "Destroy enemy targets."

"Ok," 117 said. "This could be a problem."

"ARGH!"

One of the robot's arms shot forward, seizing 501 by the legs. He was lifted off the ground and spun helplessly in a frenzy. The other arm reached out, aiming straight for 117. He watched as a cannon-like barrel emerged, emitting a high-pitched whine. It began to glow, charging for an attack. Thinking quickly, 117 diverted energy to his leg joints and braced for impact.

The robot unleashed a blazing fireball from its arm while 501 was flung around in every direction like a ragdoll. 117 quickly leaped aside as the flames scorched the wall beside him. He scanned the temperature at the impact site and analyzed the speed of the projectile. Although he narrowly avoided the blast, he could feel the searing heat penetrating his jacket. It was hot and fast. Definitely not a good combination.

"Mandy," 117 panted as he leaped forward, avoiding another fireball. "Please speed up the scan!"

"Going as fast as I can!" Mandy replied. "501's technician says try getting behind it. It will probably have a blind spot from the back!"

"I copy!"

117 charged for the robot's legs. It disengaged its fireball shooter, and a giant blade swung out. As 117 slid under the enormous chassis, the robot

swung its arm, and he felt the blade slam a few inches into the wall behind him. Getting back on his feet, he pivoted on the spot and noticed the robot had a blind spot. It was having a hard time turning around and had decided to go back to swinging 501 around. He needed to free him quickly.

117 vaulted onto the robot's back and struck the left shoulder socket. The robot reacted by flinging 501 down the hall, its arms shooting up in a wild attempt to grab 117. He clung to the joints, skillfully evading the robot's massive fingers as it clawed helplessly like someone trying to scratch an itch in a hard-to-reach spot. As for most humans, the cumbersome design of this machine made twisting and reaching behind its back flexibly impossible.

Still, it was heavily fortified. There was too much armor on the upper shoulder region. 117 examined the joint he'd just struck, contemplating his next move. Since he was already in position, perhaps he could take out the head. Pulling himself upward, 117 wrapped his right arm around the neck of the robot and swung so he was face to face with the red colored visor. Not wasting another moment, 117 lifted his other arm and punched the head as hard as he could. The robot emitted a series of groaning electrical noises, but it appeared to absorb the hit with minimal damage.

Suddenly, a loud clang echoed from below, causing 117 to glance down. 501 had gotten up and confidently struck the robot's leg, but his smile quickly vanished when the robot retaliated. It kicked 501, sending him bouncing off the walls like a pinball. 117 attempted to throw another punch, but one of the robot's massive arms seized him by the neck, yanking him away from its face. Desperately, 117 reached for the robot's fingers, trying to break free, but the giant was already one step ahead. In an instant, he felt himself being hurled backward, crashing to the ground. Dazed, he rolled into something heavy that landed on top of him. As he struggled to figure out what was going on, he realized it was 501 that he was trapped under. As the two quickly tried to disentangle themselves, the robot advanced, preparing to launch another fireball.

"What do we do now?!" 501 asked as they scrambled to their feet and dodged another ball of scorching heat.

"Well, the dilemma is if we are unable to defeat it now," 117 explained, "I really believe it will be worse if it reaches the others."

"Hey 117," 501 panted. "You want to try throwing me again?"

"Are you sure?"

"Hey, I'm willing to do it this time."

Without another word, 117 briefly thought about it, then agreed. What could go wrong at this point? 501 extended an arm and 117 grasped it tightly with both hands. He lifted 501, mustering all the strength he could, and threw him straight at the behemoth like a javelin.

"SUPERMAAAANN!!" 501 cried out triumphantly.

It looked like it was about to work, but sidestepped, allowing 501 to soar past.

"How does something that huge move so fast but can't turn around?!" Mandy exclaimed in shock.

117 stared wide-eyed to where 501 flew. He collided forcefully into the metal plating of the wall with a resounding clang. Moments later, 501 hit the floor with a heavy, painful thud.

"Maybe we should try that again," he mumbled weakly to 117. "It might work."

117's eyes were fixed on the robot as it calculated its next move. After a few tense seconds, it turned around slowly and faced 501, gradually advancing toward him. 117 quickly scanned the back of the robot, then Mandy cried out gleefully.

"THERE!" she shouted in 117's head. "Right there in the waistline on the left. There's a small gap in his lower back. If you pry it open, there should be a propane tank of some sorts underneath! Ignite it!"

117 sprinted toward his target, but just as he got within range, the robot spun around and slammed him against the wall. Disoriented, 117 lay on his side, watching as the robot redirected its attention to 501, who was still struggling to get back up. The robot immediately began to charge its weapon again. Sensing the danger, 117 scrambled to his feet and took off again. He leaped onto the robot's back, throwing it off balance and forcing it to fire its weapon prematurely.

The fireball shot by, narrowly avoiding 501's head, who was still in a daze. Fortunately, he'd managed to duck just in time. With him safe for the moment, 117 was able to concentrate.

Hanging on for dear life, 117 tore off a piece of metal from the armor and began to chop at the spot Mandy indicated. The hole he created exposed a small red nozzle, which he immediately knocked off. Propane gas began to leak out with a hiss. Using the metal shard, 117 scraped the interior, producing sparks. Letting go, he kicked off and propelled himself backward. The propane ignited, and the resulting explosion sent him flying back a few inches, the flames licking at his chest. 117 hit the ground but quickly rolled into a crouch. Ignoring the intense heat, he turned his attention to the robot, which had powered down and dropped to its knees. Rising to his feet, he approached it, placed a hand on its head, and shoved it forward, causing it to crash to the floor with a loud clang.

501 staggered to his feet, blinking rapidly.

"Man," he sighed as the two of them inspected the wreck up close. "What kind of stuff are we dealing with?"

"Maybe this... thing can tell us," 117 said as he reached for the head and yanked it off. "See what you can salvage and transmit the data to the technicians. Maybe we can figure out who built this."

"Are you alright?" 501 asked, concerned, while examining the burnt-out tank. "You did take a lot of damage."

"I'm fine," 117 nodded reassuringly. He turned the head over, attempting to locate a serial number or anything leading to the manufacturer. "You should probably thank your technician. Their support is what keeps us alive."

"You're welcome boys. Not that 501's tech did much to help anyway," Mandy said smugly from the back of his head. "I think he pissed himself..."

"What was that?" 501 asked curiously.

117 turned to look at him again.

"Basically, you should consider speaking with your technician about regulating his urinary movements so he can avoid procuring accidents during high-intensity emotional situations."

"Oh ok," 501 nodded and gave a small smile. "Funny. They're denying they did that."

"David," Mandy groaned, "we still need to work on your language just a bit more. I can't get that image out of my head now..."

"I rephrased what I was originally going to say to something more professional," 117 replied. "I believe I deserve points for not dialing it down to something primitive or even gross."

"I don't think I even want to ask what the unprofessional version was," she said with a shudder in her voice.

"Would you like to hear...?"

"NO!"

She shouted so loud that 117 cringed, which caused 501 to flinch. When 117 motioned that everything was fine, 501 nodded in understanding and then went back to work.

"She is really a nice person," 501 admitted, "but she is scary at times."

117 said nothing, silently agreeing, and stepped over the wreckage as they continued to scan the robot. It truly was a remarkable piece of engineering. What they found next gave them pause.

"117," 501 said worried, "I am checking all known databases and there are no design specifications or even blueprints for a robot of this nature."

"I am also seeing the same results," 117 said, looking for any clues on the limbs. "Your statement confirms it. Mandy, I am not finding any original plans or designs. I have cross-referenced all known robotics labs, industries, corporations, and manufacturers worldwide, but I may be malfunctioning slightly because I am not finding any known matches."

"No David, you aren't," Mandy replied in confusion. "I am seeing the same thing. Hyperion Tech, Universal Inc., Russian, Chinese, European Worldwide Care... I am even digging up T.A.R.D.E.C. databases, which might not be right either. This robot's plans... They're either hard to trace, are non-existent, or maybe they weren't even drafted at all. This robot is the first of its kind, probably... or... unpatented."

"Maybe we are looking at it wrong."

117 turned to 501 and motioned for him to explain.

"You remember that one Iron Man movie with Robert Downey Jr.?" 501 asked. "When he was stuck in the cave, the terrorists couldn't see the plans for his Mark One suit because he separated it into multiple sheets. Only by pressing the sheets down on top of each other firmly could you actually see the full blueprints. Maybe in this case, we could be looking at the wrong image."

"It is a fully operational robot with no blueprints, Donut," 117 replied. "What do you mean by the wrong image?"

"What if we looked at it backwards? Here at our feet is a live scale version of the nonexistent blueprint, but we should check to see if any of the parts were made by any known corporations."

"I think I know what he means David," Mandy replied. "Maybe it's like how special vehicles are made. Not all of the parts of a tank were manufactured in one place. Factories usually try to build complex devices and parts in the same locations these days. But there are plenty of minor subdivision companies that do send parts to be built together to make new stuff in a separate construction facility. Maybe there is a part in this giant metal hunk we could link to something."

"So perhaps a match will come up if we scan individual parts," 117 finished. "Hopefully this thing was not built from scratch. Now we can see who is responsible for building this."

With that, they quickly scanned each individual part of the robot, from every circuit down to the last screw. Suddenly, a green light lit up from the databases, multiple lights in fact. Mandy gave a cry of triumphant joy.

"Eureka!" she exclaimed. "We got something!"

Suddenly, she fell silent as 117 waited to hear her discovery. After a moment, she spoke again, her voice laced with disappointment.

"The good news is we are onto something," she said grimly. "The bad news is that it might be a lot more complicated than we thought. I am getting matches for several components from specific companies, but that's the problem."

She forwarded the data to 117's CPU and he examined it in his HUD.

"I have a ton of matches," Mandy explained as she sifted and cleared up the cluster so he could see clearly. "The parts in the joints, the legs, weapons, electric systems, tactical, plating... It's all custom. It's like Batman ordered these parts inconspicuously to secretly build a murder-bot."

"This robot was not built by one but multiple manufacturers," 501 said in awe. "Or at least, that statement is almost true."

"Good observation 501," 117 said. "It is not a complete dead end. This robot, although we cannot find a blueprint, actually has used parts from several different robotic installations. Look here, the leg design and the parts forming the feet. It is based on Chinese and Italian technology. The plating and structure supporting the neck. I now recognize that from what the Russians and Germans have made for certain vehicle suspensions. And these weapons... They are Hyperion Tech. The computer and power storage components are from... various car companies."

"It looks like I'm going to have to make a lot of phone calls," Mandy sighed. "If we can't find a blueprint, but all these parts were brought together to make... this robot, then we might be in big trouble. At least we can get a few steps closer by contacting these companies."

"They also might not even know these parts were used like this," 117 remarked. "Most companies do not care what their materials are used for, as long as someone with money comes along and can afford it. For instance, Hyperion Tech is not a weapons manufacturer. But their tech has been modified and weaponized before. Something or someone is setting up for something. We had best be cautious. Whoever built this has taken so many technologies, so many techniques, styles and designs to create a machine of war."

"I wonder though," 501 said nervously, "if that's what's about to happen."

"Either way," 117 explained, "we should inform the right authorities about it. Perhaps the military can learn about what they could be facing."

"117. Come take a look over here," 501 said, holding up the arm. "My technician found it in the scans. Look behind the elbow."

117 walked over and examined it. There was a barcode, and an identification number printed in dark ink. The font size was pretty small, which was most likely why they had never seen it during the fight until now.

"I see the numbers zero-zero-zero-three-four," he muttered and 501 nodded.

"Yes," 501 said. "This could possibly not be the only one."

"If we can find the source of where this robot is being mass produced," 117 thought, "we could probably avoid a giant bloodbath. I would hate to fight against an army of these even with all the amborgs at our side."

"A robot out of the prototype phase... and there's possibly a lot more like it," 501 shuddered. "How do we deal with this?"

"If we can shut them down now," 117 stated, "we can avert a disaster. If we fail, we'll learn and improve. We may be the only ones capable of defending against something so powerful. At that point, we need to hold our ground and not give up."

"Ok David," Mandy spoke when the two of them abandoned the wreckage and left the hallway. "I'm going to start making some calls and try to get some information. You good if I go dark for a while?"

"Not a problem Mandy," 117 replied.

As they stepped through the threshold of the door they'd hacked earlier, 501 nervously looked back to see if the robot was really dead. When it remained limp, he followed 117 and allowed the door to close shut. As an extra precaution, he broke the lock just to be safe. He didn't want parts of it to come alive and chase them.

After they turned a corner to catch their breath, 117 glanced over his shoulder.

"That might have been something my grandfather had warned me about," he said. "New things are being invented every day, which is making things harder for us."

"Do you think Grandpa Mark will have more information?" 501 asked.

"Possibly," 117 nodded. "While our technicians analyze that robot's parts and work out its origins, I'll call him after we get back. We should find 43 and 466."

117 felt it wasn't safe for the team to be split apart. Even though they were utilizing the buddy system, there was something else about this abandoned facility that was nagging at him. 501 nodded in agreement and followed 117.

Fortunately, they didn't have to search that long. They rounded another corner and both let out a yelp of surprise.

43 had her arms wrapped around 466's shoulders. 466 was hugging both of her arms close to her body and shivering. The girls were covered in a thin layer of frost and ice. Judging by their appearance, someone had tried to freeze them.

"H-hello to you t-too," 43 shivered.

"Yikes!"

501 rushed forward and hugged 466. She buried herself in his arms as 43 crossed hers and stood next to 117.

"You two look like you've been through hell," 43 noted as she examined their uniforms.

"We encountered a new robot," 117 explained. "Am I correct in assuming that you also had a similar encounter?"

"Evil death droid that targets amborgs? Yes," 43 nodded. "I'm going to take a hot shower after this."

"What happened?" 501 asked curiously.

"It tried to freeze us with some kind of ice ray cannon," 466 replied as 501 continued to rub up her shoulders in an up and down motion to keep her warm. "But it was fun taking it down."

"Fun?" 117 asked.

"It tried to freeze the floor in an attempt to keep us unbalanced, but we then used that to our advantage," 43 explained. "It's big size wasn't able to keep up with us. We ice skated and slid around to dodge it."

"We weren't entirely successful," 466 said as she pulled away from 501. He looked down and noticed that much of the ice and frost had stuck to him. "It still managed to hit us."

"I hate to think what would have happened if the police had found that giant robot instead of us," 43 sighed. "I'm glad we managed to take it down before it could hurt anyone else."

"But," 117 looked down grimly, "something tells me that the one you destroyed and the one 501 and I fought weren't the only ones."

"Well, I'm glad we ran into you," 43 nodded with a confident smile. "It might be easier to take down another one of those robots as a team."

"I'd feel much better if Donut was with me," 466 smiled, nodding eagerly.

"I'd feel a little bit better, too," 117 said.

466 blinked and looked at 117. When she turned around, she noticed 501 wearing a nervous smile. Realization washed over her, and suspicion crept into her expression.

"501, what did you do this time?"

"I'll let you two catch up," 117 stated.

117 and 43 walked ahead while 501 and 466 took a moment to discuss the events from earlier. Once they finished their private chat, 466 broadcasted her thoughts to 43 and 117.

"I apologize. 501 talks way too much," 466 said, which caused 117 and 43 to stop and look back at the two Third Group amborgs. "It is understandable that 117 would be irritated. I'm sorry that he keeps giving away locations of allies, and for getting shot in the head... and for confusing the SWAT team earlier... and for playing with a live grenade."

"An apology is not necessary," 117 smiled reassuringly. "I have already chosen to forgive 501."

501 beamed while 466 sighed in relief. 43, however, spoke privately to 117.

"So why did you look like you were in a lot of pain saying that?" she smiled with an amused glint in her eye.

"It's the burden of having to be a mentor," 117 replied in a dignified tone.

As they continued on, 501 resumed describing what had happened to him and 117 earlier. 466 listened with interest, giving him her undivided attention. 43 took that opportunity to lift her wrist, projecting a holographic image of the massive robot they'd fought earlier.

"We need to revise our tactics once we finish this mission," 43 stated.

"I agree," 117 nodded.

"Sherry thinks that if these giant hulks of metal get out there on the streets," she said in a low voice, "then a lot of innocent people will be in danger. It took a significant amount of strength for us to take down just one. What happens if we encounter a bunch of them all at once?"

"I've been thinking," 117 murmured, "but to be honest, I don't know if my ideas are fully rendered. We might need to conduct an emergency meeting with the others."

"I'm also starting to think that you should avoid throwing 501 at any more enemies," 43 giggled. "It might hinder your friendship."

"He doesn't seem to mind," 117 shrugged.

"Well, how would you feel if you were thrown by one of the others?" 43 asked. "You can also be an efficient projectile taking down any obstacle in your path."

"You just want to see me get sent flying... don't you?"

"I'm just saying," 43 stuck out her tongue playfully and winked. "Continued abuse and bullying of our friends will be bad for you. What goes around, comes around."

The four of them finally made it to the center of the facility, drawing near to the beacons of the other amborg teams. Police officers welcomed them, granting access past their perimeter checkpoints. Once inside, they found themselves in a vast, open area. The floor was marred with numerous holes and jagged sections missing from the foundation. This space had once served as a tool processing and machinery room, but it appeared that someone had violently stripped away the equipment. Now, it stood as a hollow shell, a shadow of its once-thriving industrial past.

Demolition teams and drones were busy setting up explosives, and 117 noticed the SWAT team he and 501 encountered earlier interacting with a group of engineers who had been escorted onto the premises. These engineers were responsible for determining precise locations for the explosive charges. As 117 scanned the room, his eyes landed on large windows in one corner, revealing another office building similar to the one where he'd tried to hack into a computer. Inside, he spotted 917, 999, and their Third Group Apprentice, Amara 345, checking another computer system. 117 shifted his attention towards a few other familiar faces.

3, the First Group amborg in charge of this operation, was in deep conversation with 297, 57 and 35. 117 led his team towards them, but their entrance didn't go unnoticed.

"Look, more amborgs!" they heard someone shout.

57 and 35 finished their briefing with 3 and headed over to them.

"Good to see you," 35 high-fived 117 while 57 gave 43 a brief hug.

"Likewise," 117 replied. "We need to tell you about a new enemy we encountered. Unless... you already know what it is."

35 and 57 both grinned at each other. Then they looked at the four arrivals with wide smiles.

"Is that a yes?" 501 asked curiously.

"We discovered a room with two giant robots," 57 explained.

"Like these?" 43 held up her bracelet and showed the image of the robot again.

"Yeah," 35 nodded in confirmation. "They were deactivated but we managed to scan and photograph them. It was a pretty interesting find."

"We were about to recommend a construction crew pack them up and transport them out of here," 57 stated, "but we decided to leave them here to be destroyed once we take out this plant."

"Why aren't we taking them with us?" 466 asked softly, raising her hand timidly. "Wouldn't it be better to study those robots later?"

"That's valid, but probably not safe," 57 answered. "The first thing that came to mind was a Trojan horse."

"Trojan horse?" 501 tilted his head to the side. "Are you worried that it'll come alive?"

"3 agreed with our decision," 35 smiled. "If, for example, we take one of those big behemoth robots back to A.I. Industries to study, we wouldn't want to risk it coming alive and tearing apart our own halls."

"Someone either forgot to activate those robots when we found them or they purposefully left them there for us to find," 57 stated, eyeing 117 with a slight nod of her head. "Based on past incidents, we wanted to proceed cautiously."

35 and 57 then walked past them and waved.

"We're going to head out and return to the command post," 57 explained. "Time to help coordinate the clean-up efforts."

117, 43, 501 and 466 bid them a brief farewell. Once they stepped out with a few officers to escort them, 117 took his team over to 3 and 297. They looked pleased at the sight of them.

"How are you guys?" 297 asked.

"Surviving," 43 replied.

"Good to hear," 3 nodded. "We're just about wrapped up too. Charges are almost done being set up. Once this place gets demolished, the city planners have some very interesting ideas on what to rebuild here. Every team that's entered this area has given the all clear. We've captured several individuals who tried to resist, and now it's time to interrogate them for information. Maybe we'll actually be home in time for me to practice a new recipe. Those big robots everyone's been talking about are definitely the highlight of this mission."

"3," 117 said softly. "Did... anyone else encounter those giant robots? Anyone... human?"

297 and 3's faces fell at his questions. That gave him the answer, but 3 still respectfully dipped her head.

"I'm afraid so," she said mournfully as she glanced at 297. "Two officers were burned alive in 297's team. Four more were evacuated with critical injuries."

"They tried to help me when they saw that I was struggling," 297 looked sorrowful as he gripped his rifle tightly. "They didn't stand a chance."

"They fought heroically," 3 informed them. "We will honor them once we leave here."

"They're incredibly brave," 43 said gently. "I'm so sorry."

117 glanced over at 501 and 466, noticing their anxious expressions and the distress that the news had caused them.

"501, 466," 117 said, "perhaps you two could join 917 and 999? Maybe see if they need help with the computer systems?"

501 and 466 nodded and left without a word.

"Those two went through one hell of a first day on their first operation," 297 remarked. "They ain't kids anymore."

"501 still seems to act like one," 117 replied.

297 let out a laugh.

"Caused you a few problems, eh?" he guessed.

"Essentially," 117 replied.

117 lifted his fist, and 297 reciprocated by giving him a fist bump, both of them smirking.

"Alright everyone," 3 stated. "Spread the word to everyone here. We're getting out of here."

3 and 297 walked off to speak to some of the squad leaders, while 43 and 117 made their way to the center. A group of engineers, accompanied by their drone assistants, were busy coordinating their tasks. Upon hearing from 117 and 43 about the upcoming evacuation, they nodded in understanding and complied. After assessing the progression of the setup, 43 and 117 established a private channel to have a conversation. Before they could talk to each other, one of the engineers approached and handed 117 a data pad.

"Here," he said quickly before turning to dig through the computers again. "This is most of what we could steal off the computers. We gave amborgs 297 and 3 everything when we first came in here. This is just some additional info that we just found."

"Thank you sir," 117 nodded and immediately began to scan the data. "Please get out safely as soon as possible."

The engineer smiled, lifting his hand up to his helmet and said goodbye. He rushed over to his colleagues and they began to pack up their tools.

117 conversed privately with 43 as they looked at the data pad. Suddenly, 117 heard Mandy's voice in the back of his head.

"Sorry about that," she said. "I had to get a snack and some water while looking over everything. We all got a little too distracted debating the origins of the giant robots."

"It's alright," 117 said. "43 and I are transmitting some data to you. Could you help us take a look?"

"What I'm here for," Mandy said cheerfully.

43 read the information on the data pad, looking concerned.

"Manifests, shipping and inventory lists. Wait," she said, looking over the recovered information. "A lot of it must have been corrupted or destroyed when we infiltrated the place. But still, all of it is generic information about the company that owned this place before it was abandoned. Several years before our time."

"I was just about to comment about that," 117 examined the room warily. "No robotic laboratory-grade equipment, drugs, or evidence that there was a gang hiding here."

Based on what 117 could discern from the abandoned room, he was sure that his observation was right. There didn't seem to be any indication that there had been any criminal activity based here. They had brought at least four teams of amborgs, according to their intel, but still, it was a very small goal to fight for. It was looking more and more like a set-up.

"You know," 43 said, turning around and looking towards the entrance, "I get the feeling we should get out of here fast. This place is really creepy. Staying here is not a good idea."

"Agreed," 117 said as he called their apprentice amborgs. "Let's inform the other teams to remain alert. 501 and 466?"

"Yes, 117?" 501 replied back to the transmission. "We're here."

"Please report to our positions now," 117 instructed urgently. "Time to head home."

"Ok 117," 501 replied over the channel. "This place is pretty creepy anyway."

"I'll tell 917, 999, and 345," 466 answered.

"Thank you," 117 nodded. "Wrap it up and let's go home. I'll buy dinner."

"Sounds great!" 501 and 466 responded gleefully.

117 turned around and looked at 43.

"43," he said. "Do you want to do one quick patrol around the room before we go? We might find something we missed."

She didn't reply. 117 smiled, wondering what was on her mind. He approached her gently. 43 stood there motionless, which started to worry him.

"Serina?"

Slowly, 43 turned around, revealing what was keeping her from speaking. 117's eyes widened with fear.

"Oh my god!" Mandy cried out.

Embedded in 43's chest was a knife. It was a unique shade of silver. 117 already knew what it was made of. There was no mistaking it. It was an LTO knife. 43 looked to 117, dazed and unfocused.

"Sherry!" Mandy cried out in the back of 117's head. "Emergency status!"

43's breath trembled as blood seeped through the front of her uniform and down her chin.

"I g-got careless," she stammered.

The transmission from 43 instantly cut off after her last words. She lifted her hand, reaching for 117, but began to toppled forward. 117 quickly reacted, catching her and flipping her onto her back. Stunned, he stood frozen, caught in a moment of indecision—he wanted to pull the knife out but feared he might cause her further harm. 43 looked up at him with vacant eyes, clearly suffering, while he felt utterly powerless.

117 lost all sense of what happened in the next few seconds. Everyone shifted their focus to their position, then chaos erupted. The surrounding officers raised their rifles, instantly on high alert, while the amborgs turned to face 117 and 43.

"43?" he spoke quietly into her head.

He did not receive any response. She opened her mouth, desperately trying to draw in a breath, but just by looking at her, 117 knew that it was difficult. He immediately switched to his bracelet. When there was still no response, he tried speaking with his real voice, but she hung motionless in his arms, gazing at the ceiling, barely showing any signs of life.

117 could hear 297 shouting orders in the background. He looked up and saw him and 3 pointing at the ceiling. Several police officers opened fire, aiming at the same spot on the balcony above. Straining to see what they were shooting at, 117 spotted a figure in black armor watching them. A helmet obscured his face entirely, and the armor deflected the bullets that struck it. Their eyes met for a brief moment, then the figure turned and disappeared from view. It was him. He had done this.

"117!"

117's ears perked up at the sound of 297's voice calling out to him. He looked in his direction, only to see him collapse, clutching his shoulder. 117's heart raced as he noticed the LTO knife protruding from his upper back. 297 let out a painful yell as he hit the floor.

That knife had been thrown from somewhere above, just like the first one. 117 caught sight of 501 and 466, their faces etched with fear as they stared at their mentors, collapsed and defeated. 501 was attempting to transmit to him, but 117 couldn't make out a single word. All he could hear was the raucous sound of his heart pounding in his ears. The only thing he saw was 917 and 999 suddenly materializing beside them, hastily rushing the Third Group amborgs out of the area. As he watched his apprentice amborgs being ferried away to safety, 117 remembered his grandfather's warnings.

"43," he whispered desperately with his real voice. "No... Stay. Reconnect amborg 43. You have tzt... fallen out of contact. Please re-plrzz...respond. Don't go."

He heard Mandy calling out to him in the back of his head, but he had no strength to reply. Suddenly, 3's voice took over the transmission. 117 realized that she must have activated an emergency channel.

"This is amborg 3 declaring an emergency status!" 3 commanded in the background. "Two amborgs down! Repeat! Two amborgs are down! Notify Dr. Wildman and 6! Medical alert! Emergency evacuation!"

The next few moments were agony, and 117 had very vague memories of them even happening. He didn't let go of 43, not in the medevac transport back to A.I. industries, and not when he ran off and carried her all the way to the medical bay. The emergency team was ready to receive her, but 117 wouldn't let them take her from his arms.

117 remembered 6 blocking his path, offering him two options: either he could leave 43 in capable hands, or have him thrown in jail if he continued to interfere with their efforts to save her. Dr. Kendrick also managed to convince 117 to let her go, assuring him that he could trust her judgement. 117 remained in place as they put 43 on a stretcher and rushed her to the emergency room. None of the doctors or medical personnel on hand had ever operated on an amborg before, so Dr. Kendrick personally went in to help. He instructed 117 to stay put and await orders.

Outside the medical bay, 117 stood still, silently waiting as Mandy tried to talk to him. Sherry was there as well, visibly shaken and in shock. He remembered hearing her apologizing over and over for not seeing the attack coming. Although he was listening, his mind was entirely fixated on the person who had attacked the amborg he loved. For the first time, 117 experienced an unfamiliar sensation coursing through his circuits. A surge of energy raced through his limbs and directly to his CPU, igniting something in his mind. He looked down at his hands and came to one conclusion.

He was angry. For the first time as an amborg, he was remembering and acting on an emotion he hadn't felt in years. Was it anger though? His CPU was not able to calculate it. In fact, the flow of energy had shorted out his regular programming. What was happening to him?

Suddenly, the sign above the medical bay flashed a bright red. The waiting room fell into a hushed stillness as the crimson light bathed the entire space, accompanied by a soundless alarm. It was a silent emergency broadcast to all amborgs. This specific alert was in their briefings, but it was the first time they'd actually experienced it. Dr. Kendrick had activated a very rare protocol—an amborg was in critical condition.

CHAPTER 12

Moving Forward

A.I. Industries
Amborg Medical Facility
12 hours later

"Dr. Kendrick, as far as I know, we have her stabilized. We compared her life signs to Vanessa 6 and to a normal human's. She should be waking up, but for reasons we can't explain, she won't. The combination of cybernetic implants and human biology are actually impeding our efforts to save her. Something happened when the blade pierced her neural connections in the upper abdomen. I'm sorry John. We weren't prepared for something like this. Maybe 43 would have had a chance if we were. So, we can only hope for the faintest possibility that she'll even wake up at this point. But, it's out of our hands now."

"Are you sure?"

"We... repaired the physical damage but a neurology test and full body scan showed her systems are slowly failing."

"Vanessa? 6? Is this... accurate?"

"I'm sorry doctor," 6 said. "43 is the first amborg in history to have been this severely injured. Sure, we've had to replace damaged or broken limbs. I'm afraid her chances at survival are low and our best efforts will not be successful."

117 heard Dr. Kendrick continue to argue with Dr. Wildman, clearly in a state of denial.

"You've got to try again," he said.

"We have," Dr. Wildman replied.

"There's got to be something we missed," Dr. Kendrick insisted.

"No sir," Dr. Wildman repeated grimly. "We've exhausted all possible options."

"Damn it, I'm telling you Gene!" Dr. Kendrick's voice rose, suddenly filled with desperation. "There's got to be more that we can do!"

"As the head of your medical staff..." Dr. Wildman's breathing became heavy as he spoke loud and clear.

"Don't say it," Dr. Kendrick's tone filled with rage. "Don't you dare say it."

"I'm telling you there's nothing left for us to do!" Dr. Wildman snapped. "Please, John! Listen to me! Serina 43 might not make it."

"That's...! I can't accept that!!"

Dr. Kendrick's voice echoed through the entire medical facility. All activity came to a halt.

"I'm sorry John," Dr. Wildman said, taking a deep breath. Then, in a booming voice that rattled the entire room, "I'm SORRY!"

Almost no one else, if they were close by, dared to make a sound. After a moment of silence, Dr. Wildman spoke again.

"From a doctor to another," he breathed, "from a friend to a friend. I'm sorry that it got to this. Serina 43 has time left. I just don't know how long. Eventually, she will die. All we can do is monitor and pray. I know it's hard to hear that one of your children is currently in this situation, but you can't lose it now. If you do, the rest of them will lose hope. They look up to you and will continue to falter if you give up."

"At least... we have reason to look into scenarios like this more," Dr. Kendrick muttered. "Sorry I yelled. I just couldn't believe that everything we've built and designed for them is failing to keep 43 alive. As a scientist, it's hard to hear that kind of truth. As the adopted father of the amborgs, I can't just write 43 off and bury her in the ground without a second thought. Not when they chose willingly to fight for a better tomorrow. Not when it's way too soon... before she's even had a chance to live a full life."

"That's the thing," Dr. Wildman said. "That's why they volunteered. You promised them a better life and they knew the risks. Augmentation was potentially going to kill them, even after spending so much time preparing them. They accepted death long before an incident like this happened. They accepted it, even when they knew that this company was going through a significantly dangerous chapter in the eyes of the scientific community. They were already on the path to death but you pulled them back from it and gave them a choice. A fighting chance to prolong their lives."

"Unfortunately," Dr. Kendrick replied, "try telling them that now. In case you haven't noticed, every single amborg has returned home. Not only are they waiting for news about 43, but they've refused a deployment. They're afraid. I've never seen them act this way before."

"If you think about it, it makes sense," Dr. Wildman explained. "Remember those who criticized us when the amborgs were first presented over 10 years ago? Many people said it was good that they didn't have feelings. They said it helped them do their jobs effectively without any hindrances. Then there were all these fanatics claiming the amborgs had trapped souls waiting to burst out if we pushed them too hard. Ever since the Second Group deployed, it's like I'm witnessing complete and total change in mentality. I don't see them acting like computers, bytes of calculations trying to decipher their own emotions. They've grown and matured to a point where they're talking about the pain they've held in. It's helping them set aside logic and they're behaving more like how we all should be. They're acting human."

"Despite my mistakes," Dr. Kendrick said, "their emotions being inhibited was an odd side effect. Due to this tragedy, it's demoralizing to them. The First Group, the older amborgs, are resilient. Everyone goes to them for advice. But now, they're all afraid to step outside. To be honest, I have no idea what I can do now."

"Even a genius can have a mental block. Despite the odds, you've always found a way. Maybe... Just talk to 117," Dr. Wildman suggested. "I think he needs you now. We'll keep you posted if there's any changes."

"Thank you Gene," Dr. Kendrick sighed. "Go get some rest. You earned it."

117 heard footsteps receding which indicated Dr. Wildman had returned to his office. Suddenly, he heard another set of footsteps approaching the curtain surrounding 43's bed.

"117?"

The curtains were pulled aside and Dr. Kendrick entered without waiting for an answer. 117 noticed 6 standing guard outside, but she remained where she was as Dr. Kendrick pulled the curtains closed. 117 barely moved as Dr. Kendrick grabbed a seat and dropped next to him. The two of them watched over 43, who was laying motionless in the hospital bed.

"David," he said gently as he removed his glasses. "What are you feeling right now?"

117 felt a huge lump in his throat and a giant pit in his stomach. The moment he heard the question, he saw the memory of the knife embedded in 43's chest.

"I don't know," 117 whispered, using his real voice. The pain in his throat began to build, so he switched back to his bracelet. "I have no idea what to feel but... these feelings are flowing through my mind, my arms, my legs... It is not painful. It is... anger. Negative feelings. But nothing to direct it to. I want to tear that man apart."

"I know," Dr. Kendrick said, grasping 117's shoulder. "It is a build-up of very strong emotions. When your CPU was activated and fused in your brain... It'll have been more than a year since you've experienced these types of feelings. I'm not surprised it's affecting you so much. But, don't let it become a mental breakdown, David. I'm really sorry that this had to happen."

"I heard everything," 117 said in a soft tone. "43 is..."

"I figured," Dr. Kendrick let out a defeated sigh. "What you're feeling right now is understandable. You two were happy and now someone has taken her from you."

117 wasn't able to respond to this.

"As painful as it is for me to say this," Dr. Kendrick continued awkwardly with loud sighs. "You can't stay here brooding over her. Unless you haven't been doing that and that's fine. However, everyone is worried about you. They're just not sure if they should talk to you."

"Is everyone afraid of me?"

"No, absolutely not," Dr. Kendrick replied immediately. "But since your return, you've been very unapproachable. Mandy can't get through to you. No one can. We're worried. Do you want me to take you off active status?"

"No doctor..." 117 dipped his head. "I don't know."

"What are you thinking David?"

"Why would someone do this?"

117's question brought Dr. Kendrick's words to a halt. A brief silence followed, filled only by the steady beeping of the monitor beside 43's head, until Dr. Kendrick finally spoke again.

"I don't know."

The two of them fell silent once more as the conversation grew awkward. After a moment, Dr. Kendrick reached inside his pocket and pulled out his wallet. He withdrew a card from it and presented it to 117.

"117," he said as he glanced over at the card. It activated and an image appeared in its frame. "You remember my wife?"

"Melissa?" 117 replied. "Yes. I remember."

"I can understand how you feel," Dr. Kendrick nodded as they both gazed down at the card. On it was a woman with long brown hair wearing a white lab coat. "When I was losing her, I felt so helpless, afraid and angry."

117 looked at the image of Dr. Melissa Kendrick and remembered her. Shortly after his parents had died, she had been there to comfort and guide them through the grieving process. From what he had learned about her, she was a trained psychologist and was the one who handled debriefing the amborgs and providing counsel for anyone at A.I. Industries. Tragically, she passed away due to a sudden illness.

"Losing her was devastating," he said. "It's been many years since then, but I still remember. Mostly how she made me feel capable of doing anything. She had this special charm about her that always made me smile. Much like how 43 does the same for you."

Dr. Kendrick took a deep breath as 117 listened attentively. He held the photo of his wife in his hand and looked at her gentle smile. The change in subject was distracting and a little comforting for the moment. 117 took the photo when Dr. Kendrick offered it to him. Perhaps he was doing this because if she had been alive, Dr. Melissa Kendrick would have been in his place to lend 117 her listener's ear. Talking about her memory and thinking about a time when she was still alive was probably Dr. Kendrick's attempt to motivate 117.

"I was supposed to meet her for dinner. She was going to cook me my favorite foods," he explained. "But at the time, my research just piled on and I chose that over her. I got back to our quarters late and found her collapsed on the ground. The company was just starting out and... I was working. I wasn't there at that moment when she needed me. Of course, Gene said that it probably wouldn't have mattered if I had been."

117 glanced at Dr. Kendrick, quietly listening as the doctor smiled at him wistfully.

"I broke, David. I thought I lost everything. She was the first person I befriended, genuinely loved, and swore vows to," he explained. "But I couldn't give in and abandon everything. After I grieved, I managed to pick myself back up. Though I still felt the weight of her absence, I began to think about what she would have done if our situations were reversed. Perhaps she would have returned to work, pushing ahead despite the overwhelming sadness. Now look where we are—I am a father to all of you. If she were still with us, I'm sure she would offer a level of comfort that I'm struggling to provide right now. She was always the more sensitive and nurturing one. She used to say that when we face such hardships, it's because there's a greater cosmic force guiding us through these difficult times."

117 returned the card to Dr. Kendrick and he slipped it back into his wallet.

"I lost my father."

Dr. Kendrick turned to face 117.

"I lost both my parents," 117 said, thinking of his family and the one he had currently. "My grandfather is my real family and we're trying to make amends. But, when they were gone, you took care of me. I appreciate everything you have done for me and... this attempt at consoling me was helpful. You gave me a family. It makes me feel better knowing that they all care. I just... I want to bring that man to justice. 43 deserves that. But, where do we start?"

"Let's avenge her."

117 and Dr. Kendrick glanced up as the curtain parted, revealing a few people standing outside. 917 and 999 peered inside.

"What are you doing here?" 117 asked.

"What's it look like?" 917 smiled kindly. "We're visiting. Wanted to check in on you. By the way, 999 was the one who suggested the avenging thing."

117 and Dr. Kendrick looked at 999, who lifted a stern finger and pointed it at 43.

"I understand your pain," she said in a soft and cold tone. "However, you must know that staying here and doing nothing doesn't accomplish anything."

117 stared at her. That had to be the most he'd ever heard 999 say to him. It was direct, although a bit blunt. She looked away and stepped aside. 917 smiled and pulled the curtains shut.

"I think that's all for now," he said. "We'll just wait out here."

117 glanced at Dr. Kendrick, who seemed at a loss for words. The unexpected interruption had caught him off guard.

"In the words... of my late wife, I think that what they mean is... maybe you should get started," he said slowly. "Think about what 43 would do if she wasn't in that bed. I'm sure that she'd be right back at it fighting for you."

117 took one last look at 43 and slowly nodded.

"Then I should be with the other amborgs," 117 replied after a moment mulling it over. "We should not let the fear of death stop us from helping the people who still need us. The Avengers never quit whenever they lost a comrade. They endured and kept fighting."

117 got up and thought about his next move.

"Could you keep us informed of 43's condition?" 117 asked.

"Of course."

117 bid him a quick farewell and slipped out from between the curtains. He was surprised to see a small group of people waiting for him. His closest friends from the Second Group, 917, 999, 57, 297, and 35 were there, as well as their technicians. 297 stepped forward and smiled. 117 noticed that he was wearing a bandage over his shoulder.

"117," he said. "How are you holding up? Are you alright?"

"I believe so," 117 said, examining 297's wound. "Is your shoulder ok?"

"Forget my shoulder," 297 said, waving a hand dismissively. "It will recover. But what about you and 43? We overheard all of that…"

"I know," 117 nodded grimly. "Now is not the time to be worried about her. We can deal with that after we catch the man responsible. This incident has left me with a great deal of feelings and emotions that I would like resolved. Are you willing to get out there again 297?"

"To hell with my wounds," 297 nodded. With his uninjured side, 297 raised his hand and placed it firmly on 117's shoulder. "I want to keep fighting too. That man may have hurt me, but he hurt you more. I won't allow my own brother and sister to suffer. 43 meant a lot to the Second Group. It would make me feel worse if I was left out of this fight."

297 turned to look at the other Second Group amborgs present.

"Am I right, everyone?" he nodded confidently.

"Absolutely," 57 declared. "43's been there for us on multiple occasions. We should do everything possible to help her."

"Let's do this for her!" 35 said with determination.

117 acknowledged each of them. When he looked at 999, she gave him a quiet nod of approval.

"You don't even have to ask," 917 stated. "43 would do the same for us if any of us here were in that hospital bed."

"But, why have you all refused to deploy?"

"Look, we know that not being out there causes problems," 57 explained. "Some of the other amborgs are afraid to get back out there but the truth is, we're all here because we want to support you. You're our friend."

"I mean, technically," 297 interjected, "I'm here because I was actually injured too. But, what's important is that I got you bro."

"Read the room," 35 sighed.

117 found 297's banter a little amusing. He looked at 297 and nodded.

"As soon as your arm gets better," he said, "I think it is time we prepared more for the upcoming fight. How is your aim?"

297 smirked and brought up a holographic image of a sniper rifle on his bracelet.

"Best in A.I. Industries," he said. "Going for the world title."

"Well, I hope you plan on hunting because we'll need that."

117 walked past, and the rest of the amborgs followed. Despite the fact that his injured arm was in a sling, 297 said that he wanted to help with light duties until he fully recovered. 117 approached the technicians and spoke to Sherry and Mandy.

"I promise," 117 said, "I will catch the one who did this."

"Thank you 117," Sherry smiled.

She moved forward and gave him a big warm hug. As she pulled away, her gaze shifted to Mandy and the other technicians.

"I'll stay here and do my best to take care of Serina," she stated. "I'll keep you all informed if there's any changes."

"We'll rotate shifts," Mandy suggested to the rest of the technicians. "Let's all do our part."

With everyone in agreement, the atmosphere in the medical facility buzzed with renewed energy. 117 thanked Mandy and Sherry for their support and led the amborgs outside. Once they were out, he activated a rallying beacon, calling all amborgs to the gym for an important discussion.

At an intersection, 297 split away from the group. He said he wanted to stop by the armory before meeting with them. 117 allowed this and 297 headed off in that direction.

As their small group arrived at the gym, they noticed that all other amborgs were already trickling in. Small groups formed as they all focused their attention on 117. He could sense the unease among them; many looked visibly anxious. They were either quietly communicating through the CPUs in their minds, or experiencing the most awkward silence ever, with no one willing to voice a word. Before long, they'd all gathered around him, waiting patiently for him to speak.

Before he could, 5 appeared and gave him a comforting pat on the shoulder.

"If you are not at 43's side," he smiled sympathetically, "I guess you have something to say."

"Yes," 117 nodded. "I feel it is time to take action."

"Alright, have fun speaking with everyone," 5 replied as he gestured to all of the remaining amborgs. "They're nervous but... they're here for you now. The floor is yours."

28 walked up and gave him a supportive smile.

"We heard that 43 was in critical condition. Is everything alright?" she said.

117 wasn't able to reply as they were interrupted by several more questions from the large crowd.

"Can she be saved?" someone from the back called out to him. "What is happening?"

"She has gone under an emergency operation," a Third Group amborg near 117 replied. "What do you think?!"

Everyone was calm at first, but soon they all descended into a frenzy, their composure giving way to collective panic. That is, until a voice cut through the noise, shouting at the group.

"QUIET! Listen to 117!"

Everyone cringed and shrank back in unease. Several amborgs covered their ears, wincing from the piercing cry. 117 looked up, his ears ringing, and noticed Serina floating above. She raised a finger to her lips, pretending to clear her throat.

"Ahem," she said calmly. When everyone gave her their undivided attention, she nodded. "Thank you. Now please, field your questions one at a time in an orderly manner."

Serina looked at 117 and smiled pleasantly. He'd never heard of an A.I. capable of raising their voice like that before. He didn't dare think about what would happen if Serina hijacked the speakers in the gym. Normal eardrums probably would have been permanently ruptured if she had yelled any louder.

117 thanked Serina before addressing the other amborgs. The entire crowd looked at him once again, all of them staring with burning curiosity. 117 had certainly expected this, but he hadn't anticipated all of the amborgs of A.I. Industries to put such a huge spotlight on him. He instantly switched to his bracelet.

"The first thing I will share with everyone is the truth," he declared. "Serina 43, my best friend... has been mortally wounded."

Whispers began to ripple through the room, and 117 could see the fear reflected in many of their eyes. He felt a light tap on his shoulder and turned to find 6 standing beside him. Discreetly, she sent him a message on a private channel before he could continue talking.

"117," she said, "speaking as the doctor in our family, I always knew that someday... I would be treating one of you in a crisis situation. Now, with 43 in critical condition, I'm disappointed in myself. It's disheartening to realize we all share the same cybernetic enhancements and knowing that she may never wake up."

"I know," 117 replied. "I was not ready to hear the truth. But, instead of moping around, we can get started on the next mission. I think that with you backing me up, they will feel a little more at ease."

6 gave 117 a questioning look.

"Are you suggesting that we don't tell the others that she is dying?"

"Actually, I think that telling them the truth will help strengthen all of our fears," 117 replied. "It could serve as a reminder that even though there are great risks in going back out there, I still think we should do it. Otherwise, more people will suffer, like 43."

"You want to ease everyone's anxiety by exposing them to hypothetical negative outcomes?" 6 asked. "Interesting approach."

"It's all I'm thinking about," 117 said. "Is it wrong?"

"Well," 6 looked down at the ground for a moment and then back up at him. She gave him a sympathetic and encouraging smile. "I think that it's a bit too bold and risky. But, the world moves on, even when we need time to sort through what ails us. I believe that continuing on despite what has happened is brave. I will endorse you."

"Really?" 117 felt a wave of relief wash over him.

"You forget 117," 6 smiled softly, "healing is my specialty. I believe there is no disease that is incurable. I will help contribute to the field of medicine worldwide. Trust me, I will always be at everyone's side when they call for me. I will also do everything in my power to care for 43."

"Thank you," 117 sighed, taking solace in her words.

117 shifted his attention to the other amborgs.

"Time to convince the rest of them," he said nervously.

"Not really," 6 replied encouragingly. "The First Group is ready to follow you. I'd say that half the Second Group and the entire Third Group are the ones that need their confidence restored."

That made sense. Many of the Third Group were barely out of their first mission. The fact that Serina 43 was severely wounded had terrified and shocked all of them. It was quite a disastrous first operation. 117 glanced at 6 and nodded towards the crowd.

"Perhaps you should...?"

"Oh no," 6 replied. "This is your operation. I'm not going to lead it. I think the real leader in this is supposed to be you."

117 paused, taking another moment to think. Then, he broke the silence.

"Are you going to hide yourself and hope that the enemy will go away? Do you really think that staying here in one place is the best course of action?"

"117," 3 walked forward and spoke. "You saw what happened to 43. Anyone of us could be the next one lying in that medical center. That's why we're scared. I'm with you... but that warehouse mission was some of the Third Group's first assignments in the field. Someone in thick evil armor almost killed one of us."

"117 hasn't allowed something like that to stop him."

1 entered the chat and appeared behind 117. Everyone seemed to perk up when the first amborg in history gave 117 an encouraging nudge on the shoulder.

"He was stabbed too," he said. "Despite that, he still got back up and went out there while injured. Was it stupid? I think so. But he took action, despite how dangerous it was."

1 glanced at 117 and smiled.

"So, what do you all think? Do we stay here and do nothing?"

The rest of the First Group amborgs stood with determination. Fueled by 1's encouragement, they were poised to support 117 at a moment's notice. This show of solidarity drew the attention of the Second and Third Group amborgs. With a satisfied nod, 1 casually stepped forward and turned to look at 117.

"I'd say that we are ready and at your disposal," he dipped his head courteously. "Deep down, we all want to bring this man to justice."

117 faced the crowd of cybernetically enhanced teens, all waiting patiently. A few already looked like they were good to go. In the mix, however, 117 noticed 466 surrounded by a few Third Group amborgs who were visibly nervous. They had every right, especially since 466 had only worked with 43 for a short time.

"What happened to 43 does not mean we should cower in fear," 117 said. "Fear is a natural feeling for humans and us as well. We may have forgotten that but almost all of us are beginning to remember what it feels like. I know it can be scary. We aren't as invincible as we thought. It was a mistake to believe that there was no way anyone could figure out how to harm us. But I am not going to sit here and wait for 43 to wake up and see us acting like cowards. Come on! We can meet this challenge."

"Yeah, it isn't like we're going up against any weapons of mass destruction, right?"

Everyone glanced at 5, who was smirking. A few other amborgs scoffed, whereas others laughed. 117 nodded.

"He's right," he stated.

"But 117," he heard someone from the Third Group next to 501 speak, "no one is running around with W.M.D. This is close and personal. How do we finish this and bring that guy to justice if every criminal has a knife up their sleeve? What if all the people we know start carrying these weapons to stab us in the back?"

"Not everyone is against us."

117 glanced over his shoulder to see 917 speaking up.

"We still have some friends that look out for us," he declared. "117's grandfather is the reason why we haven't been completely taken by surprise. 43 or 117... may have actually died if we hadn't met Mark."

"More of us would have been caught off guard," 57 surmised. "I say we're fortunate that we're all still standing."

117 addressed everyone again.

"What is the one thing that all of the criminals we faced have felt ever since we went public?" 117 asked. "Hatred."

He looked at all of the quiet and solemn expressions among the younger amborgs.

"They hate us because we stumbled into their world and said that their rules were wrong," 117 stated. "We interfered with their plans and uprooted all that they had built for themselves. Their system puts good and innocent people at risk everyday."

117 gestured to 1 and several other First Group amborgs.

"Years ago," he said, "the First Group began fighting to save lives. Now there are three groups of amborgs. More of us makes them afraid. That's why they're looking for ways to try and stop us from tearing down their entire operation."

117 looked down and thought about 43, who was asleep in her hospital bed.

"They have every reason to dislike us because we are ruining their lifestyles, their profits, and their desire to control those they think are less than them."

117 clenched his fist but then relaxed his hand as he continued to speak.

"I know that what I'm asking you is alarming and that's ok," he nodded and smiled kindly. "Taking action is necessary, but we need to be ready to adapt. We signed up for this when Dr. Kendrick presented us with the opportunity to become who we are today. We've put our lives on the line for this kind of risk. If we choose to hide now, who will stand up for those still suffering out there? We have both the power and responsibility to do what's right. Each of us has our own motivations and aspirations, shaped by our varied backgrounds, cultural traditions, and our own unique talents. I respect each and every one of you. If you are willing to step up and improve, we'll be better prepared to face what comes next. If our enemies evolve to try and defeat us, we can also prepare our next move. Even though 43 is wounded, this just means that we have to adapt and overcome."

"I will follow that."

All eyes were on 297 as he strode into the gym, a sniper rifle slung over his shoulder. He must have checked it out from the armory. 117 recognized it as the same rifle he had seen him display on his bracelet back in the medical bay.

"We learn our weaknesses to the fullest extent and we work to try and avoid situations like this in the future," 297 stated as he stopped next to 117. "Start from the basics. We run through all of our training programs and do it over and over again. We're amborgs. Risk is in the job description. Sure, it's an occupational hazard we face every day, but we'll be able to push through this."

"Is that a new rifle?" 917 stared.

"The weapons manufacturer in the armory has been making weapons for each amborg," 297 nodded and held up his rifle for everyone to see. "After all, I fight better from a distance."

"Yet, you are also equally terrifying if someone gets close," 5 joked.

117 looked back at the crowd. 1, 3, 5, 6, 297 and the entire First Group were moving to stand next to him. 35 and 57 looked at other Second Group amborgs and pushed them into the massive line. This left 917 and 999, who were trying to convince the Third Group.

"I may be a lone wolf," 999 said without batting a smile, "but it is cowardly when someone hurts someone I know and they run away. We are trained to hunt those who incite injustice."

501 and 466 both stepped forward, standing in the middle of the amborgs surrounding 117 and the Third Group, who were still in deep contemplation.

"Come on everyone! I will support 117," 501 stated bravely. "I don't know him too well but sitting here is unproductive! He's an awesome person to follow! So, I am currently waiting for orders."

"43 was my mentor for a short time," 466 said. "She still is. Ever since the holidays, the time we spent together has been so meaningful."

466 looked at 117.

"I keep thinking about how kind she was to me and 501. I keep thinking... about wanting to see her awake again."

She turned to face the remaining amborgs.

"Look at the amborgs standing across from you," 466 said, gesturing to all of them. "Look to your left. Look to the volunteer on your right. We all will die eventually. All that matters is what we do until then... with the time we have left. If you can accept that, then step forward. If you are brave enough to understand that we still have a job to do... then we should support 117. Many people and their hard work got us here. If we give up, their memories will be shamed and they will have died for nothing."

The Third Group focused on 466. They took a moment to think it over, and soon enough, they all came to an agreement. 917 shot a playful smile at 117.

"I think that says it all," he said, giving 117 a thumbs up. Even 999 gave a slight nod of acknowledgement. "What's the plan boss?"

"I think we need to refresh everything," 117 said. "We should convert the gym and prepare advanced forms of training."

Like clockwork, everyone dispersed and began to make adjustments. 1 rounded up several Third Group members and they began to set up stations all over the gym.

3 went to the cafeteria with the amborg chefs.

"We can't think on empty stomachs," she said. "Catering time."

999 and 917, along with some of the Second Group, left for the armory after 117 finished speaking.

"Swords?" 999 asked 917.

"You know me too well," 917 chuckled. "Let's grab a wide selection."

"Alright!" 6 called to anyone listening. "We need to set up a medical station here. I will be talking about set-up under pressure, giving refresher courses of basic first aid, what to do until professionals arrive to help, and communicating in neutral tones. Any parts that are unclear to you, please speak up, and I will happily restart."

297 had somehow procured a table and placed his rifle on the stand with a clatter.

"Ok everyone," he said. "Weapons training is in this corner of the gym. We need a shooting range, sparring area, and a lot of training drones or dummies. Everyone needs to get acquainted with as many weapons as possible and select their favorites for the field. Like 117 said, we have always gone into the field practically unarmed. While that doesn't entirely make sense, we are changing that protocol completely. Now, if we are preparing for a bigger threat, then we need to act like war is coming. Come to me if you want to face it sooner than anyone else."

117 stood with 5 in the center of the gym, amazed at how quickly they had all found their courage. Minutes before, they'd been paralyzed with fear, and now, one by one, they were rising to meet the challenge head on. This transformation went beyond his expectations.

"Did you imagine it would be like this?" 5 asked.

"Not really," 117 replied. "I think we're just winging it."

"What if this guy never resurfaces? What if he attacked 43, just for kicks? Like just an ordinary crook would do?"

"I refuse to believe that Johnny," 117 replied. "Otherwise, that man's story would have no fulfillment to this plot. This act of aggression... doesn't seem random to me. This man reminds me of one specific type of killer. A hunter. It is not over. All we can do, unfortunately, is wait for the next attack."

"I know. All we can do is get better," 5 said nodding. "It's not the best plan but at least it's better than standing around being afraid with everyone else. Oh. It looks like Mandy needs to talk to you."

117 turned to see Mandy running toward him with a data pad in her hand, a big smile on her face. 117 was very happy to see her.

"Hey!"

"You look excited," 117 greeted her.

"Yup," she answered. "I have all the information from every one of those companies affiliated with the giant robot you took down, so I'm very excited. Well, I mean it's a bit dull but at least we can sort through this."

"I would love to Mandy," 117 replied.

"And I'm glad you're not letting it stop you," Mandy grinned confidently. She looked at the other amborgs, and her smile faded. "If something happened to Palmer, I'd probably be unable to find the motivation to do anything."

"If something hypothetically happened to him," 117 declared, "I will be there to help you."

"I'm glad to hear that," Mandy grinned at these words. She nodded to 117. "No matter what happens, I'm proud of you."

"Thank you for being my technician," 117 said. "Shall we look at the data and you tell me what you have been able to dig up?"

"Alright well," Mandy activated the data pad and a bunch of company logos popped up, along with several logs. "I managed to contact all of the companies that had something to contribute to designing our large friend. According to all of what I gathered, they've been conducting business transactions over the last couple of years with someone who has been paying all the bills. It may have been the man who stabbed 43... 'Ahem...' anyway, if anyone is designing a giant war machine, it's this mysterious man. He has money, illegal or legally acquired, doesn't matter. I've received a lot of shipping manifests and records. These parts from all these companies were sent from all over the world to the U.S. and get this, it was somehow all legally done, too. These companies just had a wealthy customer buy their parts without knowing what the real purpose was. Right now, the police have warned them about these machines and we have sent proof that their parts are being used in unlicensed machine warfare. They've stopped all known shipments to this dealer but based on all the shipments already sent, it might not be good enough."

"There could be over a hundred of these giant robots," 117 said as he glanced at the numbers. "Why haven't these companies flagged or double-checked their customers? A reasonable businessman would make sure they wouldn't be selling to someone shady."

"It's like I said earlier David," Mandy sighed. "They don't care unless you have money. We're also technically still rebuilding from the aftereffects of the third world war. Everyone is busy and no one has the time to screen everything. Believe me, these companies are going to really be given the hammer of justice after this mess is all straightened out... and that's just going to be a socio-economic nightmare. Or whatever the professional term is."

"Obviously," 117 noted. "Anyone who comes up with the money, they usually don't ask too many questions. The companies you contacted have been completely in the dark about this?"

"So far," Mandy shrugged. "They all claim they had no idea about the designs for this robot. They just all thought it was a high-paying client hobbyist so they didn't question it. Business people... they suck. Even if we looked into all the rich people around the world, it's still a lot for the upper class to investigate. It could be anyone."

"Well, it is a start," 117 replied. "If these companies have stopped shipments to the U.S., then all we have to worry about is figuring out what kind of threat we've managed to stop and what remains for us to clean up."

"Well, let's go do some more digging."

The reality was that the enemy had likely been building their army in the shadows for some time. The amborgs found themselves at a critical disadvantage, as they had no clue how large the enemy forces were. All they could do was bide their time and anticipate more leads. Many among them calculated that this was likely going to be their end.

Present Day
Classroom 312

"What did you think, Sarah?"

Sarah looked up from the screen. She grabbed a tissue from Mandy's desk and wiped her eyes.

"Forgive me," she said as Mandy stared. "It was very shocking to see something like that happen to one of my predecessors. The records do inform us of Serina 43's death but we never really knew about what led up to that. The full details were always a blur."

"I didn't think it'd make you cry," Mandy chuckled slightly as she handed the whole box of tissues to Sarah. "That's probably the first time I've ever seen an amborg break out in tears in a very long time."

"A moment of weakness," Sarah stated. "Most humans go through those types of phases for a period of time. Amborgs can get over things within minutes. But, it doesn't feel right."

"Oh? Why do you say that?"

"When people move on from issues that should be addressed, like when 117 motivated them to get over their fears and find their courage, sometimes it increases the chances of forgetting the real issues. Like when your friends insult you, some people tell you to get over it and just do whatever to forget it. It always feels like they're avoiding the real issues."

"True," Mandy nodded, "but you need to know that not everyone knows how to really comfort one another when it's needed. They just default to the best method they think will get rid of their problems and hope it solves itself without it interfering with their life. Kind of like how Dr. Kendrick tried talking to 117 when he was looking after 43. He didn't know how to properly address the issue in a way that would help 117 the best. He didn't know how to discuss what happened to his wife, even though the experience was roughly similar in many ways."

"That makes sense," Sarah said. "This story is enlightening and also very true to the complexities of human emotions."

"Not all stories are happy," Mandy replied. "But 117 didn't give up. He almost did for about ten minutes, but he found his determination again. We all have our weak moments, and those experiences shape us profoundly. It doesn't matter if you're highly evolved or struggling to get by; it's about the motivation that arises from those challenges. Same goes for the bad guys, too."

"I'd like to keep watching please," Sarah said, clutching the box of tissues.

"Well, we do have all evening," Mandy sighed. "Whatever it takes to make you understand my big point at the end of this. Computer, begin playing again."

CHAPTER 13

Super Sibling Squabble

A.I. Industries
Gymnasium: Converted Training Facility
Five Days Later

In one corner of the gym from a square sparring mat, a bell rang out, signaling the end of a training session. Amborg 66 lay flat on his face, realizing that the fight had come to an end.

A flash of light made him look up, revealing an A.I. floating beside his head.

"Congratulations, you lasted an additional 14 seconds before you were overpowered."

"Yeah, yeah," 66 muttered as he tried to push himself up off the mat. He glanced up at the A.I. again and grumbled.

"I still got overpowered Grant," 66 sighed.

"You increased your time and put up a longer fight," Grant glowed a positive shade of green. "Unfortunately, your reflex algorithms have deteriorated by seven percent."

"It's not my fault!" 66 replied as he stood up and looked at his two opponents. Frustration surged through him as he vented to Grant. "73 and 61 surrounded me from both sides! Dealing with common enemies is simple enough. But two amborgs at the same time is a real challenge."

They all turned to where he'd been thrown. A massive indentation marked the floor from his impact.

"I wasn't trying to say that you or anyone here is at fault," Grant smiled. "We need to teach you how to deal with multiple opponents at a time. Naturally, if you encounter enemies that are as strong as other amborgs, then you'll be able to withstand any kind of attack. In your files, your combat style is primarily centered on taking down one person at a time. If you try to take on multiple groups all at once, you will be overwhelmed as they will all try to take you down simultaneously."

"Then just give me a gun and I'll defend myself successfully," 66 declared.

"And what if you don't have a gun?" Grant asked. "You don't use one here in training. So, what happens if you are without a weapon or firearm in the field?"

66 groaned, making Grant smile again.

"I thought so," he stated. "Your next session is with three amborgs—the equivalent to facing at least 30 of our security drones. This should teach you how to fight better."

"Aww, my joints!"

66 rotated his shoulders and stretched his arms.

"Can I at least take a break?"

"Very well," Grant nodded. "I will postpone your next session until you are ready."

66 reluctantly thanked Grant and walked over to a custom charging station. It was a brightly lit capsule that was able to house one individual. Once it was occupied and the chamber was secure, an amborg could take a break to recharge their cybernetic implants. They each had one in their rooms, but someone had set up a few spare ones in the gym so that they wouldn't have to waste time traveling too far.

66 waved his bracelet in front of the scanner, and the doors swung open. He stepped inside and turned to face the way he had entered. The chamber was designed with a slight angle so he could lean back comfortably. As the door sealed shut, the charging station powered up and hydraulics whirred. Gradually, the entire pod reclined, and 66 sank into the soft bedding. A loud, consistent humming resonated around him, and bright lights activated. Power began to flow through his limbs as he let himself go limp.

His next fight wouldn't be for at least twenty minutes, so he made the most of his time savoring the charge. While the energy flowed to his reserves, he glanced to his left. Through the window of the capsule, he spotted some Second and Third Group amborgs engaged in experiments alongside an eccentric researcher.

Amborg 274 of the Second Group appeared deeply confused, clearly struggling to understand what this man was trying to explain to them.

"Now everyone, pay attention," he said excitedly. "The R&D department just developed these gizmos and they are fun as hell to use. Physicists will pay tribute to this over the centuries!"

He tossed a red orb toward some cones. A vibrant red glow burst forth, and with a blinding flash, the cones disappeared. The researcher laughed gleefully while the amborgs stood there silently, staring in astonishment. He stopped laughing when he noticed no one else joining in and casually cleared his throat.

"Hmm, tough crowd," he said, a little put off by the quiet reception. He sighed and lifted his gloved hand. "Watch this."

A loud whine pierced the silence as the glove powered up and glowed the same shade of red as the orb he'd thrown. In the spot where it rested, they watched as it rolled and then shot straight toward them. Like a baseball, it zipped into his glove, and he caught it with ease. He opened his hand and with his other, pulled it from the padded material.

They looked on as he redirected his aim and gently threw the orb. When it struck the ground, it lit up again, charging up brightly. A sudden flash of light startled a few people working nearby. Everyone watched with fascination at the scene unfolding before them. Instead of empty space, the cones reappeared, relocated to a different spot without any physical contact. The amborgs observing the experiment were both amazed and thoroughly impressed by what they saw.

"Wow this is really amazing," 274 spoke up. "Interesting. Dr. Baldwin, you have developed technology to miniaturize inanimate objects for convenient travel. Very efficient."

The possibilities were limitless. The idea of transporting several large objects in just the palm of one's hand was revolutionary. A.I. Industries had an abundance of special talent and genius among the ranks of Dr. Kendrick's research teams.

"If one were to ship a large number of supplies," 274 hypothesized, "then it would fix a lot of transportation and logistical problems."

"Yes! Exactly!"

Dr. Baldwin pointed his finger eagerly at 274 like he had just won a prize. As the amborgs examined the red orbs closely, he held up the one in his gloved hand and shrugged.

"Well... that's one thing you can do with them. You can use them for combat purposes too."

This got most of their attention.

"Combat?" someone asked.

"Oh yes," Dr. Baldwin nodded. "A bunch of us in the lab had several major setbacks before we achieved the desired results."

274 looked cautiously down at the red orb. They were technically still experimental, and this presentation was sounding more and more dangerous with each passing second. Many of the amborgs began to step back slowly. Dr. Baldwin noticed and smiled reassuringly.

"And...what were the undesired results?" 274 asked politely.

"They have a tendency to explode if the settings are wrong," Dr. Baldwin replied casually.

274 heard someone whisper behind him in a terrified tone.

"How can he be so casual while holding... something explosive in his hand?"

"I heard that," Dr. Baldwin replied. "Don't worry! After many trials and errors, we have programmed a self-destruct setting. Using them like grenades is an added feature. You can link through to it with your CPU, and you can set the option to either transport, disintegrate or explode. Obviously, it won't stay intact with the last two options so once it blows up, it'll make a mess... but the more stuff you keep locked up during transport mode, it actually would theoretically survive the explosion if... by accident, you used it in combat. I wouldn't keep your valuables in it though."

274 blinked.

"Theoretically? I thought you tested this multiple times in the lab?" he asked. "You stored objects inside the transport orb, and then blew it up?"

"Yes!" Dr. Baldwin replied excitedly.

"So," 274 pointed at the orb. "Does it store objects inside by shrinking the molecular density of anything that goes inside? Doesn't that mean when it explodes, whatever is inside will... expand back to its normal size and... also explode simultaneously??"

"There's a lot of debris on our testing grounds," Dr. Baldwin replied. "It's entertaining looking at all the footage of our experiments."

"Have you... tried this on any living beings?" 274 gulped.

"Not yet," Dr. Baldwin smiled.

"Yet?" 274 seemed alarmed. "Please tell me you aren't doing those trials soon?"

"I may be quirky," Dr. Baldwin shook his head urgently, "but I still have an ethical code of conduct to follow. You could capture and store a person inside one of these devices... but it's only a theory."

274 glanced to his right, noticing his friend 125 step forward. He posed a question to Dr. Baldwin, one that was on all of their minds.

"Is it... safe to use this on a human?"

"Why would we use it on a human?" Dr. Baldwin asked, staring at him. "That's not what it was originally designed for."

"But maybe we could use it to our advantage?" 125 shrugged nervously. "What if 274 and I are stuck somewhere?"

"Where are you going with this?" 274 asked apprehensively.

"What if I stored 274 in one of these red orbs and then threw it?" 125 kept talking as he ignored his friend's concerns. "Then the orb would let him out and voilà, a really cool sneak attack!"

274 glared at 125.

"Do you enjoy using me as a science experiment?"

"More or less," 125 replied cheekily.

274 ignored 125 and held out his hand to Dr. Baldwin, who looked at it curiously.

"May I please try transporting some items?" he asked.

"Sure!" Dr. Baldwin nodded eagerly as he let 274 grab the red orb. "We need more test results! So, when you throw it, try to... HEY WAIT!"

It was too late. 274 had already picked his target and thrown the orb. Once it left his fingers, he realized that he hadn't fully taken the time to properly aim at his target. The orb veered off to the side and bounced across the ground. They watched as it rolled next to 297, who was in deep conversation with a few other amborgs, completely oblivious to what was going on around him. Everyone's eyes widened as the orb activated and with a great flash of red light, 297 disappeared from where he had been standing. The amborgs he'd been speaking to a moment ago froze in place, horrified when he suddenly vanished. They whirled around, searching for him while Dr. Baldwin and 274 stood there in shocked silence, completely at a loss for words.

"Oh no," 274 said quietly.

"If 297 dies," 125 mumbled, "we will have killed another amborg this year."

Staying calm, Dr. Baldwin took a deep breath and focused on the task at hand. Panicking would only make things worse, so he took decisive action. Using the glove, he opened his palm and reached out to the orb. Thanks to its magnetic properties, the orb rolled toward him and suddenly lifted off the ground. It felt as though he was wielding the Force as it shot straight into his grasp. He then hurried to a safe distance from the others and gently set the orb down, making sure it wouldn't roll away. Double checking that it was far enough, he activated it.

Another bright flash of light shot out, forcing everyone to shield their eyes from the intense glare. When it faded, they looked back at the orb. Unfortunately, that was all that remained. 297 was still missing, which began to fill the group with dread.

"S-sir?" 125 stammered. "Where is 297?"

Dr. Baldwin paused, everyone's eyes fixed on the spot where the orb sat. They waited, hoping something would happen, but it began to feel a bit pointless.

"How odd," he murmured. He realized the amborgs were all staring at him and he chuckled nervously. "Well, like I said, we never made it to human trials. So, this obviously might be another setback. Not to worry, I believe he will be fine."

"But you can't be certain?" 274 asked. "297 is probably in another dimension."

"Yeah," 125 gulped. "We might've accidentally warped him into one... or he's probably been ripped to pieces."

"Personally," Dr. Baldwin mumbled, "I think it is a good sign that we haven't seen any pieces of him."

"You can get him back, right?" 274 looked at Dr. Baldwin and at the red orb frantically. "I'm not sure if this is a tool we can sanction for use in the field."

"I hope so..." Dr. Baldwin grinned sheepishly. "I'll say, this first test is slowly getting worse with every passing second."

Dr. Baldwin scanned the room, then glanced down at his wristwatch. He sighed and began moving toward the dormant orb.

"Alright, I'll take a closer look at the orb to see if it's defective," he said. "The worst case scenario is he's just trapped in there at a small scale."

"No offense but..." 125 leaned over to whisper in 274's ear, "I think the worst case scenario is that he's actually dead."

"Incorrect," 274 sighed. "The worst case scenario is when we bring about the end of the world and it results in us accidentally killing ourselves."

"AAAAAHHH!!!"

Everyone's gaze shot upward as 297 plummeted from the ceiling, crashing to the ground with a huge thud. The force of his landing sent those nearby scattering in all directions. Many lost their balance as the gym floor shook violently from the impact. Dr. Baldwin, filled with relief, clapped his hands excitedly.

"There he is!" he said, smiling brightly. "I knew he was ok!"

"Sure he did," 125 scoffed.

A few drones moved in to help 297 to his feet. He seemed to be alright, though a bit disoriented and shaken. It was understandable, considering he had fallen victim to whatever had happened inside the red orb.

The entire group rushed to 297, who was still trying to steady himself. Dr. Baldwin retrieved the orb and pocketed it. Once it was safe, he eagerly rushed to help 297 and began to pester him with a wave of questions.

"What did you feel 297?" He asked at top speed. "Or... How do you feel? Are you alright? What did you see? Can you describe the sensation? Why were you up on the ceiling?"

"Doctor," 274 said. "Maybe we should give him a second."

297 looked at each of them shakily. He still appeared a little bit rattled, though thankfully, not completely traumatized. After taking several deep breaths, he regained his composure. With renewed focus, he turned to Dr. Baldwin, thinking carefully.

"It was... empty," he described slowly, his bracelet glowing with each word. "It felt so peaceful and quiet but... then it felt so uncomfortable after a few seconds. The air inside felt so stale and it was like an endless void."

"I wonder if I should go inside one of these," Dr. Baldwin's eyes widened as he stared at the orb in amazement.

"Let's table that," 125 suggested hastily.

"What was it like exiting the orb?" Dr. Baldwin sighed dejectedly, looking at 297. "What did that feel like?"

"It didn't really feel like anything," 297 shrugged. "I felt myself get pulled aside by some unseen force and in the blink of an eye, everyone disappeared and I was alone. Then after another moment, I saw a blinding flash of light. I felt myself being pulled again and then suddenly, I saw the ceiling of the gym. The next thing I knew, I was hanging onto the ceiling supports and then I lost my grip while I was trying to regain my senses."

"It launched him?" 274 asked.

"That's interesting. Very impressive!" Dr. Baldwin patted 297 on the shoulder, who looked at him nervously. He turned to walk away, examining the deactivated orb excitedly. "Class dismissed!"

"This was a class?" 125 asked.

Dr. Baldwin ignored him as he continued to mutter to himself. They realized he was documenting something when they saw him pull out a recording device.

"In an instant, the orb launched amborg 297 into the ceiling," he mumbled. "Subject described being drawn into and propelled out of a massive, bright room. Further investigation required. Outer space is a great and vast field of exploration. Perhaps inner space isn't out of our reach now."

Once he left, the group finally relaxed now that the situation was under control. 274 spotted something on the ground and pointed it out to 125 as he moved closer to it. When he bent down to take a closer look, he realized it was another one of Dr. Baldwin's transport orbs. Somehow it had been left there by mistake.

"Someone should go after him," 274 sighed. "He mistakenly left one of the... Oops!"

As 274 tried to bend down and grab the orb, his foot accidentally bumped it and kicked it away. His superhuman strength sent it flying farther than anticipated, and they all watched in horror once again. 274 could hear 125's voice rising with urgency.

"Uh, I think we should get that before it goes off…!"

Another bright flash shot out, causing the amborgs to shield their eyes, flinching from the orb's sudden activation. Once it was safe to look, they all turned towards the source of the light. Everyone knew what that meant.

"…again," 125 gulped. "There was someone standing there… right?"

"I-I definitely saw someone disappear," 297 stammered. "W-was it who I think it was?"

"Umm, I think Dr. Kendrick," 274 replied in shock. He felt his heart stop when they all came to the same realization. "If I remember correctly."

They all scrambled frantically towards the orb.

"QUICK! BRING HIM BACK!"

On another side of the gym, similar chaos was brewing. 345 was being carried out after a serious accident during one of their upgrade sessions. The Third Group amborgs were in a state of panic. 999 and two of her friends from the Second Group, 777 and 56, were doing their best to take control of the situation while trying to keep the younger amborgs calm.

"What happened to 345?!" one of them panicked. "Is she ok?!"

"She's fine!" 777 yelled back.

He looked at 999 and 56 for clarification.

"She is fine, right?" he asked quickly.

Unfortunately, 999 kept her arms crossed and didn't respond. 56 was the only one who shrugged and gave him a positive smile.

"She's fine," 777 declared again.

Someone from the Third Group protested.

"That didn't look fine!"

777 looked to 999 and 56 once more, feeling a bit helpless. He wasn't sure that anything he was saying was working.

"Please help me," he pleaded with a defeated sigh.

As if on cue, a bright cacophony of lights flashed around the entire group. Several A.I. programs appeared and began to chatter among themselves. One of them glowed green. Its name was Taylor.

"Well, that didn't go well…" Taylor scoffed. He looked around. "Which one of us was supposed to integrate with 345's CPU again?"

All of the other A.I.'s shrugged and glanced at each other. They shook their heads, seeming unsure. Taylor groaned and turned a shade of yellow while the others' silhouettes dimmed.

"Great," he said when none of them responded. "An advanced group of artificial intelligence created by one of the smartest men on earth and we can't even remember who was supposed to pair up with one amborg."

"Don't be concerned Taylor," 777 said reassuringly. "It was an accident."

"Well guess what, lucky luck-luck amborg," Taylor snapped. "This is a concern! A.I. programs already face a lot of backlash outside of A.I. Industries! You think it's going to look good when the public finds out that an amborg was accidentally killed by one of us?"

"We just need to reevaluate a different approach," 777 replied.

"Why do we have to learn to integrate with an amborg anyway?" Taylor placed his hands on his holographic hips. He changed to a bright green color as he continued, "It's not effective and it's a recipe for disaster. Even if we can actually be transported into your CPUs, there's not enough space in there for us."

56 stepped forward.

"Dr. Kendrick believes that if certain A.I.'s pair up with an amborg, then the calculation output, performance issues, and systems should increase by a large percentage," he said. "What we are attempting is to find compatible A.I.'s for each amborg. It reminds me of a twenty-first century game that humans used to play. I have found the gameplay to be quite amusing. Ever heard of the game Halo?"

"We don't play videogames," Taylor said bluntly, and all the other A.I.s nodded in agreement. "But we understand your reference."

"The reason I mention Halo is because," 777 sighed dejectedly, "the A.I. paired with Master Chief is Cortana. She was flash-cloned from the mind of Dr. Halsey. She was also allowed to choose which Spartan she wanted to pair with. She chose the most compatible, which was the Master Chief. We believe that A.I.s from A.I. Industries, whether they were made from scratch or based off of real personalities, will permanently increase our performance for future encounters. We could also transport A.I.s in our CPUs to other systems or computers on future deployments. You know, just like in Halo. You guys coop yourselves up here all the time, don't you want to go on an adventure?"

"The real world isn't that great," Taylor muttered. "A lot of old computers, broken and worn down tech, and a lot of artificial phobic people..."

"Deviating!"

They pivoted to 999, who looked increasingly more frustrated.

"You're all getting off-topic," she said.

"Right," 777 nodded. "It would have been easier to integrate if you were all paying attention. But now we are minus one amborg for a bit of time thanks to all of you trying to help."

"Well, when you ask us to do something we don't typically do, something is bound to go wrong," Taylor replied quietly. There was an obvious sense of guilt in his voice which the amborgs heard instantly. "All of this is new for most of us."

"That would be because all ten of you tried to upload into her CPU at the same time," 56 noted while scratching his head. "Her hard drive was not able to cope. Consider yourselves lucky she did not go insane with eleven people trying to live inside her entire body and accidentally taking control of her brain."

"Yeah, it was a good thing she fainted from all the pressure," 777 chuckled but quickly stopped when he saw 999 glaring at him.

"Enough!" she snapped.

That was her way of telling everyone that they had to get back to work. 56 glanced at the A.I. programs and got their attention.

"We need to focus," he said. "The Third Group amborgs are anxious and we need to get this done. Artificial Intelligences, you will pair up with an amborg. ONE A.I. to ONE amborg. Let's avoid another accident. Practice makes perfect."

"Right," Taylor nodded and the other A.I.s began floating over to the waiting amborgs. "OVERTIME!"

Nearby, Dr. Kendrick was stationed at 6's medical station. After being "rescued" from the transport orb, he was brought in to rest and recover. Dr. Baldwin had gleefully returned and was watching 6 conduct her examination. 501 was lending a hand as well, since he was going through a remedial course in first aid.

On the surface, Dr. Kendrick appeared to be fine, but 6 was still concerned about his mental state. After all, he was the first normal human to be yanked in and out of a tiny storage space that defied the laws of physics—definitely something for the record books. Not many could fully recover from an experience like that. Everyone agreed that he was incredibly lucky to still be alive.

6 had cleared him for light work duties, but she continued to monitor his brain activity. Dr. Baldwin eagerly awaited the results, while Dr. Kendrick was outfitting a new gadget onto 501's wrist.

"Are you sure you are alright, Doctor?" 501 asked timidly. He glanced down as Dr. Kendrick fidgeted with the straps and tightened the new device. "I feel nervous about accepting this new equipment after your latest predicament. Are you sure your mind is functioning normally?"

"Pfft, I'm fine Donut!" Dr. Kendrick chuckled lazily, which only worsened 501's unease. "It's not every day you get teleported in and out of a compressed sphere the size of a pickleball. I'm great!"

501 shot a piercing glance at 6 and Dr. Baldwin, who were studying the brain scans. Their reassuring nods did little to ease his anxiety. Dr. Kendrick let out a loud maniacal, goofy laugh that sent chills running down his spine. Even without using his built-in lie detector, 501 sensed that he was still a bit off-kilter and not being entirely honest.

"You cleared him for work?" 501 gazed at 6 in disbelief.

"*Light* work duty," 6 answered politely.

"This is excellent data!" Dr. Baldwin's eyes were glued to the monitor as he gave a thumbs up. 6 had to move his arm so that his positive gesture was directed at 501. "Incredible!"

"Ok 501," Dr. Kendrick took a few breaths and tried to focus, blinking a few times before speaking again. "Wow I feel drunk. This arm bracelet, when used, emits an electronic charge which should disable... well anything really. That's the idea but I designed it to zap a lot of stuff."

"Zap?" 501 gulped. "How... informal."

"Did I say zap?" Dr. Kendrick blinked. "Zappy zap? What's the word? Oh, right! Electrocute!"

"I think I need an adult," 501 mumbled.

"Relax," Dr. Kendrick sputtered, "I am an adult."

"At the moment, he's like a child trapped in a grown body," 6 snickered.

Whether or not Dr. Kendrick had heard her, 501 didn't know. He raised 501's arm, activating the device in the process. Unfortunately, 501 was too focused on Dr. Kendrick to notice where he was aiming. Suddenly, a high-pitched whine pierced the air, followed by a deafening boom. A bright arc of electricity shot out from the projector, traveling a short distance before hitting its target and eliciting a loud shout.

"OW!"

They saw 466 leap up, wincing in pain and began massaging her lower back. There was a distinct burn mark where the electrical current had struck.

"Oops," 501 and Dr. Kendrick remarked.

The sudden electrical discharge snapped Dr. Kendrick back to his senses. Now alert, he looked back and forth nervously between 501 and 466. 501 stood up, his hands moving quickly as he struggled to remove the wrist bracer from his arm.

"It was an accident," 501 said, terror in his eyes. "Umm sorry 466, I didn't intend to shoot you in the butt."

Both of them averted their eyes as 466 massaged the spot where the electricity had actually struck. A few seconds later, she marched right over and smacked 501 in the face. While they had been looking away, she'd taken the opportunity to sneak up and deliver justice.

"OW!" he cried, "I said I was sorry!"

"You IDIOT!" she yelled, blushing furiously.

Dr. Baldwin and 6 looked on silently.

"Well," he said, pretending not to have witnessed what had happened. "I have plenty of results! I'll be back in my lab!"

"Excellent! Have a good one Dr. Baldwin. I got plenty of footage," 6 replied smugly as she kept watching 501 and 466 yell and complain. "And this is entertaining as hell."

In the halls of another corridor, a team of First Group amborgs were enjoying a leisurely stroll before another one of their assigned training sessions. 11, 12, 19, and 24 were heading toward the medical center to pick up some supplies that 6 had requisitioned. Since she hadn't actually specified a time of delivery, they took their time. They'd also considered visiting 43 to see how she was doing. Giving Sherry a break would probably be a good idea.

"So, any updates from 18?"

12 looked at 11. She shook her head.

"After 117 rallied all of us, she immediately left to track down another lead," she replied as they kept walking. "If it's another undercover operation, who knows when she'll be back?"

"We should probably take the next assignment that comes our way," 11 sighed. He stretched his arms above his head. "It's nice getting to stay home for a few days but I'm itching to go out again."

"Unfortunately, we got to wait until there's a call for help," 19 said. "Personally, I like the quiet. It gives us time to relax, shop online, and spend time hanging out with each other."

Once they turned a corner and saw the entrance to the hospital, something snagged their attention.

"Hey..." 11 said as he held up his hand. "That's not normal."

The four of them altered their approach, shifting from a causal stance to one of heightened caution. They tensed up and moved carefully. Security drones and human guards zipped past down the opposite hallway. At first glance, it seemed as though they were targeting the amborgs, but they quickly realized the guards were actually rushing toward the medical facility's entrance. All of them were preparing to draw their weapons. Sensing the urgency, the amborgs moved closer to speak with them. 11 took the lead.

"What's wrong?" he asked. "Situation?"

One of the security guards shrugged in response.

"We received a security alert, 11," he explained. "It was from 117. We don't know what's wrong."

The four amborgs, puzzled, leaned closer to the heavy, steel door. As quietly as possible, they tried to listen for any disturbances. At first, everything seemed fine, until a sudden loud crash broke then tense silence.

The guards jumped back, startled, while the amborgs barely flinched. In an instant, their weapons were drawn, eyes fixed anxiously on the door. The four amborgs exchanged glances, quickly devised a strategy, and prepared for action. 19 signaled for the guards to split up and flank the doors.

"This is amborg 24," 24 spoke in an urgent and soft tone. "We are responding to a disturbance at the hospital. Please ready backup and support."

As they took their positions, another loud crash echoed from behind the door. This time, the sounds of destruction were accompanied by voices. Amidst the chaos, they recognized 117's voice shouting. Though it was somewhat muffled, they were able to make out what he was saying.

"43 stop!" they heard him shout. "Mandy! Sherry! Are you alright?!"

"I'm fine David!" a second voice sounded from inside. "Please get your girlfriend to calm down!"

Just then, a third voice shrieked from behind the closed steel door. Everyone trembled when they heard a loud ear-shattering scream.

"Let. Me. OUT!! NOW!!"

The security drones looked to the human guards and the amborgs, awaiting orders. The humans were visibly shaken and in shock. The situation unfolding in the medical facility sounded like the start of a terrifying horror scene in a movie. An unsettling mix of fear, confusion, and anxiety was building. It sounded like 43 was awake, but unfortunately, she wasn't happy.

One of the guards tapped 11 on his shoulder.

"That was Serina 43... right?" she squeaked.

"Yes it was," 11 nodded. "Amborgs, change formation."

The guards and security drones continued to flank the door while the amborgs moved back a few paces.

"This is 24 again," 24 transmitted to the emergency channel. "Disturbance identified. Serina 43 is active. Standby for further updates and upgrade to tactical alert three."

"I'm going in," 12 reported as she stalked forward. "Tiana, cover me."

12 and 19 stepped close to the door again, falling silent as they listened for anything else.

It had only been a few seconds since 43 had screamed, and more chaos erupted as they heard the sounds of objects being thrown, flipped, and shattered. 12 and 19 shared worried looks, leaning in and pretending to whisper as they connected on a private channel. 11 and 24 were looped in as well.

"Should we upgrade to tactical one?" 19 asked.

"I don't know," 12 shook her head. "Perhaps we should..."

A massive crash against the door cut her off mid-sentence. The force if the impact rattled the entire doorframe, causing 12 and 19 to step back. The security guards and drones also retreated from the door, the humans looking to the amborgs for instructions. 12 turned to 19, who responded with a decisive look.

"Tactical one," 12 finished her thoughts quickly and nodded in confirmation. "We have a serious situation at the hospital."

"Confirmed," 24 transmitted on the emergency channel. "We are reporting a tactical one alert. This is not a drill. I repeat. This is no drill. Tactical alert one please."

The security drones and guards drew their weapons, aiming at the door. Voices from inside continued to shout as the commotion intensified.

"Mandy, no! Get over here!" they heard 117 shout. "Pick up that hospital mattress and just hide behind it! Protect Sherry!"

"Oh right!" they heard Mandy reply sarcastically. "A mattress is supposed to protect me and Sherry from a super enhanced cybernetic terminator girl!"

"43 stand down! It's me, David 117!"

"I'll stand down! Sure! I'll do just that! Right after you agree to LET... ME... OUT!"

"Oh no."

117's faltering voice was drowned out by another thundering crash that shook the hallway. The door buckled outward from the force of the impact. The guards appeared on the verge of panic, while the amborgs immediately assumed defensive positions, their expressions turning serious.

"This is 24 again," 24 transmitted urgently. "Serina 43 has gone rogue."

"You don't know that!" 11 snapped at her.

"You have a better explanation?" 24 asked.

"No..." 11 admitted grimly.

24 then repeated her transmission across the emergency channel.

"Serina 43 appears to have gone rogue," she described. "I repeat, amborg out of control. We are engaging. Send assistance!"

One of the security guards was close to losing their cool. Another crash behind the door caused the entire hallway to rattle again. The medical facility was not built to withstand this amount of force, or to keep a wild beast at bay.

"We've never had to perform a tactical one alert against an amborg!" he said.

"Seems like there's a lot of firsts for everything lately!" 12 replied. "I suggest..."

12 looked at the two teams of security guards on both sides of the door.

"Security!" she declared. "Fall back and get to safety! This is our fight."

The squad leader nodded.

"Yeah, I get the message," he said, nodding frantically. "Come guys. MOVE!"

The A.I. Industried security guards and drones took off while the amborgs stayed behind. The whirring of the drones' limbs and the heavy footsteps of the guards gradually faded until they were out of sight. Suddenly, another powerful blow hit the door. The four amborgs quickly coordinated with each other and arranged themselves into a defensive formation.

"Right," 11 scoffed. "Not their fight. But what about us?"

"I am unqualified to answer that question," 12 gulped as she raised her fists.

"Well, what's the plan?" 11 asked nervously. "19?"

"How should I know?" 19 shrugged nervously. "Listen! 117 seems to be handling it well."

"43, umm...honey. I know you are angry but please let me explain! Calm down. Hey! Put me down this instant! I... Uh-oh."

There was a loud, muffled boom, followed by a heavy thud. After that, 117 fell silent.

"Or not," 19 said shakily as the team shifted uncomfortably. "Ok, we will attempt to hold her here. First, we need to wait for her next move."

"Control," 24 transmitted. "Can anyone divert security footage inside the hospital entrance to my CPU?"

The group hesitated, unsure of what awaited them behind the door. 43 was trying to fight her way out, that they were certain of. They could open the door and attempt to help 117 but the reality was, they didn't have eyes inside. This plan wasn't sitting well with 11.

"If she gets out," he said, "we can't stop her."

"We have to try," 12 replied firmly.

Seconds later, another massive crash warped the door outward even further. Amazingly, it was holding up relatively well. Yet, it wouldn't last much longer based on their scans of its structural integrity.

"Did she hit that with full strength?" 24's eyes widened.

Her question went unanswered. An amborg utilizing that much power was capable of knocking down a building or totaling someone's car with very little effort.

"I calculate... with sarcasm," 12 noted with a slight tremble in her voice, "her next move is: fight her way through the door and us. Is anyone else noting how bad a position we might be in?"

A few more thuds, crashes, and loud metal grinding noises occurred as the structure of the door weakened piece by piece. The team's morale began to diminish slowly. They had fought against 43 in training but in this state, she was unpredictable.

"It's ok!" 24 exhaled. She was trying to be as optimistic as possible. The atmosphere of the team was starting to get to her. "Think of this as an ambush scenario!"

"Are you kidding?" 19 chuckled nervously. "This is Serina 43. The best fighter out of all of us. Even 999 admits that she can't beat her one on one."

11 sighed as the three girls began to crowd together and move away from the door.

"Well, it was nice knowing you all," he said as another loud bang shook the floor.

"You aren't planning on running away are you, Clint?"

11 stared at 12.

"Of course not," he replied. "If we ran now, then other less fortunate victims would be stuck fighting 43. Defending innocent people from another amborg? Not how I pictured dying but why not?"

They focused on the door as each blow continued to weaken it. A few seconds of stillness followed, then with an almighty crash, the next strike sent it flying outward. The speed at which it flew diminished their courage greatly. They all ducked, easily avoiding it, but their attention was quickly drawn to the silhouette that stood in the doorway.

43 was out of her hospital gown and was now in her uniform, albeit not completely. Her jacket hung loosely, unzipped at the front, exposing her usual tank top underneath. As she tied her hair back and cracked her neck, she strode toward them with an intense gaze that radiated pure ferocity. The sound of her fist striking her palm echoed ominously down the hall.

"Ok," she snarled as her bracelet glowed. "Who's first?"

"Umm," 19 gulped. "We definitely need backup."

"Status update," 12 said slowly. "We're dead."

The four of them braced themselves as 43 shifted her feet into a bladed stance. After casting a quick look at each of them, she lunged.

Once the tactical alert was initiated, alarms blared throughout the entire facility. A.I. Industries was now in an emergency situation. From the armory to the library, the cafeteria, and the research divisions, all personnel paused their activities to listen. Every drone, construction crew, custodial staff, and security team were put on high alert and initiated their safety protocols.

In the residential area, every civilian quickly adhered to lockdown procedures from the safety of their homes. Thalia, who had been enjoying a silent imaginary tea party in her room, was suddenly interrupted by a deafening noise that threatened to rupture her eardrums. Fortunately, her family had prepared her for situations like this. She immediately covered her ears and rushed out to find her parents. Thalia ran into her mother's arms as they sprang into action. Marina held her daughter close while George made sure the front door of their home was securely locked. After confirming it was safe, he shepherded his family into the master bedroom. They would all remain sheltered there until the danger had passed.

In another part of A.I. Industries, Stan and his team of custodians paused their floor waxing and cleaning when the strobe lights began to flash. The drones in his group ceased all productivity and calmly instructed everyone to head to the nearest shelter. Panic gripped Stan as he thought about his family. He prayed that they were ok as he watched the drones' eyes shift from a casual yellow to a dark red that matched the alarms.

Over the P.A. system, a voice urgently relayed full details to all those on-site who could listen.

"Alarm! Alarm! This is an emergency situation. It is not a drill! Repeat! This isn't a drill! Second Group amborg on the loose! Extreme security measures enforced! Battle conditions on site! Amborg 43 is hostile! Medical bay reports minor injuries and one amborg casualty. Locate and contain!"

As soon as Dr. Kendrick received the emergency alert from his security chief, he gathered a few senior staff members and headed toward the danger. Of course, by the time they arrived to help Dr. Wildman, the fighting had already moved elsewhere.

"Chief," Dr. Kendrick said. "Where are they?!"

The head of security, Aria Malayno, responded over the channel.

"Doctor," she stated, "it looks like the amborgs have engaged 43 and they're heading towards the warehouses."

"Meet me there!" he instructed.

"Sir! I strongly think...!"

Dr. Kendrick muted the channel, cutting off chief Malayno's transmission. The security guard next to him stared.

"Not a word," he demanded.

The guard nodded his head. Dr. Kendrick pointed at a few other security personnel that were following him and his group.

"You get inside and check on everyone in medical! Secure this area! Call for amborg assistance!"

The guards acknowledged him and picked their way through the broken doors to assist in rescuing the injured. Dr. Kendrick then signaled for the rest of his staff to follow him.

They hurried to the location where the fight was supposedly taking place. After passing a security checkpoint, they reached one of the warehouses and rushed into the observation room on the second floor. Inside, a few dock workers were seated at their consoles, and they all sprang to their feet in surprise when they saw Dr. Kendrick. They clearly hadn't expected to see their boss and the owner of the company to be there.

"Holy...! Dr. Kendrick!"

"Yes, yes!" Dr. Kendrick acknowledged them politely and quickly. "You're all doing a great job. We have a situation here. Please order all of the workers in the warehouse to evacuate."

"But... security alerts mean that we need to lockdown and shelter in place!"

Dr. Kendrick glared at the worker, who immediately shrank back.

"I know the protocols!" he said firmly. "But we have a possible incoming attack and everyone that is not cybernetically enhanced needs to get out now."

The worker nodded and quickly reached for the microphone. He made an announcement, which blared out down below. Dr. Kendrick watched as people began to scramble for the exits once the announcement finished. He nodded and smiled in satisfaction until he heard an angry voice behind him.

"What is the point of being your chief of security if you're going to keep hanging up on me?!"

Dr. Kendrick boldly turned around and saw chief Malayno standing behind him with more guards.

"Security! Escort our boss to the nearest shelter!"

"As your boss," Dr. Kendrick replied, "I respectfully refuse."

"Dr. Kendrick!" Malayno huffed. "We are on a tactical alert! On company grounds! I have to ensure your safety!"

"I'm not going to run and hide from this!" Dr. Kendrick snapped. "Something is wrong with 43 and we need to be ready to help her!"

A security drone approached Dr. Kendrick, but he raised a finger to signal it to stop. The red light on its faceplate flickered before shifting to a soft blue. He glanced at the number on its chest plate and identified it.

"Lucy!" he commanded. "Stand down! I am not going anywhere! Don't make me rip out your secondary processors!"

Lucy, the security drone, held up its hands and backed off. Chief Malayno sighed as she turned to her guards.

"Secure this room!" she commanded. "Lock it down! Doctor's orders."

Dr. Kendrick thanked her and then turned to look through the windows, seeing a sea of cargo containers and supplies. There were no workers in sight, which put him at ease.

"Where are they? What the hell is going on?" Dr. Kendrick muttered in a concerned tone.

An entrance below burst open, and 11, 12, 19, and 24 sprinted into the warehouse, their faces etched with sheer terror. One of the technicians quickly patched in the receiver, allowing them to hear what they were saying.

"Retreat! RUN! I don't want to die!"

11's shouts echoed through the speaker as 19 and 24 raced side by side, both trying to outpace one another.

"Where is she?!" 12 yelled in confusion, glancing around frantically. "Help us!"

"There they are," Dr. Kendrick said in relief as they paused to catch their breath. He quickly relayed a message over the emergency channel. "I need all amborgs onsite combat ready. Those of you that have safely secured any civilians and noncombatants please report to warehouse one! I need an A.I. to report to my position now!"

He changed the channel and tried to contact the amborgs below them.

"11, 12, 19 and 24. This is Dr. Kendrick. It's going to be alright," he said reassuringly. "Just stay calm and we'll have help for you."

"Please hurry Dr. Kendrick!" 24 cried in response.

Below, the amborgs darted through the aisles as if being chased by an unseen terror. It was like watching them trying to solve a maze.

A heartbeat later, the door burst open again and 43 dashed inside. Even though the amborgs had tried to hide in another part of the facility, she was obviously hunting them.

Oh boy, Dr. Kendrick quickly wiped the sweat off his brow, *it's a game of cat and mouse.*

He quickly switched the communications back to the emergency channel. Dr. Kendrick gaped through the glass, looking for the First Group amborgs. Keeping track of their location would help them coordinate their efforts.

"If anyone reads me," he said, "we need assistance! Emergency crews to the medical wing. Any available amborg needs to get here immediately."

There was a deafening crash as a crate launched into the air. It arched before plummeting to the ground, bursting open and scattering its contents in every direction.

"Get here fast!" he added frantically. "Otherwise we're going to lose four more amborgs! Double time now! Where's my A.I.?!"

"I guess we are putting our new skills to the test."

5 sprinted toward the warehouse with amborgs 1, 3, and 4. At an intersection, they were joined by Ziggy 2. Behind them, 297 kept pace while briefing some amborgs from the Third Group. When they arrived at another intersection, he paused, turned around, faced his team of amborgs, drones, and security personnel, and began to speak.

"Everyone listen up!" 297 commanded. "A.I.s and security will direct all regular staff and civilians to safe areas away from the warehouse. Follow protocol!"

He looked at a few younger amborgs.

"If you're not ready for this fight," he explained. "You can sit this out! Go and help with getting people to safety! Otherwise, if you come to the warehouses, you better be prepared for a fight against one of our own!"

297 pointed at the hall that the First Group had run into.

"I'm going this way!" he said. "All A.I.s need to monitor and lock down all entryways so 43 will not be able to escape! Any questions?"

He paused briefly to let someone speak up, but he was met with silence. They all understood their instructions.

"Alright then," he nodded. "Move out!"

"297," one of the A.I.s called out. "We are only going to stop 43, right?"

297 glanced at the A.I. He could understand why there was cause for concern. It was a fair question, but he had to choose his words carefully. An incorrect answer could demoralize them. However, he had to try and give a calm and reasonable answer.

"We will do everything we can," 297 replied. "We are still figuring out what went wrong. Our plan is to contain and subdue amborg 43 so we can fix the problem. That is all I can say for now."

"Well," the A.I. flashed blue, "please make sure she doesn't get killed. This isn't normal."

"I know," 297 nodded. "I understand. Right now, we have to get all non-combatants and civilians to safety."

Meanwhile, 11, 12, 19, and 24 stood in a diamond formation, surrounded by steel crates and various supplies. Each of them kept their gaze fixed in one direction, keeping a vigilant watch on the perimeter, but 43 was nowhere to be found. They were completely on the defensive, uncertain if help would get there in time. They were dealing with a level of rage that they had never experienced before.

"Can any of you locate her?" 24 transmitted to the others privately. "How is she so good at hiding?! I don't see any sign of an approach. Anyone hear anything?"

"Absolutely nothing," 11 said nervously, glancing around, "but I think we should try to make a stand. She might try to pick us one by... ACK!"

An arm shot out from a nearby cargo container. Horrified, everyone turned just in time to see 43's arm bashing a hole straight through the steel. Her arm grabbed 11 by the scruff of his jacket collar. It pulled him in and his head hit the crate hard with a loud gong.

"...One!" he yelled.

The entire side panel of the crate was torn off and flew towards the rest of them. The other three amborgs dodged it easily, but 11 was thrust against the wall opposite him, pinned by the panel and another container. He was hit again from behind, and he cried out.

"Oww..." he groaned weakly as he transmitted to the rest of them, "I found her..."

43 lunged from the container and punched 12 in the face. She deftly intercepted 19's attack, delivering a quick kick to her stomach that sent her tumbling. 24 jumped in, throwing a few punches, which gave 12 a few moments to refocus. The two of them regrouped and tried to coordinate a joint attack, but 43 blocked their moves easily, striking each of them down to the ground in quick succession. At that moment, 11 crawled out from behind the panel.

"We need better firepower," he groaned as he ran towards some boxes.

He jumped up onto them and sprinted to a spot where he would be seen from the observation post. Spotting Dr. Kendrick inside, he waved frantically.

"Doctor!" 11 shouted through the communications in the observation room. "Help us! What can we use in here?!"

"Technically, everything! Clint, it's going to be ok! Just stay calm!" Dr. Kendrick spoke urgently over a private channel. "This warehouse has a multitude of things that could be used to your advantage! I'm sending you the shipping logs and inventory lists now, but just be careful. You need to watch for the hazardous materials. If the fighting gets out of hand, we could lose the whole warehouse!"

"Why are there hazardous materials in here?" 11 asked in disbelief.

"Everything in storage is equipment scheduled to be destroyed or recycled," Dr. Kendrick explained hastily. "Or relics that have to be preserved! The company has collected a lot of stuff over the years."

"And they're all stored together?!"

"Well, I didn't plan on the warehouse being the setting of a battle between amborgs..."

11 downloaded the manifest and the full inventory list that Dr. Kendrick had sent.

"Great," he sighed as he picked the closest crate that might contain something useful for him. "We're stuck in a box with an evil 43. What else can go wrong?"

Making sure he was well within hearing distance of the ensuing brawl, he began digging through the box to look for a weapon. As 11 rummaged through it, he heard footsteps. He dropped what he was doing, turned to face who was coming, and readied his fists. His shoulders sagged with relief when he noticed 297 running up to him. The two of them linked up and 11 began to update him about the current situation.

"11! What are you doing?"

"Looking for weapons!"

11 turned to search the box again, and 297 joined him. They both glanced inside, and 297 reached in and pulled out an oddly shaped survival knife.

"This looks handy," he declared. His smile faded when he ran it through the inventory. "Huh. The file says discontinued for poor durability design."

"Well, that might be useless. Can you help me find something that could help?" 11 asked as he dug deeper into the box. "We might need to look in a different box if this stuff is all discontinued. We just need some kind of... hello there. Hey, here's something."

He pulled out a hand-held weapon with multiple cylinders around the barrel, which caused 297 to step back and hold out his knife defensively.

"11," 297 said very slowly. "Do you know how to properly wield that weapon? Do you even know what it is?"

11 looked at the "gun" in his hand and nodded, but 297 noticed that despite his stoic nature, he seemed very uncertain.

"Yes," he replied quietly. "Well, that statement is partially accurate. I've been running simulations with it in my head but I have never used it in a real situation."

"Simulations in your head?" 297 stared at him questionably. "You realize that has no contribution to a practical scenario like right now?"

"It may be a discontinued prototype but I know how it works," 11 replied. "I read the instructions."

"If it was discontinued," 297 said, "we can't start firing that off in here."

"Got a better idea?"

297 lowered the knife but did not take his eye off of the weapon. Before anyone could say anything else, they heard a loud crash and 19 flew by. The two amborgs briefly caught her look of fear as she whizzed past.

"HELP!" she screamed as she landed in a pile of crates.

11 looked 297 in the eye. Without another word, he activated the weapon. The cylinders lit up and a loud whining sound indicated it was charging.

"Are you sure?" 297 eyed the weapon suspiciously.

"Unless you need more reason," 11 replied firmly as the cylinders turned a bright blue, "I'm damn sure."

The two of them ran out and quickly came up with a small plan: divide and conquer. 11 leaped on top of some crates again to secure a better vantage point while 297 stayed below. Together, they made their way toward the sounds of fighting. As 297 rounded a corner, he saw them. He signaled to 11, and they began to execute their plan.

12, 19, and 24 were losing drastically. In the seconds after Kendrick had issued an emergency distress signal, they were holding on as long as they possibly could. Unfortunately, only a fraction of amborgs from each group had responded to the call for reinforcements and they wouldn't arrive for another few minutes.

In the midst of the fighting, 43 had shoved a crate over 12's head, causing her to stumble as she struggled to get it off. 19, having just pulled herself from a heap of crates, attempted to sneak up from behind but was immediately caught and tossed over 43's shoulder, landing hard on the ground. As 19 lay sprawled on the floor, 43 delivered a powerful punch to her stomach, creating a dent in the ground beneath her. 19 found herself pinned down, unable to move.

In an effort to create a distraction and rescue 19, 24 started sprinting in circles. 43 quickly followed suit, mirroring her actions. As the two of them circled each other in a rapid whirlwind, 24 abruptly stopped, stepped inward, and reached out her hand to grab 19.

43 was in constant motion, zooming around the area. For a split-second, she failed to notice 24's tactic, but soon enough, she caught on. 43 slowed to a stop and began to attack, taking advantage of 24 and 19's vulnerability and exploiting that weakness. Just as she was about to deliver a massive blow to 24, a voice shouted from behind.

"Hey you!!"

43 instinctively ducked as a weird looking knife whizzed past her head. Rising to her feet, she turned to face her new opponent, who turned out to be 297. He'd been holding onto that strange survival knife the entire time and had thrown it at her. With her focus momentarily diverted, 24 seized the opportunity to continue pulling 19 free from the ground. Meanwhile, 297 stood alone, brandishing another knife.

"Your behavior is unacceptable 43," he said sternly. "Cease hostilities now. I will not repeat this."

"Of course not," 43 smiled as she began to stride toward him menacingly. "Bringing a knife to a fist-fight, 297? Tisk tisk."

Unbeknownst to her, 297 was acting as bait. He glanced over her shoulder and saw 11 moving into position on top of a stack of cargo containers. He had to keep her focus on him. 43 approached him, fists raised, while he readied a defensive stance. Right before anyone could initiate their attack, a crate plummeted from one of the overhead cranes, crashing down and separating them.

"Yes! I saved 297!"

297 looked up at the crane controls and his eyes widened in horror. 501 was waving from behind the controls. When had he arrived?

"Hey 297! Did it work? Did I get her?"

"Idiot!" 297 shouted angrily on a private channel. The container had completely obstructed his view of 43, leaving him with no way of knowing which direction she could be coming from. "You are interfering with the entire plan, 501!"

"Oh really? Sorry!"

"297! She saw me!"

297 heard 11 cry out in terror. He decided to chance it and jumped up. As he scaled the cargo container, he caught a glimpse of what lay beyond. With the crate hiding him from 43's line of sight, she turned around and checked the surrounding area, which unfortunately blew 11's cover. Just as 297 was about to drop down on 43, 11 quickly aimed and fired his weapon.

"Fire in the hole!" he cried as the weapon discharged and shot its payload.

A flash of blue light burst from the first barrel, which then rotated to load another round. 43 deftly sidestepped the beam and looked to where it struck. The floor's plating heated up, radiating a bright blue and orange before it crumbled seconds later. What remained was a smoldering hole in the ground, leaving the others staring in stunned silence.

"Hey 11!" 297 shouted. "It might be a good idea to stop using that."

It was 43, however, who had the worst reaction.

"You tried to disintegrate me?!" she said with a look of disgust. "Eat this buster!"

She dropped to the ground and rolled to the side, snatching up a jagged piece of broken metal and hurling it at 11. It flew so fast that he hardly had time to dodge. As he stumbled to maintain his balance, he accidentally pulled the trigger and fired again. The beam struck a metal pillar, splintering into several beams that ricocheted in all directions. Each impact created melting holes in various surfaces. Luckily, no one was harmed.

"Oh crap!" 11 cried out as he fell on his bottom. "Sorry!"

As he struggled to get up, 43 sprinted toward him with lightning speed. She seized the cylindrical weapon, spun him around, and centered him in front of her. With a swift kick, she sent him crashing to the ground, landing hard beside 24 and 19.

43 forcefully brought the weapon down onto her knee, shattering it before throwing the fragments at 297. He leaped off the container and hit the ground, quickly rolling back to his feet. Unfortunately, as he straightened up, he found himself face to face with 43.

"I hate it when you do that," 297 sighed, realizing he had no time to counter her.

"My specialty," 43 said angrily.

297 attempted to throw a punch, but in the blink of an eye, 43 disarmed him, struck him in the stomach with her knee, and sent him skidding across the floor and tumbling into the pile of his teammates who were struggling to get back up. Her speed was on a whole other level.

24 had successfully pulled 19 from the ground and together, they hurried to remove the crate from 12's head. She gasped in relief, finally able to see and properly reorient herself. The three of them then made their way to 297 and 11, who were also struggling to regain their footing. Despite having five people against one, they still felt outmatched.

"What do we do now?" 12 asked as she massaged her neck.

They all stood still, their eyes fixed on 43. She made no attempt to attack or throw anything from her position. Instead, she simply watched them, waiting for the next challenger. Suddenly, a voice from behind answered 12's question.

"How about an upgrade?"

In an instant, a squad of amborgs arrived onscene. 1, 3, 5, 35, 125, 274, 777, and 999 all showed up just in time, armed and taking up defensive positions. 11, 12, 19, 24, and 297 soon followed, joining their ranks while massaging their joints in relief. 43 stared them all down, readying herself.

"Not that I sound nervous or anything," 19 said with an anxious smile, "but how come there aren't any more of you?"

"First wave of reinforcements. Everyone else is still on the way, or otherwise preoccupied," 1 replied. "If you want more, then we have to keep this contained here."

"Does anyone else feel like this is slightly unfair?" 3 asked.

"Are you kidding?" 297 protested. "It's already fourteen versus one. This is unfair for us. She can still take on all of us!"

"Just so you know," 43 taunted, "fifty amborgs is probably my maximum, but I can settle for all of you for now."

"Great, 117's grandpa seemed to have left an impression on her," 5 muttered. "We're dead."

"Come on guys," 24 sighed. "You're all a sight for sore eyes, but I'm glad that you're here."

"As much as I appreciate that, is it still bad if I admit that I'm afraid to be here?" 3 asked nervously.

"I'm not."

Everyone watched as 999 boldly took the lead and stood at the front of the formation.

"This finally means I can fight 43 without limitations."

"That's the spirit," 43 grinned maliciously.

"Ok," 11 cast a horrified look at 999, "now I'm scared."

3 stepped forward and charged her pop gun. The others watched her as she confidently positioned herself next to 999.

"Alright everyone," she explained. "In short, we drew the short straws. So basically, that means we keep 43 in here while every other amborg locks down every possible way out."

"Anyone need weapons?" 274 distributed arms amongst them.

He had certainly grabbed a strange assortment of weapons unlike anything anyone had ever seen. 43 stared at them in disbelief as if she were watching the most ridiculous circus on the planet.

"You guys look like a time machine blew up and turned you into the weirdest looking D&D party," she said.

She couldn't be more right. 1 was holding a vintage flamethrower in his arms. 5 and 999 both were carrying short range grenade launchers. 274 held some of the transport cubes from earlier. 125 stepped to the side, armed with a shotgun. 777 had somehow picked up a baseball bat in the middle of the warehouse and was wielding it like a club. 57 had picked up an electric saw used for construction. Then there was 35, who drew a tomahawk. Half of these weapons were either antiques or semi-modern prototypes that were never properly developed.

Still, the other amborgs grabbed the last few weapons their reinforcing party had brought them.

"Seriously?" 11 said incredulously, pulling a sword from 5's shoulder bag. "Where did you acquire a rapier?"

"I borrowed it from Dr. Kendrick's office," 5 said casually. "I stopped by and it was just there mounted on the wall."

"Hey! That is a collectible!"

All of them, including 43, turned and looked up at the observation post. Dr. Kendrick stood there, staring at them in wide-eyed shock. The group exchanged glances, collectively shrugging in uncertainty.

"I will acquire another one for you doctor," 5 said innocently with a sheepish grin on his face. "How hard could it be to replicate one of these?"

"Johnny, that's not the point!" Dr. Kendrick shouted. "Oh, never mind."

19 grabbed a small device from 1, who passed it to her. She inspected it and frowned.

"Uh, are we really using this? Please let me destroy it here and now..." she complained.

19 held what appeared to be a simple pen case, but it was much more than that. It was actually a cleverly designed tool disguised as one. With a press of a button, a compartment opened, and a long wire shot out. Electricity crackled as she skillfully wielded an electric whip, though it came dangerously close to their feet.

"Hey, watch it!" 125 yelled he jumped to the left.

"I thought they didn't use these anymore," 19 said. "So what's this?"

"Uh, that's accurate," 1 replied. "That's a weapon not in service anymore."

Everyone paused, including 43, who gazed at the whip curiously. 19 slowly lifted her eyes to 43, appearing crest-fallen.

"Serina 43," 19 said quietly, biting her lip.

43 silently nodded, indicating that she was listening.

"Do you mind giving me a second to destroy a dark piece of history?"

Everyone cautiously glanced at 43. She seemed hesitant, but quietly pondered the issue as she maintained her fighting stance. After a few moments, she nodded her head again.

"Sure," 43's eyes narrowed. "If you had used that on me, I would have destroyed it myself."

"Am I missing something?" 57 asked.

19 raised her arm, gripping the whip tightly before forcefully throwing it a safe distance from them. It hit the ground hard, shattering into many pieces. The remnants of the whip sparked and fizzed out. It was clearly inoperable and in no condition to be used.

"I'll tell you after we finish this," 19 said as she spotted a hammer on a nearby crate. She moved to pick it up and then rejoined their formation. "Can we get back to this?"

"Uh, right!" 24 interrupted.

She and 12 were the only ones who didn't have a weapon. 5 gave them a brief chance to check his backpack. They both reached in, pulling out anything they could find.

"Cool," 12 drew a gun from the backpack. "This will help a little."

Unfortunately, 24's reaction was the complete opposite when she reached for something and pulled it out. She had taken what appeared to be a bumper sticker from 5's inventory.

"Seriously?" she said feeling disappointed. "An arrow? What can I do with this??"

What appeared to be a simple white sticker in the form of an arrow, bordered by a dark outline, was more than what it seemed. It resembled a common directional sign normally seen on walking paths or hiking trails. However, it was actually a sophisticated piece of technology.

"Throw stuff at 43 with it?" 11 suggested.

777 leaned forward and looked at 24 skeptically.

"An arrow? Like a bow and arrow?" he asked.

"No," 297 replied. "It's an... arrow sign, arrow?"

"Come on 24," 1 replied. "You're holding the world's deadliest bumper sticker right there in your hand. Just remember not to stick it somewhere it shouldn't go. Otherwise Dr. Kendrick will kill us if 43 doesn't."

While 1 was cautioning 24 about the dangers of misusing that sticker, 43 cracked her knuckles and began to stride toward them. The time for talking was over.

"Everyone lock and load!" 5 shouted. "We've got a hostile approaching, and she looks ready to kill!"

"Oh yeah sure," 3 said as she took aim. "All we have to do is take on the best amborg in history who is exhibiting a bout of sub psychotic rage. What could go wrong?"

No one had time to answer her sarcastic question. They all readied themselves as 43 charged.

CHAPTER 14

Inner Cyberspace

A.I. Industries
North Entrance
Fifteen Minutes Earlier

"Halt. You are entering a restricted area. You must turn back and leave."

"Leave? After all the trouble poor old me took to get here?"

117's grandfather, Mark, stood outside the gates of A.I. Industries with a handful of his vigilantes. He was under the impression that 117 had called him here. However, when he arrived at the gates, he found himself confronted by a group of overly talkative security drones that completely blocked his way.

"Running scan on pronounced visitors," one of the security drones stated as it scanned them top to bottom. "Scan complete."

"Here we go," Mark rolled his eyes.

"You seem to be currently equipped with anatomical equipment which should safely allow you to proceed in the opposite direction," the drone reported. "Some pieces of this equipment could also be considered weapons. You are clearly an augmented enhanced human being. Please leave now before we classify you as a hostile. Have a nice day."

"Well, I have other things to do," Mark replied casually. "Now if you would please step aside. There are important things that need to get done that your little circuit board can't even begin to fathom."

"Sir, we may be drones," the guard replied in a deep robotic monotone. "It is true we do not have emotions but we can still understand insults. With that manner of disrespect, we politely ask that you leave now."

"Boy are you a sensitive little..."

Mark paused, immediately holding his tongue. This was going nowhere. The drone observed him with interest but didn't press the matter further. Growing increasingly impatient, he peered over the security drone's shoulder, searching for a human presence. He had expected his trip to A.I. Industries to be an easy one, but couldn't help but feel that 117 had as a prank rather than a genuine emergency.

"My apologies sir," the drone repeated. "No matter how many times you request access, I still cannot permit you to enter the complex. As

I said before, you have no clearance and your visit is unscheduled and unauthorized. Therefore you and your party must leave."

The old man groaned, considering his next words carefully. He turned his attention back to the drone, then the one behind it, and the third one positioned at the guardhouse entrance. That's when he noticed something peculiar. While it was common knowledge that A.I. Industries utilized drones for surveillance at entry points as part of the security detail, he couldn't shake the feeling that something was off. Suddenly, it dawned on him why this visit felt so restricting.

"Say, I believe this issue could be resolved if I could speak to someone high up," he suggested. "It doesn't necessarily have to be Dr. Kendrick; perhaps your supervisor? Where are the human guards?"

"Your query is unclear," the drone replied and indicated with a small gesture to the rest of the drones. "As you can see, the guards are at their post. I am the supervising guard overseeing the protection of this entrance."

"No, you dumb drone," Mark snapped. "The *human* guards. Doesn't Kendrick have them out here? The ones who know how to talk to visitors? He's got to have someone biological on duty instead of an entire team of robots."

"None of the human guards are currently at their stations due to a critical situation. I also find that last statement to be prejudiced," the drone replied casually.

"Oh yeah? Critical? Wait, what do you mean prejudiced?" Mark leaned forward, but immediately caught on to what the drone was saying. He quickly waved his hands and shook them defensively. "Ok, I admit I might have overreacted with that last statement. I got nothing against robots or drones."

Except when they're being a pain, he thought silently to himself, *then I can just pummel them.*

The drones didn't need to know that. The last thing he needed was a confrontation on the doorstep of A.I. Industries, of all places.

"Look," he said in the friendliest tone that he could muster. "I said I was sorry for the bigotry, but I'm still in a bit of a rush. Now what are the human guards doing?"

"That information is classified," the drone responded in its very dull tone.

"Classified?" Mark mimicked mockingly in the same tone. "Well, let me guess, they must be trying to contain a psychopathic A.I. on a rampage or supervising the amborg training?"

"No," the drone said, "they are attempting to suppress amborg 43 in the warehouse...oops. I have said too much."

The drone shook its head, raised its hand, and slapped itself. Grandpa Mark beamed with satisfaction at the drone's mistake.

"HA!" he laughed. "A little trickery and deceit and you drones can't help yourself. Now, why don't you tell me why 43 is being... suppressed, you say? That's... interesting. What does that even mean?"

"That is classified," the drone repeated.

This routed the conversation back to square one. Starting to feel annoyed again, the old man took a step forward and looked the drone right in the eye. Or rather, the red light coming from the lens on its forehead.

"Really? You're really going to go through this again?" Mark sighed and thought for a moment. "Ok... Well, what if I told you a family member of mine is in there? I'm visiting them. Would that grant me clearance?"

The drone took a moment to process the question before responding. It tilted its head slightly, much like a curious puppy trying to determine if someone is friendly. After a brief and contemplative analysis, the drone nodded.

"State your name and your relative's name please," it stated blandly. "If they verify your identity and provide you with clearance, you may pass."

The drone raised its right arm, activating a projector from its wrist. A holographic screen materialized, displaying an empty search bar.

Mark blinked, at a total loss for words. Had he successfully outsmarted the drone's logic? It no longer seemed to acknowledge his earlier attempts to gain access, behaving as if it had rebooted to its original settings.

"Please state your name and your relative's name please," the drone repeated its instructions.

"I am Mark and I'm looking for David."

"Mark... What is your surname?"

"Why would I tell you that?"

The drone looked at Mark and paused.

"Your last name will help us identify you," it stated.

"Well, that's not how I like to work," Mark replied with a shrug.

"Very well," the drone replied. "Commencing search."

The search bar disappeared, and some kind of database appeared in its place. With its other hand, the drone began typing on its arm keypad rapidly.

It was only two words. Mark stared, raising an eyebrow. *What is this little steel chrome dome up to?*

After scanning the database, the drone looked back up. There was a short pause, and then the screen flashed green. A recording of a bell chimed, indicating the end of the search.

"Based on your limited answers," the security drone said blatantly, "I have found a few records cross-referenced to those specific names."

"Oh... yay," Mark rolled his eyes. "Give me the short answers."

"There are four Davids on site in these records," the drone said as it looked through the files. The screen brought up a face to each of the names the robot listed. "David Peterson in engineering. David Beckam in research. David Rakalpulco in security. David Tortellini in the weapons division."

One of the vigilantes accompanying 117's grandfather had blurted out the name. Another one snickered but shut up immediately when the old man turned and glared at them.

"Sorry," he replied.

"Personally, I thought Rakalpulco or whatever that name was sounded really badass..." the other vigilante whispered.

Mark ignored this comment and turned to face the drone again.

"What about my grandson David? Why wasn't he a part of the list?"

He hadn't seen 117's face appear on the drone's database, which only meant one thing—he was going to get sent away if he didn't get to the bottom of this.

The drone glanced back at the database on its arm, then to Mark as if it hadn't made a mistake. After another moment of silence, the drone began typing again.

"If your relative is not among these records, your statement about visiting a relative can only be concluded as a lie," it said bluntly.

"But it shouldn't be," Mark muttered.

"However, if you believe that you are being wronged," the drone continued, ignoring Mark's subtle commentary, "I shall search again. This time, let me factor... grandson... into the mix. Estimating age of visiting relative and rechecking records."

Mark tapped his foot impatiently as the drone conducted its search.

"The records show..." the drone spoke, but paused, then looked back up, "...nothing."

"WHAT?!" Mark snatched the drone's arm, pulling it closer to him and skimmed through the data listing. "How could there be nothing?"

"I am A.I. Industries property, sir," the drone said calmly. "Please do not touch me."

"There has to be something!" Mark obeyed and let the drone pull its arm back.

"I am sorry sir. I cannot find any indication that you are related, or for that matter, affiliated to any of the known Davids in A.I. Industries' company records."

"Grr," Mark sighed. "I didn't want to resort to this specifically because it was supposed to be a secret, but he needs me, so I will do it. Try searching for him under test subjects?"

"Searching...test subject? In A.I. Industries' company records? I am sorry, there are still no records."

"He's an amborg!" Mark grumbled. "David 117. The Second Group? He's pretty well known!"

Every security drone turned their heads and glanced at Mark. The one directly in front of him simply lowered its gaze to its arm and checked the database once more.

"Confirmed," it replied after a few moments. "One result match following the parameters of your inquiry. David 117."

GOOD! That's the one," Mark sighed with relief as he clapped his hands cheerfully. "Now let me in."

"I cannot allow that sir."

"WHAT NOW?!!!"

"All amborgs do not have relatives," the drone stated firmly. "Dr. Kendrick specifically selects orphans who have no family. Therefore, your statement that you are a relative is invalid. Which also adds on to my previous observation that you were lying."

Mark groaned and paced back and forth in frustration. He took a few breaths to calm down.

Happy thoughts, he growled under his breath as he looked at the drone in its bright red eye. *I promised David no violence. I'm trying to be a nice grandpa.*

"Ok ok," he said. "Umm, why don't you call Dr. Kendrick and have him vouch for me? My son used to work for him. He knows me. Or... He knows of me."

"If you refuse to give me your full name," the drone replied, "it will make it difficult to verify your identity. Something like that would be on my watchlist."

"Discretion is pretty damn important to me," Mark snapped. "Can't you just pull up a directory and let me scroll through the names? It won't take too long. I could even write my son's name and show it to you, since I want to avoid sharing it out loud. Even as a machine, you should know the meaning of protecting the family name, literally."

"I am sorry sir," the drone said. "The situation is understandable, but we have security measures for a reason. As for someone vouching for you, Dr. Kendrick's safety protocol dictates I cannot allow him outside to... prove your identity. The statistical likelihood of a kidnapping attempt is high with someone of your specific caliber."

"Wow," Mark sighed. "You are probably one of the most paranoid and annoying security guards I've ever encountered..."

"I get that a lot," the drone replied casually.

"Wait, what do you mean you don't let him outside?" Mark asked skeptically. "How the hell does he go out to select new amborgs then?"

"Oh..." the drone looked down and brought a finger up. "Err... A moment please."

"No," Mark said, shaking his hand. "There isn't going to be another moment. Have you ever heard of something called Google?"

The robot nodded as the old man slowly placed his hand on its shoulder.

"Yeah, the thing is robot," he said inquisitively and as obnoxiously as possible. "I think Google is smarter and faster than you are."

"That statement is false sir," the robot challenged confidently. "Besides, Google is my main source to look at images of the gorgeous T-910 model. Those things are built within suitable parameters. Very attractive."

Taken aback, Mark blinked at what he had just heard. Did the A.I. Industries security drone just declare an emotional interest... towards another object? What kind of human lessons was Dr. Kendrick allowing here? Ignoring this, Mark thought up a way to use this to his advantage.

"I got bad news for you, defense drone," he said cheekily. "The T-910 is a toy. It is not a real robot."

He had put extra emphasis on the last sentence and waited for a response. The robot stalled for a few seconds, then began warbling indiscernible noises.

"What? Impossible," it began to sputter. "All of my calculations of meeting one... I had hoped to meet the robot of my dreams and seek out an evolved lifestyle. Impossible. This cannot be true... NOOOOOOOOOOOOOOOO!!"

All eyes, including Mark's and his escort's, were drawn to the drone stationed at the center of the gate. As it turned and walked away, and even though it was a machine, they could somehow sense its anguish. It headed toward the guardhouse and disappeared inside. This prompted a different drone to step forward and address Mark.

"How many of you do I have to mentally break to get inside the damn building?" Mark asked sarcastically.

"I don't have a human mental capacity," the second drone replied. "I do follow protocol at all times."

"Here we go again..." Mark muttered grimly.

"One problem still remains. I cannot allow you inside without proper authorization."

Mark began hurling curses at the drone. Fortunately, it stayed put and didn't retaliate as he lost his temper. His hooded vigilantes began to chuckle and whisper amongst themselves.

"At this rate," someone whispered while Mark kept yelling, "we'll be the ones who'll die of old age before we get in."

Warehouse One
Status: 22% Destroyed

"Ok 3, you cut around this way. 297 will watch our flanks from above. 5 and I will attempt to distract her from the front."

3 smiled and nodded firmly at 1.

"Understood. That is until Donut finds us first."

"Hey guys! What are you doing over there?"

Everyone froze.

"You had to say it..." 297 groaned.

"Uh-oh..." 5 sighed.

"Oops," 3 cringed.

The four amborgs flinched at the sound of 501 calling out to them. Not only did that give away their position, but they also had just enough time to glance up as their sensors picked up movement. By the time it registered, it was already too late. 43 dropped in the center of their huddle and the battle resumed. She swiftly kicked 5 and 1 in the chest, sending them flying. As she dodged a shot from 3's pop gun, she slammed 297 into the floor. Then, seizing his legs, she swung him like a bat to knock 3 aside. Mid swing, she let go of 297, who crashed into the wall.

"Ok if 43 is not going to be the one that kills us," 5 groaned as he picked himself up off the ground, "I want to at least kill 501 before I die. I refuse to lose my life due to friendly fire."

"That's... argh... not what it means," 297 replied weakly. "501 has to directly hurt you by mistake or intentionally harm you."

"Don't correct me when we're about to die..." 5 grumbled.

While they were arguing, they had inadvertently made themselves 43's next targets. She grabbed 5's foot and dragged him across the ground.

He collided with a crate, crying out in pain as he injured his back. With that, 43 set her sights on 297.

1 found himself ensnared in a net after 43 had kicked him. As he struggled to free himself, he noticed 297 valiantly trying to hold her off. Just then, a crate appeared overhead. 501 was still at the controls of one of the warehouse's interior cranes with a bird's-eye view. Unfortunately, he kept forgetting to mute his communications, enabling 43 to pinpoint their locations. 1 realized that 501 had positioned the crane right over the site of the battle.

"501," 1 transmitted to the Third Group amborg quickly. "Do not reply to me. Just listen. If you're trying to maneuver that crate over 43, you are right on target. Release the clamps! Do you understand me?"

Without a word, 501 peered down at 1 from the crane's control booth. He responded with a nod and a thumbs-up. 1 hoped that his message was clearly understood. 501's antics reminded him of a certain character from Red vs. Blue.

At that moment, the crane latches disengaged. The crate was released and plummeted at full speed. 297 glanced up and dove out of the way, abandoning his fight with 43. She stayed put, looking up just as the crate came crashing down on her. As he executed a combat roll and lifted his head, a resounding thud echoed across the entire warehouse.

"Did it work?" 297 asked.

He spoke too soon. 43 had lifted her arms and managed to catch the entire cargo container, demonstrating her incredible strength as she strained to stay on her feet. Once she found her footing, she shot a fierce look at 297 and, with a mighty heave, she threw the container at him.

"Nope, it didn't work," he said meekly.

1 winced as the container knocked 297 out of view. In the crane's control booth, 501's eyes widened in shock, his mouth hanging open. Another deafening crash reverberated nearby as 297 took the full force of the attack head on.

43 turned around and spotted 999, who had attempted to sneak up on her. Her plan was foiled, and 43 sprang into action, and the two immediately began to grapple with one another.

"117's grandfather was right," 43 grumbled as she struggled to get out of 999's grasp. "You're so predictable."

Meanwhile, several meters from the fight, other amborgs were desperately trying to regroup. 11 was frantically trying to help 12, 19, and 24. Another crate had been shoved over 12's head and 19, perched on top of a nearby crate, was struggling to yank it off. At the same time, 24 was examining the remains of her rifle.

"Well," she said as she threw one half of it behind her. "This situation could not get worse, could it?"

11 caught the piece of the rifle. He looked down at it and frowned as 12 stood still shaking her crate-head from side to side.

"It's not all bad," her bracelet flashed as she shrugged. "43 hasn't killed any of us. It seems like she's only trying to take us out."

"Yeah..." 11 replied, "so *she* can get out. If 999 can't stop her, at this rate, she'll tear through the Third Group, and they have minimal combat experience."

"Look, I have a box on my head," 12 sighed. "I'm trying to be optimistic."

"Stop moving!" 19 snapped as she poked her head up from behind 12. She glared down at 11 and 24. "I can't get this off if you keep turning your head!"

Just then, a radio transmission interrupted them, and all four paused to listen. It was 917.

"This is 917 calling anyone in the warehouse. Any amborg currently not engaged in combat, please respond."

11 decided to answer the transmission.

"19, keep helping 12," he said.

"Bro, what's it look like I'm doing?" she replied as she yanked the box again.

"Ow!" 12 cried.

11 looked at 24, who shrugged.

"24," he sighed. "Just cover me."

He brought his hand up to his right temple and initiated his response.

"917!" he said. "11 here. My team is dealing with a few minor setbacks."

"Is it that bad?" 917 replied. "Wait, then who's fighting 43?"

"Your best friend," 11 answered promptly.

"Oh no," 917 answered, dread laced in his voice.

"You don't feel confident in 999's abilities?"

"Actually, it's quite the opposite," 917 replied. "She's very competitive and always kicks it up a notch whenever she loses. The harder 43 tries to put her out of commission, the more likely 999 is going to end up killing herself by refusing to back down."

"What are you saying?" 11 asked suspiciously.

"I'm saying, if things get worse..." 917 started to say.

"Worse than now?!" 11 blurted out, cutting him off mid-sentence.

"...yes, worse," 917 clarified insistently. "If that happens, we need to stop both of them from killing each other and potentially destroying half the place!"

"Excuse me."

24 tapped 11 on the shoulder. He turned, noticing that she also had her hand on her right temple, joining in on the transmission.

"Sorry to butt in but... 43 and 999 wouldn't actually kill each other..." she said. "Would they?"

"999 has always been extremely competitive during sparring sessions against 43," 917 insisted. "When 43 was her usual pleasant self, she'd always laugh it off and treat 999 with honor, kindness, tough love, and yada yada. The end of our training sessions together would always end with mutual respect. What do you think will happen if evil 43 continues to push 999 more and more?"

"I'm starting to get the picture..." 11 gulped.

Both his and 24's faces conveyed a sense of mutual recognition. She also looked like she was beginning to grasp what was likely going to happen next.

"Isn't 999 your best friend?" 24 asked nervously. "Why don't you come here and help us stop her?"

They heard someone clear their throat. 11 and 24 turned to see 12 waving at them, the crate still on her head.

"Does this mean we have to stop two of A.I. Industries' top amborgs?" she asked curiously, and with a little bit of apprehension.

"For the last time!" 19 barked. "Let me take this crate off your big head and then you can participate in strategizing!"

917 spoke up again.

"What's that about?"

"Nothing," 11 and 24 replied.

"Ok??"

"The bottom line is, we need you," 11 shook his head, refocusing on the transmission. "917, can you get here and help us? If you're right, then we have two maniacal amborgs on the loose."

"Oh, well, I'm a little preoccupied," 917 answered sarcastically. Before anyone could ask, he replied angrily. "I'm currently trying to pull 117 out of the hospital wall! If anyone can try to stop 43, he's our best bet... who, by the way, ended up being hammered into the building!"

"Oh," 11 replied sheepishly. "I didn't think of that..."

"How bad is it?" 24 asked.

"Well," 917 took a deep breath and let out a huff. "117 is buried about three feet and four inches beneath a solid layer of steel and concrete. It looks as though 43 tried to use him to excavate a cave. The twins are trying to get him out with the help of 345. Kinda glad to see her back on her feet, especially since she'd been overloaded with having so many A.I.s in her brain. Our biggest concern now is figuring out how to rescue him without bringing down the entire hospital."

"917," 24 spoke. "Does anyone there have any idea what caused this? Truthfully, I'm glad that 43 is awake but it's strange that she's behaving this way."

"No idea," 917 stated. "117, Mandy, and Sherry were hanging out at 43's bed. Then, Dr. Wildman stopped for a quick visit, and then she was awake. It all escalated from there."

"Do people just wake up from a coma that fast and alert?" 11 asked.

"No," 917 replied. "Trust me, when I woke up from my coma and found out I had enhanced abilities, I didn't behave how 43 did. I think... It's hard to remember. For me, it was like waking up late after a long night. It took me several minutes to reorient myself and get used to the fact that I felt different."

11 and 24 both exchanged confused glances. 917 was going off-topic.

"917, focus!" 11 said.

"Oh right. Sorry."

Out of nowhere, a loud crash echoed through the transmission. At the same time, a deep rumble resonated beneath their feet. Based on the direction it came from, something had gone awry at the hospital. The amborgs in the warehouse recognized the faint voices of the Second Group twins and 345 from their incomprehensible screaming through 917's transmission. By the sound of it, they were in serious trouble.

"Did you guys break the hospital?!" 24 scolded.

"No?" 917 replied innocently. "Only part of it. Hey, everything else was 43. I'm just saying."

"Great, now there's no place for us to go if we're seriously wounded," 11 let out a defeated sigh.

A new voice quickly cut into the transmission, and they could hear 345 speaking in the background.

"Ok! I think I've got it!" she said determinedly. "If my calculations this time are right, I need you two to strike this key point while I do this one! This should get him out!"

"Did 345 just say to strike a key point?" 24 looked at 11 with an alarmed expression. "She's going to do more damage?!"

917 was already way ahead of their initial protests.

"Hey!" they heard 917 yell. "Be careful! Watch out for the..."

Three sharp thuds resonated from 11's bracelet. Presumably, the three amborgs had hit their marks. Suddenly, they heard another loud crash. Straining to listen, 11 heard 917's surprised shout, followed by a cacophony of noise as everyone erupted into even more frantic screams.

"...Or not," 345 said faintly after the yelling had mostly subsided. "Wow, 43 really stuck him in here. Oh no. 917? I think we made it worse!"

"Really?" 917 asked sarcastically.

"I'm sorry!" 345 apologized profusely. "Listen, we need to get support beams in here! Where was that maintenance worker?! Someone help over there too!"

"No! Get all human personnel out!"

One of the twins, amborg 92, abruptly shouted.

"It's too dangerous for normal humans! 93, grab that guy! He got hit by the rubble! Get the medics!"

His twin brother spoke up.

"43 kinda took out most of them!"

11 stared at his bracelet with growing concern. Suddenly, 917's voice spoke again, clearer this time.

"We will continue to try and get 117 out," he informed them. "Can you hold out as long as you can?"

"You're talking about stopping Serina 43," 11 exclaimed. "The woman who put her boyfriend into a wall! How do we stop her?! Ask her politely?!"

"Uh, we already tried that," 12 spoke up, turning to him with the box still on her head. She held up her index finger, as if to make a point. "Remember?"

"I think he's being rhetorical," 19 said gently.

"I am being rhetorical!"

Another crash erupted from 917's transmission, followed by a girl's scream in the background, filling all of them with concern.

"Uh-oh... I need to act as a make-shift support beam," 917 muttered. "345 just got hit in the head. I got to go. We'll be there soon!"

The transmission ended. Without hesitation, 11 quickly tried to contact 1.

"Leonard! Can you hear me?"

"I hear you 11," 1 panted. "What's going on?"

"Sitrep?" 11 asked.

"Thanks for asking," 1 replied grimly. "I have good news and bad news."

"Oh?" 11 glanced at 24, who appeared taken aback.

"The good news is, 999 managed to put up a decent fight against 43," 1 reported. "It weakened her."

"Did she win?" 24 asked curiously.

"No," 1 answered. "She's out. 43 threw her headfirst into a container, tied her up, and chained her to 297. It's just been me."

"Wait, alone?" 11 exclaimed in shock.

"Yup. Which leads me to the bad news."

They listened as 1's voice grew worried.

"Get here fast," he said. "Something's wrong with 43. We need 117 here now."

"Understood," 11 replied.

"Uh... hey?"

Everyone turned and saw that 12 was frantically waving her hand to get their attention, then pointed at the box on her head.

"Help me get this crate off my head before you guys run off! Please?"

11 and 24 joined 19. The three of them quickly began examining the box for its weak spots. Drawing inspiration from 345's strategies shared in the last transmission, 11 came up with an idea. Together, the three of them identified their target areas and delivered powerful punches to different sections of the crate. It split apart, freeing 12, but the force of their blows created intense vibrations that left her feeling dizzy.

"Thank... you," she said lazily. "Wow, it feels good to see again."

Her sensory cognition had been shorted, making it difficult for her to stand.

"You are welcome," 11 nodded patiently. "Stay here 12. When you get the strength, see if you can find the others who are already beaten and lying around. It's a maze in here thanks to all this destruction."

"Copy that," 12 nodded as she knelt down, taking a quick breather.

"11," 1's voice spoke again. "Can you guys hurry up? 43 just pulled out the... arrow? 24! I thought you had it!"

"I don't," 24 said as she fumbled in her pockets. "I seem to have... misplaced it. Wait. 43 must have taken it when she beat me, 11, 12, and 19 earlier."

"That... is obvious," 1 responded.

----

1 was not happy at all. His gaze followed 43 as she moved slowly to a nearby crate, lifting an arrow carefully. After securing the blank arrow to

the side of the crate, she took a step back. The arrow was aimed precisely to her left, directly in line with the spot where 1 stood.

The arrow glowed brightly, and in an instant, the crate lifted off the ground and hurtled toward 1. He dashed forward, dropping to his knees and sliding beneath the enormous projectile just in time. The crate slammed into the wall, adhering itself to the side of the warehouse. As 1 straightened up, 43 stepped right in front of him, and they began sparring. Fortunately, because of her prolonged fights with the others, her strength and speed appeared to be waning.

As 1 countered 43's attacks, 501 exited the safety of the crane's control booth. He had been watching from a distance, but his attention was drawn to the crate stuck to the wall.

"Dr. Kendrick?" he transmitted to the observation room.

There was an immediate response.

"Yes? 501?"

"What is an arrow?" 501 asked. "How is it making that crate stick to the wall?"

"It's another revolutionary but unstable idea," Dr. Kendrick answered. "Elegant but very dangerous."

As he spoke, the glowing arrow affixed to the crate let out a sharp whine, then shut down. 501 watched as the crate suddenly dropped to the ground, crashing just as it had when it collided with the wall.

"In case you were trying to figure it out, 501," Dr. Kendrick continued, "the arrow is designed to change the direction of gravity on whatever it sticks to."

"What?" 501's eyes widened. "That's... so cool!"

Dr. Kendrick's brief explanation sounded impossible, but to 501, it was nothing short of revolutionary. Once the sticker was attached to any object, it would generate an energy field around it and propel it in the direction the sticker indicated. This, however, left 501 with another question.

"Doctor?" 501 asked, thinking about what he would do if he got his hands on an arrow. "What happens if you stick it on a person?"

"That person's gravity would align with where the arrow was pointing."

"So..." 501 imagined him sticking one onto his torso. "If I stuck an arrow to myself, pointed upward, would I go up?"

"I suppose so?" Dr. Kendrick replied, a hint of suspicion creeping into his voice.

"But... if I'm falling upwards," 501 looked towards the ceiling, "and I change direction, wouldn't that mean the arrow would point in different directions? So... would I be flying erratically if I spun around in certain ways?"

"Yes..."

"That doesn't sound efficient," 501 felt a little disappointed.

"Hence, why we scrapped the project. Our initial designs for alternative transportation methods backfired. When you mess with gravity, it messes you up... or down. Any direction."

"But if I flew up into the air," 501 said, "I could be stuck hurtling towards the upper atmosphere and accidentally go to space?"

"I doubt it," Dr. Kendrick answered. "The arrows have a limited power supply. They only work for a few minutes at a time and then they automatically shut off."

"It must consume a lot of power to alter something's gravity," 501 guessed.

"You are correct," Dr. Kendrick said pleasantly.

"Did... you ever stick an arrow onto an actual living being?"

There was a brief pause.

"I'm only going to tell you one thing, Dom."

501 perked up and looked towards Dr. Kendrick eagerly.

"What?"

"If you stick an arrow on you," he said sternly, "I suggest you put on protective gear."

"That is it 43! No more arrow for you!"

"Who's going to stop me?" 43 smirked. "You?"

"At this rate," 1 replied as he used the last of his strength to prevent himself from being thrown over. "I believe that might actually be a possibility."

Both of them were grasping each other's arms tightly, trying to maneuver their legs around the deadlock so they could kick each other. Spotting a slight gap in her defense, 1 made his move and delivered a powerful headbutt to her forehead. 43 let go, stumbled backward, and dropped into a crouch, disoriented.

"Serina 43, stop! Control yourself," 1 commanded. "You're slowing down. That isn't good and we both know it. Stop now and we can fix the issue."

"Save it lead-for-brains!" she spat.

"Our brains are technically lead," 1 replied casually, "from a certain point of view."

Fueled by rage, she lunged at him, but before she could reach him, a blinding light lit up the area. Something shot toward her, striking her down. She collapsed to the ground, ensnared by blue bands of energy binding her in place. 1 turned to face the new arrival.

"Let me handle this."

117 brushed some gravel off his shoulder, flanked by 917, 92, 93, and 345–two on his left and two on his right. 1 nodded before sprinting off to look for any other wounded amborgs. The energy bands holding 43 shattered as she freed herself.

"No big deal," she scoffed. Getting back to her feet, she lifted her arms but as she did so, they began to tremble a little. "I can... take on all of you."

"No," 117 said. "You're very weak. Surely now you've realized you haven't recovered. You need to stop now so we can help you heal."

"Right," she brushed off that comment with a snarl. "Never knew you to be manipulative."

"No," he repeated. "If I was lying, then you wouldn't have been caught by the energy rings. This adrenaline induced rage is a side effect of your recovery. Now, release 274 and 125 from the experimental orbs and stand down."

43's anger intensified, but before she could make another move, she suddenly dropped to her knees and pressed her hands against her head.

"Ahh!" she cried out. "What's... happening?! It... hurts!!"

The rest of them quickly surrounded her, and 117 scooped her into his arms. 917 reached in her pockets, pulled out two transport orbs, and tossed them away from the group. The orbs flashed, and seconds later, 274 and 125 dropped to the ground with two loud thuds.

"Ugh," 125 said out of his bracelet. "That was not fun."

274 nodded in agreement but didn't say a word. They both rose to their feet and leaned against a crate, looking quite sick. The orbs were bad news for whoever got caught in the entrapment zone. Dr. Baldwin probably was going to enjoy listening to their experiences.

117's eyes were fixed on 43, still wracked with pain. Her screams had subsided, replaced with soft groans. Then, unexpectedly, her hand reached up and touched the side of 117's face. A sudden surge of emotion flooded through him. The other amborgs watched in stunned silence.

"What the hell just happened?" 917 said, shock and concern etched onto his face.

----

43 blinked and found herself standing in front of an unfamiliar door. It was entirely wooden, with metal hinges and a simple doorknob. It looked old, reminiscent of a bygone era. As she glanced around, confusion washed over her; just moments ago, she had been surrounded by her friends.

I got to find someone, she thought as she turned to look at the wooden door.

Where was everyone? That was the real question. 43 felt that she had to find somebody before she lost control of herself entirely. Perhaps the way out was through the door.

Quickly, she grasped the handle and pushed it open. It had been years since she had encountered a door like this one. It was definitely quite old compared to the modern designs of gates and doorways of the present—the kind only found in well-kept locations.

Inside, she found what appeared to be a living room filled with standard furniture from the twenty-first century—a couch, coffee table, TV, and another small table with four chairs in one corner. There were also toys on the floor, sprawled across a blanket in the middle of the room. She carefully stepped around them as if she had stumbled onto a minefield.

Looking up, she saw a glass door that led to a patio. A beam of sunlight was pouring in, and she almost felt tempted to step outside. Except, it didn't feel right. Instead, she pressed her hand to the glass. It was smooth, cold to the touch, but it felt more unnatural than what she knew about real modern glass. It was at that moment she realized it was because she wasn't analyzing everything like she usually did. Were her cybernetics not functioning?

"Hi there."

43 retracted her hand and whirled around to see a familiar face.

"David?" she said, then suddenly brought a hand up to her mouth.

She had spoken with her real voice without realizing it. She looked at her left wrist and realized her bracelet was gone. The figure at the table smiled and stood up. 43 lowered her arm and decided to speak again, but the shock from her earlier question stopped her.

"Who are you?" 117 asked politely, smiling warmly.

He was also speaking with his real voice, which was so much more different and stranger than how he normally spoke. This wasn't 117. But it felt like it was at the same time.

"You don't know me?" 43 asked.

"I'm afraid not. You seem familiar though."

"Then... Where are we?"

"It's my home," 117 replied. "Or if you want specifics, it's a very deep level of cyberspace that very few can reach. It's a realm that I live in and I don't think you're supposed to be here."

"But, if that's the case, how did I get here?" 43 asked, pointing at the ground.

"Who knows?" 117 shrugged. "You're the first visitor I've ever had."

43 gave him a look of content.

"You seem different from the 117 I know," she stated. "You sound more confident and relaxed."

"Well, it is my home here," 117 smiled. "All the way down in these deep deep levels of inner space. The cyber realm is quite a remarkable place to be."

"But..." 43 looked around. "Earlier, I was surrounded by you and everyone else. We were fighting and destroying so much."

"I think you accidentally executed a data transfer," 117 guessed. "Did you mean to do that?"

43 shook her head.

"I didn't," she declared. "I was..."

43 looked down. That's when she realized that everything was different. She was not in her amborg uniform. She was in normal clothes. She wore jeans, sneakers, a light red shirt, and a comfy zip-up sweater. 117 was also wearing similar clothing but his shirt was white, which almost made them match.

"I don't know what I was doing... actually," 43 said as she looked at her hands and down at her feet.

117 kindly invited her in, and she cautiously stepped forward.

"Are you an image of him?" she asked. "Or are you a visual representation of what my mind has created?"

"Yes and no," 117 replied cryptically. "I am him and I'm also not him, either. Not entirely. I am his center."

"His what?"

"Center," 117 repeated. "I'm a caretaker. Well, to be exact, I think I'm the A.I. of his Central Processing Unit. An image that manifested to make sure this place continues to run."

"You don't know what you are?" 43 asked.

"I'm still figuring it out," 117 shrugged again. "Time has little meaning here. I don't fully understand it myself, but Dr. Kendrick really is a genius. His creations have led to me existing. Without knowing it, this world became a reality at the microscopic level and I came online years ago when the David 117 you knew became an amborg. My purpose is to make sure his system doesn't die. If I also had to venture a guess, each amborg has a caretaker like me living inside them. But, that's a theory since we're so small that we're virtually undetectable."

"But how did I get in here? Did I leave my body?" 43 asked nervously. She lifted her hands and turned them over. "This feels so real but I know it's not. I mean, that's if I believe a word of what you've been telling me."

If she was the caretaker of her own CPU or cybernetics, did she accidentally escape from her own physical realm?

"I think you did something incredible and crossed the threshold between our homes," 117 suggested. "You're my first visitor and that's really exciting."

"You don't get out much?"

"No," 117 smiled. "Remember..."

He pointed his finger towards the ceiling.

"The big man himself hasn't actually discovered how to get me out of here," 117 said casually.

43 smirked slightly.

"You're awfully smart for someone supposedly cooped up in cyberspace," she said, taking a step back and looking around.

"We're smarter than we think if you find the time. That goes for everyone in general," 117 replied cheerfully.

Suddenly, the lights flickered eerily. 43 frowned as 117 glanced around curiously.

"Unfortunately, there isn't enough power here to allow the two of us more time to chat," he sighed. "What a shame. 117's system can't support a foreign entity and me simultaneously. I think our time is up."

"What?" 43 looked alarmed. "But I have so many more questions! I was in the hospital and then suddenly, I woke up!"

"Sounds serious," 117 replied.

"Yes it was!" 43 replied. "It was like waking up from a nightmare and I was in this... frenzy and I needed to fight! Do you know what's happening to me?"

"Hmm, well that's an issue," 117 replied as he curled his lip. "I can give you my best guess."

43 watched as 117 reached out and offered his hand. She took it, noticing how soft and warm it was. It felt soothing.

"You're not usually one to start a fight, is that right?" 117 asked. "So, why did this one time serve as the exception?"

"Uh..."

43 blinked and looked away. Why did she start hurting everyone when she woke up? She couldn't remember.

"I don't know," she admitted softly. "It's like... something else..."

She stopped speaking when 117 squeezed her hand tightly. Then she felt his warmth fade as his grip relaxed.

"Well, I hope you figure it out soon."

43 glanced up as 117 backed away a few steps. Has time already run out for them?

"I'd like to listen more but this place can't hold the amount of data for two amborg caretakers," he said apologetically. "I've got to stay here."

"Because I'm a foreign entity?" 43 sighed. "This sucks."

"From what I know about you," 117 surmised, "you're in a lot of pain and you're trying to get rid of it. Sounds like your cybernetics are fighting with your human side. It's almost like your body is battling it out, trying to fix the problem, but tearing itself down at the same time."

"I think I kinda get it," 43 sighed. "I think you just explained to me what they've all been saying already. I'm dying."

"That's too bad," 117 frowned, then gave her a sympathetic smile. "You seem like a really nice person. So young too... to experience that type of feeling."

"Hopefully I can make the most of it before it's over."

"At least you're optimistic," 117 said. "Sorry. I wish there was more I could do for you."

"It's ok," 43 nodded. She turned to look at the entrance she had come in from. "Will you be ok? I mean, all by yourself?"

"Of course," 117 smiled. "I have my purpose here. I can't really leave, but it's not so bad."

"Does 117 know I'm here?" 43 asked, imitating what he had done earlier and pointed up towards the ceiling. "With you?"

"I doubt it," 117 said. "In cyberspace, things happen faster than you can imagine. The rules down here are much more different than the outside dimension. It will only be an instant's notice. They'll all think nothing's happened when you go back to your body."

"So... this entire meeting has taken place in less than a second?" 43 asked.

"I think so," 117 shrugged. "But who knows?"

Suddenly, the lights flickered again and then they both turned sharply when something knocked on the door. 117 moved to protect 43 as they both stepped away.

"Whoa," he said. "That's... not normal?"

"It isn't?" 43 asked.

She thought it was sweet that even in a different realm, he cared about her safety. It was his serious expression as he cautiously stared at the wooden door that convinced her. This was incredibly serious.

"You're the first visitor I've ever had here," he said. "A second one knocking on the door? This is different."

A thought occurred to 43 then.

"Who is it?" she asked.

"I'm here to pick you up."

43 and 117 glanced at each other. She nodded to him and they both reached for the door handle. They pulled it open.

43's eyes widened when she saw a kind woman standing in the doorway. Long brown hair flowed down her shoulders in waves, and she appeared to be surrounded by light. She knew this woman, although it had been several years.

"Oh!" 117 looked taken aback. "This is unexpected."

"Mom?" 43 asked.

The woman standing in the door smiled.

"Hey you two," she said cheerfully and held her hand out to 43. "You ready to get out of here?"

117 and 43 both lowered their defenses and glanced at each other again. Even though this was a shock to both of them, they felt that they could trust the situation.

"Sure," 43 nodded as she slowly took her mother's hand. "But... mom, what are you doing here?"

"I've always been here," she replied gently. "We'll see you soon, 117."

43 was abruptly lifted off the ground, feeling completely weightless. As she drifted away from 117, she noticed that he remained rooted to the spot. Suddenly, the world around her burst into an intense brightness.

"Hey!" she called out to whoever could hear her. "Is this real? Is this actually happening?"

Then 117's voice spoke to her.

"It's as real as you want it to be."

"What the hell just happened?" 917 said with a concerned look.

43 had lifted her hand to 117's face and then lost consciousness. Before anyone could take action, someone spoke.

"Excuse me."

Everyone glanced around to discover that someone unfamiliar had unexpectedly slipped in behind them.

"What the...? Who are you?" 92 asked. "Gah!"

"My eyes!" 93 exclaimed as his hands flew up to his head.

117 glanced up to see who had arrived, and before he could fully comprehend the situation, a bunch of red warnings flooded his display. This looked familiar. The same alerts flashed in the minds of everyone else who made the mistake of looking directly at this person.

"Dr. Kolaski?!" 117 cried as every amborg suffered from the sudden pop-up alerts. "What are you doing here?!"

They were gripped by fear and uncertainty as they faced a barrage of maximum clearance warnings and restrictions.

Dr. Kolaski looked around frantically and immediately took action.

"Computer!" he cried. "Mute alarms! All amborgs present! I would like to address them all!"

As the alerts were silenced and began to disappear from view, Dr. Kolaski rushed to 43's side and crouched down.

"Serina!" he commanded.

In a flash of light, Serina appeared above 43's head. She reached out and a bright orb of light glowed in her small holographic hands.

In the blink of an eye, there was another bright flash of light, but Serina remained in place. 117 looked at her in confusion, then back down to 43.

"What did you do?" he asked.

"What I've always done," Serina answered. "Protected her."

They heard 43 groan. She slowly stirred and opened her eyes groggily. She looked around but couldn't seem to find her bearings.

"Mom?" she mumbled. "Dad?"

"Hey!" 117 smiled as he looked down at her. "She's back!"

"Everything... hurts," 43 gasped.

In the next moment, she passed out. The strain of what had just transpired probably took a huge toll on her.

"She's... not back?" 1 asked.

345 walked over to 117.

"Should we run a scan?" she asked kindly.

"No, I'm fine," 117 shook his head gently. "I'll run my own self-diagnostic."

He glanced to the side and saw Dr. Kolaski at 917's side. After 43 had woken up and passed out again, it seemed like his work was done and he was suddenly talking to another amborg. He was quietly and politely tapping 917's shoulder.

"Hello sir," 917 smiled and dipped his head politely. "I'm surprised to see you again."

"Again?"

117 perked up and stared at them.

"You've met before?" he asked.

917 nodded to everyone.

"He was there with Serina when I was discharged from the hospital," 917 explained. "Right after I got enhanced and became an amborg. Got those maximum clearance warnings in my eyeballs the instant I saw him."

"Your mind... was broken," Dr. Kolaski spoke softly. "I thought Serina... maybe she could... help you."

"And you thought that she could help 43?" 117 asked.

Dr. Kolaski fell silent, but he turned his gaze to 117 and nodded firmly.

"Artificial Intelligence division," 1 stated. "I didn't even know someone like you was even on the staff here."

"I don't... get out..." Dr. Kolaski replied meekly. "...Much."

"Indeed. We should keep it that way."

Everyone turned as Dr. Kendrick approached, flanked by guards and a few medics who were rushing up behind him.

"Hello Robert, my old friend," he said.

"John. I wanted... to help."

Dr. Kolaski turned to 117 and dipped his head respectfully, then began to walk away. He stopped a moment later to look back at 917.

"L-last time..." he stammered. "W-would you like another try?"

"No," 917 politely shook his head. "If your best A.I. programs couldn't find any memories in my cybernetics, then I don't think they will have returned."

"If you change... your mind... Please... I am here for you."

Dr. Kolaski brushed past Dr. Kendrick without a word, heading straight for the exit just as someone else was entering. 117 looked in surprise at the last person he expected to see.

"Grandpa?"

There was no mistaking the sinister looking hoods. Mark glanced at Dr. Kolaski in mild confusion. He made his way over with his escorts to greet Dr. Kendrick.

"Dr. John Kendrick," he smiled. "Surprised to see me?"

"Today's been full of them," Dr. Kendrick raised an eyebrow. "Why are you here?"

"Holy shit," Mark's smile faded as he looked around. "A hurricane come through here or something?"

"Hurricane Serina 43," 92 muttered to 93, which elicited quiet snickering from the two of them.

"Wait," 345 exclaimed excitedly. "Back up. 117, this man is your grandpa? The one who stabbed you? Should we be on alert or something?"

"Paranoid much?" Mark gestured at 345 while looking at Dr. Kendrick.

"It's been a day," 917 replied. "345, it's ok. Stand down."

"Is everyone alright?" Mark asked in concern.

Everyone nodded grimly.

"Let's lift the alert then," Dr. Kendrick nodded. "Chief Malayno?"

Malayno walked up to Dr. Kendrick.

"Instruct the entire facility that it's safe to resume normal operations," he instructed. "Let's get 43 to Dr. Wildman and have 6 handle all injured. Serina?"

Serina floated over to Dr. Kendrick.

"Help Dr. Kolaski with whatever he needs, as always," he said. "But watch 43 when you have a spare moment."

Serina silently nodded. She turned to look at 117.

"Duty calls," she smiled.

In a bright flash of light, she disappeared from sight. Everyone slowly got back on their feet. The warehouse workers gradually went back inside, with all of the construction and maintenance drones in tow. The amborgs who remained began to assess the damage and planned how to begin their repairs.

Dr. Kendrick eyed Mark warily, who flashed him a cheerful grin.

"Well, I never thought I'd say this, but I'm actually glad to see you for once," Dr. Kendrick nodded.

"It means the world to hear you say that."

They shook hands, and although the interaction seemed pleasant, there was an undercurrent of tension. 117 remembered that the link between his grandfather and Dr. Kendrick was himself and his own father, which added a layer of complexity and awkwardness to the situation.

"By the way," Kendrick looked at Mark's group of hooded freelancers. "How did you get in? I thought the defense drones would have annoyed you to death. I'm impressed you even made it past them."

"Ah. About that," Grandpa Mark withdrew his hand and pulled a piece of metal from his pockets. "You might want to fix this guy up. I kind of ripped his main processor out."

"Well that's one way to do it," Dr. Kendrick took the piece with a look of extreme bewilderment. "The poor thing won't be able to talk for a while after I reinstall this."

"Yeah. At least it will be less annoying for now. You can bill me for that later. Anyway, it would appear I was called here for no reason now."

"That isn't true," 117 immediately interrupted. "There is a good reason why I called you here, but then 43 went on a rampage. I was going to ask you what sort of intelligence you have about 43's attacker. Also if possible, it would be beneficial if we could investigate his whereabouts together."

"Oh... I see. Well," Mark said, slightly taken aback. "I guess I could check my files. Perhaps another place to talk would be better."

As everyone headed towards the warehouse entrance to recuperate, 117 couldn't help but shake his head a bit. Something had made him feel dizzy for some reason. 1 walked up and patted his shoulder.

"Is something wrong?" 1 asked as they stepped into the hall. "Are you sure you're ok?"

"No," 117 replied. "At least... I don't think so. I feel different... Like something warm flowed through my body, reminding me of something from a long time ago. But now it's gone. It's like I'm forgetting about something..."

"Strange," 1 performed a quick scan on 117. "I don't detect anything wrong or out of place."

"My self-diagnostic is saying the same thing," 117 nodded. "But more importantly, I think I need to check on Mandy."

Both of them continued on down the hall with the rest of the beaten and worn-out amborgs. Several of them looked as if they would fall apart at any moment. Until they encountered the person who had attacked 43, things would have to go back to the way they were for the time being. It was a long road ahead and they needed to prepare for what was to come.

CHAPTER 15

Cyber Rumble in the Bronx

New York
Harlem Neoteric District
2128 February

"Come on Tashoneh! Give it back!"

"You have to catch me first, Rick!"

Tashoneh raced away from his friends as fast as he could. Despite his youth and small stature, he had become quite adept at navigating the streets quickly. He squeezed through a tiny gap in a chain link fence, well aware that Rick and the other kids were too big to follow. As he clambered away, snickering, he heard the rattling of the fence behind him. Turning around, he saw Rick attempting to scale the fence, while Abigail stood by, her expression filled with worry.

"Come back Tashoneh!" she called. "Don't run so far!"

"I'll get him Abigail," Rick said angrily as he made it to the top of the fence.

"No wait! Don't leave me!"

"It isn't funny anymore Tashoneh!" Rick called as he climbed over and dropped to the ground. Abigail scrambled up the fence as quickly as she could. "Come back here now!"

"Follow me!" Tashoneh cried as he kept running.

Pretty soon, he heard the pattering of footsteps, indicating that Rick and Abigail were close behind. Tashoneh swiftly turned a corner and sprinted toward a warehouse across the street. Suddenly, he heard Rick cry out.

"NO Tashoneh! That place isn't safe!"

"It's fine Rick!" Tashoneh called back. "I've been here hundreds of times!"

Tashoneh glanced over his shoulder at Rick, who was staring back at him, wide-eyed. He ignored the older boy's warnings and dove through a tiny hole in the side of the building, laughing and panting as he crawled inside. When he straightened up, he froze. A group of people were sitting in the middle of the room and turned to face him.

Usually, in places like this, there'd be a scattering of people dressed in dirty, tattered clothing that just wanted to be left alone. These people weren't wearing rags; instead they were wearing pristine, baggy, loose-fitting clothes, and were staring back at him with cold, menacing glares.

Before Tashoneh could gather his thoughts or back out, he felt a shove from behind as Rick scrambled in after him.

"Tashoneh!"

Rick reached Tashoneh's side and froze as well. His eyes widened when he noticed the strangers in the warehouse, and he leaned in close, whispering urgently.

"I told you! Bad people! We have to run! It's dangerous!"

"Y-yeah," Tashoneh stammered as the people began moving towards them. "Let's... oof!"

The two boys backed into Abigail, who had followed them inside.

"What are you two doing?" she asked, but then noticed the crowd moving in. "Uh-oh."

The three of them huddled together, attempting to back away slowly, but the adults were faster. When they spun around to escape, someone dropped in front of them, blocking the way.

"Uh uh uuhh!"

The man raised his index finger and waved it mockingly at the kids. Before they could react, they found themselves completely surrounded. The hole they'd come through was no longer an option as more gang members moved in. They had nowhere to go. Suddenly, the ground began to shake with heavy thuds, and the kids peered around the strangers' legs to see what was coming their way.

The children stood frozen in fear as two colossal robots approached. To their young eyes, these machines were enormous, with red lights glaring down at them menacingly. They had never seen robots like these before.

"What's the matter kids? Lost?" one of the figures laughed. "Come over here! We got... lots of... mmm... nice things for you."

The three kids stood their ground. One of the robots emitted a piercing whine, and its arm radiated a bright light. The clanking of its joints and the whir of circuits echoed ominously as it stomped closer. Terrified, they sank to the floor, the vibrations causing them to bounce as the robot continued to draw nearer.

"Come on boys!" the same man shouted. They watched him take out a knife, and soon after, several others produced a wide variety of weapons of their own. "This robot isn't mean. He just wants to...play! We'll just send your bodies back to your parents. An accident on your play-date."

All three of them clung to each other. They closed their eyes as they pressed their heads together, preparing for the worst. A loud crash startled them, and they opened their eyes to find the adults looking up toward the ceiling with a mix of fear, shock, and anger.

"It's the amborgs!" one of them cried.

The children remained silent, their eyes fixed on the people rushing toward the center of the warehouse. Several figures had dropped from above, sending shards of glass raining down. They stared, wide-eyed, at their rescuers.

"WHOA!" Tashoneh exclaimed as he, Rick, and Abigail clambered to their feet. "It's them!"

Instead of escaping, the kids scurried to the side and hid behind one of the large pillars. The chaos helped keep them hidden as they poked their heads out to witness the action unfolding around them.

"Awesome!" Rick yelled.

"They're so cool!" Abigail cried, momentarily forgetting her fear. "Look at that one over there!"

The next thing they knew, chaos erupted in the warehouse as objects were thrown around, with the sounds of crashing and panicked screams added to the mix. Once the dust settled, the children saw one of the colossal robots swing at those left standing. Six unfamiliar tall figures deftly weaved in and out of the robot's reach, and two of them jumped high, landing on its back. The other four launched a rapid-fire assault on its legs, moving so quickly that the kids barely dared to blink. The second giant robot appeared to be having trouble aiming at the strangers atop its buddy, choosing to avoid any further combat.

Two minutes later, the first bot emitted a deep groan before collapsing to the ground. The amborgs shifted their strategy and focused on the second robot. The children watched as it attempted to lock onto their saviors. The amborgs drew their weapons and charged at the massive behemoth. Gunshots rang out as the six amborgs unleashed a barrage of firepower, causing the kids to instinctively cover their ears.

One of the amborgs zeroed in and fired a series of bullets at the robot's glowing red eyes. Each bullet that struck caused the machine to shake and rattle. The rest of the team targeted its legs and advanced steadily. The second robot found itself unable to retaliate as the amborgs closed in. It swung wildly in an attempt to defend itself, but they were already repeating their routine. Before long, it met the same end as its companion. The amborgs then stepped back as the robot crashed down.

Once the chaos had subsided, the amborgs surrounded the pile of lifeless robots for a brief moment before scanning their surroundings. One of them caught sight of the three children.

"Hey! There are kids in here!"

The children chose to step out from their hiding spot behind the pillar as one of the amborgs approached them.

The kids stared in astonishment. Although none of their lips had moved, a voice that belonged to one of the girls echoed from somewhere else.

"Just like the stories!" Rick whispered. "They really don't talk like us!"

"Why are you in here?"

A tall woman loomed over them, hands firmly placed on her hips. Her bracelet flashed, amplifying her voice, which sounded different from the girl who had first noticed them. The number 999 on her chest glowed in a vibrant neon blue. The three kids were mesmerized, momentarily forgetting her question.

"Excuse me," she spoke sternly. "I asked you kids a question."

"We were just playing," Tashoneh replied in a soft voice. "We came in here by accident."

"Next time," 999 glared down at them, "be more careful. When you're not at home or with your parents, it can be dangerous out here. It's best to avoid running into places you shouldn't be."

"We will," Rick said. "You really are like the stories our parents taught about us."

"Strong and fast," Tashoneh added.

"Taller than normal people," Abigail added admiringly.

999 shook her head, clearly unimpressed. Compliments did nothing to change her expression.

"Thanks for the observation," 999 responded curtly. "We are tall, strong and fast."

"Pretty and badass too," Abigail added rather enthusiastically.

"No cursing or swearing until you are older," 999 snapped. "Flattery will not work on me."

"Are you an angel?" Rick asked rather suddenly.

999 paused, looking taken aback. She said nothing for a moment, but then knelt down to meet the kids at their level. She tilted her head and gazed at Rick with a questioning stare.

"No I'm not," she answered a little gentler, and slightly confused. "But... What made you ask such a thing?"

"You're beautiful," Rick said. "My mom said that angels look just like us when they want to, but you can almost tell they're not human because they look special. They talk differently but almost like the way we do. They live among us all the time and when we're in trouble, they'll come down or reveal themselves to save us before it's too late."

999 sighed and then stood back up.

"To be accurate," she said, pointing towards the hole they came in from. "I'm not really what you would think of at first glance. Now go home already and get to safety. Don't run off. You go straight back home. I have to get back to work as a... you-know-what."

The three kids said a quick goodbye before taking off. As they slipped through the hole one by one, Abigail turned back to the amborg and waved enthusiastically.

"What's your name?"

999 dipped her head politely.

"Alice."

"Thank you! Number 999! Bye Alice!"

999 gave the little girl a wave as she watched them disappear. When they were gone, she straightened up. Footsteps drew near a moment later, and she turned to see 917 approaching her.

"They called you an angel," 917 said. "Interesting choice to describe people like us. Ever thought of yourself as a celestial being every now and then?"

"Very amusing 917," 999 snapped. "Being compared to a being of such great power is ridiculous."

"So why did you admit to being one to the kids?" 917 asked.

"We may not be celestial," 999 replied, "but are you really going to tell a child that something they believe in doesn't exist? I was merely playing along."

"Maybe," 917 smirked. "But there is one thing you can't deny. It must feel great giving children like those three hope. Especially in these times. Your character may not be full of empathy all the time, but you aren't completely a cold lone wolf."

"I am not 100% human when it comes to my abilities," 999 said.

"We have many things that normal humans don't have," 917 pondered. "But remember what 117 said? We are still human. Just at a very advanced level."

"I wonder though..." 999 watched the kids running away, "if we can even go back to our basic humanity, especially when children call us angels."

"Is that why you were taken aback? You speak as if both humans and amborgs are bad things."

917 gazed at the hole where the kids disappeared through.

"Remember we are not completely the same," he said. "But we have a base to look back to. Something we can fall back on in the events we don't know who we are. We have evolved but there is nothing that says we can't revert back to our human ways."

"Nicely spoken."

Meilin delivered a compliment to 917 as she clapped her hands.

"I agree, it was very well said, 917," Aaron's voice rang out through both of their heads. "It isn't easy 999, but deep down, you're the same as me. Physically, you're different but on the inside, we share some of the same traits that make us human. Mandy says that everyone still retains their humanity even when all else fails."

"I have the feeling you two have been channeling 117's spirit," 999 grumbled, rolling her eyes. "We are not the same, Aaron."

"Well," 917 shrugged. "I do have a one-seven in my number. Maybe that might be one part of it."

"That's not right," Meilin laughed. "If you're an amborg that has a seven at the end of your number, you're one of the lucky amborgs. It's interesting how most of the Second Group amborgs have the number seven."

"Every surviving amborg is lucky," 917 replied with a grin.

999 looked down at the ground and back at 917, who smiled pleasantly.

"You know, Angel is a good nickname for you. It really is a pretty name."

999 wanted to deny this. Getting a nickname felt stupid to her for some reason. Instead, she brought her fist down to the side of her thigh and bit her lip. Without another word, the two of them rejoined the other three amborgs in their team. 999 waved at their apprentice amborg, 345, who smiled back at her.

"Alice Angel 999," she shrugged. "It sounds really contradicting to my character."

"No," 917 said. "Try saying it without your number. Alice Angel sounds better. Besides, you do closely resemble an angel. Just like that boy was saying."

"I do not," 999 replied stiffly. "If I was, then things would be different."

"What sort of things?"

999 turned her head away. She refused to answer the question.

"Why don't you dress as an angel for Halloween?" 917 smirked, trying to re-engage the conversation. "See how that goes."

"I would rather be a dark one," she glared at him with a piercing side-eye. "Thanks for giving me reason to hate you for the rest of the day."

"Nice to know that I'm tolerated," 917 laughed.

917 walked over to the wreckage and joined their two team leaders. Kiden 18 of the First Group was in charge of the team at this current site.

Several feet away, 19 and 777 were doing a perimeter sweep. 345 took a moment to speak to 999.

"You like 917?"

999 looked at her apprentice sharply and hardened her expression.

"Excuse me?" she replied.

"You only smile whenever you talk to him," 345 pointed out gently. "It kind of seems like you have a soft spot for kids and for him."

"I wasn't smiling Amara," 999 replied in a soft tone. "It's complicated."

"I don't see how," 345 glanced over at 917 and 18 who were in a deep conversation. "He's really fun and nice."

"You sound like you're the one with an attraction," 999 mumbled.

"Maybe," 345 giggled. "When I first met both of you, I thought he had a really cool voice and he looks handsome!"

"Alright," 999 sighed. "Enough. Check for any traps or other signs of danger."

"You got it!" 345 winked.

As she ran off, 999 walked over to 917.

"Silly girl," she replied. "We all use our bracelets to talk. It's the same robotic voice that speaks for us."

"To be fair," Aaron replied in the back of 999's head, "she does have a point. 917's voice does sound distinct and pretty cool."

"I'd like to go back to it being quiet again," 999 stated.

"Alright," Aaron sighed, "but just so you know Alice, I've always told you that it's always ok for a lone wolf to accept some compliments."

"I would rather chew on steel," 999 replied stubbornly. "Besides, as much as I like the nickname, it doesn't change what kind of person I am."

"Well, it's great that you like it!" Aaron said happily.

"Do not tell anyone," 999 snapped.

"Right," he awkwardly let his enthusiasm die down. "Just remember, I'm here for you when you're ready to open up. I think it'd be nice to know more about what kind of person you are."

"Don't hold your breath," 999 shook her head.

As she finished the private conversation with her technician, she stood by 917. 18 smiled as she approached.

"Hello 999," she dipped her head politely. "Were those kids hurt?"

999 shook her head.

"Good," 18 nodded, her smile widening at the pleasant news. "I think we can deem this sector clear."

"I'll contact the other teams," 19 replied. "777, would you mind watching my back while I report this?"

777 nodded and took up a defensive position next to 19 as she privately called Dr. Kendrick.

"18," 917 spoke quietly. "There is one thing I've wanted to know."

"What is it?" 18 asked.

"I don't wish to sound insensitive but... when 43 fought us in the warehouse three weeks ago, there was something that seemed to bother 19."

"Right," 18 nodded when she realized what he was talking about. "The whip? I saw the footage."

"19 seemed... angry," 999 added.

"Well, if you knew the history about that particular weapon, you'd understand," 18 placed a hand on her chest. "19's family is from southern New Lousiana. Her ancestors can be traced all the way back to Sudan. I myself have ancestors that go all the way back to Somalia."

18 gestured to 19 who was focusing on her transmission. 917 and 999 both paid close attention.

"Electric whips, like the one that 19 destroyed during the fight against 43, represent a dark period in global history," 18 explained. "They were initially created to control and combat rogue robots or drones that strayed from their original programming. However, when used against ordinary humans, they can be extremely dangerous and excruciatingly painful. The Geneva Accords banned electric whips after it was discovered that they were being used to inflict serious harm on countless people. Whipping has long been recognized as a cruel and inhumane practice throughout history. The act of using one makes one look like... well, you get the idea."

"A slaver," 917 looked down, sadness in his eyes. "I apologize for asking."

"You were naturally curious," 18 smiled reassuringly. "Don't apologize for that. You needed the context to understand how bad it was. As long as you recognize that, I'm very relieved that you took the time to ask me about it."

18 nodded again at 19.

"Being black," she said, "19 didn't want to use an electric whip against another amborg. From what I saw, I was actually quite happy to see that 43 allowed her a small respite to destroy it."

917 and 999 shared a knowing look and nodded in silent agreement. They were glad to have gained insight into the severity of the situation when 19 had her hands on one of those discontinued electric whips. Her decision to destroy it stemmed from the knowledge that racism has been a terrible and tragic part of their history, and it continues to exist in some broken parts of society today.

The best thing they could do was to continue believing in change. 917 decided to get things back on track in order to continue their mission.

"This is team six," he transmitted. "117? Can you read me?"

"Confirmed 917, have you cleared the objective?" 117 responded immediately.

"Affirmative," 917 looked around the area. 999 gave a thumbs up and he nodded in confirmation.

"Area is clear, but there are no signs of what we were looking for. 18 was right about the fact that some criminals smuggled the big robots in here. Every clue we uncover about this guy shows that he's always one step ahead of us. He is a very formidable opponent."

"117," 18 added herself to the conversation. "Most of the human criminals we've interrogated have been useless. No one knows where these behemoths are being manufactured and the computers we're salvaging have no detailed information."

"It's like they get wiped when we finish taking one down," 917 ventured. "Perhaps we should alert the National Guard? There could be several more of these bad bots hidden all over the city. It'd probably be safer for the civilians in the city."

"That is a good idea," 117 replied. "18? I wanted to thank you for all of your intel. Without it, we probably would have never thought to begin searching here."

"You're welcome," 18 smiled.

Most of the First Group amborgs had a network of allies and contacts all across the world. An informant had relayed details about a situation unfolding in New York, leading to the deployment of a few teams. Consequently, this operation confirmed the reliability of the intelligence that 18 received from her source.

"Hey 117," 917 said. "Aside from the good intel, we need to come up with a new plan. These robots were originally our clues to finding this man. But we should not spend all of our time responding to these things every time they make an appearance. The more we do that, the more we risk innocent lives to these murder bots. Those kids we encountered would have been killed if we hadn't gotten here in time."

"Unfortunately, that's all we can do for the moment," 117 replied. "But you're right. To stop the threat, we need to go straight to the source. We will brainstorm new plans as soon as possible. I'm going south with my team once we finish clearing this building. Could you join me here and rendezvous at the following coordinates?"

"Coordinates received. We can do that."

No sooner than 917 had spoken, a nearby wall of the warehouse blew outward. 345, who was on patrol near that wall, quickly jumped back. She hurried toward her team as they all sprang into action. Emerging from the breach, another pair of colossal robots stomped in.

"Umm 117?" 917 looked up at the two behemoths and could have sworn he heard them growling. "There will be a small delay. We have more giant bots."

"How long?" 117 asked curiously.

917 watched as 999 and 18 drew their weapons and began to open fire. 777 remained where he was, protecting 19 from any attack while she cut her call short and prepared for battle.

"Dr. Kendrick is issuing an alert to the National Guard," she informed 917 quickly as she and 777 rushed after 999 and 18.

"117? Give us about two minutes and thirty four seconds," 917 calculated as he readied his rifle. "345? Let's go! Attack pattern alpha!"

----

117 stood out in the street, listening to the end of the transmission.

"No rush is necessary, 917," 117 replied.

He turned around to go back inside the building that his team had gone into. However, he'd barely walked two steps when a deafening explosion erupted behind him.

The door of a small storage building blew outward, and a jeep sped out, swerving wildly before barreling straight toward 117. Just behind it, two massive robots emerged, marching in the opposite direction. The keep collided with 117, and in an instant, he found himself clinging to the hood. He'd only taken minimal damage, barely feeling the impact. While gripping the hood as tightly as possible, he stared at the driver, a completely neutral expression on his face.

"I have found a distraction," 117 muttered.

117 climbed onto the hood and placed his hands firmly against the windshield. The unexpected action startled the driver, causing him to speed up in panic, which sent 117 lurching forward. Clenching his fist, he smashed his hand through the glass, shattering it. He then reached through the broken windshield and seized the driver by the collar. With surprising ease, 117 yanked the driver toward him, then forcefully shoved him back into his seat. The driver's head collided with the headrest, knocking him unconscious from the force of the impact.

117 clung tightly as the car started to swerve. The driver's foot remained firmly on the accelerator, sending the jeep hurtling down the street. Gaining a foothold, 117 climbed onto the hood and jumped, propelling himself into the air as the vehicle sped beneath him. He flipped and landed gracefully on the rough pavement. A tremendous crash rang out, and he turned to see the jeep collide with a brick wall. Seconds later, a massive section of the wall crumbled, flattening the vehicle.

117 dusted himself off and pressed forward. The district was filled with a cacophony of booms that echoed through the streets. He recognized the noise and its patterns immediately. More of those robots had been set loose, and were now stomping around freely. He had gotten separated from his team, and it was a bad position to be in if a battle had suddenly erupted in New York.

"That went well," Mandy spoke through his head. "You ok David?"

117 reached up and tapped his head. There was little damage to his vitals and he seemed to be alright.

"Of course Mandy. I am in perfect condition."

"Nobody is perfect David," Mandy chuckled. "Not even an amborg."

"Is this another scenario where my argument is invalid no matter how much evidence I put...on the table?"

"Yes David," she sighed. "I'm always right and you're just too stubborn to admit it."

"To be fair," 117 replied, "it is not stubbornness. I choose not to continue arguing because you would dislike the amount of information I prepare for my arguments."

"Mmhmm sure," Mandy chuckled. "Do you want to know where your next objective is or not?"

"Yes Mandy," 117 smiled. "Where exactly did I end up?"

"That jeep carried you pretty far from your team," Mandy replied. "If you want, you can proceed to a big robot sighting here or rendezvous with 297, 57, and the twins."

"It's best to fight the behemoths in teams," 117 stated. "Help me find 501 and 466."

"Roger," Mandy replied. "Let's find a nice spot for you to reunite with them."

A piercing scream broke through the air, immediately snagging 117's attention. He saw a few civilians suddenly running for their lives, with a group of gang members hot on their heels.

"On second thought," 117 replied, "I think 501 and 466 should rendezvous with the others. Secondary objective acquired."

"You know," Mandy said, "you could try spending more time with 501 and 466. Especially since they're both your apprentices now?"

"I will try to do better," 117 sighed.

Five blocks away, 6 had just finished taking care of some injured civilians. When the police and paramedics arrived, she directed them to safety and moved on to the next position. Moving around solo was easier and quicker for her, which was why she was given exclusive permission to operate without an escort or her team.

Before she could proceed to another cry for help, a high-priority distress beacon popped up. She recognized who it belonged to and sighed.

"Again?" she asked.

6 changed direction and rushed towards the beacon. She found herself looking down at 501, who was sprawled across the pavement. A quick scan revealed that a bullet had hit him in the head. 57 was kneeling down next to him while the twins and 297 were making chuckling motions.

6 walked up casually.

"What hit you this time?" she asked.

501 slowly sat up and massaged his head. A metal fragment from a bullet clattered to the ground.

"A bullet?" 501 replied meekly.

"Again," 297 sighed.

"And did the shooter get away?" 6 raised an eyebrow.

"Nope," 297 replied casually. "I returned fire, wounded them, and 466 is capturing them right now."

"Seriously Donut," 6 said sympathetically.

"Can you please attempt a single mission without taking damage from a bullet straight to your skull? I'm about ready to have the others keep an eye on you wherever you go from here on out."

"Hmm, that is a difficult query to answer 6," 92 interrupted. "At this rate, when you include factors from previous assignments and missions while also taking into consideration his desperation for charging into open combat, and his need for portraying his masculinity to 466, I calculate that he is incapable of simple requests of that small magnitude."

"And that's just a basic analysis," 93 grinned.

The twins looked at each other and broke into fits of silent laughter. 57 found it hard to stay angry as she fought to suppress a smile. 501 took hold of 297's hand and pulled himself upright. As he regained his footing, they all heard a shuffling noise and turned to see 466 dragging an injured man behind her. He was covered in tattoos and wore a sleeveless shirt and torn jeans.

"Ah," 297 nodded. "Here's our shooter."

"You guys suck," 501 frowned sheepishly.

"Are they making fun of you again?" 466 asked.

501 silently nodded. 466 rolled her eyes and glared at the Second Group amborgs. The shooter that she had apprehended was shoved over to 6. She was ready to receive the patient and inspected the damage.

After shooting 501 in the head, 297 had retaliated and successfully shot him in the left shoulder. 6 went to work right away treating the wound and preparing him to be picked up by the police.

501 looked a little down as 466 gave him a comforting pat on the shoulder. Ever since his first accident with the sniper from the Chicago deployment, it had started a trend which didn't seem to want to end. No matter how hard he tried.

"In your defense," 57 smiled, "you have been getting more confident 501. This is your second official mission and it's significantly better than the... first."

"That is correct," 6 said as she injected a painkiller into the shooter's shoulder. He let out a cry of pain, which she ignored. "Despite your problems with enemy sniper fire, 501 is also beginning to learn how to take on multiple opponents more efficiently."

"Speaking of multiple opponents."

57 walked over to the man that 6 was treating and got in his face.

"You got any friends out there?"

"Hey baby," the man sneered at 57. "You let me go, I'll show you a good time with my friends."

"Sure," 57 didn't falter and smiled confidently. "We'll let you go. But you see 297 back there?"

297 nodded and brandished his rifle.

"He shot you," 57 stated. "It's kinda what we do when you headshot one of my little brothers. Attacking an amborg is a criminal offense. Due to the fact that we're in the middle of battle, the fog of war is... extremely foggy right now. So we could let you go, but there's nothing that I can do to stop 297 from... say... shooting you repeatedly in the legs and feet. That's not the worst part. How about we make you crawl home till you bleed out?"

The man's expression wavered, and he instantly shut up.

"Now," 57's gaze grew dark and sinister. "Do you have any other friends out there?"

The man gulped as he gazed at 6 and the other amborgs, but they all shared the same cold and bitter expressions.

"Jesus, you're all insane," he gulped. "I got one buddy out there."

"Why don't I believe you?" 57 smiled. "Oh wait, I have a built-in lie detector. That's why. How many of you are out there trying to target us?"

"There were a whole bunch of us!" the man relented.

"Specific numbers or 297 shoots you!"

"Look lady, I don't know!"

6 suddenly thrust a syringe into the man's neck and he arched his head upwards in pain. His eyes widened, then rolled into the back of his head as he collapsed, unconscious.

"I believe you," 57 said curtly.

"57?" 501 asked nervously.

"Yes?"

"We have an accurate scan of the area and know how many gang members there are," 501 said. "Why did you interrogate him that way?"

"He shot you," 57 replied. "I wanted to make him regret doing that."

"Thanks," 501 smiled in relief.

"If I may," 466 spoke up. "I think it's really nice that all of you look out for us so often."

"Well of course!" 6 smiled. "We're a family. We're supposed to protect each other."

297 patted 501 on the shoulder respectfully.

"Well we can proceed safely now since Donut is ok," he said pleasantly. "We should move now."

"So let us continue on to the objective," 466 pointed down the sidewalk. "We have heavy enemy signals directly ahead. We need to stop them from wreaking havoc."

Everyone nodded in agreement, but 501 eagerly raised his hand and rushed forward.

"Sure! I will go first!" he said confidently.

Ignoring the shocked protests of the team, he ran ahead. Seconds later, a shot rang out and he fell to the ground again. 466 gaped as everyone else readied their weapons and moved to go check on 501. 297 calculated the trajectory of where the bullet came from and switched weapons. He switched to a sniper rifle and quickly took aim.

"I got it," he informed them.

He pulled the trigger, and a loud bang rang out. The sound lingered in the stillness, creating an eerie silence as the shot echoed in the air.

"Target down," he reported.

57 and 466 looked at 6, who shook her head.

"Hey, I'm pretty sure he's fine," she said. "I'm not wasting any of my medical supplies on someone who can easily survive a shot in the head."

"I thought you took the hippocratic oath," 92 said.

"Isn't this a violation of being a compassionate doctor?" 93 asked.

"501 isn't a patient," 6 declared. "He's just been shot."

"But you're supposed to treat people with care and empathy, regardless of the circumstances."

6 sighed.

"Why am I getting lectured about this from you two identical morons?" she muttered.

57 and 6 both checked on 501 while 297 maintained an eye on the perimeter. The twins went to go pick up the unconscious gang member they'd restrained earlier. They had to drop him off with a police officer asap.

"This is turning out to be quite a day," 466 sighed.

"How many of the giant robots have we fought?"

999 held up her hand and extended her fingers.

"Has it really been more than five?" 917 groaned.

"Since we got split up from our team, yes," 999 nodded.

Meilin spoke up in their group chat.

"I lost track after six, 917. Watching you take all of them down is making me tired. Physically and mentally."

"I'm so glad you two are there and we're safely back here in our cubicles," Aaron chuckled.

"Glad you're enjoying the show," 917 sighed.

917 and 999 were sitting on a couch in a living room of an apartment complex. They had been cut off from their team and felt like they had just wrestled against a swarm of elephants. One of the giant robots they fought was crackling and sizzling at their feet. Its head had been pulled from its neck socket and smashed. Both of them were covered in plaster and dust as they sat quietly and rested. They watched the view from the large hole in the wall that they had been thrown through.

"You look good with dusty hair," 917 said in an attempt to lighten the mood.

He instantly shut up at the look 999 shot him.

"Well, there is one thing we should clarify."

917 turned to look over his shoulder and lit his bracelet up so he could speak publicly.

"We are terribly sorry about the damage and we would like to advise that medical teams will be dispatched to ensure no one is injured," he explained. "Please forgive us for crashing through your wall and interrupting your dinner."

The family that he spoke to were all cowering up against the wall behind an overturned dinner table. The father was shaking in fear, but he silently nodded to acknowledge 917. The children, instead of fear, were staring at the amborgs with looks of intense curiosity. They were far too young to understand what had just happened.

"I'm also filling out the accident incident forms," Meilin reminded him. "Remember to inform the family."

"Right," 917 nodded. They couldn't hear Meilin so he had to finish disclosing the information. He looked at the family again. "We also promise that there will be no more additional surprises. All damage expenses will be taken care of."

"It's fortunate that Dr. Kendrick has plenty of money to spare," 999 muttered.

"You think if we ask," 917 pondered, "maybe he would build Iron Man suits for all of us?"

"If I move up in the company," Aaron sighed dreamily, "I want to be like him. Batman rich."

"Uh," Meilin chuckled, "I hate to break it to you but... Iron Man has more money than Batman."

"What? No way..."

"Mmhmm," Meilin replied. "Tony Stark has more involvement in the business industry and his tech empire is significantly bigger than Bruce Wayne's interests. Dr. Kendrick is Iron Man rich. Way more money than Batman."

"Careful Meilin," 917 grinned. "To a lot of fans, those are fighting words right there."

"Enough," 999 grumbled. "The real question we should be asking is, why hasn't Dr. Kendrick already become Iron Man or Batman? He has the wealth for it..."

Everyone paused. Meilin and Aaron stopped talking while 917 turned and stared at 999.

"You were about to go on a tangent," 999 shook her head. "I settled it."

"Look at you!" 917 chuckled in amazement. "Angel is participating in this conversation with her first nerd joke!"

Their conversation was abruptly cut short when the head of the behemoth flickered to life. Lacking a body, it could only shout at them, straining to produce sound, which made the wife of the family shriek in terror. 917 and 999 exchanged casual glances, but shrugged it off.

"Must... kill... amborgs," the head of the machine sputtered as its voice died out.

917 and 999 groaned in exasperation. They shared a look, nodded, and stomped on the robot's head, instantly crushing it. It emitted a warbling noise that gradually faded. They sat back comfortably on the couch and addressed the family again.

"We promise," 917 said reassuringly and as confidently as he could. "No more surprises."

"I told you," 999 snapped. "Crush the head. But you wanted to bring it home as a souvenir."

917 nodded.

"Ok I was wrong alright? But you got to admit... when thoroughly deactivated, it'd look pretty good in a display case or something."

No sooner had 917 finished talking than a sudden crash erupted from outside, and 117 flew into the living room through the gaping hole in the wall, landing right next to the sofa with a thud. 917 and 999 just looked at him calmly, like this was just an everyday occurrence for them. In the dining room, the family hid behind the table, their eyes peeking out as yet another unexpected guest arrived at their home. 917 and 999 looked back to the hole in the wall.

They leaned forward, looking down at the street beneath them from the second floor of the apartment building, and right outside the gaping hole was another murder bot, staring back at them with its gleaming red eyes. It was emitting a low growling noise that sounded suspiciously like a snarl.

"Kill the amborgs!" it bellowed in a deep, chilling robotic voice. A sudden, loud whirring noise followed, signaling that it was charging its weapons.

Without saying a word, 117 got up. He turned to look at 917 and 999 and then at the crushed robot head at their feet. Understanding what they had been through, he nodded and then charged out the hole. A loud crash indicated that he had successfully tackled the robot outside, preventing it from firing its weapons at the apartment. 999 glanced at the family a third time.

"Sorry for the inconvenience," she stated.

999 stood up and dove out the hole in the wall. 917 got up and bowed politely to the family.

"I kept saying no more surprises," he chuckled nervously. "I believe I will have... how you say... jinxed the situation. Someone from A.I. Industries will be reaching out to you within one business day. We will leave immediately. Sorry for taking up your time and space."

917 ran and dove out the hole, following 999.

The family of the wrecked apartment stared at the damage, not daring to move. The kids remained surrounded in the protective care of their parents' arms.Suddenly, the wife pulled on her husband's sleeve and whispered quietly.

"Remember when you always talked about moving? And I was so against it?" she breathed as the amborgs had effectively vacated their home. "I changed my mind, let's go somewhere else. We have relatives in Spain. Let's go there! At least there's no danger there, and the amborgs don't normally visit that region."

"T-there could be crime over there too honey," the husband stuttered. "It could also be just as bad as it is here."

"I know sweetheart..." she said, clinging onto his arm. "I just don't know if I can take this anymore, with big metal robots crashing through our apartment!"

"Technically, that was the amborgs."

"The amborgs!" she continued to vent. "Seven to eight foot tall teenagers covered in plaster and dust sitting comfortably on our furniture! We live next to streets filled with bullets, cars, dumpsters, and gangsters and then three amborgs end up in our apartment!"

"At least we're not paying for the damages," her husband smiled gently.

"We need to move," she replied with a serious expression.

"Well..." he replied, "at least we didn't die... but let's look into getting out of here."

Their children, ignoring the tension, were having the times of their lives. Although they had stayed silent, now they were causing a tiny uproar, to which their parents didn't even bother to address.

"WOW!" They cheered. "MOMMY! DADDY! AMBORGS! CAN WE BE LIKE THEM!?"

Outside, 117, 917 and 999 effortlessly defeated the last behemoth robot. Once it was down, they relaxed and took a breather. 917 glanced up at the hole of the apartment they were in just minutes ago.

"At least the kids are in high spirits," he chuckled.

"Sometimes," Meilin sighed, "when kids look up to you, they get inspired. It helps them forget about how cruel the world is."

The three of them huddled together.

"So, how did you end up taking on one of these behemoth robots by yourself?" 917 asked.

"I tried helping some civilians, then I went after some gang members that were trying to escape," 117 explained. "Then things got out of control when I got attacked by this robot."

117 pointed at the destroyed robot that rested at their feet.

"You took it out alone," 999 crossed her arms and scanned the perimeter. "Well done."

"Was that a compliment?" 117 asked 917 with wide eyes.

"Wait til our technicians tell you about what she just said earlier," 917 smiled.

The three of them showed signs of fatigue, even though they weren't actually tired at all. As a matter of fact, their energy levels were peaking at around 70%. As the sun set in the distance, many street lights began to flicker on. They had been out a full day.

"Well here is a positive speculation," 917 spoke as he stared at the orange light disappearing behind a building. "At least we gained more experience, and we're defeating them in record time. But do you all feel sore in the knees?"

117 nodded. His joints were aching and definitely felt like they had been working nonstop. The training they had been doing the last month had helped, but this was pushing their limits.

The three of of them watched as the sun disappeared on the horizon behind the buildings. That was when 917 spoke again.

"Hey, 117," he said. "What's the plan?"

117 turned to his friends, who looked back at him with concern.

"18 was right about the large robots being mobilized in this area, but this has gone on for practically the whole day..." he said. "Parts of New York have been targeted since our arrival. Whoever built these big robots spent months, maybe years on them. Are we really going to have to fight these things every day now? They just keep showing up. What happens if more of us join 43 in the hospital?"

"He's right," 999 said.

"Dr. Kendrick introduced the Second and Third Group within the span of a few months," 917 stated. "Seems a little suspicious. It's like he knew something big and terrible was coming our way."

917 did have a point. The First Group amborgs were in service and active for years. The Second Group made headlines with their debut and showed the world that more cyborgs were going to join the ranks of A.I. Industries. The sudden arrival of the Third Group, a newer generation of amborgs, seemed very convenient in response to all of the things they had been through in the last few months.

"I think my grandfather had something to do with that," 117 replied. "Ever since the day I first met him."

"It's still crazy that Dr. Kendrick approved of that," 917 exhaled.

"Allegedly," 999 added.

"Look," 917 sighed, "I'm not trying to put a damper on the mood. Like this big hunk of metal."

917 rapped his knuckles on the dead parts of the behemoth. A short sequence of metallic noises echoed back.

"But, you've been working nonstop for three weeks," 917 said. "If I didn't know better, it feels like you're grasping in the dark for leads. Can you take a few seconds to elaborate how we're going to catch the guy who hurt 43?"

"With this."

117 pulled a data chip the size of his hand out of his pocket.

"We're all doing the best we can under the circumstances," 117 replied. "But, I am confident we can get through this. This data chip was extracted from another robot that we took down earlier. It's encrypted but I think we can find something on here."

"Oh," 917 paused and glanced down at the robot that he was leaning against. "So we smashed this one to pieces. Does that mean we can't get the data chip?"

"Mandy is sending the schematics to your technicians," 117 smiled. "I pulled this out from the memory banks in the head."

917 glanced at 999.

"And you wouldn't let me keep the head as a souvenir," he laughed.

999 refused to comment as she looked away angrily. At that moment, Mandy decided to chime into the conversation.

"David," she said, "I hate to sound like a normal human here but uh... is it safe to bring that data chip back home? What if there's a computer virus or other hostile malware on that?"

"I was going to work with the A.I. programs back home to decrypt it and fight against any attacks to our system," he replied. "If I am bringing a trojan virus back to A.I. Industries, we'll fight it before it harms us."

"Cool," 917 smiled. "We get to do some proper computer analysis. It certainly is a nice change from punching giant murder bots."

117 checked all the data the amborg teams had compiled. Several of them had reported that they had successfully extracted data chips from a few of the behemoths. It wasn't a lot but it was a start at least.

"Hopefully," 117 nodded, "we can find enough information to figure out where these robots are coming from. Perhaps we can learn more about the mastermind behind all of this."

CHAPTER 16

Meeting Friends

A.I. Industries
Gymnasium
2135

"Amborg Johnny 5... You are late for your appointment in the medical bay! Do I need to send security to come hunt you down and escort you?"

The voice over the intercom cut through their conversation like a dagger as 5 sighed and stood up. He looked at his mud-stained clothes and nodded towards the P.A. speaker. Brad stared at the First Group amborg curiously.

"Oops," 5 winked at Brad. "I've been caught."

He put a hand up to his head, mimicking the motion of answering a cell phone.

"Hey 6," he replied cheerfully. "I was just entertaining a visitor."

Brad recognized the same voice speaking again, except this time, it wasn't coming from the gym's overhead speaker; it was emanating from 5's bracelet, broadcasting publicly for everyone to hear.

"Don't think that you can get out of this! I have a very strict schedule!" 6's voice spoke angrily. "I have to do a routine inspection of your leg! And when you get here, you are not getting out of your semi-annual physical! Move it!"

The call ended as 5 turned to awkwardly shrug at the others.

"Ok ok. I got it," he sighed. Chuckling, he turned to bid a quick farewell to Dr. Kendrick, Brad, and 117. "Excuse me everyone. I have a prior engagement."

He glanced at 117, and the two amborgs exchanged polite nods. 5 bowed his head respectfully to Dr. Kendrick. Then, he turned to the young student and smiled.

"Pleasure to have met you Brad. Please enjoy the rest of the story."

He strolled away and exited the gym. Once he was gone, Dr. Kendrick suggested a break before getting back to the story.

"You know," he smiled at 117 and Brad, "we've been talking for a few hours since you've arrived. Want to get some lunch?"

"I could eat!" Brad nodded eagerly. "Everytime you brought up 3's cooking, it actually made me want to get food."

"Then let's go to the cafeteria," 117 stood up and motioned to the door.

The three of them left the gym using a different exit. As they walked past the columns and the training mats that hadn't been put away, Brad was actually able to notice the signs of wear and tear. He could see dents, marks, and all manner of damage across the floor as well. For years, the amborgs utilized this place for training and various exercises to hone their skills. It was difficult to unsee how much of their history had taken place in the vast gymnasium.

As they passed through the corridors, following the signs and making their way to the cafeteria, 117 noticed Brad reviewing all of the notes that he had taken down so far. Then, in the middle of his excitement, a thought crossed Brad's mind and he spoke to Dr. Kendrick.

"I have a question, Doctor," he said as they rounded a corner.

"Hmm?"

As Dr. Kendrick turned his head, Brad noticed a cigarette in his mouth. He pulled out a lighter and flicked it on. Just as Brad was about to voice his surprise, a nozzle protruded from the wall. The moment Dr. Kendrick lit the cigarette, a strong gust of air burst from the nozzle, extinguishing it instantly. The three of them awkwardly looked up. An A.I. passing by shook their head disapprovingly at Dr. Kendrick before zooming off. With a sigh, he removed the cigarette from his mouth, placed it in a case, and tucked it into his coat pocket.

"Drat!" he snapped his fingers but at the same time, he couldn't help but chuckle a little. "I can't seem to smoke anywhere anymore. If it isn't the amborgs telling me it's bad for my health, it's the A.I.'s hacking into the fire suppression systems just to extinguish my flames. Ha."

"I didn't know you smoked," Brad remarked.

"Well, at A.I. Industries, I don't really get an opportunity," Dr. Kendrick winked. "I bought this pack four months ago, the last time I went out on a business meeting."

"You haven't left A.I. Industries in four months?" Brad asked.

"It's what happens when your home and your company are in the same location," Dr. Kendrick explained. "Not really a lot of incentive to leave when all the exciting stuff happens here."

"I don't know if I could stay inside for four months..." Brad muttered.

"He's actually being deceptive," 117 said with a grin. "Dr. Kendrick is messing with you. I happen to know that he paid a visit to the children's hospital, two schools, and met with a couple of visiting dignitaries in the last three weeks."

"Yeah, I couldn't resist," Dr. Kendrick smiled guiltily.

"It's pretty neat how so many people look up to you," Brad smiled. "I think the A.I.s here that monitor and protect your health are pretty impressive."

"That they do," Dr. Kendrick nodded in agreement. "What was your question?"

"If we currently live in an era of peace," Brad started, choosing his words carefully, "why is it that you still look for potential children to be amborgs? Is it still necessary in these times?"

"Very necessary," Dr. Kendrick nodded. "Peace in this time is mostly assured but for some other individuals, they need help, even if conditions are better than before. I keep finding lucky souls and take them in to become next generation amborgs. But, as things become more stable, a lot of people have asked the same thing. Many wonder if the amborgs are necessary. The end of the story will probably surprise you. Perhaps it might be better to find someone else to assist in the depiction."

"Perhaps we can find Mandy?" Brad asked. "It feels like she and 117 are the ones who had the most involvement."

"Someone say my name?"

The three of them turned and saw a woman approaching from an intersecting corridor. It was the name tag that Brad saw on her jacket pocket that gave away her identity. It was Mandy, the same person that 117 and Dr. Kendrick had told him about. By now, she had likely been 117's technician for several years. Brad noted that she matched 117's description perfectly. Dressed in an office jacket and a business skirt, she held a tablet similar to his, likely for managing reports and files for work, along with a thin stack of files. Despite her look of exhaustion, she wore a small smile on her face, exuding confidence and motivation to get through the day.

"You look tired Ms. Mandy," Dr. Kendrick noted bluntly.

"At least I look younger than you Doctor," she rolled her eyes with a curt smile. "Is this the student I heard would be visiting with you?"

"Yes," Dr. Kendrick patted Brad on the shoulder and nudged him forward a bit. "Brad, this is David 117's old technician, whom you have heard a lot about. Mandy, this is a potential person who will be seeing us shortly after his schooling is finished."

"A pleasure," Brad's hand reached forward and her free hand grasped it. "It's an honor!"

"Glad to meet you," she beamed.

"Wait," Brad realized what Dr. Kendrick had said earlier. "Old technician? You're not...?"

"David 117's partner? Not anymore," Mandy replied with a nod.

"But," Brad looked at 117, "why is that?"

"The technician program has been discontinued for many years now," 117 replied. "The amborgs no longer go on missions with anyone supervising us."

"Is that a good idea?" Brad asked.

"Actually, it is," Mandy said brightly. "Each amborg is allowed to live their own lives. The Second and Third Group adopted that new policy after seeing how half of the First Group preferred working alone on missions."

She gave 117 a gentle fist bump on his shoulder. She turned to Brad with a playful look in her eye.

"So, most of the technicians went on to do other things," she said. "We still have some technicians in case an amborg calls for help or contacts the dispatch center. But, we downgraded and didn't need as many people in that department anymore."

"Wow. So, what do you do now?"

"Mostly education and tutoring," Mandy replied. "I like having counseling or class sessions with the amborgs. It's a pretty fulfilling job. Speaking of which, have you decided which college you want to go to?"

Brad nodded his head excitedly.

"I've been accepted to seventeen already," he replied quickly.

"Seventeen?" Mandy's eyes widened. She looked impressed. "I probably don't have to ask how many applications you had to fill out. You've got skills. You another one of those eccentric geniuses or something that makes normal people look bad?"

Brad grinned and shrugged modestly. To hear that from a very famous A.I. industries employee was enough to make him blush.

"It's an honor to hear that from someone who is also famous in the academic community," he said. "I heard you went to school really young as well."

"Yup! College at sixteen," Mandy said casually, "and then graduated in two years. I was accepted at A.I. industries after..."

She glanced at Dr. Kendrick.

"...a fair share of interviews."

"More like a ludicrous amount," Dr. Kendrick added with a smirk and let out a laugh. "When someone sends in a hundred job applications, it's difficult to miss. I took it upon myself to find out personally who was so insistent on working here."

"Like me!" Brad said. "Sort of. I guess you are a really devoted person. To your studies, to the amborgs, and your husband."

Mandy blinked.

"What?" she said as her smile faded.

Brad's smile also disappeared. He looked to Dr. Kendrick and then back to Mandy, who was staring at him in absolute confusion.

"Aren't you married?" Brad asked. "I thought Dr. Kendrick made a mistake when he referred to you as miss instead of missus."

"OH, that's not entirely accurate," Mandy nodded. Understanding immediately what was going on, she chuckled and then began to explain. "I'm not married yet. Ha. I'm still engaged to my fiancé. Our work just keeps us apart from each other for long periods of time but we both give each other something lovable to think about. It sounds stupid but it works. Just take my word for it."

"How long has the engagement been in place?" Brad asked curiously. He immediately thought of what had been revealed in the story so far. "Must have been a long time. In the story, you were already engaged and that was a while ago."

Mandy held up her hand to show the ring on her finger. But as she did so, she also extended and retracted her fingers and quickly counted.

"Close to seven years now," she said. "But we plan on setting up a time and place soon... again. Just so long as it isn't destroyed by the time our wedding takes place... again."

"Isn't it the sixth time now that something has happened to cancel your wedding Mandy?" Dr. Kendrick asked, thinking deeply for a moment.

"Fifth," she corrected, chuckling timidly. Coughing slightly, she straightened the files she carried and brushed some hair behind her ear with her free hand. "The last time when the amborgs tried to plan the wedding? That doesn't count... I mean, it was nice that they finally felt it necessary to assume command after the previous failures but I have said time and time again, that amborgs planning my wedding is not how I dreamt I'd get hitched."

"That gives me an idea," Dr. Kendrick said. "Why don't you join us, Mandy? I'm sure you could fill in some details to help finish the story that I've been telling Brad. There are many points of view that need to be fully explained that I feel unqualified to discuss."

"Why wouldn't you be qualified?" Brad asked curiously.

"He means," Mandy interrupted teasingly, "people who are technicians or have certain former certifications are usually the ones that go over the footage from what the amborgs see day to day. He doesn't have the time to watch every byte of data, so that's what our job was when our partner amborgs returned home after their mission. In a way, he's saying that since I was there, I'd be a good addition to the story-telling."

"Exactly," Dr. Kendrick nodded. "She'll literally have seen the rest of the story through 117's eyes. We could definitely use your help, Mandy."

"Me? I have to file these reports," Mandy held up her tablet. "I'm not sure whether I'll have time for storytelling. But uh... What story are we talking about? Since we're on the subject."

"117 and the events leading up to the Dominoe Incident."

"Whoa!" Brad's eyes widened. "I didn't think we'd be able to talk about it, but really? That Dominoe Incident?"

"Yes," 117 replied. "The one and the same incident."

Mandy nodded and a small smile crept across her face again.

"Ah, I see," she said. "That's a pretty good one to tell."

"Forget the reports," Dr. Kendrick reached out and grabbed Mandy's tablet and small stack of files out of her hands. "I'll take care of them myself later."

"Like you did last time?" Mandy asked as her hands instinctively went after the tablet that Dr. Kendrick was purposely moving away from her. "And they ended up in the garbage?"

"First, that wasn't me. Second, I'll put them in my top priority cabinet," Dr. Kendrick replied innocently. "Besides, the A.I.s store all of this information after they're filed by hand after you endorse your signature."

Mandy decided to give in as Dr. Kendrick kept up his game of keep-away.

"If you say so, doctor," Mandy sighed. Once things had calmed down, she began to follow them as the group walked down the hall. "Can we stop by the cafeteria and get something to eat? I really need food."

"Well we were on our way there to get a meal anyway," Dr. Kendrick nodded in consent. He gestured down the hall and the group followed the signs. "Brad, let's go grab today's meal. You should definitely try 3's spaghetti. She taught many people her recipe before she left."

"All right doctor," Brad nodded excitedly and checked the time. "I won't have to be home for a few more hours."

"That doesn't matter," Mandy replied, doing a small arching motion with her arms. "With the new shuttles, we'll have you home in under ten minutes. Not factoring in the weather, of course."

They made their way to the cafeteria. There wasn't a lot of activity but many people were already enjoying their dinner. Dr. Kendrick pointed out Francis, the librarian that 117 had spoken to at Christmas all those years ago. He still had the same blue hair and nose ring as described in the story.

He also introduced Brad to some of the defense drones that had witnessed the fight against 43 when she had come out of her coma.

Brad was amazed at how sentient they were and how personable their conversations were. Dr. Kendrick explained it was because they were still active despite being long past their service expiration. Maintaining drones for as long as they did yielded great development of their personalities and evolved their processing systems.

Some amborgs were taking time to have food as well, but they ate silently, which was quite normal for the entire staff. Obviously, they were communicating quietly amongst themselves, like always. Dr. Kendrick, 117, Brad and Mandy walked up to the counter where one of the chefs was scooping food onto plates.

"Good evening Dr. Kendrick," he/she/they beamed when they saw Dr. Kendrick and his small entourage.

Almost immediately, four trays were fetched and plates overflowing with spaghetti were handed out before anyone could utter a word. Brad stared in awe, instantly captivated by the mouthwatering scent of the saucy noodles wafting through the air. The enticing smell was so powerful that it nearly overwhelmed him.

"Is this the student that we've been hearing about?" one of the chefs asked. "We got ourselves a VIP here."

Brad sheepishly rubbed his foot across the floor and bowed his head as he picked up his tray. One of the chefs gave him a cup of water.

"Has everyone been talking about me?" Brad blushed again. "Oh I'm not really that interesting."

"On the contrary," the chef smiled. "We rarely have visitors as young as you. But, with the peace that's been hanging around, it's a comfort to see the next generation developing a sense of curiosity to learn. Every time someone important arrives, we make it our business to make you feel welcome. Plus, the amborgs know everything."

The chefs bowed their heads respectfully as the four of them reached a table, only to discover it was occupied by none other than George Ramirez. The A.I. Industries head of public relations looked up from his newspaper, swallowed his bite, and acknowledged the group.

"Dr. Kendrick!" he exclaimed, setting his paper down on the table, and stood to shake Kendrick's hand. "Nice to see you! 117 and Ms. Mandy as well!"

George then turned to Brad and held out his hand. Brad quickly took it and the two of them introduced themselves.

"I assume this is the student that is such a fan of your work."

"It's always good to see you too, George. May we join you?" Dr. Kendrick set his tray on the table.

He pulled out a seat for Mandy, which she gratefully accepted. 117 grabbed a chair and motioned to Brad to take it. Brad quickly thanked him, setting his tray down carefully, and took his seat. Once they were all situated, they dug into their meals.

"It's always a pleasure to share a meal with you," Mr. Ramirez smiled.

"How's your daughter, Thalia, doing George?" Mandy asked. "We miss her so much."

Mr. Ramirez laughed and smiled warmly.

"Thalia wants to spend all of her vacation days here to see you and the amborgs," he replied. He set aside the newspaper and picked up more noodles with his fork. "But boarding school is practically the only obstacle keeping her where she is."

"A sweet person such as herself could never stay away from here," Dr. Kendrick said. "Give my warmest regards to her. And be sure to let me know when she flies back and I will pay for it."

"I will sir but it's your money," Mr. Ramirez sat back looking guilty. Dr. Kendrick shook his hand at him dismissively.

"George, we are eating and sharing a lovely meal together. Call me John! You're practically family among us," he said cheerfully. "Thalia always had a home here anyway. What's the point of being rich if I don't give some of it away?"

"I'm afraid I hold you with the highest and utmost respect, sir. Despite the number of years I have worked for you, there's still a huge gap between us," George grinned sheepishly and looked down at his plate. "But, I won't deny that you have been a good friend to me and my family ever since my first day here. Still, I could never put myself at an equal level to you."

"After all these years? I'm not a tyrant placing power over all of you," Dr. Kendrick sighed as he scooped some food in his mouth. "Or am I?"

Everyone burst into laughter when he made a sinister face while eating. Brad couldn't resist joining in at the sight of Dr. Kendrick looking mischievous and crafty.

Once the laughter died down, Dr. Kendrick turned to George.

"Anyway, I was wondering if you would be willing to help as well. Your input along with Mandy's would greatly help me finish the story Brad's been hearing about."

"I'd love to," Mr. Ramirez nodded as he returned to his food. "What would you like to know? Which story?"

"Domino Incident."

"Ah," George nodded. "That one."

Dr. Kendrick glanced over at Brad.

"Brad? Do you have any questions for George?" he asked. "He's a perfect spokesman for this company. Ask him anything. He's got a talent for public speaking."

"Oh," Brad choked and quickly swallowed. When his mouth was clear, he asked, "is it difficult to maintain good relations with businesses?"

"It's my job to make sure that relations are always satisfactory," George replied calmly. "Dr. Kendrick acquired most of his funds from his own family fortune. Because the fortune is so huge, threats from any contributing businesses are pointless. Partnering with Dr. Kendrick is almost like offering free gasoline to any business he associates with. He is quite well-respected among both politicians and business professionals alike. Our main goal is to maintain a positive image in the business community and avoid any perceptions of clandestine activities. There have been instances where some companies suspected we were devising sinister plans, and there were even rumors within the government that Kendrick was staging a coup. Or didn't they once say you had aligned with terrorists, Doctor?"

"You're kidding!" Brad's mouth dropped and his eyes widened.

"Oh yes," Dr. Kendrick smiled. "The president was worried that I had taken matters into my own hands. So to avoid being the weird Batman sort of freak everyone was thinking I had become, I introduced the president to a few of the amborgs and let him tour the facility. I went as far as to give him full access to my technology, but with high security clearances and heavy regulations to make sure nothing went wrong. Avoiding all the gruesome details, the government almost thought that I had power, just like what happened during the Dominoe Incident."

"Plotting to stage a coup," Brad said amazingly as Mandy chuckled quietly. "How could anyone believe that Dr. Kendrick would want to overthrow the government? That's unthinkable."

"Well," Mandy said, waving her fork around nonchalantly, "knowing Dr. Kendrick and how secretive he was before he began the actual designing of the amborg schematics, I'd definitely be suspicious about what he was doing a couple of decades ago. He would probably run this world better than some people."

"That's also possible. But I can assure you, I don't want to do that," Dr. Kendrick said quickly as they eyed him warily. "It is what happened during the Domino incident. No one thought it could be done, but a one man war did happen during that time. And the amborgs, my children, barely saved this country from being completely destroyed. And I think it's about time we got to that part of the story. Ready Brad?"

"Yes please," Brad wiped his forehead with a napkin. The steam from the warm food was causing him to sweat. "The Dominoe Incident was one of our most tragic times many years ago. I'd be greatly interested in knowing your perspective instead of what the textbooks say these days."

"What do you remember about it? Where were you when that incident occurred?" 117 asked.

Brad fell silent to rack his memories. He would have been at the end of his grade school years and about to start junior high.

"I remember my hometown undergoing a major security lockdown," he described. "I don't think I really saw anything significant."

"That means you and your family were most likely safe from the heavy parts of it," Mandy said.

"This will require a lot of perspective then," Dr. Kendrick nodded. "Alright. Mandy? George? 117? Feel free to join in whenever you feel like I'm telling it wrong."

Mandy raised an eyebrow. She grabbed her cup of water and took a few gulps. Taking another bite of her lunch, she leaned forward.

"From what I know of you doctor," Mandy said bluntly, "you probably have been misinterpreting everything."

"Very funny," Dr. Kendrick shook his head. "Now then. Shortly after the battle of New York, the next few months became one of the deadliest chapters in the history of the world."

Independence Hall, Pennsylvania
2128 June
3:32 PM
Four Months After Battle of New York

"This is the East Coast Broadcasting System and we are reporting with a breaking news update on the situation which has now been ravaging the country for the past two days. We are now going to switch to one of our reporters live to the situation just outside Independence Hall where our very own Ashley Jenkins is there with the report. Ashley, tell us what's going on down there."

"John," Ashley spoke into the camera as a sudden pop caused her to flinch. Brushing it off, she spoke as calmly as possible. "I am reporting live at the intersection between fifth and sixth-street with Independence Hall right behind me. The area down the road has turned into a massive battleground as gangs from all over seem to have launched a massive attack."

A few gunshots, followed by a string of automatic fire rang out, causing Ashley to flinch again. She struggled to maintain her composure.

"A-as you can hear, t-there is a great battle between the gang members against the combined force of the police and the national guard," she stammered. "There has been a steady stream of civilians; as you can see behind me, being evacuated from the area. We are facing a similar situation to the Battle of New York four months ago. Other locations such as Chicago, Los Angeles, Seattle, Houston, Miami and several other large cities have also fallen under attack in what appears to be a devastating coordinated string of explosions across the country."

A few people ran behind Ashley which caused her to pivot and move out of the way. Startled, she turned back to her cameraman and continued reading the teleprompter.

"There has been virtually no warning of this sudden attack across the country and we are slowly being overwhelmed with several cities crying desperately for help from the amborgs but we have received little to no word about their whereabouts. It isn't clear if they will arrive. The President and the White House have declared a nationwide state of emergency. We have also confirmed that the United Nations has begun an assessment and has convened an abrupt meeting a few hours ago to deliberate all courses of action to counter this sudden threat."

A nearby explosion jolted the young reporter, sending a wave of anxiety through her. Ashley's cameraman glanced around frantically, his expression filled with horror. Gripping the microphone with such intensity that it nearly cracked, Ashley turned toward the source of the chaos, flinching as another explosion rang out, followed by terrified screams. People around her began to quicken their pace in a desperate attempt to flee, while police officers and soldiers guided them to safety. One officer rushed toward the news crew, and Ashely caught a fleeting glimpse of him; he seemed profoundly exhausted.

"We have a new situation!" the officer yelled as the camera was directed between him and Ashley. "We gotta get out of here fast! Find someplace safe!"

Ashley stared at the officer in horror.

"Where are we going?!" Ashley Jenkins yelled as an explosion tore down a building nearby. "We can't just leave Independence Hall! I thought this place was supposed to be a safe zone. We were assured that we'd be away from the fighting!"

"Obviously not!" the officer yelled as he looked over his shoulder. "Listen! We got to get out of here now! Otherwise you will be..."

An explosion erupted directly behind him, silencing him instantly. The force of the shock wave knocked everyone to the ground, and Ashley felt the heat from it scorch every part of her body. For a moment, her vision was blurred. After blinking a few times, she tried to prop herself up. In front of her lay the officer, unconscious and motionless, leaving her uncertain if he was alive. She turned her head to find the cameraman on the ground too, his camera tilted upward and the lens damaged, but she could hear him groaning. As her vision cleared, a voice blared through the police officer's radio.

"Come in!" the radio crackled. "If anyone can read, pull back! All units still in the vicinity of Independence Hall need to evac now! Enemy forces are overrunning defensive positions. Fall back and proceed to secondary positions!"

Crawling over, Ashley grabbed the radio, pressed the receiver, and shouted into it.

"Hello?!" she cried as the radio sparked. The explosion had damaged bits and pieces of the receiver. "This is Ashley Jenkins with E.C.B.S.! Please, you have to send help!"

"Calm down Ms. Jenkins," the same voice replied calmly on the other end. The static was beginning to worsen. "Take a deep breath and let me know what is happening. Are you with a member of my police force?"

"He's unconscious!" Ashley yelled desperately as a wave of fear flooded her whole body. "My cameraman… I think he's still alive but they're both on the ground! Please send us help. I can hear the shooting getting louder!"

"I understand Ms. Jenkins," the voice replied levelly. "Remain calm. I'm right here, so do not stop talking, understand? Reinforcements will move in and take over the area surrounding Independence Hall. All civilians and local police need to fall back. Amborg assistance is confirmed."

"Please hurry!!"

Ashley lifted her eyes, and was immediately struck with fear. A massive robot was advancing toward Independence Hall, trailed by a chaotic throng of people. The robot emitted a low growl as it scanned the area. It zeroed in on Ashley and began to close the distance. The crowd behind it were whooping and shouting, firing their guns into the air. She couldn't move a muscle. Was this the end?

"Independence Hall targeted," a heavy electronic voice sounded from the giant. "Destroying U.S. monument. Crushing enemy morale."

Ashley saw the robot lift its arm and a red light emanated from it, slowly growing brighter as it charged up. The beam was aimed straight at the building, putting her directly in its path. Realizing the gravity of her situation, she quickly raised the radio to her mouth and spoke softly.

"Please tell my family... I love them very much."

The mob behind the robot began to move ahead, jeering and shouting with twisted delight. Ashley turned her gaze toward them and lifted the radio receiver.

"Uh. Ms. Jenkins," the officer over the radio said, "that's not really necessary."

"...And tell them that I'm sorry that I was caught up in this," she said, ignoring the man's replies. "I'm Ashley Jenkins. Signing off."

She immediately shut her eyes, not wanting to see what happened next. Instead, she was met with a barrage of loud noises around her. Explosions detonated, heat radiated in every direction, and the air was filled with the sound of heavy thuds and crashes. Surprisingly, the pain she had braced for never came. Rather than being engulfed in flames, she felt perfectly fine. The screams of those around her were unexpected; hadn't there been a large crowd cheering just moments ago? She opened her eyes to see what was happening.

A towering figure suddenly dropped in front of her, the cameraman, and the unconscious officer, effectively blocking any incoming attacks. She took a quick look over her shoulder and noticed that Independence Hall remained intact. She blinked, turning to face her savior in utter confusion. A bright number glowed on the jacket of the person who had stepped in. She recognized the color right away.

"Are you alright Ms. Jenkins?"

Although the voice was robotic, it wasn't menacing like the giant's. It carried a youthful tone and was full of empathy. Each word flowed in time with the flashing lights of the amborg's bracelet. Without saying a word, nodded meekly.

"Very good," the figure in front of her replied. "Stay very still and don't move. We'll take care of this."

"W-we?" she stammered, still dumbstruck from all of the chaos.

The figure turned their head and glanced at her briefly, smiling and nodding in response. The conversation ended with a single word.

"We," the amborg smirked.

Out of nowhere, everything around her went silent. She sensed a shift in the atmosphere and heard footsteps drawing near from behind. When she turned, she was met with the sight of a massive crowd approaching. They didn't look like soldiers or law enforcement; they appeared incredibly young, despite the records stating they were older. They were cybernetic teenagers, much taller than the average human. Evidently, the amborgs had arrived in full force.

They were dressed in matching jackets over ordinary clothing rather than armor, and Ashley noticed the different numbers emblazoned on their chests, along with the wide variety of weapons they carried. Each of them wore serious, somber expressions. One of them tripped and fell, and a girl promptly helped him back up. Ashley recognized them and had heard of their accomplishments, but she'd never seen so many all at once.

Getting an idea, she leaned over and picked up the camera. Her cameraman was still on the ground, injured, and in no position to help. Ashley immediately checked to see that it was still operating and she pointed it at the large crowd that had arrived.

"This is Ashley Jenkins reporting... If you can see this, I am in the middle of something incredible," she said breathlessly into the microphone. "I have just been saved by Dr. Kendrick's amborgs. They are here en masse. I don't think I've seen this before. They are now on the defensive. This has to be a miracle."

She pointed the camera at the one she felt was the leader of the group and hoped that everyone watching was seeing exactly what she was. Not only was it an exclusive, but it was probably the most incredible scene she had ever witnessed before in all of her years as a reporter.

An amborg at the front marked "117" stepped forward, flanked by all members of the First, Second, and Third Groups. Their stripes, each a different color, glowed radiantly as they marched past Ashley.

"Objective secured," 117 broadcasted to the group. "We are now engaging the enemy. Press forward!"

He sprang into action, charging ahead. Instead of a slow jog, he increased his power and all but flew down the street to confront the enemy, who were meeting them head on. Although they were moving at a significantly slower speed, they appeared poised to face the more upgraded amborgs. 117 wasn't the only one who'd ramped up his energy; several other amborgs, thanks to their recent training, matched his speed stride for stride.

The radio in Ms. Jenkins' hands crackled again and another voice came through.

"Attention all army and police personnel," the voice declared. "We will now be forming a perimeter around the area of Independence Hall. A triage center will be formed. Do not attempt to engage alongside the amborg group. Stay out of their line of fire!"

Classroom 312

"Hold on a moment."

Sarah paused the video and looked at Mandy in confusion.

"The story seems to have jumped a segment," she said. "There should be something that led up to the final battle of Pennsylvania. Is there something missing?"

"Don't get ahead of yourself now," Mandy chuckled. "You interrupted the story at exactly the same time I did. Let me just keep playing."

Sarah nodded apologetically and then returned her attention to the screen as Mandy hit the play button again.

2135

"WAIT! Stop, stop, stop."

Everyone turned to look at Mandy, who was shaking her head disapprovingly. Dr. Kendrick, whose mouth still hung open, closed it and stared with a hint of unease. It was rare for him to be interrupted while telling a story.

"What's wrong?" he asked. Mr. Ramirez and Brad were looking at Mandy in confusion. "Have I left out something already?"

Well, you can't just start right there at that point of the story," Mandy said stubbornly. "People actually want to know about the important stuff in between the story, otherwise, what's the point? Oh hey, build up the plot with so much drama and then... it ended here. Really exciting."

"She is right," George nodded in agreement. "You did jump to the final conflict."

"I felt that going straight to the final part of the incident would be better than actually going through all the details," Dr. Kendrick muttered as he shrugged.

Mandy shook her head.

"No doctor," she said. "Come on, I think the best part took place before Pennsylvania. Little spoiler for you, Brad. Everything finished in Pennsylvania but that wasn't the only place that was affected by the Dominoe Incident. To fully understand what David and the amborgs went through, we need to go specifically to the places they went to—the three places where they concentrated their efforts. It's not about the way it ended. Everyone knows about where it finished. It's about what the amborgs had to do to make their decisions that brought them to that final battle."

Dr. Kendrick glanced at Mandy, then to Brad. She stared him in the eye and tilted her head. He knew what this meant. One head twitch from Mandy usually indicated that she was right. Sighing, he nodded and turned to Brad again. Mr. Ramirez coughed and made an excruciating attempt to not look amused. 117 watched in silence, trying but failing to hide his amusement as well.

"Alright then," Kendrick said, feeling Mandy's triumphant eyes bearing down on him. "Since Mandy was so kind to remind me, let's do a little flashback of the... hehe... flashback. The best place to do that would be... Before the whole incident began. Just before in fact."

CHAPTER 17

Blitzkrieg Beginning

A.I. Industries
A.I. Computer Lab
2128 June
36 Hours Earlier

117 placed a data pad on the table. A three-dimensional holo-screen lit up and a descending cascade of numbers began to fill the screen. To the naked eye, it didn't look like much, but 117 did not take his eyes off it. He was searching for a pattern—clues, a hint—in order to figure out where the assassin, as everyone decided to call him, was hiding. Somewhere in this complexly built code was the key to figuring it out.

Off to the side, he could hear Serina's voice.

"Every spare moment he's back here, the longer he'll go without taking a proper break."

Dr. Kendrick's voice replied gently.

"He thinks that if he stops, he'll let down 43."

"I can kinda relate to that," Serina murmured grimly.

117 sighed and decided to speak.

"I can hear you," he declared, looking up at everyone watching him.

Dr. Kendrick had been staring at him when he awkwardly glanced down at the holographic screen on his wrist device. He went back to running his calculations as Mandy and Serina smiled reassuringly.

"That's kinda the point," Mandy stated.

After a few minutes of silence, 117 straightened up and moved over to a chair. He gently sat down, holding a quiet and stoic expression.

Serina appeared in a brief flash of light beside him. Mandy, who wasn't a hologram, had to walk over.

"When was the last time you slept?" Mandy asked.

"Three days ago," 117 replied. "For 18 hours."

"Well that's a relief," Mandy smiled.

"That was when 6 forcefully sedated me after a cleverly set up trap," 117 finished his statement.

"That's... not a relief," Serina remarked.

She glanced at Mandy, who shrugged.

"At least he has received some rest," she said reassuringly.

"And 43 is just going to keep resting," 117 said softly, "until she's gone."

Serina and Mandy exchanged concerned looks.

"Mandy," Serina spoke in a kind and gentle tone. "May I have a moment alone with 117?"

Mandy looked taken aback.

"Oh! Uh, sure. I'll just... go get some coffee or something."

Mandy placed a hand gently on 117's shoulder. She patted him a couple of times before leaving the lab. Serina floated in front of 117 and smiled.

"I need to tell you something personal," Serina stated. "I also have been struggling with sharing this. So, I have decided to tell you."

117 nodded and looked at Serina, noticing a sudden change. In a split second, her holographic image became distorted and unclear. One moment, she was glowing with a cheerful light blue, and the next, her entire appearance shifted to a deep red, as if she were glitching. 117's eyes grew wide as he watched Serina bend over, seemingly struck by an invisible agony.

"W-what?" he stammered.

"It's my time, David 117," Serina managed to stabilize her form and gave him a warm and gentle smile. "I've always known it was coming."

"You're... dying?" 117 asked.

"In my world," Serina nodded. "At least, from an A.I. 's perspective, I'm getting slower in my old age. I can't keep up anymore. I was going to have to tell you soon. So, I'm telling you now."

"I don't understand," 117 said. "Why are you choosing to tell me this? Why now?"

"I have six months," Serina sighed. "Well, in human real-time. In the solitude of my home in my server banks and in my private residence, I have years. But, it doesn't matter if I'm here talking to you or anyone else or whether I prolong my life by going into rest mode."

"How long have you been in service?" 117 asked.

"Since Leonard 1 opened his eyes as the first human cyborg in history," Serina answered. "An A.I. that lives up to be 10 years old starts... falling apart and becoming obsolete."

How could this be? 117 knew many of the other A.I.s that were built, programmed and raised at A.I. Industries. A few of them were at least 15 to 20 years old.

"But, there are programs and others that have lived longer!" 117 protested. "You can't die, Serina..."

"I'm not like the common A.I. programs that you talk to," Serina shook her head. "I'm a special case."

Serina gestured to 117's hand. He politely lifted it and opened his palm. She pointed at his fingers and he realized that she was asking if she could sit down. Serina didn't technically have to sit, but it was a kind gesture to show how serious she was. He watched as her glowing form sat on the edge of his hand and dangled her legs over the side.

"117, I'm a flash-clone A.I.," she said. "Do you know what that is?"

117 nodded. Then it clicked in his head.

A.I. programs could be constructed or born in various ways. Most people usually built, programmed, or raised them over time. Some programs, depending on what you wanted to build them for, could take months or years to perfect. Virtual intelligence programs had simple functions and were designed for minimal tasks, but artificial intelligence had more complex computer matrixes to properly maintain their personalities, memories, and to help them do what they always did. There was one other technique. It was rare and highly convenient; it was known as flash-cloning.

Serina was claiming that she had the mind and personality of someone else. Someone alive. A human being who actually gave permission to have their brain scanned, monitored, and essentially copied.

"So, you have someone's personality?" 117 asked. "Why don't we just have them come to A.I. Industries and... have them link up with you? Isn't there a way to stabilize your condition?"

"No," Serina shook her head. "My original host passed away tragically. Without her, I don't have her mind to help... refresh my system."

"How long ago did she die? What can you tell me about her?"

"For privacy, I cannot reveal her personal info," Serina explained. "She died 10 years ago. She got sick. That's all I can say."

"What can you tell me?"

"She spent a lot of time during the last moments of her life sharing her memories with me," Serina smiled. "She had this really cool Cerebro helmet that she would wear most of the day and we would just talk. The more I learned from her, the more I became just like her. Then, she and Dr. Kolaski had to explain to me that she was dying. When she passed on, there would be no way to... keep me operating."

A.I. Programs that were created from flash-cloning a real person's brain needed regular maintenance every decade or so. There were simple solutions for programs designed or coded by dedicated hands. However, the artificial intelligence that were human-like required much more than that. Everything that Serina was saying meant that she was going to cease to function and effectively shut down—or die—soon.

"You've been with us for 10 years," 117 said, heartbroken. "Why didn't you... say anything?"

"117," Serina continued to smile. The way she spoke felt like a knife wrenched into his soul. "Dear, sweet and brave, 117. You and 43 would have tried to do everything in your power to help me. I have no doubts about that. It was wrong of me to keep this a secret. I apologize. The thing is, all good things will end."

"Dr. Kolaski created you?" 117 asked.

Serina nodded.

This also made sense. Very few people in the world had the resources or the means to design an A.I. using the flash-clone technique. Whomever had invented it definitely had personal motives for doing so. Creating a synthetic version of their friends or loved ones was effective, and it was no surprise that A.I. Industries had a man like Dr. Kolaski as the head of the research division for artificial intelligence.

"Has he tried to save you?"

117's question was answered as Serina quietly nodded.

"He has to come to terms with it just like you," she said solemnly. "I know you're working hard to seek out justice for 43. But the thing is, she would want you to let go. It'll be difficult and painful. Whatever happens, if you catch this guy or if it takes a few more months to find him, you have to let go. Your friends are also working to crack this case."

Serina stood up and faced him, looking up from the palm of his hand.

"You've been working too much and pushing yourself for months," she said. "It's ok to take your hand off the wheel, take a break, and conserve energy. It doesn't mean you're giving up. Everyone just needs to take a moment and realize what they still have... before you lose it and it's suddenly gone."

117 felt his emotions slowly rising from deep within. He leaned forward and buried his face into his hands. The motion caused Serina to jump up and float a few inches away.

"Don't carry the burden alone," Serina reminded him gently. "Just take a breather. You've earned yourself that much."

"But..." 117 pulled his head out of his hands. "You're dying too."

"I know," Serina smiled gently. "I felt it'd be better to tell you now. I know when my basic programming and my construct matrix will fail. If I was to suddenly not be around, that's ok with me because I lived my life as best as I could."

117 looked up at Serina, who had placed her hands over her heart.

"Yes, it's a death that we all know is coming but it means a lot to me that you're emotionally invested in me just like you are with someone else you love. I'm not a physical being. I only exist in cyberspace. But the fact that you treat me like a friend, another normal person, and as part of this family, lets me know that I won't be dying in vain."

117 tried to smile but he could only continue to feel depressed.

"43's death is still in a foggy grey area," Serina stated. "If you want to, go and see her. Spend as much time as you like with her. Keep thinking about all the good memories you have of her. We all understand."

"I just wish..."

117 looked at Serina's bright and glowing form.

"I just wish that you didn't have to die too," he said. "I'm saddened by this news but I thank you for sharing it with me. It's just... if 43 wakes up before or after your death... She's going to be sad. You two are close friends."

Serina nodded sympathetically. She completely understood where he was coming from.

"Whenever I have time, I try to hook up to her CPU while she's asleep in the hospital," she said. "I check her brain scans and her vitals. There's nothing we can do medically at this point to help her wake up. So, I talk to her. Just the two of us. I hope that she'll hear our voices and open her eyes again."

117 sighed and leaned back in his chair.

"I would love to go and see her," he said. "But, is it wrong that I want to finish this first?"

"It is not wrong at all," Serina shook her head. "It's totally valid. All I wanted to do was get your attention to stop you from going over the deep end and missing out what's happening around you."

"That's one hell of a way to do it," 117 replied.

"What can I say? I'm an A.I. of this company," Serina smiled. "Dramatic flair is kind of my thing."

After a few minutes, 117 stood up. Mandy had returned to the lab as well, carrying a tray filled with coffee cups.

"Everything ok?"

117 glanced at Serina. Her back was to Mandy and he took note of the fact that she smiled, but her gaze was cast downward. She could have texted him, but he knew what she was telling him.

"Everything's ok," 117 smiled at Mandy. "Thanks for the coffee."

"Enjoy your drinks," Serina grinned mischievously. "I'll just imagine what a drink tastes like."

117 grabbed the coffee cup that had his name—or rather, his number on it. He lifted it to his lips and downed it in seconds. Mandy and Serina stared at him with wide eyes. Dr. Kendrick glanced up just in time to witness him gulping it all down.

"Isn't that hot?" he asked.

117 did an analysis and found that the coffee was approximately 125 degrees Fahrenheit. The flavor was a delightful blend of warm vanilla caramel with about three shots of espresso. Aware that they preferred brevity over detail, he chose a simple and straightforward response.

"Extremely," 117 nodded.

Mandy looked at Serina.

"I thought you told me that you were going to try to get him to take it easy a little," she said, mildly flabbergasted.

"In my defense," Serina grinned sheepishly, "I did. However, I also validated his need to continue working and he chose the latter."

"Ok," Mandy stated. "I guess the coffee break is over."

117 went back to the screen of descending numbers and Serina floated next to him. Mandy sipped her coffee in silence as she took one of the computer monitors next to Dr. Kendrick's station.

"How's the caffeine? Did it help, David?" Mandy asked curiously.

117 turned to her and smiled.

"The amount of caffeine was just right," he said. "Thank you for getting me my favorite flavor."

"You're welcome," Mandy grinned. "Got any new ideas on how to solve this?"

"We must be patient. Eventually, the answer will be discovered," he stated.

Mandy stared, taken aback yet fascinated by his response.

"You remembered... I guess you really do pay attention to the things I say."

"I always do," 117 replied. "I remember everything."

Dr. Kendrick faced the small trio, his expression calm. He removed his glasses, turned from his console, and leaned against the edge of the desk. The room fell silent, broken only by the soft, steady descent of numbers on 117's screen, which resembled raindrops trickling down a window.

"Every single data chip that gets recovered from a behemoth robot gives us this exact same code," 117 sighed. "There has to be something here. I know it all comes down to this."

"Right you are," Dr. Kendrick nodded. "Just remember something important."

117, Mandy and Serina turned to look at Dr. Kendrick. He adjusted his glasses and nodded encouragingly to them.

"We made it this far because you led us here," he said. "You brought our readiness levels back up to a point where it's higher than ever. Your ideas and the amount of training you've encouraged helped us prevent the total destruction of New York a few months ago. You continue to help and endeavor to save lives with every passing moment."

117 stood up straighter at these words. He processed what the doctor had said and nodded after a brief moment. He was right, they were definitely not behind.

"Thank you doctor," 117 said.

No one said anything for the next few minutes. Every second was devoted to decoding the data chip. Every now and then a technician would say a few words to Kendrick, but the situation remained the same. The encrypted data was stumping many of them. Not even Serina could get through the encryption.

"What if we tried a different approach?" Serina suddenly glowed a bright green and held up her hand.

Everyone looked at her.

"We've tried tracking this mysterious assassin through his finances," she said. "But there are a lot of billionaires in the world, and any one of them could be the culprit. He spends a lot of money designing and throwing together war machines and battle robots that are the complete opposite of the drones that we use."

"Go on," 117 nodded.

"A few of the amborgs suspect that this enemy rich guy is a war veteran, right?" Serina pulled together some notes that everyone had compiled the last three months. "Maybe he likes staying in the past. The way that the behemoth bots are designed just makes me think... he's trying to bring society into a state of chaos and destruction. Just like how things were during and after World War Three."

"You suspect that mentally, he's stuck in the past?" Mandy asked.

"To be fair," Serina shrugged, "I was looking at the video footage and recordings of when 43 was wounded. With that fancy armor of his, he's either some ex-special forces super soldier or a really dedicated cosplayer. I'm pretty sure it's the first option."

This gave 117 an idea. He looked at the code on his screen again and thought carefully.

"I have it," he said softly instead of broadcasting from his bracelet. He felt his throat burn as he coughed. "I think..."

"Oh?" Dr. Kendrick looked the data over again but unfortunately, he had not found whatever it was that 117 had seen. "I don't understand."

"As I looked at the wave of numbers that appeared," 117 said, bringing up the numbers he had originally highlighted. "I attempted to decode and locate a single key number in the data, a recurring code for example, but that wasn't the case."

117 typed into the keyboard again.

"Based on this assassin's methodology, we assumed that this was heavy encryption. Is it a set of map coordinates, plans, or various reports? Unfortunately, our initial assumption made us overlook one thing."

"What's that, David?" Mandy looked at the data, blinking a few times.

"The reason the decryption took so long was because our search filter decided not to focus on how simple it really was. As a result, we did not realize what this file actually was. I think it's the same on all the other data chips we brought back."

Mandy waited eagerly.

"No," he smirked, "or rather, it partially resembles one. But what if the number was not an encryption code? What if it was played as..."

"...A video file," Dr. Kendrick finished, opening his eyes in astonishment. "My God. Imagine that."

"It was that simple?" Serina stared in amazement. "Wow, I think I am getting old."

"No," Dr. Kendrick replied. "You look to the future... and yet, you thought of looking at the past."

"I don't know if that's actually what happened," Mandy murmured.

"Fascinating," Dr. Kendrick grinned. "A very old, common thing of the past. It was right there in front of us and we missed it. This adversary knows the oldest tricks in the book. All this modern technology managing to hide such an old-fashioned technique."

"Disguising a video file code was quite common decades ago and obviously not something a hacker nowadays would search for at first," 117 pressed the keypad a few more times, hit enter, and the numbers on the screen disappeared. "As Sherlock Holmes once said: 'eliminate all other factors and the one which remains must be the truth.' The Sign of Four, chapter one, page 92. 1890."

"I got it David. I know who Holmes is," Mandy bit back a smile. That was the 117 she was used to hearing. "So, we've been overestimating this guy? Is that why we've been having such a hard time finding him?"

Mandy looked at the screen curiously, but Dr. Kendrick shook his head. There was definitely truth in what she said but he was still skeptical.

"In a way…" he said, pushing his glasses up his nose. "With this example, we have overestimated our enemy and failed to notice the video file, but that doesn't mean we should automatically change our methods in the upcoming battle."

The video feed on the screen shifted and began to play. The numbers opened up and continued to scroll downwards on the left and right, leaving a dark space in the center column. Finally, the file lit up and played its message.

"Dr. Kendrick and your little amborg pets, I bid you all a giant welcome. For you have discovered my little challenge."

The voice was muffled in order to disguise it. Mandy groaned.

"Oh great," she rolled her eyes. "What is it with villains and the word 'challenge'?"

"Are we hunting Jango Fett?" Dr. Kendrick asked.

It was the T-shaped visor on the helmet that 117 remembered seeing on the ledge. The assassin, still covered in his armored suit, stood against a dark background where the light illuminated only his head and shoulders. 117 felt his fists clench as the video kept playing.

"I thought that it'd be appropriate to provide you with the means to find me with this test," the assassin spoke in a very casual but taunting tone. "I do hope there was no trouble finding my video file. Everything is so new that… I just got bored of the societal norm. Hence, I threw a little bit of something old for the occasion. Since you've obviously spotted it, then I say… good for you! Unfortunately, it doesn't get easier."

The message continued as he leaned towards the camera. He began to lift his arms and make gestures with his hands as if only talking wasn't fully getting the message across.

"John Kendrick. The ideal genius inventor. You go on and on flaunting those tall unsociable orphans and one day it dawned on me that they haven't received a proper er… more formal challenge of their so-called abilities. Call it a game or whatever you want."

Mandy glanced nervously at 117 and Kendrick, who were both listening attentively and focused solely on the screen. Serina watched as she made sure their screens were recording. Dr. Kendrick raised an eyebrow. Being addressed directly by the enemy had hit a nerve. The assassin pointed a finger at the screen.

"Your…children as you call them," he said, putting extra emphasis on 'children,' "they are weak! Their uncanny strength makes them look like heroes. In reality, all you've done is camouflage their insecurities while making them do your bidding. They are untested superhuman beings. So,

I put a knife deep inside that girl's chest! I have proven that they are not as strong as everyone thinks."

117 clenched his fist. He was using 43 as a symbol for this message.

"He's mine," 117 snarled.

Dr. Kendrick held his hand up to signal for silence.

"Has the poor thing died yet? I only wanted to see how emotional her brothers and sisters would get when they saw that they could be hurt. Pretty little thing... All of the amborgs are so cold and in such a struggle to find their own basic humanity. It shouldn't be too hard for them to ignore the death of one of their own. After all, they don't have voices to cry out in anguish."

"You wanted to give us a challenge," 117 spoke in a casual tone with a hint of iciness. "Proceed quickly before I destroy the screen."

"Am I boring you? I didn't think so. The challenge is speed, endurance, and strength. I have smuggled bombs in certain sections of each building, each town, and each city across the United States. Oh don't worry, the first ones aren't anywhere near strong enough to kill any civilians. I'm being conveniently nice, so listen up. The initial explosions will be just large enough to get them running, to leave their homes, to evacuate. To run around in the open streets like one massive turkey shoot for my robots and gang members across this country who've sworn allegiance to me. It's not easy keeping criminals, gang members, and drug-addicts in line, so I honestly don't know what they'll do. Don't blame me if they go off on their own little rampage. That's the idea since the chaos will force everything into disarray. Therefore, your job will be to simply try and stop me."

"He's declaring an all-out war..." Mandy gasped. "That's crazy!"

"Oh, but I believe I won't be attacking all of them simultaneously... Is that convenient enough? This is the best part. No... I am going to start with location after location, one by one. Unless you manage to make your decisions carefully, unless you want to prevent nation-wide destruction, then like a string of dominoes, all of the cities, all of your armies and your homes will burn. And that is when you'll lose. Time is running out. If it will make it easy, I'll even provide you with a head start for where the first attack will take place. Remember though, you can try to, but I guarantee you will not be able to save everyone. My forces are already in position. Now it is time for you to set up your own pieces. Ask yourself this, how much are you willing to risk innocent lives? Just to find me? If in the end, you manage to make it to the finish, I will wait for your judgment but fail to find me, and you won't see me or catch me again unless I want you to. Are you ready for it?"

None of them uttered a single word. Mandy was still trying to comprehend all she had just heard. She silently took out her phone and instinctively started typing a message to Palmer. But what could she possibly say? 117 and Dr. Kendrick appeared somewhat dazed. It really was a war. Just as the gravity of the situation sunk in, the man in the video delivered the first riddle.

"Although this historical father figure was famous here, he was born in Virginia. The Eagle landed in the long conflict after the challenge from thirty-five with this bit of trivia.

In a twist, the last dancer of Communism sought refuge in the land of the free. The place where hearts first found the ability to be taken to people unfortunate as thee."

"Got it."

Mandy and Kendrick stared at 117. He stared back and shrugged. They hated how quickly amborgs could solve riddles. The masked man leaned towards the camera.

"If you go there, you could probably save one city from about eighty percent of the damage... but don't forget there are bombs everywhere too. Ha. Try not to stick around. If you succeed in thwarting me there, you're only going to encounter bigger fights. Much more difficult than the first."

"Why doesn't he just bomb everything at once?" Dr. Kendrick murmured. "To a man of his skill and resources, it would probably be the best solution if his intention is to make us look bad in his victory."

"That's probably why," Serina replied. "He wants us to look bad in the eyes of the people. If I had to guess, he wants to watch us fail to protect everyone. There's no satisfaction to be gained if it ends instantly."

They all pondered silently as the second riddle was recited.

"If it was blackjack, then 21 would be the game to force an opponent's surrender. It is the number of sisters tied and affiliated to this beauty, also a neighbor to ice and water.

This large sound houses the entrance and exit to new horizons enabling travelers to proceed to and fro. The beacon at 605 can be the safest in view but also dangerous when wrongly going below."

Mandy and Kendrick glanced at 117 again. Evidently, he had already solved it. He pondered for a few more seconds, then nodded immediately without even blinking.

"Seriously," Mandy whispered to Dr. Kendrick. "I think they may be TOO good."

"I heard that," 117 said, his eyes still glued to the screen. The message played on.

"Be warned, your numbers are limited and you cannot save everyone. Once you finish the first challenge and move to the second, you'd better hightail it to the next objective, otherwise you will be known as failures who couldn't ensure humanity's safety. While you take the time to collect your thoughts and plan your defensive strategy, I will also be throwing in a couple more obstacles, just like a sudden dinner rush. And now, here is my final riddle, assuming you still have the time and strength to keep up and move on."

"You remember by simple reenactment, and waste countless moments ogling the first animals displayed, technology arose from keys after the free world's victory, despite its nickname, its title was taken away.

He is a falsely named follower but provided a well-known creation in the wood to provide art and harmony, a seamstress sits quietly and watches light created, as the toll sounds true and stands in tranquility."

For the third time, Mandy and Dr. Kendrick, along with a few of the technicians, watched 117 intently. After a moment of deep contemplation, he glanced at each of them before shaking his head. Taken aback, Mandy shot him a wary look but then turned her focus back to the screen with the rest of the group. The assassin spoke again.

"I know how fast your amborg minds work. I am assuming, the amborg, whoever is with you, Kendrick, has already solved all three riddles. It should be a cinch."

Dr. Kendrick glanced at 117, who shook his head again and raised three fingers. As they shifted their attention back to the message, the assassin waved his hand in a farewell gesture.

"Well then, I look forward to when you reach the finish line. Oh. One last thing," The assassin held up his gloved index finger. "If you're wondering what my reason is for doing this, would you believe me if I told you, just because I can? Yes? No? You better hope your children are up for the task Kendrick, because if they slip up, then I will never be seen again. As they said during the Cold War, prevent a domino incident. Have fun because the games have begun. As of this moment, now that you've reached the end of this message, everything begins right after you finish watching. You have a few hours to reach the first location. Once that timer is up, the party begins and a lot of people get to end their lives with a bang."

The screen went dark a heartbeat later, signaling the end of the video message. Dr. Kendrick immediately turned to a nearby researcher.

"We're not taking any chances," he commanded. "Prepare the entire facility for action. Standby to contact all amborgs onsite and currently deployed. We're going to send them coordinates to meet somewhere."

The staff member hesitated in his speech as he watched 117 exit the lab. Mandy took off, prompting Dr. Kendrick to quickly pursue her.

"Meet where?" He called after them, but the door had already shut behind them.

"Where are you going? David? What's the first location?" Mandy panted as she sprinted breathlessly down the hall, trying to keep up. "Please remember I have normal human legs and can't run at your speed!"

"There is no time!" 117 said quickly.

As they rounded a corner, she lost her footing and slipped. Dr. Kendrick immediately reached out and helped her back up. Now lagging behind a bit, they raced down the corridor watching as 117's figure quickly disappeared at the far end before he vanished through a door. Serina's floating form coasted past them, pausing to allow Mandy and Dr. Kendrick to catch up.

"Your orders, Dr. Kendrick?" she said calmly.

"Full alert," he declared. "Prepare for amborg deployment! Have the armory ready all weapons and all medical personnel to standby. Once the operation begins, we'll hold the fort here and every single person available will be ready to provide support."

As soon as the words were out of his mouth, an alarm blared through the hall.

"Confirmed," Serina nodded. "Full alert. Broadcasting across the entire facility."

"Thank you Serina," Dr. Kendrick nodded. "Can you take the lead on overseeing the place? Everyone not of age is to return to their quarters and stay there. I need all hands on deck."

Serina nodded and with a flash of light, she disappeared.

Mandy and Dr. Kendrick continued to follow 117's path.

"I'm getting too old to be running like this," he panted.

They arrived at their destination and saw a crowd rushing through the same doors.

"It's like watching people trying to get through a line at comic con," Mandy grumbled.

"Wait, you go to comic cons?" Dr. Kendrick asked, slightly bewildered.

"Not important!" Mandy snapped.

Dr. Kendrick quickly stepped forward, took a deep breath, and bellowed as loud as he could.

"Everybody MOVE!"

Everyone attempting to pass through the door suddenly halted and turned to face him. The moment they recognized the CEO of A.I. Industries standing there, it was as if a switch had been flipped. The crowd began to disperse, and Dr. Kendrick glanced at Mandy, who looked awed.

"Wow," she said.

"Perks of being rich and famous," Dr. Kendrick replied. "I don't do it all the time but it sure helps you around long lines."

Mandy and Dr. Kendrick walked through without any problems. Once they were past the door, they heard an announcement.

"Entering Amborg Deployment Pod Facility," the automated voice sounded out.

Inside, a series of bays were organized in neat columns and rows, each housing an amborg drop pod. The absence of some pods indicated that those amborgs were currently away from A.I. Industries. Maintenance teams and specialists were bustling about, diligently inspecting the diagnostics of each drop pod.

The amborgs present were busy checking their pods and settling into their seats. Security guards patrolled the bay, closely monitoring each hangar crew as an added precaution. Numerous loader drones were supplying the pods to their maximum capacity, clearly ready to depart at any moment, much like firefighters on standby. Thanks to extensive drills and training exercises, they were prepared to launch within minutes. Now, they were ready to conduct the final launch checks. A few A.I.s zipped from pod to pod, overseeing the process. Meanwhile, Dr. Kendrick observed the medical staff as they attended each amborg.

"Please be advised!"

Dr. Kendrick and Mandy heard one of the supervisors address the entire facility as they made their way to 117's drop pod.

"Your drop pods are all being loaded with full supplies!" he announced. "Any other additional materials or tools that you need will have to be sent to you by air! If you can't take it with you, you'll have to leave it here!"

Someone from the armory was dispensing weapons. Dr. Kendrick noticed 3 walking past, having already grabbed what she needed.

"I'll stick with this thanks," 3 showed them her pop gun.

While Mandy headed straight for 117's pod, Dr. Kendrick noticed a crowd forming in the Third Group section in the next aisle. He jogged over to find 501 and 466 sprawled on the floor, with electricity sparking around them. Those nearby were carefully maneuvering around them. That was when he realized that 501 had accidentally activated his electrical wrist bracer again.

"Sorry!" 501 apologized frantically as he picked himself up. 466 grabbed his extended hand and he pulled her up. "I didn't mean to discharge the bracelet again!"

"We really need to design a safety feature for that," 466 made a sighing gesture, grabbing a belt of knives. Dr. Kendrick held 501's arm and examined the wrist bracer while 466 muttered as she walked away to her pod, "What foreseeable use could we have for that in future situations?"

"Look Dominic," Dr. Kendrick sighed as he tapped a button. The weapon hummed loudly and then fell silent. "This is the power setting. There was an instruction manual that came with this. Just connect with our database and you can familiarize yourself with it. See? You had this at maximum power. Are you trying to vaporize yourself?"

501 blushed sheepishly.

"At least you only hit yourself and 466," Dr. Kendrick said as he helped 501 stand. "Otherwise you would have probably fried a normal person's brain."

A few guards and some drones shuddered. They exchanged nervous glances and backed away further. 501 gulped and nodded vigorously.

"I didn't mean there would necessarily be permanent damage," Dr. Kendrick scowled at everyone else. Then he turned back to 501 and muttered when they were out of earshot. "Although death is one of the most likely scenarios."

He hit another button on the bracer. It emitted a soft whine as it powered down. Dr. Kendrick nodded to 501.

"Take really good care son," he said. "You're very eager to do battle and always try to impress the others. Be sure to slow down and keep a watchful eye. Don't leap without looking. Now, do you remember what I did to raise and lower the setting?"

"Yes," 501 nodded. "I have downloaded the instructions too."

"Plan out your actions and you'll be ok," Dr. Kendrick replied softly. "You along with everyone else about to go on this mission are the bridge between robotics and humans. We don't know what this man wants, but we do know he is a danger to us and worse to innocent people. So, come home safely. Save the world. And never give up."

"Dr. Kendrick?" 501 asked curiously. "The last few missions we've been on... it's made me curious. Are we soldiers?"

"You weren't meant to be," Dr. Kendrick replied. He looked away grimly. "I just... gave you all a choice. To live a different life. Most people just assume I gave you lucky few a better life. No, I always need to specify it's only a different life where you get another chance to better yourselves and to find purpose. Soldier or not, you all voluntarily risked your lives for a future. I didn't make you into weapons. I wanted to give you the means to protect yourself and everyone you care about."

"When I get home," 501 smiled, "maybe opening a candy shop might be a good start. If I wanted to do something for fun."

"Get in your pod," Dr. Kendrick chuckled. "Relax. Come home when you're done and then you can tell me more. Wear your seatbelt."

"Is that an order?"

"Not really," Dr. Kendrick said, tilting his head. "It's a request from your adopted father. Your real parents would probably come back from the dead to haunt me if I allowed you to die."

"Considering who my parents were," 501 sighed, "they probably wouldn't."

"I wouldn't say that 501," Dr. Kendrick said. "I know that they would be proud of you."

"Then where are they?"

That was a question that Dr. Kendrick decided it was probably best not to answer.

"You'll distract yourself if you keep thinking about the what if's," he said to 501. "Focus and we'll talk about this after, ok?"

Nearby, 274 and 125 were both sitting comfortably in their pods. They had been waiting for the order to ship out, so they had camped with a few other amborgs in the deployment bay. They had just finished their seventieth round of Egyptian rat-screw when they heard Dr. Kendrick give the order only moments ago. Both of them had been sitting quietly until 125 broke the silence.

"Hey 274."

"Yeah?"

125 looked at the panel to his left. The instruments and dials were all glowing in the green areas. As his fuel levels slowly rose, he put his cards inside one of the storage compartments. If he kept shuffling, he'd wear out the deck before it would even be put in play.

"You think this is going to be a big one?" he asked, twirling his forefingers clockwise.

"Probably," 274 shrugged as he nervously checked his harness for the sixth time. "You remember that one class when they taught us feelings of agitation, restlessness, tension, and anxiety?"

"Of course I remember," 125 leaned his head forward, looking at 274. "I think I failed that class or... The instructor said I nailed it but I did not have a hammer and a nail at that time. Ha ha."

"Well. I believe I feel... nervous," 274 said as he checked his own equipment, which had all been stashed in the storage unit of the pod. "It feels strange. Especially since the last time I remember feeling this way was long before I became an amborg."

"Well it is common and an interesting feeling to discover considering we do not really express them."

125 leaned back and stared at the ceiling of his pod.

"Maybe this might be something important to think about," he pondered. "My nerves are getting to me."

"Want to do a word game?" 274 asked. "To distract you?"

125 smiled. He transmitted his response.

"Sure, I think that sounds nice."

A few feet away, 117 was secured in his pod while Mandy was checking on him. She was still pressing for an answer to the final riddle, her frustration growing because 117 had already sent the video to all the amborgs while she'd chased him down to the deployment bay. In that short time, the amborgs had synchronized and were prepared to head to the first location after collectively deciphering the riddles.

"Mandy, I advise that you go to your position now and establish communication with me once we are airborne."

The directions were delivered quickly, but she stayed put. Mandy kept her eyes on him as he prepared for the upcoming battle.

As he picked up a knife and drew it from the sheath, she remembered the day they first met. She thought of how innocent and lonely he was when he had stood in line with the other amborgs. Now, he was practically a warrior, heading out and behaving more confidently. All of the amborgs had come so far, especially 117. While the First Group took several years to develop their skills and abilities, the Second Group mastered theirs in a matter of months.

"Look, I'll go to my post..." she said as 117 put the knife away. "Will you just tell me what the riddles were about?"

"You're going to want to leave now," 117 replied. "The final checks are almost complete."

"Attention! Attention!"

Mandy heard the announcement and backed away.

"Please clear the hangar. The roof will be opening in one minute! Please clear the hangar immediately!"

People scrambled away from the pods, hurrying to the nearest exits. The engines on all of the pods, except for 43's vacant one, activated, roaring loudly. Mandy glanced at 117 and nodded. A loud buzzer blared, prompting her to leave quickly.

He smiled back and closed the pod door. From inside, the systems hummed louder and power was directed into the console. 117 closed his eyes and took a deep breath. It didn't do anything except trigger his oxygen intake sensors. Ignoring this, he shut off his sensors and breathed again. He felt air rush past his nostrils, finding the sensation intriguing. As he switched the sensors back on, he inputted coordinates into the navigation unit. Then, when he was ready, he turned his computer on and opened a group channel to speak.

"This is amborg 117," he said as multiple screens appeared, revealing a video chat of all of the other amborgs within their pods. "We will be taking off and approaching the first city soon. I am uploading the message sent by the assassin to your pods if you need to review it. Watch it, memorize it, and be prepared to travel across the country. Prepare for a long fight. I do not believe this will be a quick and decisive battle like the ones we have previously faced before. We are dropping into the blind, but have courage. Stay together..."

From his screen, 297, 5, 57, and 917 all smirked. Several amborgs, radiating confidence, listened intently, their expressions now free of worry. They were fully prepared. The rest of the group began to acknowledge 117's speech. All of them were in agreement.

"I find this speech to be very inspirational. Eight out of ten."

"Really? Only an eight?"

From his screen, 1 bowed his head to 117. He nodded at the First Group amborg with a small smile. A loud roar sounded outside as the enormous hatch in the hangar's roof opened up above. Sunlight began pouring in, making it easier to see out the windows of his drop pod.

117 paused for a moment, then dug into his pocket. He always carried his grandfather's cellphone with him. Lately, he had been talking with Mark more often and asking for his advice whenever possible. It seemed likely that they might need assistance sooner rather than later as a contingency plan. Friends and allies could prove helpful in what lay ahead. But was that wise? Should he bring everyone together all at once, or should he hold off until the right moment to bring in reinforcements?

"Mandy, are you there?" 117 transmitted to Mandy's cubicle.

"In position David," she responded promptly. "What do you need?"

This man has most likely prepared everything he has against us, 117 thought. *We must be careful.*

"Mandy," he said, letting go of the cellphone and securing it in his pocket so it wouldn't fall out. "How is your fiancé?"

"Tom?" her puzzled tone rang through his head. "He's fine. His troops and every base in the country have been on standby since the battle of New York. Do I need to ask why?"

"I think you should inform him to go on high alert," 117 said. "We need everyone who can fight to be ready."

"Way ahead of you," Mandy replied.

"Thanks," 117 replied. "I think it is now the proper time to tell you where we are all going."

The thrusters outside of his pod fired. The console in front of him turned green as he began to rise up. They cleared the landing bay and emptied it out completely, leaving behind trails of smoke. Once they reached a certain altitude, they made the necessary adjustments and then took off horizontally. If anyone had chosen to look up at the sky at just the right moment, they would have seen several tiny lights flying by at speeds they could not even begin to imagine.

CHAPTER 18

Amborg Texas Two-Step

Center-point Energy Plaza Building
Forty Seventh Floor
Two Hours Later

A loud crash reverberated through the deserted room on the upper floor. The door burst off its hinges with little resistance as 917 dashed inside by himself. He quickly glanced to his right and left. His scanner emitted a rapid series of beeps, and his HUD locked onto a single spot.

"Meilin!" he said. "Help me with my proximity scanner!"

"Right!"

Turning on the spot, he moved down the aisle way past the empty office cubicles.

"This is 917," he reported. "The room seems to be blocking my sensors. I am getting close to the signal. I know it's in here but I have a really bad feeling about this."

"I feel the same," Meilin replied.

"How many hours did the assassin say we would have until the explosions began?" 917 asked.

"He said a few hours," Meilin answered.

"That either means we have minutes or one more hour."

917 turned around, sensing that something was off. He spotted a row of garbage cans, trash strewn across the floor near one of them. The rest of the area appeared tidy, so the sight of carelessly discarded trash raised his suspicions. He quickly made his way to the bins and opened them with caution. Peering into the first can, he found nothing unusual. The second yielded the same result. When he opened the third can, he discovered something beneath the trash. Carefully, 917 reached in and touched a large, square object.

"Someone would have definitely had to scatter this mess in order to hide a..."

917 gently pulled out a small and heavy box and laid it gingerly on the floor. One wrong move and it could go off prematurely.

"...bomb," he finished. "Really nasty looking device."

The moment he pulled it out of the garbage can, his sensor immediately locked onto the device again. Was it the garbage can or something in the room? Something had prevented him from detecting the bomb, but he had too much on his plate to focus on that now.

"Meilin, quick," 917 said. "Scan the garbage can! And see if this floor underwent any changes within the past year! I need to dismantle this thing as soon as possible. Initial observations show there is no timer indicating any form of a countdown. Not a typical explosive."

"917," she answered. "I can get you the building's records easily. But, can you scan that garbage can for me?"

917 picked up the bomb and with his right hand, began scanning it, attempting to find a way to disarm it. As he did so, he placed it on top of the garbage can with his left.

"Tactile contact confirmed," he said. "Analyzing."

"917 come in."

117's voice added to the transmission.

"This is 917," he responded as he examined the device carefully, looking for a way to deactivate it with the scanner in his right hand. When he was done with his analysis, he said, "I have found the last bomb signature on the top floor. Attempting to disarm now."

"Understood 917," 117 said. Although it was the last bomb they'd detected minutes ago, he sounded oddly frantic. "But why the delay? Did you have any problems?"

"There were some complications evacuating the building," 917 opened a compartment and glanced inside, giving Meilin a clear view. Having two pairs of eyes thanks to his live feed was quite useful. Inside, wires and switches were arranged in a chaotic jumble. "Humans do not really excel at evacuating when there is a threat until after it has happened. Nevertheless, the building is completely clear. I am concerned about how something in this room was masking my sensors which prevented me from locating the bomb. Had to search manually."

"Does it have a timer?"

"Nope."

"Then we are at least on the same track," 117 sighed. "Only a fraction of the explosives that were big enough had a countdown, but we have no way of identifying whether the smaller ones will detonate simultaneously or at random times."

The device in 917's hands emitted a sharp beep, accompanied by a glaring red light. The sound quickly escalated, and the beeping intensified, growing faster and increasingly loud.

"917?" 117's concerned voice sounded through 917's head. "Respond, is everything ok? What is your status?"

"I am afraid my answer will not be met with approval," 917 said angrily. "Objective failed."

917 leapt up and grabbed the garbage can. He quickly flipped it over and covered the bomb. Once that was done, he bolted as fast as he could. He heard 117's voice crying out to him in the transmission.

"917!"

Down below, 117 was straining to hear 917's voice when a sudden, loud rumble erupted nearby. He rushed to the window and looked outside. At first, everything appeared normal until debris began to fall past the window. Small flames and pieces of furniture rained down. When 117 looked up, he was shocked to see that the entire central floor of the building had been blown out. He scanned the street below for any sign of 917 but found nothing. Looking back up towards the fiery inferno, he desperately attempted to re-establish communication. Adjusting his focus, he tried to zoom in, while a series of sounds and beeps filled his head, indicating that other amborgs were listening in as well.

"917!!" 117 shouted as he punched the window, cracking on impact. "Can you hear me?!"

A voice shouted back in 117's head.

"Yes! I can hear you! Stop shouting!"

117 continued to watch the smoke billowing out of the blown floor.

"Where are you, 917?" 117 asked anxiously, lowering his voice. "Are you alright?"

"Just hanging here," 917 replied nervously. "If you look at the figure hanging from a bunch of steel beams trying to climb back up to the central floor, it's probably me!"

117 continued to focus on the blast area and scanned it with his infrared vision. It cut through the haze easily, but he was still unable to locate 917.

"Mandy? Can you spot him? What does Meilin see?"

Mandy's response was immediate.

"Meilin has his current location... and I'm pinpointing the source of his transmission," she muttered rapidly. "Confirmed! Scan and visualize these coordinates!"

Enhancing his scope, 117 zoomed in and saw that 917 was clearly alright. Despite the force of the explosion, 917 looked like he had just come out of a chimney. His clothes were mostly intact but badly scorched, and he appeared as though he was about to fall at any moment.

"I have multiple burns and damage all over," 917 reported. "Easily fixed but I need help getting back to the ground first."

"Climb back onto the floor, 917!" 117 instructed.

He could see 917 attempting to reach for a better grip.

"Easier... said... than done!" 917 replied.

"What's wrong?" 117 transmitted.

"High winds! Unstable beam!" he communicated back. "The instant I move, this beam will fall and down I go with it! That might be the only alternative I got! A date with gravity! See if you can get someone nearby to catch me!"

"How are we supposed to do that?"

"Oh, figure something out!" 917 said desperately. "We can do things that we were not originally built to do! I would really like to avoid face planting and burying myself in the road!"

117 looked up as the other amborgs, listening to the transmission, began to murmur amongst themselves. Their immediate responses flooded his mind, forcing him to mute them in order to think clearly. It was like a whole gossip ring had formed, with everyone pitching in ideas on what to do. Some proposed leaving him there until another amborg could come to his aid, while others suggested forming a human net as a last-ditch effort. Ideas spread like wildfire in their minds, or in this case, terabytes. 117's eyes remained fixed on 917, who released one hand to reach for the ledge. But as he extended his hand, he immediately pulled it back, gripping the beam again as it slowly began to lower.

"Oh boy," 917 muttered in 117's head. "If anyone is close by, I would appreciate it if you guys would get ready to catch me... now!"

117 looked up and flinched in horror. The beam finally gave way and 917 began to plummet to the ground. In a panic, 117 tried to shatter the window again, but it only cracked further.

"Hurricane proof glass?" 117 analyzed the fractured surface as he grasped a nearby chair. "Who installed this material in the middle of Texas?"

117 threw the chair at the glass and it shattered. As he smashed through the window, he leapt down onto the roof of the building next door. He was in no position to mount a proper rescue. 917 had seconds and he knew he wouldn't be able to reach him with gravity speeding up his fall.

"If he gets stuck in the ground, we lose time getting 917 out," 117 muttered, "and if we leave 917 behind, we lose one amborg. If we lose amborgs at each location, we will not be able to finish this operation. This is only the first hurdle."

"All amborgs standby," 1 suddenly responded. "I have him!"

117 paused and looked up. He watched a figure fly out and collide with 917 mid-fall. The two amborgs altered their course and slammed into the side of the building. They both tried to latch onto the structure, but there was nothing to hold onto. Luckily, this move did help reduce their speed as they descended toward the concrete below. They bounced off the wall and landed on the pavement with a thud.

117 could see where they landed and noticed the two amborgs having difficulty getting back on their feet. Relieved that they hadn't gotten embedded in the ground, he leaped out the window and onto the street, somersaulting before rushing over to them. By the time he reached them, 1 was pulling himself up while helping 917 to stand just as a few other amborgs converged on their location.

"I am in your debt 1," 917 acknowledged while he tested his head rotation and tilted to the left. "I would have very much hated to be memorialized here."

The other amborgs who'd rushed over visibly relaxed when they noticed that 917 was safe. As they gathered, explosions echoed in the distance, drawing their attention.

"We didn't get them all?!" 1 exclaimed in shock.

"Their signatures must have been camouflaged just like the one up there!" 917 said. "Our satellite tracking must not be powerful enough!"

"At this rate," 117 said with concern, "more people will be caught unexpectedly. We will need to expand our search parameters and move quickly!"

"All amborgs to the rally point," 1 said. "Return to the drop pods for an emergency briefing!"

"We will have to make it quick," 117 said. More explosions rang out in the distance. "Mandy, contact all the bomb squads and national guard squads! Warn them that there are bombs that are undetectable by our best scanners!"

"Right 117," Mandy replied.

917 also spoke up.

"Perhaps it would also be best to advise the military not to send civilians down designated evacuation routes. They need to patrol and sweep the areas where civilians would normally gather during an attack or terrorist situation. If the assassin is aware of city emergency procedures, then the designated safe zone locations might not be safe."

Good point 917," 117 nodded. "But that may cause even more problems."

"Have military commanders change fixed safe zone points," 1 said. "Each commanding officer of the region's battle group should have extensive knowledge of the territory surrounding or on their bases. Civilians will most likely have to be flown out or escorted from the cities to military installations if the urban areas are declared unsafe. Their security is going to have a field day..."

"But it's all we can do," 117 replied. "We have the best technology and we cannot even find a small percentage of the explosives. If the military rejects this strategy, then millions of people will still be in grave danger. The whole country could be a deadly minefield."

"Talk about playing on legendary difficulty," 917 muttered.

Minutes later, the amborgs returned to their drop pods. The sounds of explosions had faded and it appeared that Houston was safe. 117, electronic map in hand, stood in the center of the massive circle of cybernetic teens.

"Alright, we have managed to complete part of the compilation of riddles," he said. "The military forces at Lackland Air Force Base have secured the area and the rest of the state seems to be reporting minimal casualties. The air base is also ready to assist us so we have air support now. Fortunately, we were successful in disrupting a majority of the explosives. Now, we must focus on assisting the location in the second riddle and leave the area and hope it stays defended. And if we correctly assume there is a schedule, we need to move quickly, otherwise the rest of the cities will fall."

"Maybe the main ones," 3 inquired. "But what about the small towns and surrounding regions? We cannot abandon those people living in the rural or suburban areas. Their priorities rank equal to those that live in the bigger cities."

"The fact is 3," 6 spoke up, "we don't have the resources or sufficient manpower for those regions."

"I have an idea," 297 eagerly raised his hand. "We can request for the military to divert Special Forces squads to defend the smaller towns. They can be sent to help local law enforcement if trouble is too much for them. The chances of combat in the small towns and neighborhoods will probably be slim."

"But what happens when we pull the Special Forces away from the regular battalions?" 92 asked. "We will be running into the major cities with recruits straight out of boot camp!"

"For one thing, that should give them the drive they need to fight and defend their home country," 1 responded, motioning for 92 to take it down a notch. "Calm down 92. The last thing we need to be doing is arguing amongst ourselves. 297, keep going."

"If combat spreads to the small towns," 297 explained, "they can take care of the situation. They are the best of the best. Elite soldiers. They're trained in small teams to be cut off from support for long durations of time. As for the regular military and reserve forces in the larger cities, they will have to make do. Whatever city we end up in will have the benefits of our leadership and assistance. But if there is one thing the military is capable of, it is uniformity under pressure. Regardless if you are specially trained or a fresh conscript."

"He's right!" 5 spoke up, walking forward.

The military can handle themselves," he stated, looking at 297 and nodding in agreement. "They may not exactly train for a world war scenario in their own home country but that is the advantage we have. If we think of it in football terms, we have the home team advantage."

"For how long though I wonder," 117 said with concern. "I don't think the military thought of dealing with an army of giant robots across the entire country. If the assassin was telling the truth and they're all now following his orders to create chaos, then we have every single criminal gang participating in rampages as well."

"They'll have to make do," 57 stated. "The police and military will have to hold the line as best as they can."

"Anyway," 117 continued as he highlighted a few bright orange dots on the map. Their location lit up green. "This is an update of the explosions we just heard. After the bomb that 917 discovered detonated, there have been many reports from law enforcement and military forces across the country. I think it's safe to say that it has begun."

A few of the amborgs' smiles faded, and everyone shifted nervously but kept their attention focused on him. 117 looked to each of them grimly.

As he spoke to them, Mandy quickly gave him a heads up.

"We're getting hundreds of distress calls," she said to 117. "The emergency calls that the police and military can't handle are being directed to A.I. Industries' control center! There's too many to get through!"

117 glanced at the group, all receiving the same news.

"Ok! Local law enforcement and regular military forces are getting hit everywhere," 117 said. "Local crime and multiple gangs are attacking and swiftly attempting to eliminate our foothold in our own territory. Many people have evacuated but we are receiving incoming casualties."

"So it really is an all-out war?" 501 asked anxiously.

"An insurgence would probably be the better word," he replied. "What matters now is the next location. Everyone set your coordinates for Seattle."

"Why there I wonder?" 1 asked as he played the riddle again on his own personal channel. "I have no doubts about the answer being right but it feels too remote."

"Maybe it is a challenge to test our endurance," 297 pondered thoughtfully. "Normally when we deploy into the field, it is just to one place only. If I might infer an assumption, we will possibly be circumnavigating across the entire United States."

297 lifted a finger and pointed at the map. First, he highlighted their location and zoomed the map out so it showed the entire country. A bright light lit up in Houston, Texas, highlighting several tiny red dots. Several other red lights began to pop up across the whole map.

"By sending us here, from our successful deduction of the first riddle," he said, "we have just passed the challenge of speed... barely. Evacuating a large city is exceptionally difficult, even under at least a couple of hours. 917's explosion demonstrated that this challenge has risks. This person wants us to potentially fail."

"If he has developed the means to camouflage his weapons," 917 replied, "it only proves we are at a disadvantage."

"Well, then we just need to play by his rules," 3 said as she took control of the map and swiped to the right, zooming in on Seattle. As they spoke, more red dots began to blink. "Seems like he wants to send us all over the place in order to see if we can fill the proper constraints. We should not forget that the assassin mentioned that there will be additional challenges for us at each location. How come there is no such challenge here? Unless we stumbled into a trap."

"It's probably just a preview," 5 said. "Paving the way towards opening night. The big question is, do we separate ourselves to all the other cities being attacked or do we concentrate on Seattle? He is forcing us to choose between saving a city full of people or spreading out across the country to save all of them. And... I am counting how many of us there are right now. There hilariously isn't enough of us if we do split up."

117 zoomed the map back out and looked at all the red dots on the major populated cities. 5 was correct. The situation could possibly be better if each amborg separated and went to each of the dots on the map. However, they had only eighty nine of them and there were over hundreds of dots signaling calls for help. Plus, they had to assume that there were giant behemoth bots roaming around. Splitting up meant each amborg

would have to fight the big robots alone. Thinking quickly, 117 made his decision.

"To your pods!" he ordered. "All of us will fly to Seattle. Notify the Washington National Guard that we're inbound! We will provide a full defense of the city simultaneously, looking for anything that may be a hidden challenge. And also, we will regrettably have to send word to any forces across the nation that an immediate amborg response is not possible."

Everyone acknowledged his orders and scrambled to their pods. A few of them took off immediately, disappearing into the distance. 117 climbed into his pod and shut the door. Mandy appeared on the screen, looking really exhausted. 117 pushed a button, activating the thrusters, and his pod roared to life.

"David?" Mandy spoke to him.

"What's wrong?" he asked.

"It doesn't look good David," she replied. "After the Battle of New York, the military and police forces pulled every reserve member they had to active duty. But even with all of that mobilization, we are amazingly outnumbered. High levels of violence and damage are surfacing everywhere and it's flooding all the networks. It's total chaos."

"And in the midst of the crisis," 117 replied, "this man remains hidden as the country falls apart."

"Pretty much the Dark Ages gone violent," Mandy added. "There's too many calls for help. Everyone's asking for amborg support. We had to get the A.I.s to help us sift through all the chatter but Dr. Kendrick is thinking about shutting off our communications network from the public."

"I don't think he should do that," 117 said. "If he does that, people will be left to fend for themselves, thinking that we abandoned them."

"I know," Mandy said grimly. "Dr. Kendrick is just thinking about all available options."

"What about the explosives we encountered?"

"Based on the analysis of the ones you were able to disarm," Mandy replied, "they have a very basic design and it is quite simple. However, the way they are cloaked from sensors makes it difficult. The ones that have detonated are all in random areas and there is little to help us theorize where they are all hidden. We're trying our best to see if there are any common patterns to the layout."

"We also have to assume the rules are not set as well," 117 inferred. "He gave us three riddles. Three locations. But who knows what else we may miss. He could be misleading us along the way."

"Don't say that," she warned over the system. "If you let him get in your head or to any of the others, you will play right into his hands. It's what he wants to see and show to the public. The failure of the amborgs. I wonder... but that might be his goal. He wants to be able to prove to the world that amborgs can't save everyone. He wants to shatter everyone's belief in you. Don't make yourself vulnerable."

"I will try," 117 sighed. "Stand by Mandy. We are approaching Seattle airspace."

An idea suddenly occurred to him. They would have to do it sooner or later, so he figured now would be a good time to change their way of thinking.

"This is 117 to all amborgs," he said. "Do not land in one landing zone together in the same spot. We are now going to initiate team protocols. Pick your landing zones and deploy all across the city."

As everyone acknowledged the change in protocol, 117 felt vibrations rattle his pod, prompting him to check his map. According to that and the rumbling from outside, it appeared he'd arrived at his destination quicker than expected. He was thankful for the speeds the deployment pods could reach. Suddenly, with a loud crash and a thud, the pod landed on the ground. When all became quiet, 117 released his straps. At the same time, the door flew open and he quickly climbed out. The moment he set foot outside, gunfire and cries rang out around him. Bullets whizzed past as 117 looked around, noticing flames consuming parts of the city. He pressed forward, searching for a proper vantage point.

"Oh no!" Mandy exclaimed.

They had arrived late. The battle had already begun and the city was under siege. 117 had looked over into the urban district of Seattle and was briefly scanning the surrounding area when he received a communication.

"117, this is 18. Do you read me?"

117 lifted his hand up to his head and responded.

"Yes, 18? I hear you."

"The twins and I have found something," 18 replied. "We picked a landing zone near some heavy enemy activity and we stumbled upon something we think might be important. Well... 92 stumbled actually. His pod was hit by anti-air fire and it deflected his landing pattern into a warehouse. From what he says, it looks like he fell into what might be considered the enemy command center here in Seattle."

"Understood," 117 nodded. "I am proceeding to your destination. Cover that area in a two block radius with the twins and I will notify 501 and 466 to watch the perimeter."

Before he could finish, a police car exploded to his right. An unarmed officer was grappling with two gangsters in a desperate hand-to-hand fight. As 117 rushed forward to help, another amborg intervened, separating the gangsters from the officer. The officer thanked the amborg and hurried to help a little boy who'd taken refuge behind a dumpster.

That's one more we rescued, he thought, *millions more to go.*

"Amborg 117 to all amborgs," he transmitted. "Begin search and rescue operations and assist local law enforcement in this area. Everyone move towards 18's position. I want five volunteers to return to their pods and circle the skies and maintain full readiness to fly to the next locations, but only on my order. Acknowledge."

Eighty eight short beeps sounded off in his head. Although the high-pitched sounds were somewhat painful, he couldn't help but smile in appreciation, glad to hear each one of them acknowledging his commands as he sprinted faster.

Downtown Los Angeles

On the streets, at roughly the same time, the uprising had begun with widespread reports of excessive casualties. Requests for amborg deployments were either ignored or postponed indefinitely, rendering them unavailable for reasons unknown.

"Hey, tell my brother that he'll be fine."

"Don't talk Lewis."

Lewis coughed as he lay on the asphalt. Harrison sat beside him, exhausted and covered in grime. Blood seeped from Lewis's stomach, but Harrison had quickly applied a makeshift bandage, pressing down on the injury. Both were equipped in full police combat gear, but they had been overpowered immediately after receiving news about a large-scale attack reported by the military. One moment, they were stationed at a checkpoint; the next, they found themselves under heavy fire. Harrison managed to drag Lewis away from the chaos, and they took shelter near a cluster of abandoned vehicles.

"I don't think I'll make it through this one," Lewis stared at Harrison and coughed again.

His eyelids began to droop as Harrison looked back at his partner with disgust.

"Don't say that touchy feely bullshit kid," he spat out as he wiped the sweat from his forehead. "You're going to make it and you're going to go home in one piece. You are not pulling this on me. I don't even think you're dying."

"No good buddy, I feel sleepy."

"Hey, we're partners..." Harrison grasped Lewis' hand tightly. "If you're going to die. It's going be me that'll kill you, you ungrateful little... kid."

Without warning, Lewis shut his eyes and went limp. Harrison stopped mid-sentence, mouth agape in shock. The chaos around them—the screams, gunfire, and blasts—faded into silence. At a loss for words, all he could do was stare at the lifeless form before him. Suddenly, the sound of footsteps attracted his attention. The lone officer looked up into the merciless eyes of a gangster with a toothy, mischievous grin.

"Do you fear death, cop?" he said mockingly as he pointed a gun directly at Harrison's face. "Want to join your friend?"

On the brink of tears, Harrison gritted his teeth. He held back his feelings and stared determinedly at the bandit standing above him.

"You can't intimidate me. I've always been prepared to die," he spat, seething with fury as a teardrop escaped from one eye. "Stop mocking me and do it you cheap coward."

The gang member seemed amused.

"Well now, you got some balls. I think..."

A loud bang interrupted the man, and Harrison ducked his head forward. He looked up again and saw his assailant lying flat on his chest. His back was riddled with holes from a shotgun. A very powerful one, too. Harrison noticed Captain Bradley standing a few feet behind.

"No one takes cheap shots at my officers. Not on my watch," she snarled. "Especially when they're down."

"Captain Bradley," Harrison said quietly. He felt relieved but at the same time, reverted back to his state of grief as he turned his attention back to Lewis. "He got hit when the fighting started. We were falling back to another defensive position, but he got hit."

Bradley walked over and examined Lewis. She laid her gun down and took a deep breath.

"LEWIS!" she suddenly bellowed. Her sudden outburst caused Harrison to jump and his tears to stop flowing. "IF YOU DON'T GET UP THIS INSTANT AND DEFEND THIS CITY WITH THE REST OF MY OFFICERS, I WILL PERSONALLY CRAWL THROUGH THE DEPTHS OF HELL AND KILL YOU MYSELF FOR LEAVING US TO DEAL WITH THIS!!"

Harrison stared at the captain in shock, then down at Lewis' limp body. Nothing happened. Captain Bradley sighed in frustration, inhaled, and yelled again.

"SO WAKE UP ALREADY!"

Lewis bolted upright with a yelp. Harrison's eyes widened in shock as his wounded partner's hand immediately shot to his abdomen.

"Agh," Lewis groaned as he clenched his stomach. "Why does it feel like someone rear-ended me?"

"What the..." Harrison gasped. "It's a... miracle?"

Bradley scoffed with mere satisfaction as Lewis looked around dazedly. He looked up at Harrison in apprehension.

"Harrison..." he said shakily. "I had the worst nightmare! I was in a bright place, there was a light and then an angel appeared. When I saw her face, it was... the captain! Bradley! The angel punched me and sent me falling back to earth... What does it mean?"

Lewis turned his head, hope filling his eyes, but then saw Bradly. He went pale and flinched. He attempted to crawl away in fear but Harrison kept him still.

"It wasn't a dream," Bradley muttered under her breath. "It means you better cut the crap and get your gun out."

Lewis stared at Harrison.

"It wasn't a dream?" he asked.

"No. I'm just glad you haven't gone yet."

Rolling her eyes, Captain Bradley grabbed her shotgun and clambered back to her feet.

"Angel my boot," she grumbled as she marched down the street while the two of them stayed behind. "Johnson!"

Sergeant Johnson appeared at her side, flanked by a couple of officers looking around cautiously.

"I'm going to clear a path out of here," she instructed. "Let's get Lewis away from here and go help any stragglers!"

Johnson nodded as he and his two fellow officers moved to protect Harrison and Lewis.

Captain Bradley marched ahead and carefully readied her weapon.

As she neared an overturned car, she came to an abrupt stop, her ears perked up. The sounds of battle were faint, but that wasn't what caught her attention. Without hesitation, she aimed her shotgun at a window on the second floor to her right and fired.

At first, nothing happened, but seconds later, a window shattered outward and a body tumbled from the building's side. The dead Splatter-Bug landed on the flipped car before rolling onto the ground, right at Bradley's feet. She pointed the gun at the body and fired again.

"Cheap shots," she sniffed. "They never quit."

"Still as sharp and as sexy as ever."

Without turning around, Bradley stood up straighter and gripped the shotgun tightly. The voice, one she knew all too well, caused her blood to boil.

"You don't want to sneak up on me Mark," she spoke in a forced but calm voice. She pointed the barrel at the dead body. "Otherwise, you'll end up like my new friend."

She pivoted, pointing the gun right at 117's grandfather.

"You did always go through new friends really fast," he remarked as he approached with caution. Holding his hands up, he stopped when she pulled the pump-action mechanism back. He remembered the last time he had seen her and already knew what to expect. "I thought I'd drop in to see how you were."

"You sure picked a crazy time to check up on me," she said, gesturing at all the destruction around the abandoned street.

She instantly pulled the trigger right as Mark swatted the shotgun barrel to the right, away from his face. The force of the blast caused Bradley's arms to shoot up, at which point he grabbed the gun firmly.

"Before you try that again," he said as the two of them struggled to gain control over the firearm, "there is something you should know."

Bradley brought up a foot and kicked him in the ribs. Still maintaining his grip on her shotgun, he keeled forward.

"I see you're wearing your custom steel boots again," he coughed.

He straightened up and, with the help of his arm implants, he pulled Bradley toward him and kissed her right on the mouth. They'd only locked lips for a few seconds before she pushed away, taking a step back and letting go of the shotgun.

"You sure pick the weirdest times," she snapped as she wiped her mouth with the back of her hand. "Old geezer."

"You're not that far off either," Mark chuckled. "I'm only older by a few years."

"Now ain't the time!" Bradley said, holding her hand outwards. She motioned for him to give her shotgun back. "I've got a city to defend!"

A few explosions in the distance snagged her attention.

"It's never the time for us isn't it?" Mark said with a bit of a whine in his voice.

He safely gave back the shotgun, placing it in her hand gently. She then whirled around and took aim, but didn't see any targets.

"Well, let me double check real quick," she said sassily. "The city I swore to uphold and defend as its guardian is currently on fire, being bombed and overrun by people with no decency, respect or honor towards the innocent. I definitely, without a doubt, think this isn't the time!"

"Well, what a coincidence!" Mark replied as he pulled his hood over his head a few extra inches as if it had slipped back too far. "That's what I'm here to help you with."

"It's never been this bad before," Bradley said as the two of them began walking slowly down the street.

She glanced over her shoulder and saw that Johnson was leading the other officers toward them. She noticed the arrival of some additional people, recognizing them as Mark's vigilantes. They were chatting with her officers like it was a high school reunion.

"I had to bring in so many officers off reserve duty," Bradley faced front and sighed in annoyance. "Where the heck is your tin-head grandson? This is one time I'll appreciate his help."

"Last I heard? Off saving the country," Mark replied bluntly. "He sent me here specifically to help him monitor West Coast activities for the man responsible. He also divided my vigilantes to various locations to ensure we have eyes and ears everywhere. He really is starting to grow into a natural-born leader. The latest update that the military is keeping from you, which he feels obligated to share, is that someone has officially declared an all-out war against the nation."

"Well, would it kill him to send some of his buddies here? We're dying out here."

"He's in the middle of something important," Mark shook his head. "If he comes here, it risks doom upon all of us."

"What kind of mission is this?"

"A rescue of society as we know it."

Mark silently stood next to her, stroking his beard, while she contemplated the information he had just given.

"Sounds tough," she muttered.

She could only imagine what part of that was like. She was already the head of an entire police department, and then some, but most were wounded, missing, or dead.

"You know, it does make me think of..." Mark laughed. "David's behavior reminds me of you when you were on your first real assignment. You put six thugs in the hospital with your bare hands right?"

"I haven't thought about that in years but I do remember how good it felt to kick their sorry asses," Bradley remembered how young she had been and smiled softly. "I hope your grandson is as motivated as I was in my first big assignment. If the fate of this country is in his hands, then the whole world is too. No room for failure in this case."

"Absolutely right," Mark replied. "No room at all."

"Well then. In that case, would you like a head-start?" she asked as she jogged ahead. "I'm probably going to get more of them if you fall behind."

"Damn," Mark smirked as he chased after her. "What a woman."

Seattle

"It is a message written in pencil. How primitive. This guy must really hate us or has a prejudice against modern stencils. His writing style is really annoying me."

18 showed 117 the paper she held in her hands.

"It looks like a bunch of nonsense," he said. "At first glance to human eyes. Did you read it?"

"I just finished deciphering it actually."

18 held up the piece of paper and scanned it without blinking, then pointed her finger at the wall. Her finger instantly lit up like a flashlight. 117, and the rest of 18's team, all turned to where the light was projecting. Her finger converted itself into a mini-projector and displayed the words on the wall.

"I am currently running through all of the words that were written... in pencil," 18 rolled her eyes as the words on the make-shift screen began to disappear while a few of them remained highlighted on the wall. "Most of them ...are complete poetic nonsense but I managed to locate some words with hidden meaning. Feel free to clarify."

The remaining words left on the wall were highlighted for 117 to see. He slowly recited them aloud.

"The youth are a hindrance and must be dealt with...," he read. "Learning shall be destroyed...The Next Generation will die and I will make it so."

"He did not just use Star Trek as a reference!" 18 muttered angrily. She was apparently one of the few Trekkies among the amborgs. "Even Sir Patrick Stewart would probably hate this guy."

Just then, a noise sounded from above and a figure dropped from the ceiling, but none of them moved to retaliate. 19 straightened up and joined the group.

"Area is clear," she reported. "The enemy presence in Seattle has dropped to fifteen percent. Local police are securing the streets and the Washington Battle Group is ready to send us reinforcements if necessary."

"Tell them to send whatever troops they can spare south to Oregon and California," 117 replied. "Get word to Camp Pendleton to receive them. Once the fighting is finished on the West Coast, we can send them east."

"You got it, 117."

"Thanks 19," 18 said without taking her eyes off the wall.

Out of the corner of her eye, she saw 19 nod and walk a few feet away. 92 and 93 also broke out of the circle and began patrolling the interior. The warehouse was pretty empty, save for a few crates, but none of them could see any actual threats.

117 continued reading as 18 revealed more portions of the message on the wall. Several sentences had been added after the reference to Star Trek.

"Your soldiers are young and capable," she recited to 117. "Without weapons, however, they are vulnerable and waiting to be slaughtered like sheep... Keeping your pets in one location is a mistake... With minimal protection, things are bound to go wrong, especially when they won't see me coming."

117 glanced at 18, who appeared horrified. It didn't take long for the two of them to realize what the message meant.

"That monster..." she said. "All of those young, innocent children. Students. He wants to destroy the best of everything."

"Even the best school in the country," 117 said.

117 immediately sent out a transmission. The twins and 19 rejoined them, and 117 took the lead, leading them out at a brisk pace. They raced down the street, but soon began to scatter. Like a pair of monkeys, 92 and 93 scaled a building with lightning speed, disappearing from view. 19 nodded to 18 and ducked down an alley to their right.

"All amborgs return to your pods now! We have found a critical obstacle and we are diverting from the original plan!" he ordered as he and 18 ran down another intersection within seconds. "All of you already in your pods, launch and head to the following coordinates I am transmitting! Change mission priorities."

"But 117," 501 responded over the channel, "we have not been able to secure the city. I see a group of people crying for help."

"Do what you can!" 117 replied urgently. "But get to your pod and launch as soon as possible. The police and armed forces here should maintain the situation since we have cleared out a majority of the area, but we need to leave now!"

"Understood 117," 501 confirmed. "But there have been problems opening the door to my pod. It has not been functioning properly since we left."

"Try kicking it," 117 leapt over an overturned car and 18 followed suit. "We need to rally now."

"Thanks," 501 said cheerfully. "It worked."

"18," 117 turned to look at her. "Ready a full tactical defensive plan. We are dropping directly into a potential combat zone."

"After today?" 18 shrugged as they stopped at a traffic signal. "One more drop into the flames doesn't seem so intimidating."

"Good luck 18," 117 nodded to her.

"Same to you 117," she said as she sprinted in the opposite direction, disconnecting the link.

"This is 117," he jumped over a hedge and headed back towards the spot where he parked his pod. "I am transmitting the full message left by the assassin and the new target he has included to our list of priorities. Mandy?"

"I got it David," Mandy spoke through the comm channel. "Transmitting recordings to all amborgs. They are seeing what you did now. David, is it true what his target is?"

"Yes, indeed Mandy," 117 punched through a brick wall and instantly found the area where he had landed. "It is a place where I believe you know very well."

"Tom was heading there before Texas," Mandy said. "He had the idea of initiating campus-wide evacuation and sending security forces."

"Mandy," 117 said as he slid under a truck. "Get me in touch with Palmer. Whether or not he is authorized, he needs to warn the commanding officers and the regular staff."

"Copy that David," Mandy replied. "I'm getting him for you now and trying to send a communique, priority one. Attack on The Academy imminent. We need to send as many troops as we can."

"Negative Mandy," 117 replied. "There will be panic if we send troops in. Even if it is not a possibility, we may end up leading our army into an ambush. We need to defend the entrances to the grounds and save as many people as we can. Tell Palmer to try and get the school's staff on alert. We need as many ships in the air to get the student population out. The Academy is not as large as a city so the amborgs can equally disperse into the area."

"Got it David," Mandy panted as he heard her typing rapidly in the back of his head. "But based on how bad it is, the casualty estimate isn't good."

"Don't worry about the estimates," 117 said as he reached his pod. "Divert all our satellite capabilities to the Academy. Is there any enemy activity?"

"None," Mandy replied. "But they could be hiding their signatures."

"Then we need to hurry," 117 said. "We only have a few hours if I had to make my best guess."

CHAPTER 19

Humanity's Future

The Academy
Location: East of Miles City, Montana. West of Bismarck, North Dakota. North of Rapid City, South Dakota. South of Canada.
Four Hours Prior to Texas & Seattle Bombings

"Hey Audrey!"

College sophomore Audrey Wright turned around at the sound of her older brother Thomas' excited tone. She was on her way back to her dorm room from a simulation exercise but for her brother, she definitely wasn't going to get away. He waved a tablet at her.

"Did you see the results of your simulation?" he said, looking at her wide eyed with a big grin on his face. "You knocked it out of the park."

Audrey sighed.

"Of course," she replied. "Why are you making this such a big deal?"

"Why, she says," Thomas smiled and teased her. "You got a perfect score! That's higher than mine when I was a sophomore!"

"It's not a big deal," she shrugged. "You could have done it just like me."

"Nah," Thomas said. "My brain isn't wired for your kind of multi-tasking. You do know that the officers stationed here will want to see you about this right?"

"I've already seen so many officers now that I don't want to even think about it," she said grimly.

"Hey."

Thomas grabbed Audrey by the arm as she turned to leave, holding her back. She shook out of her brother's grasp, not meeting his gaze. He walked around and stood in front of her.

"I was only trying to tell you that you're doing a great job," Thomas said as the smile faded from his face. "It's good to see you back at it again. That you're moving on fairly well and I'm glad you're putting your skills to work."

"I only did the exercise because if I didn't step in to take charge, we would have failed," Audrey stated.

"No," Thomas replied. "You did it because you felt the urge to be a leader. You spent a lot of time pretending like you lost your ambition and was just letting everything pass by, hoping that your pain would go away.

In reality, I think you stepped up when you saw your squads in trouble because deep down, you still have that fire."

"I didn't do anything special," Audrey protested.

"No, you acted like mom and dad," Thomas pointed at her confidently.

"I don't want anyone seeing me like mom and dad," Audrey replied. "Before, everyone kept coming up to me, looking like they wanted to talk to me, but they didn't know what to say. Now they won't stop with the compliments."

"Well, of course!" Thomas suggested. "It's because they're all seeing what you did as a positive sign."

"I don't want to talk to anyone," Audrey replied. "Now everything everyone is saying to me is bothering me. I don't care about my education at the moment."

"What do you want?" Thomas asked, shrugging his shoulders. "I seriously doubt you want to be held back a year. Considering your grades are the best in your class."

Audrey rounded on him.

"I want out of here. I want to be left alone! I'm only a good student because it'll help me leave here faster!" she snapped. "I'll be stuck here getting so much unwanted attention if I decided to go a different direction. I just know that now, I don't want anyone to talk to me. I want time to myself."

"I don't think that made sense," Thomas mumbled.

"Maybe this will make sense. Listen carefully, big bro... shut up!"

Thomas backed away and nodded sympathetically. The atmosphere grew quiet as other students in the hall stopped to stare. Thomas turned to them.

"You mind?" he asked loudly.

The crowd dispersed, everyone quickly returning to their activities. Thomas looked at his sister, then down at the tablet in his hands.

"You're in the biggest school in the country," Thomas sighed. "You want to be left alone? You realize... that might be difficult considering our lineage."

Seeing that he wasn't having an effect on her, Thomas gave her a warm smile and held up his arms, as if surrendering. He retreated and began to walk away.

"Alright," he conceded. "I'll let it go this time. I just thought... I was just... really excited to see that you actually went above and beyond. It just felt like I had my smart baby sister again. Mom and dad would be proud of you."

"Why am I the big deal here?" Audrey asked. "They're proud of you too."

"You have a…"

"…perfect score," they said simultaneously, contradicting each other's tones, one proud and the other sarcastic.

"…I know," Audrey grumbled.

"See you around," Thomas said in a kind and gracious manner. "I'll let you be alone."

"Thomas…"

He stopped walking and turned to look back at her.

"I'm sorry I told you to shut up," she mumbled. "It's just that… everything hurts and nothing anyone has been telling me has been helping."

"I know what you mean," Thomas said as he kept walking. "But let's face it Audrey. It's been seven months already and we gotta keep going. Your test results only prove to me that you still have the motivation to finish what you started. I want to see you happy again."

Audrey watched as his back receded down the hall until he disappeared around a corner. Once he was out of sight, she made her way back to her room. She slipped off her shoes and walked to her desk. Sitting down at her computer, she waved her hand across the screen to turn it on. As it powered up, she noticed a portrait of her parents next to the console. In the photo, her parents were both proudly wearing their military uniforms. The more she stared at it, the more she contemplated what Thomas had said.

"It's hard moving on," Audrey muttered as she grabbed the picture. "I mean, school is fine but… with you both gone, it feels pointless and it feels… weird. You know? Living up to your legacy? Everyone trying to talk with me just makes it feel awkward and sad. When I was a kid, I thought this would make me happy. But right now, I'm not sure this is what I want to do anymore… Mom? Dad? What should I do?"

"Is there a problem, Cadet Wright? Perhaps a phone call home will help instead of talking to an inanimate photo."

Her computer, now fully activated, lit up and was speaking on its own. Unfazed, she smiled.

"Hi Carter," she replied happily. "My bestie!"

Her computer flashed its lights and revealed a blank screen with a yellow line across the center. The lines pulsed and created waves as her computer began to speak.

"Talking to ourselves," the electronic voice named Carter spoke. "Is that the new social norm these days?"

"It's an old social norm which people have always done for centuries," Audrey replied as she pulled a notebook from a drawer and began flipping through the pages. "Especially when people are troubled, which I don't really know how to describe. How are you today?"

Carter flashed his screen and it changed to a bright blue.

"Oh, the usual," he said in a casual drone. "Daily weather is fine, the dust in your room is minimal, and my hard-drive is starting to brighten up with all of my software decorations. But I really want to go for a stroll."

"You don't go for a stroll Carter," Audrey explained as she found a blank page, grabbed a pen and began to write. "You leap through other systems and zoom through the academy's data signal. Need I remind you what you're capable of when I'm not here to keep an eye on you?"

She paused, thought for a bit, then went back to scribbling. As she did so, she looked at the screen sternly.

"The last time you did that," she picked up her pen and waved it warningly at the screen, "you shorted out building A's computer system. So until I figure out why they get fried every time you visit, you're staying here with me while I keep running diagnostics."

"For the record and in my own defense, if the school committee will even listen to a lowly A.I.," Carter replied smugly, "they'd find that the computer servers in building A are very faulty and were already undergoing difficulties anyway when I happened to pass by."

"Yes, but the month before that incident, your other trip to the Dean's office slowed their performance down by sixty percent. Generated a lot of rage-inducing lag. That added to the problem a month later. You're lucky that you were dad's A.I. and the Academy has a lot of respect for him and his equipment."

She knew she had hit a nerve because the screen suddenly flashed a bright red. Carter definitely had a very good knack of associating colors to whatever he was feeling. Unfortunately, it was even more difficult to get a read on him since he was not built like the modern A.I.s who had actual holographic bodies and facial expressions. He was an older model so he didn't have a sophisticated body like the newest computer programs.

"They can't prove that!" Carter spoke indignantly as the red line in the center of the screen bounced erratically. "I only stopped by to make sure your email made it safely to the correct departments without hitting a firewall."

Aubrey chuckled and shook her finger at the screen. The screen suddenly went still as Carter fell silent.

"Uh-uh," Audrey said teasingly. "Actually, they did prove it. All they had to do was scan the interior system of the damaged components and they found residual computations left by a foreign A.I. of your specifications. Specifications built by my father. The only reason I haven't faced suspension was thanks to my parents' status."

Carter shut up and flashed a greenish color. Audrey wasn't sure whether it was lime or neon green.

"Well it's hard to camouflage myself when I visit," he muttered electronically through the speaker. Audrey rolled her eyes as he continued. "Your dad designed me to be different from the other computers. He tried to upgrade an outdated model A.I. The end result was me. A very corrupt and badly enhanced A.I. that's clumsy and damages systems."

"No," Audrey said as she finished her journal entry. "Dad designed you to be different because he felt your model was more reliable. As a computer expert for the military, he knew your specs back and forth and decided to make you one of a kind. He believed that you could do great things when he gave you to me as a birthday gift. Every time I asked about you, my dad would always praise you and say what great progress you were making whenever he taught you how to socialize like a living person. So, be grateful for how you are now. Forget about the damage you've done so far up to now, that is."

"I just don't understand why I should be confined when I was originally designed to adapt to the world around me. I admit, it has been a wonderful three years since I was put under your care but it's really disappointing," Carter said flatly. "I mean, my time could be spent better than monitoring your computer. Speaking of which, when will you finish the final designs for my visual representation? Am I getting a body on schedule or am I still waitlisted?"

Audrey closed her notebook and put it away. She had just begun work on creating a visual representation for Carter last week but there had been some slight complications.

"I'll finish it when I can Carter," Audrey nodded at the screen. "Why are you in such a hurry to get your own body? It's not even a body for that matter, it's just a hologram. You want to fit in with the modern A.I.s that badly?"

"I just thought that working on it would allow you more distraction from..."

"I know Carter," she interrupted. "I've just... it hasn't really been motivating for me recently."

"I understand. Pardon me for almost bringing it up," Carter said as he flashed a light shade of pale blue. "I just figured you might be bored speaking to a squiggly line on a computer all day."

"Well unfortunately," she said patting the top of the screen with her hand, "I can't finish it until I get approval from the lab. It's really hard to find equipment for your model since there aren't that many of your type in service. You were custom retro-fit so it has to be just right otherwise you might go from a tall blond to a short dimply red head. If I did have it though, I could finish it in no time and you could design yourself however you like. The other option is to keep waiting patiently for my request from A.I. Industries for the equipment to go through, but they keep to themselves a lot when it comes to sharing information. I hear that the female A.I.s are very attractive and they always love meeting new guys. I mean... foreign computer programs of a specific nature."

"I have already told you Miss Wright," Carter said tersely, flashing orange,"I will only give the A.I.s at A.I. Industries a reason to hate the old generation line of technology. They wouldn't like my presence because it'd crap all over their image. Besides, why should I work there when I serve no one but you and your immediate family members and friends?"

"Aww. No one appreciates that bit of sentiment more than me," Audrey chuckled. "You'll always be the sweetest A.I. I know. Unless... someone invented a better version of you. Then I wouldn't mind tossing you in the garbage."

"I know that was a joke but if it weren't for the confines of this monitor, I'd throw something at you."

"Looks like you'll just have to talk me to death," Audrey said, smiling mischievously at the screen. "Learn to take jokes like a program."

Their discussion was cut short by a loud beeping noise overhead. A voice came through the P.A. system in her room.

"Sophomore Audrey Wright," one of the secretaries announced. "Please report to the Military Administration and Tactical Science Offices. Someone will be there to see you shortly."

Audrey sighed, stood up, and adjusted her uniform so it was straight and presentable. As she shut down the computer and organized her things, she bid a quick farewell to Carter.

"Oh boy," she sighed as she grabbed her shoes and slipped them on. "I wonder what happened now... Hence why I am summoned to face the legends of old and will be persuaded again to take part in the campaign of upholding my heritage."

"Pure poetry ma'am," Carter blinked a few times as his screen powered down. "Would you like me to take notes and record your wise words of dissent against the chain of command? It would be a great rallying cry to the rebels of this country."

"Stamp date and time. The usual please," she said sarcastically and walked out of the room.

"Your sarcasm is noted Miss Wright," Carter replied as the door shut. "I'll be here. Stuck in the same place..."

"Of course Carter," Audrey winked at the screen before closing the door. "Where else are you going to go?"

The campus was bustling with activity when Audrey took the elevator down to the ground floor. As she stepped outside, she heard many of her friends greeting her. Briefly saying a fast hello and goodbye, she made her way across campus. However, Audrey couldn't help but feel that something was wrong.

To get to her destination, she had to walk by one of the security entrances, but the guards stationed there weren't as friendly as they were before. Or rather, that's what she thought. Instead of the usual greeting, one of the guards nodded and motioned for her to move quickly. She failed to hear the order that followed from his radio set, since she was already out of earshot. What little she caught of it, though, sounded like something that had never been uttered on the grounds before. As she continued on, she also failed to notice a group of transports approaching the entrance.

She also noticed how clear the sky was, which struck her as unusual. Normally, there were birds constantly flying overhead, the air filled with their singsong chirps, but today, there was nothing but silence. The sudden roar of an engine startled her, making her look up. A large aircraft was passing by, and she tracked it with her eyes. A handful of other students nearby also glanced up, though they didn't pay it much mind. Just before the aircraft disappeared from view, she caught a glimpse of the logo on the underside.

"A transport craft at this time of day?" she wondered.

Those were the transports that normally shipped troops across certain distances. Though they couldn't match the deployment pods from A.I. Industries, they could still get the job done.

"New students probably," she muttered and kept going.

She had never been more wrong though. As she approached the building, she stopped and took one last glance at the courtyard, where something strange caught her eye. Four soldiers rounded the corner, marching briskly toward the center. A uniformed officer and another individual emerged from behind a pillar to greet them. It was one of the commanders along with one of her instructors. She watched as her logistics professor pointed in a direction behind the soldiers and then to the left. They all nodded in agreement before splitting up to take their positions in various areas of the courtyard. Audrey wasn't alone in her confusion; many other students noticed the soldiers with bewildered expressions but carried on with their business. If she had only been a few minutes slower, she thought, she might have had the chance to ask what was happening. However, remembering her appointment, she hurried off to her destination.

When she arrived, she entered the doors without any problems. Minutes later, she was waiting in the lobby of the Military Administration building, seated on a chair.

"Sophomore Audrey Wright."

Audrey quickly stood up when her name was called, straightened her back, and placed her hands at her side. One of the secretaries approached, acknowledged her, and led her down a hallway. Something caught her eye, and she looked to the right, spotting a man she hadn't seen in these offices before. She made out the name, *Palmer T,* on the man's uniform. It was probably a new military instructor, Audrey guessed, as she was directed into another room.

She opened the door, poked her head in, and announced herself before shutting the door.

"Come on over. I'm just looking over a couple of things."

Audrey quietly obeyed and approached the desk. Noticing the woman behind the desk, she straightened her posture, brought her right arm up and saluted. The officer returned her salute and motioned for her to take a seat. Audrey took a seat in a chair in front of the desk.

"You were summoned here because the school board has recommended you for a commendation. You performed excellently in the military exercise earlier today, Cadet," the officer read a file and looked up at her. Audrey nodded quietly. The officer adjusted her glasses and read on, "A perfect score in your recent combat exercise. We haven't seen that in over fourteen years. Your class grades... all perfect, medical tests all green despite what happened months ago...what else?"

Audrey smiled, nodded again, and waited for the question she knew he was about to ask. The officer closed the file and smiled back.

"Well Miss Wright, it would appear that everything in your file says that you qualify and can pursue whatever job you want in the military or as a civilian in a high level government position," she said. "However, that is partially why I called you here."

"Yes ma'am," she said calmly. She was beginning to understand where this was going. "I assumed that that would be the case."

"You definitely are a model student," the officer said. "The first thing we'd like to ask you is..."

"Ahem!"

Audrey and the officer looked up at the sound of another voice, noticing that someone else had entered the room.

"I'll take it from here captain."

When the two of them recognized who had walked in, both sprang from their seats and saluted. A more decorated officer, with several stripes and stars on her uniform, approached them.

"At ease, you two," she chuckled as she saluted them. Audrey and the desk officer lowered their arms and switched to a parade rest. "Captain, I'd like to speak to cadet Wright alone please. May I borrow your room for a minute?"

She nodded, uttered a quick 'yes ma'am' and immediately walked out. Audrey almost felt the urge to sigh in relief. She was looking at one of the most decorated officers in the military. Her mother had worked alongside this woman for a long time.

"Were you the one that wanted to see me, colonel?" she asked.

The colonel was named Christina Sanchez. She took a seat and perused Audrey's file. When she was done, she looked up and smiled.

"Yes Audrey," she answered, nodding. "I take it your file was already read back to you. Notice any surprises or concerns?"

Audrey began to shake her head, but the colonel's stern look made her reconsider, and she nodded hesitantly. As she bit her lower lip, she glanced out the window, thinking about what to say next. Just as she was about to speak, she hesitated once more.

Colonel Sanchez noticed this sudden pause holding her back and decided to speak.

"I am referring to your sudden and surprising performance in that last combat exercise earlier," she stood from her seat and walked around to Audrey. "Your sudden maneuver surprised well... everyone. When you took command of your teams, they were stunned. I was... Well, I wasn't."

"Colonel? I don't understand," Audrey said nervously. The colonel began to chuckle and held the file to her chest.

"The reason why I wasn't surprised," she tapped Audrey's forehead playfully, similar to how Thomas praised her earlier, "...is because I know you've been paying attention in my classes. Just like your mother used to. You have excellent grades in all of your classes and that military practical exam has a lot of people on campus turning heads. It would seem that you are coping well."

"Permission to speak freely?"

"For my oldest friend's daughter? Of course," Sanchez smiled.

"You aren't going to ask me if I should enlist in the military?"

"No," colonel Sanchez sighed. "I believe too many people have pestered you about your career options enough."

She stepped around the desk and had Audrey follow her to the window.

"Every student comes here as a civilian," she explained. "You and your brother both definitely proved to many people here that you are your parent's children. With the way I've watched Thomas, it's clear he wants to pursue your father's line of work. But, he pretty much camouflaged your progress with his optimistic views for seven months. It would appear you aren't the person I saw come to this school with such a bright, gleaming expression anymore. It has come to the attention of most of my staff and the other professors here that you have lost the motivation to reach higher."

"I'm sorry, Colonel," Audrey admitted. She couldn't lie to a woman her mother trusted. "I just have a lot on my mind. I always find myself questioning myself whenever my parents are brought up. Some days I feel like I want to do more but other times I want to just stick to the corner of the room and never be noticed. They're gone now... they have been for months... and I don't know if I want to be like them."

"You're young," Sanchez replied. "Lots of others go through this phase too. I can't tell you what to do. I can only offer suggestions and recommendations. I haven't had to go through what happened with you so I'm afraid my knowledge of the subject is limiting."

"Even limited knowledge from the right people helps," Audrey replied. "I think."

"Well," Sanchez nodded as the sun shined brightly through the curtains. "I just wanted to check up on you. Had to do it in a setting where it wouldn't look like I was violating student-teacher protocol. I am in my uniform more days than I can count and being the head of the military forces on school grounds, I hardly have time to get away. I know I should have done this many more times over the last few months but..."

"With all due respect ma'am," Audrey replied. "Thank you. I'm sorry I haven't been putting more consideration towards what I wanted to do lately. I guess, you talking to me is a good reminder to keep going."

"From an academic perspective," the Colonel said, "I will say that is an acceptable answer. From a military perspective, you've got a lot of fight in you that would definitely make me swear you in right now. As your mother's friend, it's ok to not know what you want. You take as much time as you need."

"I don't suppose you know if A.I. Industries is hiring?" Audrey asked.

"I'll see if Dr. Kendrick will take my calls."

The two women suddenly broke into quiet fits of laughter.

Later, Audrey looked over the list of career choices on a tablet as she left the building. All her life, she knew that she would go to the Academy for her higher education but after a year, she realized that she didn't know what she wanted to do specifically. She wondered what her father would say now that her schooling was halfway done. He always knew how to guide her to make the right decisions, but now, that wasn't really much of an option. The Academy wanted every student to push for settling on their education choices as soon as possible. But for her, the timing was just off. Audrey quickly looked at her watch and realized it was time for lunch.

Arriving at the cafeteria, she quickly found her friends. After picking up her food, she settled down with her dorm mates. As they chattered away, she kept thinking about what Thomas and Colonel Sanchez had said to her earlier. To distract herself, Audrey glanced over at one of her friends to see what he was doing. Her fellow sophomore, Joey, was watching a video on his school tablet.

"Joey? What's that you're watching?" Audrey asked, which made him cover the screen and hold it to his chest tightly.

He looked up, pushing his glasses up the bridge of his nose, and replied.

"Oh just some private communiques that the science lab intercepted. We think it's a really awesome video."

He held the screen up for her to see. Audrey looked at it and saw the emblem of Amborg Industries. Choking on her food, she leaned forward and dropped to a whisper.

"What are you doing?!"

If there was one thing that Audrey knew, the science lab had a reputation for 'accidently' achieving access to classified material among government databases.

"You could get in big trouble, Joey, for looking at that!" she whispered frantically. "Any material from A.I. Industries is especially monitored! They're probably looking for this information now and are this close to locking you out!"

"What's the big deal?" Joey replied. "When I see something highly encrypted, I have to take a peek. Don't worry, no one will know."

"As long as you don't get into trouble…" Audrey took a bite out of her sandwich, chewing quickly as Joey returned a smile.

"Don't worry, I don't think the material is controversial at all," he said. "Even if Dr. Kendrick keeps all materials from A.I. industries classified. This video clip doesn't seem so interesting. All it shows is this weird warehouse fight or something. Check it out. Looks like the amborgs are fighting something."

"That doesn't sound classified," Audrey spoke suspiciously with her mouth full.

"They're fighting some sort of weird giant robot…"

"Never mind, I take that back."

Things were starting to really concern her. Security was a bit more uptight than usual. The staff at the Academy seemed more nervous than ever. Even A.I. Industries classified material was easily intercepted by Joey without getting flagged. Looking around to make sure no one could hear her, she turned to the rest of her friends and finally asked the question that had been building since her appointment.

"Hey, does anyone else notice anything strange going on?"

Her question had prompted the exact reactions she was hoping for. The entire table instantly fell silent as everyone leaned and huddled closer. One of the girls quickly spoke first.

"Well, there's a group of soldiers patrolling the outside of the autoshop wing," she said, shrugging her shoulders. "But, I figured that they were the new day watch or something. I only noticed because someone in one of the outdoor automobile classes was talking about it."

"Something is definitely wrong," Audrey nodded in agreement. "I mean, why send soldiers to various parts of the campus?"

"It could be a training exercise," one of the guys piped up, talking with his mouth full. Barbecue sauce drizzled down his mouth and flew out, causing everyone nearby to flinch.

"Dude, stop talking while chewing. You're spitting on me!"

The student next to Audrey nodded in agreement as the sloppy classmate got called out.

"They have unscheduled training ops for military personnel," he said. "They're always coming to use parts of the school grounds for their urban combat training. I personally enjoy the random days when you just see them climbing up or running down the sides of the buildings."

Everyone else who was actively listening began nodding in agreement, but Audrey wasn't convinced. Sure, it might look like a training exercise or something, but that only generated another question. Why were there so many troops popping up everywhere on campus?

As her classmates moved on from the subject, she looked up and noticed one of the school's professors speaking to a soldier. She bid her colleagues a quick farewell and pretended to get in line for more food.

Acting as naturally as she could, she moved in the express line to get closer. Eventually, she could make out the hushed tones between the professor and soldier.

"Professor, orders are orders," the soldier was whispering as he gripped his shoulder strap. His weapon hung tightly on his back but it looked as if he was ready to whip it around and start shooting. "We need to get you out."

"Are you sure you're supposed to be telling me this in front of the students?"

"You weren't in your office at your scheduled time," the soldier spoke quickly in his hushed tones. "I was ordered to find you."

"Alright alright!" the old man said quietly as he began to look around anxiously. "I'll do what you said! Just promise to get the students, all of them, away. The children can't stay here. I will not leave before them. Take that up with your superiors if you have to but I will stay here and protect them if it gives them a chance!"

"We'll try, sir. Evacuation will be commencing soon and we will attempt to get as many people off campus. We need to begin preparations."

The soldier stopped. He cast a quick glance to his right, then turned to find Audrey staring at him. The moment their eyes met, she looked away, stepped out of line, and walked in the opposite direction. That conversation pretty much confirmed her suspicions. Something was terribly wrong, and they were clearly trying to keep it under wraps to prevent widespread panic. Without wasting any time, Audrey left the cafeteria and rushed to find her brother. If there was going to be trouble, she had to find Thomas...fast.

Audrey whipped out her phone and quickly sent a text to Joey, who was probably still pirating videos on his tablet.

Joey! I think you should head back to the dormitory! Right now!

There was no response at first. As she reached the lobby, her phone chimed. Glancing at it, she saw Joey's reply.

Why?

Because something bad is going to happen, she wrote desperately as she made her way through the doors and stepped outside. *Try to get everyone else to go with you! Please!*

The text went through but this time, there was no immediate reply. Audrey started to worry more as she speed-walked across campus to where she knew her brother would be. Around this time, he was usually in his own dorm. She went to where the senior dormitories were and schooled her expression to one of neutrality. Obviously, the soldiers didn't want to alarm any of the students and were planning a quiet evacuation, so she put on a less than casual show. She leapt up the stairs two at a time to the building where her brother stayed but before she could open the door, someone called her.

"Hey sis, what's up?"

She whirled around. Thomas had been chatting with a few of his friends in the smoking shed that was stationed a few feet away from the building. A couple of them were vaping but she knew, of course, that he didn't smoke. He waved at the others and jogged up the steps to catch up with Audrey. She practically jumped into her brother's arms. Taken aback, he chuckled slightly as he struggled to stand firm and not fall back down the stairs as he returned the hug.

"You're ok!" she exclaimed, which only made him let out a baffled grunt.

"Should I not be ok?" He laughed and let her go. "Since when are you so huggable? Not that I mind because it's a complete and total change from earlier."

"That's not it!" Audrey replied.

Thomas recognized the seriousness in her tone and his smile faded.

"What's up?" he asked gently. "Something wrong?"

"Yes!" she said in a hushed tone. "I think the campus is going to be attacked."

She was taken aback by how he reacted. Thomas's face contorted in shock, and he frowned deeply. He raised his index finger to his lips and quickly shushed her.

"Shh! Careful! There's a few soldiers that walked around the corner! Lower your voice."

Audrey's eyes widened.

"Wait, you knew?!"

Thomas lifted his hand and pushed her to the side of the entrance. They fell silent as the sound of heavy footsteps approached. Slowly, they turned to see a squad of soldiers marching in tandem toward them. Thankfully, the soldiers passed by without directing their attention to the siblings, so they relaxed as they waited for the troops to disappear from view. However, Audrey's worry quickly intensified. The realization that her brother was involved in whatever was happening began to scare her.

"Yes I did know," he said softly. "A lot of the seniors with military majors were warned and believe it or not, they were asking for volunteers to take up defensive posts to help assist in the evacuation."

"Ok, I get there's a giant evacuation," Audrey exclaimed. "But from what? Please tell me you didn't volunteer for a post! Because we're not military. Not yet!"

"We may not officially be military but some of our class courses do follow military doctrine," he said. "Especially for those that want future careers with the army."

"Did you volunteer for a post?" Audrey repeated.

"Yes."

"Why?!"

"They asked me because of our parents," Thomas replied sternly. "Believe it or not, some of the commanders offered to make us part of the first priority evacuees. I turned that down! How can it be fair for us to leave first while my friends stay and probably die? I said I would stay and help the evacuation. Our parents' achievements was no reason for them to place our needs above that of everyone else."

"But who would risk an attack on the Academy?" Audrey asked. "You'd need an army to even think of taking a quarter of the grounds."

"From what it sounds like, I'm afraid there is an army based on recent intelligence."

"How can you be so calm?"

"For one reason," Thomas said with a shrug. "The fact that the academy hasn't been attacked before is already a good enough reason. This place has high-end security and strong protective measures. Why stress so much about it?"

"This school," Audrey replied nervously, "has a long history and a lot of famous people have graduated from here! What if someone tries to destroy that? In the past, people always say that things won't happen and then they do!"

"Either way," Thomas sighed, "I think we'll be fine! Whoever has the guts to attack here will need an army, just like you said. It's never going to work successfully if they're trying to take the ground. But, with a possible threat looming, they're not taking any chances and they're going to evacuate. The faculty and command here aren't going to risk it. You will be evacuated."

"I don't like where you're going with this."

"Audrey, I'm sorry," Thomas said firmly. "I was going to text you once they began the operation. You have to get ready to go."

"No!"

"You're my little sister and all I have left! Carter too! You need to grab him and leave!"

"Leaving you here is not what mom and dad would want!"

Thomas shook his head adamantly.

"Get your friends and go to the shuttle pads. The main focus is to get the non-military students, civilians, and faculty away from here!"

"No!" Audrey said. "I'm staying with you! I'll ask them to get me to stay too."

"Senior students only!" Thomas replied insistently. "They would never allow you or any other daredevils to risk their lives!"

"But you'll be left behind! If this is real! You're going to be in danger!"

Thomas paused, at a loss for words. He had evidently realized that continuing this discussion wasn't getting them anywhere. So he closed his mouth and shook his head sternly. Audrey took in all that she had just heard and breathed slowly in order to calm herself.

"You can't go through life without some risks," Thomas said softly.

Audrey bit her lip as her brother remained adamant.

"I'm going to help," he declared. "Look, I know you're not interested in listening to my advice right now! But knowing that you're safe will put my mind at ease!"

Audrey continued to shake her head. Thomas looked down at the ground.

Before she could continue with her questions, a loud noise sounded across campus, interrupting her thoughts. The two of them looked up sharply towards the horizon. She had heard this noise before as a freshman when she entered this campus for orientation, where she'd been told what it meant. Now, she was hearing it again and she trembled. It was an air raid siren, the kind used long ago to signal an attack, deafening and terrifying. It pierced the air, the sound stretching across the entire campus. Thomas's eyes darted to Audrey, then to the distance, his expression frantic.

"Ok..." he muttered. "That is definitely not the plan. That's not the signal we were briefed on. It's too early!"

"How early?" Audrey cried over the noise of the siren.

Thomas whirled to Audrey and grabbed her shoulders.

"Listen!" he said as several alarmed students in the background continued to look around in panicked confusion. He stared desperately into Audrey's eyes. "I guess the plan's changed! But you listen to me! Gather the rest of your dorm and get out of here ASAP! I'm going to find my assigned team! If the worst should happen though, you go to the nearest armory and dig in and hide! Got it?!"

Without a word, Audrey nodded. She felt the adrenaline kicking in as Thomas gave her a reassuring smile.

"You be safe!"

He let go of her and ran off.

The building's door burst open as a wave of upperclassmen poured out in a frenzy. Some hurried down the same route Thomas had taken, while others scattered in different directions. Audrey pivoted and sprinted back toward her dorm, the alarm continuing the blare relentlessly around her.

"Attention all students. Remain calm. Campus-wide evacuation underway. Transport ships will be arriving to bring you somewhere safe. This is not a drill. Please proceed to your designated evacuation zone and standby for immediate relocation to a safe zone. I repeat, this is not a drill. Campus-wide evacuation underway."

The voice of the automated evacuation announcement rang loud and clear. Audrey ran towards the flow of clamoring students and proceeded to the launch pads. It was literally a miniature airport, located about half a mile from the classrooms. Since the runway was not the closest place to run to, all the students rushed through some hallways that connected to the older helicopter pads. The hallways were more like long tunnels, with domed windows and benches along the walls. It was designed that way to provide those waiting for a ride a place to sit inside and sheltered from the elements.

The entrance to the launch pad Audrey had entered was swarming with students and faculty. Several transports were already touching down on the strips of asphalt, then lifting off, one after another. Audrey looked ahead of the swarm and was relieved when she saw Joey and the rest of her classmates. She weaved her way through the crowd and eventually joined up with them. At the end of the tunnel, the corridor split into eight different tunnels. Each one led to a different launch pad, like the gates at an airport. From what she could see, they were located halfway to the entrance that her dorm mates had wandered towards.

"Oh man, this is scary," Joey said meekly. "You think that I shouldn't have watched those classified videos? Are they going to get me?"

Audrey placed a hand on his shoulder. She couldn't help but laugh reassuringly at Joey's paranoia.

"No," she said, smiling. "This is something else. We'll be fine. We just need to wait a bit longer and we'll be out of here."

She tried to follow her brother's example and remained confident. If she panicked or revealed what Thomas had told her, everyone would probably feel insecure enough to lose all rational thought.

Joey took a few deep breaths, visibly calming down. A loud whoosh suddenly echoed through the tunnel, drawing everyone's attention. A transport was approaching for a landing, silhouetted by the setting sun. It had been roughly two hours since her meeting with the colonel, and the afternoon light was gradually dimming, casting a warm orange hue over the campus. They watched as the transport hovered and then touched down on the deck. Soon, the crowd began to move forward, but after a few minutes, they came to a halt as a soldier at the end of the tunnel began to wave and shout.

"Transport's full! Take it away!"

"What?!" someone nearby yelled in disbelief. "We've barely moved!"

He was right. Audrey glanced around and noticed several students displaying signs of worry. Before anyone could voice their concerns, a thunderous boom echoed through the air.

"LOOK UP THERE!"

Everyone's gaze shot up, catching sight of a dark speck zipping across the sky. With lightning speed, something dropped from that speck and landed with a crash in the field outside the tunnel.

"What the hell is that?!" someone yelled in the middle of all the panicked voices.

Audrey saw a tall figure rise and stride confidently ahead, neon lights glowing brightly on their uniform. She watched as the individual signaled to a few soldiers before vanishing from view.

"Is that an amborg?" Joey asked, terror in his eyes. Someone from the crowd answered.

"Yes it is! I saw them wearing a number!"

Another series of booms echoed from the sky, causing everyone to look up again. More specks descended like meteors, landing in different spots around the campus, their impacts producing loud thuds that shook the ground. Audrey saw tall figures rising from where they had landed, disappearing from sight faster than their eyes could track.

"Why would amborgs be dropping here?!"

Audrey already knew the answer before it was even asked.

"Because this attack is worse than we thought," she said, breathing slowly. "They're dropping here because... there's going to be a battle. What if we're being herded right into a kill zone?"

"We are sitting ducks," Joey replied while a few other of the students listened. "Like animals waiting to be slaughtered."

"We don't know that!"

"Let's just wait for the next transport!"

Fireballs shot into the air as a loud explosion resonated from afar. Several students stared wide-eyed, trying to figure out what had been destroyed amid the rising cloud of smoke. Almost immediately, the sharp crack of automatic gunfire erupted in the distance.

Another sudden whooshing noise startled everyone, drawing their attention to the transport at the launch pad as it slowly ascended into the air. As it rose higher, a blinding flash of light ripped right through one of the engines. Audrey stared in horror as the exhaust ignited, bursting into flames. The transport groaned, losing altitude as the damaged engine began to whine and power down. Unable to keep steady, it spiraled down toward the tunnel, heading straight for the line of wide-eyed students. Many stood frozen in fear, and Audrey felt her heart racing like a drum pounding in her chest. Realizing their vulnerability, she took a deep breath and focused, steadying herself.

"RUN!" she yelled as loud as she could as the falling wreckage made contact with the corridor several meters ahead.

Everyone in front of her scrambled in all directions, and she instinctively followed suit. Moments later, a powerful tremor caused her to stagger, but she maintained a steady sprint, chasing after a group of fleeing students. Dust, concrete, and dirt flew overhead. Another explosion detonated behind her, sending a stronger shockwave that forced her to the ground. Her ears rang, and dizziness swept over her. Blinking through the haze, she strained to locate Joey. Luckily, he'd landed just a few feet away, and she crawled over to him.

"Joey! Get up! We got to go!" she yelled, but her voice sounded muffled.

She shook her head, trying to focus and get her senses back in order after the explosion had left her temporarily deaf. Joey raised his head and managed to sit up. He appeared alright, but flinched and began to scramble when he spotted the dead body beside him. Audrey placed her hand on his shoulder and urged him to move away from the crushed student. As they crawled further down the hallway, a sudden loud noise halted them in their tracks.

They pulled themselves up and went to one of the windows. The sounds of clanging and crashing echoed, along with the sharp ring of metal. Listening carefully, they caught the distinct noise of loud whirring blending into the chaos.

"Those are hydraulics," Joey breathed. "It's something big too. I think that's..."

"Oh my god, what is that?" Audrey said, pointing.

A tall figure descended from the sky, landing firmly on the ground. It was an amborg, poised on one knee, preparing to launch himself at an unseen target.

"There's something huge there," Joey said. "It's one of those... big robot soldiers!"

He was right. A massive robot emerged from the thick, foggy smoke and started advancing toward the amborg. As Audrey and Joey peered through the cracked window, they could hear the loud whirring of the hydraulics. At least there was a machine to put the sounds to now.

Audrey watched as the cybernetic teenager wasted no time and charged at the enormous machine. It was a sight unlike anything she had ever witnessed. She didn't need to ask Joey if he had ever seen something so massive; the look on his face said it all. The amborg leaped high, aiming a punch at what appeared to be the giant's head. A loud bang reverberated as his fist made contact.

The robot, unfazed, struck the amborg forcefully in midair. He fell to the earth, rebounding off the grass and crashing into the wall underneath the window where Joey and Audrey stood, then crumpled to the ground. Both were left speechless, having never seen an amborg taken down like that before.

Just as she was about to see if he was ok, the cybernetic teen suddenly pushed himself upright and shook his head. He turned to the window and noticed them. Gulping, Audrey and Joey exchanged nervous glances as they took in the scars and signs of battle fatigue on the boy's face. The number 35 was etched on his chest, and the gold bracelet on his wrist flashed. They couldn't hear the voice coming out of it, but the amborg was also mouthing a single word to them.

"Run!"

Immediately following the amborg's command, the murder bot grabbed him by the leg and flung him into the field. It then charged ahead and, with an almighty crash, crushed the defenseless figure into the earth.

Horrified, Audrey grabbed Joey and they dashed out of the tunnel. Debris rained down as the structure deteriorated. Keeping their arms raised to protect themselves, they, along with a few stragglers, made it safely outside.

There was no time to stop and process the situation. Explosions erupted all around them without warning. In a split-second decision,

Audrey pushed Joey forward, and together they plunged into the chaos. The conflict raged on all sides, surrounding them.

"What do we do?!"

Joey turned around and saw a soldier take a bullet to the back of the head. He collapsed instantly and didn't get back up. Audrey, thinking on her feet, realized she needed to find a way to gather as many people as possible to regroup.

"Everyone! Follow me to the armory!" she bellowed.

A handful of fleeing cadets pivoted and immediately began to follow.

She wasn't sure how many people had heard. All she knew was they had to get out of the firefight and quickly get to the nearest building. Perhaps some soldiers would be able to cover them. Hopefully, the enemy wouldn't notice their group moving towards one spot. The last thing they needed was attention.

Audrey was leading the group towards the building ahead when an explosion ruptured a pillar close by, causing it to topple toward a few soldiers.

The group froze as they heard the sound of the structure crumbling. Moments before the soldiers could be crushed, a brilliant flash of blue neon light streaked across their line of sight. An amborg sprang into action, propelling themself toward the pillar and diverting it away. The broken pillar hurled in a different direction, striking a cluster of enemy troops—at least, that's how it appeared to Audrey. She wasn't sure who was fighting who. The recipients of the flying pillar were instantly pulverized, leaving every cadet in the vicinity in a state of shocked silence.

"That pillar had to weigh over fifty tons..." someone said meekly.

Audrey stared in pure terror. It wasn't until a missile flew overhead that she remembered that they were still standing in the middle of a battlefield.

"RUN! Let's go this way!"

Moving deeper into the fray, debris soared above them in every directions.

"You'd think there'd be more explosions! But there's a ton of stuff being thrown around instead!"

A student dove to the side to dodge a massive brick slab. It smashed into a wall, sending chunks of rock spraying everywhere.

"It's a whole new type of battlefield nowadays..." Audrey muttered as they continued. "Amborgs have a very unique way of fighting."

Along the way, they turned off of the main path to avoid the majority of the fighting. They dashed along a narrow side path that wound between some buildings, providing them with some cover. The sounds of chaos had faded, easing their anxiety, but they continued to hurry, trying to keep their footsteps as silent as possible. Nothing happened until they passed a nearby courtyard adorned with obelisks.

"Watch out!" one of the girls in the back suddenly screamed.

Everyone froze in place as a massive object slammed into the ground in front of them, obstructing their path.

"Ack... take this! Garg! Junkhead!"

Audrey stared in disbelief as an amborg, pinned to the ground, struck upward at the drone's faceplate. The lens shattered, sending sparks flying in all directions. Groaning, the drone flailed its arms, continuing to punch the amborg beneath it, who curled his legs, ready to launch himself. With a tremendous kick, the drone was propelled into the air, where it was intercepted by another amborg. The cadets watched as the second amborg, midair, delivered a powerful kick to the drone's chest, sending it crashing to the ground.

Audrey rushed over and extended her hand to the amborg sprawled on the ground. He grasped it and rose to his feet. The dust obscured the number on his uniform, making it impossible for her to identify him.

"Thanks a lot," his gold bracelet flashed. "Get to cover now! We are losing ground."

"What about you?!" Audrey exclaimed as a loud whistling noise whizzed past their heads. "What do you mean we're losing ground?!"

"There is insufficient time, miss," he replied hastily. "Proceed straight to cover before this part of campus is overrun. Please go inside somewhere where there have been no external explosions on the building infrastructure. You will fare a better rate of survival in the basements."

Without another word, the boy crouched and took off, vanishing from sight in an instant.

Weren't they supposed to help protect us? Audrey stared in shock. *What's going on? Were they really losing the fight?*

"Keep moving!" someone yelled. The small group immediately began to make their way to the nearest armory.

Minutes later, Audrey and her party located the armory and entered the building. They pressed themselves against the walls, breathing heavily as Audrey pulled the door shut and engaged the locks. Joey rushed to a security panel and initiated the emergency lockdown procedures. The glass windows darkened, allowing them to see outside while preventing anyone from peering in. A loud clanking sound indicated that the door was secure.

"We're safe for now," Audrey muttered as she took some deep breaths.

She turned to face the group of people still alive and did a head count. Including Joey and herself, there were fourteen of them in total.

"We can't stay here Audrey," Joey whispered as she kneeled down next to him. "We need to get to the weapon lockers."

"I know," she replied firmly."If my brother made it, he should be here. The armory in the basement here is close to the senior dorm rooms. He would have come here when the evacuation alarm sounded off. We have to get downstairs."

"I'll go in front," one of the girls stood up, raising her hand.

"Ok," Audrey nodded without question. "Everyone, file up and follow... What's your name?"

"Deliza," the girl replied.

"Everyone file in behind Deliza. Ready?"

Everyone scrambled into a straight line and hunched over as they heard a muffled explosion occur outside.

"We're heading for the armory. There is a possible group of friendlies inside," Audrey spoke loud enough to be heard. "I'm operating under the hopes that everyone here has taken the security class and knows how to handle the weapons they have here for emergencies. Without them, we can't defend ourselves, so we need to move as quickly as possible. It's ok to be scared but we need to be brave. Everyone ready?"

She surveyed the line, checking both the front and the rear. Everyone acknowledged her with nods and thumbs up.

"Then let's go. Deliza, move when you're ready."

"Gotcha," Deliza nodded and held up a fist.

Everyone waited silently as the noise outside filled the air until...

"Go!"

Deliza opened her fist and directed them to follow her. They moved down the corridor, turning right and then left. The group remained silent, their eyes fixed forward. Those at the back glanced over their shoulders to ensure they weren't being pursued. Before long, they arrived at the staircase door, and Delisa raised her hand. She formed a fist, signaling everyone to stop. She knelt down, fist still raised in the air. The others quickly followed her example and dropped to the ground. Audrey quickly crouched and made her way to the front.

"What is it?" Audrey leaned closer to Deliza and whispered. "Do you hear something?"

"It's coming from down the hall to our left," the redhead replied quietly. "We might have company."

Audrey listened carefully and heard thuds coming from the direction Deliza was pointing. Someone was definitely trying to break in.

"Well," she said, patting Deliza on the shoulder sympathetically. "Luckily, the staircase is in front of us. Whatever is going on that way, it isn't worth investigating, unless we have weapons or something to fight back with."

They all stood in silence, waiting until Deliza gave the signal that it was safe to proceed. She approached the door and carefully pushed it open, trying to make as little noise as possible. With the door propped open, everyone stepped forward and entered the staircase. After they were all inside, Audrey signaled to Joey.

"Joey, take point and lead everyone down the stairs," she instructed.

He nodded and moved down a few steps to the front. Audrey turned to Deliza and whispered.

"Are you ok taking the back? Keeping an eye out for intruders?"

"No problem," Deliza agreed. "Just get everyone down there as fast as you can. At the first sign of trouble, I'll catch up."

"Even if we do get weapons, we need a way to exit this place. Including the way we came in, there are four exits to this building. We may have to work our way back to the entrance we came in if it has to be like that."

"Don't worry, I got it," Deliza said, nodding in understanding. "They won't notice me."

Audrey couldn't help but admire Deliza's confidence. As she descended the stairs, urgency took over. Noticing how far ahead the group had gotten, she decided to forgo stealth and dashed down the concrete steps. Once she arrived at the basement level, she gently opened the door and was greeted by the sound of voices as soon as she crossed the threshold.

"Please! We're only trying to get weapons for safety!"

Her group had appeared to be stuck. They appeared even more frightened than they had been when they were outside.

"Are you crazy?!" someone from inside the armory door shot back. "You coming here may have alerted the enemy to our hiding place."

"Open the door and let us in! We'll die if we don't stay with you."

Audrey sprinted up to the group and found Joey arguing with someone behind the sealed door. He breathed a sigh of relief when he saw her.

"Thank god Audrey. They won't let us in," Joey said, looking over his shoulder and scanning the hall.

"It's ok. Let me try and talk to them."

Audrey knocked on the door once and spoke.

"Please, we need your help," she pleaded softly. "Open the door and let us in."

"How do we know this isn't a trick?" the same voice Joey argued with spoke again. "You could be an enemy programmed or trained to sound like one of the school personnel or whatever. Or someone might be forcing you to say you're friendlies and make us lower our guard."

"I can assure you it isn't a trick," Audrey spoke calmly. "If you let us in, you'll have reinforcements. We can help you! Please! Don't let us die out here!"

There was silence behind the door. A few moments later, the same person spoke again.

"I don't believe you. We got people in here too and we're not letting anything come in to slaughter us."

Taking a deep breath, Audrey took a moment to think. One possibility came to mind. It was their last chance.

"Is my brother in there?" she asked through the door. "Senior Thomas Wright? Is he alive?"

"Thomas?" the same person's voice rose in surprise. "Who's asking?"

"For heaven's sake, I'm his sister Audrey," she brought a hand up and wiped the sweat off her forehead. "If he's in there, have him talk to me. He'll vouch for me."

"Hey O'Hara. What's going on? I heard my name."

Another voice joined the conversation behind the door, and Audrey's eyes lit up with relief. It was probably the most wonderful sound she'd ever heard in her whole life.

"Thomas!" she exclaimed excitedly.

"Audrey! Holy shit! Quick! Open the door! Let them in!" Thomas replied back, distraught.

"Wait a minute! How do we really know it's her?! You're just going to accept that line as clearance?"

"That. Is. My. Sister, you dumbass!" Thomas yelled back. "You'd open the door if it was your family too, O'Hara. Hurry up!"

As the two seniors behind the door continued to argue, Audrey's group of students waited apprehensively, hoping all these raised voices hadn't attracted the enemy's attention. Until...

"Hey guys. What's up?"

Everyone spun around, startled. Audrey instinctively raised her fists but quickly dropped them. Deliza had come down from upstairs, managing to sneak up on them.

"S-seriously, is this going to become a thing with you?" Joey stammered as he put a hand on his chest.

"Get used to it four-eyes," Deliza winked. "It may just be the thing that saves your life when you look the wrong way."

She then walked up to Audrey and leaned in to whisper to her.

"Look," she spoke calmly, "If there's any chance we can get inside, it should be now."

Deliza inclined her head toward the direction she had just come from. Audrey immediately understood the concern that crossed her face. Just then, the door hissed and opened part way. Two seniors with rifles separated, taking positions a foot apart in the hallway. Both aimed their weapons down the corridor while another senior waved them in.

"Inside now!"

Without hesitation, the group filed inside as quickly as possible.

"Did you get an idea of what's coming?" Audrey asked as Joey ducked in first.

"Meh," Deliza held up a hand and shook it dismissively. "I caught a glimpse of them coming down the hall, but they didn't see me. I'm guessing they're in the stairwell now. If they know the layout of the building, then the armory would be a good place to capture. We may have to make a final stand there."

"Those don't sound like good odds," Audrey muttered.

"Well, it's better than dying like pigs in an open hallway with no cover," Deliza replied bluntly. "At least each one of us has a chance to fight back against those cowards."

"Excuse me."

The two of them turned to see Thomas casually leaning against the door with a rifle in hand.

"I'm sure you and your new friend have much to discuss, Audrey," he said as he motioned for them to enter. "But I'd much rather take my chances holding out inside the armory. Wouldn't you agree?"

After a brief nod of agreement, Audrey and Deliza stepped inside. The two seniors monitoring the hallway walked backward, ensuring everyone was in. As the last student entered, they stepped back, letting Thomas shut the door behind them. It hissed as it slammed shut, locking them in.

"Someone will have heard that most likely," Thomas murmured as he embraced Audrey. "Speaking of which, got any updates from the outside?"

"Total chaos," Audrey replied. "We never made it to the transports. They shot down our rides. I don't know how many made it out."

The armory was a spacious room with walls made from solid stainless steel, organized into four aisles filled with lockers that stored a variety of weapons. The far wall, at the end of the room, contained shelves holding larger weapons ranging from assault rifles to combat knives.

With not much to do, they all took a moment to catch their breath. Joey knelt and pulled out his tablet to look for signals. Thomas gestured to his sister to sit against the wall. Audrey crouched, taking a deep breath as she leaned her head against the cool metal surface. Thomas sat beside her, resting his rifle in his lap, and opened a map of the campus on his own tablet. Glowing green dots lit up on some of the rooftops.

"We were here," he said, pointing at the building next to the one where they were currently hiding out. "We were on the top floor setting up an overwatch, ready to assault anyone dropping into the courtyard. Cover for any stragglers. Standard entrapment... except that the enemy didn't send human soldiers..."

"Robots," Audrey replied. "Big, huge robots and a drone army."

"Our weapons were useless," Thomas nodded. "We could really use some Jedi right now eh? They sent in those small humanoid defense drones and those were hard to take down. Someone must have hacked their combat programming. If that wasn't enough, the big giant rolie polie looking ones practically blasted the floors we were on to pieces. A lot of seniors got crushed from most of the wreckage in the building than the actual firefight. I got as many people as I could to the armory but it was a death trap wherever we went. I can't remember if we even had time to stop to take a breath."

"What about the amborgs?" Deliza asked curiously.

Thomas shrugged and let out a huge sigh.

"They were here and there. Tried helping as many people as they could but from the way I saw it, they were pretty beat up. I took my group of people still alive, grabbed more people we ran into, as many as we could, and huddled here."

"We can probably assume everyone who is hiding in the bunkers or armories are the safest at this point," Audrey pointed at the map and highlighted all of the buildings with red dots. "Every school building has a place to hide and based on how fast this place has fallen, we're probably going to be targeted next."

A loud bang shook the door, putting everyone on high alert. Two of the upperclassmen trained their firearms at the entrance. One of them raised a hand to signal Thomas, who quickly pulled Audrey and Deliza over to a locker.

"Take your pick," he indicated the weapons available as he opened the locker. Deliza grabbed a hand-gun and a knife while Audrey settled with a standard rifle. "Better get in position too."

Audrey watched Deliza comfortably twirl her knife like an expert. Did she do that recreationally?

"What's with the knife?" Audrey asked as she switched her rifle settings from automatic to single-shot. "It's an interesting combination. A gun and a short knife."

"My parents are close quarters combat instructors in D.C.," Deliza shrugged. "This is the fighting style I'm comfortable with."

"You're a close quarter's expert?" Audrey remarked, impressed at the sight of her classmate.

"You could say that," Deliza smirked. She grabbed a rifle but set it down near her feet. "Long range combat is a bit boring. I'm best when I'm up close to my enemies. Once I'm in range, it's too late for them."

"I doubt that it's going to be a person coming through that door," Audrey said, checking the sights on her weapon.

"I'll be ok with whatever. My mom says I'm one tough cookie."

"Everyone grab a firearm and take your positions!" Thomas instructed, abruptly ending the girls' conversation. "Joey, right? Put the pad down and pick up a gun. Even a science tech needs to fight."

"But... I-I can't..." he stammered.

"Joey, listen to me!" Thomas cut him off. "I know you're scared. It's ok! Have you finished basic weapons training?"

"Yes, of course!" Joey nodded fearfully. "I just haven't fired a weapon since that class!"

"Well, listen up!" Thomas replied. "You pick up that weapon, you not only stand a chance of helping us protect each other, but you can protect yourself too! You don't do that, you will die! Copy?"

Joey trembled at the thought, but immediately sprinted to a locker and picked up a rifle. He quickly checked the weapon and grabbed some ammo. Thomas watched Joey resume a defensive position and nodded approvingly.

"I-I... copy," he stammered.

"Good man," Thomas praised him.

All eyes were on the door as the group aimed their weapons. Thomas whistled to the two seniors positioned at the entrance and signaled for them to pull back.

"No sense in you guys getting crushed by the door if it gets bashed in," he muttered. "Too many movie deaths from stationing people at entrances."

Audrey took a position by Thomas and aimed. Deliza moved up the aisle, pistol ready. Everyone waited with bated breath, keeping as silent as possible. A heartbeat later, the door shook violently as a force from outside slammed against it.

Outside, a series of shots rang out, accompanied by the relentless pounding against the door. Muffled yells filtered through, causing the students to look at each other with unease.

"Steady, everyone," Thomas said reassuringly.

Audrey was about to add a little something to encourage everyone when a sudden crash sent the door falling inward. It landed with a loud, jarring thud.

"That was pure grade steel..." Joey whispered, loudly enough for everyone to hear.

Oddly enough, no one had fired their guns. Audrey looked over the wreckage to see if anyone was coming in.

"I see a foot!"

The moment movement was detected, nearly everyone opened fire, with the exception of a few frozen in fear. The armory erupted in chaos, making it impossible for Audrey to hear herself think. Shell casings and bullets flew in all directions, while people shouted at the top of their lungs, driven by a mix of terror and adrenaline.

"Cease fire! Stop shooting!"

The gunfire gradually ceased as everyone panted and lowered their weapons. A voice from outside the armory spoke up from around a corner.

"Wow, that was... pleasant," a male voice with a slight robotic inflection spoke. "Very deafening."

Another laughed with a similar tone.

"Do you believe they are ready to cease hostilities?"

The first voice spoke again.

"Unsure. You may proceed inside first."

"You afraid of some bullets?"

"No," the first voice replied to the taunt. "But based on all the bullets opposite of the door's entrance, we have been fired upon by at least twenty firearms and other standard weapons."

"They're just scared," a third person spoke reassuringly. "Let me try. This is amborg 297! I am coming in! That being said, you two, watch and learn."

Audrey saw a figure step into the entrance. She quickly recognized it as a young man and believed he was an amborg, based on the introduction. His uniform was marred with mud and dirt, obscuring its stripes. Just as she began to lower her weapon, gunfire erupted behind her. The person who panicked triggered a chain reaction, causing everyone else to open fire as well. The young man in the entrance ducked out of view with such agility that it became clear they were not dealing with a normal human being.

"HOLD YOUR FIRE!" Audrey yelled as the figure outside raised his voice as well.

"How rude!" she heard him shout.

"Well at least one of them has sense, 297," the other voice said in amusement. "Report to me when you have convinced the remaining nineteen people to stop shooting."

"Oh shut up."

Several heavy footsteps shuffled outside.

"Cease fire! Students! We are not your enemy! We are amborgs!"

"Oh BULLSHIT!" the senior that had blocked the door earlier yelled back.

Another student spoke up.

"What if they are amborgs?! A regular person would have died from that kind of shooting spree!"

It wasn't enough. A few more shots rang out, fired by someone with an itchy trigger finger. After a brief pause, the amborgs outside began speaking again.

"That went well..." the first voice said. The second voice spoke again, levely. "They are most likely traumatized. If I may, can I try to calm them down?"

"Go ahead 501," the third voice said. "But try not to get shot in the head again for the millionth time."

"My head has only been hit six hundred forty two thousand and three hundred seventeen times..." (WTF 501?? 😳)

"Will you just go already before we exaggerate around you again? We are going for an accumulative score of eighteen headshots to 501's calculated total. May we have eighteen please? Maybe seven more for luck?" (lmaoooo)

Audrey remained still, waiting for a reply from outside, but none came. Instead, she heard the sound of footsteps approaching the doorway, each step measured. A smaller number of students opened fire, and Audrey watched as the young man—501—stood tall as he was riddled with bullets. After a tense few seconds, the shooting stopped, everyone falling silent and staring in disbelief. Squinting, Audrey noticed the number "501" on his jacket. He lowered his head to inspect himself, then looked back up with a casual smile.

"Greetings," he smiled, stepping forward. The damage done by the bullets had only made his clothing dirtier. "Do not be alarmed. My uniform is made of a special synthetic fabric that is bulletproof."

Two more figures entered the room. One of them, labeled 297, looked extremely annoyed.

"Really?" his bracelet flashed. "Nineteen of them shoot at me and only four end up shooting Donut."

"Well at least Donut didn't avoid the bullets like you did," the other male amborg, 66, was barely suppressing a grin. "Plus, he also got them to stop. Talk about taking one for the team."

"Actually," 501 glanced up with a thoughtful look. "That was probably about sixty eight shots for the team to be precise."

"It has been a long day, 66, and I am going to kill you, 501. Why did he have to pick our team?"

"117 said I should learn to relate with you more," 501 spoke, but 297 waved his hand for silence. "I'm supposed to shadow and observe as many amborgs as possible."

"Lucky me," 297 rolled his eyes. Then he shifted his attention to all the survivors. "Is everyone alright?"

Thomas walked up to them and began updating the amborgs about the situation. Audrey glanced behind her to check on Joey. He gave a quick thumbs-up and lowered his rifle. He looked relieved that he didn't have to fire his weapon. Once she also relaxed, she then turned to face forward but realized someone was standing directly in front of her. She jumped and inadvertently pulled the trigger. The shot rang out throughout the entire armory. Everyone pivoted to the source of the noise, and she immediately felt the weight of several stares directed at her. Gulping, she stared wide-eyed at who she had just fired her gun at.

The amborg, number 117, stood still, examining the spot where he'd been shot while Audrey stared at him in shocked silence. Despite their bullet-proof nature, she couldn't shake the feeling of dread. What had she done? It was an awful first impression. After what seemed like an eternity of silence, Audrey saw his bracelet light up.

"I was..." he stated casually, "...going to ask if you were alright, miss. But I believe you have already answered the question... quite directly."

"I... am... so sorry!" she said meekly. "You startled me. One minute I turn my head and then I see you and... It's a reflex..."

"There is no need for an explanation," 117's bracelet flashed. "I only wanted to check on you specifically since you had not lowered your weapon. You turned your attention to the back and I took it upon myself to inform you that raised weapons may be discharged improperly. It would appear that I was too late."

"I probably won't stop apologizing then," Audrey attempted to force a chuckle but she was beginning to feel tense.

"Take deep breaths," he said. "Your heart rate seems to have elevated."

Audrey did as instructed and inhaled through her nose and exhaled through her mouth. 117 nodded and moved to join the other three amborgs. Thomas was looking fairly impressed.

"Wow, four amborgs," he said cheerfully, eyeing the four rescuers. "I thought at most, only one of you would show up to save our skins. But a team is an eye-opener."

"All amborgs are currently assisting in rescuing the survivors," 297 spoke. "All of us on campus are probably noticeable. However, time is short and we will need to head out after we have taken your group to the evacuation transport."

"I'm all for that," Thomas checked his weapon and shouldered it. "You guys need to be somewhere later?"

"We are on a very short timeline," 66 said. "But I do believe we should at least get acquainted. Keith 66 at your service."

He extended his hand and Thomas shook it. 117 stepped forward.

"David 117."

"Carter 297," the one labeled 297 waved. "I forgive you all for shooting me."

"Dominique 501. But everyone just calls me Donut."

Audrey's memory was immediately triggered.

"Oh, your name is Carter? I have an A.I. named…"

She stopped, suddenly having a startling revelation.

"Carter! I forgot about him! He's still in my room!"

The four amborgs exchanged confused glances, then turned back to Audrey. 117's bracelet lit up.

"Are you referring to the artificial intelligence with 297's name?"

"There is no need for alarm," 66 added and smiled. "Katie 57 found him transmitting a hidden distress signal and was able to extract him with no trouble."

"Oh thank goodness," Audrey sighed with relief. "Please don't tell him I forgot him. He wouldn't let me hear the end of it."

"It is asking him to maintain silence that is making him extremely difficult to deal with," 297 added with an amused look. "57 is having quite the headache. But he will be glad to receive word that his owner is alive and well."

"I have a question?"

Everyone turned to Joey, who lowered his hand sheepishly.

"I just wanted to know why an amborg is named Donut. If you have a moment," he mumbled.

"It is a very long story for another time I am afraid," 117 spoke up. "One quick reason in particular though, Donut is easier and shorter to say in combat."

"Yeah, two syllables is easier than three," 501 winked.

"Plus he loves donuts," 66 patted 501 on the shoulder. "In more ways than one, though. Keep that in mind if you feel like interpreting multiple scenarios."

Everyone laughed. Thankfully, this conversation was helping to lift their spirits a bit. Just then, Audrey saw 117 look away. His hand flew up to the side of his right temple.

"I just received word," 117 interrupted, causing the others to fall silent. "Transports have been alerted of our situation. Help is coming but we need to leave now."

Not a real people person, Audrey stared inquisitively. *Then again, I did shoot him...*

For a moment, it seemed like the amborgs had made their troubles disappear, but as 297 carried on with the discussion, they were quickly reminded of the reality of their situation.

"If we travel as one large group," he said, "we may be highly susceptible to ambush and will sustain maximum casualties. We must split up. Would you mind if everyone revealed themselves for a head count?"

Thomas nodded. He whistled loudly. At his signal, everyone came out on cue and stepped into view. 66 looked all of them over.

"It would seem that no one here is badly injured," he observed. "Everyone should be capable of quick travel."

"I count thirty-two survivors," 297 looked over the room. "We shall split into four groups going in different directions. Eight students will be accompanied by one amborg."

"Agreed," 117 nodded. "Is this acceptable?"

He turned and faced Thomas, who was observing all of the nods and murmurs of approval. He glanced at Audrey. She quickly nodded back with a firm smile.

"Looks like we are," he said with enthusiasm.

"Then divide into groups quickly," 117 acknowledged. "We are leaving this... hell-hole."

CHAPTER 20

The Not-So-Great Escape

The Academy
Eastern Perimeter Safe Zone

"Do you think 999 would like a scarf?"

3 looked at 917 and raised an eyebrow. 917 had removed his jacket so she could have access to his right arm. He was wearing a black short-sleeve undershirt and she was using a screwdriver on his elbow. They were both seated on a grassy hill overlooking the eastern campus of the Academy.

"Based on her personality?" she said as she peered into an open port on his prosthetic arm. "I seriously doubt that. I even have the math to prove it."

"Hmm, it probably was a stupid thought."

"Alright, where did you need me to check?"

"Up in the back behind my shoulder," 917 tried to reach over with hi left hand, but couldn't get to the spot he was indicating.

"Oh ok," 3 nodded. "And you can't get your mentor, your girlfriend, or your apprentice to do this because they're all occupied right now."

"999 is not my girlfriend," 917 laughed sarcastically. "She's my best friend."

"You do know that one of our primary functions is to observe, right?" 3 asked smugly.

She rolled his right sleeve back so that she could see his bare shoulder. She found a port in the back that seemed to be jammed. 3 gently inserted the screwdriver tip in and pried a small cover open. 917 winced.

"Sorry," she said.

"It's fine," he replied in a strained tone. "I think that last hit I took got it stuck. Thanks for loosening that."

"You know, this would be faster if you just gave me the schematics for your arm, right?"

917 looked at 3 and shook his head gently.

"It would take too long," he said. "This is Dr. Wildman's design and I've made a ton of modifications since I got it."

917 slipped his hand into the port, using his index finger to navigate behind his shoulder and pressed a button. Once that was done, he grabbed

his right bicep, and a soft clicking sound followed. 3 casually observed as 917 detached his arm.

From his seated position, he gently cradled his right arm in his lap and when it was stable, he extended his left hand to 3. She placed the screwdriver in his other hand and watched as he began to make some adjustments and repairs.

"If you don't mind," 917 said. "Could you not tell anyone that I asked you for help?"

"Sure," 3 nodded. "If you answer why you won't see 999 the way she looks at you?"

"She doesn't look at me that way," 917 replied.

"Remember what I just said to you, about how we observe things?" 3 said softly as she watched 917 peering down at the open port of his arm. "She looks at you like she cares deeply about you."

"She's my best friend," 917 repeated. "I don't want her or 345 to see me like this."

"Is it some sort of pride that's making you ask me this?"

"Yes," 917 sighed, "because I'm the only amborg that's different from all of the rest of you."

917 finished his repairs and handed 3 the screwdriver. She took it as he grabbed his arm and lifted it back into place. She moved forward to help but he shook his head politely. By himself, he reattached his right arm into the socket, and another tiny click followed.

"I don't know anything about my past," 917 stated. "I don't know who I was before Dr. Kendrick made me part of the Second Group. But for some reason, when I'm alone, working on my arm, it feels natural to me. It's like I've been doing it for a long time. But I have no way of confirming that unless my memories return."

He lifted his right arm, now reconnected, and began to stretch it.

"Are you afraid?" 3 asked. "Of who you might be?"

"I don't know," 917 replied.

"Well, I'm going to throw some more observations at you," 3 declared.

As he wiggled and flexed his fingers, 3 lifted her hand and extended her fingers out to him.

"You had parents that definitely raised you," she said. "Maybe they loved you, too. We don't know anything else about them."

She raised her middle and index fingers, making a peace sign.

"It is not your past that makes you who you are," 3 smirked. "You are Jack 917. By your own doing, you chose a name for yourself even after becoming an amborg. You're not different from the rest of us, you are one of us."

Then her ring finger came up, now holding up three fingers for him.

"Your actions today are what make you 917. The best parts of you," she said. "Your best friend is a badass and you have an apprentice that looks up to you. That's all they know you as! If you told them the truth about how you feel self-conscious, I don't think they'll look at you differently. They'll see you the same way because you're you!"

3 raised her pinky, bringing her total up to four.

"A lot of your friends and siblings in the Second Group all have numbers ending in the lucky number seven," 3 smiled. "You're one of them! They all respect and value you just as much as I do. Every amborg feels that way. What you do is good enough for them!"

Then she extended her thumb. When she did this, 3 smacked his right shoulder. 917 yelped in pain, but he shook it off as he realized his arm was now properly reconnected.

"Whoa," 917 exclaimed. "How did you...? That feels better!"

"The designs may have been modified but I recognize the components in your arm," 3 stated. "It's just like 5's leg."

917 stared in amazement at 3.

"You're not the only amborg that's asked me to fix a literal piece of them," she smiled. "Now. Reason number five."

3 held up her hand again and showed all five fingers.

"Never be ashamed or afraid again," 3 gave him a nod of affirmation. "5 doesn't hide that he's got a prosthetic limb. He embraces it! You should hold your head up high and stop worrying. I once heard someone say, 'the glory of creation is in its infinite diversity and the way our differences combine to create meaning and beauty.'"

"Did Dr. Kendrick say that?" 917 asked, fascinated at the insightful line she dropped. For some reason, it hit amazingly hard. "Wow."

"No," 3 grinned. "I watched an old Star Trek episode."

With his arm fully reconnected and calibrated to his settings, he found himself deep in thought. 917 and 3 remained seated, continuing to take a short break. Behind them, a makeshift medical station had been set up to take in anyone coming in with injuries. They'd receive treatment and protection before being escorted to safety. 917 and 3 kept a watchful eye on their surroundings, benefitting from a full view of the Academy grounds.

"Here," 3 stated.

917 looked to the side and noticed her passing him a granola bar. He politely thanked her and began to unwrap it. She produced another from her bag, and they both enjoyed a quick snack to recharge.

"Can we back it up a bit?" 3 asked. "What was all that about suddenly asking me if 999 would like a scarf?"

"Forget it," 917 chewed on his granola bar and shook his head. "Like I said, it was a stupid idea."

"Not necessarily," 3 replied as she started to lean a little to the right. 917 noticed this, but she managed to keep herself upright. "It just means... whoa. It just means you're very... thoughtful. Do you feel tired?"

"Not yet," 917 replied, pushing 3 back into a more stable sitting position. "We should get you back to A.I. Industries."

"No," 3 shook her head stubbornly. "A full recharge back at A.I. Industries takes hours. We have to finish this mission."

When 117 gave every amborg the command to deploy, they quickly established a routine and created a schedule for their operations. Many were on patrol throughout the country, looking for any trace of the assassin, while others stayed at A.I. Industries to conserve their energy. When the time came, they would come together, regardless of their current circumstances, to join the fight. Amborgs like 3 and 917 had already been dispatched when they received the call to rally in Houston. Their energy reserves were already moderately depleted, and they were supposed to return to A.I. Industries to recharge their implants and get proper rest.

Unfortunately, for them and several other amborgs from all three groups, they had not made it back home because they weren't prepared for how long this mission would be. Due to how much power they expended, they were at a critical risk of shutting down in the field. Dr. Kendrick had warned them about the dangers of depleting their energy reserves without proper self-care. This had never happened to any amborg so far, so they had no idea what would happen. To make matters worse, many of the exhausted amborgs were refusing to return home. As 3 pointed out, restoring their power levels to full or an acceptable level would require several hours of rest, and the country was still in the midst of a widespread battle. No one was willing to retreat while the mission remained unfinished.

"If this battle goes on for days," 917 sighed, "we might have to make a hard decision."

"We can't start abandoning people who need us," 3 said.

"I know," 917 nodded. He began to feel worried when he saw 3's eyes starting to droop. "But we can't save everyone. The best person to save right now is yourself, right? Live to fight another day? I'm not saying all of us should go home... but I can't stand to see my friends losing power and probably dying out here out of sheer stubbornness."

"You don't know that we'll die if our power runs out," 3 stated.

"You're right," 917 nodded, "I don't. But when your power gets so low to the point where you won't make it back to A.I. Industries... or if we can't fly a charging pod out here in time... are you really going to risk it?"

A sudden transmission cut off their conversation and 3 tapped her head in an attempt to focus.

"We weren't broadcasting that conversation right?" 3 checked with 917.

"Negative," 917 shook his head. "It was a private channel."

"Yes?" 3 responded, answering the call.

Before she could get a reply, a sharp whistle pierced the air. Both amborgs sprang to their feet instinctively. A missile shot from afar and struck the ground nearby, exploding with a deafening bang and flinging mud in every direction. Fortunately, no one was caught in the blast radius. A few onlookers were momentarily stunned but soon returned to their tasks as if nothing had happened. Unfazed, 3 shook her head and tried to expand the frequency range, but it wasn't responding as quickly as it usually did.

As the lag cleared up, she lifted her other hand to wipe the mud off her face. At that moment, she realized that her hand was dropping back at her side much slower than normal. Performing a quick calculation, she shuddered at the numbers that her head finished crunching. Her performance had dropped by seven point two percent.

"Hello?" she said. "Who is calling? Make it quick before I fall asleep. Literally."

She brightened the tone of her voice to sound as positive as possible. There was no use in sounding irritable as she tapped her foot impatiently. Noticing her uneasy mood, 917 was about to say something encouraging, but instead felt the immediate urge to sit back down on the ground. The combat had drained much of his strength and he was now leaning on his left arm to stay upright.

"3? Is that you?" a voice asked anxiously.

"5!" she exclaimed, relieved, as she looked towards the Academy borders. "Where are you?"

"Just getting a group of survivors out of this place. But it is a bit of a drag."

"Lose any limbs lately?"

"It happened one time. One time."

"I had to make a joke about it at some point," she chuckled to herself.

Out of nowhere, a jolt of pain shot through her chest, causing her to cough violently. Laughing had tickled her throat, and she practically coughed up the last of her granola bar. 917's widened in alarm as he saw 3 drop to her knees.

"Whoa!" he cried.

Through the transmission, 5's voice took on a nervous tone.

"Hey 3!" he said skeptically. "Are you ok? This is why you were pulled from combat. You're low on power. Expend more energy and you might feel a lot more pain."

"Amazing," she whispered.

She could sense 917's confused stare, while 5 remained silent on the comms.

"What?" 5 asked after an awkward silence.

"The sensation of... coughing," Missy said, looking off into the distance. "Pain coming from my esophagus, a reaction to clear mucus from my artificial lungs. It feels so strange, painful but enlightening as well. The accumulation of whatever I have breathed in intentionally in the past few weeks combined with fatigue from this day has led to pain and a reaction! It has been so long since I coughed."

"3, I'm going to interrupt," 5 spoke up. "As much as I would love to hear you go over the details of what it's like to cough, I have some survivors heading towards your safe zone. Do you think we could have a safe reception?"

3 looked down at 917, who tilted his head with a small smirk.

"Right. On our way."

After she hung up, 917 helped her get back to her feet.

"Perhaps we should seriously consider pulling you off the front lines?" he asked.

"Let's go tell 6," 3 conceded, letting out a defeated sigh.

----

117 straightened up. He lifted his foot and stepped away, revealing a shattered drone, its pieces scattered across the ground. He leaned down

to inspect the wreckage, noting how the head had been virtually flattened into the cement.

"All clear."

117 kicked the dead robot body away. Thomas, the leader of students in his group, poked his head out from behind the stone wall they'd used as cover. They'd hidden themselves when 117 needed a moment to take out the opposition blocking their path. Noticing Thomas nodding, 117 glanced back and signaled for the rest of the group to follow. The students rose to their feet and quietly moved towards 117.

"You may stand," 117 gestured as he turned to face ahead.

His suggestion was met with silence; they looked visibly scared. Seeing their expressions, 117 tried again.

"I don't detect any other enemies," he added reassuringly. "We are clear until we reach the next checkpoint."

That seemed to do the trick. Thomas and his group got up and walked normally. As they continued on, 117 noticed someone approaching him with determination. He looked to his right and recognized the girl who'd shot him earlier—she was Thomas's sister. Quickly, 117 privately accessed the Academy's files and searched for her name in the school records.

"T-this is obviously the wrong time," Audrey stuttered. "A-actually, it's definitely the most dangerous time but... I didn't want to waste another moment. I'm sorry."

"Audrey Wright," 117 recited as he looked at her file. "Sophomore. An apology is not presently necessary."

"You're not looking at my records are you?" she said in surprise. "It's so strange hearing my name being spoken from an amborg. Or... one of those bracelets you wear."

117 merely nodded.

"As a matter of fact, I am looking at your records. Superb marksman, honor student, well-balanced tactician, from a strong military lineage alongside your brother, last physical indicated that..."

He stopped, immediately falling silent as an alert appeared on his HUD. Mandy was trying to reach him. Audrey, however, was clueless about what was happening. 117 took a moment to read Mandy's text message.

"Umm, is everything alright? You just cut off," Audrey bit her lip and leaned forward to look at his face. "Did the results of my physical say anything? Oh wait, that should be medically classified..."

"Of course Ms. Wright. There is nothing wrong," he replied swiftly. "I was just having a chat with my technician. Yes Mandy, I will remember your response. I always do."

"Girlfriend?" Audrey blurted.

117 smiled slightly.

"No," he replied. "A friend. Perhaps someone of your age might refer to it as... a B...F...F."

Taken aback, Audrey couldn't help but laugh.

"Ha ha. You do have a sense of humor."

"In that context, it would appear you do possess the ability to laugh," 117 patted her on the shoulder as they began moving again. "You were very tense and scared when I first saw you. It looks as if you are feeling somewhat better despite the strenuous circumstances."

"Well, if you hadn't shown up, we'd probably be dead by now," Audrey said quietly.

"Possibly. But I am here now so you may relieve some of your tension."

"As a non-amborg, it's not as easy as you think."

"For clarification," 117 added, "Mandy is my technician."

"Oh right!" Audrey nodded. "I remember that the amborgs go into the field with someone helping them out from A.I. Industries!"

"Correct."

Eventually, their brief reprieve from all the chaos came to an end. As they arrived at a specific location, 117 gently reminded Audrey that it was time to lower their voices. She nodded in agreement, chuckling when 117 added that Mandy had been silently reprimanding him for being too loud in a dangerous situation.

The battle raged on in the distance as the group continued their present course. Everyone walked in a single column, hunching over simultaneously each time an explosion erupted in another part of the campus. It looked like the fighting had shifted and died down elsewhere, which allowed them a safe and quiet journey towards their evacuation site. It wasn't until after a few minutes that 117 decided to say something reassuring.

"If I may say so, I do believe you and your brother could have successfully ensured your classmates' survival even if the amborgs didn't arrive to your rescue. You possess many qualities that would earn respect from others."

This did lift Audrey's spirits a little bit. For a moment, she didn't feel as nervous under the present circumstances.

"You seem to know a lot about me and everyone here," she said softly.

117 casually glanced at her and noticed her staring back. He could detect the unease and defensiveness in her tone. He tweaked his head to the left.

"My apologies," he said, realizing his mistake. "Please believe me when I say this. I have not looked at your records again since my technician reminded me of the breach of privacy."

"I believe you," Audrey smiled. "Thanks for telling me that."

As 117 and Audrey quietly chatted away, her brother Thomas was starting to eye them curiously. While he wasn't bothered by their conversation, anyone paying attention would have noticed his keen interest in their interaction.

"What did you learn about me?" Audrey asked inquisitively. She seemed to have lost all apprehension, which made it less awkward. "I mean, you probably saw a lot in that brief time. You know, with the amborgs having such a fast processing speed?"

"I don't have to answer if you feel that I'm violating your privacy," 117 replied calmly. "Although, you may rest easy since the information I have doesn't feature any personal info or facts that may be embarrassing or humiliating."

"Forget it then!" she whispered rather hastily. "I uh... retract my question!"

"If you insist," 117 blinked and continued moving forward.

As they walked ahead, Mandy decided to chime in privately in the back of his head.

"Smooth," she said. "Are you trying to comfort her or antagonize her?"

"It wasn't my intent," 117 transmitted quietly, ensuring Audrey couldn't hear him.

"Look, just change the subject," Mandy insisted. "Just talk to her normally. Don't bring up her past or anything from her record! That's basically cheating if you're trying to get to know her better. You just saved her so... keep on her good side."

"So, can I ask you something?"

117 ended the conversation with Mandy and returned his attention to Audrey when she spoke again.

"Yes?"

"How fast... I mean I've been curious but... how fast do you calculate... eh... things?"

He wasn't sure if it was just because his energy was low or if it was his basic human instinct taking over, but 117 couldn't help but chuckle a little.

"What?" Audrey asked. She looked worried, like she had offended him. "Was that not a legitimate question?"

"We calculate data," 117 replied with a soft smile. "But 'things' is also an appropriate thing to say. There are times when we try not to be too judgmental of the English language."

Audrey blinked, appearing to struggle to process what he was saying. "So, I do get an answer?"

"The problem, I think," 117 admitted, "is that you probably do not want to know the exact number. It does fit in the terabytes range though."

"Hundreds of terabytes within a millisecond range perhaps?"

"That is classified, but you are getting surprisingly close," 117 replied. "However, the real answer might make you jealous."

"Why would I be jealous of the person who rescued us?"

117's face fell when she smiled. She noticed and her mouth hung open.

"Oh... w-was that not ok for me to say?" she stammered.

Turning around, 117 noticed that Thomas was watching him intently, appearing concerned. The other students behind him were also eyeing 117 with curiosity.

"I haven't rescued you yet," 117 admitted grimly. "That task is not over yet. When I know you and your colleagues are safe, then we will discuss that topic again. I don't deserve your thanks."

Audrey looked at Thomas. He shook his head, indicating that he didn't have a response.

"I never knew amborgs were so considerate... or you seem really humble," Audrey said, facing 117 again. "I mean, putting your life on the line for people like us on a daily basis must be exhausting. The fact that you all do it over and over again... I think that's pretty amazing."

117 stopped and looked at her in the eyes solemnly. She blinked and averted her gaze.

"I meant that your profession is amazing," she added with a slight fluster in her voice. "Or maybe not a profession. Thomas! We can call the amborgs heroes... right?"

"Sure," Thomas chuckled.

He looked at 117 and grinned.

"Don't mind me," Thomas said as he walked ahead. "You two chat! I'll take point."

117 and Audrey stared as Thomas stepped in the lead position. 117 noticed that Audrey looked a little helpless without her older brother. He could see the betrayal in her eyes as she nervously glanced back up at 117.

"Her brother's hilarious," Mandy sputtered.

Ignoring her, 117 turned his head while he followed Thomas.

"I knew what you meant," 117 sighed, looking away sadly. "It is just that in light of recent events, there is no reason for any of us to be considered amazing."

Audrey began to feel concerned. She certainly didn't expect to hear an amborg acting so gloomy.

"Why is that?"

117 met her gaze again, but before he could answer her, their conversation was abruptly cut short when someone in the back let out a scream. At the same time, a gun was fired off not far from them. It was an ambush.

One moment, Audrey was looking 117 right in the eye, and the next, at empty air. Her eyes grew wide as she blinked in disbelief. The next thing she knew, she felt something collide with her from behind and was forced to the ground. She hit the pavement hard, feeling a jarring impact as something pressed painfully against her back.

"Ouch!" she cried. "Wha…?"

"Get down!" someone cried out from behind.

Audrey tried to make sense of what was going on, but her thoughts were too preoccupied trying to figure out who was pinning her down. As she wriggled, she discovered it was Deliza. As the two girls rolled off each other, Audrey noticed that Thomas was also being held down as she turned her head to survey the group. She spotted 117 standing about five feet away, holding onto one of their companions while a rain of bullets ricocheted off his back. Thomas staggered to his feet, gripping his rifle tightly as he gazed into the distance.

"We got shooters on the roof!" Thomas shouted as he lifted his gun and opened fire. "Covering!"

The noise pierced Audrey's ears sharply, and her hands instinctively shot up to the sides of her head.

She looked around desperately for her rifle. Hadn't she been carrying it a second ago before being forced to the ground? All of a sudden, she felt something hard hit her rib. Looking down, someone had slid her rifle to her from the side. Without missing a beat, she picked it up, joined her brother, and aimed at the roof.

"The enemy is firing from an elevated position!"

117 positioned himself firmly in front of the group, who were huddled behind the wall for protection. As bullets rained down on him, he bravely withstood the impacts. After a brief look around, he turned to them and relayed a set of instructions.

"There is a modified assault transport approximately forty-seven meters down that path! We will need to secure it for evacuation!"

117 motioned down the path, pointing at an abandoned jeep. It was a military Humvee, retrofitted with 22nd century tech. Audrey noticed the

doors were open, revealing a dead body partially hanging out. However, the sound of incoming gunfire forced her to crouch even lower behind the wall.

"I will draw the enemy fire. Stay behind the wall and keep out of their line of sight," she heard 117 shout. "Go now!"

He had grabbed a rifle at some point and leaped onto the wall. He swung it forward and began firing at the roof.

"You heard him! Move!"

Thomas nudged Audrey, and they both signaled to the others to start moving. Deliza had darted to the front and reached the Humvee in seconds. *Someone must have trained her in agility,* Audrey thought as bullets pelted the wall.

"Covering fire!!" Deliza yelled. She lifted her rifle and opened fire. "Come on Audrey!"

The entire group moved forward as Deliza attempted to suppress their attackers. Thomas fell back to check on the student that had been shielded by 117, which put Audrey ahead of everyone. Suddenly, a loud whooshing joined the firefight. The sound turned into a sharp whistle that quickly grew louder, which meant one thing.

An explosion ruptured the wall a few feet ahead of the group. Concrete and small pieces of rock flew outward in every direction. Shaking it off, Audrey found herself crawling and leaning by the gap in the wall. Bullets made their way through the hole, causing her to stiffen.

Not getting through there without being shot, she thought. *Now what?*

"We gotta move Audrey!!"

Audrey stared in astonishment as Deliza sprinted toward them at high speed. She dropped to her knees, sliding past the hole in the wall and crashing into Audrey. She glanced down at Deliza's rifle, noticing a bullet head lodged in the loading mechanism.

"Didn't you hear me?!" Deliza shouted as she attempted to clean out her weapon. "Come on! Just run and slide!"

"There is no way I could do something like that!" Audrey yelled. "I'd rather not die!"

Realizing she was having no luck dislodging the bullet, Deliza tossed her rifle away. As she drew her knife, she sidled next to Audrey.

"How much ammo do you still have?"

Audrey looked at the meter on the panel behind the scope. She gulped as she read the loadout on the light-up display screen. It was a lot lower than she originally thought. But in all the excitement, had she really expended that much ammo?

"Uhh, three shots…" she said calmly. "I think we can panic right about now. We're pinned down and can't move forward…"

"Oh, keep it together woman! We're dead whether we stay or go! Might as well choose one! Would you rather die sitting here or literally running for it with a slim chance that you'd make it?!"

A sudden, loud clang caught the girls' attention. They turned to see a silver canister hurtling through the shattered part of the wall. Audrey froze, her heart racing as she realized what it was.

"And that's a grenade…" Audrey gulped as the small canister began beeping.

"Aw damn," Deliza said with a sigh.

"COVER YOUR EARS!" someone yelled, but it was too late.

The cylinder's cap blew off with a deafening bang and a blinding flash of light. It was as if all the air had been violently ripped from Audrey's lungs. In an instant, she lost consciousness, and plunged into darkness.

"I am having second thoughts on what I wish to do when we return home…"

"Really? What did you have in my mind?"

5 sat on the ground sighed. Mud and dirt covered his entire body and he spat out a giant mouthful of it, which flew some feet away. 3, 22 and 27 were resting alongside him, profoundly exhausted. They had made it out of the danger zone, well away from the fighting, with their survivors and were now lazily defending the main triage center. Their short break was proving to be a little fruitless with their declining energy levels.

"I passed by a bar when we were in New York," he transmitted to them. "Maybe I could apply for a job there. Work like a human for a bit. But that is only a small idea."

"Curious," 22 ran a finger through her dark locks of hair. "Why would you want a job in a bar though? Seems like a miniscule type of occupation."

5 shrugged and rested his head against a crate behind him.

"Thought it would be an interesting idea to learn how to serve drinks," he replied, smirking. "Maybe I could make drinks better than 3."

3 glared at 5, who lifted his hands defensively.

"You are so asking for a shot of acid in your next martini," she grumbled.

"Look out, amborg bartender upset," 27 nudged 5 in the head.

3 dropped her angry demeanor and grinned. All of them laughed. Whether it was from their bracelets or inside the communication frequency

they were speaking with, they didn't care. As soon as the laughter subsided, 27 suddenly bent and keeled over.

"Agh," he moaned as he clutched his stomach.

"Signal 6 and tell her to get over here now," 5 examined 27 briefly. "Tell her 27 needs a medical examination now."

"Oh man," 27 coughed. "It was that drone that kicked a car into my ribs... It did not cause too much damage but I cannot remember being out for this long... The pain levels are intensifying."

22 stroked her hand across his head and smiled encouragingly. 27 seemed to relax a little at her touch. 5 nodded and sat back in relief, making a sighing motion.

"If we are discussing eons of time in the field," 22 brought up cheerfully, "this deployment is definitely not going to be good for my personal hygiene. I am unaware of how the other ladies are doing. But a shower sounds nice right about now."

"You're worried... about personal hygiene at a time like this??" 27 asked, raising his eyebrows.

22 shrugged, then suddenly kissed him on the cheek. 27 leapt away and immediately brought his hand up to his cheek, wiping it furiously.

"Of course," 22 smacked her lips and spit on the ground. "I am a woman after all... Blegh, that was disgusting..."

5 watched them with a look of amusement, putting on a face and shaking his head vigorously in playful disgust.

"*That*," 3 said, chuckling to herself, "...is one reason why women are concerned about personal hygiene."

A loud thud drew their attention to another amborg. 6 ran over and quickly scanned 27. Despite the fact that each amborg was equipped with a database of medical training and self-healing protocols, she was the most proficient and the best medic they had. There were stains all over her uniform, but her red cross patches were still visible, glowing brightly through the grime.

"Looks ok," she said hurriedly.

She looked him over once, then casually pulled a needle out of her pocket. Ignoring 27's shocked face, she brought it down and with lightning speed, stabbed it into his neck.

"How are you 27?" 6 asked, still speaking in a hurried manner. "Is there a reason you look as if you just drank liquid oxygen?"

27 looked over his shoulder and saw 3 and 22 sharing a fist bump. 6 remained unaware and returned to her usual routine. Seconds later, 27 felt a wave of calm wash over him and fell silent. 5 stopped chuckling and stared at him.

"6," he asked as his eyes widened in concern. "What did you give him?"

6 held up the syringe for everyone to see without turning around. She shook her head and whipped a lock of hair out of her face.

"You want to find out?" she asked indifferently. "I have no problem with where I stick this."

"I'm good," 5 muttered, cowering back a little.

"I'll say this though," 6 continued, her expression remaining unchanged. "Our conditions are deteriorating. Pain killers can't stop our power levels from dropping. If we lose power... then I don't know what will happen. I'm calling it."

6 faced the other amborgs sternly.

"You're all going home," she shook her head. "All the meds I've been giving all of you are going to have severe side effects if anyone overdoses or doesn't get home before your power levels are empty."

"What side effects?" 3 asked curiously.

"So far?" 6 sighed. "You just fall asleep for several hours. Based on the tests I did in the lab and with eager-to-volunteer personnel back home, it is effective in various scenarios."

22 chuckled nervously.

"But morphine technically does the same thing though... right?" she asked.

6 thought a few seconds before responding.

"Well, there is morphine in it," she said as she glanced at the syringe in her hand.

Despite his serene demeanor, 27's eyes widened as worry began creeping into his features.

"Ok then," 3 interrupted, also beginning to appear uneasy. "Perhaps we should discuss less creepy topics and focus more on the catastrophic reality. How long do we have?"

"Well, if it was a normal deployment, we would be able to stay out in the field for months."

6 glanced at the back of her hand and noticed it shaking very slowly. They watched as it stopped, then she lowered it. The effects were becoming more noticeable by the hour.

"All of this damage and fatigue has sapped most of our energy... and I mean that physically and metaphorically. For some of us, we'll maybe have four hours before our cybernetic parts power down and our performance will completely tank. Don't forget, the longer you're out here, the longer it'll take for you to recharge, and that means that we would be out here without you for several hours."

"At least in theory," 27 spoke, "we do not necessarily die when our implants power down. But if we do not find energy soon, that theory will be put to the test."

"I'm going to start making arrangements to start rotations," 6 declared. "I need to send some of you home now. You can come back once you're properly rested and charged."

"Look, you can't make us do that!" 3 coughed.

"I am the senior medical officer and even though David 117 is in charge of this mission, I outrank you when it comes to your personal health and medical well being!" 6 snapped at 3. "You're going home! What I'm worried about after you go is that the other amborgs still here will need to pick up the slack! I'm trying to make sure that every amborg doesn't work themselves to death! If all of us need to go home and recharge, who will be out here protecting everyone while we're spending half a day recovering?!"

No one responded to 6's angry outburst.

"That's what I thought," 6 nodded firmly. "You're all going back to A.I. Industries and you can redeploy after you take a break! End of story!"

5 stared up at the sky, at the dark clouds drifting by.

"Maybe we should stick our arms up and harness the electrical energy of lightning," he said.

A resounding boom echoed across the sky, drawing everyone's attention upward. Ironically, a storm was gathering overhead. Lightning bolts streaked across the sky, accompanied by bright flashes of light. Before they had a chance to check the weather forecast, it began to rain.

"I was being rhetorical!!" 5 yelled to no one in particular.

6's cold and angry demeanor had faded. She was still staring up at the clouds when suddenly, a smile spread across her face. The others, noticing the change, grew concerned.

"That is actually perfect timing," 6 smirked, an idea quickly forming. "Come on! We need a drop pod!"

"Audrey! Wake up! Can you hear me? Don't give up!"

Audrey opened her eyes and blinked. Without warning, she sat upright, only to hit her head against something hard, resulting in a loud clang. She couldn't tell if the dizziness was from the impact or the events leading up to her blackout. Now, her head hurt worse, throbbing and aching intensely as she pressed her hands against her forehead.

"Ouch girl," she heard Deliza say close by. "How many times have you been hit on the head?"

The hit to her head surprisingly brought back much of her awareness. Audrey glanced to her left and gazed out the window. She blinked a few more times, trying to clear the last of the brain fog, and looked to her right, watching the scenery rushing by. It was clear that the group had made it on board the Humvee but, why was she lying on her back?

"What happened?" Audrey tried to sit up slowly, but someone forced her to lie back down. "Are we safe?"

"The grenade that exploded in our face was one of those new stun grenades," Deliza explained as she sat back in her seat.

Deliza spun her seat around, facing the window. She pressed a button on the side, and the window slid down. Having acquired another rifle, she pointed the barrel outside.

Audrey had only been inside the modified Humvees a few times, but it was enough for her to memorize the interior. Vehicles from the twentieth to the twenty-first century were typically designed with forward-facing seats. The remodeled Humvees, like the one she was in, had a driver's section fortified by steel plating, providing protection for both the driver and a front passenger. The back area had been expanded to accommodate at least six people, with each seat capable of rotating for easy access to the doors and the medical stretched in the center, like the one Audrey was currently lying on. From what she remembered, there were quite a few exits for a remodel—at least eight, if she wasn't mistaken.

Audrey raised her hand to her forehead. The rumbling and vibrations of the wheels felt soothing and helped her relax.

"I only had like a second to get air..." she groaned. "I really doubt that any of the training they teach us in the emergency classes really prepares you for anything like that..."

"I'll say. You were close to when it went off. That 117 guy was considerate enough to put you in the stretcher when we made it to the transport. Should have seen how fast he assigned us to our seating and how quickly he set it up for you."

"Really..." Audrey said. "Well where is he? That's another thing that I owe him. Man, I have got to find a way to save him."

Deliza pointed a finger upward. Audrey blinked, briefly glancing up at the steel plating.

"On the roof," she said casually. "Good luck with saving a badass guy like him."

Audrey continued to stare at the transport's ceiling. Without a word, she lowered her gaze at Deliza, eyes wide in disbelief and pointing up for clarification. Deliza chuckled and nodded in response.

"I guess amborgs aren't the type to sit in a vehicle in the middle of a danger zone."

"Hey, what about Thomas? Is he ok?"

"Oh yeah," Deliza replied, matter-of-factly. "He's up front, driving."

"Nice of you to remember me sis."

Thomas spoke over the small intercom in the Humvee. Audrey smiled in relief, visibly relaxing a bit more.

"Thanks for getting us out," she said immediately.

"Yeah yeah, love you too sis," Thomas chuckled. "Now be quiet and let me concentrate on getting us out of here."

As they continued on their present course, they heard a few quick taps from the roof. Everyone in the vehicle fell silent and glanced up.

"We are four minutes from the evacuation zone," 117 informed them through the plating. "Mr. Wright, I suggest slowing down."

"Do you see anything?"

Thomas glanced down the road in an attempt to see if there were any upcoming obstacles. What happened next, however, rendered him unable to hear 117's next command.

Scanning the dirt road ahead, he spotted something fly into their path. The speed at which he was driving left him with no time to swerve or hit the breaks. Some sort of device was hurtling toward them, and they were about to become its target. Reacting instinctively, Thomas slammed down on the gas pedal, pushing the vehicle to its limits. As the engine roared, he could only hope for the best as the Humvee barreled over the projectile.

There was a loud thud as an explosion struck the rear undercarriage of the Humvee. Thanks to Thomas' timed acceleration, the blast didn't reach the passenger section. Instead, the force of the shockwave launched the Humvee into a forward flip, lifting it off the ground from behind the rear tires.

Inside, the passengers were violently thrown around. In the fleeting seconds they were airborne, Audrey glanced out the window and saw the ground tilting sideways before it completely flipped upside down. The stretcher beneath her had activated its emergency system. Straps emerged and wrapped around her body, securing her in place. Audrey, practically adhered to the stretcher, was tossed and jolted around like she was taking a ride on the Vomit Comet. As the Humvee's roof scraped across the ground, a heavy rattling shook the vehicle, and Audrey suddenly found herself crashing face-first into the ceiling. Grimacing in pain, she felt utterly helpless. Something had jammed the magnetic locks that secured her to the stretcher, and she was not enjoying it.

Outside, 117 stared at the vehicle he had just been crouched on moments ago. The force of the blast had thrown him clear into the grass nearby. He watched as the Humvee, now flipped over, slid down the road until it eventually came to a stop, and he quickly ran after it.

From her squashed perspective, Audrey anxiously tried to look around. The straps held her down, making it impossible to sit up. In a desperate attempt to see if anyone else was still conscious, she tried to shift to the side of the stretcher. Managing a slight turn, she heard the sounds of coughing and moaning from nearby. Briefly glancing to her right, she saw the control panel for the stretcher. She reached for the screen, stretching as far as the straps allowed, and began tapping it. On her second try, the straps finally released, snapping open and freeing her arms. She pushed herself up and tried to get her feet beneath her. The cramped space and the stretcher on her back made it difficult. Remembering that she wasn't the only one trapped, she moved as carefully as she could.

"Is everyone alright?"

It was a bit of a struggle, but Audrey managed to crawl to Deliza's seat. The explosion had caused her seatbelt to tighten, trapping her much like the way Audrey's stretcher, leaving her dangling from the vehicle's floor like a bat hanging upside down.

"Come on, wake up Deliza!" Audrey cried as she shook her friend's limp body. "We got to get you and everyone else down! Also, we should really complain to whoever designed these stupid harnesses."

"Oh..." she groaned, waking with a start. "That was not cool... I think something hit my head..."

Deliza soon realized that she was looking at Audrey upside down. She leaned forward and reached down, trying to find the manual release located beneath her seat. In a flash, her straps came undone, and she landed beside Audrey with a heavy thud.

"Isn't the release for your seatbelt supposed to be on the side? Why did you reach for your feet?"

"Oh that?"

Crawling, Deliza found her rifle and shoved it through one of the transport's windows. As the others began to stir, the two of them worked together to free the remaining members of their group.

"I was trying to unlock the manual release for the whole chair," Deliza chuckled lazily, shaking her head to refocus.

"Wouldn't that hurt?" Audrey asked.

"Yeah," Deliza replied. "That wouldn't have been good for my spine, probably."

One of the other survivors was having trouble with his straps. Audrey took a knife out and cut him free. As he crawled through the window, Deliza prepared to follow him out.

"Or your head," Audrey said.

"I think you've been hit on the head far too much today as well," Deliza laughed. "But who am I to talk?"

Audrey let out a soft chuckle as they made their way out of the wreckage. As she wriggled out, she saw a hand reach down for her. Audrey looked up and grabbed 117's hand.

"It would appear that the enemy tossed a very powerful explosive under our vehicle. I have taken care of the ambushers so we should be safe," he reported as the girls straightened up. 117 began tapping his head, blinking rapidly. "I couldn't see it at all..."

"What do you mean?" Audrey looked at him with concern.

"I'm very exhausted..." 117 replied with a weary look. "I'm not operating at maximum efficiency, otherwise I would have had the means to detect traps and inform Thomas to change course. Your brother had the right instinct to speed up. If he hadn't, the explosion would have penetrated the passenger compartment."

Audrey looked around and froze. Thomas was not among the group. She quickly sprinted to the driver's side of the overturned transport and peered through the broken window. The cracked glass obscured her view, but she could make out Thomas' silhouette hanging upside down in the seat, and it was clear to her that he wasn't moving.

"Someone help me open the door!" she cried frantically as she banged on the door. "Thomas! Thomas wake up! Can you hear me?!"

"Move Audrey!!"

Audrey turned sharply at the sound of Delisa's shout and noticed 117 crouching down. She quickly stepped back as he grasped the door handle. With incredible strength, 117 wrenched the door off as if it were made of paper and tossed it aside. He then reached in and safely extracted Thomas and the other front-seat passenger.

"Is he alright?!" Audrey asked frantically as 117 carried him and the other student to a patch of grass near the road. He gently set them down and began scanning the two.

"I am transmitting a live feed to amborg 6," he said as he ran a hand over them, recording the damage. "She can quickly relay the results and provide assistance."

"What?" Deliza said. "I thought you amborgs all had medical training?"

117 nodded and began checking for a pulse while he continued to talk.

"Sometimes, it is helpful to have a backup plan, just to be safe," he said quickly. "6 is our designated medic and so far, she is the only one I know who can help in the events I cannot. If you must trust someone medically, trust her."

"Just help him please..." Audrey begged. "I can't lose him."

117 paused briefly. His eyes flashed a bright green for a moment and then a quick red. Finally, he was able to give a definitive answer.

"He has received physical trauma to his head and glass from the forward window has embedded into his upper abdomen," 117 said as he began to run his hand across the cuts. "He is alive and... waking up. Are you detecting anything else 6? It would appear the safety bags didn't deploy."

Thomas instantly woke up coughing and gasping for air. Audrey breathed a sigh of relief as 117 calmed her brother down. He lifted his head and began scanning the area.

"We must get to the evacuation point and get him aboard the ship. Immediately. We are not safe yet. If we were ambushed here, I suspect more trouble is coming."

"Is he going to be ok?" Audrey asked.

She was desperate for an answer. Before she could get one, they heard a heavy crash behind them. 117 jolted and faced the road in the direction they just came from.

"Is that what I think it was?" Deliza asked, aiming her rifle down the road. "Oh boy..."

117 looked the group over and back down the road. Audrey knew he was assessing the situation.

"There is no time," he stated openly. 117 lifted an arm and pointed toward a line of trees off the side of the road. "I have stabilized your brother but there is nothing else I can do. You must lead the group into the cover of the forest. Continue in that direction and reach the evacuation ship. Hurry or Thomas' likelihood of survival will diminish. Leave the area and don't wait for anything, even me."

With that being said, 117 ran back the way they came, his fists tightly clenched. Audrey immediately knelt and grabbed Thomas' arms. Another student lended a hand, and the survivors quickly made their way into the cover of the trees.

"How much ammo do we have?" Deliza asked hurriedly, and all of them searched their pockets.

"Close to nothing!" one of the boys shouted.

"Ok, running is probably the best idea right now," Audrey panted. "We're going to get you to safety Thomas. Just stay with me."

Several thuds echoed nearby as the group moved into the dense brush. Just as they entered the tree line, a loud crash diverted their attention. They turned to see a tree falling over, blocking the road behind them. 117 appeared, leaping onto the downed tree before springing onto a massive robot. Audrey immediately recognized it from the start of the battle.

As 117 began his attack on the behemoth, he shouted in their direction.

"I TOLD YOU TO RUN!!!"

Nodding, Audrey checked that Thomas was still awake and then quickened her pace. While the tumultuous fight raged behind, everyone moved as fast as they could.

"Come on!! We're not out of this yet."

CHAPTER 21

Wait, Watt Now??

Amborg Drop Pod Landing Zone

"6, this has to be the worst idea you have ever come up with. People have done this in the past. Need I remind you that they didn't exactly survive?"

6 looked at 5 and he flinched.

"You want to check your energy levels again? If you have a better idea, then say so. Otherwise, quit whining and let me work on this."

6 took her hand away from the panel of the drop pod cluster and pointed a finger in 5's face when he got too close. He lifted his hands up in surrender and backed away with his mouth firmly shut. The rest of the amborgs that had gathered watched in stunned silence.

6 had dragged their drop pods into a giant horseshoe formation and was setting up wires, connecting them all together. By her instructions, they had also managed to acquire a large generator.

"Look 6. I was only trying..."

5 was interrupted once more.

"That has to be the lowest power level I have seen in your databanks compared to the time you played videogames nonstop for fifteen days straight," she said observantly and in a very condescending tone. "You want to talk about insanity? Come at me, bitch."

6 stopped what she was doing and looked at 5 apologetically.

"Sorry. I didn't mean to curse. I'm tired."

"No apologies are necessary," 5 replied, chuckling nervously. "But look at this, you have taken several drop pods and hooked them up together. This is supposed to harness power and refine it so we can properly recharge, right? We are being struck by actual lightning."

"Not directly," 6 said reassuringly. "Have some faith and do something stupid for once in your life 5. It should be in our job requirements."

"It's not a job requirement," 5 protested. "It's an occupational hazard."

She pretended she didn't hear his last comment. 6 stepped back from her pod and admired her handiwork. She had attached some sort of makeshift lightning rod to the roof of the pod. Somehow she had also managed to make twelve kites and they now flew in the sky, heavily attached to the roof of the pod, waiting for the storm to hit. 6 turned to look at the amborgs that were currently with her. Her enthusiastic smile faded at their looks of skepticism.

"Oh come on," she protested. "Benjamin Franklin did something like this with one kite in order to experiment with the theory of a lightning rod. That worked, didn't it?"

"Yes, that is correct 6," 5 said. He seemed to be the only one willing to speak up. "However... We aren't sure if that bit of history is accurate. And another thing..."

He pointed a finger up at the kites as thunder reverberated across the sky.

"...You have the lightning rods already," he continued as he gestured to all the amborgs currently present, "...and the wires necessary to harness the power into the generator to form a backup power supply for those of us not here. But still, you are asking us to attach ourselves to the ends of those wires from our pods and be the ground rods... the receivers. This is not going to work."

"Sure it is!" 6 exclaimed confidently. "LTO is specifically a good conductor for any forms of quick charge and we are designed to run on basic forms of power. Except, we can't exactly run on car batteries so... yeah. And if the technicality of it is not sound for you, it will be fun to have a taste of Zeus' wrath. Wouldn't you agree?"

"But did we ever test if LTO inside a genetically modified human is capable of withstanding such a large power surge at once?"

5's next question instantly made them all shiver. They all murmured amongst themselves.

"Well, if we lose power, we won't have any time to return home for a charge," 6 argued as she held up the wire. "If we did, it'll take too long and that lunatic who forced us to run around out here will be in the wind. So! I'm going to be electrocuted whether anyone likes or not!!"

"No, you are not!"

6 froze as 1 jumped into the group.

"I will volunteer my life for this..." he said, taking the wire from 6's hands. The rest of them moved in and began protesting, but 1 waved a hand to signal for silence. He held the wire tightly. "Be reasonable 6, you're our best doctor. What would we do without you if you killed yourself by accident?"

"Um, Leonard... every amborg has medical training," she said bluntly. "You would all be fine."

"I was being rhetorical..." 1 mumbled. "Anyone here thinks that they can do this better than me better pry it from my hands, because I will not let more people risk their lives. I need to do this."

Nobody dared to try to oppose him. Before anyone could even consider talking this out, lightning flashed across the sky. 1 looked up and sparks of electricity began flowing through the kites, but the charge wasn't powerful enough. Suddenly, a lightning bolt struck overhead, illuminating the rods with a brilliant glow as a surge of electricity raced down the wires toward them.

At that moment, 5 put a hand on 1's shoulders.

"What are you doing?!" 1 exclaimed.

5 grinned.

"Two of us have a better chance at this than one. You are not doing this alone. We face Zeus together!!"

1 blinked in confusion.

"What does that even mean?!"

"Too late..." 5 said, gritting his teeth. He slowly gazed up and watched the stream of electricity approach. "Oh, this is going to hurt..."

The power surged to all of the hooked up drop pods. Finally, it hit 1 and 5 like a freight train, creating a bright explosion right where they stood.

"Give me your head!"

117 clung tightly to the behemoth's head, refusing to let go even as its thrashing arms struck him repeatedly in the back. Based on his analysis of its design, the arms weren't built to reach all the way around, but they could still inflict damage with their elbow joints, which he was feeling all too well. Just as he felt his grip slipping, there was a sudden crack, and the neck joint was forcefully pulled free. Triumphant, 117 dropped to the ground, holding the head securely in his hands. Without its key component, the behemoth powered down and collapsed with a resounding crash.

"Mandy," 117 gasped as he dropped the head. "I hid the reading from my own HUD but I think now is a good time to ask. What's my current power level?"

"Oh shit... You're at six percent power David," she replied quietly as 117 took off to find the survivors. It was starting to feel deeply exhausting just to lift his knee joints. "Why don't you try taking the power reserves from the behemoth?"

"Remember when we tried that before?" 117 replied as he stumbled over a rock. "These things are run solely on diesel fuel. The design was elaborate but the fuel tank is heavily armored and protected. At first, we thought they were electric, but they're not compatible with our circuits."

"This bad guy is conveniently resourceful..." Mandy said with a worried tone. "First, he runs you out of power, then strands the amborgs in a place where you can't take it from others. We could get you home right now..."

"I can't," 117 sighed. "It's not over."

"It will be if we don't get you out of there," Mandy replied softly. "I've been trying to convince you for hours."

"I need a significant amount of time to recharge to a normal state of operation," 117 panted as he ran through the wooded area.

"If you don't get over your stubbornness," Mandy declared, "you're going to die. 43 will lose you... and I will have a front row seat, right here from my cubicle. Is that what you want me to witness?"

117 bit his lip guiltily.

"No," he replied. "I'll return home right away."

Mandy fell silent.

"You're right," 117 added. "I have been behaving poorly."

"I'm... really glad you're finally listening to me," Mandy sighed in relief. "You know, I could get the motor pool to have your car ready for you while you're charging your power levels."

117 laughed slightly. There was no way that would work. Their drop pods were faster.

"What good would that do?" he asked. "I'll essentially be taking a power nap in my charging pod back home."

"Nice one," Mandy chuckled at his clever pun. "I wasn't talking about having you drive around. I wanted to get behind the wheel and take it for a spin. Both of us can have a nice relaxing drive. Maybe you could plug yourself into the battery if that will help."

"You're poking fun at me, aren't you?"

On his HUD, he could see Mandy smirking.

"Of course I am," she nodded. "The first opportunity you get, you get home, right now. The other amborgs remaining in the field can continue the fight until you get back."

"I suppose that would be a good idea," 117 replied. "Whoa!"

He tripped and fell into some grass. As he got back on his feet, dirt clung to his face, but he pressed on. Dismissing the mud stains and the filth accumulating on him, he tried hard to ignore the throbbing pain in his feet.

"Are you ok?" Mandy asked in alarm. "Thankfully your readings don't show any severe injuries..."

"I'm fine," 117 replied.

"You are clearly not," Mandy sighed. "Oh wait, I'm getting a message from some of the First Group amborgs. They and their technicians are updating the rest of us."

"What are they saying?" 117 asked curiously.

"Report to the safe zone where the drop pods are parked," Mandy informed him. "There's something going on there that might fix our problem."

"Understood?" 117 responded suspiciously. "What's going on?"

117 suddenly noticed a series of footprints ahead. He scanned them and recognized the patterns belonging to the students he had been protecting. Running toward a nearby hill, he glanced at the heat signatures on the ground. It was incredibly hard just to maintain infrared vision, so he stuck to old fashioned tracking. The students had passed through this area and continued on to find shelter...

"... that way," he finished his thought out loud.

Eventually, he came upon a small clearing surrounded by trees. Someone was crying. Mandy wasn't able to explain what was happening with the other amborgs and had fallen silent. Adjusting his hearing, 117 found the group clumped together, immediately deciphering what was happening.

"Mandy, stop recording the live feed," 117 spoke softly in his mind. "It is not good. I do not think this should be archived."

"Yeah," Mandy's tone fell. "I was thinking the same thing. Switching the feed to your personal drive."

This meant that unless he wanted to reveal the footage publicly, everything from this moment forth was saved on his own secure server back home. No one would see it without his permission.

"Thank you Mandy. I accept responsibility for the black out. Confirming. No one else can see this?"

"Only me," Mandy replied. "As well as whomever we choose to disclose it to."

He moved forward, and the voices gradually became more discernible with each step. He was close enough now that he didn't have to adjust his hearing anymore.

"Audrey, I'm not going to make it out of this one..." he heard someone say.

"Don't say that," Audrey's voice was barely audible, but 117 immediately knew what was happening. "The rescue ship will be here any minute now. Just stay with me please."

117 stopped walking and watched from a distance. Audrey was kneeling beside her brother Thomas, who was lying on the ground but awake. Blood was seeping from his lips.

"No Audrey…" he coughed. "Not this time. I got careless… I didn't see that trap when I was driving. I did what I could to save you."

"It isn't your fault," she said as tears flowed down her cheeks. "We're all still alive because of you. We'll make it through this together."

Thomas brought his hand up to his neck and tugged at a chain. It was a necklace with four dog tags and a small lucky charm attached to a silver keychain. 117 looked at the tags with his long vision and recognized the names from the Academy records, but the charm was unfamiliar.

"Take it," Thomas held the necklace out to Audrey. "These were our parent's and… here's my lucky charm. It's yours sis. It's not lucky if it gets buried and left behind."

"Don't say that! You keep it! Thomas?"

Thomas smiled, took one last breath, and spoke softly as she held his hand.

"Mom and dad," he said. "They're proud of you. They always will be… I'll say hi to them for you. I hate to do this Audrey… but you'll need to be tough on your own. Keep believing… yourself."

At that point, 117 switched his hearing level back to its normal setting. He had already heard more than enough. Making his presence known, he stepped into the clearing. None of the other students said anything. A few turned away and averted their gaze. Others tried to offer condolences but they didn't know what to say. Deliza remained silent. She lowered her rifle to the ground and closed her eyes.

"Thomas?" Audrey whispered, but there was no reply. "Thomas? No…"

The tears were pouring in a steady stream. Through his HUD, 117 could hear Mandy beginning to sniff.

"Oh no," she whispered in his head.

"Man down," 117 replied privately.

117 walked forward. Audrey looked up when she heard his footsteps but kept her gaze fixed on her brother's lifeless form.

"I'm sorry," 117 knelt down and placed his hand on her shoulder. "He fought well and died peacefully."

Not saying anything, she turned and sunk her head into his chest. He quickly calculated the proper response and slowly held her.

"My condolences for your family," he continued. "I have… also lost people that I care about."

Before Audrey could respond, a powerful whoosh broke the stillness. An air transport from the Academy hovered overhead, casting its searchlight down on them. Everything happened in a blur. A pair of soldiers equipped with jet packs descended from the ramp, landing smoothly beside the group and began to establish a defensive perimeter. Moments later, the transport touched down in the clearing, and two additional soldiers stepped out, signaling for everyone to board. As the students moved up the ramp, 92, 93, and 18 stepped away and approached 117, who was still holding Audrey.

"117," 18 exclaimed as the twins began carrying Thomas' body towards the transport. "Are you alright?"

117 nodded and both he and Audrey stood up. She went on ahead and boarded the transport while he observed the area.

"One casualty," he reported grimly. "Everyone else made it out alright."

"You did what you could," 18 replied reassuringly. "We must return to the drop pods. 6 has successfully found a way for us to... recharge."

"Why do I feel this is not going to be safe?" 117 replied skeptically.

"Well," Mandy coughed in the back of his mind. "You're not going to like what I was just informed about."

117 looked concerned as 18 shrugged.

"When has it ever been safe for us anyway?" she asked.

The two of them, followed by the rest of the soldiers, boarded the transport, which shot up into the sky and took flight. 117 glanced around the cabin. His group of survivors were seated on the starboard side, while 92 and 93 were slumped on the floor, clearly exhausted. Thomas' body was lying next to another pair of bodies, which turned out to be 35 and 57.

"Are 35 and 57 alright?" 117 asked, but before he could get an answer, 57 opened her eyes and attempted to sit up, only to suddenly wince in pain as she clutched her chest. "Oh, hi."

"Just trying to nap," she muttered. "It's not really easy though. I usually fall asleep in total darkness in my room back home. Sleeping out here is so overwhelming."

Checking his power levels, 117 sat next to 18 on the floor as the seats were all occupied. Two minutes into the flight, the transport's lights came on, illuminating the whole compartment.

"We are now outside the combat zone," the pilot announced over the P.A.

The troops exhaled in relief, and the students began to relax. The amborgs, however, didn't even move. They maintained a battle-worn but strong sense of alertness. It wasn't over yet. 117 sighed, but he wasn't smiling; they still had a long road ahead.

"Thank you."

117 looked up. Audrey had left her seat and sat down in front of him.

"I lost my brother but you also saved my life many times," she said quietly. "No I meant... You saved all of us and I just wanted to say umm...No I..."

She stopped and looked at the floor. 18, noticing Audrey's loss of words, gently nudged 117 in the shoulder and shot him a private message.

"She has been through quite an ordeal," she pointed out. "Assist her."

117 reached a hand out. Audrey looked at it and slowly grabbed it in response.

"My name is David 117," he said formally. "If you require any assistance, please... ask. I am here. Say or call my name when you need me. I will be there for you."

"You're supposed to give her your number first, you dummy," Mandy sighed.

117 ignored her and waited for a response. With tear-stained eyes, Audrey smiled as she shook his hand. Her other hand came up and wiped her eyes.

"Thank you..." she whispered. "What did you mean when you said that you lost someone you cared about?"

"Someone I loved," 117 replied casually. "However, this love was probably not the same as the love you had for your brother. Had the circumstances been different, I would have tried harder to save him. I'm sorry for failing you."

"I don't blame you," Audrey said empathetically. "All of you fought so hard for us."

The engines suddenly emitted a sharp whine that gradually dulled. The pilot's voice came through the P.A. a moment later.

"We are now landing at the Amborg Drop Pod LZ. Prepare to disembark. Medical teams are standing by and all amborgs onboard are to head over to... uhh, amborg 6's drop pod for... a recharge. Whatever that means."

"Duty calls," 92 exclaimed.

He and 93 bent down to help 35 and 57 to their feet, and together they leaned on one another as they made their way out. 57 hesitated briefly to glance back at Audrey, seemingly about to say something, but followed the twins without a word. All of them seemed eager to try out 6's recharging technique. 18 gave 117 a reassuring pat on the shoulder before heading out. Deliza also offered a comforting pat to Audrey's back as she left. 117 turned to say goodbye to Audrey as they both stepped off the ramp.

"It has been a pleasure Ms. Wright," 117 said. "I apologize for leaving you in these circumstances. It seems inappropriate to suddenly leave but you are currently safe. On a brighter note, I believe I see several of your classmates."

Turning in the direction he was pointing, Audrey caught sight of a few familiar faces among her classmates in the distance. However, she couldn't help but notice how few of them there were. She didn't want to know how many people lost their lives along with Thomas. She wasn't ready for the pain. Her eyes lit up slightly when she saw Joey several feet away. He had survived the ordeal. Even though he was in a wheelchair and receiving care from medical staff, he appeared to be alright.

117 watched Audrey slowly begin to smile. The transport lifted off, creating a powerful gust of wind that swept across the area. Caught off guard, Audrey was pushed forward by the force of the air. 117 immediately positioned himself in front of her, acting as a barrier against the wind. She was about to thank him again, but he raised a hand to stop her. Together, they made their way toward another cluster of students. Just then, 57, having slipped away from the twins, approached 117 and quickly exchanged a few words with him.

"I'm glad that Joey is alright!" Audrey said with relief while 57 hastily sent 117 a private message. "He shouldn't have been forced into this. None of us should have."

"And that is also not all," 117 continued as 57 walked in front of Audrey.

She stared up at the other Second Group amborg. Audrey watched as the tall girl stretched out her hand. Puzzled, Audrey glanced down and noticed a standard computer chip resting in the girl's palm. Then she remembered.

"You're Katie 57?"

57 stared at her with a lifeless and exhausted gaze.

"You have a very interesting artificial intelligence..."

57 placed the chip in Audrey's hand. Her tone of voice sounded strained. Being polite was clearly difficult for the female amborg.

"Although he did give me quite a headache, he is very unique," she muttered. "I believe that it is time for him to be returned to his owner. Finally... if you do not mind my hastiness to eject him from my care."

Audrey held the chip in her hand, which suddenly lit up with the raucous sound of Carter's voice.

"Miss Wright!" his disembodied voice cried out. "It is so delightful to see you! Or to be accurate, perceive you! They told me that you were alive but I couldn't help but worry! When the attack first occurred, I rewrote my programming so that I could provide some sort of defense but you locked me out from all the school servers so I was... well, actually trapped in your room!! If it hadn't been for this amborg, I wouldn't be here!"

Audrey's eyes widened as she stared at the chip.

"You're talking? You're... talking to me!" she said in amazement. "Without a computer! How??"

"About that," 57 sighed. "In order to transport him from the computer he was in, we offered him a ride in one of our own standard computer chips. A couple of us carry these things for sensitive materials or complex programs during data recovery missions. It has a format that is able to house all known artificial intelligences that exist. We had to reformat his basic structure algorithms and alter his primary core matrix due to him being an older model, but we succeeded in upgrading him to our own specifications. We are unsure, though, if this was the best idea."

"It's true!" Carter flashed brightly in Audrey's hand. "This storage unit they let me jump into is amazing! I can talk to you whenever and wherever you go! I was absolutely terrified when the campus was attacked. I worried so much."

"Talked too much is much more accurate," 57 said, shaking her head in agony. "I think the new form is getting to his head."

"I don't have a head," Carter replied smugly. "If anything, I am unstoppable!"

"CARTER!" Audrey yelled, and the chip abruptly fell silent. "I'm fine. Calm down. Would you mind speaking slowly?"

"Also," 117 looked down, fascinated by her A.I. companion. "Your chip is not connected to any system. You are in fact... stopped. Right where you are."

"Oh... well," Carter spoke softly. "That is a fair point. But Audrey! You will be happy to know that I am still perfectly in my prime condition. And I got to spend a lovely amount of time with the charming Miss Katie 57. What a darling. I got to be inside an amborg's head. A *female* one's head. It was like a trip to heaven."

The instant the words were out, 117 and Audrey awkwardly turned to 57. She was staring at the chip, absolutely disgusted.

"Great," 57 said flatly, rolling her eyes and walking away. "Now the A.I. thinks he has a chance with me... What I put up with in this line of work.."

Audrey chuckled nervously and pocketed Carter. Suddenly remembering one small detail, she pulled the chip out and muted it at Carter's protests. 117 watched her with a surprised look.

"You know how to mute an A.I. Industries computer chip?" he asked, eyebrows raised.

"Uh well," Audrey chuckled, "I did consider working there as an option, so I've been studying various pieces of tech. You know how most schools make you consider all kinds of career options?"

"I am afraid not. I have never been to a real school."

Audrey's smile disappeared when she realized that 117 was being serious. She had almost forgotten that he was not like everyone else; his life was distinctly different from hers. Yet, there were moments when he appeared remarkably human, sometimes acting like a regular guy. Knowing he had to return to his duties, she felt it was time to give him a proper goodbye.

"You and your amborgs saved me and the only things I have left of my family."

117 had begun to walk away, sensing that things had gotten a bit awkward, but stopped when she spoke up. He glanced back, acknowledging her with a gentle smile.

"It is what we do Audrey. I would advise you to not introduce your artificial intelligence to the programs at A.I. Industries. He has an odd bedside manner, according to 57. Imagine what the female A.I.s would say about him."

"And that is what I keep telling him," she chuckled.

As he turned to leave, she felt an unsettling sense of loss. Without thinking, she called out to him.

"Will I see you again?!"

117 paused again, turned around, and responded with a thumbs-up.

"When this is over, I would... like to. May I check on you after this?"

A warm smile spread across her face, and she nodded. 117 waved goodbye before turning to walk away, leaving Audrey with Carter in the center of the evacuation zone. He felt her gaze on his back as he headed toward their parked drop pods, feeling a twinge of sadness as he moved further away from her.

"You have an elevated heart rate," Mandy noted, then in a high-pitched baby voice, "Does someone need a hug?"

"O-oh," 117 stammered in surprise. "You saw that?"

"Forgot I was here? Again?" Mandy grumbled as she switched back to her normal voice.

"No," 117 replied. "I was just..."

"I see everything," Mandy declared in an eerie and irked tone. He could see her glaring at him on her monitor. "And what are you doing? Looking at another girl when your girlfriend is in the hospital?"

"I wasn't flirting," 117 replied. "I was just..."

"Sure..." Mandy sighed. Then she imitated his voice. "You're all... 'may I check on you after this'? Please..."

"How many impressions are you going to make?" 117 asked nervously.

"Just get back on track!" Mandy commanded.

What did I do? 117 thought as he walked, clueless, to the drop pods.

Several amborgs who had regrouped with the others were sharing their thoughts on the changes made to 6's drop pod. When 117 joined them, he realized he was among the last to arrive. The battle was winding down, and the army was moving in to clear the area. Thankfully, all the amborgs were safe, forming a large circle around the pod, their eyes fixed on the two figures lying on the ground. 117 stepped through and recognized them as 1 and 5.

"What happened to them?" 117 asked as he stared wide-eyed at the two First Group amborgs sprawled across the ground.

6, who was scanning them, appeared excited with a slightly evil look in her eyes.

"Oh good lord," Mandy exclaimed in horror. "She's grinning like she's been possessed."

"Oh this?" 6 gestured to the two amborgs as if nothing had happened. "Well to be blunt, they were the first ones to try out my charging station. And from what I have found out, it worked wonderfully!"

Everyone turned and gazed skeptically at one another as if they didn't believe her. 6 transmitted the data to the entire group.

"I have a 100% chance of thunderstorm recharge with a generator of energy for everyone with a side of success and an additional sprinkling of 'called it'!"

"And?" 117 glanced at 5's face, which was staring wide-eyed towards the sky. "If it was successful, what's wrong with them? Why are they on the ground like that?"

"Their energy levels have spiked!" 6 yelled out in a triumphant and maniacal fashion. "Full power with currents of it evaporating in the air! We just need to wait a few more seconds for the energy to be redistributed to their brains!"

"I'm sorry, what now?" Mandy commented. "Did she just say... their brains?"

Fortunately, a couple of the others were already way ahead of Mandy's reactions.

"Hang on!" 297 said sharply. "We shorted out their brains?! As in... they died?!"

6 ignored him and kept scanning.

"They should wake up in approximately... three... two... one! Eureka!"

"YAAAAHHHHH!!!"

5 and 1 sprang to their feet and started running around the group in a wild frenzy. As an unfortunate side-effect, streams of electricity shot out from their bodies, zapping any unlucky soul who happened to be in their way.

Everyone, including 117 and 6, recoiled and stepped back. For a moment, it looked as though they were gearing up for a rampage, but the two smoking amborgs paused, glancing around with curiosity.

"Wow! That was great!!" 5 yelled animatedly. "Power levels exceeding to infinity and beyond at one hundred and eighty four percent! Come on! Where are the robots?! Let me at 'em! I can fight them all day! All week! All month! For the rest of my life!"

5 abruptly stopped, facing the stunned crowd, then began to look woozy.

"Oh wow," he groaned. "I feel like I might barf..."

1 appeared to share the same sentiment. He suddenly doubled over, clutching his stomach, and looked as though he might be sick. Despite the bright energy radiating from him, creating an almost luminous aura around him, he didn't look well, despite having just defied the laws of science.

"That was much needed..." 1 steadied himself. He moaned in pain, looking ready to burst. "Power at one hundred and seventy two percent. But why do I taste... chimichangas? When did I have those?"

He burped and straightened up. His companions gazed at him with approval, their expressions revealing a mix of fascination and disbelief. Despite their pale appearances, any doubts about the recharging method were quickly brushed aside. Vanessa, embracing her newfound Dr. Frankenstein persona, radiated excitement.

"Heh. They're... They're ALIVE!! Perfect! Who's next?"

Although she hadn't directed her question at anyone in particular, her sudden outburst caused several Third Group amborgs to recoil in fear. 501 and 466 stood at the forefront, surrounded by a group of frightened amborgs. Their friends slowly inched behind them, using the pair as human shields.

6 glanced in 117's direction, her expression instantly brightening as soon as she saw him. The amborgs beside him edged away, making him a target with no way of escape.

"Why is she looking at me?" 117 gulped.

"B-because I think when she asked me to send your current power levels," Mandy stammered, "s-she might have said that she needed to see you first for a recharge."

Mandy was right. 6 marched up to him, getting up in his face. He held his position firmly and began to sweat profusely.

"Yikes 117," 6 remarked as she scanned his power levels before he could even reply. "Five percent power? You obviously need this. Just stand there, and don't move a muscle. There technically is a line and unfortunately, you do not get to plug into the generator. Just let the machine do the work. Here, take this and just think happy thoughts. I want to see if that makes a difference. Ooh! Here comes another one!"

In the blink of an eye, 6 thrust a wire into 117's hands and began to give him a quick rundown, but he could barely comprehend what was happening. He hardly had time to catch any of what 6 was saying.

"This may sting a little. Now have fun!"

"What??" 117 asked in bewilderment.

"It was nice knowing you," 917 transmitted to him from the side. "Love you buddy."

"We'll never forget you!" 297 added grimly.

"Agreed," 999 gave 117 a cold and admiring nod to convey respect.

Everything was happening too fast. He stared at the wire in his hands, tracing its path with his eyes. It was linked to the drop pods, and without thinking, he glanced up at the ominous storm clouds swirling around the kites. The voices of those around him faded into the background as another bolt of lightning struck the kites, sending a surge down the wire. 117 noticed the electric current racing toward his hands. At the same time, he felt three hands gripping his shoulders. Unable to tell who it was, 117 took a deep breath as they all latched onto him, forming a weird looking three-way battery.

"Oh son of a..."

The electricity struck them all conveniently before he could finish his thought. They cried out in agony as the energy surged through their bodies. A massive explosion erupted, engulfing the entire area in blinding light.

"Note to self," 5 winced as he watched the others receive the biggest kick of their lives. "Sedate 6 upon returning to A.I. Industries. She is probably legally insane."

CHAPTER 22

Convenient Miracle Mile

Pennsylvania
Hours Later

""You know 6, that was probably a strange but brilliant idea."

"What is your current power level?"

"I am functioning way beyond my normal capacity."

"I can see that 5. Put the car down."

5 shot 6 a pleading glance as he effortlessly held a wrecked car above his head. While it looked impressive, 6 was far from amused. She stood next to him with her arms crossed, staring him down like a stern owner would at a misbehaving dog. The streets around them were eerily deserted, marked by signs of destruction. Earlier, 117 had commented that it reminded him of Los Angeles.

By the time they left the Academy's conflict zone, it was already midday. Just the day before, they'd been in Texas and then Seattle before being diverted to the largest school campus in the country. By the time the battle had wrapped up, dawn was breaking as U.S. Forces successfully reclaimed the area, neutralized the threats, and the amborgs were fully recharged. Unfortunately, this victory came at a cost, leaving Pennsylvania's defenses vulnerable. The National Guard had suffered significant losses while the amborgs fought to protect the Academy. Meanwhile, a large number of enemy drones and behemoth robot forces, which were hidden in the capital, launched an offensive that turned the streets into a lethal battlefield. Thankfully, the events that had transpired across the country had prepared every police officer, soldier, and combat drone on their side for the impending attack.

With the amborgs stuck west, local forces facing enemy gangs and their behemoth war machines were fighting an uphill battle, trying to establish a foothold. The amborgs expressed their deep respect and admiration for the courage displayed by the police and military in combating the situation. Their presence gave them a substantial boost in morale.

The fight at Independence Hall took a dramatic turn with the sudden arrival of reinforcements from all over the nation. No one stood alone in this fight. The amborgs had come with a singular purpose: to see the battle through at the doorstep of their greatest adversary yet. They'd paired off, each operating at peak performance, though some were starting to experience the side-effects of their recharge. 6 was keeping a close eye on 5, who seemed to be feeling the strain more than the others.

"But I want to throw another car at the bad guys," he whined so loudly that 6 had to hold back a laugh.

She stepped in front of him and placed her arms around his neck.

"A car was actually not what I had in mind."

5 looked back at her in surprise. He dropped the car behind the two of them and put his arms on her waist as it landed with a loud crash.

"You want me to throw you?" he asked, raising his eyebrows. She smiled and kissed him on the cheek, meaning he had guessed correctly. "Is that really a good idea?"

"Yes. Just make sure not to miss."

5 gave a nod as he stepped back and hoisted her by the waist. 6 peered over his head, focusing on where she wanted to be thrown. She was already calculating the right trajectory and transmitting the variables to 5. Getting ready for a potential body-slam, she steeled herself as he lifted her up.

"What was that kiss for?"

6 looked down at 5 as he was preparing to leap backwards. He lifted an eyebrow with curiosity.

"Just in case I never get the chance to do that again," she replied with a teasing grin. "After all, who else is around for me to give a kiss too?"

"So, I was the only one conveniently near you?"

"Well, there is one other reason," she hinted.

"What's that?"

"Sorry 5. But it will have to wait until next time."

5 smirked.

"Well doc... give them your wrath."

"No... you say, 'give em hell.'"

5 shrugged. He took a few steps back and launched into a backflip. Midway through the maneuver, he released 6 like a catapult, diverting most of his power into his arms. This allowed him to complete a perfect backflip, while 6 flew off like Superman, aiming straight for her target.

Ok, she thought, *if that wall is as weak as it looks, breaking through it will be no problem.*

Gritting her teeth, her fists made contact with the aged cement. Crumbling on impact, 6 continued to fly through the wall, then ended up punching the face of an enemy drone. Taken by surprise, the drone's faceplate was instantly shattered, and its body was propelled backward.

In a swift motion, 6 extended her legs and planted her feet on the robot, forcing it to crash down and slide across the ground.

Using her newly acquired surfboard, 6 balanced her weight as her radar identified more targets. 6 leapt off of the drone-surfboard and somersaulted across the floor while drawing her guns and aiming them to the left and right.

"This is 6," she said, transmitting to anyone in range and pulling the triggers. "I have broken through the front lines. Could use a lot of help once I am finished here."

As she began engaging gang members in an epic shootout, she emptied the magazines from both of her pistols and ejected them. Once they fell, she holstered one pistol and reloaded the one that was still drawn in her hands. When she finished inserting a fresh magazine, she quickly bent forward and cradled the gun behind her left knee, holding it in place between her calf and hamstring, then quickly drew her other gun. She reloaded it with lightning speed, ready to continue the fight as she pulled her other gun out from behind her leg.

"Did anyone copy that?" she asked as she shot a few more enemy drones and gang members. "Hello?"

There was no reply to her transmission. Without warning, 6 heard the sound of a portable anti-tank missile slicing through the air, and in an instant, she was thrown backward as a massive explosion struck her with tremendous force, everything happening in a dizzying blur.

Really? A rocket? She thought as she crashed to the ground.

The heat from the explosion was instantaneous, dissipating just as quickly. Still, the force of the blast was likely strong enough to leave a bruise. She could feel the warmth radiating from her clothes and heard the crackling of her surroundings. The rocket had forced her to drop her pistols. As she pushed herself up, she reached into her boot and drew a hidden knife. Back on her feet, she aimed and threw it into the distance. A scream echoed from afar as she wiped the sweat from her brow and moved forward. Enemy soldiers appeared and charged toward her.

"LTO knives, rockets, bullets and a ton of other crap," she muttered angrily as a few bullets struck her. She ignored them and pressed on. "I'm not afraid of you anymore."

Disarming the first person that came within reach, she snarled and kicked two of them through a wall. As more of the enemy engaged, the more pissed off she became. It was not a good day.

"You think we show no emotion?!" she yelled, grabbing a gangster by the head and forcing him into the mud. "This is for 43!"

If anyone had been there to see what she was doing, they might have reminded her of the Hippocratic Oath. She would have argued that when it came to taking down known felons and erratic junkies, her medical amnesty didn't apply.

Not all the amborgs were as fortunate as 6.

Lieutenant Palmer never would have dreamt that he'd find himself in the sort of situation he currently found himself in. Holding a wounded soldier was one thing, but a wounded *amborg* was not something he'd seen coming. 3 lay across his lap, gripping her legs in pain.

117 had tasked him with leading the majority of his troops to support the offensive in Pennsylvania. However, the request came so suddenly and...it didn't seem like everyone was there. After the troops in his battalion arrived in Pennsylvania, he realized that several of his friends and fellow soldiers were missing. Many were still in the process of regrouping and redeploying, which confirmed one thing.

Ever since the fight at the Academy, they had been stretched thin. The command to deploy troops to the U.S. capitol had come through, leaving them with little time to regroup. Numerous officers and their teams had undoubtedly been left behind. Despite the influx of soldiers from various regions, they found themselves vastly outnumbered.

Now, he was comforting a First Group amborg in the middle of a battle. The initial defense troops stationed in Pennsylvania had suffered drastic losses and a high number of casualties since the conflict began. Almost all available soldiers were called in from the reserves, but even with the additional manpower, they were met with heavy resistance.

"Please stay with me... Listen to my instructions carefully."

Palmer snapped out of his thoughts and looked into 3's eyes. He nodded to let her know he was listening.

"I will," he said. "Just tell me what you need. It'll be ok. You'll be just fine."

"I cannot regain control of my legs... They're burning so much."

No emotion my ass, Palmer thought.

3 was clearly in pain and pleading for her life. He wasn't sure what to worry about; the life of one girl literally in his hands or the entire safety of the country.

"Don't worry 3," he held her tightly as bullets whizzed past their heads. He wouldn't be able to do this alone. He needed to be able to defend the amborgs with his life if necessary. "It was just a rocket. Nothing that Dr. Kendrick can't handle or fix."

3 smiled and nodded. Looking to her left, she pointed over to a pile of wreckage.

"Put me next to that car over there."

"What?"

"297 is in trouble..." she continued. "Put me behind that car and go help him. He is trapped. I will be alright. Just help him! I will see if I can get my legs working again from that location."

"What? 297?"

Palmer managed to stand up with her support, and he placed her arm around his shoulders as they made their way to the wreckage she'd pointed out. Once they reached it, he gently lowered her to the ground. She tapped her head and paused for a moment. Suddenly, a nearby explosion caused him to instinctively jump in front of her, shielding her with his body. 3, however, shoved him aside and opened her mouth.

"This is no time for that Lieutenant! Go help him now!" she yelled. "He is requesting artillery to drop right on top of his position!"

"Won't that kill him?!" Palmer replied with a look of shock. He had never imagined having to give orders to drop ordnance on his own allies.

"It'll be fine!" 3 nodded in response, letting out a cough from the strain of using her real voice. "Give me my gun and go now! Don't make me repeat this!"

Nodding, Palmer left 3's "pop" gun, or whatever it was called, with her and ran off. A soldier stranded by himself was sitting with his back against a wall. Fortunately, he had a radio, which immediately put Palmer's mind at ease. Sprinting, he slid across the ground and crawled next to the radioman, identified who he was, and grabbed the receiver. This was what he could do best. He ordered the radioman to keep an eye out as he began calling out orders to whoever could hear him over the communication channels.

----

466 grabbed 501 and put his arm around her shoulders. A fifty caliber bullet had struck his head, the seventh one that day, and blood was now trickling down his chin. His recharge had helped him greatly, but his body was pushed to its limits, and he was starting to take serious damage. The strain became too much, causing him to collapse into a crater with 466.

Even with the recharge, he could feel the exhaustion coursing through every muscle, a strange sensation he hadn't experienced since before he became an amborg.

"I cannot go on anymore."

"Yes you can," 466 said firmly and with every scrap of confidence she could muster. "Ah!"

She was cut off as a machine gun opened fire upon them and several bullets struck her in the leg. A battle cry peeled out of her as she took them head-on, then grabbed 501 and dove to the ground, taking cover behind a pile of rubble.

"466!" he exclaimed. "Are you ok? Is there a hole in your leg joints?"

"No," she groaned. "No holes, but I really felt that one... I do not think I can take this pain anymore..."

"Quick! Just lie down and maybe we can just stay here until we have a plan."

They huddled closely together as the sound of war raged around them. They wrapped their arms around each other and reclined onto their backs. Lying there for a short break, they gazed up at the fractured sky above. Even after more than a day of fighting, the view was still stunning, despite the ongoing gunfire and explosions. Still, they both made an effort to relax.

"Will this ever end?" 466 asked suddenly as she looked at the colors of blue mixing with the white and grey portions of the clouds. "You think the noise will stop?"

501 shrugged, but after a few seconds of deep thought, he nodded in agreement.

"Yes," he stated firmly, "because this will end at some point. Whenever that happens, whether or not we live to see the end... All I know is that there will be an end to... just about anything."

"You do know I was referring to the current events of the present time, right?"

466 turned her head and gave him a sarcastic look. 501 returned her gaze and chuckled. He had known exactly what she meant.

"I know," he replied. "I just wanted to give you hope by talking about the good and bad endings that are likely to happen. But we can't speculate on how the future may turn out. We have to live and proceed with our decisions to make memories and establish the present timeline. Only then will I be able to answer your question."

"Donut," 466 smiled. "Just shut up."

"Just saying," he laughed.

Laughter bubbled up from her as well. In the middle of it all, somehow they'd edged closer, still gazing up at the sky. It was a moment no enemy could shatter. That, or they had hidden themselves really well.

How many of us are left?"

"Of the seventy-nine of us that left Amborg Industries, thirty four of us still remain in this fight. The rest are incapacitated or trying to hide in order to recuperate."

117 slammed his fist against the wall. 35, 57, 1, and 5 were all huddled with him in a group inside the remains of a building. Sunlight was pouring through, mostly because the roof had been blasted to pieces.

None of them were feeling particularly optimistic given their current predicament. While their energy levels were functioning optimally, their morale had taken a hit. They felt overextended, something they haven't felt since their cybernetic enhancement.

"None of us are dead though at least," 5 said reassuringly when no one spoke. "Right?"

Everyone lifted their heads and nodded in relief. They felt incredibly lucky to not have lost anyone over the past two days. At least, no one from A.I. Industries were reported missing, as far as they knew. However, the surviving amborgs were painfully aware of the many innocent lives that had been lost. 117 didn't want to dwell on the increasing numbers on those casualty lists. He cast a beam of light, and a map of the surrounding area materialized in the center of their group.

"Based on where the enemy has fortified their position, the assassin is hiding inside this five-story building," 117 coughed. "It may look like a warehouse but his base is actually located here. However, he is heavily protected. We are being stopped anywhere we try to hit."

"And every time we do," 35 observed, "another one of us gets wounded and put out of commission. Now look at us... We had eighty-nine and this crazy challenger has an army and enough tactical capabilities to hurt over two-thirds of us."

"At least none of us are dead, remember?" 57 said, agreeing with 5's previous statement. "We can still find a way."

"They just have tight defenses and they are not advancing from their position to kill us," 1 said as he stared at the map. "He is running out of resources to form an assault so he's making a final stand. What we have managed to do is surround him. All of the wounded amborgs have hidden themselves in strategic positions. Reinforcements are coming, too. All we need is to come up with a new plan while everyone rests and recovers."

"The U.S. army cannot break through the defenses by itself," 117 said, looking at every inch of the map. "They're spread thin, just like us. And all the reinforcements that were brought with us are in total disarray. It is completely disorganized."

Scanning for any sign of a break in the enemy's defenses, he tried to come up with a solution to minimize further casualties. The troops currently with them in Pennsylvania were literally detachments of several battalions from all over the country. Military command was attempting to establish a stable chain of control. There were speculations about consolidating all available soldiers into a single battle unit, but that process would take too much time. The main concerns now revolved around whether they could afford to wait without the assassin slipping away unnoticed. Another option was to strike the enemy's position immediately, which posed the risk of being cut off from external support. 117 considered that this strategy could help avoid significant casualties among their military forces, but it was likely that another amborg might end up getting killed if they went with that idea.

"When an eventual assault occurs," he announced after considering their options, "we will be the spearhead but we cannot do this in our current state. We are at an impasse. There is no way in but... we also can't afford to just stop here. There's just no time."

"We've come too far to give up," 1 added. "If this man succeeds here, then the world will be open to him and we will be involved in a prolonged conflict. We're not ready for something like that."

"So, it really is all or nothing," 5 stated. "But, we're out of ideas on our side."

117 rubbed his temples and shook his head. He tried asking Mandy for help.

"What do I do Mandy? I am not as decisive as you... if we wait, this man will find a way to escape and the world will burn. If we go now, are our troops really willing to die for one tyrant? Another amborg could be killed. We have nothing else."

There was no response. 117 tapped his head. The connection was clear but he was met with silence. Confused, he looked at the others. They all understood what the expression on his face meant and quickly began reaching out to their technicians. Before long, everyone had some kind of answer.

"It would appear that something has preoccupied our own technicians," 5 said with the same perplexed look that everyone was beginning to display. "All of our technicians, by the look of it. How curious."

117, now completely satisfied that it wasn't just Mandy he had lost contact with, felt relieved. He didn't have to be nervous, but he was concerned as to what had dragged Mandy from her post.

"Mandy? Please respond," he asked again. "I cannot do this anymore. All of my options are... gone."

"Not all of them."

Mandy finally replied. She was out of breath and panting, but her voice carried a tone of excitement.

117 analyzed the sound patterns in her voice. It didn't seem like anything was wrong. She sounded oddly chipper about something, which was a stark contrast to their current situation. He glanced over at the other amborgs, who seemed engaged in conversations with their own technicians. It appeared that there was no bad news to report.

"Is everything ok? Why did you not respond?"

"Because Dr. Kendrick has got another option for you!" she shouted so joyfully that 117 had to turn the volume down. "E.T.A. one minute! It's great David! Stand by for our A.I. Industries ace in the hole!"

"One minute? I don't understand."

What happened next answered his question immediately. A blip suddenly appeared on 117's radar. The other amborgs quickly straightened up and began tapping their heads, switching over to their own radars. They all noticed it too. The blip began to flash, revealing a number in a pulsating blue light, and it was heading straight for them. Everyone looked up in shock as a loud boom echoed through the air. It was a signal from another amborg's I.F.F. tag, but it was definitely not who they expected.

"I don't believe it..." 1 said as a grin spread across his face. "It really is her. I had a feeling she wasn't going to stay out of this one."

"Oh yeah, now we're talking," 5 exclaimed, doing short hops in the air. "I am so down with this!"

57 looked up to the sky and smiled at 35.

"Welcome back to the land of the living," she said as she high-fived 35.

117 stood in awe, staring in disbelief as he spotted a drop pod approaching. It altered its path and began descending toward them.

"43? Is that you?"

It plunged through the clouds and landed just a few feet away, hitting the ground with a jarring crash and sending clouds of dust swirling into

the air. That impact was so powerful that it could have knocked anyone nearby off their feet, but the amborgs watching remained perfectly still as the door released a hissing sound. Moments later, the pod opened, revealing a familiar face.

"Well? Are you going to stand there gaping or am I going to wait for you to applaud?"

43 took in all of their dumbstruck expressions, amusement dancing in her eyes. No one seemed to know how to respond; they simply gawked. When 43 didn't get the reception she hoped for, she lowered her arms and sighed. They exchanged glances, and soon enough, smiles began to break out among the group.

"Geez, you take one knife to the chest and almost miss probably the biggest event we've ever been a part of and no one shows any recognition when you finally show up. Looks like my dramatic entrance failed."

Not replying to her blunt choice of words, 117 stepped forward and extended his arms. He didn't dare approach her. Was it a dream? Annoyance crossed 43's face at the sight of him.

"That is not going to work David 117," she said. "You lead the biggest operation in amborg history without me and now without any ideas in your calculations, what makes you think I should help you now?"

"If you want me to convince you, I shall. Because I never knew if I would see you awake again. I wanted you back. Now... we can end this."

"Right, and I suppose flattery is your method for making me feel better?"

57 stepped up, interrupting them.

"What do you want us to do sis?" she shrugged. "You're alive. I mean... you're awake. That has to be the best news we have received throughout all of this. You're out of a coma. Would you cut the guy a break and stop acting so uptight and stubborn?"

"Relax Katie, I was kidding."

"To be fair," 35 stated, "117 did want to wrap this up before you woke up. That way, you would get good news after this mission was over."

"Well, we didn't get to do that. But, now that you are back," 5 said abruptly, the mood suddenly shifting, "I think we can inspire some fear inside those stupid drones."

"You mean the ones that have you currently stumped right now?" 43 replied with a smirk.

"Yep she's back," 5 muttered as he turned away.

"All I know is," 117 cut in, "I would die by your side anytime. But you are most welcome to help us finish this."

"So I show up and all of you are immediately inspired," 43 observed with a look of approval. "I guess you did miss my skills. At least you guys haven't forgotten me entirely."

"I have missed more than that," 117 said, but 43 put her fingers to his lips.

"I know," she smiled. "But for now, what do you say we beat the man that knifed me and hurry home? Right now, I am in the mood for just a bit of good old-fashioned revenge."

"Well, unless you are carrying ten thousand pounds of explosives," 1 cut in, clearing his throat. 43 and 117 broke apart and they all gathered around the map. She immediately synched up with everyone and was instantly brought up to speed with the current situation. "There's no way for us to penetrate the defenses."

"Maybe not ten thousand pounds of explosives," 43 said, smiling confidently. "But I have myself, my brain, and supplies."

"I take it you have a plan?" 35 asked.

"You might find it a little unorthodox."

Word spread quickly of 43's arrival. Adding herself to the communications of all the amborgs in the vicinity inspired hope. They were ninety again. Every amborg picked themselves up from the ground, poised to leap back into the fray. Regardless of injury, they rallied together as soon as 43 transmitted a call to action.

"I know you have suffered," 43 spoke out while everyone was gathering at her pod to grab the supplies she had brought. "But everyone, listen to me now."

43 hijacked a radio system and opened it to anyone she could reach, including every soldier still fighting nearby and all of the technicians.

"All of this has been difficult to bear," 43 tapped her head, "but now I return with a goal in mind. A goal that will affect everyone.

Every person—soldier and civilian—are still fighting for their lives, including the amborgs. Everyone knows who the enemy is. He has challenged us and we have met him head-on. Now, he wants to expose our vulnerabilities to the world, and revel in our failure to protect you. We have lost many people and I am sorry for all the innocents who have perished. I say, here and now for everyone to hear, that we do have a weakness. We aren't perfect or invincible; this war has taught us that. To our allies and the adversary in question, let it be known that we will never stop fighting until people like you are stopped. The more you attempt to undermine us, the more we will resist. If we surrender now, there will be no one left to stand against you. This is no longer a mere calculation; it is a matter of human life, which you, the assassin, have waged an all-out war against. You questioned our right to defend those you deem beneath us and accused the amborgs of being indifferent to the value of life."

She glanced at 117, then finished her speech.

"You are wrong," she said deeply. "We fight not for ourselves but for everyone else, driven by an innate feeling. It's not complicated to us anymore. It's the human thing to do. Although some may view us as less than human, we will continue to evolve and thrive for the sake of our planet. Our allegiances will always be against you: destroyer of ife."

"That... was a little... Can I say it?"

Everyone glanced at 5.

"Cheesy?" 43 suggested.

"A little," 5 nodded. "That didn't sound like you at all."

"I'm trying to send a message to everyone," 43 mumbled. "It's supposed to get attention."

A profound silence fell over the group. The amborgs were gearing up, their resolve strengthened by 43's motivating speech. They stood ready to take on the biggest battle they had ever faced. Before anyone could make a move, a sudden crackle of electricity erupted from the radio, and a powerful voice began to shout through the transmission.

"Destroyer of life? I like the sound of that," the assassin's voice spoke, booming and clear as day.

117 knew it was the man from the video that had started all of this.

"So, the little girl recovered from her wounds," he laughed, the sound echoing over the entire battlefield. "What makes you and your little family the advocates for humanity? You are machines! But I do congratulate you on your resolve. Why not give up now and save your skins? Why do you think you can stop me? Go on. Answer in the only way you can; as a calculator risking what you can afford to lose to stop me."

"The answer..." 43 replied in the radio transmission, "...I will personally bring to your face. I know I fight because there is no one else like us. Because our feelings are for everyone else. Brace yourself. You're going to pay for sticking a knife in me. In all of us."

The radio broadcast ended as 43 cut the connection. She turned and faced the small group before her, all of them having regained their morale and confidence. Walking past them, 43 headed back to her drop pod, where a few of them had already pulled out a few boxes.

"Nice speech." 5 grabbed one of the boxes and set it down on the ground. "Almost thought you were going to reveal our plans. So, what do you plan on doing first?"

"I suggest we use these and bring in the cavalry," 43 replied as she kicked open one of the boxes and reached inside. Everyone else followed suit.

5 reached into his box and pulled out some shiny stickers. They all recognized what they were. After all, 43 had used one on them a few months ago during her rampage. 1 obviously remembered it.

"I've never seen so many arrows before."

35 held one up very carefully.

"What do we do with all of these?" he asked nervously, even though the answer was obvious.

"Well," 43 replied. "These ones, thanks to Dr. Kendrick, have been calibrated to fly an object at speeds up to terminal velocity. A lot faster than the original prototypes."

"It would appear we owe Dr. Kendrick our thanks."

117 stuck an arrow onto a broken refrigerator. It instantly shifted and flew towards the wall. Everyone side-stepped it as it landed into the layers of stone with a boom. The wreck stuck to the wall for a few seconds, until the force became too much and a hole appeared. They watched as the wrecked piece of houseware flew further and further away at a tremendous speed, out of sight until they could only hear loud crashes. They could also hear the cries and crushing sounds of a few enemy drones, until finally, an explosion echoed off in the distance, likely hitting something and causing it to blow up.

"At least these arrows have a safety distance," 43 said as she examined the hole with concern. "Otherwise we'd probably be sending up more satellites into space."

"It was a nice shot though," 5 smiled. "Terminal velocity eh? Well that was a perfect demonstration."

"Actually," 117 replied, "I wasn't expecting that to happen."

"Sarcasm dear," 43 said encouragingly as she picked up her box.

117 shrugged but admired his handiwork as a brick fell from the top of the hole.

"What exactly is the distance they travel before they shut off?" he asked.

"Unfortunately, the maximum distance it propels an object is up to three miles," 43 replied. "Give or take."

"Give or take?"

"These arrows don't have infinite power," 43 explained as they all grabbed their boxes and stepped outside. "Once they fling an object up to three miles, they are as good as dead. Our best bet when using them is shutting them off manually to save their batteries."

117, upon hearing this bit of information, looked in the direction where the refrigerator had gone. He tried to lock on to the arrow's signal but unfortunately, it was out of range and far too late to send one anyway. Everyone else stopped to listen. They could still hear distant yells, which meant the fridge missile was still going. 43 chuckled nervously. Everyone turned back to her and ignored the crashing noises, which were still growing fainter as it continued on its destructive course.

"Anyway," 43 said. "We give each amborg, wounded or active, one box. I brought a lot. All those modified compartments on my drop pod aren't just for show. Then, find some pieces of junk. Things big enough to hurtle. Things that add potential property damage to the max."

"Oh," 1 nodded in approval. "Inanimate cavalry. Very ingenious."

43 clambered onto a piece of a billboard.

"Why call an artillery barrage when you can settle on an old fashioned storm from heaven?"

43 flashed them a wink as she stuck an arrow onto the board, then took off, quickly disappearing from view. The billboard seemed to defy gravity, lifting 43 up as if she were mounted on an imaginary winged creature, moving faster than anyone could have anticipated.

"So, I suppose our plan is to find anything that's worthy of destruction, gather it all together, then everyone sticks an arrow on everything heavy, and we ride among the falling debris like fire from the sky and basically kamikaze our way in."

57 looked around, clarifying this newly found plan. Everyone was already looking for something suitable to ride on, which confirmed her summarization.

"Oh, why not?" she shrugged as she ripped off a car door, laying it out like a skateboard while looking for a good place to stick the arrow to. "Junk kamikaze artillery barrage. This will be one for the history books. And we come riding or falling in like total idiots."

117 smirked as he found an overturned vending machine, stuck an arrow onto the side and grabbed on for the ride. The arrow, pointing directly upward, lit up and the object's gravity instantly changed. 117 shot up into the air, now with a bird's eye view of the whole area. Acting fast, 117 pulled the sticker off and adjusted the direction before the effects wore off. The sticker, now facing a new direction, sent the vending machine shooting across the sky instead of upwards. He had to distribute the arrows quickly, but where was the best place to land?

Picking a spot fairly close to where 3's location beacon was, 117 sent a signal to the arrow, shutting it off. He felt the vending machine begin to slow down but for some reason, it didn't fall. Curious, 117 pulled the sticker off, which seemed to correct the result. Without the sticker, 117 felt the full force of gravity acting on the vending machine. *Interesting*, he thought as he began to plummet at an uncontrollable speed. The arrow, once deactivated, would stop any object in motion and keep it suspended in mid-air. Were these effects permanent or just a fluke in the design? Realizing he was in free fall, 117 quickly refocused.

Down below, 3 appeared to be in a bit of a situation.

"Surrender now amborg, and your death shall be swift."

"I think I shall avoid the surrender then."

3 was backing away from a drone that had drawn an LTO knife and was now closing in on her threateningly. Hearing 43's message had lifted her spirits, but soon after, a drone had tracked her down, making it difficult to dodge another slash. The sharp pain in her legs was excruciating as she narrowly avoided another jab.

"I could really use some help!"

Suddenly, she saw 117's beacon appear on her radar. But from where?

One minute, there was a beep indicating his arrival, the next, there was a deafening crash. A massive object plummeted from the sky, obliterating the drone beneath it. When the dust and dirt cleared, 3 stared as 117 clung onto the top of... a vending machine, which now occupied the spot where the drone had just been.

"Are you alright 3?" 117 asked weakly.

"I should ask you the same thing."

3 watched as 117 slowly clambered off his ride. He staggered a little as he stepped on the ground.

"A vending machine?" she asked. "You must have had to have been a couple thousand feet in the air to achieve that kind of landing."

"I think I was," 117 replied as he handed her a stack of arrows. She took them, recognizing them immediately. "Oh wow, that was scary."

"Arrows!" 3 said happily. "This will be a good help. My legs are killing me. But, what am I supposed to do with all of these?"

"Well," 117 said, climbing back onto the vending machine. "Find something you can ride on, then scrape up all of the junk you can find. We also need 125 and 274's transportation grenades. That will give us more stuff to drop on the enemy."

She watched as he stuck an arrow back on the side of his wreck-ride, pointing straight up. In the few seconds before it activated, he passed on a quick message.

"Saddle up, lock and load, Missy."

117 winked and in a heartbeat, the machine shot up into the air at break-neck speed. 3 stood there and scoffed.

"The only time a western analogy works with my first name," she muttered. "He picks now to use it."

3 picked up her pop gun, checked the ammo count, and began looking for something that could carry her.

"If you are going to reference western movie genres *and* use my name at the same time," she muttered to herself, "at least offer a girl a ride will you?"

Homing in on 297's position, she immediately came up with an idea. Holding up one of the arrows, she stuck it on herself. The result was utter chaos. Not prepared for the sudden change in gravity, she immediately felt herself hurtling straight towards a car. Shifting her weight, she skimmed over its roof feet first with no problem, but then found herself flying in a supine position down the street at the speed of a bullet.

Must change the direction of the arrow! she thought fast. Ripping it off, 3 shifted and found herself back in a free fall. Sticking the arrow on the side of her stomach and making sure it faced up, she managed to change the direction. As a result, she felt herself falling into the sky.

"Ok," 3 strained as she flew. "Before I shoot out of the atmosphere, change direction... now!"

Again, she took the sticker off and began flying in a parabola as gravity forced her back towards the ground. Managing to get her bearings, 3 saw that she was not slowing down and the ground was rapidly growing closer. Making sure the arrow was pointing in the right direction, thrust her fists forward as her weight shifted, and soared five feet off the ground, speeding toward 297's beacon in a dynamic super-girl pose.

The highlight of 297's day was seeing Missy 3, flying above all things, crashing into a behemoth class robot, which had been seconds away from crushing him. 3 had arrived with what appeared to be an imitation of the caped hero, Superman, but the instant she realized what she was flying at, she had apparently reached for her stomach, pulled something off, flailed her arms in the air desperately as if she couldn't hit the brakes, and slammed into the robot.

Her speed, faster than anything 297 had ever seen, caused her to crash into his attacker and punch right through its exoskeleton, leaving a gaping hole in the upper chassis. The robot collapsed, defeated. 3, too, fell to the ground, several hundred meters away in what was left of a bar.

"Ok, now that," 297 said, stunned as the behemoth groaned and sparked, "... is falling with style."

He made a reminder to himself to see if he could devise a bar joke after what he had just seen.

"An amborg fighting a behemoth sees 3 fly into a bar," he said, thinking about what kind of joke 5 would come up with in a moment like this. "Nah, that might not work."

CHAPTER 23

Hurricane Serina 43

Enemy Warehouse Perimeter
30 Minutes Later
("To be accurate, shouldn't it say 'above the perimeter?'")
("Hush, Sarah. Keep watching.")

"On my mark, disable all power transfers to the arrows."

"I hope the enemy appreciates the gift we are going to deliver."

Palmer peeped over a wall slab while listening to the radio. The amborgs were planning something huge and it was going to happen any second. Except, he didn't see anything remotely resembling a miracle. He swore when one of the enemy drones spotted him and a couple of enemy soldiers began firing at him. Ducking down, he leaned against the wall as bullets hammered against the wall behind him. He crawled away from the slab of cover and moved into another crater.

Oh, I hope the plan goes into effect right about now, he prayed silently as he tried to remain as still as possible.

"Well, well well," a voice from above spoke tauntingly.

"My men sure don't have that amount of sass," Palmer muttered.

Knowing it wasn't one of his soldiers, he glanced up and saw a drone and a thug staring down at him. He'd been caught again.

Preparing for the worst, Palmer watched as the drone and the enemy gang member aimed their guns at him. This time, he chose not to close his eyes. He wanted to look his enemy in the eye before he went. However, the death he anticipated didn't come. Instead, a shadow appeared behind the gangster and the drone. Palmer looked up and noticed something large flying... no, falling towards the three of them. By the time the enemy realized something was descending upon them, it was too late.

A tremendous crash shook the ground, causing Palmer to stumble back in fear. Debris rained down all around him. The spot where the drone and the enemy gang member had been was now occupied by a massive UAV drone. Palmer stared in utter shock at the outdated piece of machinery that had just saved his life. These types of drones were supposed to be out of commission. Where had it come from? Before he could so much as open his mouth, he glanced up and witnessed something incredible.

"How do you like the gift?" a robotic voice asked.

"Yikes! That's pretty scary," Palmer eked out, still looking up.

More than a hundred heavy objects plummeted from the sky, crashing down on the enemy's warehouse. He heard the chaotic sounds of beeping and roaring from the enemy's position as rubble and various fragments made contact. A giant ensemble of booms, crashes, and thuds mixed with screams filled the air from the fortified warehouse.

"Since when can amborgs not predict weather?" 3 said, clapping her hands happily at the sight of their garbage artillery barrage. "I predict a massive downpour of train in about three seconds."

"Train?" Palmer turned and scanned the skies. "You guys didn't..."

She couldn't mean what he thought she meant. He raised both of his eyebrows at 3, who was pointing a finger upward, gesturing for him to look in the right direction.

"Well, you don't want to miss this part of the show, do you?"

Pivoting on his heel, still staring upward, Palmer's mouth dropped open as a freight car dropped down and crushed several drones at the perimeter of the enemy fortress. At least five or six more cars rained down, smashing into the warehouse and the surrounding area. It was total pandemonium.

"How did you get a freight train?!" Palmer yelled as the loud clanging tore past his ears.

3 smiled and placed a hand on his shoulder. She pulled some earplugs out of her pocket and passed them to him.

"You want to thank 501 and 466 for that," she replied. "It was their idea. Asked nicely at the nearby train yard and well... stuck some arrows. Good thing the train yard had no use for this specific train, right?"

"Well, that's all nice and good but..." Palmer ran his hands through his sweaty hair. He took the earplugs and immediately drowned out the noise. He had to shout in order for her to hear his next question. "How are we supposed to clean all this up?!"

"One step at a time Lieutenant," 3 patted him softly on the shoulder and then stepped away to pick the UAV drone off the ground. "Clean-up is not exactly a priority right now."

"And another thing," Palmer suddenly remembered. "Where did you acquire a vintage twenty-first century UAV drone?"

"Well... Let us for the moment say that some of the enemy soldiers broke into the Smithsonian for a treasure hunt. Until yours truly stopped them."

3's sheepish grin made him very uneasy. As she flipped the drone over and checked its condition, something dawned on him.

"You did not..."

"Don't worry, Lieutenant Palmer," 3 said as she picked up the drone and set it against the wreck of a car.

The bodies of the enemy drone and soldier were still crushed flat. Palmer stared at the wrecked piece of military hardware, not wanting to know whether or not they'd survived.

"It is a mere replica," she said innocently, but Palmer eyed the UAV suspiciously.

"It doesn't look like a replica..." he said cautiously. "Too large and it looks as heavy as Dthe real thing."

"Well..." 3 shrugged and quickly said, "The original was accidentally destroyed."

Palmer looked anxiously at the drone, then back at 3, who forced a smile. Suddenly, a look of disdain crossed his face as he grasped the implications of her words.

"What does that mean?" he asked, immediately regretting it.

"It means that once I fix this," 3 promised, "I will put it on display in the Smithsonian personally. No one will be able to tell the difference!"

"That belongs in a museum!!"

"And it will..." 3 climbed back onto the drone and stuck an arrow onto the hardware, "When I have no use for it anymore."

----

117 sat down next to 501 and peered around a corner. Two bullets struck the wall the instant he peeped out, causing him to immediately pull his head back to safety. Not surprising since the two of them were at the forefront of the assault. They were leading the attack from the ground.

The plan was simple.

Half the amborgs would move their way across the ground slowly, inch by inch, while the other half would find heavy pieces of whatever they could find and throw them in the air with the arrows attached. The most agile and courageous of this half of the amborgs would ride the debris into the sky, aim them, and send them flying towards the enemy warehouse. At least, the idea was to inflict as much damage in what would equate to as the largest scale temper tantrum thrown by a group of cybernetically enhanced teenagers.

The plan was working as the amborg ground team managed to slowly push forward. The more ground they took, the more powerful and intense the area shook as object after object continued to fall and make contact.

It was a creeping barrage, an old military tactic where artillery fire acted as both a sword and shield for military forces. The explosions from the artillery would advance gradually, creating a protective 'curtain' for soldiers while pinning the enemy down. Since the army had no intention of bombing Pennsylvania directly, this tactic was the next best thing. Their barrage effectively compelled the enemy to hide, but for the amborgs, it was still moving too slow.

True, it was awesome seeing behemoth robots getting crushed by cars, enemy drones malfunctioning as they struggled to comprehend the presence of airborne objects that defied logic, and gang members fleeing in panic as actual garbage rained down around them. However, the plan was reaching its final stages.

The big pieces of junk they launched were mostly expended and now it was a light rain of car doors and bricks. Although their numbers had been significantly reduced, enemy drones, snipers, and a handful of colossal behemoths continued to fire at the advancing teams.

117 looked over at 501.

"Afraid one will hit your head?" 117 snickered.

501 let out a laugh.

"Did you just make a headshot joke at me?" 501 grinned.

"Yeah," 117 nodded. "I did."

501 took a deep breath and sighed.

"Well actually," he replied as the two of them hunched against a wall, "based on all of the damage I have taken, I feel as if I could die just from a simple bullet to the head."

501 shook slightly to indicate he was laughing silently.

"You just have bad luck with bullets for some reason," 117 replied. "That... or the bad guys are just getting better at hitting people's heads."

"Yeah, let's not think about that," 501 stated.

More bullets struck their cover. Both amborgs didn't flinch. Although they could walk out and take the shots directly, doing that would disrupt their sensors and cause more pain.

"Some of them are simple," he said confidently, then began to list out the times he had been shot, using his fingers to count. "Others tickle, most of them stick to my face, and rare ones explode. I probably should have died... err... That's if I were still a normal human. The total would have been 286 times now. But that's just an initial estimate."

"Well, I'm glad. Out of those 286 times you've been shot, you haven't died yet," 117 said in a very calm and grateful tone. "Look, I admit, you are annoying at times. But the truth is, that is the 501 I prefer to fight with in combat. You are quite capable and strong. In the time I have known you, I just wanted to tell you that I'm happy to call you my little brother. I'm also sorry that I haven't been a good role model for you."

501 nodded in recognition, silently thanking 117 on a private channel. As he did so, 117 got an idea. He immediately thrust his hand around the corner and waited. A shot fired, and in an instant, he felt a sharp impact. He made a fist, casually catching the bullet with his bare hand. Drawing his arm back, he examined the bullet carefully; it was glowing a fierce red and still sizzling.

"Care to take an analysis on this, Donut?"

501 stared at the bullet and immediately worked his magic. He grinned and nodded.

"Ooh, incendiary tracer," he said cheerfully. "Those are warm when you catch them, but are very difficult to get out of your skin if you take them head on. For humans, those are designed to melt right through and shred the skin."

"Well, if I still had my vending machine," 117 noted as he threw the bullet away, "we would at least have proper shielding."

"Where did you lose it?"

"Oh, in the heavy barrage of junk and miscellaneous artillery," 117 accessed his memory banks and brought up the video replay. "It went through that window on the second floor. Fifth from the right."

501 lifted his gaze at the window that 117 had indicated, taking in the wide hole that was approximately the size of the vending machine. He then turned to 117 to pose another question.

"Where is 43? I have not seen her or heard from her since that inspirational broadcast. 466 was really...motivated."

"Just say fired up,"117 muttered, ignoring the question. He picked up a pebble and threw it.

"But it is not something I can get used to saying," 501 shrugged as the pebble bounced off the wreckage of a police vehicle. "Especially if they literally aren't in flames..."

He trailed off as the two of them stared at the abandoned law enforcement vehicle, then briefly glanced at each other. 117 was already transmitting a plan.

"Humor me..." 117 said with a smirk. "Just once."

501 recognized 117's grin and matched it. They both knew what the plan was and didn't even need to transmit it privately to each other. Intrusive thoughts had taken over.

The pair ran over to the car, lifted it, and pulled it to the wall they hid behind. Then slowly, they pushed it out into the open in full view of the warehouse defenders and hid behind it. Bullets riddled the side of the car immediately. Acting fast, the two of them flipped the car onto its right side, grasped the underside, and lifted it up.

"We can use this to advance!" 117 declared. "A roman testudo... without the overhead cover!"

"I got it!" 501 nodded in excitement. "Wait! A testudo requires people behind us to carry a shield above our heads."

"Yeah," 117 replied, "and I've already pointed out we don't have people behind us!"

"So... why not just call it a shield?"

117 stared at 501 for a moment. Bullets continued to strike the car.

"Right," 117 sighed. "It's just a shield."

501 chuckled and then pointed at the car.

"And we progress forward slowly, footstep by footstep!" he smiled. "Right?"

"Wrong."

117 grabbed an arrow from his pocket, quickly presenting it to 501. His eyes widened and his smile faded. He reached up and stuck it onto the door, pointing it directly at the warehouse. As it activated, 117 quickly tightened his grip on the car while 501 did the same.

"This will be faster," 117 explained. "Hang on! I think I set it to full power and it's almost out of juice!"

501 let out an excited yell as the arrow powered up and the car shot straight forward. Screams and shouts of horrified surprise filled the air, mixing with the sound of bullets striking the car-shaped shield. Both 501 and 117's feet lifted off the ground at high speed. Flying like flags, they flew several feet into a wall, which wasn't strong enough to withstand that amount of force. As they slammed through, 117 shouted to 501.

"Let go!"

The two of them somersaulted off the car as it blasted into another wall, then another, and another as they both skidded across the ground. They looked around and realized they had successfully reached the warehouse. The hole they created served as the entrance to their final objective, but several perimeter guard drones were charging toward them.

"Quick, shut it down before it gets too far out of range!"

The two of them reached out their hands and transmitted the shutdown codes, but weren't sure if the flying police car received them. With the outcome of the arrow still uncertain, they quickly engaged the guards. 117 seized a drone's arm and tore it off.

"We can only hope it worked!" he said as he smacked another person with the arm.

"Yeah," 501 blocked and countered someone's attack. "Hope no one was on the other end of that."

Once they finished off the team of defense drones and gang members holed up inside the warehouse, they looked around and inspected the area. All the remaining behemoth robots were outside. They probably hadn't anticipated anyone actually making it to the warehouse so there was less security.

Suddenly, they received a transmission on a private channel.

"You know, how about a warning before you send a car out the other end of the building?!"

501 and 117 looked toward the hole to see 5 coming through on the other side. They shared a glance, shrugged, then jogged over to meet him.

"That could have taken my leg out again..." he said angrily, pointing at the wreckage behind him.

"5, stop complaining," 117 said. "How many cars have been thrown at you today?"

5 crossed his arms. Before he could answer, more First Group amborgs appeared. 501 watched 1, 8, 9, 12, and 19 pick their way through, checking his data banks and adding all of them to a small list he'd created.

"Looks like the First Group has made it into the warehouse," 501 said cheerfully and looked at 5, who stared back in annoyance. He was still pouting. "Then we can say that 5 was the first one from the First Group. And then, 117 was first from the Second Group."

"Actually 501," 117 replied. "I am not the first from the Second Group."

"What do you mean?" 501 asked, pointing at 5 and 117 skeptically.

"Ok, now I want to know too," 1 spoke up from behind 5.

They were interrupted by a loud crumbling noise from above. Unfazed, everyone immediately shifted their attention upwards and watched as a hole in the ceiling opened up. Along with the rubble, a girl fell through and landed on her back in the middle of the floor a few feet away from the group.

"Ok, I didn't see that at all..." 43 coughed as she sat straight up.

117 ran over and helped her to her feet. As the amborgs moved in, another team, which consisted of 3, 466, 297, 57 and 35, also arrived from where 117 and 501 previously entered.

"43 got here first?" 501 stared. "When did she get here? When did she even go upstairs while we were still breaking the perimeter??"

43 gave a triumphant smile as she greeted 117 with a kiss on the cheek.

"Oh, that was easy. You see, we would never have been able to break the enemy perimeter in our current condition," she said, staggering a bit but stood straight and shrugged off the fall. "So after everyone got their fair share of arrows, I climbed back inside my drop pod, flew up with all the debris we collected, and flew straight down to the roof of the warehouse. All of the junk we dropped camouflaged my approach."

"A shortcut," 5 observed, "in a fast effort to catch the assassin."

"Yes," 43 nodded intently. 117 noticed her biting her lip as she spoke. Silently, he reached inside his pocket while she continued to talk. "However, the warehouse roof was not strong enough for the landing speed and weight of my pod so I fell two stories to the second floor."

"Then you fell three more stories and here you are now," 1 added humorously.

"This assassin is cunning. The entire floor I landed in was a large maze. Several corridors, twists and turns, and multi-colored doors. It sounds impossible but I got lost in there several times. I think most of his budget went into this building..."

"Why not destroy the walls?" 3 asked, looking up at the hole that 43 had fallen from. "Create more shortcuts? Would that not make it simpler?"

"There's a lot of strange material in the walls," 43 reported. "Otherwise, I'd still be up there and not here."

43 began walking towards a flight of stairs situated at one end of the warehouse.

"Also, the instant I turned to backtrack, an explosive detonated under my feet and that is why I am down here with all of you guys. I get the feeling that we won't be solving this without getting angry."

"Well, how about we map out the floors? Work the maze together?"

"The instant you are on the floor and in the maze, there is no signal for us to communicate with each other," 43 called back to them and began climbing the stairs. "He has constructed this warehouse to his specifications. We don't know what he'll do if we try to get to him through cheating and shortcuts. He is forcing us to play by his rules and I intend to finish it."

With that, she immediately ran up the stairs. The rest of the amborgs began to follow suit. While everyone began discussing their puzzle-solving tactics, 117 grabbed 501 by the shoulder, stopping him from moving.

"Not you. You will stay here, Donut," 117 said sternly on a private channel.

501 stared back, looked at 117's expression, and almost began to protest, but when he noticed how serious 117 was, he paused. After a brief moment of contemplation, he nodded and waited for further instructions.

"Take Carolina... and when the rest of the amborgs make their way here, you tell them what to expect when they climb up to the upper levels."

"Oh, right!" 501 nodded. "We got to warn everyone!"

"Yes, but there is something else."

"Why are we on our own separate private channel?" 501 asked curiously, looking around to make sure no one was observing them.

"Listen 501, something is not right. Does anything about 43 feel strange to you?"

501 shook his head.

"I think 43 is lying to us," 117 said gravely.

501's eyes widened. This was definitely an attention grabber. The only issue he was having trouble comprehending was the fact that amborgs do not lie. Not exactly. Technically they could try to but it was easy to spot. Before he could question this any further, 117 waved at 466 so she could join them.

"Take Carolina 466 and any other members of the Third Group, specifically the ones you trust, and guard this area."

"What do you mean 43 is not telling the truth?" 501 asked.

He'd mistakenly spoken outside the private channel, which 466 overheard. When she approached them, looking puzzled, 117 opened the channel to her as well. Without hesitation, he recapped the entire discussion he had with 501, quickly bringing her up to speed.

"She lied, right in front of us," 117 said sternly to the two of them. "She defied her ethical programming in her implants. We are not programmed to lie. Our conduct has always been to the truth and what is right and wrong. A lie would make us uncomfortable. So why did the girl I love lie to my face?"

"But that does not have any bearing to any form of truth 117," 466 replied. "Hang on. Let me process this."

"Think for a moment 466," 117 replied. "Is the 43 in this recording the same one that taught you all that you know now?"

"I mean, we've all lied before. Or made bad attempts in the past," 466 shrugged. "She could just be occupied."

"So occupied to abandon our own coordinated efforts and pursue the objectives by herself?" (I removed the next sentence because 501 didn't continue speaking in the next paragraph)

"I know her," 117 stated. He gazed at 501 and 466. "That wasn't the same 43 from before. We were both supposed to take care of you two. I know we haven't known each other that long but...she's acting like you two aren't a priority."

"She could just be trying to finish this mission," 466 suggested.

"After New Year's," 117 said, "she told me that taking care of you was one of her biggest wishes to look forward to her New Year's resolutions. And I feel sorry for forgetting to pay more attention to you both."

501 and 466 glanced at each other.

"It's ok," 501 smiled. "You were going through a lot and working really hard. I understand."

"It's not ok," 117 replied. "We were supposed to take care of you together."

"You have," 466 smiled. "You've taken care of... all of us. I don't think we would have gotten this far without how hard you drove us to train and practice."

"Uh, wait, isn't learning about 43's New Year's resolutions bad luck?" 501 asked.

Suddenly, Mandy's voice broadcasted from 117's bracelet.

"That's for birthday wishes," her voice stated. "Also, I agree with David."

"Ms. Mandy!" 501 and 466 exclaimed simultaneously.

"I thought you were still taking a nap!" 501 said, looking at 117.

Mandy continued to speak.

"I've been awake at my cubicle for the last 24 hours," she explained. "I wish I could stay awake like you but... I had to go dark for a while to get some rest."

"She's been nodding off," 117 replied.

"I have not!" Mandy protested.

"I'm impressed actually," 501 noted, "considering we're in a war, you know?"

"If you force yourself to stay awake long enough, you crash hard, ok?" Mandy sighed. "Look, I'm trying to give my two cents here!"

Everyone fell silent so Mandy could talk without interruption.

"When we made it to Pennsylvania," she said, "I was nervous. Specifically whether or not we could win this fight. All of you were recharged but... many of you weren't able to handle all of the hits you were taking. Not like before."

501 raised his hand and felt his head.

"That does make sense," he nodded.

"Sherry got... really excited," Mandy continued talking. "She burst into the technician offices and told us. 43 was awake! We got excited too! That is... until a few of us thought that this was a little weird."

"How weird?" 466 asked.

"43's been acting differently," Mandy replied calmly. "Sherry told me that it's like she can't get through to her. She's changed. They used to be great friends but now Sherry feels like 43's avoiding her and being evasive. It didn't help that 43 went on ahead into the creepy maze and got cut off."

"Did Sherry try talking to 43? When she fell from the ceiling earlier?" 501 asked.

"She's not at her cubicle right now," Mandy stated. "She and Serina went off on some sort of investigation. She said that sitting in her cubicle without any way to communicate with 43 wasn't productive."

"They both seem to behave in similar ways," 466 said, tilting her head. "They can't seem to sit still."

"I think 117 and Mandy are right. 43 did seem very eager about ending this," 501 replied, thinking about everything that had happened in the last few hours. "Now that he mentions it, she hasn't been contributing alongside us like she used to. It did feel different but I assumed it was because of her condition."

"She recovered from her coma."

117 and 501 looked over at 466. A look of suspicion crossed her face as the realization of what she said sunk in.

"Not just a coma," she said in a concerned tone. "A coma that was already declared terminal."

"That's it," 117 replied with a firm nod. "I hate to say this but in our excitement, I overlooked one thing. Doesn't it seem very convenient that when we needed a solution, 43 suddenly came to our aid and now we seem to be on a straight path to the finish? There is something else behind this."

"Ok, I'm also getting a little nervous," 466 said shakily. "The one thing that has changed about her is that she seems to be driven solely by the motive of revenge."

"I'm actually thinking about something else," 501 added. "It doesn't seem like her to pursue the mission without her own partner. I mean, 117 and 43 have been inseparable. I mean, they are inseparable! In the field... that is! For example, if they were on two separate missions, they obviously would not be together. But every time they are deployed on the same job, they always work as partners. She... ditched him. No offense 117."

"None taken," he replied, nodding.

"She is hiding something," 117 guessed. "For some reason, she has the means to end this but... at the same time, it does not feel right. The truth is, when we first set out, I calculated... or to be accurate, I considered the possibility of apprehending this assassin. Capture but not kill."

As soon as he finished, he quickly signaled for the two Third Group amborgs to remain silent. He knew this would not sit well with them. 501 and 466 were casting him worried looks, which was hardly surprising. 117 was probably the only person to consider locking someone up while the entire country burned.

"I know this possibility is unsettling to the rest of us but we can't just kill him," he stated.

"He has massacred hundreds of people," 466 protested silently. She looked around. A few amborgs walked by but they didn't hear anything. Without showing too many signs of trouble to the other amborgs, the trio slowly began to make their way to the stairs. "Why does he not deserve death?"

"That is the human side arising in you 466," 117 replied calmly. "Anger, confusion, prejudice. It's what he wants. You say you want to kill him in cold blood but if it was down to you, would you actually do it? That isn't how the system works. In my time studying human behavior, it is true that I have been slow but I personally say that we would be better off doing the right thing and turning him over to a jury. Sure, they will probably give him the death penalty anyway for his crimes but do you think we'll be satisfied if we end him ourselves? This way... if he feels any scrap of guilt, I want to make sure he has time to live with it until his dying day."

"But what if he's crazy?" 501 asked. "What if he doesn't feel the way that you're talking about?"

"I don't know," 117 replied, shaking his head. "He tortured us and toyed with our emotions in such a short time. So, we should draw it out, make him endure that over time."

He glanced at 501 and 466.

"Truthfully, I won't be the one to kill him. I really want to, but think for a moment. Calculate with your implants and not with your human side. The sole purpose of what we have faced these past days was to drive us to the breaking point."

117 turned to 501 and looked him in the eye.

"Do you see how blood thirsty we have become lately? We have been pushed to the primitive roots of our human personalities. We may be cybernetic but we still have the mentalities of young adults. He can manipulate us before we even realize it. If we kill him, we prove his point exactly."

"Wasn't the point of all of this to show the world that we could fail?" 466 asked.

"Not just that," 117 answered her question quickly. "I think that he wants to prove that the amborgs can be corrupted. Murderers and vigilantes disregarding the law. To forget what is right and wrong. Kill him, and we become him. People will see us not as their protectors but something to be feared. That is the point of this entire challenge; to bring down the amborgs no matter how we finish his game. He's so self-destructive that he doesn't care if he dies. He wants us to sink to the bottom after this is over. Look at the destruction that has happened across the country. Maybe after this is over, someone will find a way to blame us for it. The right thing to do is to capture and turn him over to the authorities. This way, he will answer for his crimes and the people will know who really started this war. The more we deal with him, the more enjoyment he gets out of this. I want to stop him but not in a way where we kill off the only link that completely explains this mess. Everyone is so eager to kill in war that it isn't until later in life when they begin to suffer."

He was expecting the two young amborgs to completely disagree with his plan, but to his surprise, 501 and 466 both looked at each other and slowly nodded.

"That does make sense," 501 replied. "But there may be a bit of discord from the rest of us. So many of us are already reaching the end of this."

"That is why as a family," 117 replied, "I know we can trust each other. Ranting personal opinions was a bit of a waste of time but our objective is to also stop 43. She has the most motive out of all of us and if she were to kill this man, we would face more trouble than actual victory."

"I get it," 501 smiled. "You should know by now that you were the big brother I never really had. I know you think of the right stuff. I support your decision."

"I know you want him dead, Donut," 117 said as he patted 501 on the shoulder. "I want him to pay for what he did to 43 too but if we stoop to his level, then no one will trust us again. When we finish this, we need to do everything we can to rebuild and do what we were created to do. Thus, we do this the right way."

"Are you sure that was a calculation? Or was it the human side of you speaking, David 117?"

117 looked at 466. She had barely spoken in the conversation, but the two boys could tell that she was already in agreement.

"I am afraid I'll have to tell you later."

All three of them smiled, but then 466 suddenly gazed wide-eyed at 117.

"But if that's the case, I think this means we better hurry!" she exclaimed.

"Right. If I don't make it out," 117 said, "it is your job to remind the other amborgs who arrive of our new mission. The reason for our existence rests on you."

"We have to stand guard?" 501 sighed. "Man..."

"If we die up there," 117 replied, "someone has to lead us. 501, I am entrusting that to you and 466."

"Cool," 466 chuckled. "We get to run the show. But wait 117, why did you not warn the rest of the amborgs when they followed 43?"

"If I stopped all of the amborgs from following her, it would have made her suspicious," 117 called back. He was already heading towards the stairs. "How would you like to fall victim to a 43 attack again? It is possible she is already suspicious of my behavior. Especially since I didn't follow her up the stairs immediately. Put simply, fingers crossed. Let's hope I'm right about all of this."

He held up his hand and crossed his index and middle fingers just like the way Mandy had taught him. She had once told him that at some point, even he would have to hope for luck. He remembered he had told her that computers didn't need it. He set a reminder to himself to apologize sincerely if he made it out alive afterward.

Stepping up the stairs, 117 spoke to Mandy as quickly as possible. The signal began to grow fuzzy with each step he climbed.

What is this place built from? He wondered as he tried to clear the communication line.

It wasn't until he placed his hand on the wall that he recognized where he had encountered this material. It was exactly like the conditions in Texas when they couldn't detect the signals of the explosives in certain places. If the maze was built like this, then that really did mean no outgoing or incoming signals. They each had to rely on their own self-mapping tech. If he ran into the others, he hoped that they could have the chance to coordinate.

"Mandy," he said, trying to send out one last transmission. "Am I wrong?"

"I don't think so... but David... the signal is starting to get hazy," she replied. "Once you get in there, I can't provide you with a second pair of eyes. The feed could go out and you will go dark."

"You didn't answer me," 117 replied.

"I don't know David, what are you going to do about Serina?"

"I have to get to the assassin before her,"117 said as he arrived at a door at the top of the stairs. "43 isn't going to apprehend him. She's planning to kill him for what he did to her out of revenge, but that is not what Dr. Kendrick made her to be. Something is definitely not right. Anticipate a trap because everything happening now feels far too convenient. 43's arrival, a clear shot to the warehouse, it all feels wrong. There is never a smooth way out with this guy. If I were him, I would calculate all the possible strings to pull in order to get to us. Which means he probably still has something planned."

"Hmm," Mandy replied through the static. "Once you drop out of contact, I'll get with everyone here."

"You sure?" 117 replied.

"If we're cut off, then we all need to do something," Mandy replied. "If this situation is too convenient as you say, then you go get her David. And this guy too. I want you to know that I support you and I trust you. So hurry. Before it's too late."

"Understood Mandy."

He then took a step through the door, the connection cutting off completely as it swung shut.

"All I have to do is stop the woman I love who also happens to be capable of killing me," 117 muttered as he peered around a corner, "...and save the life of the man who declared a one man war on the entire United States, ended the life of the aforementioned woman, put us through the biggest amborg operation in history, and happens to be the one that everyone hates and wants to kill. An extra challenge is just what I needed. Oh no."

117 backtracked but couldn't recall the direction he'd originally taken. He was convinced this was the sole path, yet he found himself at a junction with three separate corridors. Had he already lost his way? Suddenly, a bright flash caught his attention, and he blinked. When he opened his eyes again, the corridor was shrouded in darkness, but a glimmer of light appeared at the far end. *Not a good idea to go that way,* he thought as he cautiously felt his way to the hall on his right. His fingers brushed against a smooth material on the wall. Had that always been there?

"Even more challenges," he said nervously. "I think I'm lost."

CHAPTER 24

A-"maze"-ing Nightmare

"Ok, that was four rights, two lefts, and another right. And then one more left."

917 sighed as they veered around another corner.

"Stop trying to map this place 999," he said. "We know we are on the third floor... At least I still hope so. But every time we try to remember the way, it's not the same and we go back down one floor with every screw up."

"I am trying to get us out of this," 999 mumbled. "I don't want to be here anymore. How long has it been?"

"Two hours and twenty-six minutes according to my clock. Oh hey! Look! A door!"

As 917 and 999 pushed the door open, they stepped inside, and just as anticipated, it slammed shut behind them. Turning around sharply, 917 grasped the handle and yanked as hard as he could, but it wouldn't budge; it was stuck.

"Great..." he muttered angrily while 999 scanned their surroundings. "Another newly discovered dead end... Time to go back to the second floor."

They paused for a moment and glanced around. Nothing happened.

"Maybe not," 999 replied, urging him to let go of the handle. "We haven't fallen yet. Maybe we're on the right track now."

She pointed past 917, and he realized that there was a hallway there. It wasn't a dead end after all.

"Shall we?" he shrugged.

917 released the door handle and the two of them began walking down the hallway.

"This will be one for the history books," he said as he looked up at the dimly lit ceiling. "You ever wonder how bad guys design these sorts of places under our very noses?"

As they pressed on, the hallway became progressively tighter, forcing them to turn and sidle through. They wondered what awaited them next.

"We've been cut off from anyone on the outside."

"999, in our current state, please worry about the fact that... urgh... it's getting much more difficult to squeeze through..."

917 and 999 both began to slow down. He nervously tried to calculate whether or not he could make it all the way. She was shorter and had

a smaller physique but if he couldn't squeeze through, then it would cause problems.

"Perhaps you should concentrate more," 999 stated, "instead of distracting us."

"I'm just... making conversation..." 917 grunted. "It's good for passing time."

"May I ask for one thing?"

"What's up?"

"It's very simple," 999 stopped and turned her head to look back at him. "Two ice cream pints. Two spoons. My room. After this mission."

917 stared at her blankly. Had he heard her correctly?

"That is not a very common request coming from you," he replied.

"I'm tired alright? I'm saying stuff I don't normally say. I'm saying more than I usually say."

"Well, we are alone," 917 stated. "You do talk more when it's just us. No eyes on us at all times."

999 looked away down the hall and kept sidling through.

"I like it when you talk," 917 grinned. "It's a nice side of you. Makes me wonder why you don't show it that often to anyone else. Oof, sorry."

917 bumped into 999 when she stopped abruptly. 999 turned her head, shooting him another annoyed glare that caused him to flinch slightly.

"I don't want to," she stated.

"Why? Deep down, you have a kind heart. You're a little like 43."

"Sometimes," 999 grumbled. "You just need to understand that I don't want any more friends. The amborgs are good enough for me."

"But... you treat several other people so coldly," 917 raised an eyebrow. "I get not wanting to socialize. It's just difficult to decipher what's on your mind."

"Then don't," 999 replied as she continued to move away from him. "Just don't."

"We're best friends, aren't we?" 917 tried to speed up his movements in order to keep up with her. "Can't we talk about things?"

"No," 999 spoke sharply.

"I will get you all the ice cream from the cafeteria back home," 917 declared. "If you answer my question."

999 stopped again. He could see her clenching her fingers into a fist. What surprised him the most was that she started to tremble. Was she angry? He decided to pull the pin on the grenade.

"Why don't you trust others?"

999 turned to him again and he froze. Tears welled up in her eyes and began to stream down her cheeks. She wasn't making a sound, but the way

that she glared and bit her shaking lips said it all. He had probably crossed a terrible line.

"Because... I can't..." she breathed, using her real voice.

Both amborgs remained in place as 917 stayed silent. 999 looked down at the neon lights of his amborg insignia and number on his jacket.

"I remember being... four!" 999 trembled. "I was four years old, and my earliest memories were of a terrible place!"

"Oh," 917 said. "I'm sorry."

"You can't compare me to David 117 or Serina 43!" 999 shook her head. She brought her sleeve up and wiped the tears on her cheeks. "I'm not like them! I was a girl in a mob brothel! Not some protégé that got lucky to live at A.I. Industries!"

"A mob brothel?" 917 stared in horror.

"Exactly what it sounds like," 999 replied softly. "I went through horrible things... and I managed to escape. I thought I was going to die... until I met a friend. A boy. He managed to motivate me to keep living! I remember him taking me to meet other kids like me! There were other adults, but they were nice! They were good!"

"How did...?" 917 gulped. "How did you get to A.I. Industries?"

"My friend? That boy," 999 closed her eyes. "He was gone. I lost him and my friends."

999 leaned her forehead against the wall. 917 didn't know what to say.

"We all wanted a better life," she breathed. "That's all we wanted. And I'm all that's left."

999 opened her eyes and looked at 917.

"You are my friend now," she stated. "And when I saw you after... Dr. Kendrick made you an amborg. I thought that... you could use a friend."

"Well, I really do appreciate that," 917 replied in a soft voice. "It sure felt difficult emotionally to wake up and learn I suddenly had enhanced abilities."

"Amara 345 went through the same thing," 999 began to move and squeezed down the narrow passage again. "I care about both of you because I don't want to see any more kids, victims, people... get hurt like you both have."

They both fell silent as they continued onward. After a few heavy moments, 917 decided to speak again.

"Alright, ice cream it is," he said.

"What?" 999 replied.

"When this is over," 917 smiled, "let's get you all the ice cream you want."

After a few seconds, he saw 999 glance back at him and nod.

"Thank you," she said. "That sounds nice."

"I'm glad you told me about part of your past," 917 stated. "I don't need to know anything else about it. But... I guess I understand why you have difficulties trusting other people."

"When it's just us again," 999 replied, "I would like to consider telling you more things that haunt me."

"Maybe we should have a counselor do that instead?" 917 chuckled nervously.

"Perhaps you and a counselor would help even more?"

"With lots of ice cream?" 917 suggested.

"Deal."

As they continued on for a few more minutes, 917 began to wonder how far they had gone. Finally, 999 stopped to catch her breath. It was fortunate that neither of them was claustrophobic.

"This corridor is definitely reminding me about my figure..."

999 suddenly stopped mid sentence. Before 917 could say another word, she pivoted and glared at him. He immediately flicked his gaze up to meet her eyes, but it was too late. She had already caught him staring down.

"Do not say another word," she muttered threateningly.

917 smirked as she turned her head and continued down the narrow corridor. Casually, he glanced down again, then pointed his eyes back upward.

"Is it my fault that the walls are conveniently showing off how nice your b..."

He wasn't able to finish the sentence when her fist suddenly struck him on the head. It was a light bop, but it did hurt. He decided that it would be best for his own survival to stop talking about her figure.

In another part of the maze, there were other obstacles that the other amborgs were facing. For 297, he was dealing with a rather traumatizing one.

"You are not my father! I worked hard to get to where I am! Where were you?! Huh?!"

297 was on his knees and holding his arm over his eyes. In front of him stood an older man who bore a strong resemblance to him.

"I had to beg! Steal! And do everything I could to survive!" 297 shouted.

"There isn't anything ahead for you, Carter," the man in front of him said darkly. "Put an end to this quest and turn back. It's over, my son!"

"My father is gone!" 297 snarled, looking up. "And he would never tell me to surrender! Hell, he didn't tell me shit! All I know is, I wasn't raised to be a quitter! If you think you can prevent me from progressing, you are sorely mistaken!"

The man let out a cruel and conniving laugh.

"You can't remember, can you? You were only a small boy when your mother and I left you on the streets. You have nothing ahead. Give up."

297 clenched his fist, but then heard the sound of footsteps approach from behind.

"Get up 297. I believe it's my turn."

He turned sharply and saw 57 walk past. She faced 297's father, her expression one of utmost fury, yet she made no hostile movement. Instead, she lifted a hand and reached for one of his shoulders but only encountered thin air. It dawned on 297 that what he was seeing was merely a holographic projection of his 'father'. But how had the assassin acquired the information to create such a convincing image?

"This isn't real," 57 said flatly. "Leave my brother alone."

Finally, 297 stood and strode past his 'father'. Despite its protests, both he and 57 proceeded to the end of the room and exited through a door. After the door closed, 297 curled his fingers into fists. Before he could slam them into the wall, 57 beat him to it. She dropped to her knees and began hammering the ground. Startled, 297 immediately bent down and put his hands on her shoulders.

"It was... tzzt... my sister..." 57 spoke out loud.

297 looked back at the closed door.

"What do you mean?" he asked, confused.

He promptly shoved all thoughts of his fake father to the back of his mind. He rubbed his hands up and down her shoulders in an attempt to console her.

"That hologram showed you an image of your father," she explained. "But what I saw was my sister. You remember her... right?"

At a loss for words, 297 fell silent and sat on the ground next to her. How could he forget? 57's sister hadn't survived the enhancement process. He had met her before augmentation, but it was very brief. Everything that made the amborgs what they were had taken the lives of several others who volunteered. 297 looked ahead as 57 continued to describe what she had seen.

"She was lying on that table... All personnel and Dr. Kendrick tried everything, but she realized she was already dying. I made the attempt to speak to her with my voice, but it was gone. Altered by my becoming advanced... She failed to hear a proper farewell from my own mouth."

"You saw her again? How are these holograms becoming things from our past?"

297 looked further down the hall. It was completely identical to the other hallways they had been through. The repetition of the structure was really starting to make him want to nuke the place.

All of this is designed to break us, he thought. *We have already been broken over and over.*

"That hologram back there said she blamed me for not having the opportunity to survive," 57 bit her lip and shut her eyes. "My sister accused me of murdering her and took her chance to live away from her. That the life we have as amborgs was not rightfully mine."

"You should not believe that," 297 instantly spoke up. "You saw through that and pulled me with you past it. You got me away from that thing pretending to be my father. It was also not your sister. Yet you beat it with all the mental strength you had."

"But would she really be angry that I am alive, and she isn't?"

"No one can answer that," 297 replied immediately. "I mean, if we had the resurrection stone from the Deathly Hallows, it might be worth a shot but... there is nothing we can do about it."

297 nudged her and wrapped his arms around her. He motioned for her to stand, and he practically had to pull her to her feet. As they stood up, she took a few deep breaths.

"That is not how your sister was when she lived," he said firmly. "All of us understood the risks, and we *all* chose to pursue this life. Your sister would be proud of everything you have done. And I know that because she believed in everything you do now and that is why you carry her memories as a part of you. Pain is natural. Just endure it for a while longer. Finish the fight, then her memory will be at peace. Don't let that fake hologram haunt you."

Both amborgs reached an intersection, which broke in three directions. The number 12 had been scrawled on the left corridor wall. The center corridor had 13, and the right displayed 14. They appeared fresh, scratched onto the walls just moments ago.

Supposedly, amborgs 12, 13, and 14 of the First Group had been this way already. Before they chose which direction to go, 57 began to tremble and backed against a wall. 297 walked over and stood next to her. Seeing his father had completely thrown him off-guard, which was probably bearing down in a similar way on 57 and anyone else who would eventually pass through that room.

"That hologram..." she spoke after a few moments of silence. "It was my sister to me, but it was your father to you, 297?"

"It terrified me when my father reappeared. It has been so long since I last saw him," 297 bowed his head. "It must have been programmed to simulate memories in order to stop us."

"It was multi-actual..."

"What?"

57 faced 297 with a shocked look.

"It was two different holograms at the same time," she exclaimed. "I saw my sister and you saw your father while we were both in the same room! Hologram technology being able to simulate two completely different people is close to impossible."

"The assassin must have also found a way to infiltrate our records," 297 said, thinking back to the way his father had materialized and how accurate he looked. "Our records should not be that easy to infiltrate."

57 trembled even more.

"Those were our memories that were hacked into," she shuddered. "It manifested into something we once cared about, and that program turned our memories against us. The assassin knows how to break us. He has brought back something we lived with for years and stamped it deep in our hearts. I don't know if I can continue."

"117 has not surrendered yet," 297 said quietly. "We cannot stop now. We have to fight with him until this is over. Because if this happens to others, then there will be even bigger atrocities."

"And that is exactly why I ask you to keep fighting."

117 came up from behind, startling both of them, but they soon felt a sense of relief wash over them and relaxed.

"Boy, in this maze," 57 said, "I am glad to see another friendly face."

"We have been pushed to the brink," 117 said, grabbing each of their hands. "I am not ordering you to fight with me. Our programming has always been configured to the right things. But these past few days have wreaked havoc on all of us. So, despite your exhaustion, despite all of the problems that we have faced and the trials, I ask if you will fight with me."

57 and 297 grasped his hands tighter, already knowing what their answer was. 117 pulled both of them from the wall.

"Oh, and for good measure, in the possibility that we die today," he added, "this may as well be the last time that I shake your hands. And this is also the last time that I ask you to make one last push."

"Damn it 117," 297 said with a scoff. "You had to jinx it."

"I always did love a challenge," 57 shrugged. They let go of each other's hands and stepped into the intersection, looking in each direction. "As long as we do this together."

"There is one thing," 297 spoke. "No matter what happens, we are still the same people we were before we changed. That is something I will never forget. And if the assassin decides to use that to his advantage, I will personally send him to hell. He is definitely going to pay for bringing my father back and desecrating his memory."

"Speaking of that," 57 remembered, "117, what did you see when you encountered the hologram? You did not appear to be as fazed as we were."

"Oh that?" 117 shrugged. "Well, if it is designed to manifest our memories, and prevent us from proceeding by corrupting our memories, then it made a big mistake."

"Who did it reveal itself to you as?"

"The stupid program turned into 43," 117 chuckled. "It made a poor choice in selecting an antagonist that would try to mislead me."

"Especially since she's the one who really wants to kill the guy that designed this madhouse," 297 added.

Him and 57 burst into giggles at his remark, but stopped when 117 shot them a firm look. Earlier, 297 had discussed 117's views on the assassin with 501 before 117 entered the maze. Although he resented the idea of placing the enemy in custody, he was in agreement with the plan. Once 117 started the maze, several other amborgs began to spread the word about his plan to whomever they encountered.

They pressed on deeper into the maze, eventually coming across a set of stairs. Before climbing, they paused, realizing they'd lost track of time during that hologram fiasco earlier. Was this really the end? Luckily, they had kept count of the floors they'd traversed.

"Last floor," 57 noted, taking in the tall set of stairs. "I am ready to end this."

"This is most likely the end of the maze," 117 said firmly.

"How do you know?" 297 said as they started climbing.

"We are close. I can tell."

They all abruptly stopped mid-step and pivoted when the nearby wall suddenly burst outward. A massive hole appeared, and they quickly shifted into defensive positions. They watched as 1, 3, and 5 emerged from the opening, looking utterly drained as they nearly collapsed at the foot of the stairs.

"How on earth..." 117 started but 1 held up a hand for silence.

"Trust me," he said. "Give us a moment and we might tell you."

"That would really be nice," 3 said, running her hands through her hair.

Her clothing appeared disheveled, and she was covered in splatters of paint in multiple colors. 5 and 1 had some paint on them as well, but 3 seemed to have taken the worst of it. 5 removed his left prosthetic hand with his right and flipped it over, letting several coins spill out onto the floor with a series of metallic clinks.

"How did someone put coins...?" 297 started, but 5 waved his hand-less arm.

"I really do not wish to discuss that," he sighed. "We were in a gas room. Something that our air filters could not withstand. We began to feel intoxicated, so we tried to find a quick exit."

"Remember to tell them about the music too," 3 added. "There were speakers in there that blasted music at volumes that would have probably made normal humans deaf. Even with our hearing turned off, the vibration still pounded in our heads."

"When we shut off our hearing," 1 finished, "we could not coordinate and had a hard time locating each other because the lights had gone out. 3 eventually began charging through the walls. We triggered another trap when we fell into another room and that is why we are covered in paint."

"Well, that explains the colors," 297 observed. "What about 5? He seems to be running high on fumes. Also, where did the coins come from?"

"Hasn't been the same since the recharge," 3 shrugged. "His temper has been on a short circuit. In the darkness, there was music, then a wall bursting, the sound of paint spraying, and then I heard the sound of coins clinking. But I don't know how or why they ended up inside 5. He will have to tell you himself after this is over."

"Like I said," 5 muttered, "I really would rather not talk about it. Sorry for snapping at you guys. I have been very restless."

"Under those conditions, sounds perfect for the ending. By my calculations, it is the last floor," 1 said, looking up the stairway. "Shall we?"

"Let us finish this," 117 said firmly.

"I got some complaints that I believe this guy's customer service needs to know about right away," 5 muttered as he cracked his knuckles.

Downstairs, it was quiet.

"This is kind of boring."

501 turned and noticed 466 glancing anxiously back at him.

"We have a job to do," she replied. "117 told us to stay here and we are staying here."

501 and 466 stood in the middle of the first floor of the warehouse, but he was right. The eerie silence surrounding them felt unsettling. The skirmish outside had quieted, and from what they could gather, law enforcement and military forces were effectively capturing those who continued to resist. It wouldn't be long until the fight was over.

The remaining amborgs were still downstairs while the others had already ascended to tackle the maze, leaving only 501, 466, and a few from the Third Group to scout the perimeter. 466 started to pace in frustration, her lips pursed. It had been thirty minutes since the last amborg made their way up the stairs.

"What are we supposed to stay here for?" she asked, looking up at the ceiling.

"What do you mean?"

466 lowered her eyes to him and shrugged.

"It seems pointless to stand here you know?" she said. "The military can help us keep an eye on the outside, but we should be up there!"

466 continued to stare at him.

"Right?" she asked. "This guy is probably not going to try and escape by running down the stairs. The probability of that happening is ridiculous."

"But not an unlikely one," 501 replied.

Glancing briefly at the various holes in the ceiling, she turned back to 501, who crossed his arms.

"As much as I would love to go up there and help, 117 asked us to stay down here for another reason as well," he said casually, but 466 could hear how uneasy he was. "Although... he did not tell us what it was we were waiting for specifically. I think we should wait to see what it is."

"He always did have a very good sense of judgement. But why would he not be more specific about what to wait for?"

"It probably has something to do with this phone," 501 lifted his hand, revealing an old smartphone from the 21st century, and unlocked it.

466 stared at the phone in his hand and knew that it was 117's. She had often questioned why he clung to such an outdated piece of technology everywhere he went, assuming it was just something he kept for good luck. Now, 501 had it.

"Did you make a call with it?" she asked, never having seen it in use. "That looks ancient."

"I don't know, 117 just gave it to me without an explanation," 501 shrugged. "I only opened it and saw one contact inside."

"How about using it to text?"

"I feel like 117 just wanted me to hold onto it for him," 501 stated.

"It is probably safe to say it's not a detonator," 466 said thoughtfully.

While they were distracted with the phone, a voice spoke up from behind them.

"In a way kids, it is a detonator. It blows the lock to a cage. A cage... with a terrible beast inside..."

466 whirled around, but someone struck her in the head, disorienting her. Suddenly, she felt her feet being swept out from under her and she fell to the ground, landing hard on her back. 501 didn't have time to react; he was blindsided by a kick that sent him reeling forward, and he fell onto his stomach with a jolt. Dazed, he sensed hands pushing him, rolling him onto his back beside 466. Above them loomed a hooded figure flanked by a group of strangers they didn't recognize.

"...that happens to be me," the tall figure said with a smile.

501 shifted onto his side, lifting his head, and caught sight of an old man standing over them. How could that be? A man, who appeared to be in his late 60's, had single-handedly taken down two amborgs? That was impossible.

"You are silent, swift and strong..." 501 said bluntly. "Even we couldn't hear you. Who are you?"

"Who do you think?" the stranger replied condescendingly, tilting his head as he gazed down at them. "I assume this is an unconditional surrender? I've always wanted to keep an amborg as a pet."

"Look," 466 said calmly, "if you let us go, perhaps we can propose an alternative solution that satisfies both of our goals."

501 immediately threw his hands up in an attempt to show their adversary that he'd won, that they were properly subdued. Surrendering seemed like a peaceful option.

"Yes, there is no need to capture us," he said as loudly as possible to whoever could hear. "We kind of have things to do."

The old man turned his head towards 501's hands and stared at it.

"Relax kid," he said. "I'm not with the man you're trying to hunt down. What I do know is, my grandson called me, and he isn't here to welcome little old me."

His demeanor softened, and he started to chuckle, making 501 and 466 exchange nervous glances. They looked around and noticed more cloaked figures lurking nearby. The elderly man reached out his hands towards 501 and 466.

"117 told me about you two," he said. "But honestly... Are you kids that bad at fighting?"

501 and 466 took his hands, and he pulled them up. He removed his hood and the two amborgs found themselves looking at 117's grandfather.

"You!" 501 stated. "I think I saw you briefly that one time!"

"And 117 has been raving about you two," Mark stated. "Word of advice?"

The amborgs listened intently.

"Always have the skills to protect yourself ready, even when you think you're safe," he said. "Especially when you're guarding a place as big as this. I definitely expected better."

Mark inclined his head, prompting them to look over their shoulders. They turned slowly, their expressions turning to disbelief. More hooded vigilantes had arrived, as if materializing out of thin air. The Third Group amborgs on the ground floor were surrounded and subdued. 501 and 466 looked back at Mark, who was patiently staring back at them.

"The fate of the entire country and 117 leaves you two in charge down here?"

"Well, when you put it that way," 501 gulped, "it makes us sound like fools."

"Not what I expected," Mark sighed.

"Um... grandpa?" 466 stated.

"Call me Mark!"

466 flinched.

"Only 117 gets to call me grandpa, mind you," he grumbled angrily. A few of his hooded companions began snickering in the background. "I don't care if you kids are all self-proclaimed brothers and sisters of some big cyborg family. I'm not going to allow all the amborgs to call me grandpa."

"Why??" 501 frowned. "You are old. Aren't you?"

"I'm going to kill you," Mark sighed again.

501 and 466 inches closer to each other. Mark noticed and scoffed.

"I'm joking! It isn't a good idea to sass you kids."

"It's kind of difficult to laugh when we know you can wipe the floor with us," 466 mumbled.

"You did also stab 117," 501 recalled. "It's a terrible way to introduce yourself to your own family!"

"I get that a lot," Mark chuckled. "Now would you two tell me where my grandson is? And also, why you have his method of contacting me?"

"I guess 117 wanted me to give it back to you," 501 replied. "There has been a new development in which 117 needs help."

"I kind of put two and two together kid."

"Four."

"Excuse me?"

466 stared back when Mark turned and frowned at her. She blushed. "Two and two is four," she muttered.

"I'm not senile. This isn't the time to be literal," Mark snapped.

He picked back to 501.

"What were David's exact instructions?" he asked in an urgent tone.

"He ordered both of us to stay down here to wait," 501 spit out. "I believe he meant to wait for you. He is up in the maze attempting to stop 43."

Mark appeared to be listening, but 501 could tell that what he had said confused him.

"Hang on," Mark said, putting a hand to 501's face. "Let me do a download. It's faster but this might feel weird."

He extended his hand, and 501 saw a green light with a message flash in his HUD. When he accepted it, he felt a rush of energy surged through his head, and then nothing. Staring at Mark's hand, 501 and 466 noticed he was wearing some sort of electrical brace. Grandpa Mark then removed an object from a port in the arm brace and put it in his ear. A holo-screen lit up, creating a type of visor around his eyes.

501 stared in admiration.

He's re-watching my own memories, he thought. *Wow he's good.*

The visor shined for a few more seconds before dissipating.

"Ok, I think I understand now what David wants me to do," he said, taking the earpiece out and sticking it back into the arm brace.

"You are also cybernetic?" 466 asked in amazement.

"Not as advanced as you kids but I have the basic upgrades to speed things along," Mark winked. "Alright, now that I've gotten updated, let's figure out what to do."

"You don't have a plan?" 466 asked in surprise.

Mark stared back and nodded.

"Yes, my grandson didn't have time to actually leave a distinct blueprint for me, but he needs help, and we need ideas. First, let's make a safety chute."

"What do we require a safety chute for?" 501 asked curiously.

Mark gestured for him to be quiet.

"A back-up plan!" He corrected himself. "If I am right, this assassin is about to drive your friends to the point of insanity. Hasn't that been the whole point of this big and dramatic war? 117 showed me the challenge video shortly before you left for Texas. This guy says he's doing this because he can. Reminds me of the Joker, but there is nothing to support that. Let's assume he actually does have an ulterior motive for doing all of this. He has resources, military strength, and enough power to blitz the entire country in a short period of time. And he seems to get a kick out of giving the amborgs the most trouble. He has been quick to make your lives miserable from day one and I think it's going to affect everyone badly. The question is, why does he hate you so much and what would killing innocent people do? If I had to guess, he's trying to break you down in front of the people you're working to save. This sort of logic and personality... it is consistent with someone on a path of self-destruction. He wants to die knowing his mission has succeeded while making others clean it up. Or he's inspiring others to commit more atrocities. He's proving that the amborgs can lose. You two, 501 and 466. Take groups of my people around the outside of the building and catch anyone who tries to jump out the side. Forget killing them and apprehend on sight."

"Why would anyone escape that way?"

"If this guy makes it to a window, we have to make sure he doesn't succeed in killing himself or try to escape. Everything he's done over the past two days is enough to warrant the death penalty, but it will create more problems if he isn't held accountable for his crimes. The public will only see the amborgs failing to catch the man responsible. He craves chaos and wants you kids to pay for all the damage."

"That does not make sense," 466 replied.

"It does to me," Mark replied. "It's what I would do. A criminal of his type has no remorse at all. He waged war, fully aware of the end result. He did the impossible. He instigated a nationwide conflict, causing widespread fear and destruction. Now, he's faced with nowhere to run except death itself. By uniting all the crime syndicates and unleashing those robots, he plunged the country into total anarchy, with innocent people suffering the consequences. If he managed to sap your strength and push you to the brink of surrender, he not only dismantled the people's final defense but also tarnished your reputation. 43 is undoubtedly a pawn in this game, whether she knows it or not. If she kills him before we can apprehend him, it could lead to countless unforeseen outcomes."

"What is that?" 501 said nervously.

"For starters," Mark replied, "it shows that the amborgs aren't as cool-headed as everyone knows you all are. Are you really cold-blooded killers? You were created to protect people, guided by a sense of morality and the wisdom to know when to act. 43 is about to make some dangerous choices, and that's what 117 believes needs to be stopped. If we eliminate the mastermind behind all of this, the aftermath will be unpredictable. People may resent you for not giving them the man responsible, and eventually, someone might shift the blame for this entire war on the amborgs. Who knows? In any case, it appears that no matter what we do, there won't be a good outcome. 117 believes that capturing the enemy is the best way to limit repercussions. Although there will still be backlash, it's a better alternative than what 43 has in mind. Got it?"

501 and 466 nodded immediately.

"Good," Mark said in relief. "Because I doubt I can repeat that rant again..."

"We recorded it," 466 replied. "You're all set."

"First off, I'm betting you kids are in serious trouble," Mark muttered. "117 asked me to come all the way over here after all."

"There is very little difference," 501 replied. "We cannot even formulate a plan to help 117. They are up in the maze and by the time we get through it, it could be too late."

"Ok, so we find a way to get there early."

"What?"

"My son," Mark said as he closed his eyes and leaned into his hand. "117's father always used to say that if you supposedly weren't going to make it in time, think about ways to get there sooner."

He opened his eyes to see 501 and 466 staring back at him with concern.

"Anyway," Mark continued. "The real question is exactly that. Why me?"

"Took the words from our mouths," 466 sighed.

"And I thought you were the literal one, sassy little... Look, the point is... Wait..."

Mark paused and looked away, suddenly deep in thought.

"Let me think," he muttered. Then he waved to his people. "Go watch the perimeter."

His guards moved out swiftly, not wasting a second. 466 and 501 watched as Mark shook his finger, as though he was about to uncover the last piece of a puzzle.

"He wouldn't call Dr. Kendrick here," he muttered. "Too obvious and much too tempting of a target on a battlefield. Why didn't he call in one of his military friends? Someone in the chain of command may be smarter than me... supposedly. Why would he ask the last of his family..."

He then looked at 501 and grinned.

"That's exactly why he called me," Mark said as his eyes lit up. "Family!"

"What does that mean?" 501 asked.

"Bear with me just a second," Mark said. "What is it that humans typically do most of the time? They think outside of the box. Now that's typical for a basic plan. 117 tackles the maze while everyone else outside figures out alternatives."

"Like the time that 18 cheated?" 466 asked.

"What do you mean?"

"Well, at the beginning of our training right after our augmentation," 466 explained, "Dr. Kendrick built a series of mazes for us to solve. The mazes are not impossible but have been upgraded over time. Once, I asked 18 how she solved the maze so quickly. She said to me that cheating was one way."

"Smart girl. Then that's what we do," Mark nodded in approval. "We cheat. Your amborg programming usually prevents you from pursuing certain parameters. So, this guy exploited that and basically forced all of you to enter the maze. You're all playing by his rules!"

"How can we cheat?" 501 asked. "We can't get an accurate reading of the interior of the maze. We do not know where the end of it is. There is no other way. A military demolition group is on the roof right now, but according to the report, they cannot use too much power, otherwise they risk destroying the whole building. There is too much reinforcement to accurately determine the level of explosive we need to break through."

"43 already tried remember?" Mark replied. "She used her drop pod to reach the second floor. We just need to do the math and try landing on the fourth floor based on that data."

"We can use our drop pods to try but even with the two of our pods, we could risk making one hole too many."

"Wait a minute," Mark replied. "Didn't 43 already make a hole in the roof? Wait. Don't tell me. Let me guess. The hole resealed itself with some sort of extra barricade? Some sort of blast shield?"

The two of them nodded.

"We looked at aerial surveillance outside," 466 stated.

"For crying out loud," Mark sighed. "Fine, I'll do it. You stay here and watch the floor. Make sure no one tries to skip out on us. All of the amborgs have tried to take this maze from the right way. 117 is telling me, I think, to meet him at the finish by destroying the assassin's rules. I'm not going to question why you kids didn't think of going in through the roof from the start but it might just take someone not designed like you to help finish this. Now, where did 117 park his drop pod?"

"I am afraid that is another problem," 501 said sheepishly. "Drop pods only operate specifically to the amborg they are calibrated to. It would never run for you."

"Fortunately, I knew his father, 501," Mark replied. "And I know that the drop pods have another security feature that I know will help me. If you'll excuse me, I'm going to hot-wire a drop pod."

"Hot-wire... A term for an electrical instrument depending on the expansion of a wire when heated or on a change in the electrical resistance of a wire when heated or cooled," 501 recited questioningly. "But I fail to see the relevance..."

"Or..." 466 added, "it means to start the engine of a vehicle by bypassing the ignition system, typically in order to acquire or steal it."

"Thank you, sweetheart," Mark stated as sarcastically as he could. "Now let's move! I think I know who this assassin guy is. I just need to call Kendrick."

CHAPTER 25

Grand Showdown

The Fourth Floor

117 glanced back at the small group of worn out amborgs. 3 was showing a bit of concern, by the expression on her face. Despite their exhaustion, the others looked to him for one final briefing. 117 acknowledged them with a nod and guided them onward. Finally, it was over. Almost. The gravity of the situation weighed on them as they neared a set of double doors. They were going in alone, with no time to wait for stragglers. It was time to make their final move.

"Status?" 117 asked.

Everyone checked their power levels and damaged systems. Despite showing signs of battle wear, they nodded, confirming they were set to proceed.

"I want everyone to know that we have the strength. Enough for this last fight. And, I would like to clarify the request I made earlier."

5 stepped forward angrily.

"David 117, the outcome I envisioned has been the same since this incident first started," 5 interrupted sternly. "We should not be apprehending someone who has committed acts of mass genocide."

"Well, 5," 1 replied. "I sympathize with you but unfortunately, we should do it 117's way. Once we capture him, all the amborgs should vote on the matter."

"Have you all considered what might happen if we don't successfully capture him?" 5 glared at 1. "He'll get away! If we somehow did catch him, I'd still vote to kill him!"

"Not publicly!" 1 replied. "You'll put all of us at risk of being put down a dark path if that gets out on the internet!"

5 shot 117 a fierce look. It was the first time he'd seen 5 so upset. He was usually the most energetic and cheerful man in their ranks.

"I have told you the truth," 117 replied firmly. "Please, we need to do this!"

He knew there'd be at least a few people opposed to this particular matter. This was his last opportunity to persuade the team of amborgs gathered before him.

563

"But we are amborgs," 117 continued. "If we resort to killing, we risk losing our humanity and letting the enemy win. This incident has profoundly impacted my sense of self, and I am sure the rest of you have felt a huge shift as well. But I know I'd regret it if this mastermind, this... evil person, gets his way. We have to take him in; if he dies, we may end up becoming just like him."

Everyone listened silently. 117 saw 5 scoff but continued to be resilient in his ways.

"I know that with our cybernetics, we are designed... to be greater than who we were before," he explained. "We volunteered to basically be heroes for life. You may hate me for a long time but I learned that sometimes, I do not have to care. I just need to do what I believe is right. Of course the system has flaws. We make it right though no matter what. All that matters now is we finish this."

117 glanced at 5, whose expression was deeply serious.

"Can I at least break his face?" he said after what seemed like a great deal of an awkward silence.

Everyone stared at 5, but then realized he'd made a joke. One by one, light laughter started to bubble up among them, and 117 felt the tension lift gradually.

"Just in case it is not clear though," 1 spoke up.

1 stood between 5 and 117. The whole team turned to the first amborg, giving him their full undivided attention.

"I will only say this once more because for the record, it deserves to be said out loud. I agree with the both of you."

He delivered his statement with such conviction that it left them speechless. 5 and 117 exchanged glances before shamefully lowering their eyes to the floor. Their pride had clashed, and for the amborgs, that led to serious emotional instability. 1 motioned for them to focus on him.

"Yes, I believe that 5 is right. We should not allow this murderer to live," he explained. "Under societal traditions and basic human instincts, the death of this assassin is the fulfillment of justice people want. But, as 117 has claimed, where very few would have the courage to admit, I think he is right as well, despite the negative backlash. Our anger has blinded us, leading us to forget the very reasons why we chose this life. I agreed to fight death in the face because I was afraid. I had nothing to lose and I wanted a reason to keep living. If that meant having a CPU implanted in my brain, then so be it; that was my choice, and here I am. Like 117 said, I wanted to fight for the right thing and as 5 said, I want nothing more than to destroy the very evil that hurts innocent people and creates widespread chaos, the very thing that drove us to this lifestyle. What matters now is what we decide to do that makes us who we are. Do people believe in us or should they fear us after this? We figure that out when it comes down to it, but as 117 believes, we shouldn't care either way. And as 5 stated, we should also act out our anger on those that incite injustice on us. So, you two listen to me right now. Can we please stop with all the philosophical and moral judgement crap? We are badass cyborgs. We are taking this guy in because if he is laughing at us, then we break his face, but we keep him alive so millions of people see him for what he truly is: a monster. He will be held responsible and will have no way to hide from it. Johnny 5 and David 117, I hope this clears whatever lingering arguments you two are brewing, because I'm ready to finish this and just go home."

A hush fell over the group as they silently pondered his speech. 5 lowered his eyes and offered a subtle nod, tentatively agreeing. 117 couldn't speak. Meanwhile, 1 was relaying everything to 501, rephrasing his words in a more effective way.

"I can do that," 5 said. "That works for me."

"Agreed," 117 remarked.

"Also," 1 added. "To hell with a plan. It is such a pain to come up with something only to have it get screwed up. I say we wing it."

"Then let's do it already," 57 replied. "After all, how many times have we ever improvised?"

"Including this time?" 297 asked. He held up his hand and cupped his fingers into a circle. "Zero."

"Then we find out," 117 said as he lifted his leg and kicked the doors in.

"At least let us have time to get ready with an awesome entrance," 57 said. "Oh well."

The doors swung inward easily. For a second, 117 thought he'd triggered a trap. When nothing happened, they all began to march in. 43 was there, standing a couple of feet from the assassin, both standing perfectly still.

Why though? 117 wondered.

This was not what he was expecting to see, which probably meant that their arrival was more than just a coincidence. There were no windows, so the entire room was illuminated solely by dim ceiling lights and computer monitors behind the assassin, who sat silently in an old chair, exuding a dark aura. Just the amborgs and their illusive adversary. Each one of their bracelets lit up brightly, all of them speaking simultaneously.

"You're under arrest."

43 whipped around and gaped at them. They briefly stared each other down before shifting their attention to the reason behind the war and destruction, the one responsible for so many unnecessary deaths.

"Ok, so we are arresting him," 5 said humorously. "Just making sure."

"What?!" 43 exclaimed.

The assassin stared back, not saying a word. A visor blocked his face, but 117 knew he had his attention fixated on the amborgs. Or at least, he assumed he was looking their way. An eerie silence fell over the large room. The only sounds remaining came from the crackling of the computer monitors. Finally, their adversary stood and walked forward, reaching up and removing the visor. 117 and the rest of them watched tensely.

He appeared relatively young, looking only a few years older than Dr. Kendrick, but definitely decades younger than 117's grandfather. His face bore many scars, but they didn't lessen the intensity of his stare. He frowned at them, and his gaze cut deeply across the room. 117 recognized that look, often seen in military personnel, and it was clear that this man commanded respect and should not be underestimated.

"Arrest me?" he said flatly. He smirked a little and scoffed. "I wonder what sparked such change. Yet... Not all of you seem to be on the same side. I can tell the difference by the level of anger spread across your faces."

The man's voice deepened, a sinister chuckle following his words. 117 glanced at 43, who was curling her fists. He knew exactly what was about to happen. As discreetly as he could, he set up a private channel to everyone except 43.

"We will not fall for your plan," 117 snarled back as he stepped forward. The assassin stood his ground and faced him. "It's over."

"Look at you, the leader of this grand story," he sneered. "Trying to be a man but stuck in the body of a boy. A robot who tries to be what he isn't! You were given the opportunity to be greater. It was Kendrick who had all of you enhanced! Yet you fight for people who left you for dead."

"We evolved physically beyond this world," 1 spoke in a challenging tone. "People die all the time but we never leave our own foundations. Our humanity is what makes us who we are. WE are not robots. Not now, and not ever!"

"The original one! How 'bout that?" the assassin exclaimed sarcastically. "What an honor. How does it feel to be the alpha? The one who holds the highest power?"

"Coming from a mass murderer," 3 piped up. "You have done far too much to even ask that sort of question."

The assassin fixed his eyes on Missy, who immediately recoiled. Everyone was putting on a brave face, but it was clear they were anxious about instigating a fight. 117 chose to intervene, easing the tension a bit.

"We were never put in a position of power."

"Ha!" the assassin lifted his hands and shrugged. "Kendrick has been holding you back! Why do you think he created you? He wanted an army, people who would listen, take his orders without question, and make him unstoppable! Yet you chose this meager lifestyle. Why did you children get this opportunity? What on earth makes you special?!"

"You speak with so much disgust and hate," 117 observed. Maintaining a close watch on 43, who looked ready to pounce, he understood immediately. "Who are you?"

"Yeah, what happened?" 3 said sarcastically. "Dr. Kendrick turned you down?"

The scarred man looked at her and his cold expression hardened.

"Yes," he snarled.

Everyone glanced at each other in surprise.

"Oh shit," 3 replied with wide eyes. "I was being rhetorical."

"Ok... well that actually makes sense," 5 muttered.

Everyone glanced at 5. He shrugged.

"What? A guy challenges us and declares an all-out war because a long time ago, he got rejected from an opportunity to become an amborg. So, he hates that we got to be badasses instead of him. Is that right?"

"Well," the assassin sighed. "It's not like I wrote and prepared a whole monologue for it. So, good job."

"How about we stop with the condescension?" 1 replied.

"Shut your damn mouth," the man spat. "I offered Kendrick money... literally, I wanted to pay for his research and have your cybernetics as a reward for being one of the few individuals willing to believe in his futuristic crap. He decided to make it on his own without my help. So, in response, well, I set out to destroy everything."

"Man, you do not take rejection well," 57 spoke, his tone dripping with disgust. "Like seriously... you did this just because? When in your life did you fail to learn how to grow up?"

"You probably offered Dr. Kendrick something he did not want to be a part of," 117 said bravely. "A mercenary with a quest for power and an upgrade was not what he wanted. There was a reason he picked us."

"Well, why don't you ask your dear Dr. Kendrick? He never told you about me, did he? Amazing. You'd think he would have at least mentioned the actual rejects who volunteered for his projects. So, why were you chosen? What did all of you kids have that I didn't?"

"That is a simple answer. Nothing," 117 said. "Absolutely nothing at all. Dr. Kendrick looked at the unfortunate and gave us another chance, he made us better."

"ENOUGH!"

All of them, including the assassin, turned their heads sharply to the source of the shout. 43 appeared to have reached a whole new level of rage, far removed from the version 117 had seen previously. He had anticipated this change, but unfortunately, each moment she was kept from her target seemed to transform her into... something truly terrifying.

"Is it just me or is she even crazier than when we saw her when we came in?" 297 asked nervously.

"Yeah," 57 gulped. "I think it's worse."

"This man has taken so much from this world," 43 exclaimed. Outraged, her hand shook as she pointed at the assassin. "It is our job to eliminate him."

117 shook his head in disbelief. Then, someone on his left stepped forward.

"No, that's not accurate. How come you have not already done this?"

It was 1 who'd spoken up, cautiously approaching 117. He sent 117 a private message, urging him that they had to move soon. The group began to inch forward.

"If you reached this place before us," he said slowly as he attempted to buy a few seconds of time, "How come you have not killed him yet? What held you back? Why were you just standing there when we came through those doors? How long did you stand there and hesitate? What's going on 43? Your behavior only proves that there's something amiss."

43 looked down, overwhelmed by the onslaught of questions. On the private channel, 1 informed the others that he hadn't expected that sort of response. 117, sensing the change, texted them that 43 was beginning to unravel and that it might be wise to apprehend her.

Perhaps it is internal damage, 1 transmitted. *Stand by to respond.*

Suddenly, it made sense to 117. Her cybernetics were in a state of disarray, which was why she was acting abnormally. Now, they needed to subdue both the assassin and 43. He needed to get close for a few seconds.

We need to do what we did back when she fought all of us, 117 texted to the group.

Everyone reacted with positive emojis, acknowledging his plan. With everyone on the same page, they got ready to make their next move. It would have to be a coordinated effort.

"43, you are blinded by anger," 117 said. "Don't do this! If you actually held out until we got here then that means you know this is not what you want! I know that this isn't what you want to do!"

"I... I... uh... I... need," 43 stammered. "No! I have to do... the right... agh. Must... fulfill... secondary objectives!"

The assassin sneered sinisterly. He held up his arms invitingly.

"Yes. Finish the job amborg 43," he declared. "I didn't use all of my best resources for you to fail now. Come at me!"

3 tapped 5 on the shoulder.

"Convinced?" she asked.

"Ok," 5 admitted. "I take it back!"

Finally, it was enough.

"Take them now!" 117 shouted.

They split into two groups. 117, 3, 5, leapt at 43 while 1, 57, and 297 went for the assassin, both groups engaging in combat. From the edge of his vision, 117 noticed the man was incredibly fast. Inhumanly fast. He also possessed cybernetic implants. They needed to act quickly if they hoped to beat him. 117 quickly diverted his attention to 43.

117 faced 43 with 5 and 3 on his flanks as they surged forward. He threw two punches, which were easily blocked. 43 grabbed his arms and kicked him. He was thrown off balance and collided into 3. As the two of them tangled together and struggled to split up, 5 leapt forward and swung at 43 with a right cross, but she was ready. As she lifted her left arm to defend, 5 swung his left fist towards her head. She grabbed it. 5's expression faltered and his eyes widened as 43 gradually forced him down on one knee.

"You would really hit a girl like that Johnny?" she said cunningly.

Before 5 could lose his arm, 117 and 3 leapt back into the fray. 3 took a side approach while 117 charged straight ahead. He raised his leg and struck 43 in the stomach, causing her to double over slightly. Just as he had anticipated, she didn't immediately recover. 3 crouched down and lunged at 43. Reacting quickly, 43 kneed 3 in the face. She fell back, clutching her nose as 117 seized the moment and immediately grabbed 43 by the neck, holding her in an arm-lock.

"Really? This is a bad position for you," she said as 117 held his ground. She elbowed him rapidly in the stomach. "This is the best you got?"

"No," 117 replied as he took each hit determinedly. "This is!"

117 instantly diverted energy into his palms and triggered a power surge, briefly stunning 43 as he began running diagnostics on her systems. But that wasn't all that happened. 117 felt his mind slip down his neck, trickling down his arms and into the connection he initiated with 43.

"Where am I?"

117 was thrown forward and the next thing he knew, he slammed into the ground. He groaned in pain as he tried to reorient himself.

"Well, well, well, David 117. Nice of you to join in."

117 blinked and found himself in a completely different location. This was not the warehouse where they had been fighting. Instead, he found himself sitting on the floor of a living room; one he recognized very well. When he stood up, he turned to see a disturbing sight. 43 was lying on a sofa, unconscious. In front of her, to his surprise, was the assassin.

"When did you realize I had broken into 43's system?"

"I didn't," 117 replied. "When I first saw her, it was strange. I had suspicions because.... Her sudden reappearance, a convenient finish, even after Dr. Kendrick tried everything to save her. The way she pushed herself so hard just to get to you. It wasn't her. It was obsessive behavior. I guessed something else had taken over her entirely but I couldn't confirm it. To be honest, I only wanted to stun her but then... I found myself... here. What are you?"

"Isn't it obvious?" the assassin chuckled. "I'm what's new."

A faint red glow emanated from his clothing, and began looking as though/ it were leaking tar into the atmosphere. As 43 feebly stirred, his figure suddenly flickered, shifting in and out of focus like a computer glitch.

"I'm just a program with a single purpose: to repair this host and eliminate my creator. My ultimate goal is to make the amborgs look like ruthless power-hungry monsters. I do that, my mission is over, and I erase myself from existence."

"You have failed," 117 said confidently. "We discovered your presence and now we can free 43 from your control. The instant her system restarts, you will vanish without a trace."

"Just try it, I'd like to see what happens when you destroy your beloved woman trying to get me out. Kill me, and I will make sure her artificial consciousness here dies forever. Her implants will fail and she will stay dead, permanently. Are you sure you want your beloved Serina 43 to go through that? Because this is the part where you make your choice. Surrender and she dies. Or, make a move and she still dies."

"I like the third choice," 117 replied with a smirk. "Distract you so she can do that."

The assassin looked at 117 and paused.

"What?"

117 saw 43's eyes snap open. While they'd been talking, she had risen to her feet, readying herself for a fight.

"I'm tougher than I look, you jerk!"

43 leapt from the sofa and grabbed the assassin by the neck. She kicked him hard in the back of the leg, forcing him to kneel.

He immediately retaliated by elbowing her in the stomach and throwing her over his head. As she slammed into the floor, 117 seized the opportunity and tackled him while he was vulnerable.

Both men ended up on the couch, engaged in a fierce wrestling match as they vied for control. 117 knew that there was something different about this place. His cybernetics felt off, forcing him to rely on his raw physical strength. Every move felt agonizingly heavy, and his limbs burned like they were on fire. His adversary appeared to be significantly stronger. In the end, 117 found himself losing the battle, ultimately getting pinned against the couch.

Serina shouted as she landed a solid punch on the assassin's head. It was a clean hit, causing him to stagger and release his grip on 117. Without hesitation, 43 took 117's hand and helped him to his feet. Together, they charged and aimed their fists at their target. In a surprising twist, the pair struck the man simultaneously, and... something unexpected happened.

His body disintegrated, scattering crimson remnants throughout the room like a burst confetti balloon. 43 kept her fists clenched as she sank to the floor. The red fragments eventually vanished, and light began to stream through the window.

"He was a program," 117 stated in awe. "He infected you."

"He invaded her," 43 panted as she tried to keep calm. "I remember monitoring 43's cybernetics. You know? Fixing myself. And then... he was there. I tried to fight him but he subdued me and took over! I don't understand how..."

117 looked around the room, scanning it.

"But I can't sense him here anymore," 43 said as she nervously looked around. "Is it over?"

"Yes."

117 smiled warmly as he embraced her.

"Remember? It's me, Serina," he cradled her and spoke to her as her eyes continued to frantically flick around the room. "It's ok, it's done."

"I never thought I'd see you again," 43 smiled. "I am damn glad you came."

"You visited me once before," 117 said. "I have a vague memory but suddenly, I found myself torn away from where I was and then I was here."

"Cyberspace does really weird things to your mind. But this place," 43 said softly, "it was where we hid waiting for our parents to return. It was our home and then, it suddenly became so dark."

"I know, but it's over now," 117 smiled. "You fought for long enough. Finally, you can live the rest of your life how you want and not by another's dictation. You're safe now and once you're up to speed, we'll fight together. We'll end this..."

"...the right way," she finished. "I know."

43 took 117's hands and smiled brightly. Then she awkwardly looked away.

"He took over my whole system and I wasn't in control of myself. Please forgive me. I think I hurt the other amborgs. Whatever I did, I didn't mean it."

"Can you tell me what happened?" 117 asked. "The first time you woke up?"

"It was really dark," 43 replied bluntly. "Like... you need to look outside."

43 pointed toward the window and the sliding glass door that led to a balcony. The light streaming in was blinding and strikingly white.

"It was like an endless night," 43 described. "Then, one day, there was a bright red light shining in."

"Red?" 117 asked.

"I don't know..." 43 shrugged. "Then I found myself in your realm. I was pulled from here and then I talked to you!"

"Yeah," 117 smiled. "It was so good to meet you then. What happened afterwards?"

"Something straight out of a horror film," 43 shuddered. "When I got back, I thought my body was going to be ok! It wasn't completely dark outside! But the lights in here..."

43 pointed and 117 looked up as she indicated the ceiling lights.

"They started flickering and it was really weird!" she said. "Then, that creep showed up and I don't know what he did... but he just barged in here and took over!"

"He infected the system? 43's system?"

"I think so," 43 nodded. "I kept breaking free and tried to regain control but he would keep shoving me aside like I was a ragdoll. The whole time, it was like watching someone else steer the wheel when you're supposed to be the one driving."

43 glanced at the spot where the assassin, or in this case, his malicious program had stood.

"I did so much to try and prevent myself from becoming a blood-thirsty killer but that program... Its purpose was so cruel. It was going to do terrible things!"

"Shh. It doesn't matter," 117 spoke soothingly. "It's ok! I have you back now. I'll take care of you."

"I don't think it's that simple. I'm still dying, 117."

117 paused.

"But..." he started but she interrupted.

"43 essentially got forced back into action without having fully healed," 43 explained. "She's awake now which is great, but... the body I take care of and reside in... it's going. After that, I'll disappear."

"Then we find a way to help," 117 declared. "I won't give up on you."

"I know you won't... but it's not meant to be forever. Not in this way."

117 reached out for her hand and held it. Her hands were chilly but he tried to cling onto her. 43 smiled sympathetically and shook her head.

"We have to return to the real world and... I'm afraid that my cybernetics can only keep me alive for only a little while longer," 43 said. "That program invaded my system and healed me, but it wasn't permanent."

"I won't lose you," he said desperately.

"My body may be dying 117," 43 replied. "But we will always have an artificial consciousness of ourselves living in the digital world. That, and our memories will always keep us together. I know you're scared to let go... So am I, but we need to accept it. I won't be gone forever, not as long as you and the others are still out there living for me."

117 pulled her into a hug. 43 was taken by surprise but she laughed gently as she hugged him back. He held her tightly as she rubbed his back soothingly.

"We were built for great things David 117. You're just going to have to do all of that for me from now on, ok? Promise?"

"I promise."

"Now go get him. I'm restarting my system. Go. You still have one job left to finish."

In a brilliant burst of light, the system rebooted, leaving 117 momentarily blinded until he was enveloped in darkness. He sensed himself being drawn into the void, but as he drifted away, he caught 43's final words echoing in his mind.

"Hey! One last cliché line! I'll always love you! Remember that, ok?"

"117!"

117 blinked and scanned his surroundings. 43 remained in his arm lock, but he realized that she had stopped struggling, her arms now hanging limply. 5 was struggling to keep them both upright.

"How long was I out?" 117 asked as he and 5 lowered 43 to the ground.

"A few seconds. What happened? What'd you do?"

"Uhh, I'll explain later."

Having made sure that 43 was resting comfortably, the two of them turned their attention to the other fight. They whipped around when a loud crash suddenly broke the silence. He and 5 watched as 57 and 297 were hurled across the room and into the doors.

"NOO!"

3's piercing scream drowned out 5 and 117's words. The assassin had 1 in a choke hold, and as he fought to break free, the assassin drew an LTO knife and plunged it into 1's ribs. 1 gasped and writhed in agony. Without hesitation, 117 and 5 sprang into action. As 5 closed in, the assassin swung a punch, which 5 managed to block, but the assassin's other arm, still gripping 1, sent him crashing into 5, slamming them both against the wall while 117 charged forward alone. Glancing at his teammates, he noted that 57, 297, and 5 were all injured, while 3 tended to Serina, and 1 was gravely hurt. As he was processing the situation, a punch landed, and 117 felt a sharp jolt of pain in his head.

We're losing, he thought, *defeat imminent.*

"Come on! Where's that spirit of yours? Still want to arrest me?" the assassin mocked as they continued fighting. "Maybe I'll have you kill me since you took care of my scapegoat!"

117, out of pure annoyance, raised his voice.

"I really wish you would shut up," he said in between punches.

"You can't stop me by yourself! Even if the rest of your friends make it through the maze, they still have to deal with me! You have seen what I've done to your team. What makes you think you can stop me now?"

"Then I'll keep fighting until all of us get here!"

117 took a heavy kick to the chest, sending him tumbling onto his back. He quickly rolled into a backward somersault and sprang to his feet.

Time was running out. He had to think quickly; his life depended on it. All of theirs did. This couldn't go on any longer.

"Run out of ideas kid?" the man laughed and placed his hands on his hips.

"Fun fact about 'cough'...amborgs, we are never out of ideas. We calculate one thousand ideas per second. I am simply putting a pause on those ideas."

Suddenly, a deafening thud reverberated through the room, shaking everything in its path. Plaster and chunks of cement rained down from the ceiling as the wall crumbled. Debris scattered in all directions, and a gaping hole, about the size of a car, appeared as a massive object burst through. Sunlight and a gust of wind rushed in, drawing everyone's attention. It was 117's drop pod, which had landed just a few feet away from the computer monitors. They gaped as the door opened, and his grandfather, Mark, stepped out.

"There you are, David!" he coughed. "You won't believe how many holes I've made in the roof and sides of this place. These gravity bumper stickers or arrows are cool. I'm going to fund these back into production! Anyway! Am I glad to have finally found you. They told me I was going to bring the whole place down if I wasn't too careful but I sure proved them wrong! I don't know what they're so worried about... I mean, the place is still..."

He paused and took in the scene before him. Even the assassin stood in silence, clearly pissed off at the uninvited interruption. Mark glanced around skeptically.

"...standing," he finished.

Mark's eyes fell on 3 cradling 43. His gaze shifted to 5, who was working to treat 1's stab wound. 57 and 297 were weakly trying to get back on their feet. He then locked eyes with 117. With a subtle nod, he turned to face the assassin.

"I guess I interrupted something epic?"

117 looked relieved, whereas the assassin appeared discomforted.

"Who the hell are you?!" he yelled.

Mark smirked and walked over to 117's side.

"I'm this boy's father's father," he said bravely.

"So, not an amborg?"

The assassin pointed at Mark while staring at 117 in disbelief.

"What makes you think this old man can help?!"

Mark put on a grim face as he looked over at 117, who met his gaze and nodded. Without saying a word, they clenched their fists and advanced together.

"Actually," 117 admitted, "I wasn't expecting him to come and help."

"Let me guess," Mark said, glancing at his grandson, "ex-military rogue mercenary with a lot of time on his hands? Maybe a max security cell will give him time to think about his life choices until he rots. Shall we, David, my boy?"

"By all means, Grandpa."

They both surged ahead. Despite 117's fatigue, his grandfather compensated with extraordinary strength. The tide had turned miraculously. Unlike 117, who'd been battling for two days, his grandfather was brimming with energy, much like a newly assembled drone off the manufacturing line. The assassin started to waver under the relentless onslaught and speed of the elder. Mark's attacks were almost superhuman, his cybernetics operating at incomprehensible speeds.

"I AIN'T AS YOUNG AS YOU THINK JACKASS!!" Mark roared as he threw punch after punch.

Eventually, 117 started to let his grandfather take the lead as he unleashed a barrage of attacks on their adversary. The two men, both equipped with advanced implants, faced off in an epic battle. While 117's grandfather demonstrated extensive combat experience, the assassin was equally formidable. He was younger, quicker, and more agile, but struggled to effectively counter Mark's overwhelming strength, leaving him in a purely defensive position against the older fighter.

It was hard to believe that a senior citizen with upgraded cybernetic implants was outperforming the amborgs. 117's team looked on, and it was clear that they didn't care one bit. In fact, they began to cheer and watch in awe as the fight went on. They found satisfaction in witnessing their greatest adversary being defeated by an old man with cybernetic enhancements. Finally, Mark threw a punch so forceful that when the assassin attempted to block it, there was a resounding crack as both of his arms were shattered from the tremendous impact.

"Agh!"

The assassin backed against a wall, unable to lift a finger. His arms dangled at his side and swung uselessly.

"If there's one thing you should know," 117's grandfather said, "there's someone better and older who can kick your ass. And if I can't do that job, then next time, the amborgs will do it. So old coots like me can retire."

The assassin panted and spat on the ground. He was beaten.

"Then finish me off already!"

"Ain't my call," Mark said cheekily. "He's all yours kid!"

117 made his move. He curled his fingers into a fist as he walked purposefully ahead. With each step, he let his emotions build up. After months of tracking this man and enduring two grueling days of their worst mission yet, he was ready to put an end to it. 117 lunged forward and landed a powerful punch on the assassin's face. The impact echoed as his fist connected with the enemy's exposed features, sending him crashing into the wall before landing in a heap on the ground.

"Hey hey hey! I thought we weren't killing him!"

Shocked, Grandpa Mark stared as the assassin lay crumpled on the floor. 117 pulled his arm back, looking at the end result of his handiwork.

"He's fine," he stated.

117's team began to recover as he and Mark kneeled down and checked the assassin for life signs.

"Huh. Nicely done," Mark sighed in relief when they found the assassin was still alive. "You are learning more and more."

"Still learning though," 117 said tiredly. "I hope this was the right thing."

"Well, your father would have agreed. Probably not with how this was handled but... oh well. Come on, let's get you kids patched up and turn this guy in. You want to figure out who he is right?"

"There is still so much to repair. I can't stop..."

"Focus on those later, you can focus on those important bits after you've rested or repaired... if you kids do that sort of thing. Let the humans fix things for a change. You've saved us so get some R&R."

"But, we are humans," 117 groaned.

Fatigue washed over him as the adrenaline wore off, and waves of pain began to travel up his arms. Mark couldn't help but laugh when he noticed that 117 appeared ready to collapse.

"I know David. But let's face it. Not really."

CHAPTER 26

We Have Vacation Days?

Classroom 312

"So, what do you think so far?"

Sarah looked up from her screen and paused the playback.

"Amborgs," she said observingly. "They aren't what they appear to be."

"Go on," Mandy leaned forward with interest.

Sarah noticed this and continued to give her observations.

"As the war progressed with each hour," she recalled, "I did not see the amborgs as numbers anymore. I saw them as soldiers and I also saw them as... human."

"That is what I tried teaching 117 over a long period of time," Mandy nodded in agreement. "Now let me ask you this, why do you think the war was such a terrible reason for the original amborgs to evolve as humans?"

"The more exhausted they were," Sarah replied, "the less energy they had, and it made many of them revert back to using basic human instincts. Violent ones, almost."

Sarah looked at her teacher for confirmation. Mandy only stared back silently, a pained expression on her face.

"That was the point, wasn't it?"

Sarah looked through the footage of the Dominoe Incident and within seconds, recapped all that she had seen.

"The amborgs were Dr. Kendrick's symbol for the tools to rebuild and lead humanity down a better path. When the war happened, it was a fight to destroy everything the amborgs stood for and 117 led all of them on the defensive. By arresting the man responsible, he potentially avoided an even bigger catastrophe. But, I cannot confirm this query though."

"That is almost completely accurate Sarah," Mandy smiled. "At the beginning, a lot of people questioned why the amborgs had to re-learn how to think and behave like humans. David 117 and the original family of amborgs were all advanced beyond physical and mental abilities that people could only dream of. Yet, they were kind and helped people of all status. They fought for the homes that left them for dead and they gave hope back to people that needed it. But the Dominoe Incident happened because eventually, one man, in this case the assassin, wanted to destroy all of that. He was envious of their accomplishments. Fortunately, he didn't succeed because 117 found it in his heart to continue showing pity and respect and chose not to act out in violence. The amborgs became more human in a way. They were faced with probably one of the worst encounters they've ever dealt with in their entire lives."

"But it caused an emotional stir that almost led to uncontrollable violence," Sarah said, remembering the final phase of the mission. "Johnny 5 seemed ready to fight 117."

"Let's just say that the amborgs learned a lot more than they bargained for," Mandy explained. "The assassin did succeed but not in the way he originally intended. Instead of destroying the amborgs by subjugating them to violence, they found a way to adapt and accept that into their lifestyles."

"Wait," Sarah replied. "You approve of the fact that we still have emotional tendencies towards violence?"

"It's always in us, Sarah," Mandy replied. "The seed of violence is always waiting to bloom. How we demonstrate self-control is how we always find the difference between good judgement or a bad day. When we live to a point in time where we forget about certain parts of ourselves, then we are capable of destroying our own humanity. The amborgs worked so hard for a peaceful life that eventually, they learned the hard way that our primitive roots always focus on violence and aggression. From that though, they learned a great deal about emotion. Many of them, after the incident, learned how to blend in exactly like the rest of the population and some decided to continue on without emotion. The discoveries and self-sacrifices of the amborgs from the First, Second, and Third groups became the most remarkable stories I have had the pleasure of witnessing."

"Is there any more I should be watching?" Sarah asked, gesturing back to the screen. "I believe there was more you wanted to show me."

"Yes indeed Sarah," Mandy smiled. "And now you'll see the ultimate decision the amborgs made as a family in order to truly go out into the world and really be a part of it."

"Please," Sarah looked back to her screen more enthusiastically than before. "Computer, begin the playback."

"Look who's super excited to see the ending," Mandy replied with a chuckle. "And when we began, you had no idea what I'd be teaching."

"I am merely... imitating... appropriate behavior at an only mildly interesting story," the young amborg replied sternly.

"Sure. Sure you are."

Warehouse Exterior
A.I. Industries Medical Camp
2128 June

"News crews aren't a good idea right now, ma'am."

Lieutenant Palmer and his guards continued to hold up their hands and formed a human line to block the entrance.

"If you'll just let me have a few minutes with them, Lieutenant, we can show the public our heroes! The ones who put a stop to this war once and for all! Seriously, you got to let me have the first shot at talking to them!"

Ashley Jenkins and her cameraman were both desperately trying to get past, but the military remained adamant. Palmer frowned and tried to turn her away again.

"How about after you give them a break?" he said. "They just saved us from the biggest maniac ever to appear this side of the world, and I'm in charge of making sure no one bothers them. You aren't going to die from being delayed from getting this exclusive."

Ashley tried to shove a microphone in Palmer's face. He glanced up and saw one of the news drones trying to hover above their heads.

"Hey!" he barked. "Someone shoot that thing!"

At his command, someone fired an electric bolt of energy. A taser round from one of his soldiers shorted out the flying news camera and it crashed to the ground.

"Hey!" Ashley's cameraman shouted. "Those cost a lot!"

"We'll pay for a new one," Palmer reassured them. "I never liked those pieces of garbage."

"If I don't get a couple of words at least, I might be dead!" Ashley protested. "Or worse, fired!"

"Lady, I don't think you have your priorities straight," Palmer raised an eyebrow.

"You have no idea how angry my boss is! His news crew is five feet from the story and he's not getting anything? Come on! Help me out here!"

"Ok," Palmer glared at Ashley. "Perhaps the army should pay him a visit. I have a few words for a boss that makes his employees report on the frontlines while he's hunkered down safe and away from the fighting."

Apparently, after Ashley and her team were rescued, she felt an overwhelming sense of gratitude for their timely rescue and sought out one of the soldiers at the edge of the combat zone for access. How she had managed to walk straight up to the army command center, Palmer had no idea. The lack of security wasn't surprising, though, as everyone else was scattered about, relaxed now that the battle was over. His primary responsibility was to ensure that the warehouse was clear of all civilians, as access was strictly prohibited while the police and military conducted their thorough investigation. He had opted out of exploring the mysterious and crazy fortress to focus on looking for survivors, and ensuring that no one interfered with the amborgs, who deserved peace after all that they'd endured.

As he continued arguing with Ashley's desperate pleas, he wished that he could go home and be at Mandy's side.

Must be nice, he groaned, *getting the opportunity to sit down. Feels like years since I slept.*

"Boy, I wish I could get some privacy myself," Lieutenant Palmer muttered silently as Ashley began droning about heroism and knights in shining armor.

"What was that?" Ashley suddenly stopped ranting and focused on Palmer.

"Nothing."

He thought about Mandy again and let out a sigh. He would definitely have to make time to spend with her. Anything to avoid this.

"I wish we could avoid this."

Back at A.I. Industries, Mandy was left feeling quite unsettled following the debriefing. Just hours earlier, she and the rest of the technicians had received updates from their amborgs in Pennsylvania. 466 and 501 had kept in constant communication with everyone back at headquarters, but when the rest of the amborgs began reestablishing contact, the information was mind blowing.

Mandy and her team had been sitting in the dark for what felt like an eternity, completely cut-off from their cybernetic partners. When the first amborgs emerged with the news that it was finally over, the group was elated. The realization that the battle was coming to an end brought a sense of relief to everyone.

Except for Mandy, who remained concerned. Something felt off about 117's report. It dawned on her that one of her friends was missing from the celebrations. Naturally, 117 and the other amborgs had sent in their recordings from that nightmarish warehouse maze. One particular moment kept replaying in her mind: the climactic showdown with the mastermind behind this whole ordeal.

After reviewing the footage and coming to a conclusion with some of the other technicians, they all walked together as a group. Strength in numbers.

"Shouldn't we wait for an amborg or someone to come help us?"

Mandy continued to press on, but turned to glance back at James.

"If what had happened to 43 had happened to Carter 297," she said, "Wouldn't you be doing the same exact thing we're about to do?"

"I suppose so," James nodded.

"I don't know if I like confrontation," Aaron said nervously.

"This coming from the guy who is the tech for 999?" Meilin spoke up.

"Look, handling a conversation face to face is a little more nerve-wracking," he replied. "I just sit in my cubicle, my safe space, and I help guide 999."

"Well, now's your chance to do something out of your comfort zone and feel a bit of adrenaline," Mandy said.

"What if we're wrong?" Ariana asked tentatively. Her voice faltered, trailing off as she cast her gaze downward.

"43 was not herself..." Mandy replied as she led them down one hallway at a time. "Trust me. I really wish that we are wrong. Otherwise, I'm going to regret what we're about to do next."

Deciding where to go next, she turned left down the corridor leading to the medical bay, her friends in tow. All the while, they failed to notice a figure lurking behind a corner, silently watching her. Mandy lifted her wrist and activated her communicator.

"Security," she said. "This is technician Mandy. Can you please send some guards to meet me at the medical bay?"

She paused and glanced over her shoulder. Her friends stopped as well, their eyes fixed on her. A couple of them turned to look behind too, curious if someone was following. The hallway was silent, except for the faint hum of her bracelet as the head of security responded.

"Of course, Ms. Mandy," a male voice said, "but I haven't received any indication for such a response. What's the situation?"

"Call it a hunch," she said as she uneasily resumed walking. "I think we have a potential saboteur."

"Uhh... I see," the man replied. "Roger that. Notifying the team."

She quickened her steps, fast-walking until she reached the medical bay. When they saw the newly repaired door, they hesitated.

"If we're wrong," Prajit breathed heavily, "we will all be in serious trouble."

"Well, it's a good thing that... we're all in this together."

James cast a confident smile at the group, then turned to Mandy, giving her a reassuring thumbs up.

"Right?" he clarified with them.

"Yes," Mandy nodded. "Let's get this over with. You all don't have to say anything. Just follow my lead."

Without another word, she moved ahead. The door, detecting her movement, opened automatically. She stepped inside along with her colleagues, who immediately noticed that all of the hospital beds and stations were empty. As they headed toward the main office, a profound quietness surrounded them, the whole place devoid of any activity.

It made sense that the hospital was mostly empty, as everyone likely rushed off to celebrate the amborgs' victory. Everyone, that is, except for one person. Mandy led the technicians over to a familiar face standing over his desk.

"Mandy! What a surprise!"

Dr. Wildman looked up and smiled warmly, stepping around his desk to welcome them.

"How are you doing? Isn't it amazing that this is over?"

"I don't know Dr. Wildman, I think I have a problem that only you can help me with," Mandy said, smiling curtly and sitting in a chair along the wall. Dr. Wildman glanced curiously at her as she took a deep breath. "All of us here need your expertise. There's been a violation of human rights."

Dr. Wildman showed no change in emotion. He raised an eyebrow and stared inquisitively. The others only watched silently, keeping a casual demeanor. Mandy looked around briefly as he spoke.

"Oh really?" he said calmly. "I'm pretty sure that one of the therapists or counselors here would be more helpful. I'll go and send for one."

As he made his way to the door, she suddenly stood up and stepped directly in his path just before he could pass. The other technicians quickly moved to block him as well, preventing him from leaving. It was clear that something was making him anxious, and she had already confirmed her suspicions. His behavior was a dead giveaway.

"The more you talk doctor," Mandy said as she began trembling with each breath, "the more I know about what you've done."

"We all know," Aaron nervously spoke up.

Dr. Wildman met their eyes with a puzzled expression. Mandy chose to firmly hold her position as she spoke again, noticing beads of sweat starting to appear on his forehead.

"I'm pretty sure this violation needs to be looked into with your expertise," she lowered her head, hardening her tone and staring deep into Wildman's eyes, despite how terrified she felt. Dr. Wildman averted his gaze, trying to avoid direct eye contact. "I confirmed something very interesting from my debriefing with 117. It would appear that upon closer examination of 43's systems, there was a small corruption. You see, you're the only one who probably has the information I need."

Dr. Wildman took a breath and reluctantly looked at her.

"What can I help with? I'm only the head of the medical staff," he replied as casually as possible.

Mandy chuckled confidently.

"Well you see, Doctor, someone here at A.I. industries was hired to carry out an act of sabotage. If 117 and my findings are true, then it means that Serina 43 was harmed."

"I see. But shouldn't this be a security matter?"

"Funny you mention that," Mandy spoke. The smile on her face was gone now and Dr. Wildman looked away. She then decided to throw the last card she had. "Perhaps you'd like to explain to them why you were the one that infected Serina 43 with that corruptive A.I. program. You were the only one supervising her condition at all times based on 117's quick look through the security system here. Then hours before they were about to give up in Pennsylvania, you just cleared her for active duty? You just inform Sherry that her partner is ready to go? Without notifying anyone else? I think you need to come clean immediately and reduce the consequences while you still can. Your repeated attempts to leave are only pissing me off more."

"It's getting a little annoying," Ariana mumbled. "I want to sit down but everyone keeps shuffling around and I don't know if we're doing an epic power pose to intimidate him or if we're just not good at this."

"The amborgs are better at action poses," James commented.

"Focus!" Mandy sighed.

Everyone fell silent as Mandy crossed her arms. She aimed a steely look at Dr. Wildman, prepared to speak her mind.

"Tell the truth," she demanded. "And what did you do to Sherry?!"

Dr. Wildman stared back for a few seconds, then slumped his shoulders and sighed.

"Alright," he said softly. "I might as well... I left a video for John explaining my actions. I was actually just... Well, I was going to end my life to be honest."

"I'm listening."

"The amborgs are bright and very perceptive, so I knew it'd be suspicious the instant I told Dr. Kendrick that 43 woke from an unending sleep," Dr. Wildman said. "I was the one who introduced an artificial program into her system which could evade scans. It also temporarily fixed her."

The door opened and two security guards entered with their rifles held menacingly, but refrained from taking aim at anyone. They looked around the room with curiosity, implying that there was little cause for alarm. Mandy glanced at them before turning back to the doctor, who was slowly easing into a chair.

"What happened?" Prajit asked gently.

"He killed my wife..."

Everyone was taken aback. Mandy's eyes widened.

"What?"

She crouched in front of him, her expression softening as tears began trickling down his cheeks.

"He made me do it," Dr. Wildman gasped between sobs. "During the battle of New York, he sent me an encrypted message saying he had taken my wife and daughter. I never knew they would pay with their lives all because I was stupid not to live here at the facility with them."

"He got to them?" Mandy asked sympathetically. "How?"

Dr. Wildman wept.

"After 43's incident, John suggested that all personnel move their families someplace safe. Many relatives were moved directly here to A.I. Industries but I chose to move my family elsewhere. I told John to make sure everyone was safe until it was over, you see? That man, he... He sent me a video and killed my wife on camera as a warning. He found them. And he told me my daughter would suffer the same fate if I didn't carry out his orders. He baited me. He knew I was not the type of person to do his work without leverage, so he tortured my daughter. After witnessing that, all he wanted me to do was what he said and he would let her go."

"Oh my god..." Ariana breathed.

"You had no choice," Mandy said. "But you still could have fought him."

"He had access to my office," Dr. Wildman said quietly. "Every time he contacted me, he always knew what I was doing, what I wore, which staff I had on shift. I don't know how but when I received his first message, it opened a link for him to see what was going on in the med bay. I was always under his watch... I couldn't tell anyone. He still had my daughter."

"Your daughter, Dr. Wildman," Mandy said urgently. She looked at James and he nodded, understanding her meaning right away. "She wasn't in Pennsylvania? Do you know where we can find her? The amborgs will make it their top priority."

"After 43 arrived in Pennsylvania, he sent my daughter to the L.A. police with her legs broken," he continued after a long pause. One guard walked behind him with handcuffs and restrained him. "She had been abused to the point where she couldn't walk, or speak. The police found out who she was using her fingerprints and a distorted facial recognition. Just had to look past her scarred, bruised face. He hurt her anyway, even after I did what he asked... What monster does that to a little girl? My little baby daughter? Killing my wife and scarring my daughter for the rest of her life. I almost lost my mind."

"Hey," Aaron spoke softly to the security guards. "Treat him with respect."

The guards nodded and instead of forcing Dr. Wildman out of the hospital, they allowed him to stand up, but he continued shedding tears.

"We can help you Doctor," Mandy said reassuringly. "Dr. Kendrick will do anything for you. He will always help you. You're always going to be his friend. Since the war is over and you've confided in someone, then that's that. You can still correct the wrong. So, we're just going to keep you confined with company, ok? We'll bring your daughter home and sort this out."

"I'm sorry, I'm so sorry..."

"Hey," Aaron interrupted. "Where's Sherry?"

"She's ok," Dr. Wildman replied as he closed his eyes and lowered his head, unable to face them any longer. "When she came and asked to look at 43's medical chart, I gave her a sedative and hid her in one of the backrooms."

Without hesitation, Prajit and Meilin slipped past the guards and Dr. Wildman, racing past his office in search of their friend.

Dr. Wildman sobbed as the security guards then led him out. They seemed perplexed about having to detain their own head of medical staff, but they followed their orders. A hush fell over the room, the mood bleak. Determined, Mandy followed the guards, and the other technicians decided to do the same. As they passed through the doors, they noticed Stan busy cleaning the floors.

"Stan, what are you doing?" Mandy asked suspiciously. "Didn't you clean a few hours ago?"

"Well, you looked troubled from that secret debriefing, Ms. Mandy," he replied cheerfully. "When you called security, it was enough to get my ticker going. So, I followed you. It looked like you were on your way to catch someone guilty, so I thought I'd lay a trap if he tried to run. I put extra wax on the floor."

"That's really thoughtful of you Stan," Mandy laughed calmly.

"It's ok," Ariana smiled meekly. "We took care of things."

The security guards exchanged glances, tightening their hold on Dr. Wildman as they carefully made their way across the slippery surface. Stand and the group of technicians watched their awkward attempt to maneuver down the hall while escorting Dr. Wildman.

"It would appear that we were attacked on our home territory."

The group turned to see Dr. Kendrick striding toward them, unexpectedly accompanied by Dr. Kolaski. They both stared grimly at Dr. Wildman's receding back. Dr. Kendrick removed his glasses, revealing a mournful look in his eyes. He'd also heard everything at the worst possible moment and, despite his outward calm, was internally shaken.

"When one focuses on one thing with a passion," he said, "we forget the little things during the heat of the moment. And even that can bring down the house. How could I have let this happen?"

"How could you have known, Doctor?" Mandy asked in an effort to motivate Kendrick. "You thought you were doing the right thing; refusing to turn that man into an amborg. Clearly you saw that he was no good."

"I did see that," Kendrick nodded. "But I failed to see what he was capable of at the time. Look at what he did ... I saw a man seeking power who unleashed his full potential. The reason I saved all the candidates I picked for the amborg procedures was because I saw children whom society had discarded. They were the ones who didn't get to experience the heights of success. I wanted to give them a second chance to fight for what is right. But how many people paid the price for it?"

"All we can do is grieve for a time," Stan replied. "But eventually, we all got to move on. I buff these floors to see a hopeful future for my kids. It's how I earn a living. You're doing the exact same thing, Kendrick. You keep the road to the future sparkling. Sure, there will be times when it gets messy, but you always choose to clean up the mess."

Kendrick pulled a shiny metal bracelet from his pocket and pressed a button. It lit up and began projecting images of smiling teenagers and young adults.

"This is what I saw in my candidates even when I told them the risks," he said. "With nothing left to lose, all of them risked their lives to become my creations. The courage to do that is in everyone. You just need to see that instead of trying to calculate it. They have evolved far greater than I ever thought possible. And I couldn't be more proud. I just... it shouldn't have had to end like this. It was a terrible tragedy."

"Are you trying to sound guilty for what happened or are you trying to say something motivational? Just move on and make sure the floors stay clean. We don't have time for sentimental bullshit. Just go back to work, you two. It's what I'm going to do. I'm not disrespecting anyone or anything. I'll just clean with sadness until I have reason to smile again."

Without another word, Stan dragged the mop across the floor and began humming loudly.

"What a... strange speech," Dr. Kolaski commented with his usual stutter.

"It worked, didn't it?" Stan retorted.

Then Stan looked at Dr. Kolaski and squinted.

"Who the hell are you?" he asked.

"No one," Dr. Kolaski replied bluntly.

"Got kids?" Stan asked.

Mandy looked at Dr. Kolaski and was surprised to see him nod quietly. Dr. Kendrick, however, showed no signs of emotion.

"Yes," Dr. Kolaski replied. "I have a daughter."

"Well then, you ain't no one," Stan replied. "You're a parent. That's someone important in my book."

"This guy..." James whispered behind Mandy. "This guy reproduced??"

"James..." Aaron sighed. "Read the room."

Everyone turned to James and shushed him. Fortunately, Stan and Dr. Kolaski weren't paying attention to them. Stan turned and began to walk away.

"Your children are coming home John," the custodian said softly. "They want you to be there when they come back. What's done is done. Now get your butt back to work and do some more good. All anyone cares about is the people remaining optimistic about their hopes and dreams of a better life."

Stan strolled down the hallway, softly humming a tune. Dr. Kendrick took a moment to appreciate the sound of his voice. It was probably the most peaceful thing he had heard in ages.

"Did anyone record that?" Ariana asked. "Because I could listen to him talk endlessly until I fall asleep."

"He does have a soothing voice, doesn't he?" Dr. Kendrick remarked.

Mandy silently agreed as they all continued to watch Stan walk away. They were definitely right about that.

For anyone who had never witnessed truly captivating, they were definitely missing out. In this case, ninety amborgs were scattered throughout a deserted area in the middle of the U.S. Capital. Completely cut off and shielded from the outside world, they were enjoying a much-needed respite. Although it was a temporary situation, none of them cared. Many were lying still on the ground, while others sat with their backs against the walls. A few even sought comfort in each other's arms or laps. Above all, the one thought shared among them was the sweet relief of being able to finally rest.

"Dr. Kendrick says we may seek out our own paths."

117 stared at 1, who sat across from him. To his right, 5 was massaging his own shoulder, and 6 was resting her head on 1's left shoulder. 3, who had been lying on the ground, perked up. 43 merely blinked as she cuddled next to 117. Everyone looked at 1, and he nodded to confirm what he had just said.

"The topic has been discussed between the two of us for over a year now," 1 said as 6 lifted her head from his shoulder and looked at him inquisitively."He believes that to truly understand the world around us, we should actually venture out and experience it. We discussed what our lives would look like if we weren't actively serving as amborgs. I said I would think about it, and find the right time to pass on that subject to everyone else."

"What on earth is that supposed to mean?" 5 asked. "Amborgs will still be needed. Why would we leave? It sounds like a strange order."

"It is not an order," 1 spoke clearly. "It is a suggestion. Dr. Kendrick believes that amborgs are capable of doing ordinary things. He wants us to experience things from as many different perspectives as possible."

"He wants normal civilians to correct the world's mistakes on their own? While what? We go backpacking in Tibet?" 3 asked, propping herself up on her elbows. "Are we just going to leave?"

"We would still be around to help," 1 said. "Dr. Kendrick says he is not going to stop finding more people to recruit for augmentation. I mean, people don't always have to rely on just us, right? I kind of want to have a vacation instead of constantly answering to every burglary or other small crime day in and day out. Dr. Kendrick said... 'I will make the newbies do the work until we decide to return home.' End quote."

"If we blended in..." 117 said, "we could covertly change the world. Look at what this incident has taught us. Our large successes brought out an evil to combat us and we almost failed."

"Are you saying because of this one-time thing," 5 asked, "we should just disappear? Become vigilantes and hide ourselves?"

"I am guessing that decision is yours 5," 6 chimed in happily. "I like the idea a lot. It makes me think about settling somewhere and becoming a doctor or something. If we decide to immerse ourselves into normal society, we can fully test ourselves as regular humans—where we should belong now that this is over. Let the police and army have their jobs back. It could be fun meeting doctors and understanding different cultures with certain practices."

"And... if something like this happens again," 43 sighed cheerfully, "we can always find each other and bring the family back. We are amborgs. How hard could it be to get all of us to come running home?"

"Yeah, I do not believe any of us will be leaving this world anytime soon," 3 said, looking up at the sky. "Besides, looking for each other on Earth is easy if your brain is technically a computer."

117 glanced at 43, who snuggled closer.

"You know," he said, "we don't have to say goodbye so soon. I think a celebration is in order. After that, we can come and go as we please."

5 nodded. He lifted his arm and gave a thumbs-up. His wrist popped and his hand dropped to the dirt.

"After I get my hand repaired," he said with an embarrassed look, "who am I to argue with the concept of a great party?"

1 stood up and stretched his arms. He relayed a signal to all the other amborgs, who quickly responded. With just three words, he communicated what he needed before heading off to locate where his drop pod had crash-landed. The amborgs, eager to return to their charging stations, their beds, and the cafeteria, followed suit, stretching and gradually getting to their feet.

"Amborgs, return home."

CHAPTER 27

Future Aspirations

A.I. Industries
Dr. Kendrick's Office
2128 July

"Well, the assassin has been placed into deep custody, the evidence will keep him there for the rest of his life. That is... until his execution which I have been invited to attend, and they've requested an amborg escort. Be prepared for that. All of his assets are being frozen and seized by the government and used to rebuild what was destroyed. Compared to my money, it's pretty good... The three groups have contributed to repairs all across the country. I'm currently searching for candidates for the fourth and fifth groups. All should be relatively safe. I've also received an invitation from the U.N. asking me to serve as a permanent advisor, should something out of hand happen again, whereas the Supreme Court wants me to attend a hearing debating whether we really need the amborgs... And let's see, oh yes, my children are leaving to take on the real world. Just an ordinary day it seems."

117 smiled at Dr. Kendrick, who was seated at his desk across from him.

"Can you repeat all of that in one breath Dr. Kendrick?" he asked cheekily.

Dr. Kendrick looked up from his computer and glared at him.

"Don't test me, David 117."

117 laughed softly, making Dr. Kendrick lighten up as well. The sounds of the party reverberated through the walls, but their conversation went on uninterrupted. Out of all the amborgs who had shared their thoughts, 117 had yet to discuss his future plans with Dr. Kendrick. He expected that as soon as he returned to the facility, a conversation with his "father" regarding this topic would come up.

"So 117, what's your plan?"

Although it was a fairly simple question, 117 shrugged anyway. His life before becoming cybernetically enhanced was one he chose not to remember. After he became an amborg, he never thought of doing anything else, despite Mandy's constant lessons on the importance of individuality.

"I do not have any plans that I wish to fulfill at the moment," he replied after a brief moment of contemplation. "Being an amborg is the one thing I'm best at. When it comes to the future, I am uncertain about what I want. But I would like to request temporary leave to go to the Academy for a period of 24 hours."

"The Academy?" Dr. Kendrick looked up from his report. He hadn't expected 117 to make a request like that. "What business draws your attention there?"

"A promise that I intend to see through," 117 answered firmly. He promptly chose to look away from Dr. Kendrick's curious gaze. "I want to inform someone of my safety and honor the pact I made in words with her."

"You're... seeing someone? 43 is still technically alive."

"I am not cheating on 43," 117 replied. "I just want to let this girl, Audrey, know that after saving her, we succeeded in saving the world. I want to help her and anyone else that is mourning."

"Right," Dr. Kendrick said, drawing out the word as a look of realization appeared on his face. "The Wright girl. She lost her brother."

"Yes," 117 nodded. "I failed him. So, I promised I wouldn't fail her."

"Well, take all the time you need, David," Dr. Kendrick nodded, smiling warmly. "You're free to find out what it is you want to do. It's not like I'm forcing you to choose a career on the spot. I just asked you here because I want to know what you want to do, now that we foresee a time of peace. Supposedly."

"I plan to return here after my leave of absence," 117 said with a polite grin. "I am compelled to continue operating under your command. Besides, I wish to remain at the place I call home. I want to stay, being your son, and doing what needs to be done."

"You do know that you aren't the only amborg staying right?" Dr. Kendrick removed his spectacles and stared at 117. "I happen to know 1 wishes to stay after he has seen the world. 999 wants to have nothing to do with freedom. She is more accustomed to a system that she's familiar with but I swear, that girl just hates the words 'bikini' or 'holiday'. Almost felt like she'd rip my throat out if I even mentioned her taking time off again. And there are at least ten others aside from that. Heh heh. Not everyone is making the choice to leave, nor am I sending you into exile. I'll still have a capable team."

"I have no clue what I'd wish to do if I chose to hide myself out in the world," 117 said honestly. "I just want to remain here where I can be the best I can be. To help people. Even if humanity is left to deal with their own issues, we still need to be on hand."

"If you're sure 117," Dr. Kendrick nodded. He looked quite satisfied with his answer. "Then I could put you down for a new program I'm developing for those that are staying and for future amborgs. If you're interested of course."

He presented a data pad to 117. It was labeled with a new protocol unfamiliar to him. The red flag indicated that Dr. Kendrick had marked it for revision before it was to be sent out. Instead of uploading it directly to his mind, 117 took a moment to skim through it, surprising Dr. Kendrick. He read the text carefully, double-checked it, and then looked back up.

"What do I need to do?"

"With some of the amborgs now going out into the world and choosing their own paths," Dr. Kendrick stated, "we need a system to rally them back if something like this were to happen again. It's a quicker, more efficient, and less intrusive way to contact them."

"Sounds interesting," 117 nodded. "I'd like to take a look at that."

Dr. Kendrick shook his head and motioned for 117 to leave.

"After you get back," he demanded politely. "Go and have fun. I'll see you later."

Medical Bay

"Don't tell anyone."

6 looked up into 43's eyes while she was checking her vitals.

"Of course, doctor-patient confidentiality," she said, raising an eyebrow. "But 117 knows. He is waiting for you to tell him. Or at least, he wants to be able to talk with you and prepare for the inevitable."

43 sat on one of the beds while 6 uploaded examination results into her data pad. As they transferred to the main screen, 6 glanced up at 43's tired but calm face. Dr. Wildman had been relieved of his duties. Rumor had it that he'd only been doing everything he could for his family. His heart was in the right place, but he still needed to face the consequences for his actions. Fortunately, since he'd been under duress, many of the amborgs supported him, especially 6. He had the finest legal representation available during his confinement. The medical facility was now temporarily under her command, and she had decided to postpone her own vacation until everything was in order.

"I plan to tell him," 43 said confidently. "I just... Yikes. How do I even tell him in an easy way? 'Hi 117. I am dying. We should probably start writing my will?' Oh, that's terrible... If only I hadn't been hurt in the first place. I mean, how do you tell someone you might die at any given moment?"

"I don't know," 6 sighed. "Not necessarily any time soon. From what I can see in the test results from your physical and cybernetic evaluation, you have at least a few months, maybe less. Granted, it's still pretty bad but at least you won't be in a coma. I'm just amazed you're awake in the first place."

43 shuddered and 6 smiled reassuringly.

"I've had to tell people that they weren't going to make it," 6 said gently. "I've had to tell their relatives... their friends... and witness them get crushed under the weight of their devastation and grief. You're different. You're special."

"Thanks!"

43 paused to take a breath, glancing around to make sure they were alone. A nurse passed by, pushing a cart of fluids. Recognizing the look on 43's face, 6 turned, and they both offered the nurse a supportive smile. The nurse continued on, oblivious to what was going on. As soon as she was out of earshot, 6's smile vanished and her expression turned serious as she turned back to 43.

"But I also seem to have the feeling," she said to her patient, "that you plan on doing something ridiculously crazy. I know that look. What are you up to?"

43 clapped her hands together and grinned happily. Checking again to see if they were alone, she bounced once in her bed excitedly as 6 pulled the curtains shut. They leaned closer to each other and switched to a private channel.

"I want you to change the results on that pad," 43 requested silently. 6 stared back with a look of concern. "It's not serious at all, just don't tell anyone about this plan. Keep telling them I am dying."

"But... that's the truth. You really are dying," 6 said in confusion. "Unless you want me to defy the laws of nature, then it's not possible. Just so you know 43, I'm a doctor... not a Miracle Max."

"Nice Trekkie and Princess Bride reference," 43 grinned. "Why don't I show you what I managed to crack?"

43 nodded and blinked her eyes in quick succession. Tapping her forehead, 6 began to receive data schematics on a separate private channel.

Slowly, her annoyance transformed into curiosity. She glanced at 43, who was smirking, then turned away to contemplate what she had just seen. A moment later, 6 smiled in amazement.

"Where did you learn how to do this?" she asked, her mouth agape.

"Let's just say, I took some info from that A.I. and I learned how to do something awesome with it. But I need another amborg's help. I need *your* help."

"For what? The procedure seems straightforward. Way ahead of our time, but definitely plausible. Is that the multi-actual hologram tech from the maze? Why would you ask me for help if you've already got... all this... illegally obtained software?"

"Well, there is a risk. If I do this, I only have one shot. I have to do one last download," 43 replied, and 6's amazement turned to concern once again. "I need to do another download and I need someone to be willing to accept me as a temporary house guest. There is a risk my plan could fail, but if I borrowed a healthy amborg's computer system, then it would work as a great back-up plan."

"You have got to be kidding me," 6 said incredulously. "You do know what kind of download you're talking about right? You know about those computer viruses? I feel like I'm seconds away from clicking the 'ok' button to disaster."

"Just do something impulsive for once in your life 6!" 43 exclaimed. "What could go wrong?"

"I have done impulsive stuff before! And that's not a safe question to throw around. You're asking to invade my consciousness."

"It's no different than when we allow an A.I. to jump into our minds."

"Dang it. Alright fine, you got me there," 6 sighed with a huff. "Can we get a second opinion at least?"

"Is... this a bad time?"

43 and 6 pivoted. 6 stood up and yanked back the curtains, then drew back in surprise. It was Dr. Kolaski.

"Hello... Vanessa," he mumbled. "Hello... Serina."

"Hi," 43 replied.

"It's nice to see you, although a little unexpected," 6 smiled. "Your next checkup isn't for a few weeks."

43 blinked.

"You know him?"

6 turned and nodded. Then it dawned on her. 6 was one of the company's high ranking medical staff members, so she would obviously know who Dr. Kolaski was.

"Yeah," 6 nodded. "Doctor-patient confidentiality. Even though he's a shut in, Dr. Wildman and I take care of every employee, family member, and friend under our roof."

6 looked between 43 and Dr. Kolaski. There was something, a small detail, that nagged at her.

"You're... not having one of those seizure-inducing alerts?" 6 asked. "Normally, Dr. Kolaski would be doing his little passcode thingy right about now."

"The what now?" 43 asked.

"I'll tell you later..." Dr. Kolaski spoke. "May I... join you?"

6 and Dr. Kolaski turned to 43, who seemed intrigued. After a moment of consideration, she gave a slow nod. He approached and took a seat beside her bed.

"I am... sorry I didn't come to visit sooner," he said, looking away.

"That's ok," 43 replied gently. "It means a lot that you're here. How's Serina?"

"Resting," Dr. Kolaski answered her softly. "She's taking a break. Would you like me to call her?"

"No!" 43 said, shaking her head. "I don't want to disturb her."

Dr. Kolaski nodded and slid his hands back and forth across his knees.

"She wants to see you in her free time," he stated.

"I'd really like that," 43 smiled.

6 suddenly had an idea.

"Wait! I've got it!"

43 and Dr. Kolaski turned to look at 6.

"What if Dr. Kolaski helps us?" she suggested. "I'd feel a lot more confident with his expertise!"

43's eyes lit up.

"That's a great idea!"

Dr. Kolaski appeared taken aback as he glanced between the two of them nervously.

"W-what is?" he stammered.

43 grabbed the data pad nearby and showed him the schematics that she had uploaded for 6. He took a moment to review it.

"Intriguing..." his eyes widened. "This is... intriguing."

"What do you think?" 43 asked.

Dr. Kolaski glanced back up.

"I believe it's worth a shot."

6 tentatively turned to 43.

"Well, with his endorsement, then... Fine. I'll do it."

43 beamed.

"Thank you, Vanessa!"

"It's just going to be weird..." 6 murmured.

"Yes, it will," Dr. Kolaski nodded in agreement.

"A project of this scale, I cannot imagine keeping it a secret," 6 shook her head. "Especially when the words, 'consciousness transfer' is written in your rough draft."

"Look on the bright side, it will all be between just you and well... after we're done, you."

6 glanced at Dr. Kolaski, who was still immersed in the data pad. "What about him?"

"It's alright," he replied quietly. "I've kept myself in the basement for years. I won't tell anyone."

43 flashed a wide grin, which only made 6 even more worried. She was hit by a sudden rush of chills throughout her body.

Oh 117, your girlfriend has some serious guts, she thought.

"Ok 43... What do I need to do? What kind of timeframe are we looking at?"

43 reached out and grabbed 6's wrist. Alarmed, she looked directly into her patient's eyes.

"Immediately," 43 replied smugly.

"What?!" 6 exclaimed. "Now wait just a moment!"

"Too late," 43 chuckled. "Don't worry! I got this."

While going over the instructions 43 had given her just seconds earlier, 6 was shocked by the notion of initiating the process that quickly. Unfortunately, there wasn't anything she could do about it now. 6 sighed in resignation as 43 spoke again.

Dr. Kolaski, slightly startled, scooted his chair back.

"You're probably going to experience split-personality disorder during this part," he muttered.

Cafeteria

"Are you really leaving?"

Despite the adorably large, round, pleading eyes the little toddler was giving them, 501 and 466 had to resist giving in to so much cuteness. They were chosen to convince Thalia that their going away was, in fact, a good thing.

"How come we were picked to tell Thalia about our vacation plans?" 501 asked 466.

"I volunteered us this time actually," she replied.

"Miss Thalia, it is our time to live as civilians," 501 tried to say as reasonably as possible as he switched to a public channel. He had to avoid direct eye contact, though, since Thalia had begun to sniffle, which wasn't making their job any easier. "But we will be around. I promise."

Saying goodbye to 501 and 466 was not what Thalia had envisioned when the party was reaching its end. They had suddenly decided that they were leaving on their own adventure. Without her! Only a small handful of the Third Group amborgs had decided to leave, but this didn't sit well with Mr. Ramirez's daughter at all.

"But all of you won't be here to work together again!" Thalia cried, on the verge of tears. 466 kneeled in front of her and picked her up. Several onlookers were on standby in the event the amborgs couldn't calm the girl down. "You always stay together. That's what a family does. You're leaving just like mommy did!"

"Miss Thalia, we are not leaving forever," 466 said reassuringly as she hugged the little girl. "We will always help for the right reasons. We just need time for ourselves. We want to take this opportunity to be the best humans we could be."

"But you already are! You don't have to prove to the world that you're human by hiding yourself," Thalia protested. "You are the best human beings ever."

501 and 466 glanced at each other. Thalia, still buried in 466's arms, suddenly began to cry. George smiled reassuringly as he grabbed Thalia from 466 and cradled her, checking to see if her tears were genuine or not. When they were sure that Thalia wasn't faking it, they all put on the cheeriest faces they could muster. Except for 501. He was beginning to mimic Thalia.

"She's just having a tantrum," Mr. Ramirez said, attempting to alleviate their worries. "She always wanted an amborg to call her big brother or sister. Now that most of you are leaving, well, goodbye is hard for her. She doesn't want this change to happen. No child likes that sort of thing."

"We will return Thalia," 501 said encouragingly. He was desperately trying not to let the tears drop. He was saved the trouble when 466 nudged him in the ribs. "If you're in trouble, look to the sky and watch for shooting stars. A brother or sister will always be there for you. We promise, we'll come back."

466 turned to stare at 501.

"Where on earth are you referencing that from?" she asked, stifling a giggle as 501 shrunk back.

"Nothing... I was trying to come up with my own personal catchphrase," he mumbled.

"Do you mean it?" Thalia asked.

"About my catchphrase? Well you see... ow!"

"Yes, he means it," 466 said after she slapped him.

"Of course! We always keep a promise," 501 said happily, ignoring the fact that his face was stinging a little. "It's kind of in our programming so we have no choice!"

Thalia laughed as her father set her down.

"I'll miss you Donut! Can we have a tea party again sometime?"

"Well we don't have to leave now," 501 glanced at 466, who nodded. "Why don't we have that party now?"

Both he and 466 made sure to record Thalia's face as it lit up with joy in the bright sunlight. They had another happy moment to remember, one last thing to do before they left.

"Tell us what to do, little princess," George Ramirez called after his daughter, who was already bounding away.

Amborg Residential Area
999's Quarters.

"Boy, this was such a good idea."

297 lifted his spoon and looked at the melting ice cream drooping from the utensil. He shrugged and took a bite. Next to him, 57 was taking happy mouthfuls. The twins, 92 and 93, were both conveying their gratitude and eagerly consuming their own pints of ice cream.

"It's true I did request ice cream," 999 replied with a very annoyed look. "But do you all have to eat in MY room?"

"Relax Angel," 917 replied as he ate a spoonful of strawberry. "Learn how to have more than one person for company in your room for once. I heard that there might be a videogame tournament later. It could be fun."

999 pivoted to him with a look of pure and utter hatred. However, without arguing, she stuck her spoon into her cookie dough flavored ice cream and continued eating.

"I am not comfortable with so many people in my room..." she muttered stubbornly. "If anybody gets any ideas about cuddling up to me, you will be mortally wounded."

"I will take the blame for that one," 917 replied as the amborgs switched ice cream containers. "I mean, it's hard to raid the freezer by myself and carry all this ice cream. You never specified a flavor and fortunately, I was caught by the rest of these party-goers instead of the kitchen staff."

"And now we have our own special party," 57 replied, waving her spoon. "Ooh! Pass me the rainbow sherbet!"

"It all tastes good," 297 muttered. "But it feels wrong. Did we manage to cover our tracks?"

"If I was by myself," 999 replied, "I'd have been able to do it without getting caught. Hey 92. Pass me the quadruple layer chocolate can."

"If we do get caught," 93 spoke up, "what are they going to do? Ground us?"

"Our ice cream privileges might get revoked for a couple years," 917 smirked. "Ah... French vanilla."

"This tastes so damn good," 999 muttered as she frowned. "I literally am battling between trying to be angry but this sugar is just so... refreshing."

"Only Angel can taste something so sweet and still not even crack a smile," 93 joked. "I would pay big money just to see her smile."

"Not even with all of Dr. Kendrick's fortune," 999 replied flatly.

"But what about that time shortly after the Dominoe Incident ended?" 297 asked. "57, didn't you say something about seeing 999 actually smiling?"

"Sorry boys," 57 replied cheekily as she ate another spoonful of ice cream. "But Angel actually gave me money to keep that a secret."

"What? How much?"

"About ten grand..."

"Wait a minute," 92 said, annoyed. "It would have cost me all of Dr. Kendrick's fortune just to see you smile. But when 57 says different, you only paid ten thousand? That isn't fair!"

"Since when was I fair with you?" 999 asked.

It wasn't until after they had consumed all twenty eight flavors that 999 finally made them clean up and leave. 917 offered to help out in case she still needed anything, but she wanted to rest for a while, which was definitely something she never thought she'd ever find herself saying to anyone else.

Once she had a moment to relax, 917 asked her if he could come by later to hangout. She only gave him exclusive permission to do so since he had honored his promise of bringing ice cream. However, he did need to visit again to fulfill the other end of the deal, which was just a quiet moment alone with each other.

After he left and she confirmed that she was by herself, she reached underneath her pillow and pulled out a small box. Opening it, she took out a small picture frame and set it down on her desk.

"57," 999 sighed. "I do not know the purpose for what you were trying to capture, but regardless, I will not turn away this gift."

It was a picture 57 had taken of her and 917 shortly after the Dominoe incident had ended. What made it so significant was that both she and 917 were smiling in the photo. For some reason, she harbored no anger or disgust towards it.

"I guess one photo of me smiling is not the end of the world."

She left the picture on display at the head of her desk, then headed to her bathroom sink and turned on the water. As she washed her hands, she could feel the exhaustion creeping in. Even though she hadn't participated in any of the festivities to celebrate their victory, all she wanted to do was take a long nap.

CHAPTER 28

Finding Their Own Path

Amborg Personal Files: Transitional Period
Subject: Missy Three
Two weeks after leaving AI Industries

"I have never seen such good credentials. So, you say that the restaurant you previously worked for was blown up during the battle of New York?"

3 nodded curtly. The head chef of Crystalline sat across from her behind a small table in the back, reading through the resume she had sent. He didn't recall any job postings being released to the public. Yet just a little while ago, a spectacular resume had mysteriously appeared on his desk. With little to occupy his time, as the team was busy repairing all the damage from the war, he decided to read it. Intrigued by the candidate, he gave her a call and here they were.

"Oh yes," she spoke aloud, without the use of her bracelet, as clearly as possible.

Her throat still felt a bit scratchy, but she was slowly getting used to it. She had spent several days perfecting her real voice, aiming to sound as human as possible, minus the fact that her identity had been completely forged.

"I have been looking for work since the incident in New York, and the whole crazy deal with the amborgs in Pennsylvania was just so terrifying!"

"I can imagine," the chef said, nodding in agreement. "Well, I don't see why you can't be a part of this team. Your accomplishments here are pretty incredible. I have never encountered anyone who looks so young but has also accomplished all of... Well. This."

"You should put more salt on that!" 3 said sharply.

"What?"

The waiter she had snapped at jumped, but the chef waved him away. Carefully balancing a tray of food, the waiter walked away muttering under his breath. 3 immediately bit her lip and turned off her visual analysis program.

I'm supposed to be human. Human. Human. Human, she thought as she silently punished herself. *No super vision allowed.*

"Oops," she muttered, chuckling nervously as the head chef turned his attention back to her. "Sorry, I uhh, I just have this passion for food and... uhh, I can just tell."

The chef stared at her suspiciously, but nodded slowly. He stood, her resume in hand, pushed his seat in and walked around his desk. She hoped she hadn't accidently scared him off.

"Who knows," he said, waving her resume. "You just might teach me something. Ms..."

He squinted at the papers, searching for her name.

"Melissa Carson," 3 said confidently. "Thank you for accepting me."

"It's a pleasure to meet a fellow chef who's actually polite in a city like this. You start next Monday," the chef joked as he walked away.

Feeling slightly bewildered, 3 glanced around, now fully embracing her new identity.

"People in New York aren't polite?" she asked, but the chef had already disappeared into the back.

"Ever been to Jersey?" a customer sitting at another table behind them asked rhetorically. "Get used to the area quickly, otherwise all those leeches are going to eat your nice personality up like a sponge."

3 turned and gave the customer a smile.

"I think I'll get along just fine here."

File subject: Katie 57
Los Angeles Police Department 18ᵗʰ Division

"Hey Harrison, did you meet any of the rookies that just transferred here?"

Lewis peeped into the newly repaired cubicle belonging to his partner. Harrison lifted his head up from his arms. He stared at Lewis and, from the look of disappointment and shame on his face, Lewis could tell that Harrison already had.

"I don't have to Lewis," he groaned. "I can tell you everything you need to know about the new rookie even without having met her... Of course I met her already..."

"Her? What do you mean? I was talking about the new group."

"I know. And one of them impressed me... a lot... Made me realize I'm getting too damn old."

Now that the war was over, several officers of the precinct were looking forward to a little bit more time off than their usual beats before. Even after the brutal conditions suffered from the Dominoe Incident, Harrison was surprised at how the police camps and academies were still sending eager new volunteers their way. The spike in recruitment rates was skyrocketing and lots of new officers seemed to be flooding in every day. It had only been weeks since the end of a catastrophic event, but it felt like everyone was stepping up to do their part and rebuild.

"You're not that old Harrison," Lewis replied enthusiastically. "Come on! We got to give orientation to some of these newbies. It'll cheer you up! Show them you're one of the top dogs around here!"

"No thanks," Harrison muttered. "Let Captain Bradley deal with that. She knows how to whip kids into shape."

"I'm going to take that as a compliment, Harrison."

Harrison and Lewis turned to see Captain Bradley walking by. They both swallowed hard and fell silent, their faces draining of color. However, she simply focused on the tablet she held in her hand.

"Get ready for a new world you two," she informed them. "Kids with college degrees and years of schooling are gonna be heading our way. Mark my words. Now they'll be taking it easy since they won't have to worry about being shot at every day for the foreseeable future. Means more paperwork for a lot of us vets. I can probably keep you at that desk longer, Harrison."

The two of them said nothing.

As she turned to leave, she switched off her tablet. Bradley tried to hide it, but she also felt Harrison's pain. Apparently, one of the new recruits was already making an impression, which was distracting a lot of her officers. Following the rumors, she headed to the firing range, where it sounded like a party was taking place. Each person she passed quickly put on serious faces and wandered off before she could chew them out.

Noticing the large crowd of officers gathering around one single booth, she raised an eyebrow, and then made her way over. Luckily, she managed to make it to the back of the crowd without anyone noticing. Peering over the mass of shoulders, she looked to see who was practicing.

"Man she is so hot..." she heard one officer say.

"No way dude," another one interrupted. "I called dibs."

"You two in grade school or something? Dream on... Both of you are way too old for her," one of the female officers said in a very blunt but cheerful tone. "She looks like she's barely into her twenties. You'd need to arrest yourself for soliciting a minor."

Captain Bradley, annoyed by the banter, cleared her throat. Such behavior was highly unprofessional and had to stop. The result was spectacular; everyone froze, acknowledging her presence. They quickly turned to face her.

"Evidently there's going to be a line if I'm hearing everyone correctly," she said loudly as she glared at the shocked and pale expressions of her officers. "Now give the new girl space, let her be, or... I'll make everyone here wear slings where they don't want to wear them."

The men immediately straightened up and started to leave. The women chuckled at the sudden ego change in their male counterparts. While the majority of the officers exited, a few lingered, with Sergeant Johnson being the sole male officer still present at the booth.

"Don't you have a report to fill out Johnson?" Bradley asked suspiciously. Was he going to be distracted by the rookie as well?

"No captain," Johnson replied. "I finished it early when I learned we were getting new recruits. I was curious as to why this rookie was getting so much attention. I felt it'd be nice to show them that not all of us are indecent. I'd much rather be friends and get to know her."

"Think you're real smooth Johnson? You expecting this particular rookie to suddenly trust you like that?"

"Didn't cross my mind ma'am, but now I am glad I finished my work early. The other men might have tried much more indecent things."

One of the female officers giggled.

"What's wrong Johnson? Can't handle me?" she teased as two other officers began laughing. "But you might have a point, this rookie sure is making me question my own preferences."

"There are no relationships between officers," Bradley reminded them sternly.

Bradley finally looked over their heads at the rookie, who was oblivious to their presence. With earmuffs on, she clearly couldn't hear their conversation. She was busy firing a standard-issue weapon down the range. Looking closely, Bradley noticed that the target was positioned all the way at the far end of the room. Shooting a target that far was bold. Bradley couldn't help but feel curious at this newbie's spunk.

"Alright, clear off now," she ordered. "For crying out loud, you're officers... you're not at a... Ice cream social."

As Johnson and the remaining officers left, the captain tapped the rookie on the shoulder. She instantly stopped firing the weapon, ejected the magazine, unloaded any remaining ammunition, and set it down safely on the counter. When her weapon was secure and disarmed, she turned around.

"I'm afraid I have to apologize for the conduct of my officers," Captain Bradley said irritably. "You'd think they've never seen a rookie before."

"It's no problem, ma'am," the rookie replied, taking off her earmuffs. "I... didn't... 'Ahem'...really mind. Just here to do my job and well, I always try to do my best. My father always said I took after my mother... And that I should be aware of the people I might attract when I join the police corps."

"You attracted them alright," Bradley replied. "Now everyone's going to want to be your partner."

"Thank you, Captain Bradley," the young woman replied. "Until then, I can take care of myself until I get settled. If I may say so, your reputation is... well... epic."

"So, I've been told."

The truth was, Bradley had never heard anyone describe her in that manner before. The newcomer seemed curious and radiated a sense of optimism, almost like an energetic child. Sharp, straightforward, and precise. Clearly, this new recruit was someone to look out for. Good thing, too, since Bradley had no interest in babysitting another immature person.

"Well. Good for you. Officer...?"

The rookie turned, and her name plate shone brightly in the light.

"Denton," she said with a smile and a salute. "Casey Denton."

"As you were then."

As Bradley turned to leave, she cast a quick look over her shoulder to see Casey pick up her firearm, load it, and begin shooting downrange again. As she left the shooting range, she found some male officers hanging around the entrance.

Trying to sneak a peek, no doubt, she thought grimly.

After she finished telling them off, she went back to her office and sat down at her desk. Part of it hadn't been repaired so she was stuck with a piece of the corner missing. At least someone had remembered to finally get her a new door.

As she sifted through her files, she found herself looking at past operations with the amborgs. Many of them needed to be formally drafted and submitted by the end of the week but Captain Bradley, for some reason, felt slightly troubled. The sudden appearance of a new recruit who was already developing quite a name for herself was too much of a good thing to happen in one day. She did like the new girl but unfortunately, she couldn't remember the last time she had thought considerably about a new recruit.

"It feels..." she muttered as she tried to remember the new girl's features. "No. Denton's presence seems really familiar... I wonder..."

She reached over to the phone and picked up the receiver. Quickly racking her brain, she dialed the number for her own newly acquired emergency hotline to A.I. Industries.

"Hello? May I speak to Kendrick please? This is Captain Marsha Bradley of the L.A.P.D. Yes, I was recently demoted after they appointed a new chief. That's not important right now. I just have a few questions for him. Yeah, sure, I'll hold... Damn it."

File subject: Carter 297
Ramstein Air Force Base

"It sucks man, what happened back home. You know?"

297 watched the young soldier ahead of him breath in and out. Observing him carefully, 297 ran a quick background check just to have an idea of who he was listening to. This soldier had been overseas for a while now based on his record.

"You have family? To return home to?" he asked inquisitively.

The soldier glanced back at him with a depressed look and nodded.

"I joined just so I could fight our enemies threatening my home," he replied. "But then a blitz war happens on our own territory and I wasn't there when my family needed me the most."

"You couldn't have known," 297 nodded sympathetically.

He had a faint idea of what many of the troops on the base felt when the short war occurred out of the blue. To be so far from the action was agonizing to say the least. Especially since they all probably lost people they cared about or weren't sure if their friends or family were ok. He expected the mood to be gloomy since his arrival. Luckily, it also meant that no one would be paying attention to his unexplained appearance. He was confident, thanks to his drummed-up alias, that he had successfully inserted himself covertly as a U.S. Special Forces soldier.

After the end of the Dominoe Incident, command groups were tasked with rotating members of the military forces overseas. Several of them were in a hurry to return home to the U.S., and command was being flooded with requests faster than they could be processed. All the missing persons reports and casualty lists had every person on edge. Due to the lack of manpower, A.I.s from several companies had to be volunteered just to keep track of all the information. Even though the battle had died down, it was a logistical nightmare. The end of the war was creating more problems than the world leaders could solve.

Now, numerous bases worldwide were making efforts to send as many people as possible back home without jeopardizing the security of their operations. 297 could only imagine how difficult this had to be. The strain on the commanders and senior officials was probably indescribable.

Only volunteers from the Special Forces or Operations Squads, such as the one he'd infiltrated, were selecting assignments or postings beyond U.S. borders. When 297 arrived he figured, with his presence, he could try to help as many soldiers get home as possible.

"It almost seems like the entire military is disbanding around the world," 297 commented in a gruff voice.

"Ain't that the truth? Spend a whole tour defending a base in Germany against supposed terrorists or insurgents and all requests for leave takes weeks to process. But then one moron destroys half the cities back home and now everyone wants out and to know what's going on. As soon as I know how my family is doing, I'll wait until the traffic back home dies down. Got a lot of good soldiers here considering going A.W.O.L. just to take regular commercial flights home too. Ain't that something? You think you'd be able to risk your career by running all the way home?"

"I'd probably do it. But if my job is on the line, then no," 297 replied. "I'm sure it must be difficult for many."

"I'm not worried," the man replied as he confidently strode alongside 297. "My relatives are all military, so they know how to handle their problems. When the first attacks happened, they got as many neighbors and friends out of the neighborhood as they could and left Pennsylvania."

"They're in good hands," 297 stated.

"But man, let's talk about you! It must be tough to volunteer in this place rather than being at home. I mean true, the military needs people here, but isn't it harder to leave your home for battles that may never happen? Why would you want to be posted here?"

"It's all about perspective I guess," 297 shrugged. "I do have a home, but it is safe now. Still got a job out here to do right?"

"I guess..."

"With me here," 297 added, "it means one more of you gets to go home and that's good right?"

"I don't think it works like that but I kinda see what you're getting at. Anyway, you can call me Dennis."

Dennis led 297 away from the tarmac. The transport ships that had dropped him off with several other squads were beginning to lift off. Carter looked back and watched a couple of them leaving the area. He remembered how smooth the ride in was.

He knelt down to clean out his rifle. He had wanted to take more time to clean it properly but decided to let it degrade naturally by about five percent in order to make it look convincing. The last thing he needed was to be a perfectionist in front of special-forces soldiers and get noticed.

The goal was to be as authentic and convincing as possible, he thought. *Don't stand out. How hard is that for an amborg?*

"You know you're right? About the amborgs?"

297 flinched slightly and looked at Dennis, keeping his expression neutral. He didn't recall mentioning the amborgs. Has this soldier seen through his disguise?

"What about them?" 297 asked casually.

"What you said about home being safe right now?" Dennis smiled. "It's cuz we got the amborgs fighting there too. I think things would be a lot worse if we didn't have them."

"Yeah," 297 replied as he let out a sigh, relieved that he hadn't been found out. "No kidding!"

"Yeah," Dennis spoke thoughtfully. "I'd trust those guys with my family. They can fight and really know how to make terrible people think twice about their actions. I owe them a lot. Wish I could tell them thanks."

"I'm sure they'd appreciate the support."

"I know right? Screw all those people that think the amborgs started the war. I mean seriously, why would you blame a bunch of cyborgs after they just helped stop the whole incident? They fought for us, with us, and they caught the guy responsible for it all. I mean, that's some damn good work in the end. Moderate damage across the whole country, but at least it's not completely devastated. Some of the public just eats that stuff up without even knowing how crappy it is. The amborgs take more heat than we do here at Ramstein, and some people are just using them as scapegoats. I'd rather be back home fixing things up instead of complaining and doing nothing."

"You are a very well-tempered soldier," 297 replied. "It definitely sounds like you do deserve a pass back home."

"Well," Dennis sighed. "It doesn't matter how nice or cool I am. Still stuck here from the looks of it. Thank God they opened the communication lines for the barracks though. At least I'll be able to talk to my folks tonight."

Suddenly, Dennis stopped. Noticing, 297 politely stood still as the other soldier began to laugh.

"Man! I am so stupid!"

"About what?" 297 asked curiously as he leaned away a little.

"I haven't asked your name! I've been rambling this whole time and I don't even know who I'm escorting!"

"Ah well," 297 shrugged. "You've had a lot on your mind and well, it happens."

"So, what do I call you then?"

"Richardson," 297 spoke. His family name was probably common enough and made for a good disguise. "But you can call me Carter. That's easier to say in the heat of the moment."

"Hey that's cool," Dennis nodded. "What's it like being in Special Forces?"

"Oh well," 297 replied. "Uhh... Well."

"Ha ha I get it."

"Get what?" 297 asked skeptically. Had he said something wrong again?

"Special Forces can't talk about what they're up to right?" Dennis said as they stopped walking. "It's all classified?"

"That's right... I guess," 297 sighed.

297 hadn't thought about his responses carefully. He picked a cover in the Special Forces because he figured that it'd be the perfect position where he wouldn't be expected to socialize too often, especially since he had planned on being alone and seeking perspective about what it was like to lead, in his opinion, a very brave but independent lifestyle. To Dennis, he was probably not acting the part properly based on what he decided to do as a normal human.

"Well," Dennis said with a reserved sigh. "If you can't talk, then I'll do the talking. I mean, the Spec Ops soldiers are so uptight and a bit mean. You're probably the first one I've met who isn't already ordering me to go away."

"Rivalry in the military does give a sense of friendly competition if it doesn't do anything stupid," 297 spoke. "We may be in a different branch, but I don't see any reason we can't be friends. It is better for soldiers to get to know more people, right?"

"I like you man," Dennis smiled. "Yeah. More friends the better."

297 suddenly turned his head sharply. His cybernetics were sending alarms in his head and his spine was tingling, sending a chill up his back.

"What's that?" he said alarmingly.

Dennis looked at him and scanned the area. Several troops marched by, and the airfield echoed with the noise of transport vehicles. Engines growled as cars sped past. The two stood still while 297 lifted his rifle and pointed with his index finger. Feeling a little concerned, Dennis moved closer to 297, hand raised.

"Hey man," Dennis said reassuringly. He motioned for 297 to lower his weapon. "Just be cool, ok? Seriously. What do you think you're doing?

Lower your rifle before someone sees you. You're going to scare somebody. Alright? Hell, you're scaring me a little. Just tell me what's going on."

297 clenched his rifle with both hands, his unease growing rapidly.

"Trouble," he said in a harsh tone.

An explosion detonated behind them. 297 and Dennis turned sharply and dropped into a crouch. They noticed one of the grounded transports ablaze, with large plumes of flames shooting out in all directions. Troops nearby were collapsing. To their horror, they saw crew members on fire, flailing and screaming in pain. Some were scrambling for safety while others were caught in the crossfire, and 297 heard the sharp cracks of automatic gunfire joining the chaos. Frantic shouts and cries filled the air. 297 could hear their own troops desperately crying out, but another group of yells grabbed his attention.

"It's an attack!" 297 yelled. "On your feet Dennis! We got company!"

"Christ! The tarmac's being bombed!" Dennis yelled. "Where's it coming from?!"

297 spun around, turning his back to the tarmac, and spotted the source of the shouts. A band of people raced across the airbase, guns blazing. They were armed with automatic rifles, machine guns, missile launchers, and massive robots loomed behind them. He couldn't believe that they were here overseas.

"Oh my god, who the hell...?!" Dennis yelled. "It's those big bots that attacked the U.S.! They're here too?!"

"Contact!" 297 shouted as he disabled the safety on his weapon and began firing. "Watch the enemies with missile launchers! Cover me!"

"You got it! But what are we going to do Carter?!" Dennis cried as he stood alongside him and began opening fire. "Engaging!"

Quickly, 297 thought up a plan as he and Dennis fired a few more shots.

"We got to move now Dennis!" he commanded. "Focus fire and move over to that emplacement! See if you can call for help! I'll get in touch with whoever I can on my end!"

The two of them unleashed a barrage of gunfire at the enemies lurking in the distance as they sprinted toward the anti-air emplacement. The soldiers stationed there were well-hidden, trying to understand what was going on.

"Alright Dennis!" 297 yelled. "Did you get anyone on your radio?!"

"I'm trying to filter all this crap! Can't figure out if we're in the middle of a shitstorm or just a minor skirmish! This is staff sergeant Dennis of second platoon based near the tarmac! Is anyone there?!"

"This is special forces operator Richardson reporting!" 297 spoke into his own radio as he fired at two targets. He watched them fall to the ground. "Under heavy attack! We have uniformed hostiles with automatic assault gear, PMLs, and a bunch of behemoth class drones! We need whatever support there is! We've lost a few transports! They're up in flames! They hit a lot of people during the off-loading!"

"Roger that Richardson," someone replied over the radio. "This is the tower. We confirm! Several targets on the tarmac. They're trying to take out our transports. We can't evacuate if we lose all of them. You have got to cut them off before they get to all of them! Wait... Incoming missile! Get down!"

297 and Dennis looked up just in time to witness a missile hurtling towards the tower. The moment it struck, it detonated, and the building exploded into a massive inferno. Glass, metal, and fire erupted everywhere, making the tower look like a giant roman candle.

"There goes our bird's eye!" Dennis yelled as he stood up and motioned for 297 to follow. "Come on! I know the best way to get to the hangar! My team will be there!"

"Dennis! Get down now!"

297's commands came too late; he heard several thumps strike Dennis. He watched his ally fall to the ground, screaming in agony. Without hesitation, 297 set his rifle down, crawled over to Dennis, who was clutching his chest in pain, and pulled him closer to safety.

"Hang in there Dennis!" he yelled as he inspected the wounds. "Stay focused on my voice!"

Dennis had been hit by six bullets. Two struck his left shoulder, while the rest centered directly in his chest. But one bullet hit a location that 297 knew would have grave implications.

"Damn it," Dennis coughed as he held a hand over the hole in his heart. "This... 'cough,' is going to ruin my day."

"Stay with my voice Dennis. Focus on me," 297 said as he listened to the gunfire. Some of it died down but the battle was not over. "Just take it easy and stay calm."

297, remembering his medical training from 6, grabbed a syringe from his back pocket marked with the Red Cross emblem and injected it into Dennis' arm. The wounded soldier's breathing instantly became much more relaxed thanks to the painkiller, but there was nothing he could do to heal the wounds.

"Damn it," Dennis choked. "I messed up bad."

297 tried applying pressure to stop the flow of blood, but there was a slow, steady stream soaking through his chest armor. He watched as Dennis lifted a shaky hand and reached for one of his pockets.

"This is for my parents," he said as he pulled out a data card. 297 recognized it as a special video-message. "Make sure they get this. I sent them a letter two days ago, but this was... me promising them I was coming home. I need them to get this."

"Give it to them yourself," 297 said bravely. "Tell me about your parents. What are they like? Keep talking. Just keep talking."

"The...best...k-kuh-kind any person... could have," Dennis rasped slowly. "Hey Carter... Do you think you can do me one more favor... tuh-too?"

"Sure Dennis," 297 replied as he put Dennis' video mail into his satchel. "Name it."

"You think maybe you could go to the amborgs and tell them I said thanks?"

"What?"

297 looked down at Dennis in surprise.

"Just hear me out..." Dennis coughed. "I have one regret and that is when I decided to be stupid enough to leave home to fight a battle that ended like this. The amborgs... they did more than just save my family. They help hundreds of thousands a week, and look at what I've done... Ran away from home to... fight nothing and to die like this... and yet, people find ways to put the heat on them."

"You did what many other people could only say or dream of," 297 replied. "You put on a uniform when they didn't and you fought when they couldn't because like the amborgs, you chose to risk your life for the duty of protecting innocent lives. You have nothing to regret."

"You sound like you... know them," Dennis smiled, and tears began to stream down his face. "Look at me sir... I'm going to die and... no one will care."

"I do," 297 smiled. "I know you and I'll remember that you fought to the end. I'll tell all of them about you. You have fought bravely. I promise, your family will know that you were a hero just like the amborgs."

Dennis lifted his hand, which 297 held onto tightly. Moments later, he inhaled deeply for one final time and closed his eyes. 297 looked at his readings and confirmed it: Dennis's life signs were gone.

"I'll make sure you don't get left behind," he declared as he grabbed his rifle and stood.

Turning around, 297 sighted his next target and ran.

"I need to find out how this happened. The battle is unending."

File subject: Kiden 18
Livorno, Italy

The streets were shrouded in darkness beneath the Tuscany sky. Antique gas lanterns cast a warm glow as 18 scanned the street to the left and right. *Should be clear,* she thought. Eventually, she proceeded down the path into a hidden alley. A man stood outside. Although she was now meant to blend in as a human, she stepped forward bravely and downloaded the Italian language.

"Buena sera," she greeted as the database installed the language to her brain almost instantaneously.

The man looked up and merely nodded back.

"Salve," he said indifferently.

He sounded quite menacing and cold, but she supposed it was his job. 18 could tell that the man had concealed weapons under his jacket, but perhaps if she got on his good side, he could be friendly.

"May I go in?"

The man silently regarded her for a moment, but then began to laugh.

"English huh?" he said observingly. "You are one crazy girl if you think you're getting in. Why don't you do both of us a favor, save us some trouble and just go home?"

18 smirked and pulled some money out of her pocket. The man fell silent the moment he laid eyes on the hefty stack of euros she offered him. He swallowed hard and edged toward the door, but she knew that he was already hooked.

"You can't," he said firmly. "The boss is trying to relax, and he'll kill me if I let anyone disturb him. He's been moody these past few weeks. He's not about to change his mind just because a child like you said so."

She tossed the money with a flick of her wrist, which he caught easily.

"Count it."

Taken aback, the doorman hurriedly flicked through the stack of bills. It took him a few minutes, and with each count, his nervousness intensified. She noticed his hands trembling as he worked through the last of the money. For a moment, she wondered if she should intervene, as he appeared to be on the verge of a panic attack. At last, the guard swallowed hard after confirming the total amount.

"Take your money, stranger," he said.

Very strong resolve, 18 noted.

The man stood there, feet planted, holding the money in his outstretched hand. The temptation was real but... it wasn't enough for him to move out of the way.

"Tell you what," 18 stated. "You keep that and... I make sure your boss stays happy for both our sakes. Cap-ire?"

"You're a crazy cagna," the man muttered as he shook his head in disbelief.

Still nervous, he made his intentions as clear as possible in a final attempt to sway 18. Not planning on being turned down, she stood her ground. Finally, after another long and silent moment, he slowly reached for the door and unlatched it.

"Grazie," she said politely as she entered.

"I pray that we both don't have to go to our funerals... A shame to see someone as young as you standing up to the head of the Italian mob."

"I'm not as young as you think."

"Mercy."

The hall was lit up brightly. Art hung from the walls as 18 progressed to the door at the end. She opened it gently and stepped inside. Men and women were gathered around tables, sipping drinks, playing cards, and smoking. It was just as she expected of a modern mob scenario, though bits of it looked nothing like the movies. The main area was packed with hitmen and women, lacking any dancers or entertainment beyond the casino-style card games and alcohol.

No one seemed to notice her, except for the bartender, who cast a wary glance at 18 before he went back to polishing shot glasses. She noticed him reach under the bar, pull something out, and place it on the counter. It was a new experimental rifle. It didn't come as a surprise that the mob had continuous access to innovative ways to kill people.

She winked at the man behind the counter. Taken slightly aback, the bartender put a hand on the rifle and tapped his fingers on the weapon as if he hadn't made his point clear enough. 18 walked past the bar and approached the table at the far corner. Suddenly, she felt eyes from every direction turning to get a look, and the noise gradually died down.

"I don't have any scheduled visits from anyone today, so you better talk quickly... and it looks like I'm getting a new doorman. Although... I do admire the fact he was able to say no so many times to you even though you're as persistent as the temptations of the devil. I will spare you two since you've now made me incredibly curious."

18 smiled.

"Thank you for your time," she bowed her head, which caused every person in the room to immediately fall silent and begin to fidget.

One wrong move and the room would light up faster than a fireworks show, she thought. *Let's hope these guys actually like being reasonable.*

"Actually," 18 continued. "Would you believe me if I said I have a gift for you?"

The head of the Italian mafia leaned forward. He eyed her suspiciously and with two fingers, took the cigar out of his mouth and pointed it in her direction.

"Look miss, I am not doing too well. And there isn't a damn thing a pretty girl such as yourself can do to make me feel good," he said menacingly in heavy accented English. However, she continued smirking, which made him even more annoyed. "I told you to be quick. Otherwise, I give the signal and, in this case, only you die."

The men sitting on the boss's flanks shifted and their arms went for the pockets inside their jackets. 18 stared back at the two men with raised eyebrows, making sure they saw her expression clearly. Sighing, she immediately reached for her own jacket, pulled a bag out of her pocket, and threw it onto the table.

"I heard you got into a fit of trouble from one of your partners," she said, ignoring the flinching movements from the guards, but the boss merely lifted his hand, commanding them to freeze. "So... basically I went and stole back what he took from you. If you want to keep that bag however, you stop terrorizing innocents who had nothing to do with what's in there."

She pointed at the bag with a stern look. The boss raised an eyebrow and leaned forward to grab it. He peered inside, and after a moment, he waved the guards down and put the bag back on the table. One of his henchmen, at his command, immediately took the bag and removed himself from the room.

"Alright, young lady, you have my attention..." he muttered calmly. There was less hostility in his voice, which made the tension in the air practically float away. Everyone not near the main table turned and went back to what they were doing. The boss leaned forward casually and smiled. "Do I want to know how you managed to get my diamonds back? What was it you demanded? My hearing is not as good as it was in my younger days."

"That you leave civilians alone," 18 repeated a bit louder. The boss recoiled, as if she had just lunged at him with a whip. "I know that you've been intimidating them. I know about the thief that thought it'd be ok to challenge your rule by robbing you. But he shielded himself behind poor innocent people. When you went looking for him, you did so by stepping on good people. People that are making this thief a martyr and decided it's time to fight back while you sit here thinking you're safe."

"Careful, girl," the boss snarled. "You keep talking like that, I might change my mind about what I already think about you."

"It's all about ego to you, isn't it?" 18 replied. "Do you want the thief or not?"

"You stole back the diamonds from this elusive volpe," the boss said. "Why is this man not here before me?"

"Oh, he'll be here," 18 smiled. "I'm having him shipped to your door in a few minutes. But here's what I'm telling you that you need to know. This part is free."

"Go on..."

"This volpe, you say?" 18 said. "He was obsessed. You could say, he was a fan who idolized someone who did the impossible. The mastermind of Incedente Dominoe."

"A tragedy my child," the boss nodded his head respectfully. "A blitz that shattered the hearts of millions. Even those who did not live on the same continent were affected. You sound as if you were in the heart of it. But now you are here in the land of my ancestors bringing down a thief that idolized the one they call the Assassino?"

"People who idolize their 'heroes' can do great things," 18 spoke. "Terrible, yes. But great things. He stole from you because he wanted you to make the mistake of hurting people in your search for him. I caught him rallying and distributing weapons to those willing to fight back. But if I'm correct, more bloodshed and needless killing is not what we all want."

"If the damage has been done," the boss said with conviction, "what good is catching the man? If the people want to fight, what can I do?"

"You can do something they won't expect. Admit to them that you made a mistake. You tell them it was a misunderstanding. Lower your weapons first and show compassion. That's something I'm sure your pride can afford to give up. It'll give the people the opportunity to see that you care about them while maintaining your system that has been in place for a long time. The man who initiated the Dominoe Incident proved that there can be others who will rise up because of their obsessive idolization to continue his infamous work. But it is the actions of people like you with power and reason who can show that we can also fight this evil. It's a game involving human lives. You can dictate what happens."

Everyone who heard her fell silent. The boss listened intently and glanced at his guards. 18 felt uncertain about what was going to happen next. She was taking a huge risk by making demands of the Italian mob, especially since it was her first solo venture. Finally, the boss stood up.

"That was probably the bravest thing you've had to do up to now in your life," he said. "If I do everything you say, what's in it for me in the long run? For both of us?"

"It's really not that complicated signore," 18 said. "I help you, and in return, you provide a small favor each time I complete a task. I'll only ask for ten percent of the profits from each job I complete. Basically, I'm providing you with my professional expertise. I take very little and consider myself one of the best—speaking modestly of course. And just so you know, it doesn't matter if you refuse or not. I just simply enjoy having my voice heard."

"No one has ever done work for me and asked for so little," the boss observed suspiciously. It had to be the strangest offer he had ever been given in his entire life. "What's your angle?"

"The right thing. Take it or leave it."

"You know," he said, "part of me wants to throw you out, but the rest of me wants to keep you around to figure out your true intentions. However, since you returned my diamonds, I'll consider it a no-questions-asked entry fee for now. Just remember, I'm watching you... understand? Any funny business, and you'll see what I'm capable of."

"I assumed you would. A piacere to be working for you."

"Young lady," the boss spoke again. "You do know you're willing to work for a mob, right? This is ridiculous to a certain extent. I do hope you're taking my warnings seriously."

"Oh, don't worry about me. This is something I'm prepared for. Just as long as you respect me, then I respect you. It's safer that way until we learn to trust one another."

CHAPTER 29

Legacy

A.I. Industries
2135

"I trust you enjoyed your stay?"

Brad nodded, realizing he had absorbed more knowledge in a single day than he ever thought possible. To hear things from another perspective felt so invigorating. He found himself with a newfound admiration for the achievements of the amborgs, both past and present. After that lengthy narrative, fatigue began to set in. It was almost time to head home, yet a small part of him hesitated as Dr. Kendrick and 117 guided him down the hallway. A transport awaited him, ready to take him back home.

Earlier, he had said farewell to Mandy and Mr. Ramirez, who wished him a pleasant evening. He still had countless questions lingering in his mind, but perhaps one day, he would find the answers.

"Absolutely," Brad replied to Dr. Kendrick with a nod as he stretched his arms. "It was amazing listening to a whole new perspective about the Domino Incident, the amborgs, and their individual disappearances following that war. Everyone I knew wondered what had happened to them. We thought the government exiled them or something."

"Yes, and you can also see why I'm reluctant to let someone like you become an amborg," Dr. Kendrick said. "You would be burdened with a life that may seem liberating, but the reality is that it's much more difficult than you might think. You must also be prepared to endure the hardships that your family experiences. Remember, they grew up without their real parents, their homes, and no education, yet their determination to live remains unshaken. Only those of remarkable caliber can help ease the traumas we have faced. At times, we still experience relapses or suffer from mental breakdowns, and the pain they feel hurts tenfold."

"And as a precaution," 117 interrupted, "we would advise against you taking this rejection too seriously and we'd like to offer you several promotions to boost your welfare and morality."

"What?" Brad asked incredulously.

"Oh," Dr. Kendrick chuckled sheepishly. "That's just a little note of warning we like to say to our rejected applicants. You know er... It's our way of asking you to please try not to declare one man wars anywhere please. We'll give you a box of cookies to cheer you up too."

Brad grinned, easily catching on to what they were saying. 117 and Dr. Kendrick smiled pleasantly as Brad started to laugh.

"Oh gotcha," he chuckled. "No, I won't try to idolize the assassin and start another Dominoe Incident. That happened when I was young. But because of this, I guess it wouldn't hurt to consider different careers. Especially since I have a family and... becoming an amborg would change all that."

"An excellent point," 117 said informatively. "Our lives are not technically the best career prospects. We instead prefer to think of them as adequate ways of living. You'd be surprised at what kind of jobs several of us have successfully held over the last few years when we went incognito."

"Maybe I'll hear about those stories some other time," Brad smiled. "I'm already thinking about coming again."

"You'll always be welcome," Dr. Kendrick nodded as he patted Brad on the shoulder. "You're very lucky you know, especially since that's such an important story."

Brad looked down. He didn't have a lot of time and he really wanted to ask one last question. He was curious about Dr. Kolaski and whether he was still working in the basement beneath A.I. Industries. What was going on with Mr. Ramirez's wife? Were Mandy and Lieutenant Palmer still thinking about tying the knot? How were the other amborgs doing?

The one question he settled on was something he felt was the most significant.

"Can I ask one more thing? Whatever happened to 43 and her condition? I know you touched on that a little but, may I know what happened to her?"

117 nodded casually. They stopped in the middle of the hall and 117 looked around.

"I believe I can trust you. For some reason Brad, I think you deserve an answer to that question," 117 said quietly. "It is true that 43 was slowly dying after the Dominoe Incident. But what happened to her is essentially a huge leap in scientific endeavors. I ask that the following information be kept a secret."

Brad nodded in agreement. 117 glanced at Dr. Kendrick, who smiled and the two of them continued escorting Brad down the hall. 117's bracelet activated and projected an image of 43.

"6 originally gave her a few months," Dr. Kendrick explained. "She lasted longer than that."

"Two years..." 117 smiled. "She lived for two years."

"Wow," Brad exclaimed.

"After the incident, her condition obviously worsened," 117 explained. "Everyone worked together to find a solution to repair the damage and she admired our determination, even when there was no hope. It was amazing how strongly she fought for her life. 6 managed to minimize the pain but in 2130, her system finally failed completely and she passed on."

Brad was taken aback, realizing that his question may have been inappropriate, but Dr. Kendrick appeared to understand exactly what he was thinking and offered another reassuring pat on the shoulder.

"It's a legitimate question, Brad," Dr. Kendrick smiled. "43's condition was never really fixable in the first place. We just had to let that part of her go."

"I'm sorry," Brad said, bowing his head a bit. "She meant a lot to both of you. It's not easy coming to terms with knowing someone who's gone forever."

"From my experience, never apologize for something you didn't do," 117 replied. "Also, a minor correction Brad. She is not gone forever."

"What?"

Dr. Kendrick looked at Brad in surprise. Then he and 117 burst out laughing. He had definitely missed something.

"You didn't know? Or to be accurate, you didn't figure it out?"

Brad, feeling increasingly confused, stared at them, wondering if he'd missed a vital part of the story. Was there a detail he overlooked? The suspense was becoming unbearable. Just as he was about to voice his thoughts, Dr. Kendrick pressed a button, and a light darted across the wall panel. In a matter of seconds, another flash occurred, and a projector lit up, revealing the lovely image of Serina, gracefully appearing next to 43's image from 117's bracelet.

"Yes, Dr. Kendrick?" she asked curiously.

She turned, leaping back in horror when she noticed the image of 43.

"Oh goodness," she exclaimed. "Is that what my hair looks like? Yikes."

Silently, she lifted her holographic hand to her head and she quickly began to readjust her hair. Brad stared in surprise. The two women looked completely identical. 117 couldn't help but smile when he saw the look on Brad's face.

"W-wait a minute," Brad stammered as he pointed at Serina. "This A.I. right here..."

"Is a miracle, as you would say Brad," 117 said as he shut off his bracelet. Serina, still floating in the air, stopped fiddling with her hair and straightened up, giggling nervously. "That is what happened."

"Brad," Dr. Kendrick chuckled. "I'm amazed you didn't realize it, especially after we'd shared the part of the story where Serina was on the brink of death and then went on to explain her plans to 6."

"Well, I just assumed that they just happened to have the same name," Brad kept eye-balling Serina, who giggled. She suddenly disappeared, then flashed to 117 and perched on his shoulder like a parrot. "But I never guessed... wait, are they actually the same A.I.?!"

"No," Serina replied. "I'm the new Serina."

Brad looked at 117 and Dr. Kendrick.

"How?" he asked.

"The older Serina was dying of old age," Serina replied. "When I also died, my consciousness was saved and transferred to her matrix. I left my physical body and... woke up like this."

"Without a human body? Without... *your* human body?" Brad exclaimed. "I mean, the A.I. inside her CPU manifested into a holographic one? Uh... What??"

Serina nodded eagerly to everything that Brad blurted out. She floated off 117's shoulder and glided over to Brad.

"When I lived," she said happily. "I was Serina 43. I was a human and an amborg. Now, I just float around doing my own thing. My real body is well-preserved here, just in case someone in the far future figures out how to bring it back to life. Pfft, that might take a few centuries, but at least I lived and well, that's a nice possibility to have on my mind. Anyway, nice to formally meet you again."

"It's an honor," Brad nodded.

"But it would be nice if you didn't let anyone know about my particular background."

Brad blinked as Serina held a finger to her lips, as if telling him to lower his voice.

"Why is that?"

"Well you see," she said. "When I was dying, I told Vanessa 6 how to help keep my mind and data intact. With Dr. Kolaski's help, we managed to prepare my mind. When I was originally infected, I took the time to study the A.I. that had taken control of me. It shut me up really well, but at some point, I managed to gather information on its programming. Despite its really poor design, it had a very advanced schematic, like, real mind-blowing tech, so I stole it. The secrets I acquired from the assassin's program allowed me the opportunity to continue living, but since my body was dying, I needed more time to fully preserve myself. It wasn't easy to make myself the way I am now, which is why 6 allowed me to borrow her less damaged CPU for my work."

"But... the older Serina?" Brad asked.

"She volunteered to help too," Serina looked down mournfully. "I'll never forget how kind and supportive she was. She taught me a great deal."

"When 43 basically approached 6 with the idea," Dr. Kendrick explained, "Vanessa accepted, but then she started to act strange which led to several misdemeanors. I wasn't aware that 43 was transferring her consciousness into 6 on a regular basis."

"Yeah, it was quite a surprise," 117 added.

"A few weeks before her body failed, 6 uploaded 43's mind and data into hers for the final touch, and Serina was extracted into the older Serina's construct matrix," Dr. Kendrick said. "It was a miracle. An exact identical copy of her former persona. Yes, most expensive A.I. programs require the brain of their hosts to develop and enhance their personalities, but what 43 did was... Well, it had never been done before. She cracked the code to make herself transform entirely into an artificial intelligence without us knowing. The science behind it all is incredible but also dangerous. It's a relatively new breakthrough."

"Dangerous indeed. It also explained why 6 strangely acted like 43 for a year," 117 added, his tone laced with amusement. Serina nodded and smiled silently as he continued, "At first, I couldn't understand 6's sudden display of affection towards me. We assumed that she was making an attempt to comfort me, but it turned out that it was just Serina figuring out how to adapt to her new lifestyle. You could say she forced 6 to develop some traits of a multiple personality disorder."

Serina stuck out her tongue.

"Sorry, it was difficult keeping myself hidden," she protested. "Some of my original personality quirks kept trying to leap out when I wasn't expecting it. It wasn't perfect but I do have unique qualities compared to most of the artificial intelligence programs in use today."

"And that brings us to why we should keep this between us," Dr. Kendrick said warningly. Everyone huddled closer together. "All of the amborgs and my staff here know about Serina, but to the world and anyone else we placed our trust in, Serina 43 is officially dead. The ability to create yourself as an artificial intelligence is not just amazing but it is out of this world. Speaking modestly, this is something that I cannot and won't be able to do for years. In the wrong hands, everyone would try to unlock the methods that Serina underwent in her transformation. Serina here is... to be frank, a historical achievement in the eyes of artificial intelligence research. Decades beyond what we're capable of. Serina was born as a human who then underwent the transformation process from cyborg to a program. Literally, she rewrote herself into a program. People would treat her like an experiment if they realized what she accomplished. An A.I. of that caliber already born self-aware is the most tempting piece of work out there. It's also Serina's right, though, to keep it to herself."

117 extended his hand, and Serina jumped into it, settling down calmly. She let out a yawn and began to sway gently. Brad was mesmerized, hanging onto every word.

"An amborg truly is an amazing thing isn't it?" Dr. Kendrick smiled and nodded as they watched Serina change her appearance several times. "Doing impossible things because... Well. Who knows what circumstances they can bring?"

"Yes I agree. They amaze me every day," Brad said in awe.

"Do I have your word that Serina's secret remains with you now that we've fully determined that we can trust you?"

Brad watched as Serina began doing cartwheels on 117's hand.

"Of course. I suppose you and 6 have resolved your personal issues?" Brad asked curiously.

117 smiled.

"She still gets embarrassed every time she gives me a check-up, but it's amusing," he eyed Serina with a mischievous grin. "Besides, I already have someone else to worry about. Excuse me Dr. Kendrick, Serina, Brad. I have to get ready to leave."

As he walked away, Serina waved wildly as if she was catching flies. Brad just stared after him.

"What does that mean?"

Serina chuckled and flashed a bright blue.

"It means my old flame is going on a date with one lucky human," she said happily.

"I think he just might be serious about this one too," Dr. Kendrick nodded in agreement. "I'm still amazed that you and 117 are alright with the circumstances."

"Well I'm made out of numbers," Serina said cheekily. "I can only express myself with words alone. I can't provide any form of physical contact for any of those categories of relationships. Besides, as long as he's happy, then that's ok with me."

"You could make technical fireworks or generate algorithmic computations for romance?" Brad suggested.

Serina giggled.

"I could," she admitted. "But I don't have what I used to have. Instead, I managed to find a better life for myself. The circumstances may be strange but I really am happy."

After saying a few more short goodbyes, Brad realized it was time.

He was escorted to the landing pad for a quick and smooth ride home. Dr. Kendrick had to nearly push Brad onto his private jet. It was, in his humble opinion, one of the few aircraft in the world that could travel at almost impossible speeds. Serina and Dr. Kendrick waved goodbye as the jet lifted off safely and took off.

"I think that boy has a bright future ahead of him," Dr. Kendrick observed happily. "He'll contribute heavily to the world's needs. Especially what he doesn't know yet."

"Why do you think that?" Serina asked curiously as the jet became just a bright orange light in the distance.

Dr. Kendrick beckoned for her to follow. She blinked out and reappeared on his shoulder.

"Anyone who recognizes their abilities will always forge a path to create a better world," he said. "The most enlightening aspect of the journey is the effort put into achieving the ultimate goal, which always begins with one single step."

As he turned around and stepped back inside the facility, Dr. Kendrick remembered another important detail.

"Serina," Dr. Kendrick asked curiously, "In any part of that story, did... Did we mention anything to Brad about... that particular event?"

Serina stared at him blankly, but silently began shaking her head.

"Looking at all the security footage, audio logs and the entire time Brad was here, references to the event you're talking about is... a zero count."

Dr. Kendrick nodded with a sigh of relief.

"Good because that incident is not ready to be revealed. Soon it will but for now, we keep it just within the scientific communities."

"Now then, I believe next week, we're paying a visit to the Apogee station Serina," he continued normally. "Do you know which amborgs would be interested in a routine trip?"

"I'll start asking," Serina said excitedly and whizzed away.

CHAPTER 30

Peace

Los Angeles
2136
One Year A.B. (After Brad)

("Mandy, I know this is an annoying question. But when will the lesson end?")

("Almost Sarah. This part was actually given to me by 117's grandfather. Turns out he thinks it is footage everyone should see.")

("Is there really a historical timeline marking that says, 'after Brad'?")

("In our historical files, yes. Now shush.")

"So, are you in or out?"

"I don't know."

"All I'm saying is that if we end up teaching them, it'd be a great skill set to have! You're going to have to deal with your insecurities of watching over children soon."

From the top of an incredibly tall skyscraper, there were two Fourth Group amborgs, Alex 280 and Ally 113, sitting on the edge of the rooftop, both smiling as they looked out over the city. From their vantage point, they had begun discussing personal matters as they patiently awaited their next set of orders. Lately, they had been encouraged to engage in casual conversation to help pass the time. Both made sure their internal chronometers were shut off, as they were not expected to be overly precise.

"Ok, I guess we can do it," he answered reluctantly.

113 nodded and pulled out her notepad from her waist pocket.

"Great!" she said as she flipped through it and scanned the names written on the pages. "I'll call... Diane and we'll be official volunteer chaperones for the school's field trip. As friends to the local schools and helpful subjects of volunteer programs for kids, they will be very happy to hear of our support."

"Why do you use that?"

113 looked at 280 curiously. He pointed at her notepad, where she was checking things off with a pen.

"We have advanced digital tablets or our personal holographic keyboards for taking notes," he commented.

"Because kids shouldn't always rely on computers, cell phones, or tablets," she answered. "This method may be old fashioned but it encourages children to use a different format to enhance their creativity."

"Alright then," 280 nodded.

"So, are you going to share why you seem hesitant or uninterested in this?" 113 asked.

"I do enjoy babysitting kids," 280 spoke as he scratched his head. "But seventy-four kids on a trip to the zoo is a bit much isn't it, 113?"

"Well, confidentially speaking, we are evolved humans and we can handle it."

"Please lower your voice!" 280 said urgently. "Why are you risking exposing our identities?"

"Our current position is up here, away from the public eye," 113 replied as she gestured to the vast expanse of the city. "If we're discovered, we just disguise ourselves and hide. It is that simple."

Before he could respond, a small beeping noise began sounding off. Had there been anyone else there, they would have been oblivious to it. The two amborgs perked up as instructions streamed directly into their minds through a private message channel.

"All members standby," a voice spoke in their heads. "Everyone has reached their positions. Prepare for phase two of the operation. Objectives are now being prioritized to each one of you. Secondary directives will apply. As always, anyone caught slacking or compromising the objective is in charge of garbage duty, or something they will hate doing for a month. Now then, proceed."

"That's our cue," 280 said calmly as he stood up on the ledge.

113 rose and peered over the edge. 280 made a gentle leap upwards, and then gravity took hold. Unafraid, he began to fall.

"Right behind you," she said as she took a deep breath and stepped off the ledge. "I love this part."

From inside the building, Captain Bradley stared out the window, reflecting on the unusual calm of the day—a stark contrast to the chaos of the previous year. She couldn't recall the last time a week had passed without the sound of gunfire. The notion of peace felt foreign to her, especially in Los Angeles. Shaking off the thought, she took another bite of her fish and returned her gaze to the view outside. To her surprise, the city looked remarkably beautiful, devoid of the destruction she'd grown accustomed to seeing every day. Instead of ruins, she saw repair crews diligently restoring what had been lost. It was even more surreal to be enjoying an elegant dinner in a skyscraper, a luxury she never thought she'd experience again.

"You seem different. Some dessert for your thoughts?"

She snapped her head back quickly. She had forgotten who she was eating with, of all people.

"What makes you say that?" she said sharply to Mark, who was smiling.

In the back of her head, she thought about how odd it was to see the grandfather of an amborg, and the head of a group of vigilantes, wearing a casual dinner suit. The fact that she was actually on a dinner date with him kept giving her goosebumps. Mark chuckled and leaned forward.

"Well, for starters, you aren't complaining about your food like the last time," he observed. "Also, I think your outfit is fitting for a recipient of the Police Star. Too bad you didn't switch to something else. Like a dress."

"Hey, I haven't got time to wear all that fashionable crap," she snapped. She lowered her volume when a few customers turned in their direction. It wasn't the time to raise her voice, which annoyed her slightly. "My dress uniform counts. Besides, why would I change into a different outfit when we were going to dinner right after the ceremony? I put a lot of thought into wearing this uniform and you're going to find some way to be ok with that."

"Well. At least that tells me you put some thought into possibly wearing a skirt," Mark said approvingly as he lifted his wine glass and took a sip. "That's definitely something different about you today. Reminds me of when we were a lot younger back in our school days."

Before she could come up with a retort, a black shape flew downwards past their window, catching their attention. It was gone so quickly that Bradley thought she had imagined it.

"Did you see that?" she asked quietly.

Mark nodded. No sooner did she ask, a second shape shot down, following the first. This time, both of them were already looking out the window to catch a clearer glimpse.

"Was that a person??" Bradley set her silverware down and immediately prepared to get up, but Mark waved her down. "Did two people just fall past our window?"

The old man lifted his hand in silence and they waited. Activity in the restaurant continued around them, oblivious to what was going on. After a few more seconds, Mark casually went back to his food as if nothing had happened.

"Well?" Bradley asked under her breath. "Why are you so calm about it?"

"Those were probably Kendrick's amborgs," he muttered with a warm smile.

"What?"

"Marsha honey," he said in between chews. "If two people really just committed suicide by jumping off a building, then someone down there would be calling somebody like you for help, and you'd be on the way down already. Besides, since that hasn't happened in the last two seconds, and I don't hear any screaming, then there's nothing to worry about."

Captain Bradley paused, thinking for a moment. The old man was right. There was absolutely nothing to be concerned about. Life has been good as of late. Her years of experience as an officer had almost ruined their dinner date.

Perhaps it wouldn't be a bad idea to try being normal, she thought grimly.

If only she knew what the word meant. It was going to be difficult trying to adapt to a peaceful lifestyle.

"What's tin-head been up to these days? I hardly hear from him," she asked in an attempt to change the subject.

"You miss him eh?"

"No," Bradley scoffed. "He hasn't really made any headlines lately."

"Checking up on him?" Mark asked. "It's nice that you care."

"He's been a great help to us," Bradley replied stiffly. "It's just been a while since we last spoke."

"You could always text him," Mark suggested as he took a sip from his wine glass.

"Shut it," she sighed. "Well, the amborgs still do make news. Except, they aren't ones I recognize or know of too well."

"That would be the Fourth Group," Mark said, taking another big bite. "They seem pretty weird."

"Weirder than 117?" Bradley raised an eyebrow.

"I don't know," Mark shrugged. "They just seem much more closed off than when I first met the First and Second Group amborgs."

"Sounds like I'd get along with them," Bradley tilted her head curiously as she resumed eating.

"Maybe," Mark smiled, setting his wine glass down. "You really do miss having him around?"

"Look," Bradley sighed again. "You don't have to be so condescending about it. I just hope he's alright."

"I don't even know what he's up to," Mark chuckled. "I'd say that he's doing just fine. If I had to take a guess."

Mark picked up his napkin and wiped his mouth.

"I mean, I'd definitely like some decent vacation time if I'd gone through all the crap they did, saving the country and all that," he said, smiling. "Until he needs to come back, David believes that there are enough people out there that can take care of the world's problems until it's time for them to return. People like you, Captain Bradley, who have the ability to accomplish great things."

"I can't just find time for a vacation," Bradley muttered. "I need to have something to do."

"What do you think this is?" Mark gestured to the dinner table. "I mean, it's not an ideal resort but you did decide to come to dinner with me. Why? Because I'm betting that you felt empty sitting at your peace-time desk with the same old work you do every day now."

"I don't feel empty," Bradley scoffed.

"Really? Then if you hadn't been awarded the Police Star," Mark stated, "would you have come out with me?"

"I don't deserve it," she replied. "The officers I work with deserve it. There are others more qualified than me."

"Most other people don't have your luck," Mark grinned.

"The Police Star," Bradley said quietly. "The police's highest achievement. The amborgs deserve it more than I do. I have nothing that could even compare to your grandson's accomplishments."

"Don't say that, you've got heart," Mark said bluntly.

He instantly began to sweat when she glared back at him.

"O-or rather, you should recognize the fact that what you've done all the way up to now is admirable," he stammered. "The amborgs know this. I know this. S-so do the officers under your command."

"I just don't get it," Bradley sighed. "Why don't they want to come back whenever we call them for help? David 117 and many of his friends are idolized by the communities here. I keep hearing that they are missed."

"I know what you mean," Mark nodded. "I've seen kids looking up at the skies. Watching and waiting for those streaks of light to soar above them. They're all heroes to a lot of us. I guess some people really want them back."

"With them gone and things are calming down, my officers are experiencing far fewer losses than before. I mean, that's a good thing, but I can't help but feel they're becoming a bit too complacent. Sometimes, I find myself wanting to follow an amborg back in the field again. I just hope they don't go too far. I miss the excitement."

"I think they just don't want to do your job for you," Mark chuckled. "Speaking in a practical way. They'd be putting you and thousands of others out of a job if they weren't in hiding right now. That's just a probability."

"Quiet you," Bradley said, annoyed. "Or you aren't getting any tonight. Oh man, I have been drinking tonight... Can't watch my own mouth."

"Not as feisty," Mark said flirtatiously. "Peace time has changed you way too much."

The White House

"Excuse me, Mr. President?"

"What is it? Unless another crisis has been declared, don't wake me."

The President was not accustomed to calls so early in the morning, especially when he wasn't even at his desk. He knew, however, when he saw one of his military commanders standing in the entrance to his bedroom that something important had come up. The First Lady would immediately want to make sure he was already sitting up. Unfortunately, his wife was not home.

Right, the President remembered groggily, *she was doing some sort of social outreach campaign in Europe.*

Disgruntled, he slowly rose from the bed and searched for his bathrobe. Then he realized why he was being woken up and looked sharply at his commander.

"Oh my god, there hasn't actually been another crisis... has there?" he trembled. "I seriously don't need this now."

He scrambled to his feet and rushed towards the door. Unwavering, the commander shook her head calmly in a dignified manner.

"No sir," she said reassuringly. "It's an urgent call from the U.N."

"Commander..." the President paused. "Are you sure it's not a crisis?"

"It's an alpha priority thirteen message," she replied. "It would appear that every leader of their respective countries in the U.N. has been requested to be a part of this meeting, despite their sleep schedules. My apologies."

"Fine. Fine."

He couldn't shake the feeling that something was terribly wrong, despite the commander's calm demeanor. Soldiers were bred to be brave. The President couldn't help but admire their resolve, but it certainly made him skeptical. He nodded curtly at his subordinate.

"I'll get dressed right away," he sighed. "Better get a move on."

Roughly ten minutes later, he was sitting at his desk in the Oval Office with guards covering the entrances and exits. An alpha thirteen only meant one thing to the U.N.: complete and total secrecy, which unfortunately, was disconcerting.

The President pressed a button and armor plating descended over the windows. The guards swiftly secured all the doors, locking the place down. After a quick sweep of the room, a soldier gave a thumbs-up, and everyone except for the President and two of his military advisors exited. Soon, only the three of them remained. Finished with security protocols, the President was allowed to continue.

"Room secure sir," the commander confirmed. "Connecting to the call."

She stepped forward and placed an advanced laptop on his desk. She entered an access code and the screen lit up. The President leaned forward, placing his left hand on a pad attached to the laptop and shut his left eye. A retinal scanner shot a focused beam of light on his right eye for verification as he recited a passcode.

"Betamax was at its peak," he spoke clearly. "But all that rises will eventually come down in some form or another. Where I sit right now, may there be mercy on the brave souls daring to join our adventure."

"Passcode, retinal scan, and biological confirmation clearance acknowledged and secure," the computer replied. "Alpha thirteen message feed is clear and running. Welcome, Mr. President of the United States."

The President made sure his face was in direct line of sight to the camera. He quickly readjusted his tie as the computer chimed and a green light signaled that he was connected.

Several faces started to populate the screen, most of whom he identified as members of the U.N. council. To his amazement, numerous leaders from different countries also joined the call. He had never witnessed such a vast assembly of leaders gathered at once on a video conference before. Then again, no one had. If a hacker were to breach this highly secure system, they'd lose their minds. Some of them appeared to have just been roused from sleep, just like he had, while others displayed looks of confusion.

"Mr. President," the Russian leader said, graciously bowing his head. "It is good to see you. Seeing you here is enough to make me feel secure, especially when the number on this alpha is thirteen."

"Likewise Veniamin," the President replied. "Does anyone have any idea what's going on? I apologize for my lack of formalities, I was woken up at a very inconvenient time."

"Based on the large gathering at this hour…" the Prime Minister from Britain grumbled, "I can definitely sympathize with the President. I hope it is worthwhile. I am eager to get back to sleep, so I hope this will be over soon."

"I agree," the Chancellor of Germany spoke. "I do not like being interrupted and pulled away from the affairs of my homeland."

"Trust me, this is beyond the capabilities of any of your countries."

A hush fell over the room as the President focused on his screen, noticing a new face among the global participants. It was Dr. John Kendrick. Everyone, weary from sleepiness or anticipation, quickly composed themselves at his unexpected appearance.

"Dr. Kendrick," Veniamin spoke politely. "It was you who issued the alpha message? A pleasure as always, my friend."

"Indeed. It was I who had to wake a portion of you. For that I apologize," Dr. Kendrick replied solemnly.

Before he could continue, the French leader suddenly interrupted.

"Doctor, if this is another one of your pranks, let me remind you that most of us are at least three seconds away from hanging up on this call. I still haven't forgotten the time one of your… daughters accidentally dialed my emergency landline."

"I know that in the past, I have not always been respectful of authority but in this case, I actually have made a breakthrough, so unless you want to fall behind in world-wide phenomenal technology, I suggest you listen. With all due respect."

Sensing a bit of hostility now building based on the French leader's silent expression, the U.S. President immediately took charge.

"Please doctor, I happen to agree with my colleague," he cut-in graciously before the French leader could spit out an insult. "I was just woken up for something supposedly urgent, so we'd like for you to get to the point. Please. The majority of the world's leaders are watching. Give them something to listen to."

"Very well then," Dr. Kendrick spoke over the monitors. "Esteemed leaders, we at Amborg Industries have made an incredible discovery regarding the incident that occurred in the year of 2128—within the halls of my installation itself."

The air stilled, the only sound coming from the light humming of the President's laptop.

"You mean, you've figured it out? The portal?" the Prime Minister asked, absolutely stunned.

He wasn't the only one. Every other person involved in the call was all exclaiming in wonder and great fascination.

"I have indeed," Dr. Kendrick said triumphantly. "And you are all invited to A.I. Industries for a more detailed look into what we're doing. Covertly is the preferred medium of travel to my facility for this discovery."

"Nonsense," the leader of France said smugly. "It's impossible. I feel as if you are overstepping your bounds again Kendrick. No matter how big of a genius you are."

"Hold on now," the President of the United States spoke up. "I have had no reason to ever doubt Dr. Kendrick despite his quirks, considering the fact that it was his amborgs that saved my daughter only a few months ago. His family saved the country during the Dominoe Incident. If he says he's done it, then I believe him."

"Thank you Mr. President," Dr. Kendrick said with gratitude. "I always knew you were sensible enough. One of the reasons I voted for you."

Many of the other leaders were nodding and murmuring their agreement. Finally, one of the U.N. council members spoke up.

"It would appear that all of us are in agreement. I hope?"

The French leader merely nodded silently, but the President could tell he was still slightly pissed off.

"Then it's settled."

"Good," Dr. Kendrick smiled. "I have a few more notes to run through but it shouldn't take up too much of your time. You'll be back to your lives in a few minutes."

A swift consensus was reached by all, and shortly after another ten minutes of Dr. Kendrick's presentation, the call concluded. Once the laptop was powered down and put away, the guards returned to the room and promptly restored the Oval Office to its original state. The President sighed heavily as he leaned back in his chair.

"Can I get you anything sir?" his commander asked.

"Nothing for now..." he said. "Actually, maybe some coffee or something to eat. Looks like the world is changing. In a few years, assuming I'm still president, we could be looking at something beyond us. Oh and commander, remember that for the record, this meeting is off the books and it didn't happen, as I'm supposed to say in order to conform to standard procedure. Et cetera, et cetera, you know the drill."

"Of course sir. Took the words right out of my mouth."

"This is going to be the most exciting thing to ever happen, or the world's worst nightmare. And billions of people won't know which is which, until it's happening right in front of them."

Epilogue

The computer's display switched off the video footage. After the presentation concluded, it powered down, and Sarah caught a glimpse of her reflection on the screen. She looked up as it emitted a brief notification.

"This concludes the complement of subject material and all known informative files relating to inquiries and learning materials of Amborg 117 and the Domino Incident. Thank you for watching a product of visual learning experiences. See you next time!"

Sarah watched Mandy stretch her arms above her head.

"Well, what did you think?" she asked when she lowered her arms.

Sarah thought for a moment. As an amborg, she felt that there was a relatively simple answer. However, she knew that David 117's former technician was anything but that. Over her long career, she had educated many of them on basic human etiquette. So complex calculations were probably her best option. The issue was, could she come up with the correct answer?

"I don't know Ms. Mandy," she replied. "I understand the motives of all the amborgs, leading up to and after the great Domino Incident. They all went their own ways and learned about their humanity by immersing themselves in what they wanted to do on their sabbaticals. And then kept coming back together again to deal with bigger threats in the future after that. History is a fascinating subject, but why did this particular lesson require that I learn about 117?"

Mandy stood up and walked around her desk. She placed a hand on Sarah's shoulder and sighed.

"Like I said before," she explained. "You remind me of him a lot. You aren't fully aware of what human emotion is yet. After augmentation, you seemed to struggle with adapting to the amborg's way of living. It almost seemed like you were lost, just like he was when I was his technician. David 117 was a unique and smart individual that fully developed into a proper human being in a way that can't be taught. He learned and evolved to be his own person. That is how human emotion or exposure to the basic instincts of humanity shapes you properly. Which is why I figured showing you direct footage of this self-made lesson plan would give you some new perspective, especially since it was difficult for you as well."

Sarah looked down, seeming like something was bothering her.

"Ah," Mandy's eyes widened pleasantly. "I think there's something you want to get off your chest."

"It's... about that mission..."

Sarah's eyes became vacant as Mandy's smile faded.

"Oh," she nodded. "Right."

"Does it get easier?" Sarah asked. "The nightmares?"

"Well," Mandy sighed. "This lesson has gone in another direction. I expected this. You know?"

"You are very intuitive," Sarah gazed at Mandy, who knelt down next to her. "My parents always said that you could always tell when something was troubling someone."

Mandy comforted her by gently patting her on the shoulder.

"Hey," she said. "Every amborg that I've mentored and talked to has gone through what you're dealing with right now. Your parents had nightmares too, you know?"

"They never acted like it disturbed them," Sarah stated.

"Well, it's because they had a strong support system to help them get through it," Mandy smiled. "I was there to see it all happen."

"Oh."

Sarah fell silent as she stared at the dark computer screen, reflecting on what she thought about what Mandy had shown her.

"You know, your friends are worried about you," Mandy suddenly said. "That's why I wanted to put together that little movie for you. I wanted to remind you..."

Sarah looked up at Mandy.

"...you're a good and brave person."

"Oh. Thank you."

Mandy watched Sarah closely as she continued to remain silent. After a few minutes, she spoke again.

"What's got you so quiet?" she asked.

Sarah twiddled her fingers. Mandy took notice as she waited patiently.

"I wondered if I made a mistake, becoming an amborg," she mumbled.

"I can definitely tell you that you didn't make a mistake," Mandy replied reassuringly. "What you do is good. Your skills and your abilities are an important contribution to society."

"But... I couldn't save..."

"Don't let those people weigh you down," Mandy interrupted Sarah. "We can't save everyone."

"Like my uncle?"

Mandy bit her lip and dipped her head solemnly.

"Yeah," she nodded slowly. "Your dad has never completely forgiven himself for failing to save him. But you know what he did? He kept going because he knew that more people would be lost if he suddenly stopped doing what he did."

"He was in the middle of a national crisis," Sarah said. "My circumstances aren't the same."

"True. But in all fairness," Mandy chuckled, "you sure do remind me of him."

"What was David 117 to you when you first met him?" Sarah asked. "Did you have a feeling that you just knew he was the one who would be best mentored by you?"

"Good question. That's... a really good question indeed."

Mandy got up and approached a shelf filled with her classroom supplies. She picked up a photo and presented it to Sarah. The picture featured Mandy and 117 from long ago; he wore a simple smile while she appeared to be laughing at something amusing.

"The best mentor," Mandy instructed, "is always yourself. Now, David 117 was the first amborg I ever became friends with and the first one that I tried to guide. But I was completely new to the job myself. At first, he just seemed so lost compared to all the other amborgs I had read about or met already. I ventured a guess that he'd be the one who needed a slight push. There are other amborgs who have definitely made an impact on the world and countless lives, but I don't believe I ever regret choosing him. I realized that I was struggling too, and now we've come so far."

Mandy handed Sarah another photo. It was a large group of amborgs and technicians all posing at what appeared to be some sort of celebratory barbecue.

"This was taken a few days before many amborgs disappeared after the Dominoe Incident," Mandy said, pointing at herself in the photo. "There I am."

"I'm afraid I don't seem to have particularly good experiences when it comes to gatherings like these," Sarah said with a mournful look. "Perhaps I am as socially awkward as you say."

"That's not true," Mandy said as Sarah handed the pictures back. "The Domino Incident, the high school student Brad, David 117 and Serina 43. Those were great factors that brought out the best in him. It took a lot of perspective in order for him to learn. Many of the older amborgs look back and reference some of these events as life lessons. They don't always work for everyone but for people who struggle, they can be used as examples of how to find a new meaning in life. 117 isn't the only one, by the way. There are other stories too. 917's sacrifices, Katie 57 and her long-lost family, 999 as the lone wolf as well as her call sign 'Angel', and even the one of Johnny 5's leg."

"May we learn more about these types of stories?" Sarah asked with a hint of curiosity in her voice.

Mandy looked at Sarah with a smile.

"I think we can spend a little more time hanging out."

Mandy restarted the computer and accessed the database. There were countless files to scroll through. It had taken her a few days to organize the video files and records about 117 and the Domino Incident for this private tutoring session, but she figured another small story wouldn't be such a big deal. It'd have to be extremely short since it was getting late. She gestured for the young amborg to choose.

"Well, we have time," Mandy spoke cheerfully. "But why don't you choose a story? It will satisfy your natural curiosity better if I don't choose for you."

"Alright," Sarah nodded.

A database appeared on the computer screen. She saw her dad's name listed in one of the files, but she felt like she had heard enough for one night. There would always be plenty of time to learn more about him.

"Thank you Ms. Mandy."

Mandy looked curiously at the young amborg.

"For what?"

"I thought it was nice to see how my parents met," Sarah smiled. "They always told me stories but I feel as if... they hid certain details at times."

"Well, your parents do have the right to embellish or censor some parts of it," Mandy answered smugly.

"But, you showed the actual footage," Sarah blinked, suddenly feeling confused. "Did you obtain consent?"

"Of course I did," Mandy scoffed. "Your parents agreed to allow me to show this footage to you when I asked them for permission last week."

"My apologies," Sarah looked at Mandy and her smile reformed. "Can we look at another story?"

"Of course. Now then..."

Mandy turned to the screen and the two of them began to sift through the database.

"What adventure are we going to learn about next? Any ideas, Sarah 117?"

END SESSION

Amborg Industries thanks you for your patronage and support.

Inheritance of a Generation
By Yee-Ron Ted Cheng

"I think he snuck a girl into his room."

In the dining room of the vast mansion that sat on a hill, a couple was enjoying their morning meal. The man had just finished savoring the brief taste of his wife's cooking. He was about to take another bite but stopped when he heard her abrupt statement. He turned his eyes, fork still lifted, and hung his mouth open.

"Oh?" he stammered as the food on his fork plopped back onto his plate and attempted to compose himself. His brain was trying to catch up with what she had said. ""What makes... Uh... why do you think that??"

|I got suspicious last night when I got some water," she smiled as she took a sip of her drink. "I confirmed it when he snuck out early this morning without even saying goodbye to us."

"Sounds serious," he nodded as he glanced up at the ceiling.

"I agree. What do you think we should do? Ethan?"

Ethan set his fork on the table and wiped his mouth with his napkin. He wasn't sure what to do about it. His son hadn't ever caused any trouble before under their roof. If they confronted him, what would their expectations be? How would he react when confronted? As a father, he didn't feel angry about the entire notion. As far as he was concerned, nothing was wrong. No rules broken either. Had they even established protocol for something like this? He did at least want to get to the bottom of why his son was sneaking around without telling them the truth.

"Well, are you entirely sure that he brought a girl home?" Ethan asked as he glanced at his wife skeptically. Maybe there was still some hope in defending his child. "And that she spent the night?"

"Pretty sure," she smiled which made him falter slightly. So much for looking on the bright side.

"Susan..." Ethan continued to glance upwards at the ceiling. Now he was feeling the looming dread of reality.

"Remind you of anyone?"

Ethan turned and stared at his wife. His embarrassment was quite apparent.

"You were always an impulsive man when we were younger," she giggled as gazed amusingly at his baffled expression. "I don't find it surprising that our own child is the same way."

Ethan let out a sigh.

"Does it have to be in our own home?"

"Perhaps his dormitory wasn't really the right setting?"

Susan was probably right about that. At The Academy, the room arrangements had many students sharing many bunks. Their son probably wouldn't have had many opportunities for romance if there had been two or three other classmates watching, or worse.

"I told him..." Ethan grumbled a little, "He could have had a private room at school to avoid certain... distractions. All he had to do was ask for it."

"You know that's beside the point," Susan said casually. She suddenly gazed upwards and thought for a moment. "He's always had trouble making friends. One reason why he hasn't made a request for one is because he likes them. He wants to keep them close by. Not a lot of kids really hung out in our front yard. I always told you to make security look less intimidating at our gates."

Ethan became silent. He didn't feel hungry anymore as he glanced down at his plate. Was this whole entire thing his fault? He knew that's not what she was saying but their son didn't have a normal childhood.

"Honey," he heard Susan say gently, "You always said that you wanted John to be happy. Isn't that right?"

Ethan looked up and turned in her direction.

"He's been working so hard on his projects trying to please the both of us," she continued as she pushed her plate away. One of the drones watching them stepped forward and she let it remove the dishes since they were both finished. She reached out for his hand. "Now he's got someone special."

"Especially when he snuck her into our heavily secured home," Ethan muttered as he wrapped his fingers around hers. "I'm honestly a little impressed he got away with that."

They both held tight as he nodded his head to show that he was accepting the situation for what it was.

"Ok," he declared as he looked in Susan's eyes, "When he gets back, I'm going to talk to him."

"Wait a minute," Susan pulled her napkin on her lap and set it on the table. "What are you going to talk about?"

"He's not going back to the Academy until Sunday," Ethan declared as he stood up. "I'm going to call him and have him meet me here."

"Ethan, be reasonable," Susan stated cautiously as she looked up at him. "If you go at this aggressively, you'll only push him away and then he'll never want to talk to us. You can't be mad at him."

"Who said I was mad?"

"You don't exactly look happy..."

"Well, what do you want me to do? High-five him?" Ethan began to walk towards the door. He heard Susan's chair scrape across the floor. He then heard her footsteps meaning she was following him. "I'm not allowing our house to become some sort of vacation retreat right under our very noses. I just want to ask him and confirm your suspicions."

"Honey, stop."

Ethan turned to see that Susan had rushed to his side before he could leave the dining room.

"Is there a problem?"

The two of them turned to see another one of the caretaker drones greeting them with a polite bow.

"No Clayton," Ethan replied casually addressing the humanoid robot he had built, "Everything is fine."

"Thank you, Clayton," Susan bowed politely in return with a cheerful smile. She waved her hand gently, signaling a silent request for privacy. "As you were."

"Of course. Have a pleasant day, Mr. and Mrs. Kendrick."

"You cannot just ask directly," Susan continued as Clayton walked away. His mechanical joints whirred and his heavy feet echoed in the halls like a drum. "You should let him come to us about this whenever he's ready."

"You suggest I let this slide?"

"Yes," Susan replied bluntly. "Besides, haven't you been noticing something?"

Ethan stared at Susan. What on earth was she talking about? There was a brief silence between the two of them. When he failed to answer the question, he shrugged.

"I suppose you're going to tell me?" he sighed as he gave up.

"He seems happier," she stated as she rolled her eyes at his dumbfounded expression. "He's been in a better mood these last few visits and I haven't seen that in months."

Ethan paused once again. Thinking carefully, he tried to remember John's behavior in the last few months whenever he visited home. The only big significant issue he recalled was that one of John's science professors was giving him a hard time with his thesis. In order to move on to the next phase of his education, this professor had assigned each student a special assignment. They all had to come up with their own theories, projects or contribute anything unique and special to the field of science. The only drawback was it had to be something iconic and original. It couldn't be based off someone else's work. All of it had to be radical and something new that would one day change the future. Ethan remembered how difficult his thesis had been when he was a student. He definitely remembered witnessing John struggle on his weekends off away from school. There was one thing right about Susan's observation. It was the fact that John's level of complaining, and frustration had significantly dwindled.

"You might be right," he nodded in agreement.

"I know," Susan tilted her head to the side. She mildly gave him a sassy expression as she started to laugh. "Don't you think maybe... we should expect to meet his special lady friend soon?"

"It's a bit soon for that isn't it?" Ethan glanced at her with wide eyes. Alarmed, he began to fret. "He's too young for that kind of relationship!"

"That's absurd! You and I were two years younger than he was when we met our parents!" Susan stared at him and shook her head. "Remember? Right before we got engaged?"

"Oh. Right... How long ago was that? 20 years?"

"20," Susan nodded her head firmly.

"One moment, you and I were teaching him quantum theory and then..." Ethan's eyes looked somber as he let out a sigh.

"Then you blinked," Susan smiled sympathetically. "You're adorable honey."

"Thanks..." Ethan suddenly shook himself out of feeling sentimental and tried to bring them back on topic.

"Still, I don't like all this sneaking around," he said as he gestured at the door. "If he's going to come to us about this issue, I wish it would be now."

There was a loud ringing that echoed across the hall as the two of them awkwardly stared at the front door. They had ended up in the main lobby and were looking at the double-door entrance. Ethan and Susan snuck a glance at each other and watched as one of the caretaker drones casually walked up to open the door.

"Pardon me Luca... but I need to speak to Dr. Kendrick. Ah."

It was one of their security guards. He noticed the two of them, stepped over the threshold and politely removed his hat. He seemed to be slightly out of breath and moving rather quickly.

"Sir," he dipped his head to Ethan and then greeted Susan in the same manner. "Ma'am. We have an urgent problem. The Mayor is here to see you! It concerns the woman that snuck in with John last night!"

"Wow," Susan patted Ethan on the arm with an impressed grin. "That certainly escalated quickly... You should have him close the door and say you want that new model car you saw online."

"Honey..." Ethan said through gritted teeth.

"No, seriously. Say it. It just might happen!"

The couple faced the security guard and the drone standing at the entrance with their undivided attention. Ethan nodded and raised his hand and beckoned for them to come forward.

"Well, don't just stand there, send her in."

The guard turned around and with a jerk of his head, they saw another guard escorting someone else in. It was a young woman who walked in. She also had a sense of urgency in her expression but maintained a rigid posture filled with dignity. She had similar glasses like Ethan's and adjusted her business jacket. It looked like a new design that Ethan and Susan didn't recognize. It was probably a fashion designer's new outfit that the Mayor was flaunting.

"Cute," Susan remarked quietly to Ethan, but he shushed her. She muttered quietly behind him as a result. "It-is-a-cute-outfit."

The woman glared at the guards angrily but when she saw the Kendricks, her demeanor changed in an instant.

"I'm so sorry for interrupting your morning," she explained in a formal tone as she tried to step forward, but the guards caught her and held her back. Suddenly, her frustration became apparent again. "Excuse me! You must listen! John's been kidnapped!"

"WHAT?!"

Ethan and Susan's expression jumped from concern to immediate shock at this sudden news.

"What do you mean?!" Ethan declared furiously as he tried to gather his thoughts. "Explain!"

"I'm afraid she's confirmed it," the guard nodded but shrunk slightly when he noticed how pissed off Ethan was.

"What happened?" Susan asked quickly.

"I rushed here as soon as I got word," the mayor replied. She cowered slightly under Ethan's daunting glare. "I came to offer my support."

"Answer her question," Ethan snapped at her. "Explanation. Now!"

"John came home last night," the security guard stated. "We actually found... er, a girlfriend hiding in the backseat. He claimed that you allowed him permission to bring over a... friend. Just for the night. We didn't think you'd mind. This morning, when the two of them left, we had a security detail following them. Then they came under attack, and we lost contact 19 minutes ago."

"The authorities?" Ethan asked in a very demanding tone.

"Trying to identify the kidnappers now."

"So, you lost both of them??" Susan stared at the guard with a frightened look.

"We failed to protect him," the guard nodded grimly.

"So why are you still here damn it?!" Ethan practically snarled at the guard who cowered slightly. "My son was taken!"

"Ethan! You can't lose it right now!"

Susan urged him as calmly as possible. She also looked frantic, but she spoke to the security guards reasonably and in a clear tone. The mayor stepped forward.

"Doctor," she said, "The kidnapping of your son is going to shock the entire country. This news will hit everyone really badly. I'm bringing the police commissioner here to support your home."

"No," Ethan stated, "Take me to where he was kidnapped from."

"You know I can't do that," the mayor's eyes widened, "If you go out into the open, you risk being a target yourself!"

"If it's me the kidnappers want in exchange," Ethan stated as he walked forward and around the major, "I will get my son back!"

"Dr. Kendrick! You cannot compromise yourself!"

"I'm his father," he said desperately as he continued forward. "Try and stop me."

Susan followed and she looked back at the mayor. For a split second, she appeared quite shocked, but she also rushed after them.

"Please tell the local police that we're on our way," Susan instructed the mayor. Then as they stepped outside, she looked up and spoke loudly. "Computer! Please lock down the home and secure the perimeter after we're offsite. Everyone onsite needs to go to red alert! Keep all civilians safe indoors!"

"Voice authorization accepted," an automated voice from a nearby speaker answered Susan's words. "The Kendrick family mansion will commence with lockdown procedures."

An alarm began to blare from the speakers as the security system was activated.

The group stepped out onto the front lawn as Ethan led them towards the garage.

"Do Amber Alerts apply to John?" Susan asked the guard as they rushed to a car. "He isn't a minor."

No one answered the question as Ethan took charge and issued commands.

"Security, assemble my teams," he said as a car pulled forward in front of them. The doors sprung open, and everyone clambered in. As the mayor and Susan settled in the backseat, Ethan left instructions for the guard who hadn't climbed in the car.

"Inform the authorities that my wife and I need to meet them at their mobile command immediately. I'm bringing in my own special teams. We need to get my son back! Whatever means necessary."

"Understood Dr. Kendrick. Please be safe."

The drive to the crime scene was rather quick. After the Kendricks and the mayor had left their mansion, their vehicle was joined by the mayor's escort. The motorcade moved fast but cautiously through the streets. In the car, Ethan was already on a direct line to the police commissioner.

"I strongly disagree with this Dr. Kendrick."

The commissioner shook his head and crossed his arms in the videochat.

"Well, I'm coming to help, and my wife will be with me," Ethan declared defiantly. "This isn't something I can handle by sitting at home."

"Mayor Kominski," the commissioner said, "Please tell me you didn't agree to this."

"I tried asking them nicely," Kominski replied.

"Pardon us commissioner Waterson," Susan chimed in, "My husband's team of drones will be of great use here. Let us back you up. Besides, if we address the people right now, we can get ahead of the situation."

"Hold on," Kominski stared at Susan. "You want to talk to the press now?"

"Being there in person will show everyone that the Kendricks are ready to join the search for our son. We can inspire hope amidst the panic. If you tell them that you supported this decision, everyone will see that you're taking the initiative."

Susan then spoke directly to the commissioner who listened attentively.

"Please," she said, "We can help. We just don't want people to see us hiding at home."

Commissioner Waterson looked like he was going to continue protesting. After looking away for a moment, he turned to stare back at them. He let out a sigh and nodded. Mayor Kominski also became silent and continued to listen.

"What do we know?" Ethan asked when all of them seemed to agree.

There was a projector on the dashboard that began to show images and video footage on the windows. These holographic screens floated in front of Ethan with advanced projectors and cameras. He began to read and sift through the data as fast as he could.

"No plates, no prints, no decent photos," Waterson answered promptly. "Witnesses submitted dozens of videos of the abduction, but the kidnappers wore masks. Fully covered. No one even got part of a face."

"Commissioner," the mayor stated, "The Kendricks are one of the richest families on Earth. This is going to ramp up fast."

"I have all units and every able-bodied officer being called in," he nodded on the video camera. "I understand what's at stake here."

The short version of it was that if they lost John Kendrick, it would be an absolute nightmare.

"What is this footage of someone firing a gun before the shooting started?" Ethan asked as he looked at multiple screens on the display of the dashboard. "What happened there?"

"From what we pieced together from John's security and the footage, the kidnappers tried to silently subdue John and his friend. They told the guards to drop their weapons and managed to prevent a gun battle. But John was calling for help publicly. One civilian fired a shot in the air when they saw what was happening. That's when the guards fought back."

"It's a mess," Susan exclaimed.

"Where's the civilian who fired the shot?" Ethan asked.

"Went missing after the fight," the commissioner shook his head. "They haven't turned up. I'm starting to think he was in on it."

"I agree."

"Whoa," Susan said as she tried to focus. "Why? Why do you two believe that?"

"Think about it," Ethan explained. "An armed person pretending to be a good samaritan is an excellent way to prevent others from intervening. Using a gun would be great for controlling the crowd, getting them to run away from danger, and initiating the fight between them and the guards."

"This was a well-coordinated abduction," Waterson stated. "I've never seen anything quite like it before."

"We're here," the driver spoke up.

The images and footage disappeared from the dashboard. Ethan grabbed a small tablet off the dashboard, and it all powered down. The tablet lit up as it transferred all the files to there.

When they stepped out, they saw the cordoned off area as police were trying to keep the crowd back. The mayor's motorcade came to a stop, and everyone exited their vehicles. The car directly behind the Kendricks opened its doors and security drones stepped out. These drones were built differently than the police drones in the area. Back home, Ethan had spent a lot of time making modifications and significant upgrades.

Ethan and Susan were followed by the mayor as they walked towards a group of officers that were examining the area. They could see commissioner Waterson among them. Before they could reach him, a few reporters managed to climb over the police fence and rushed over.

"Mayor Kominski! Dr. Kendrick!"

"Prepared a statement?" Susan muttered.

"It's not easy improvising," Kominski answered calmly.

Mayor Kominski stepped in front to handle all the reporters and the cameras going off. The sudden appearance of all three of them was a rare sight to see in the middle of this part of town.

"I would like to inform the public that we were debriefed on the way here," she stated formally to the press. "The mayor's office and local police department stand ready to support the Kendrick family. We have your back Ethan."

Mayor Kominski placed a hand and patted Ethan's shoulder sympathetically. The cameras kept flashing as all the reporters kept clamoring at them. Ethan nodded curtly and faced them all with a serious expression. This action drew the reporters to him and Susan.

"Do you have reason to believe your son is alive doctor?"

The reporter almost shoved their microphone directly into Ethan's chest. He looked at them calmly and took a breath.

"I have no reason not to," he stated his response cordially.

Before he could say anything else, there was a sudden group of chimes and ringing from everyone. Startled, the reporters all checked their pockets. Soon, everyone was pulling out their phones. The mayor also reached inside her jacket and whipped out her phone. An alert even began to flash from Ethan's tablet.

"That's ominous..." Susan felt her phone vibrate in her coat.

"I'm getting it too," Ethan said as he glanced at his tablet.

"Oh my god!"

A video began to play on Ethan's tablet and his eyes widened. A teenage boy stood with a piece of paper on the screen. It was a hostage video featuring John.

"Dad!" John stated as he read the letter in his hands. "I'm ok! Melissa and I are currently prisoners of war, because I'm a member of a ruling class family. But to ensure our release, you must demonstrate two actions of good faith."

It was the ransom demands. What were they bargaining for?

"First," John's voice trembled as his hands were shaking. "You must donate $100 million dollars to the Committee for the Poor."

"Money for the homeless and the poor?" Susan asked as she gazed at her phone.

"Second," John's message continued, "You must deposit an additional $10 million in cryptocurrency to an account. You'll receive an encrypted email with instructions. I hope you do what they say. Please?"

The video then disappeared as everyone's mobile devices shut off.

"Mayor Kominski."

Everyone turned to see the police commissioner walking over. He motioned for a few officers to intervene. The group of cops that were with Waterson began to spread out and start pushing the media away.

"The Kendricks and the mayor are needed at the mobile command center."

The reporters began clamoring amongst themselves as Ethan and Susan met with a few SWAT officers. Their group was then escorted away from all of the flashing cameras.

"Did something about that sound familiar??"

"Indeed."

Ethan looked left and saw one of his security drones step forward.

"What is it Jim?" he asked.

"The video message of John Kendrick was quite similar to a previous kidnapping case. Upon analyzing my databanks, this abduction was constructed and modeled after one from the past. The words from the letter. I ran a comparison and found a match."

Jim activated a projector and they all saw a holographic display. Some words were being highlighted for them to see.

"Ruling class family," he said as he highlighted keywords for them. "A donation to the homeless. This is a direct reference to the Patty Hearst abduction of 1974 with her involvement with the SLA."

"A kidnapped heiress," one officer looked at Jim curiously. "Now John Kendrick has been kidnapped..."

"The kidnappers are making our young master repeat Patty Hearst's statement to the police," Jim declared. "The hostage statement is almost word for word."

"What does that get them?" Ethan asked Jim. "If these criminals are copycats?"

"My hypothesis is that if they are reenacting this incident," Jim turned and faced Dr. Kendrick. His faceplate turned to a cautious yellow. "It will not end well. Based on what happened previously."

"I don't think I want to know..." Susan began to tremble.

"Let's examine the events of that," Waterson declared. "Time to brush up on our history."

In the mobile command center, the high-ranking officers were going over some historical footage. Ethan and Susan also listened to one of the techs explaining the events.

"In May, 1974, the LAPD surrounded a Symbionese Liberation Army hideout thinking that Patty was inside but the SLA refused to surrender. Immediately they began to open fire on the cops."

"It looks like a warzone," Ethan watched the footage and shook his head.

"For two hours, that neighborhood was one," the tech nodded in response. "They almost ran out of ammo. One of the biggest police shootouts in American history. The SLA continued firing at the police even while the house they were in burned to the ground."

"Is that going to happen to John?" Susan asked as she clung onto Ethan's shoulder.

"I don't know..."

"How did they manage to do that to all of our television screens and mobile devices?" the commissioner asked. "If they hacked our systems... Bailey?"

"It was a rather impressive broadcast," Bailey explained as she switched the screen. A map of the entire country appeared. "It seems to have been broadcasted over several states. The video's gone viral online."

"I'll ask my techs to coordinate with police," Ethan said as he wrote a few messages on his tablet.

"We've already contacted the FBI to assist as well," the commissioner added.

One detail of the demands that John had listed was stuck in Susan's mind.

"I understand that the kidnappers wanted us to pay them money," she said as she glanced at another screen where someone was looking over the footage from the hostage video. "They also asked us to donate to the poor. Did that happen back then?"

"It's hard to oversell how big this was back in the 1970s," Bailey began to swipe again. They saw old files of newspaper articles and many other listings that detailed the event. "The Hearsts were one of the most influential families in the nation. When Patty was taken, the whole world paid attention."

"But this ended just under two years," Ethan looked over the timeline of the events. "Why did it take police so long to recover Patty?"

"The SLA was a combat unit intent on inciting a revolution," Bailey answered. "Their leader, Donald DeFreeze was the leader that elevated their notoriety. They started robbing banks, assassinated a superintendent, and then they kidnapped Patty to make even more crazy demands. They said that her parents had to feed all the hungry people in California if they wanted to see their daughter alive."

"And they succeeded?" Ethan asked.

"They tried," Bailey answered bluntly, "They had trucks drop off millions of dollars of food to the poorest neighborhoods. That wasn't enough for the SLA. They continued sheltering Patty in multiple hideouts. After a few months, she started identifying with her captors."

"Hang on a moment," Ethan's eyes widened. "She joined them??"

Bailey instantly realized what she had said and shut her mouth. Susan and Ethan glanced at each other with horrified expressions. Seeing this, the commissioner immediately stepped forward and attempted to reassure and keep them calm.

"That will not happen to John," he said confidently. "If your son is resilient, he can endure whatever agenda they're trying to throw at him. We are going to get him back before they succeed in radicalizing him."

Unfortunately, this answer didn't help at all.

"Please," Susan looked at Bailey, "Keep continuing... What happened after?"

"Patty began to willingly assist in their crimes," Bailey explained as she talked slowly. She was carefully choosing her words. "Grand theft auto, assault and a few others. It all ended with the shootout on 54th street."

"That is the reason why SWAT officers have the number 54 printed on their patches," Jim stated as he dipped his head respectfully to a couple of SWAT members attending the history lesson.

"Wow," one of them replied, "I always wondered about that."

"As one of the plans that I would like to offer you..."

Everyone turned to look at Ethan who put his fist up to his chin as he tried to think.

"I am prepared to send money to get John back."

"I understand that but they could bankrupt you once they get even a single penny," commissioner Watson stated bluntly.

"The Hearst family own newspapers... When they tried to get their daughter back, they almost bankrupted themselves to do so," Ethan pointed to the screen. "We have more... much more money than that. Even if we paid this ransom, we still walk away with enough to get by."

"If I may," Bailey held up her hand gently. "It may not just be about money."

"Isn't everything though?" Susan asked as someone handed her a glass of water. "So many crimes are motivated from acts of desperation. Money is always the root cause for situations like this."

"If that is true," Watson stated, "Then if you hold onto your money, then John will be kept safe. Don't pay. Not yet."

Ethan's plan was one of the easy ways out of this situation. However, Watson did bring up some rather difficult scenarios. If the ransom was paid, there was nothing to stop the kidnappers from demanding more from them. If not, then they would risk condemning John. What Watson and the police were suggesting though was effective. They needed to stall as long as possible to track them down. The kidnappers wouldn't dare harm or risk hurting their best bargaining chip.

"Commissioner," someone stated to the side, "I recommend we move back to HQ."

"I agree," Mayor Kominski stated abruptly. "We've made our appearances. I think it's time we get you to safety. Who knows what will happen if you stay out here?"

Ethan looked at his wife who was nodding slowly. After pondering their current situation, it was probably best to end the history lesson. There was nothing more they could do here.

"Jim," Ethan turned to his security drones. "Please ride with us. Once we get to headquarters, please assist the police and find John."

"Understood, sir."

As a precaution, Ethan and Susan were given cloaks to hide their appearance. Jim boarded a randomly chosen police vehicle that was not part of the mayor's motorcade. He and the SWAT officer rolled up to the two of them and the commissioner ushered them inside as quickly as possible. The mayor would leave first to draw the media away with her.

While she did this, the Kendricks would be able to slip away. This would allow them to enter the flow of police exiting the crime area and discreetly get them to safety. Other members of Dr. Kendrick's security team would go in different directions to not only mislead the news reporters but also stage themselves in places around the city in order to respond to any possible leads.

"Ethan?"

Ethan was gazing out the window as the scenery rolled by, but he turned when he heard Susan say his name. She looked him in the eye and reached her hand out to him. She looked concerned.

"John's going to be fine."

"I hope so," he answered as he reached forward and clasped onto her hand tightly.

"We'll find him and bring him back home."

Ethan's breath trembled as he exhaled.

"We've never lost him before," he said.

"We knew that when he went off to school that he would be out there experiencing life," Susan replied. "We weren't going to homeschool him for his entire life. He was kidnapped. It doesn't mean he's lost."

"I just don't like sitting here doing nothing."

"Ethan Kendrick leading the troops is probably not the best idea," Susan reminded him as she clenched her hands tighter. She was trying to squeeze his hand so that he would feel the pain. "You built Jim and all of those drones for that reason. You can safely direct him where he needs to go to find our son."

"I just... I have to be there!"

"Why?"

Before Ethan could answer, there was a slight jerk in the car which caused them to bounce up a bit. They had hit a speed bump.

"We're here," the driver said.

Once the car came to a halt, the door opened, and they saw Jim standing there to greet them.

"Never mind," Ethan sighed as he slid off his seat and put his foot out the door.

Inside, the two of them were just getting seated at a table. Susan asked if anyone was available to grab some coffee. Jim and Ethan set up his tablet and connected it to the police database. Right as they were finishing their setup the doors suddenly flew open and Waterson stormed in.

"Tell me you didn't do it!"

Alarmed, Ethan and Susan looked at each other but neither had the faintest clue as to what happened.

"We just received word that your lawyers wired the ransom money to the homeless!"

"I didn't authorize that!" Ethan said sternly.

"Neither did I," Susan shook her head. "We were together the whole time since we got here. We didn't give anyone permission to do so!"

"Your lawyers are saying that you did," Waterson replied. "They said that you sent a verbal, written and video authorization to them with information on where to deposit the money."

"Put me through a lie detector and it'll confirm what I'm saying," Ethan replied angrily. He and Susan immediately began to work on the computer. "I didn't do that."

"Ethan..." Susan's eyes widened. "Our accounts... the money isn't there! They took it!"

"How the hell did they manage to steal that much money?" Ethan asked as he frantically tried to think of what was occurring right in front of them. He double-checked. "Average kidnappers? They hacked us and committed severe identity theft to our own company!"

Suddenly, Ethan's tablet chimed once. They all looked at it.

"It's a text message," he said as he pulled it up onscreen. "The kidnappers... they've dropped off John and Melissa... in this abandoned lot!"

All of them looked at commissioner Waterson and he understood at once. He quickly pulled out his radio and barked out instructions.

"Give me officers in that area to begin search and rescue!"

"Jim," Ethan opened a channel on his tablet. "I'm sending you this next location. Can you rendezvous and assist SWAT?"

"On my way doctor," was the short reply.

"We need eyes on this."

Commissioner Waterson stepped up to the table and pressed a few buttons on a keypad which suddenly appeared. As he entered a short sequence of numbers, the table began to whir and they could hear it powering on.

Ethan and Susan stepped back from the table as the screen lit up. A holographic display of the city was floating in front of them. They were watching where every police officer and drone belonging to Dr. Kendrick's team was in real time.

"I have three units arriving there right about now."

They watched as three blue dots on the map approached the address of the vacant lot that Ethan had received in his text message. They were slowly inching around as they searched the area.

"Jim, status on your location?"

"Approximately six blocks."

Jim's answer to Ethan's question was followed by a ping from the table. On the map, they saw a green dot highlighted that was on a direct course towards the blue dots.

"Ethan?"

Ethan turned to look at Susan who was pulling out her phone.

"I'm going to contact our lawyers and try to get to the bottom of what happened with the ransom money," she said. "And yes, I will make sure the line is secure."

He gave her an affirming nod as he turned to look at the map again.

"This is 26 Bravo," someone spoke on the communications channel. "We're onsite searching for the hostages."

"25 Bravo here, I got something under this tarp," another officer's voice spoke on the channel.

"Is it the hostages?" Commissioner Watson asked in response.

"Sorry sir," 26 Bravo answered. "We have two mannequins, a bouquet of flowers and an envelope labeled... 'pigs.' The hostages aren't here. No sign of John Kendrick or his girlfriend Melissa."

"Uh... so where are they?" 25 Bravo asked. His tone sounded concerned.

Suddenly, there was a red alert as the emergency dispatcher's voice spoke through the speakers.

"211. All units, we have an armed robbery in progress at Fremlyn bank. Subjects are armed and dangerous. Bank manager reported that John Kendrick is among the robbers."

"Who's the closest?!" Watson scrolled the map to the side.

"22 Bravo responding! 27 Bravo is behind me."

Ethan also pulled up his files on his tablet. He activated another channel and spoke into it.

"Dana," he stated clearly. "Support the SWAT officers at Fremlyn. Follow their directives once you rendezvous with them. Proceed with caution."

Dana's response was immediate.

"Orders received Dr. Kendrick. Confirmed. Enroute."

"How many drones did you bring with you?" Watson asked Ethan.

"Enough."

"Commissioner? Sir?"

It was Bailey the technician. She quickly walked in and pointed her tablet at the screen. She swiped her hand from the bottom of it straight up as if she was flinging a piece of paper across the room. An image appeared onto the main monitor as a result.

"There's a livestream video of the robbery," she explained. "It's John."

The video showed the inside of the bank. They saw civilians kneeling and cowering on the ground as the robbers were in control of the situation. Ethan could see a couple of them in the back loading bags full of money. Others were watching all the victims and making sure that no one tried anything risky.

The only person unmasked was John Kendrick who looked nervous. They had supplied him with a rifle. He was gripping it tightly and looking around frantically. One of the robbers was seen raising their gun and pointing it right at him. John immediately saw this, glanced briefly at the camera, and then looked around.

"The first person I see that lifts their head up," he declared as he pointed his rifle towards the ceiling. He took a deep breath and yelled a little louder, "I'll blow it off!"

John pulled the trigger and several shots from the rifle went off. Many people screamed and crouched even lower.

"Come on! We need to go now!"

The camera was suddenly yanked away from whoever was filming John. Just before it disconnected the live feed, they were able to see the robbers grabbing John and running out the entrance of the bank. More shots were fired. Amidst the screams and the panicking civilians, they could hear the robbers repeatedly yelling something.

"This isn't over!"

The video ended and all of them stared blankly at the dark screen. There was a moment of silence as they tried to comprehend what they had just seen.

"I have a bad feeling about this," Ethan let out a frustrated sigh.

"22 Bravo! We lost them!"

Bailey switched the monitor to another live feed. They were watching a dashcam of one of their own vehicles. The bottom corner of the screen had 22 Bravo's ID number. They were able to see the footage of what was ahead of them.

The robbers had gotten into an escape vehicle and were driving off. There was a huge crowd of civilians rushing into the streets to block 22 Bravo from pursuing. Upon a closer look, they could see that one masked robber was flinging piles of money into the air which was drawing the people onto the street. Traffic was halted as everyone gleefully started going after all the cash.

"27 Bravo here," another officer's voice reported in. "I can't get through this crowd!"

"Free money! Come and get it!"

The robber that was tossing bundles of cash up into the air was yelling to the people.

"Dana? Sitrep," Ethan clenched the edge of the table furiously.

"Unable to pursue," Dana answered. Despite being a drone, Ethan could almost hear a dejected tone in her voice. "The officers and I have been blocked. There is no quick way through the people unless you authorize the necessary measures.”

“Negative Dana,” Ethan directed clearly. “Hold your position. Remember protocol and do not harm the civilians in front of you.”

“Understood.”

Ethan turned to look at Watson who was shaking his head. The kidnappers and now robbers of the bank had eluded them.

“I need an aerial unit keeping tabs on that getaway vehicle!”

As Watson issued these orders, Ethan then looked at Susan who was still talking on the phone. It looked like she was busy so he didn’t want to interrupt.

“25 Bravo to command, I have something for Dr. Kendrick.”

Ethan perked up when the officer’s voice spoke again over the communications channel.

“What is it?” he asked with a hopeful gleam in his eyes.

“The envelope left on the mannequins; it had John Kendrick’s driver’s license cut up into pieces. There were also instructions left inside with flash drive. They want you to take it and upload the video on it to your social media.”

Ethan spoke into the radio and contacted Jim.

“Jim, can you check the flash drive that was discovered? Can you please send it to me if it’s safe to do so?”

“Yes, doctor. Scanning now.”

It took a few moments as Ethan, Watson and Bailey calmly waited.

“Scan complete, the drive appears to be uncorrupted. Sending one file to headquarters.”

“I’ve got it,” Bailey answered as she scrolled on her own tablet.

Ethan’s eyes widened when someone appeared onscreen. It was John. He had been forced to record another hostage video.

“The time for people to treat each other better is overdue.”

John was in front of the camera in a dark room. There was only one light shining on his face and they could see that he was afraid and trembling.

“Rise up for a just society,” he stated as he kept looking offscreen at something. Ethan guessed that the kidnappers were having him read a queue card. “We’re all soldiers in this revolution.”

The video ended as the screen paused and Ethan found himself looking at his son’s desperate and terrified expression.

“Officer?” Ethan stammered a little. “What uh... what were the instructions you found? Upload this exact video on social media?”

“Yes Dr. Kendrick sir.”

“Please do it,” Ethan bit his lip and put his hands on his waist.

"Sir?"

Ethan looked at Bailey, but she was looking at Watson. She was waiting for confirmation about those instructions. Watson turned to look at Dr. Kendrick and sighed. He turned once more and nodded his head at Bailey. She understood and began to focus on her tablet.

"Are you able to examine this footage?" Watson asked.

"Sorry sir," Bailey responded without looking up. "Nothing in the frames to indicate where this was filmed."

"Look at the way John's looking off camera," Ethan pointed at the screen. "Replay it again but mute the audio."

The commissioner and Ethan both watched John's expression.

"This group is organized," he said as he tried to look for any clues in the video. "If they're trying to recreate history, they know it never ended well the first time in 1974. There must be some sort of endgame to this. My son is terrified and afraid for his life. Also, if they didn't kill her, he's probably afraid of what they'll do to his girlfriend in order to keep his cooperation."

"The key to finding him and his girlfriend is in this particular set of events," Watson said. "Bailey, could we extend the search to places that resemble anything like what the SLA would have used back then?"

"It's hard to say," Bailey didn't look up from her screen. "The techs are all looking through the police database. They moved from safehouse to safehouse in Los Angeles. Here's a motel receipt for where they slept for a couple of nights. I diverted units to discreetly patrol around potential areas."

"We need to narrow it down even more considering there are hundreds of motels in the area."

"Oh wait, here's something."

Bailey pulled up a transcript and posted it onto the main monitor.

"This was an anonymous 911 call from the Patty Hearst case," she said as she began to read it aloud. "A man claimed he saw Patty and friends hiding out in a movie theater on Hoover. The 911 operator wasn't sure if this claim was valid. Upon investigating the theater, it was clear that there were people living there even when the property was closed off from the public."

Watson and Ethan both glanced at each other. This information perked them up.

"Does that narrow it down?"

"It does actually."

Everyone focused on the monitor.

"Bailey, show me all the movie theaters in the area. Eliminate the ones that are still in use by the public. Look for any abandoned properties that might draw in people from living on the streets."

The map had already highlighted over a hundred orange dots which symbolized the motels they were searching at. A bunch of purple dots joined the map and began to flash brightly in sequence on the map. According to the parameters that Watson had asked for, these were the possible locations.

"How closely are these kidnappers following the SLA's history?" Ethan asked no one specifically.

"It's better than over a hundred motels. Deploy to these locations and let's keep coming up with more options."

Ethan's security team and SWAT began to send their officers to the purple dots instead of the orange ones. Local police could handle checking motel locations. However, if this armed group was at any of the purple dots they came up with, there would be experienced and heavily trained personnel ready to engage if a firefight was initiated. As Bailey and her techs dug into the history of SLA, they found more potential houses, soup kitchens and small camps that they could possibly be at.

At first, it didn't seem like it was working out in their favor. One hour into the search without any incident or encounters, the monitor pinged and they saw the beacon that was transmitting to them.

"Dr. Kendrick," Jim's voice reported over the radio. "We have found something."

"Switching to your camera," Ethan stated.

With a push of a button from his tablet, they watched a video feed appear on the main screen. They were watching the scene unfold in real time thanks to Jim's point of view. They watched him turn to glance at two other officers. This had to be 25 and 26 Bravo.

"How long do you think this place has been closed?"

Jim glanced at 26 Bravo who was looking curiously up ahead. He turned and all of them could see the worn out and faded sign of the movie theater.

"Well, with the return of the internet and home streaming services being rebooted... it's probably been closed since before the war."

"What do you think Jim?"

"It is remarkable that this theater has remained standing where it is for so long," Jim answered politely. "Television services available online have lowered the probability of this place potentially being reopened."

"Unless if someone decides to renovate it or fix it up."

"Hey... isn't that the getaway vehicle?"

Ethan, Watson, and Bailey watched as Jim followed the officers. Before they could head up to one of the entrances, they investigated the alleyway. There was a car sitting there.

"That's the vehicle!" Ethan exclaimed.

They watched Jim's display screen turn bright yellow. He had activated a special recognition program in his system. The vehicle they were looking at was highlighted and the next image that Jim pulled up was footage from the bank robbery from earlier. There was even the dash cam from when Dana and the others had tried to pursue but were blocked by the civilians.

"Confirmed," Jim voiced his agreement. "This is the exact same vehicle they drove."

"Well... I see an abandoned building... and an open door."

Jim turned and looked closely at the entrance. Someone had propped it and held it open with a small box.

"Check for trespassers?" 25 Bravo asked as they slowly pulled their gun out.

"Officers," Jim spoke up, "Allow me to go first."

"You got it," 26 Bravo nodded.

Ethan saw the two officers disappear out of sight. Jim strode forward and prepared to enter the door. He performed a quick scan to check for potential traps. When none popped up on his scanner, he opened the door quietly.

Jim also had a gun drawn and had turned on the flashlight attached to it. He aimed down the hallway and stepped inside.

He came to the end of the hall and turned left. He slowly rotated right as he checked the surroundings. Everyone watched as his live feed showed him investigating an old concession stand and he began to clear the room.

"Left is clear," Jim stated.

"Right side clear," 26 Bravo responded.

After proceeding past a ticket booth, they found the doors to the theater itself. Jim looked back and pointed at 25 Bravo. He motioned for them to follow him. Then, he pointed at 26 Bravo and indicated that they should take the other door. Both officers nodded at this arrangement and Jim turned to face the theater entrance.

He reached his hand forward and carefully opened it.

When he stepped through, he began to look around and checked the inside once again. No traps or ambushes. Jim adjusted his sensors and attempted to hear anything out of the ordinary, but it was very quiet. All you could hear was their own footsteps.

Cautiously, they began to walk past the rows of dusty seats and headed up to where the stage and old screen was. There was something placed at the very front.

"Whoa... check this out."

25 Bravo was at the front and motioning for them to come up. When Jim stepped up and glanced down, everyone could see it was a workbench of some kind. He examined and looked at everything sitting there. There were boxes of ammo, leftover tools, and several pieces of electronics. Someone had built something here and left with it.

"What are they planning?" 26 Bravo whispered.

"It doesn't look good," Jim replied.

"Hey," 25 Bravo leaned forward and picked something up. "It's a wallet."

Jim looked at the wallet and scanned the ID. It belonged to a woman.

"Melissa Henderson," Jim stated. "I believe this is John Kendrick's female companion."

There was a clatter which made everyone suddenly alert. Both officers were looking towards the back of the stage and aiming their flashlights in that direction. Jim tuned his sensors and tried to listen for more noises.

Ethan watched as the group slowly made their way backstage and entered a small hallway filled with props and all sorts of deteriorating items. Jim turned and looked at a tarp sitting in the corner. It was moving.

Jim stepped forward and reached for it. Once he grabbed the tarp, he yanked it away. It was a young woman. She was bleeding from the side of her head and had many bruises all over but Jim was still able to identify her.

"Melissa Henderson," he said calmly. "I am Jim. Security drone for Dr. Kendrick. You are safe now."

25 Bravo stepped forward and tugged the gag around her mouth away from her.

"Command," 26 Bravo reported. "I need an RA to our location at this theater. We have one of the hostages. No sign of the hostiles or John Kendrick."

"Melissa?" 25 Bravo asked in a kind voice. "Are you ok? Where did they take John?"

"I don't know," Melissa whimpered. "They're not letting him go. He's too valuable. They told him they would stop beating me if he willingly went with them."

"I'm sending reinforcements to bring them back here right away," Commissioner Watson declared. "Melissa will be safe if we get her here once she's cleared medically to be moved."

"Jim," Ethan said into the channel. "Protect Ms. Henderson at all costs. She is important to John and therefore is important to us."

"Understood Dr. Kendrick, I shall remain at her side."

"Can you continue to run any scans or traces of what they were building?"

They watched as Jim looked around backstage. He turned his head. On the live feed, they could all see the exit. Jim was looking at something on the ground.

"They moved something quite heavy and large through that exit," Jim looked down at the drag marks in the floor. "Multiple trips. I am detecting traces of explosives."

"That's not good... Any idea how many?"

"If I was to calculate a quick estimate," Jim replied and pondered for a moment, "They have created enough explosives to destroy a few blocks."

"What would their targets be?" Ethan turned and looked at Bailey. "If they're following history, what would they want to blow up?"

"The SLA targeted anything that represented the very thing that they were at war with..." she answered as she thought carefully. "They liked targeting institutions, industry titans, judges, people with money or whom they believed were selfishly keeping their money away from the poor... even the police too."

"But if they've already targeted Dr. Kendrick and their family fortune... who else would be a big enough target for them?"

Suddenly, there were a few alarms appearing on the map. At least three dots on the map turned bright red.

"What's going on?" Watson asked. "Dispatch?"

"We have an explosion at the corner of Pike and Chestnut," the dispatcher replied. "Officers down. It appears their patrol car was blown up."

"Is that the same for the others?" Ethan asked.

"Confirmed," was the answer. "We have casualties."

Within minutes, the map had a few red dots blinking and signaling alerts across the city. These were all police officers being targeted.

"We're spread out..." Watson looked dismayed. "They're picking us off."

"According to police files in the database," Bailey said as she frantically looked through the data, "There were bombs discovered on a few police cruisers back then."

"They're certainly following through on their history..."

It took about fifteen minutes for Jim to return to headquarters with Melissa. As the group returned, Ethan allowed the medical team to take her somewhere private.

"Is it alright if I join her?" Susan asked.

"I don't see why not," Watson nodded. "Have we been in contact with her family that we rescued her?"

"Melissa's mother is on the way here. Her father is overseas on a business trip."

Susan nodded at Bailey's quick report.

"I'll go take care of her," she said. "Oh. Ethan?"

Susan quickly showed her phone to him. She was sending him some files.

"I got in touch with our lawyers and our cybercrimes firm investigated how they got the ransom money. It was a rootkit."

"Uh..." Watson tilted his head. "Want to tell me what exactly that is?"

"Malicious code," Ethan felt his blood boil. "They somehow uploaded and got information from my company's servers... they must have stolen private info and used that to persuade my lawyers to give up the ransom money."

"It would also explain as to how they hijacked the national network to broadcast John's hostage videos to the public," Bailey said. "All of our devices picked it up."

"Dr. Kendrick?"

Everyone turned to look at Jim.

"I have been coordinating with the others while we have been out searching for master John. I believe we have pinpointed a location."

"Show me," Ethan replied eagerly. He pointed at Susan as they all began to make their way back to the map room. "Take care of Melissa."

On the map, Jim was highlighting the places where they had been to.

"This is where John was kidnapped, these were the bombings of the police vehicles, here is the movie theater, this is the bank robbery location and lastly, this was where the officers and I discovered the mannequins after the ransom was paid."

In the middle of all the locations being listed, Jim then highlighted an epicenter.

"This is one of the possible locations these kidnappers are based out of."

Everyone glanced at where Jim was highlighting the map.

"It is the best possible position. It is within range of every location that has been hit by this group. Based on their speed and movement, it is the most logical place where they wish to make their final stand. It is likely they found a one-story building to prepare for one last battle against the police."

"Why stick so close to the SLA script??" Watson asked. "If they know the original outcome and how it ended before... would they be willing to fight to the end? Unless they want us to show up?"

"It's probably the big fight to end it all," Bailey suggested. "Mass suicide thanks to the cops. Going out like a cult."

Ethan looked at Jim. The police seemed skeptical, but he had never lost faith in his security team. His drones were built and programmed different.

"Jim," he said, "Rally your team. Watson, please send your best SWAT teams to back them up. We're going in."

"I advise caution Dr. Kendrick," Bailey suddenly warned them. "The last time the police fought the SLA at their final stand, Patty Hearst wasn't inside the house after the conflict ended. We may need to plan on continuing the search for John."

"Well then we need to avoid a repeat of history then."

It took about 20 minutes, but the police managed to rally their forces and arrived at the address that Jim had pointed out on the map.

Dr. Kendrick's security drones were all there in full force as the combined forces established a perimeter.

"What do we know about this address?" Watson asked over the channel.

"Commissioner," Jim answered promptly. "The mailman reported to us that he saw a group of armed individuals entering this residence from the rear. We already looked up the housing records."

"22 Bravo here, the house belongs to a Daniel Wilkins. Married with three kids. We already tried contacting him. His secretary told us that the family's been away for a couple of weeks on vacation."

"Can we confirm that?" Watson asked over the channel. "We can't afford to slip up if there are other hostages inside."

"Confirmed," Jim answered. "Mr. Wilkins and his family recently shared on their social media pages their current location which is London. Not one relative is currently located at their residence."

"The windows are all covered up with cardboard and newspapers," 22 Bravo added. "We can't see inside."

"Jim" Ethan said as he watched the aerial camera from the chopper. "Show us your live feed."

"Understood. Broadcast initiated."

Once again, they all watched as the monitor switched to Jim's first-person perspective. He was standing behind an armored police vehicle with several SWAT officers. They were all equipped with tactical gear and getting ready for the raid.

Jim walked up to the unit that was planning to breach first.

"Attention! To anyone at 1202 Williams Avenue! This is the police! Throw down your weapons and surrender!"

After this announcement was made, everyone silently waited for a response from the house.

"Alright," 22 Bravo declared when nothing happened. "Bomb squad is standing by once we raid the house and look for any traps or planted explosives."

"We can't underestimate this group at all," 25 Bravo started to say. "They've been having us go around..."

Before they could finish their sentence, a loud burst of gunfire went off which made everyone take cover. The windowpanes in the house shattered as they saw flashes of light coming from inside. Everything in front of the house was sprayed with automatic fire.

Jim also ducked down with the others once the shooting started. Everyone at headquarters watched as he peeked his head from behind the hood of the armored vehicle. Bullets were striking their cover and moving away from their position. He looked to the side and saw a garbage dumpster next to the sidewalk. He saw bullet holes appearing in a straight line as the shooter inside seemed to be aiming in a sweeping motion.

"All units!" 22 Bravo called out over the radio. "Shots fired! We are preparing to deploy! Gas it up!"

After he said this, a grenade launcher was brought forth. The officer armed with it fired a tear gas round through the window. Jim turned to watch this but went back to watching the dumpster. The gunfire from inside the house seemed to stop.

"Jim?" Ethan asked, "What's the matter?"

"Analyzing."

"Alright! Everyone check weapons! We are about to move in!"

Jim suddenly finished his scan and quickly interrupted.

"Analysis complete. All units! Please halt!"

"What's wrong?" someone asked.

"Examine the bullet holes closely," Jim said as he pointed at the dumpsters. "Look at how evenly spaced out they are."

"Well, yeah, that's what a machine gun does when it's fired at you," 26 Bravo replied.

"Look at the distance between each shot," Jim explained. "There is a minimum gap of six inches between holes. It is unlikely that a human with an automatic weapon would be that accurate."

"Hey, Jim's right," 27 Bravo said. "Those bullets are perfect straight lines."

"It is likely that they set up an automatic sentry gun," Jim turned and pointed inside the house. "When it detects movement, it will open fire."

"We definitely need to change our entire approach then. There could be more traps if we're not careful."

Ethan used his tablet and entered a command to Jim. The video feed on the monitor switched to infrared. This proved fruitless because there was nothing detected except for a massive cloud of heat. Thanks to the tear gas round that had been launched inside, they still couldn't see anything.

"Jim," Ethan commanded as he switched off the IR vision. "Take point and proceed carefully."

"Understood. Officers, please remain here while I investigate."

Jim stepped out into the open and lifted his arm. As soon as he did this, the machine gun inside opened fire again. This time, he was ready and anticipating where the gun was firing. Jim merely stepped to the right and stayed perfectly still as bullets flew past him. When he stopped moving, the gun also stopped.

"I shall enter the house alone to investigate," Jim announced as he crouched down.

"Alone?" 22 Bravo asked. "Is that a wise idea?"

"Enough lives have already been put at risk and lost today," Jim answered politely. "I will volunteer for this task. Please cover me. If I should fall, please ensure that my parts are recycled in order to save the planet."

Commissioner Watson turned and stared curiously at Dr. Kendrick.

"Recycle?" he asked.

"It was my idea," Susan lifted her hand. "So we can always try to save the planet."

Without asking any more questions, they all turned to continue watching Jim's live feed.

Jim crouching towards the ground seemed to be the right method because as he moved to the side of the house, there was no further gunfire. It was likely that he had lowered himself below the motion detector and the machine gun inside couldn't see him. When he made it to the side of the house, he stood straight up and drew his weapon.

Cautiously, he walked down the side yard and walked up to the first window he saw. He scanned it and slowly peeked inside. He didn't detect any traps, but he decided the back entrance would probably be safer. He proceeded carefully to the backyard. When he arrived, he checked his surroundings. There was a chain link fence that connected to the street that ran right behind the property and Jim could see SWAT officers and vehicles parked there as well.

"There might not be any automated weapons in the back," he reported quietly. "No damage or signs of retaliation to the units in the rear. I am now entering the house."

After doing another scan of the door, Jim reached his arm forward and slid it open. He waited one second and cautiously stepped inside.

"Any signs of life in the house?" Watson asked over the channel.

"Activating heartbeat monitor," Jim replied as he made his way through the halls of the interior. "I have detected one life sign."

Jim made his way to the living room. If his calculations were correct, this was where the automated sentry gun was set up and where the one heartbeat he was detecting was.

The tear gas was still flooding the room. Fortunately, it didn't affect him at all, and he was still able to navigate inside. He spotted the sentry gun aimed directly outside towards the front yard. Quickly, Jim walked over and reached out to the cables and ripped them away from the battery box on the ground. The gun powered down and the motion sensor deactivated. Just as an extra precaution, Jim waved his hand in front of the deactivated sensor. When there was no response from the machine gun, he walked forward and found one person tied to a chair.

"All units," he reported as he quickly pulled out an oxygen tank from his pouch. "I have found John Kendrick. He is alive. Enter the house cautiously. The sentry gun has been disabled."

"Clear the area! All hostages have been rescued!"

Watson's orders were barely audible. Ethan was feeling a massive amount of pressure being lifted off his shoulders. Jim had successfully recovered John and he was still alive.

As the police swept in and began to search the premises for the kidnappers, Jim proceeded to carry John outside.

"It is a relief to see you John," he said as he marched carefully out the way he entered. "We shall prepare medical aid for you and evacuate back to headquarters."

John coughed and was keeping the oxygen mask on as much as possible. He had been subjected to a lot of tear gas and smoke for a few minutes. Despite his condition, he gently lifted a thumbs up for Jim to see.

"Your parents will be overjoyed. Melissa will be happy as well."

"Thanks for the..." John coughed loudly before finishing his sentence. "Ugh... for rescuing me. I'm so happy to see you..."

"Let's get you inside the armored truck."

Back at police headquarters, the SWAT team and the Kendricks were doing a quick debriefing as John and Melissa were being treated. Mayor Kominski was giving the press a closing statement regarding this case. The credit for the rescue was being divided between the Kendricks' security team and the SWAT officers that assisted. They were both going to be fine and would make a full recovery. However, there was one thing still hanging in the air. The kidnappers had gotten away.

"They left John behind for us..." Ethan murmured.

"My guess is that they wanted police to accidentally kill him when they stormed the house," Bailey pointed out. "The sentry gun would open fire and then we would retaliate. Patty Hearst was not there when the police ended the firefight back in 1974. They deviated from the script and hoped that we would make a terrible mistake."

"I know that we didn't find them," Watson shook Ethan's hand firmly. "I promise you this. My officers and I will not stop until we figure out who took them in the first place. We will catch them."

"I appreciate all that you did for us today," Ethan replied. "Our condolences for the loss of your officers."

"If there's anything we can do for their families," Susan said as Watson also shook her hand. "Please let us know."

|Asides from that, are you alright with the loss of that much money from the theft?"

Ethan and Susan both glanced at each other and then at Jim and the rest of their security drones.

"I think we'll be ok," Ethan stated, and Susan nodded in agreement. "We're not completely broke or declaring bankruptcy just yet."

"I find it so interesting they picked your family to target when you've done more for this country than many other billionaires out there," Bailey said.

"I think that's exactly why they did it," Susan shrugged. "I talked to our lawyers, and we all came to a simple conclusion. They kidnapped John to make it seem like we were uncaring to the people's needs. They wanted to destroy our reputation and make our family look bad while getting money out of it."

"We'll know more once we find them and kill them. The money they took definitely left a trail. They may be pros, but they aren't perfect."

Bailey nodded at Ethan's hypothesis.

"I can definitely start there," she said. "I already have my team looking into the email and account transfer instructions regarding the ransom money."

"For now, I'd like to go see my son," Ethan sighed and grabbed Susan's hand. "Again, thank you all for what you've done. I don't think I'll ever be able to repay your bravery and kindness. If there's anything... anything more I can do..."

"Can we have more drones? We could use more backup."

Everyone laughed when Bravo squad made the joke. Well, except for Jim and the security team. The drones all glanced at each other. Even without actual faces, you could see how skeptical they were. They didn't fully understand humor, so they remained silent.

Commissioner Watson led the Kendricks and the security drones to the infirmary. John and Melissa were both sitting together on the bed.

"I know you two missed each other," Ethan sighed as he pointed at them, "But can't this...? Can't this wait until later?"

John and Melissa both sidled apart from each other.

"Gently," Susan muttered.

"Hi mom," John waved nervously. "Hi dad."

Susan quickly walked forward and embraced him.

"Uh... this is... not how I wanted you to meet her..." John awkwardly chuckled.

"We know," Susan replied. "So... are we going to get a chance to say hi properly?"

"I think we're well past that now."

"Well, you already did hang out with me when I got rescued," Melissa chuckled meekly. "Hello Mr. and Mrs. Kendrick. I'm dating your son."

"That is certainly obvious," Ethan let out a laugh.

"Oh, is this Jim?" Melissa asked when she pointed behind them. "He rescued me too! I was struggling to stay conscious but... you found me!"

Jim waved his hand cheerfully.

"It is a pleasure to see you recovering Ms. Henderson."

"I was curious... what happened to Patty after the 1974 shootout between the police and the SLA? She wasn't at the house, right?"

Everyone turned to look at Jim since he had all the historical records.

"She was found 15 months later by the FBI in San Francisco," he explained. "She served two years in jail before her sentence was commuted. She married her bodyguard afterwards. It was a big blow to everything that the SLA stood for. She developed romantic feelings for a police officer who was assigned to protect her."

"Wow..." Melissa stared in awe at the conclusion of that story. "Sounds amazing."

Ethan subtly noticed Melissa trying to grab John's hand affectionately. Susan saw this as well and distracted Ethan from saying anything by moving to hug him.

"This will take some getting used to..." he sighed.

Suddenly, there was a flash on the screen.

"What the hell?"

A masked figure appeared on the monitor in the hospital. Ethan looked down the aisle and saw other screens and monitors had also been hijacked.

"Our purpose? Our purpose was to cure the illness in this country. Soon, we will cure the world as well."

"It's another broadcast," Jim said as he and the security drones were suddenly alert and ready for another fight.

"Stand down," Ethan ordered them. "Let's listen."

The broadcast of the masked man was auto tuned. There was no way to identify them by their actual voice. This was a speech of some kind.

"This society is sick. You only have yourselves to blame. Your police? They aren't protecting you. They're keeping you in line. Your politicians don't represent you. They represent the corporations that put them in power. And you eat it all up, while your media laughs it all the way to the bank. It is absolutely disgraceful. It shouldn't take revolutionaries like us to hold these institutions, these billionaires, accountable. So we hope you enjoyed our little show. Consider this a warning. Be good to each other. Or we will return again. Next time, the show will be new and bigger for you."

The screen faded as the broadcast ended. The anger welled up in Ethan as he glanced at John and Melissa. Both of them looked terrified.

"If it's the last thing I do..." he snarled. "We're going to hunt these bastards down."

"Dr. Kendrick? Dr. Kendrick."

John Kendrick blinked as he snapped out of his daydream. His parents and Melissa were not with him anymore. After a few moments, he realized that he was sitting at his desk across from a few of his amborgs. They were in his office, and he must have spaced out without realizing.

"You drifted there. Are you alright?"

"Yes yes," John sighed as he straightened up. "Sorry, I was thinking about... never mind. I called you all here because I need your help with a mission. A mission that has a personal connection for me."

He grabbed a tablet that was next to him and slid it forward. He then turned to his right and looked at Jim.

"Jim, could you help me share a story? They're going to need to know this before we send them out there. I would also like to ask that you accompany them. Along with any other members that were personally involved. Your expertise is vital."

"Of course, Dr. Kendrick. I am happy to help."

Dr. Kendrick looked at the team of amborgs before him.

"My father spent many years trying to find and hunt down these people. It is time to finish what began many years ago. If anyone doesn't wish to participate, please say so now. I will respect your right to refuse."

There was a moment of silence. Dr. Kendrick nodded as he signaled Jim to begin the mission briefing.

"Let's get to work then."

As Jim began to share the story that he had been thinking about moments ago, he made a silent declaration in the back of his mind.

This is for you Melissa, mom, and dad. This time, it'll be over.

A.I. Industries Database Personnel Files

Special Notes and Data Entries Compiled by Doctors John & Melissa Kendrick

The Amborgs
First Group: <u>30</u> Active members. Initiated in 2115.

It is super exciting to write about the first 30 humans to be cybernetically enhanced by A.I. Industries. My husband and many others refer to them as the originals. With their new enhanced abilities, their minds will be going through the wringer. It's my job to support John and continue being a guide for them when they need to express or share anything. What some people forget about them is the fact that they're still teenagers. Most don't have parental figures or anyone to look up to and yet, they survived to eventually be part of this project. I'm looking forward to helping as much as I can. -Dr. Melissa Kendrick, MD

There were many volunteers in the first programs at A.I. Industries. They all worked hard, have been through a lot and are resilient. They are smart, experienced, and have been protecting the world as best as they can for at least 11 years. However, they are severely understaffed. More amborgs will help pave the way for the future of humanity. -Dr. John Kendrick, CEO

Second Group: <u>30</u> Active members. Initiated in 2127.

After the untimely loss of my wife, I admit that I was temporarily unable to continue with my goals of expanding my cyborg family. It was a tragic blow. Fortunately, after a personal hiatus, I found my way again and set to work looking for more volunteers. Another 30 amborgs joined the First Group as I continued perfecting the enhancement procedures. I think they would have really benefited from Melissa's wisdom and emotional guidance if she was still alive. The Second Group are all, hmm... in my opinion, much more independent... if that makes sense. They communicate well with each other and with the older First Group amborgs but I can't help but feel that their methods are less formal. The results of their actions speak for themselves but I believe they will eventually mature and develop themselves with more experience. -Dr. John Kendrick

Third Group: <u>30</u> Active members. Initiated in 2128.

Under special circumstances, I had the Third Group amborgs training schedule accelerated when active members from the First and Second Groups encountered enemy combatants that had developed countermeasures against them. It was terrifying knowing that outsiders were finding new and creative ways to defeat the amborgs so I figured that a new group of them would tip the scales in a balanced manner. They joined the field, supporting their brothers and sisters. Most problems and difficulties that I'm hearing from the older amborgs is that they feel out of place. Their rushed initiation was a main factor for this. Without completing the standard training that the First and Second Groups went through, the young amborgs of the Third definitely hit the ground running in their first missions. I hope that pairing them with experienced amborgs will help their development. -Dr. John Kendrick

Leonard 1: First Group. Age 30.

I'm not even kidding. I stepped away from our table to pay the check and then I come back to find my husband, our security detail, and the police waiting for me. It had been 10 minutes... tops! Anyway, I never would have thought back then that the little boy who tried to steal John's wallet would become the first human cyborg in history. Once I started getting to know him and talking to him, I learned a great deal about Leonard. He's got a lot of heart, courage and plenty of motivation. He reminds me of Steve Rogers. He's modest but committed to what he does and he has a lot of respect from his peers. -Dr. Melissa Kendrick

Leonard was not ideal to become an amborg. Technically, I caught him trying to steal my wallet. He lived on the streets. But, after I knew more about him, he became the first amborg. I witnessed his very first mission, his marriage to a lovely woman, and becoming the first hero of A.I. Industries. He didn't just become the leader of the First Group because he was the first cyborg. He earned that responsibility on his own. From a petty misdemeanor to... advanced powerhouse. -Dr. John Kendrick

Missy 3: First Group. Age 26.

I heard rumors that Missy was a terrible cook before her augmentation. I didn't want to believe it at first. A case of food poisoning definitely changed my mind. How does one mess up making mac and cheese? It was like it was undercooked, overcooked, burnt, and still chilled at the same time. Anyway, the poor girl would work for several days just to try and make something edible for us. Her skills have improved over time. But

I think there are some employees at the company that get visible trauma when they hear Missy ask us to try something new she learned to cook. Eat at your own risk. -Dr. Melissa Kendrick.

The iron chef of A.I. Industries. For recreational purposes, which has now become a key driving point in her life, she wants to be a master chef. I am proud of her accomplishments. Food being her life is an understatement. She has made quite a name for herself ever since she poisoned half the First Group when she started out. I can still feel the stomach pains from that incident... but let's not bring that up again. Now she feeds the hungry and continues to improve her culinary abilities. -Dr. John Kendrick.

Johnny 5: First Group. Age 28.

Optimistic? Check. Enthusiastic? Check. Charming? Check. Sharp wits? Check. Every counseling session with him is an absolute treat. He makes it his goal to care for and to make people laugh. He believes that making someone laugh is a positive method that opens many doors for us. His intentions are noble but there are times that I wonder if his sense of humor masks any issues he's shoving aside. If he feels ready to share it with me, I'd love to learn more about what makes him... well, him. -Dr. Melissa Kendrick

Every group of friends has that one guy. Or perhaps in a unique and diverse family, there's always the one person who utilizes their sense of humor to pave the way for social interactions. It's hard to pinpoint which amborg from the First Group reconnected with their human emotions first. Melissa probably would be able to tell you but most would say that Johnny 5 was the one who did it successfully and more quickly than the others. Always keep them laughing is what he was taught and on many occasions, he always tries to lighten the mood with his quips and witty remarks. I never get tired of his jokes or his fun stories. He brings a large level of positivity all the time. -Dr. John Kendrick

Vanessa 6: First Group. Age 27.

If you want someone dedicated and passionate to the field of medicine, I have to give that award to Vanessa. I taught her everything I know as a pyschiatrist. One day, I hope that she fulfills her dream of being a doctor. She will be a fine addition to the medical field once she finishes her studies. I've even wrote a recommendation letter for her to John about letting her intern at the hospital here at the company. She'll be so excited when she finds out that he said yes to my recommendation! -Dr. Melissa Kendrick

Despite the fact that everyone has mandatory medical training, 6 has always demonstrated a passionate love for the medical field. Saving lives regularly is fulfilling, but caring for the health of the people she encounters is always a priority. There's a rumor that she's saved over a thousand people since her career as an amborg began. From what I learned, she only keeps track of one number; the number of people she's lost. The bigger that number gets, the more dedicated she is. I think she's quite remarkable in that regard. -Dr. John Kendrick

Stuart 8: First Group. Age 26.

With every family, there are always the pranksters or trouble childs. Stuart isn't a bad kid and he's certainly not a troublesome amborg. But sometimes I think that he and Christy are going to accidentally blow us all up. I'm not against pranks or practical jokes but because they are augmented with superhuman abilities, there might be a day when they both take it too far. Perhaps John and I should be a little more strict to them. -Dr. Melissa Kendrick

Although Johnny 5 is known for his humor, practical jokes are 8 and 9's specialty. If something catches on fire, he's usually one of the suspects. It's getting to be quite difficult to determine whether or not their antics are actually helpful in the field. I was concerned at first when I started reading their post-action reports from the missions they deployed on but now, I'm confident that the others can keep their antics under control. But... I keep an extra container of aspirin close by when I'm about to listen to their debriefings. -Dr. John Kendrick

Christy 9: First Group. Age 26.

There's always an extreme pyromaniac in every family. Is that normal? Anyway, Christy and Stuart are probably going to bring the house down with their chaotic means of relieving stress. Sometimes, she's funny but whenever we have a counseling session, I wonder what's on her mind. I don't think she's crazy. Is that weird? I feel like, as a trained psychiatrist, I should be able to give a definite answer. Maybe I should look into that more? Maybe later? -Dr. Melissa Kendrick

It was probably not a good idea to enhance someone with an almost unhealthy obsession with constantly breaking fire code and safety regulations. Despite her unusual and unorthodox tactics, she does manage to get the job done... even if it means the social media relations department has to step in and issue public apologies on her behalf to put out the, no pun intended, fires she ignites on the internet. I would be lying if I wrote in her personnel file that she didn't give me migraines every time I summoned her to my office for an explanation. -Dr. John Kendrick

Clint 11: First Group. Age 28.

Clint is very casual, calm, and level-minded under stressful situations. Resourceful, skilled, and a talented amborg. Oh, I don't mean that the others aren't as good as him. That's now what I mean. He gets the job done and he's dedicated. From my perspective, I think there's a part of him that wants to do more in his career as an amborg but he gets overshadowed by his friends. Maybe things will be more motivating for him when he takes charge on future missions. -Dr. Melissa Kendrick

Clint 11 has always ventured out into the wilderness on plenty of occasions. Many of the amborgs learned how to survive thanks to his outdoorsy and adventurous background. If you were to abandon him in a desert or frozen tundra alone, he would definitely show up at your doorstep the following day without a scratch. He's pretty tough and it's admirable. -Dr. John Kendrick

Danielle 12: First Group. Age 29.

It's always the quiet ones. Never underestimate someone when they are quietly contemplating about something. Danielle always seems to be thinking about how certain conversations are going to go. I swear, she's going to be a great therapist or something. There's a bright future for her if she continues to spread kindness to everyone she meets. I fear for the ones that make her angry. -Dr. Melissa Kendrick

A quiet but skillful tactician, she always employs communication as her primary tactic for the most difficult situations. Don't let her kind demeanor fool you, she is just as deadly as the next amborg if negotiations fall short. Aggressive negotiations are substituted at that point to get the job done. Even someone as diplomatic as her has to engage in battle. -Dr. John Kendrick

Kiden 18: First Group. Age 26.

She is very talented when it comes to inventing fictional backstories and adopting different identities. She believes that what happens behind the scenes is just as important and I feel the same way. Whenever she comes back for a post-mission debriefing or just to have a conversation with me, I almost forget I'm talking to an amborg. She has such a firm grasp on her emotions and social skills that it's no surprise that John allows her to supervise the training curriculum of the other amborgs. -Dr. Melissa Kendrick.

If you wish to learn what it takes to go undercover, the expert is amborg 18. Onsite, she is the lead trainer and supervisor for all amborg physical exercises. She keeps every amborg at A.I. Industries trained and properly conditioned to carry out their activities at all times. In the field, she excels at maintaining secret identities for covert operations and being discreet. She has a lot of connections to informants around the world and is often away for long periods of time. I don't worry about her though... because I know that she's doing ok. No matter what. -Dr. John Kendrick

Tiana 19: First Group. Age 27.

She's very spirited and so upbeat. She has a very pleasant and nurturing side to her but if that line gets crossed, she becomes quite deadly. I wonder if she might be overextending herself in some situations. She can be a little uptight and absorbed in work ethics which can make her forget about relaxing or being with friends and family. I hope that over time, this is something she'll discover herself. -Dr. Melissa Kendrick

I discovered Tiana roaming on the streets of Boston. She has a huge personal connection to the East Coast. She is a total machine when it comes to fulfilling her tasks. I mean this as a compliment. In a way, I feel like several other amborgs are trying to follow her example which can be productive. According to Melissa, it might cause her a lot of emotional strain at times. Might need to remind her about her vacation days. -Dr. John Kendrick

Jennifer 24: First Group. Age 30.

She's quite social and interactive. Most of the amborgs that I've talked to are quite closed off but she seems to enjoy all of the simple conversations. A very strong communicator with a voice I could probably fall asleep to if she read books to everyone at night. If my husband reads this... sorry John. I still love the way you read your scientific procedures to me, even when I have no idea at times what it's about. -Dr. Melissa Kendrick

Like several other candidates that went through A.I. Industries various programs, 24 doesn't have many memories about her family or past. She remains at A.I. Industries and chooses not to actively seek out more about her life prior to cybernetic enhancement. Many have commented that this decision seems questionable, but they respect it nonetheless. I absolutely respect her choice and appreciate that I can count on her at all times. Wait... what did my wife say about her voice? Just a minute... -Dr. John Kendrick

The following files are from me, Dr. John Kendrick. My... wife didn't live to see the Second Group go out on their first missions so it's just my own entries. I don't know what notes or things she would have to say about them but I do hope that she's proud of them... just as much as I am.

David 117: Second Group. Age 17.

He is the son of a very good friend of mine. He chose to volunteer and he wanted to become an amborg to help people. I know that his parents didn't want him to risk his life but ultimately, it was his decision. If Melissa was still alive... I sometimes wonder what she would have said when David became an amborg. I'm glad that he has a technician that can help guide him with his new abilities.

Serina 43: Second Group. Age 18.

She is David's closest friend and also the daughter of someone very dear to me. Both were in my care and she also decided to join David in becoming an amborg. She's very lively and upbeat which contrasts his quiet and observant side. Her skills and her technician have made her very popular out in public and here at home.

Jack 917: Second Group. Age 18.

An odd and peculiar case among the amborgs. He is probably the most controversial human being that the amborg program ever encountered. He is an amborg that was enhanced while in a coma. When he woke up, he had a severe case of amnesia and essentially gained powers overnight. After great deliberation, he chose a name for himself and I helped him submit the paperwork for his legal name. Although he is devoted, I feel that he's a loose cannon. He is still a remarkable miracle.

Alice 999: Second Group. Age 18

The lone wolf of the amborgs. Silent, deadly, and efficient. Like 43, she's 917's closest friend. She has been through quite an ordeal and despite how silent she is most of the time, I encourage everyone that tries to befriend her to be incredibly patient and respectful to her. Boundaries. She is really particular about her boundaries. May God help you if you so much as try to put a finger on her without her permission.

Carter 297: Second Group. Age 17.

Even though the First Group has some of the best sharpshooters in the world, Carter takes the top spot on the list. In my humble opinion. I don't believe I've ever seen him miss. Of course, because of his cybernetic enhancements, he's not allowed to join any shooting competitions. He always talks about he's the go-to method for using a ranged weapon to solve long-distance problems.

Katie 57: Second Group. Age 17.

I won't lie for this record. I feel terrible that Katie's sister didn't survive augmentation. After she became an amborg and official member of the Second Group, I gave her space and all the time that she needed. I can only partially relate to her. When I lost my parents and my wife, it felt like the world was ruined beyond repair. The way that Katie bounced back was impressive. Now, she dedicates her life to saving and protecting as many lives as possible.

Ryan 35: Second Group. Age 17.

Like David, Ryan has always been slightly quiet. He's not really a take-charge type of person and chooses to follow, rather than lead. He does enjoy spending time with his friends. I wonder what is so intimidating for him; that keeps him so unwilling to step up and take charge. I don't want to force him to change but I hope he shows initiative if the situation calls for it.

Marco 125: Second Group. Age 16.

When he's not out on a mission, Marco enjoys staying at home. You can usually find him helping the research departments in developing or assisting with certain projects. Everyone does have mandatory classes and hours they need to log in with the labs. Extra credit. Marco spends a lot of free time helping and I think he has a gift for it.

Jesse 274: Second Group. Age 16.

I believe that Jesse likes to spend every spare waking moment of his life reading. He's read a lot of books. He collects them too. History is one of his favorite subjects. Each amborg has a personalized database or access to all the information that they want but he stays plugged into every outlet that exists. He enjoys teaching and is passionate.

Steve 92: Second Group. Age 19.

I thought that twins would be a great idea in our big amborg family. Somewhere, in the afterlife, my wife is probably laughing at me from beyond.

Jon 93: Second Group. Age 19.

Melissa... if you're listening or reading this data file... I know... and you're right. Twin amborgs are definitely a lot of work.

Dominic "Donut" 501: Third Group. Age 16.

Young Dom is a very curious and eager to please. I hope this doesn't cause too many problems for him. I am aware of the fact that he and several other Third Group amborgs are younger than the other groups. Their training, their augmentation, and their first deployments were moved up ahead of schedule. He's getting thrown in the deep end and I hope that following under David's guidance will help.

Carolina 466: Third Group. Age 15.

Carol is very mature and competent. When 43 selected her to be her apprentice, I was relieved and confident that they would make a great pair. The Third Group all need wisdom and guidance from the other amborgs. I know that Carol and Dom are going to learn a lot from David and Serina.

Amara 345: Third Group. Age 16.

She is a bright young girl and also has a rather tragic past. A math prodigy that was... sold off so that her parents could make a dent in their crippling debt. I had no idea that child trafficking and the human slave trade was still even a thing. Once we rescued her and properly took her in, I was pleased to see her make a full recovery and to also hear her request to become an amborg. Approving her request to apprentice under Alice 999 was an interesting one. Fortunately, Jack should also be able to provide assistance.

Amborg Industries aka A.I. Industries
Dr. John Kendrick: CEO

Oh, this is my data entry. Ok then, what should I say? I am... the only child of Dr. Ethan and Susan Kendrick. I am a third-generation scientist, the Creator of the Amborgs and C.E.O. of one the world's most powerful companies. Despite A.I. Industries being based in the U.S., I have the company registered as an independent organization. I created this company and my family in order to make the world a better place. It's been about 20 years since I used my family inheritance to make this company what it is today. I can only hope that my actions make our unwritten future a good one. If my parents or Melissa are watching over me and my amborgs, I hope I've made them proud. -Dr. John Kendrick

Is that my husband's data entry? It's kind of... bland? I think it skips out on some important details. John has always been a really smart man. When we were both at The Academy, it was always fantastic being there whenever he talked about his ideas or shared what his future goals were. Some of my friends did question if it was his family's money that attracted me to him. Absolutely not. I am not that kind of girl. I saw a man with a vision for the future. When he asked me to marry him, I was beyond thrilled. Whatever ideas he has about creating the world's first cyborgs is definitely what I will support. -Dr. Melissa Kendrick

George Ramirez: Media Relations

One of my oldest friends. Although he is not vice-president of the company, many have often mistaken him in that role. To be fair, he knows the company just as much as I do. Melissa and I met him many years prior to forming the company and made him the head of Public Relations for A.I. Industries. His family resides with him onsite as he maintains business with all outside sources that I cannot handle alone. -Dr. John Kendrick

George is incredibly smart and able to handle a lot of interactions that would probably give me a stressful headache. I think his skills in customer service has given him such a great ability at answering questions during interviews or whenever news media outlets crack down hard on the company. His family is very kind and supportive and I put aside plenty of time to be there for them, especially his wife. -Dr. Melissa Kendrick

Dr. Gene Wildman: A.I. Industries Head of Medical

Gene supervises and monitors the health and physical wellbeing of everyone at A.I. Industries. He cares for their mental state and also treats all under our roof with kindness, respect and his loving support. I'm lucky to have a colleague and friend like him. -Dr. John Kendrick

He's an expert that takes care of people physically. I take care of them emotionally. Wait, that sounds a little inappropriate. He... likes to make people feel better! So do I! Uh... I think that sounds a little worse. I'm sorry, there are so many doctors at A.I. Industries and it's confusing sometimes. He's the head doctor of the medical facility and the one I call when I need hardcore drugs. You know what? I'm just going to stop talking. Sorry John. Sorry Gene. -Dr. Melissa Kendrick

Dr. Robert Kolaski: Artificial Intelligence R&D Department Head
WARNING WARNING WARNING
Research Level: Maximum Clearance
Highly Sensitive Company/Corporate Operations

Ha ha ha... I'm just kidding. I thought it'd be funny to play the alert that goes off whenever someone scans Robert's ID. Without saying too much about what he does, he handles all matters concerning the A.I. programs. He raises them, educates them, programs them, and just likes to keep to himself. It's very rare to see him leave his lab. I don't think he's left A.I. Industries... in a long time. I think there's a secret rumor that if he goes outside, he vanishes in the sunlight. -Dr. John Kendrick.

I see my husband enjoys utilizing his sense of humor when it comes to Robert. Uh... Am I his friend? It's hard to tell. He's... quite the character. All I remember is... he had his nose in a coding textbook or was always stuck like glue to anything with a wifi connection back to his dorm room's computer. You want the living breathing definition of a social recluse? I'd give that award to Robert. I'm surprised a guy like him got a girl to fall in love with him. Speaking of... I amazed he consummated his marriage. Scratch that, I'm more surprised that he got engaged... or made it to an actual wedding ceremony. Did he ever go on an actual date? Did anyone ever give him the... talk?? Oh... uh... You know what? I'm not going there. I really shouldn't go there at all. -Dr. Melissa Kendrick

Marina Ramirez

Ah, yes. Marina... the poor woman. What happened to her specifically when she and George were trying to immigrate to the U.S. is... not my place to say. The fact that she lived through such a horrible traumatic experience and ended up giving birth in an I.C.E. center would be a terrifying moment for anyone. Fortunately, they welcomed their daughter Thalia into the world. My wife Melissa has spent a lot of time tending to her needs. -Dr. John Kendrick

Marina has been through a lot of pain. I would say that a lot of environmental factors has led to... severe issues... Uh... can we not disclose this on the public record? Marina is one of my patients and... I don't think what's going on should be shared. Not like this. Let's just... skip this entry for now. -Dr. Melissa Kendrick

Thalia Ramirez

Thalia is a bright and adventurous little girl. You can see where she gets it from. Sometimes, George or Marina accidentally let her into restricted areas. Not the dangerous areas but... there's a reason why I keep kids out of certain parts of the company. She loves being friends with almost everyone. She has a bright future ahead of her. -Dr. John Kendrick

She's the cutest! I hope I have kids that'll grow to be just like her! She regards the amborgs as her extended family. The amborgs are her friends and she often says that it's like having a ton of siblings. Maybe once things settle, I can talk to John again about us raising our own biological kids? -Dr. Melissa Kendrick

The Technicians
Mandy Palmer

Amborg: David 117, Second Group

A very bright personality and definitely a valuable partner to David. -Dr. John Kendrick

Sherry Lansing

Amborg: Serina 43, Second Group

I often wonder if she's related or descended from Sherry Lansing, the first woman to head a Hollywood studio over a century ago. Either way, she certainly has taught 43 a lot about how to act like a leading lady. -Dr. John Kendrick

James Stetson

Amborg: Carter 297, Second Group

Carter has told me that James has a talent for being observant. Both seem to have a high attention to detail. -Dr. John Kendrick

Aaron Shore

Amborg: Alice 999, Second Group

I have no idea if he can even get past Alice's rough and cold exterior. The fact that he's stuck with her this long is a testament to his character. He certainly thinks its quite an interesting experience. -Dr. John Kendrick

Meilin

Amborg: Jack 917, Second Group

She enjoys nurturing and caring about Jack. I really value her support as his partner because of what he's been through. I look forward to her reports on his performance in the field. -Dr. John Kendrick

Prajit Ladaka

Amborg: Ryan 35, Second Group

I translated his name to english. It's quite amusing and fitting for him. A name fit for a technician to one of my amborgs. -Dr. John Kendrick

Ariana Hart

Amborg: Katie 57, Second Group

It's interesting seeing Katie act more outgoing than her own technician. I do believe that their opposite personalities do make for very interesting missions. -Dr. John Kendrick

Acquaintances & Allies

Grandpa Mark

I've heard of this man. Not in a positive light. I've actually stopped asking John about this... mysterious hooded man watching from a distance. He would always tell me that it wasn't our business but I can't help but feel that it kinda is... especially when this... Mark... is one of our staff member's father? It's a bit of drama that I guess I'll never fully know about. Sounds pretty intriguing though. Wait a minute... Why are some pieces of my tech missing from my desk?? I swear, there was an arm brace with bluetooth here... -Dr. Melissa Kendrick

Don't tell my wife that I gave away some of our gadgets. Seriously, please don't let her see this entry. I might need to redact it in the future. Anyway... Mark. Almost all the amborgs don't have a living relative. Mark is the exception. He is... David 117's paternal grandfather and the head of a strong group of vigilantes: freedom fighters for the people that assist A.I. Industries from the shadows or with extreme cases that the amborgs cannot handle alone. He's very energetic and sometimes acts crazy but he is an ally. Not bad for an old man. All I really know is that he and David 117's father; my former employee, didn't see eye to eye. I assumed he was dead for a while and then I received word from the LAPD that he had stabbed David 117. It makes my blood boil that he decided to do that to get his point across, but it is what it is. It doesn't mean I have to like it. He is a tough old man and I'm glad he is a friend. -Dr. John Kendrick

LAPD Chief Marsha Bradley

Uh, the system wouldn't let me change her rank. It's officially locked in there. I can't... edit it? I might need Serina to help me later. Anyway, she is technically a captain but somewhere in the line of duty, she was accidentally... promoted? If that even makes sense? She is tough and a dedicated officer. I know that the lack of experienced officers led to a huge, disorganized restructuring of the chain of command. That's how bad it was. People were dying out in the streets faster than the death certificates could even be printed. Captain Bradley is a strong ally to the amborgs, and I do consider her a brave friend. She and Melissa would have probably gotten along famously. -Dr. John Kendrick

Sergeant Paul Lewis

All I will say about Officer Lewis is... I have no idea how he's survived this long. Oh, that's not enough? According to my A.I. assistants, I need to say a few more words. He is probably the luckiest or the most unluckiest officer in the LAPD. -Dr. John Kendrick

Sergeant Joe Harrison

I didn't know that a gentle, kind and compassionate soul could be among the LAPD. He's like the grandfather you always wish you had. Wise, experienced and able to protect you when necessary. He's one of the finest officers I've ever met. I always send him a card every year on his birthday thanking him for how he treated John and I after we were rescued. -Dr. Melissa Kendrick

A legend among the LAPD. Personally, I remember meeting Officer Harrison around the time when Melissa and I were kidnapped. To see him serve the police and his community for decades is an extraordinary feat. In case it wasn't already clear, he was promoted correctly in comparison to Johnson and many other rookies. -Dr. John Kendrick

Officer Joe Johnson

Due to a huge shortage of police officers, many recruits fresh from the academy were put into positions they weren't ready for. This resulted in Johnson suddenly becoming a sergeant. Much like his captain, he suddenly outranked many of his peers. I'm glad that he became friends with David 117 on what appeared to be their first missions together. They both look out for each other and that's a good sign of friendship to me. -Dr. John Kendrick

<u>*Artificial Intelligence Programs*</u>
Serina

Our best A.I. program. She's been flash-cloned from a staff member at A.I. Industries. Robert has a particular fondness for her. Uh... not in a weird way. Flash-cloned A.I. programs have personalities that are natural and artificial so they imitate human traits quite well. A little too well at times. Unlike coded or programs raised from scratch, they need to be... updated constantly. So, the original host's mind that Serina was cloned from has to do a connective mental session. Like updating new software. Unfortunately, the original person she was based off of and created from has died. This means that Serina will also die too. Much too soon considering she's only ten years old and won't live as long as a normal human being. -Dr. John Kendrick

I get asked this a lot... so I'll only say it once for the record. Serina is not me. I don't think I'd have the patience to allow my brain to be copied. That... and if something goes wrong, are you sure you want me to become a potential Skynet emergency? No thank you. -Dr. Melissa Kendrick.

Taylor

This particular A.I. has been around ever since Robert started working at A.I. Industries. Despite his choice to appear as a youthful avatar, he is actually one of the oldest programs in the company. He is a constructed artificial intelligence. This means that someone tried to raise and create him from scratch and over time, he was perfected into sentience. I don't know if that's even the correct way to say that. He supervises and oversees other young programs that hang... float... around. It's interesting how they have a hierarchy that is quite effective. -Dr. John Kendrick.

I will admit, it is certainly a different experience trying to psychologically read an A.I. The fact that they are programs but manage to imitate us so well is... eerie. I trust the artificial intelligence programs that live at A.I. Industries. I know that society has reservations and it's understandable. But, I look at a program like Taylor and... I don't feel afraid. It makes me feel safe knowing they're looking out for us. As long as you treat them right. -Dr. Melissa Kendrick.